They were three brothers who did things *their* way...the Justice Way....

One signed up as a temporary, in-name-only husband—but soon found himself coveting a permanent position, in *Ryder's Wife.*

One came to the rescue of the pretty stowaway in his mountain cabin, with a duffel bag full of cash and no memory of her past, in *Roman's Heart.*

And one was looking for his daughter's angel— and ended up finding his own, in *Royal's Child.*

* * *

THE JUSTICE WAY:
Brothers Ryder, Roman and Royal.
They would do anything for each other...
and for the women they loved!

"Sharon Sala knows just how to steep the fires of romance to the gratification of her readers."
—*Romantic Times*

SHARON SALA

THE JUSTICE WAY

Published by Silhouette Books
America's Publisher of Contemporary Romance

SILHOUETTE BOOKS

ISBN 0-373-18512-X

by Request

THE JUSTICE WAY

Copyright © 2002 by Harlequin Books S.A.

The publisher acknowledges the copyright holder of the individual works as follows:

RYDER'S WIFE
Copyright © 1997 by Sharon Sala

ROMAN'S HEART
Copyright © 1998 by Sharon Sala

ROYAL'S CHILD
Copyright © 1999 by Sharon Sala

CONTENTS

Dear Reader,

I am so pleased that Silhouette Books has chosen to reissue my JUSTICE WAY trilogy. The Justice brothers, Ryder, Roman and Royal Justice, generated a lot of positive mail. Family is very important to me, as it is to the Justice brothers. They are "Musketeers" in the true sense of the word in believing "one for all and all for one." They live their own lives without family interference, but let trouble come and they are instantly there for each other.

Ryder Justice got lost from himself after a family tragedy, but when he finds love in an unexpected place, he also learns how to forgive himself and grow.

Roman Justice is the youngest brother but in many ways the hardest to understand. His lifestyle has taught him that emotion can get him killed, so he's learned to turn it off. But when he runs into a charming young woman with a life-size case of amnesia, it's no holds barred as he falls head over heels in love, and in the process saves her life.

Royal Justice is the eldest, a widower trying to raise a little girl alone. It's the impending maturity of his five-year-old daughter, Maddie, that forces him to rethink the "I can do it by myself" attitude. And it's the unexpected arrival of a housekeeper who becomes an angel in disguise that changes his world.

I hope you enjoy their stories as much as I enjoyed writing them. I can be reached by e-mail at sharonsala@romanticfiction.com or by snail mail at P.O. Box 127, Henryetta, OK 74437.

Sharon Sala

Ryder's Wife

Magic comes to us in myriad forms.
There is magic in the beauty of a sunrise,
in the reflection on a dewdrop hanging
from the petals of a rose. A mother's touch is magic
when it soothes a crying child. And laughter is
a magic that no medicine can match.

There have been many magic moments
in my life that are mine alone to keep.
But I would like to acknowledge two people who
have made their own kind of magic in helping me
create this world in which I write.

To Meredith Bernstein—
an agent extraordinaire who
stands behind me faithfully and
does not know that meaning of the word "no."

To Jan Goldstoff—
a publicist with a golden touch,
whose visions are exceeded only by her persistence.

Prologue

December—on the plains near Abilene, Texas

Heat penetrated the black void of unconsciousness in which Ryder Justice was drifting. Even in the depths from which he was trying to escape, he smelled the hair burning on the backs of his arms and knew another level of fear. He moaned, and the movement of air through his lungs yanked him rudely into the now. Gritting his teeth against the pain racking his every breath, he struggled to sit upright. Acrid smoke drifted up his nose, mingling with the coppery taste of fresh blood as he fumbled with the latch to his seat belt. That which had most probably saved his life was now holding him hostage.

A sheet of rain blew in the broken window to his left and into his eyes. It was as effective as a slap in the face. Cognizance returned full force.

Just beyond the crumpled cockpit, he could see flames licking at the metal and eating their way toward him, and he remembered being up in the sky, and getting caught in the storm. A stroke of lightning lit up the night sky and he flinched as he remembered another bolt of lightning and how the plane had shuddered, then rocked. And afterward, the sensation of an electric free fall.

An instinct for survival pushed past the misery of broken ribs and bleeding cuts, past the bone-jarring ache that came with every movement, every breath. He'd survived being struck by lightning. The plane had crashed and he was still alive to tell the tale. By God, he would not sit here and burn to death when he still had legs to crawl.

And at that moment, he remembered he was not alone. He turned.

"Dad?"

Another streak of lightning snaked across the sky, momentarily illuminating what was left of the cabin. After that, Ryder had only the encroaching fire by which to see, but it was more than enough. Stunned by the horror of what the crash had done to Micah Justice, he refused to believe what his mind already knew.

The straps holding him in place suddenly came free and Ryder struggled to get out of his seat. Ignoring wave after wave of pain-filled nausea, he freed his father from the seat and managed to get them both out of the wreckage and into the falling rain.

Sometimes crawling, sometimes pushing, he dragged himself and his father's lifeless body until he found himself beneath some sort of overhang.

Shivering from pain, shock, and the chill of rain-soaked clothing, he scooted as far back as he could get beneath the outcropping of rocks, pulling Micah's body with him, then cradling his father's head against his chest as he would have a sleeping child.

A gust of wind cornered the overhang, blowing rain and a peppering of hail on Ryder's outstretched legs, and at that moment the fuselage blew, erupting into the night in an orange ball of fire. Ryder closed his eyes against the blast, and held his father that much tighter, refusing to accept the motion as wasted effort.

"Dad?"

Again, Micah Justice did not answer. There was no familiar, sarcastic chuckle, no awkward pat from a strong man's hands for comfort. Ryder buried his face against the back of his father's shirt and took a long, aching breath. He knew, but his heart wasn't ready to face the truth.

"Dad...come on, Dad. You can do this. You've told me time and time again that it takes a hell of a lot to put a Justice man down."

Thunder rumbled across the sky, and the deep angry rumble sounded like his heart felt as grief began to settle. His arms tightened around his father's body, and for the first time since the accident had happened, tears began to fall, mingling with the raindrops clinging to Ryder's scorched and battered face.

Holding his father close, he began to rock, muttering beneath his breath and in his father's ear, although Micah Justice had already moved beyond the sound of his second son's voice.

"Please, Dad, talk to me." Ryder's voice broke. "Dad...Daddy, don't do this," he pleaded. "Don't leave us. We need you. All of us need you. Roman will go to hell without you on his case...and Royal, think of Royal. What will happen to the ranch and Royal if you don't wake up?"

A second explosion followed on the tail of the first— smaller, but still powerful in intensity. Bits of burning metal shot up into the sky and then fell down upon the ground nearby. Another flash of lightning, this time closer, revealed more of the truth Ryder Justice had been trying to deny. Micah was dead. Probably upon impact. And he was left with an inescapable fact. His father was dead, and he'd been piloting the plane. This time, when thunder rumbled overhead, it drowned out the sounds of Ryder Justice's grief.

Chapter 1

"Casey, darling, you should never wear black. It makes you look like a crow."

Before Casey could take offense at what her half brother, Miles Dunn just said, he took a seat with the rest of the Ruban family, who were gathering for the reading of Delaney Ruban's will.

She picked a piece of lint from the skirt of her black silk dress and tilted her chin, reminding herself that she wasn't going to cry. Not now, and especially not in front of Lash Marlow, her grandfather's lawyer. Although he was sitting behind his desk and watching each arrival with a focused, predatory gaze, Casey was aware that he was also watching her every move. And it had been that way with them for more years than she cared to remember.

In spite of her love for her grandfather, Delaney Ruban,

and in spite of Delaney's hopes that she and Lash might someday marry, Casey had been unable to bring herself to comply.

She'd been a willing student of Delaney's tutorial with regards to the Ruban empire, but she refused to give up what passed as the personal portion of her life. It didn't amount to much, but it was all she had that she could honestly call her own. Even more important, she didn't love Lash Marlow and had no intention of spending the rest of her life with a man who measured the value of a person by monetary worth.

She shifted nervously in her seat, wishing this day to be over. As Delaney's closest living relative and the heir who had been groomed to take over the vast Ruban holdings, she knew the task that lay ahead of her, right down to how many family members would be looking to her for sustenance.

Not for the first time since her grandfather's stroke six weeks ago did she wish her father and mother were still alive. And, if Chip Ruban hadn't taken his wife, Alysa, to Hawaii for their tenth wedding anniversary, they might still be. But he had, and they'd drowned in a boating accident off the coast of Oahu, leaving their only child, six-year-old Casey, as well as Alysa's ten-year-old twins from a previous marriage, to be raised by an absent and overbearing grandfather who quickly pawned off those duties to someone else.

Alysa's mother, Eudora Deathridge, was moved into the mansion and given full authority and responsibility of her daughter's children. And although she was Casey's grandmother as well, Casey found herself grasping for space in a lap already too full for one more small, six-year-old girl.

With the instinct of a child who knows where she is loved, she turned to Joshua Bass and his wife, Matilda. The butler and the cook. The kitchen became the center of her universe. In Tilly Bass's loving arms, she learned to trust and love again. On Joshua's shoulders, she saw the world in which she lived from a new and different angle, and in doing so, learned not to be afraid of reaching for the stars. They became the surrogate parents she had needed, and now, twenty years later, they were the anchors that kept her life on a straight and honorable path.

And while Tilly and Joshua nurtured and loved her, at thirteen years old, Casey suddenly became the focus of Delaney Ruban's world. He had looked up one day and realized that he wasn't getting any younger, and since Casey was his son's only child, she was, of course, to be his heir.

He looked for the child he'd all but ignored and found a girl on the brink of womanhood. Elated that she'd grown up so well without much of his effort, he decided that it was time she branched out past the familiarity of her school, her friends and Tilly Bass's kitchen.

And so it began. The treat of accompanying him on business trips became the first step in a lifelong education. Before long, Casey was spending all of her summers with him at his office. At first, she blossomed under his tutoring. Her grandfather had never given her anything but presents, and now he was sharing his time with her. It took the better part of Casey's teenage years before she realized Delaney's reasons for spending time with her were selfish. Someone must step into his shoes when he was gone. He'd decided it would be Casey.

And now, at twenty-six, Casey was about to become CEO of a multimillion-dollar corporation with holdings in everything from cotton mills to racehorses. Thanks to the last ten years of Delaney's coaching, she was more than up to the task.

A low murmur of indistinguishable voices hummed behind her like a worn-out motor, rising and falling with the advent of each new person to enter the room. She closed her eyes and took a deep breath. It wasn't the job that daunted her. It was those who were gathering. They were the ones who would be waiting for her to fail.

Someone else touched her on the shoulder. She looked up. It was her sister, Erica.

"Nice dress, Casey darling." Erica's eyes glittered sharply as she fingered the fabric. "I suppose it has a silver lining, too. Just like your life."

"Erica, really," Eudora Deathridge said, and gave her eldest granddaughter a none-too-gentle nudge as they moved past Casey to take their seats.

Casey let the comment roll off her shoulders, and as the women passed by her Eudora squeezed Casey's arm. It was nothing new. Miles and Erica had begrudged Casey everything from the day she was born—from being a Ruban, to being the one Delaney had chosen to follow in his footsteps. In all their lives, they had shared a mother, but little else.

Lash Marlow cleared his throat, well aware that the sound added to the building tension. "I believe we are all here now. Shall we begin?"

Casey's pulse accelerated. She gripped the arms of the chair, focusing on the man behind the desk and was struck by an odd, almost satisfied smile on Lash's face. Reluctantly, she accepted the fact that he was privy to secrets about their lives she wished he did not know. It made her feel vulnerable, and vulnerability was a weakness Rubans were not allowed to feel. She watched as Marlow shifted in his seat and straightened the papers in front of him. It was the will. Delaney's will.

Fresh tears spiked her lashes as she struggled with composure, trying to come to terms with the fact that Delaney was dead. He'd been such a large and vital man that overlooking his age had been simple. But nature had not been as kind. Despite his ebullient personality and lust for life, the past eighty-two years had taken their toll. And no matter how hard he had tried to ignore the inevitable, he had failed.

Ultimately, Lash began to read and Casey's mind wandered, only now and then tuning in on his voice as it droned into the ominous quiet of the room. Once in a while a low murmur of voices became noticeable behind her, and she supposed Miles and Erica were voicing their opinions of the bequeathals being read.

"And to my beloved granddaughter, Casey Dee Ruban..."

Casey shook off the fugue in which she'd been hanging and focused.

"...the bulk of my estate and the home in which she's been residing since her parents' death, as well as the controlling reins of Ruban Enterprises. But to inherit..."

Startled, her gaze slid from the papers in Lash's hands to his face. What did he mean...to inherit? Have mercy, what has Delaney done?

"To qualify for the entire aforementioned inheritance, my granddaughter, Casey Dee Ruban, must marry within forty-eight hours of the reading of my will, and must live with her husband, in his residence and under his protection, for the duration of at least one year, or she will forfeit her birthright. If she chooses not to adhere to my last request, then the bulk of my estate will be deeded to my step-grandchildren, Miles and Erica Dunn."

Casey stood. Rage, coupled with a shock she couldn't deny made her shake, but the tremor never reached her voice. She looked at Lash: at his cool, handsome face, his blond, wavy hair, his pale green eyes. Her eyes darkened as she leaned forward, bracing herself against his desk.

"Surely I cannot be held to this!"

To his credit, Lash's gaze never wavered. "I'm sorry, Casey. I know this must come as a shock, but I can assure you it's legal. Your grandfather was of sound mind and body when this was written. I tried to talk him out of such an unreasonable clause, but..."

When Lash shrugged, as if to say it was out of his hands, she looked away.

Someone choked in the back of the room. Casey didn't have to look to know that it was probably Miles, reveling in his unexpected windfall.

A red haze swam before her eyes and she willed herself not to faint. Marry? She hadn't seriously dated a man in over five years. The only man who persisted in being a part of her life was...

She looked up. The expression on Lash's face was too calm, almost expectant. How long had he known about this? Even worse, what had he and Delaney planned?

She swayed, staggered by the idea of being bound to Lash Marlow by law, as well as in the eyes of God, even for so much as a year.

Lash stood. His voice was low, his touch solicitous as he tried to take her in his arms.

"Casey, I'm here. Let me help you—"

She stepped back. The selfish glitter in Lash's eyes was too obvious to ignore.

Damn you, Delaney, damn you to hell.

She walked out of the room, leaving those behind to wonder what the outcome might be.

Hours later, the sun was about to set on the day as a low-slung black sports car rounded the corner of an unpaved road down in the flatlands. The trailing rooster tail of dust was evidence of how fast the car was traveling. The skid the car took as it cornered was proof of Casey Ruban's desperate state of mind. She'd been driving for hours, trying to think of a way out of her dilemma without having to acquiesce to the terms of her grandfather's will.

By naming Miles and Erica as the recipients of his estate should she default, Delaney had been certain Casey would comply. He'd been well aware of her disdain for the sycophantic life-style her half brother and half sister had chosen to live. They were thirty years old. Both had college degrees. Neither saw fit to use them.

Therefore, he had surmised that Casey would ultimately agree to his conditions. And he also knew Casey had no special man in her life, which would most certainly make Lash the prime candidate to fulfill the terms of the will. But he hadn't counted on Casey's total defiance, or the wild streak of rebellion that had driven her deep into the Mississippi Delta.

A short while later, the sun was gone and it was the time of evening when the world existed in shades of gray, faded by distance or muted by overlying shadows. Ahead, Casey could just make out the blinking lights on what appeared to be a roadhouse.

The fact that Sonny's Place was in the middle of nowhere was of no consequence to her. What mattered were the number of cars and pickup trucks parked outside the building. It stood to reason there would be a large number of men inside.

Blinking back a fresh set of angry tears, she gritted her teeth, focusing on the decision she'd made. As she accelerated, her fingers gripped the steering wheel until her knuckles turned white.

She turned into the parking lot in a skid, slamming on her brakes and barely missing a truck parked beneath the widespread limbs of an ancient oak. Gravel spewed, spit out from beneath the wheels of her sports car like a bad taste.

Casey killed the engine and was out of the car before the dust had time to settle. There was a defiant tilt to her chin and determination in her stride as she started toward the entrance, yet when she stepped inside, a moment of unrefined terror swamped her. Dank air, thick smoke and the scent of stale beer hit her in the face like a slap. And then Lash's smirk flashed in her mind and she let the door swing shut behind her.

Ryder Justice sat with his back to the wall, nursing the same beer he'd bought over an hour earlier. He hadn't really wanted the drink, he'd just wanted a place to sit down.

The months and the miles since he'd walked out on his family and his business had long ago run together. He didn't know what day it was and didn't really care. All that mattered was staying on the move. It was the only way he knew to stay ahead of the memories that had nearly driven him insane.

A few words with the man at the next table had assured him he'd be sleeping on the ground again tonight. He was too far from a town to rent a room, and too nearly broke to consider wasting the money.

A grimy ceiling fan spun overhead, stirring the hot, muggy air without actually cooling it. He lifted the long-neck bottle, intent on draining what was left in one swallow when the door flew open and the woman walked into the room. Her appearance was sudden, as was the swift jolt of interest he felt when she lifted her hand to her face, pushing at the black tangle of her windblown hair that had fallen across her forehead.

She was taller than average, and the kind of woman who, at first glance, seemed on the verge of skinny. Except for the voluptuous curves of her breasts beneath the black, clinging fabric of her dress, she appeared shapeless. And then she turned suddenly, startled by the man who came in behind her, and as she did, the dress she was wearing flared, cupping slim, shapely hips before falling back into loose, generic folds.

Ryder's interest grew. It was fairly obvious that she wasn't the kind of woman who frequented places like this. Her movements were short, almost jerky, as if she were as surprised to find herself here as the men were to see her. And although he was some distance away, he thought she looked as if she'd been crying.

Who hurt you, pretty girl? What drove you into the flatlands?

The beer forgotten, he leaned forward, studying her face as one might study a map, wondering what—or who—had backed her into a corner. And he was certain she'd been backed into a corner or she wouldn't be here. He knew the look of desperation. It stared back at him every time he looked in a mirror. And like every other man in the place, he sat with anticipation, waiting for her to make the first move.

A half dozen dirty yellow lightbulbs dangled from a sagging fixture in the middle of the room. Only four of the bulbs were burning, cloaking the fog of cigarette smoke and dust with a sickly amber glow.

Heads turned and the understated rumble of voices trickled to a halt as Casey's eyes slowly adjusted to the lack of light. When she was certain she'd seen the location of every man in the place, she took a deep breath and sauntered into the middle of the room, well aware that each man was mentally stripping her—from the black silk dress flaring just above her knees to the opaque black stockings on her legs.

Behind her, she heard the bartender gasp then mutter the name Ruban. She'd been recognized! Her lips firmed. It would seem that even down here in the Delta she was unable to escape the power of Delaney Ruban's name.

Smoke drifted, burning her eyes and searing her nostrils with the acrid odor, yet she refused to move away. She turned slowly, judging the faces before her, looking for a man who might have the guts to consider what she was about to ask.

The bartender interrupted her train of thought.

"Miss, is there something I can do? Are you having car trouble? If you are, I'd be more than glad to call a tow truck for you."

There was nervous fear on the bartender's face. Casey knew just how he felt. Her own stomach was doing a few flops of its own. She shivered anxiously, and at that point, almost walked out of the room. But as she turned to go, the image of Lash Marlow's face slid into her mind. It was all the impetus she needed. She turned again, this time putting herself between the men and the door.

"I need something all right," Casey said, and when she heard her voice break, she cleared her throat and took a deep breath. This time when she spoke, her words came out loud and clear. "I don't need a tow truck. I need a man."

The bartender grabbed a shotgun from beneath the bar and jacked a shell into the chamber as the room erupted.

Wide-eyed, Casey spun toward the sound.

The appearance of the gun was enough to quiet the ruckus she'd started, but only momentarily. When the bartender began to speak, she knew her chances of succeeding were swiftly fading.

"Hold your seats, men. That there is Casey Ruban. Old Delaney Ruban's granddaughter, so unless you're real tired of living, I suggest you suck it up and stay where you're at. This shotgun won't do nearly as much harm to you as the Rubans can."

"I heard he's dead," someone muttered from the back of the room.

"But the rest of them aren't," the bartender said.

Casey spun toward the men in sudden anger. "Let me finish."

At that point, they were so caught up in what she'd said, they would have let her do anything she asked.

"I need a husband."

Someone cursed, another laughed a little nervously.

Casey chose to ignore it all. "I'm willing to marry the first unattached man who's got the guts to stand with me against my family."

When no one moved or spoke, hope began to die. This was a crazy idea, as crazy as what Delaney had done to her, but she couldn't bring herself to quit. Not yet.

With an overwhelming sense of hopelessness and a shame unlike anything she'd ever known, she lifted her head, selling herself in the only way she knew how. She started walking, moving between the tables, staying just out of reach of the daring men's grasp.

"I'll live with you. Cook your food. I'll even share your bed."

Total silence reigned and Casey could hear their harsh, rasping breaths as they considered taking her to bed and suffering the consequences. If this hadn't been so pitiful, she would have smiled. It would seem that Delaney was going to win after all.

A sound came out of the shadows. The sound of chair legs scraping against the grit and dirt on the old wooden floor, and the unmistakable rap of boot heels marking off the distance between Casey and the back of the room. She squinted against the smoke and the harsh, overhead glare, trying to see, and then when she did, felt an overwhelming urge to run.

The man had *don't care* in his walk and the coldest eyes she'd ever seen. Their deep gray-blue cast was the color of a Mississippi sky running before a storm front. An old, olive drab duffel bag hung awkwardly on the breadth of his shoulders, as if it had to find a place of its own somewhere between the chip and the weight of the world.

He was tall, his clothing worn and ragged. But it was the still expression on his tanned, handsome face that gave her pause.

Before she had time to consider the odds of winding up facedown and dead in a ditch at some murderer's hands, he was standing before her.

Casey took a deep breath. Murderer be damned. Her grandfather had already signed her fate. At least she was going to be the one who controlled the strings to which it was attached.

"Well?" she asked, and surprised herself by not flinching when he reached out and brushed at a wild strand of hair that had been stuck to her cheek.

Ryder Justice was surprised by the vehemence in her voice. He'd been around long enough to know when someone was afraid. From the moment she'd walked into the room, her fear had been palpable, yet just now when he'd touched her, she hadn't blinked. And the power in her voice told him there was more to her backbone than the soft, silky skin obviously covering it. He also knew what it felt like to be backed into a corner, and for some reason this woman was as far in a hole as a person could get and not be buried. And, he was tired of running. So damned tired he couldn't think.

"Well, what?" he asked.

Casey's breath caught on a gasp. His voice was low and deep and an image of him whispering in her ear shattered what was left of her composure. Hang in there, she warned herself, then lifted her chin.

"I asked a question. Do you have an answer?"

Ryder touched the side of her cheek and felt an odd sense of pride when, once again, she stood without flinching.

"About the only thing I have to my name is guts. If that's all you need, then I'm your man."

"Hey, man, you don't know what you're getting yourself into," the bartender warned.

Ryder's gaze never wavered from Casey Ruban's face.

Once again, his voice broke the quiet, wrapping around Casey's senses and making her shake from within.

"I know enough," he said.

"My name is Casey Ruban," she said. "What's yours?"

"Ryder Justice."

Justice! Casey took it as a sign. Justice was exactly what she'd been searching for.

"You swear you are free to marry?"

He nodded.

"My grandfather always said his handshake was as good as his word," Casey said, and offered her hand.

Without pause, Ryder enfolded it within the breadth of his own and once again, Casey felt herself being swallowed whole. Her gaze centered on their hands entwined and she had a sudden image of their bodies in similar positions. She bit her lip and stifled a shudder. Now was not the time to get queasy. She had an empire to save.

"Come with me," she said shortly. "We have a little over twenty-four hours to get blood tests, apply for a license, and find a justice of the peace."

At the mention of haste, his gaze instinctively drifted toward her belly partially concealed beneath the loose-fitting dress.

Once, being an unwed mother might have horrified Casey. Now she wished that was all she was facing.

"Wrong guess, Mr. Justice. It's just that I've got myself in a race with the devil, and I don't like to lose."

Ryder followed without comment. He'd been on a first-name basis with the old hound himself for some time now. He never thought to consider the fact that the devil was giving someone else a hard time as well.

The room erupted into a roar as they stepped outside, and Casey found herself all but running toward her car. Only after she slid behind the wheel and locked them in did she feel safe. And then she glanced toward the man beside her and knew she was fooling herself.

His presence dwarfed the sports car's interior. He scooted

the seat as far back as it would go and still his knees were up against the dash. The duffel bag he'd had on his shoulders was now between his feet, and Casey imagined she could hear the rhythmic thud of his heartbeat as he turned a cool, calculating gaze her way.

"Buckle up, Mr. Justice."

He reached for the seat belt out of reflex, then gave Casey another longer, calculating look.

"I have a question," he said.

Casey's heart dropped. *Please stranger, don't back out on me now.*

"I have one for you, too," she said quickly.

"Ladies first."

She almost smiled. "Do you have a home? Do you have a job?"

His expression blanked, and Casey would have sworn she saw pain on his face before he answered.

"I don't have an address or a job. Does it matter?"

She thought fast, remembering the conditions of the will. She had to live in her husband's residence and under his protection. This was good news. It was something she could control.

"Do you have a driver's license?" she asked.

He nodded.

"Good, then you're hired."

He cocked an eyebrow as Casey started the car.

"Exactly what have I been hired to do?"

"You're going to be the new chauffeur for the Ruban family. You... I mean...we...will live in the apartment over the garage on Delaney's...I mean, on my estate."

Ryder frowned. "Lady, I have to ask. Why marry a stranger?"

She backed out of the parking lot, the tires spinning on loose gravel as she drove onto the road, heading back the same way she'd come.

"Because I will be damned before I let myself be forced into marriage with a man I can't abide."

He wondered about the man she'd obviously left behind. "You don't know me. What if you can't abide me, either?"

Her gaze was fixed on the patch of road visible in the twin beams of her headlights.

"Living a year with a total stranger is better than living one night under Lash Marlow's roof. Besides, I don't like to be told what to do."

So, his name is Lash Marlow. This time Ryder did smile, but only a little.

"Casey."

Startled by the sound of her name on his lips, she turned her gaze from the road to his face.

"What?"

"I think you should try calling me Ryder. I've never gone to bed with a woman who called me Mister, and I don't intend to start now."

Gone to bed with...!

Almost too late she remembered what she was doing and swerved to avoid the ditch at which she was heading. By the time she had the car and herself under control, she was too desperate to argue the point.

First things first. Marriage. Then rules. After that, take it one day at a time. It was the only way she knew.

Chapter 2

There was something to be said for the power of the Ruban name. It had gotten Casey and Ryder through blood tests without an appointment, gotten a court clerk out of bed and down to the county courthouse in the middle of the night to issue a marriage license, then dragged an old family friend out of bed before sunrise to perform the impromptu ceremony. The waiting period most people would have experienced was waived for Delaney Ruban's granddaughter.

"You all take yourselves a seat now," Sudie Harris said, and pulled her housecoat a little tighter across her chest. "Judge will be here directly."

Casey dropped into the nearest chair, well aware that Harmon Harris's wife had taken one look at Ryder Justice and found him lacking in both worth and substance. When Ryder refused a seat and walked to the window instead, something about the way he was standing made her nervous. What if he was already sorry he'd gotten into this mess? What if he was thinking about leaving? Nervously, she got up.

"Mr. Justice, I—"

He turned and she choked on her words. He was so big. So menacing. So much a stranger. What in God's name had she done?

"What did you call me?" he asked.

She swallowed and the lump in her throat seemed to be getting larger by the minute. Oh, Lord. "Ryder. I meant to say, Ryder."

His eyes narrowed thoughtfully. Casey Ruban was on the verge of a breakdown. She might not know it, but he recognized the signs. Her eyes were feverishly bright and the knuckles on her fingers had gone from red to white from the fists that she'd made. Add to that, a breathing pattern that was little more than a series of short, quick gasps, and he figured it wouldn't take much for her to fall apart.

"That's better," he said shortly. "Now sit down before you fall down."

Casey did as she was told and then tried not to look at his backside as he turned away. It was impossible. In a few short minutes she would be tied to this man as she'd never been bound before, not only by law, but in the closest of proximity. Wife! Dear God, she was going to be that man's wife.

She watched as he shrugged his shoulders in a quiet, almost weary gesture, rubbing at his neck and massaging the muscles with long, brown fingers. She couldn't quit staring at his hands. Out of nowhere a random thought came barreling into her sleep-starved mind. *I wonder if he's a gentle lover.*

Startled, she shuddered and looked away, wishing Judge Harris would hurry. She doubted there was little about Ryder Justice that was gentle, and the tension between them was making her crazy.

Torn between the fear that she was jumping into a worse mess than the one she was already in, and fear that at the last minute he wouldn't go through with the ceremony, she wanted to cry. Instead, she closed her eyes. All I want to do is go to bed and sleep for a month, then wake up and find out this was all a bad dream, she thought.

Somewhere in another part of the house a clock chimed

five times. Startled, she glanced at her watch. Five o'clock!
In a little over an hour the sun would be up. Footsteps
sounded on the stairwell behind them. She stood and turned
to face the man who was entering the room.

From Harmon Harris's expression, he was none too pleased
to see who awaited him. "Casey Dee, what on earth are you
doin' here in the middle of the night?"

"Getting married, and it's not the middle of the night, it's
almost dawn."

Regardless of whether it was night or day, Ruban women
did not sneak around to get married, and Harmon knew it. He
stared at the man near his living room window, then glared
at Casey.

"Not to him?"

She gritted her teeth, preparing herself for a fight.

"Yes sir, to him. We have blood tests and the license right
here." She thrust the papers into the judge's hands.

When he noted the dates he frowned, staring at her hard
and long, from her head to the middle of her belly. Like Ryder
before him, Harmon was assuming the only reason a woman
would rush into marriage was to give a bastard child a name.

"Hell, girl, the ink is hardly dry on this stuff. What's the
big rush?"

"You can get that look off your face," Casey muttered.
"I'm not pregnant. I haven't even been exposed."

Bushy eyebrows lowered over his prominent nose as Harmon Harris laid the papers to one side and took Casey by the
arm.

"I've known you a long time, Honey, and this isn't like
you. Before I perform any ceremony, I want an explanation."

Casey's gaze never wavered. "If Delaney were alive, you
could ask him yourself. All I know is, I had forty-eight hours
to find myself a husband or forfeit my inheritance to Miles
and Erica."

The judge's eyebrows rose perceptibly. "You're joking!"

Her shoulders slumped. "I wish I were."

He glanced over her shoulder to Ryder. "I don't understand."

Then his voice lowered. "Why not marry Lash Marlow? You've known him nearly all your life. Why this man?"

"Because he's not Lash."

The judge didn't comment. He didn't have to. Casey's answer pretty much said it all.

"Who is he?"

"His name is Ryder Justice."

"I know that," the judge said. "It says so on the papers. What I'm asking is *who* are his people?"

Casey shrugged. "I haven't the faintest idea, and quite frankly I don't care. What I do know is I will not be coerced, especially by a dead man, into marrying someone I do not even like, never mind the fact that I don't love him. Do you understand that?"

Suddenly Casey and Harmon realized they were no longer alone.

"Is there a problem?" Ryder asked.

There was something about the look on the big man's face that made Harmon Harris release his grasp on Casey's arms.

Harmon sighed. "No, I don't suppose there is. Casey is of age and enough of her own woman to do as she chooses." He turned. "Sudie, go next door and wake up Millard Shreves. We're gonna need ourselves another witness."

Casey relaxed as Judge Harris's wife hurried to do his bidding. It was going to be all right.

"It will take Millard a bit to get out of bed," the judge explained. "If you two want to freshen up before the ceremony, the guest bath is down the hall on your right. However, you're going to have to excuse me for a bit. I'm going to be needing some coffee."

Having put the wheels in motion, he left Casey and Ryder alone in the Harris parlor with Sudie's crocheted doilies and silk flower bouquets.

Casey put a hand to her hair, feeling the disarray. She started to the bathroom for a quick wash then remembered

Ryder. Was it safe to leave him alone, or would he bolt at
the first chance he got? She glanced back at him, and to her
dismay realized he was watching her. It was almost as if he'd
read her mind.

"Go on," he said. "I'll be here when you get back."

There was something compelling about this man, something she couldn't quite name. There was a strength within
him that a couple of days' worth of whiskers and a faded
T-shirt and jeans could not hide. Right now his eyes seemed
blue, although at first they'd seemed gray. Their color was as
changeable as the weather. She hoped his disposition did not
seesaw as well and knew she was staring, but she couldn't
help it. Although she was afraid of what he might tell her,
there was something she needed to know.

"Why did you agree to go along with this madness?"

His expression hardened. "Don't dig too deep, Casey. You
might find worms in the dirt you're taking out of the hole."

Startled, she pivoted and headed for the bathroom, telling
herself it was exhaustion that was making her shake, and not
the implied warning in his words.

"...pronounce you man and wife. What God has joined
together, let no man put asunder."

Judge Harris's clock began to chime.

Once. Twice. Three times it sounded.

Casey exhaled slowly.

Four times. Five times. Six times the gong echoed within
the silence of the room.

She went limp, and were it not for the firm grip Ryder had
on her arm, she wouldn't have been able to stand. But she'd
done it. It was over! The Ruban empire was safe, but dear
God, could she say the same about herself?

"Congratulations. You may kiss your bride," Harmon
added, although he doubted, considering the reasons for the
ceremony, there was much to celebrate.

Both Ryder and Casey stared, first at Judge Harris who'd
just granted permission for something neither had been pre-

pared to act upon, then at each other as they contemplated the deed.

To Casey's dismay, her vision blurred.

Ryder had intended on holding his ground until he saw her tears. It was her weakness, rather than the bulldog determination with which she'd gotten them this far, that made him do what he did next. He'd entered into this farce without giving a thought for consequences, much the same way he used to go through life. But that was before he'd killed his father and lost his nerve to fly.

Intending only to assure her, he cupped her cheek with the palm of one hand, gentling her much in the same way his brother, Royal, tended the horses on his ranch, giving them time to adjust to his presence.

"Easy, now," he said softly, and when he felt her pulse beginning to slow, he lowered his head.

Casey saw him coming. Her lips parted. Whether it was to voice an objection or to ease his way, Ryder didn't know and didn't care. His focus was on her mouth and the woman who now bore his name.

Casey's breath caught at the back of her throat and this time, had Ryder not been holding her up, her legs would have given way. Whatever her intent had been, it stopped along with her heart when Ryder Justice kissed his wife.

It should have been awkward—their first joining—but it wasn't. The ease with which they touched, then the gentleness with which the kiss deepened felt right, even familiar. At the point of embracing, the judge's voice broke their connection.

"Well, now," he said, and made no attempt to hide a yawn. "I suppose you two are as hitched as a couple can be."

When Ryder moved away, Casey felt a sudden sense of loss, and then reality intruded and she felt nothing but dismay. She had no intentions of pursuing the intimate part of a marriage and the sooner Ryder Justice realized that, the better off they would be. She stepped back, then turned away, unwilling to let him see how deeply she'd been affected by what he'd done.

"It served its purpose," she said shortly, and started looking for her purse. "What do I owe you?"

While she was fumbling for cash, Ryder was dealing with uneasiness of his own. The kiss was supposed to have been nothing but a formality. He hadn't expected to feel anything because it had been months since he'd allowed himself the luxury. But something had happened to him between the time her breath had brushed his cheek and their point of contact. Left with nothing but a lingering dissatisfaction he couldn't identify, he, too, turned away. It was almost as if he'd left something undone. He hadn't been prepared for what the kiss had evoked—what it felt like to hold someone close, the pleasure that comes from lying in a willing woman's arms.

He inhaled slowly and considered the woman who was now his wife, if in name only. He had agreed to marry her and no matter what, he was a man of his word. But he didn't want to like her. There was already a time limit on their relationship. God forbid his feelings should ever go deeper.

Casey said something that made the judge laugh and Ryder turned to see what was funny. Instead of an answer, he found himself watching as Casey peeled five twenty-dollar bills from a wad of cash in her handbag and handed them to the judge. He frowned, then looked away, uncomfortable with the fact that a woman was paying his way for anything, and more than a little bit anxious as to how he was supposed to fit into her life. He had already suspected she came from money. Her car and her clothes had given her away, and the money she stuffed back in her purse only confirmed his suspicions.

For the first time since he'd run away, he thought about what he'd left behind, yet not once did he consider confessing his true background and identity to Casey.

She thought she'd married a bum, a no-account drifter without a penny to his name. His eyes narrowed as he stared out into the burgeoning dawn. Part of it was true. He didn't have two quarters with him that he could rub together. At this point, the fact that he owned four airplanes and a helicopter, and that his charter service had been in the black for nearly eleven years didn't matter. Nor did the fact that the deed to nearly fourteen hundred acres of prime real estate on the outskirts of San Antonio was in his name.

Sick at heart from an accident he couldn't forget, he'd walked away from it all. Things of monetary value had become unimportant to Ryder. If he could have, he would have given up everything just to have his father back alive and well.

But there would be no trading with God...or the devil. Micah Justice was dead and buried, and no matter how far Ryder went, he couldn't outrun his guilt.

Someone cleared their throat. He looked up. It would seem that Sudie was patiently waiting to lock them out. Casey held the front door ajar. Her posture and the tone of her voice gave away her impatience.

"Are you ready to go?" she asked.

Something inside him snapped. The quiet in which he'd encompassed himself over the past few months suddenly seemed too confining. Sarcasm colored his answer.

"I don't know, Mrs. Justice, are you?"

Her bossy, managerial attitude disappeared like air out of a punctured balloon. He had the satisfaction of seeing her pale as he walked past her and out the door.

The air was muggy, a promise of another long, hot July day. Sweat was already rolling down the middle of Casey's back and there was a snag in her stockings. Since yesterday when she'd made her exit from Lash's office, her hairdo had been windblown and finger-combed a dozen times. The last time she remembered putting on makeup was right before she'd gotten out of the car to go into the office for the reading of the will. She felt like hell and figured she looked a shade or two worse. She was exhausted and couldn't wait to get home and into a bed.

But thirty minutes outside of Ruban Crossing, Casey's plans were about to change. The flashing red-and-blue lights of a Mississippi highway patrol were an unwelcome addition to the events of the day. She had expected complications, but not quite so soon, or from the state police. She looked at Ryder, then began pulling over to the side of the road.

"I wasn't speeding," she said.

Ryder glanced over his shoulder, then started unbuckling his seat belt. The highway patrolman was already out of his vehicle with his gun drawn, and although the air conditioner was on and Casey's car windows were up, they could hear him shouting for them to get out of the car.

"I don't think that's the problem."

"What do you mean?" Casey asked, and turned. There was a gun pointed straight at her head.

"Get out of the car!" the patrolman shouted again. "Do it! Do it now!"

Stunned by the order, Casey began fumbling with her seat belt, but couldn't seem to find the catch. The harder she tried, the worse her fingers shook, and the longer she delayed, the louder and more insistent the officer became.

"Let me," Ryder said, and to her relief, the latch gave way, freeing her from the straps.

She opened the door. "Look, Officer, I don't know what…"

"Get out and put your hands on the hood of the car! You!" he shouted, pointing the gun at Ryder. "On the passenger side! Come around the front of the car with your hands in the air!"

Ryder didn't argue. He'd learned years ago never to argue with an armed man, especially one wearing a badge.

By now, Casey was out of the car and furious. "What's the meaning of this?"

Handcuffs snapped. First one on her right wrist, then the remaining cuff on her other.

"Sit down," the officer ordered, pushing Casey none too gently to a seat beside the rear wheel of her car before proceeding to cuff Ryder in the same smooth manner. He hauled Ryder off to the back seat of his patrol car and shut him inside while Casey watched in disbelief.

"This better be good," Casey said, as the officer returned and helped her to her feet.

"You're driving a stolen car and the woman who owns it has been reported missing."

Casey couldn't believe what she was hearing. "*I* am not missing, and *this* is my car."

The officer took a long, slow look at the disheveled woman in black and didn't bother to hide a smirk.

"That car belongs to Casey Ruban. Her family reported her missing when she didn't come home last night."

"I repeat, this is my car, and I didn't go home because I was out getting myself married," she said.

"Excuse me?" the officer asked.

She closed her eyes, counted to ten, then glared at the patrolman, derisively enunciating each syllable.

"Married. Capital *m*—little *a*—double *r*—*i*—*e*—*d*... Married. Last night...no, actually it was early this morning that we got married. You might say I've been on my honeymoon and you..." she frowned against the glare of early morning sun, peering at the name tag on the front of his uniform "...Officer Howard, have just stuffed my groom in the back of your patrol car. I want him out, and I want the handcuffs taken off both of us now, or I swear to God I will have your badge and all that goes with it."

Her adamancy startled the cop, and for the first time since he'd pulled them over, he began to consider the possibility of having been wrong in his first assumption. But he'd been so focused on being the one to get a lead on the missing heir that he hadn't followed protocol by asking for their identification first.

"I'll need to see some identification," he said.

"It's in my purse in the front seat, along with a copy of my marriage license. Want to see that, too?"

He unlocked her cuffs and opened the door. "No funny business," he said shortly, as Casey leaned inside.

She handed him the marriage license, her driver's license, as well as the title to her car. "There's nothing funny about

any of this, and when I get home, I'm going to have someone's hide for this.''

The officer looked long and hard at the picture on the
driver's license and then at Casey. There was little resemblance between the cool, composed woman in the picture and
the fiery-eyed hellion standing before him.

Casey could see he still wasn't buying her explanation, but
she wasn't about to explain the mess she was in, thanks to
her grandfather's will. She opted for something he would
probably believe.

''Oh, for God's sake,'' Casey snapped. ''I've been on my
honeymoon, okay? You try a wedding night in the back seat
of a car and see how good you look!''

The patrolman flushed with embarrassment as he began to
realize the seriousness of his situation. Unless he made peace
with this woman now, he could be in big trouble. The Ruban
name carried a lot of clout.

''Sorry, Miss Ruban…I mean uh…''

''Justice,'' Casey said. ''The name is Justice.'' She pointed
toward the cruiser. ''About my husband…''

Moments later, Ryder found himself standing by the side
of the road, watching as an officer of the law did everything
but crawl as an excuse for his overzealous behavior.

''Thank you for being so understanding,'' the officer said,
as Casey brushed at the dirt on the back of her dress.

''We'll call it even if you just don't notify my family,''
she said. ''I want to surprise them on my own.''

''Yes, ma'am. I'll just call this in to headquarters so you
won't be stopped again.''

''Fine,'' she said, and didn't bother to watch as he drove
away. When she glanced up at Ryder, he was grinning.

''What's so funny?'' she asked.

''You're hell on wheels, aren't you, wife?''

''Don't call me that,'' she said, and slammed herself bodily
into the seat behind the wheel.

Ryder was still grinning when he took the seat beside her.

"Want me to drive?" he asked. "After all, I'm going to be your chauffeur."

Her bottom lip slid slightly forward as she started the car, leaving the side of the road in a flurry of flying dust and gravel.

"I guess not," Ryder drawled, and then settled back into the passenger seat. The longer he was around this woman, the more he liked her. She reminded him a little bit of his brother, Roman, who chose to believe that laws and rules were made by men with too much time on their hands.

There was a pasty white sheen on Lash Marlow's face as he hung up the phone. He glanced at the clock over the mantel and swiped a shaky hand through his hair. It was almost noon. Time was running out.

His thoughts were jumbled as he considered the possibilities of where Casey might be. Damn Delaney for insisting on that forty-eight hour time frame. He'd told him from the start it wasn't a good idea, but Delaney had insisted, claiming he knew his granddaughter better than anyone. He'd sworn she would never adhere to the terms of the will unless pushed.

Lash felt sick. It seemed obvious that he and Delaney Ruban had pushed too much.

"Any news?" Eudora asked, and not for the first time wished she'd sat beside her youngest granddaughter during the reading of the will. She was still convinced she might have been able to soften the blow Casey had received. If she had, maybe they wouldn't have spent a sleepless night expecting the worst.

Lash shook his head and reached for another antacid. Instead, his fingers closed around the rabbit's foot in his pocket, and he rubbed it lightly, making a bet with himself that everything would be all right.

Taking comfort from his superstitious gesture, he decided to forego the antacid. It probably wouldn't help anyway. He was long past worry and far past panic. From the way his gut was burning, he was either starting a new ulcer or about to have a heart attack. He'd expected Casey to be difficult, but he hadn't expected this. If she didn't show up soon, it would be too late.

Miles lounged near the window overlooking the tennis courts, contemplating the party he would throw when he got his hands on the money. He was sick and tired of pretending to be worried about Casey. As far as he was concerned, she could stay gone. For the past six years, even if she was his sister, she'd been nothing but a judgmental little bitch, always harping at him and Erica to get jobs of their own.

Eudora paced back and forth, fanning herself with a dampened handkerchief. "I just can't bear this suspense. Oh dear. Oh dear."

Miles rolled his eyes. "Oh, let it rest, Grandmother. She'll come home when it suits her."

Eudora frowned as she fanned, although the small square of fabric did little to stir the air. "I'm just sick about this. What if something awful has happened?" When no one echoed her concern, she sank into a nearby chair, dabbing at her eyes. "Poor, dear Casey."

"Poor, dear Casey, my ass." Erica muttered, and sloshed a liberal helping of Jack Daniel's into her iced tea and sat down near her twin. Ice clinked against crystal as she swirled the liquid before lifting the glass to her mouth.

Lash glanced at his watch and dug his own handkerchief from his pocket, mopping at a fine line of perspiration that kept breaking out across his brow. Time was running out. If she didn't show soon, his worst fears would be realized. Miles and Erica would be in control of the Ruban fortune and Lash's dreams to resurrect the Marlow estate to its former glory would be dashed. At this moment he didn't know whom he hated worse—Delaney for causing the fuss, or Miles for the possum-eating grin he'd been wearing all day.

Never one to let a good silence extend itself, Eudora tucked her handkerchief into her cleavage and rang a small bell near her chair.

Moments later a tall, dark-skinned man dressed in virgin

whites entered the room. Still straight and handsome at sixty, the only evidence of Joshua Bass's age was the liberal dusting of gray in his hair.

"Yes, ma'am?"

Eudora pointed toward a nearby table. "Joshua, we're all out of tea."

"Yes, ma'am."

He picked up the tray and started out of the room when Eudora remembered.

"Oh, Joshua!"

He paused. "Yes, ma'am?"

"Have Tilly put some lemon in the tea this time. I do believe lemon helps cut the miasma of July."

Casey entered on the tail of Eudora's order, countermanding it with one of her own. She took the tray out of Joshua's hands and set it down, then to the continuing dismay of her family, gave him a huge, breathless hug, which he gladly returned.

Casey smiled up at Joshua, taking comfort in the love she saw there in his eyes. "Forget the tea, Joshie. Bring a bottle of Delaney's best champagne instead. We're going to toast my marriage."

Joshua looked startled, and his first thought was what his Tilly was going to say. Casey was as close to their hearts as if she'd been born of their blood and here she was about to drink to a marriage they knew she didn't want.

Miles's face turned an angry red. Erica choked on a piece of ice, and Eudora clasped her hands to her throat and started to cry.

As for Lash he went weak with relief. Not only was Casey back, but she seemed willing to celebrate their upcoming union with no remorse. He went toward her with outstretched hands.

"Casey, darling, I'm so glad you..."

And that was the moment they realized Casey had not come alone. The unexpected face of a stranger at Casey's back, never mind his trail-weary appearance, startled them all into sudden silence.

"Everyone...this is Ryder Justice." She glanced at Ryder. To her surprise, he seemed calm, almost disinterested. "Ryder—my family." She pointed them out, one by one, starting with Eudora. "This is my Gran." She glanced at Miles and Erica and the expressions on their faces said it all. She sighed. Some things never change. "The two beautiful blondes with the fabulous scowls are my brother and sister, Miles and Erica."

As she smiled at Joshua, her voice softened. "And this is Joshua Bass. He and his wife, Tilly, helped raise me."

Ryder nodded. "It's a pleasure, sir," he said quietly. "And, I'd say you and your wife have done a fine job. Casey is quite a woman."

She gave Ryder a quick look of surprise. The praise was unexpected.

Joshua grinned, pleased to have been recognized as part of the family.

"Casey, really! He's one of the help," Eudora said, and then flushed, embarrassed that she'd been put in the position of having to remark upon the differences in their stations in life.

Casey's chin jutted. "Unlike the majority of this family, Joshua has a job. I have a job as well. I fail to see the difference." Then she softened her rebuke by winking at Joshua. "Joshie, hurry and bring that champagne. We have some celebrating to do."

Lash had more on his mind than sipping champagne and social niceties. He glanced at his watch. There were a million things to do and so little time.

"Casey, dearest, we've been so worried. When you didn't come home last night I even called the state police. We all realize the will came as a terrible shock to you, but if you'd just waited a bit, I could have saved you from all this turmoil. You know how I feel about you. It was only a matter of time before you came to your senses and did what was best for everyone.''

When he reached for her hand, Casey took an instinctive step back, right into Ryder's arms.

"Easy," Ryder said softly, and Casey shivered. That was what he'd said earlier, right before he'd kissed her.

"I don't need saving," she told Lash. "And I've already come to my senses. I saved myself."

A nerve jerked at the side of Lash's eye, causing it to twitch. "What do you mean?"

Although Ryder was no longer touching Casey, she knew he was still behind her, and, oddly enough, it was his solid presence that gave her the courage to say what had to be said. She pulled the copy of their marriage license from her purse and handed it to Lash without batting an eye.

"Ryder and I were married this morning. I suppose you'll need this to confirm the legalities and finalize the edicts of the will."

"Married?"

The shriek came from across the room. Casey wasn't sure whether it was Miles or Erica who'd come undone, and she didn't much care.

The paper fell from Lash's fingers and onto the floor as shock spread across his face. Speech was impossible. All he could do was stare at the woman who'd dashed his last hopes. She seemed calm, even smug about what she'd done, and as he looked, he began to hate.

At this point, Joshua came back into the room with an uncorked bottle of champagne and a tray full of glasses. Casey took it from his hands.

"I'll pour while you go get Tilly. This won't be official until you two are in on my news. Also, will you please tell Bea to get the apartment over the garage ready. When it's cleaned, have someone move my things out there, okay?"

Joshua left with an anxious glance.

"Why on earth would you be doing such a thing?" Eudora asked.

Before Casey could respond, Ryder stepped to her side. For a moment, Casey had the sensation of what it would be like to never stand alone against this family again.

His voice was cool, his manner calm and assured. "Because a wife lives with her husband, and as of yesterday, I'm your new chauffeur, that's why."

Miles's snort of disbelief was echoed by his sister. "My God, Casey, marrying some ne'er-do-well is bad enough, but a chauffeur? Have you no shame?"

Ryder's expression underwent a remarkable change, from calm to quiet fury. He never took his eyes from Miles. "I don't care if he is your brother—do not expect me to like that little pig."

Casey almost laughed. The look of shock on her brother's face was priceless.

"You don't have to," she said, and then felt obligated to add, "but you can't hurt him."

Ryder gave Miles another cool stare, then took the champagne Casey handed him. "There's more than one way to skin a cat," he drawled, and gave Miles a cool, studied look. Then he lifted the glass toward her in a silent toast, pinning Casey with a stormy gaze that left her stunned.

"To justice," he said, letting them decide for themselves what he'd meant.

Chapter 3

After the family accepted the shock of Casey's news, there was one more person Casey needed to see. While Ryder was prowling through the garage and the cars that were to be under his control, she slipped into the kitchen in search of Matilda Bass. The need to lay her head on Tilly's shoulder was overwhelming. She hoped when she did, that she would manage not to cry.

And Tilly wasn't all that hard to find.

"Come here to me, girl," Tilly said, and opened her arms.

Casey walked into them without hesitation. "You didn't come drink champagne with me."

Tilly ignored the rebuke. She had her own idea of her place in this world and in spite of the money the Rubans had, she wouldn't have traded places with them for any of it. She had more self-esteem than to socialize with people who chose to look down on her because she cooked the food that they ate.

"Well now, what have you gone and done?" Tilly asked.

Her sympathy was almost Casey's undoing. "Saved us all, I hope," Casey replied.

Tilly frowned. She'd already heard through the family grapevine what a burden the old man Ruban had heaped on her baby's head.

"If you ask me, that old man needed his head examined," Tilly mumbled, stroking her hand gently up and down the middle of Casey's back.

Casey sighed. "Well, it's over and done with," she said.

Tilly stepped back, her dark eyes boring into Casey's gaze. "Nothing is ever over and done with, girl. Not while people draw breath. You be careful. I don't know why, but I don't like the feel of all this."

Casey managed a laugh. "Don't go all witchy on me, now. You know what Joshie says about you messin' with that kind of stuff."

Tilly sniffed. The reference to her mother's and grandmother's predilection for voodoo did not apply to her. "I do not indulge myself in the black arts and you know it," Tilly huffed.

Casey grinned and then gave Tilly a last, quick hug. "I know. I was only teasing." Then her laughter faded. "Say a prayer for me, Mammo."

Casey hadn't used that childhood name in years. It brought quick tears to Tilly's eyes, and because it was an emotion in which she rarely indulged, she was all the more brusque with her answer. "Knowing you, I'd better say two," she said, and gave Casey a swift swat on the rear. "Now you run on along. I've got dinner to fix before Joshua and I go on home."

Casey paused on her way out the door. "Tilly?"

"What, baby girl?"

"Have you ever regretted staying on here as cook? You and Joshua are so smart, you could have done a lot of other things besides wait on a small, selfish family."

Tilly turned, and the serious tone of her voice was proof of her sincerity. "Maybe I could have, but not my Josh. You've got to remember, he only hears good in one ear. That handicap lost him a whole lot of jobs early on in our marriage. By the time we landed here with your grandfather, he was glad to have the work. And Mr. Ruban was more than fair. Our pay is good. We have health insurance, something a lot of our friends do not. And, because your grandfather did not like change in his household, the incentive he gave us to stay on was to set up trusts for our retirement. Actually, we're better off than some other members of our family who have college degrees.'' And then she smiled. "Besides, I like to cook, and who else would have raised my baby if Josh and I hadn't been here?''

This time, Casey didn't bother to hide her tears. She wrapped her arms around Tilly's neck. "I love you, Mammo.''

"I love you, too, girl. Now run on home. You've got yourself a man to tend.''

Startled, Casey did as she was told, and after that, the day went surprisingly well.

Although Miles and Erica no longer had any hopes of attaining control of the Ruban fortune, their circumstances were still the same. Before, they had come and gone as they pleased, spent and slept at Delaney Ruban's expense. For them, nothing had changed.

As for Eudora, she'd sacrificed much for her dead daughter's children. Years ago she'd given up a suitor who could have made her golden years something to remember. She'd left her home on Long Island and came to Mississippi with the best of intentions. She refused to consider that she'd contributed to the ruination of her eldest grandchildren by coercing Delaney to leave their upbringing in her care when he'd begun to focus his attention on Casey.

She hadn't meant to make them so dependent on others, but it had happened anyway. And now that their life-styles were pretty much set in stone, she felt it her moral obligation to see that their comfort level stayed the same.

Yet when it came to sacrifices, it was Casey who'd sacrificed the most. Whatever dreams she might have harbored with regard to her personal life were gone. She was married to a stranger, and for the next twelve months, had resigned herself to the fact.

At her demand, Ryder had been sent into Ruban Crossing with a handful of money and orders as to what to buy, while she went in to the office. There was a merger pending and an entire factory of workers in Jackson, Mississippi who were waiting to learn if they still had their jobs. She didn't want another day to pass without assuring them. In fact, everything was running so smoothly it should have been the warning Casey needed, because when the sun went down, tempers began to rise.

Casey climbed the stairs leading to the garage apartment and tried not to think of her spacious bedroom across the courtyard; of her sunken bathtub and the cool, marble floor, or of her queen-size bed and the down-filled pillows of which she was so fond. Her stomach growled and she wondered what feast Tilly was concocting across the way for the evening meal. At this point, she began to consider the benefits she was losing by having to live under Ryder Justice's roof. Who would cook? Where did she put her dirty clothes?

Caution forbade her to use any of the services available across the way. From the expression on Lash Marlow's face when he'd left the house this morning, she knew his anger would not easily disappear. It would be just like him to try and catch her cheating on the terms of the will.

Oh, well, she thought. I can always order takeout and take my clothes to the cleaners.

She took out her key to open the door then found it already unlocked. Her pulse skipped a beat. That meant *he* was home. Quietly, so as not to alert the "tiger" who lurked within, she shut the door behind her and then stood, absorbing the sight of what was to be her home for the next twelve months.

The entire apartment consisted of three small rooms, the accumulation of which were still not the size of her bedroom inside the mansion. But it was clean, and blessedly quiet. For today, it was enough.

Just when she was beginning to relax, she noticed a man's shirt draped over an easy chair and a pair of dusty, black boots on the floor nearby. Reality set in.

Never one to put off what had to be done, she reminded herself that the sooner the confrontation began, the sooner it would be over. She sat her briefcase by the door and looked toward the bedroom. Since he wasn't in here, he had to be in there.

She walked inside. Several pairs of blue jeans lay on the bed, along with a half dozen white long-sleeved shirts, a new sport coat and a broad-brimmed black Stetson. A pile of her best lingerie was on the floor next to the dresser. She frowned, wondering why her things were on the floor.

She stared at the clothes. Where were the uniforms she'd told him to get? She'd given him the address of the place where they'd rented them before. Ruban Crossing was a fair-size city, but he'd had all afternoon to find one simple address.

She opened the closet. It was full of her clothing and nothing else. She looked back at the bed. That explained why he hadn't hung his up. Obviously, there was no place left for them to hang.

She turned around, eyeing the small room with distaste, then shrugged. Tomorrow, she'd go through her things and have Bea take part of them back to the main house. It was the least she could do.

A door creaked behind her. She spun and then froze. Ryder had obviously just had a bath. Steam enveloped him as he stepped out of the doorway and into the room with her, giving him the appearance of emerging from a cloud. His hair was spiky and still dripping water as he began to towel it dry.

Her thoughts tangled. Most men would appear smaller without benefit of clothing. But not him. He enveloped the space in which he moved, almost as if he took it with him as he went.

Casey frowned again, biting at the inside of her lip and wondering why she hadn't had the foresight to wait outside.

How would she ever get past the memory of this much man covered with such a small, insignificant towel?

"Sorry," Ryder said, and gave his hair a last, halfhearted rub before tossing the wet towel back into the bathroom floor. "Didn't know you were here."

Casey tilted her chin, determined he not know how shaken she was.

"Obviously," she said shortly, and then pointed toward the clothes on the bed. "I gave you money to get uniforms, not all this."

Ryder's eyes narrowed, and Casey knew the moment the words were out of her mouth that she'd ticked him off. He walked to a bedside table and withdrew a handful of money, then stuffed it in her hand.

"What's this?" Casey asked.

"Your money."

"But how did you pay for all this?"

He didn't answer, and she glared. But when he spun and started toward her, she took an instinctive step backward. When he bypassed her for the dresser beyond, she caught herself breathing a small sigh of relief. Determined to get to the bottom of his behavior, she struck again, only this time with more venom.

"I asked you a question," she snapped.

Her relief was short-lived. When he turned, the anger on his face almost stopped her heart.

"Don't go there," he said quietly.

"Go where? I don't know what you mean."

"There's one thing we'd better get straight right now. I don't take orders from you, and I don't take your money. I pay my own way."

She couldn't imagine how he'd obtained the clothes. For all she knew he might have stolen the stuff. She would have been shocked to know he had a gold credit card with an unlimited line. And, if she'd known, would have been even more surprised to learn he hadn't used it in months.

"But the uniforms...why didn't you do as you were told?"

As far as Ryder was concerned, what was in his past was none of her business. Suddenly he was right in front of her. His breath was hot, his words angry.

"Because you're not my boss, you're my wife. I gave you my name, and I'll drive you and yours anywhere they please for the next twelve months, but I'm not wearing a damned monkey suit to do it."

Casey's mouth dropped. Never in her entire life had anyone had the gall to defy her in such a manner. Before she could think of a comeback, he turned away, opened the top drawer of the dresser, withdrew a brand-new pair of white cotton briefs and dropped his towel.

She bolted, taking with her the image of a long-limbed body that was hard and fit and brown all over.

A few minutes later he emerged from the bedroom in his bare feet, wearing an old and faded pair of jeans and no shirt. The casual are-you-still-here glance he gave her made her furious.

Disgusted with herself for not standing her ground, she watched from across the room as he sauntered into the kitchen and opened the refrigerator. When he bent down to look inside, the urge to hit him was so strong it startled her. She was not the type of woman to resort to violence. Then she rescinded her own opinion of herself. At least she *hadn't* been. But that was before she'd driven into the flatlands and brought out a husband.

He set a package of raw hamburger meat on the counter then went back to the refrigerator. She didn't know what angered her most, the fact that he was being deliberately mutinous, or that she was being ignored.

Smoothing her hands down the front of her blue summer suit, she tossed back her hair and slipped into the sarcastic mode she used to keep Miles and Erica at bay.

"Are you finished?" she drawled, wanting the bathroom all to herself.

Ryder straightened, looking at her from across the open refrigerator door. He stared at her, from the top of her hair to the open toes of her sling-back pumps. A slight grin tilted the corner of his mouth as he stepped back and closed the door.

His thoughts went to the year stretching out before them, considering which one of them would be the first to break. "Finished?" he muttered. "We haven't even started."

With that, he moved toward her.

Panic came swiftly and Casey wondered if the family would be able to hear her scream from here. She held up her hand in a warning gesture.

"Don't you dare!" she said, and winced at the squeak in her voice.

She was scared! The fact surprised him. She'd walked into a bar with a roomful of strange men and offered herself up as a golden goat without batting an eye. She'd roused a doctor, a county clerk and a judge out of bed to do her bidding. She'd stared down a roomful of antagonistic relatives and kept a lawyer out of her pants who seemed to have had his own hidden agenda, and she was suddenly scared? And of him? It didn't make sense. He hadn't done anything to warrant this. Yet when he might have eased her fears, he found himself letting them grow.

When he got within inches of her stark, white face, he realized why. This woman, who was his wife, was damned pretty. In fact, if a man didn't get picky about that little bitty mole at the left corner of her lips, she was beautiful.

Sexually, he was a starving man and this woman was legally his wife. Although he'd cut himself off from everyone he cared for, he'd been unable to cut off the emotions of a normal, red-blooded man. Keeping her slightly afraid was a safe way of keeping her at arms' length. Yet when her eyes widened fearfully and her color rose, he relented.

"Easy," he said. "All I need to know is how you like it and do you want more than one?"

She would have sworn that her heart shot straight up her throat and she had to swallow several times to work up enough spit to be able to speak. *More than one? Oh my God!*

"I don't think you understand the situation here," she stuttered.

"What? Don't tell me you don't eat meat."

Her face flushed as she thought of his lean, bare body. "Eat? Meat?"

"Do you like hot and red, slightly pink, or hard as a rock?"

Her eyes widened even more and her voice began to quiver. "I don't do things like that," she whispered, and put her hand to her throat, unconsciously stifling that scream she'd been considering.

He frowned. Things like what? All he needed to know was if she wanted... And then it dawned on him what interpretation she'd put on their conversation. He stifled a grin and pointed back to the counter.

"Are you telling me you don't do hamburgers?"

"Hamburgers?"

He went straight past her and out a small side door onto the attached deck above the driveway, opened the lid to a smoking barbecue grill, checked the coals, then let the lid drop back down with a clank.

"The charcoal is ready." He headed back toward the kitchen, pausing at the package of hamburger. "One last chance. Do you want one hamburger or two, and how do you want it cooked?"

There was a silly grin on her face as she slumped to the floor in a dead faint.

Ryder sat in the room's only chair, watching as Casey began to regain consciousness. The sofa he'd laid her on was a small, two-cushion affair, and he'd been forced to make the decision as to whether her head would be down and her feet up, or vice versa.

He'd opted to lay her head on the cushions and let her legs dangle. No sooner had he done so than one of her legs slipped from the arm of the sofa and onto the floor, leaving her in an indelicate, spread-eagled faint.

Ryder stifled a grin. Waking in such a compromising position would embarrass anyone. For Casey, a woman obviously used to nothing but the best, it would be the height of humiliation. In a considerate move, he removed her shoes, then lifted her leg back in alignment with the other. But when it slipped off again, he decided to leave it, and her, alone.

As he watched, he couldn't help but stare at the woman who was now his wife. He was still a little shocked at himself for going along with such a hare-brained scheme. The Justice men were not impulsive. They had always considered the consequences and then lived with their decisions without regrets. Until now. While it was too late to consider anything, it remained to be seen if there would be regrets.

He kept looking at her, separating her features in his mind. It wasn't just that she was pretty, though he couldn't keep his eyes off her thick black hair and those big green eyes. And her skin—it looked like silk, ivory silk.

And Ryder remembered that when she smiled, her mouth had a tendency to curl at one corner first before the other decided to follow. It gave her an impish expression, which he knew was deceiving. If this woman had an ounce of playfulness in her, he hadn't seen it. The devil maybe, but nothing so frivolous as an imp.

While he was watching, she blinked. And when she groaned and reached for the back of her head, he grimaced. It had been thumped pretty good when she'd fainted. He felt bad about that. She might be touchy as hell, and they might not agree on anything, but he didn't want her hurt.

Casey opened her eyes. The ceiling didn't look familiar, and for a moment, she wondered where she was. A whiff of charcoal smoke drifted past her nose and, all too swiftly, her memory returned.

Seconds later, she became aware of the implications of her less than ladylike sprawl. What had that man done to her while she'd been unconscious? Better yet, where was he?

She turned her head and caught him staring at her from a chair on the other side of the coffee table. When he grinned and winked, she swiveled to an upright position, grabbing at her skirt and smoothing at her hair. When she could think without the room spinning beneath her, she glared at him.

"What did you do to me?"

He arched an eyebrow. "Not nearly as much as I wanted," he replied, and knew he'd scored a hit when she doubled up her fists. He stifled a laugh. "Easy, now. I was just kidding. I've been the picture of decorum. I picked you up from the floor, laid you on the sofa, and have been waiting for you to come to."

Her southern manners forced her to thank him. "I appreciate your consideration."

His grin widened. "Honesty won't permit me to accept your compliment. I have to admit it was hunger that kept me waiting for you. I was taught that it's bad manners to eat in front of people without offering them some, too. And, you never did answer my question. How do you want your hamburger?"

If she'd had a shoe, she would have thrown it. As it was, she had to satisfy herself with a regal, albeit shaky, exit from the room, slamming the door shut between them with a solid thud.

"Does that mean you don't want one?" Ryder yelled.

She yanked the door open long enough to give him what was left of her mind.

"You're a swine. A gentleman would have covered my legs and bathed my head with a cold compress."

"If you wanted a gentleman, you shouldn't have gone shopping for a husband down in the Delta."

She glared and slammed the door again, this time louder and firmer.

"I suppose this means no to the hamburgers?"

The door opened again, but the only thing to come out was the sound of Casey's voice at its most dignified. The shriek in her tone was gone and she was enunciating each word, as if speaking to someone lacking in mental capacity.

"No, it does not. I will have a hamburger, well-done, light on the salt, heavy on the pepper."

This time when she closed the door, it was with a ladylike click. The glitter in Ryder's eyes was sharp, the grin on his face sardonic.

"So you like it hot, do you, wife? That's interesting. Very interesting indeed."

He reentered the tiny kitchen and began making patties from the hamburger meat before carrying them out to the grill. As he slapped them on the grate, smoke began to rise and the fire began to pop and sizzle as fat dripped onto the burning charcoal.

Oddly, it reminded him of Casey in the midst of her family, putting up a smoke screen to keep them from knowing how scared she was, and popping wisecracks and issuing orders before anyone could tell her what to do.

He closed the lid and sighed. He had married a total stranger for the hell of it, but he hadn't counted on the family that came with her. In fact, they reminded him of snakes, writhing and coiling and biting out at each other in some crazy sort of frenzy.

He thought of his own family, of how loud and rambunctious—of how close and loving they'd been—of how empty and scattered they now were. And how the world as he'd known it had ended because of something he'd done.

He went back inside, leaving the hamburgers and his memories behind.

"Want another one?" Ryder asked, indicating the two remaining well-done patties congealing in their own grease on a pea green plate.

Casey eyed the plate. Besides being an atrocious shade of green, the plate was chipped. She'd never eaten from a chipped plate before. She suspected this night was the beginning of many firsts. Dabbing at the corner of her mouth with a paper towel, she shook her head.

"No, thank you, I'm quite full." Grudgingly she added, "It was very good."

Ryder nodded and continued to stare at a ketchup stain near

his fork. What now? Conversation with this woman had been nearly impossible. Every time he opened his mouth to speak, she jumped. And she watched his every move with those big green eyes, as if she expected to be pounced upon at any moment. Hell, she was beginning to make him antsy, too.

He glanced at his watch. "It's almost nine."

She paled.

He sighed.

"Easy now, lady."

"Casey," she said. "My name is Casey."

His expression darkened. "Yes, and my name is Ryder. Unfortunately, that's all we know about each other." When she looked away, his frustration rose.

"Casey, look at me."

She did, but with trepidation.

"There's something I think needs to be said. This is going to be a long haul for both of us. I suppose we each had an agenda for even considering this situation, but it's done, and for your sake, it has to work, right?"

She thought of Miles and Erica, and then of Lash. "Yes."

"Okay, then there's something I think you should know about me."

Her head jerked up and she was suddenly staring at him in a still, waiting manner. Oh dear, what was he about to reveal?

Again, he sensed her fear. "Dammit, don't look at me like that. I am not a dangerous man. I do not taunt women. I do not hurt women. I do not force women to do anything they do not want, and that includes the issue of sex."

Startled by his bluntness, Casey blushed. "I've been meaning to talk to you about that," she said.

"I'm listening."

"There won't be any."

Her announcement came as no surprise, but Ryder was unprepared for the sense of disappointment he felt. He chalked it up to several months of denial and let it go at that.

He shrugged. "I will abide by whatever rules you feel comfortable in setting, but I have a couple of my own. I am not your servant. I don't take orders…but I will listen to suggestions.''

He watched her swallow a couple of times, but she remained silent.

''Well, do you have any?''

Casey blinked. ''Any what?''

''Suggestions.''

''Uh…no, I don't suppose so.''

''Okay, then that's settled. Why don't you start the dishes? I want to make sure the fire is out in the grill.''

He got up before he had time to see her panic again.

''Ryder?''

He turned.

She waved helplessly over the table and the dirty dishes. ''I've never done dishes before.''

''You've never…!'' Then he muttered beneath his breath. ''Good grief.''

''What's wrong?''

''You've never done dishes.''

She hated him for that dumbfounded look he was wearing. ''That's what I said. I also don't do windows,'' she snapped.

''And I don't suppose you can cook, either.''

She had the grace to flush. ''No.''

He groaned.

Casey was surprised at her feelings of inadequacy. She hired and fired with the best of them, bought and sold corporations without batting an eye. How dare he consider her lacking in capabilities?

''It's not my fault,'' she argued.

''Then whose is it?''

She had no answer.

''If you ask me, it's high time you learned. Soap is under the sink, the dishcloth is in it. You're a smart lady. Figure the rest out for yourself.''

''Where are you going?'' Casey asked, as he started out the door.

"To put out a fire then take a shower."

"But you already had a shower," she said, remembering the steam…and the towel..and the bare-naked body.

"Yeah, so maybe I have more than one fire that needs quenching, okay?"

It took exactly five seconds for the implication of what he'd suggested to sink in, and another few for her to be able to move. After that, she was glad to have something to do besides think about what he'd said…and why he'd said it.

The air was thick and muggy from the lingering heat of the day. It was that time of the evening just before dusk and right after the sun has passed beyond the horizon. A family of martens swooped grass-high in daring flight then soared heavenward, constantly feeding on the mosquitos in the air.

Graystone, the home that had been in the Marlow family since before the War of Northern Aggression, loomed large upon the landscape. It was a three-story monolith which had seen better days. Its regal structure and the land upon which it sat was sadly in need of repair, yet at a distance, the charm of the pillared edifice was still imposing.

Lash reclined in an old wicker chair on the veranda of his family home, nursing his third bourbon and water and surveying all that was his. This was his favorite time of the day. It wasn't because the workday was over and he was taking a well-earned rest. It was because Graystone looked better at half-light.

He tossed back the last of his drink, trying to pinpoint exactly where his plans for glory had gone wrong. The liquor burned and he silently cursed the fact that he could no longer afford the best. He was drinking cheap bourbon, living in the servant's wing while the rest of the mansion was closed off, and down to doing for himself. He didn't even have the funds to hire a housekeeper and made only enough at his law practice to keep the taxes paid on his home and himself afloat.

His belly growled. Without conscious thought, he pushed himself up from the chair and entered the house, taking care to lock the door behind him. Just for a moment, he stood in the great hall, staring up at the spiral staircase gracing the entryway, remembering another time when the house had been alive with laughter and people.

Something moved in the far corner of the hall. He winced as the sound of scurrying feet scratched on the marble flooring, then disappeared behind a breakfront. It wasn't the first rodent of that size he'd seen inside these walls, but tonight, it would be one too many.

He started to shake, first with rage, then from despair. It was over! There would be no more dreams of bringing Graystone back to her former beauty, or of returning dignity to the Marlow name. And it was all because of Casey.

A red haze blurred his vision. He drew back and threw his glass toward the place where he'd last seen the rat. It shattered against the wall, splintering into minute crystal shards. Only afterward did he remember that it had been part of a set, but regret swiftly faded. What did it matter? His only guests wore long tails and came on four feet…in the dark…in the middle of the night.

Startled by the sound of breaking glass, the rat that had taken refuge behind the breakfront made a run down the hallway for the deeper shadows beyond. As it did, something inside of Lash snapped. He grabbed at his grandfather's ivory-handled walking stick that had been standing in the hall tree for more than forty years, and ran, catching the rat just as it neared safety. He swung down with deadly force and the sound shattered the silence within the old walls as well as what was left of Lash's reason. Glass splintered on the wall behind him as he drew back the cane, but he didn't notice.

Even after the rat was dead, Lash continued to hail it with a barrage of blows until gore began to splatter on his shoes and the cuffs of his pants.

But in his mind, the rat had been dispatched from the first blow he'd struck. He was oblivious to the overkill, or that he might have lost more than his control. He kept venting his rage on a woman who'd dashed his dreams. And it wasn't the rodent who was coming apart on the cool marble floor. It was the beautiful and complacent surface of Casey Ruban's face.

When he finally stopped, his body was shaking from exertion and the muscles in his arms were burning from the energy he'd spent. He stared in disbelief at what he'd done, then tossed the cane down on the floor, disgusted by its condition.

Weary in both body and spirit, he turned and then stared at the wall in disbelief. The mirror! The glass in the ornate, gold-rimmed mirror that had hung in this hall for as long as he could remember, was shattered. His heart began to pound as he looked at the broken and refracted image of himself— a true reflection of his life.

He stepped back in horror and reached for the rabbit's foot in the pocket of his pants. All he could think as he backed away was, Seven long years of bad luck.

Chapter 4

Casey roused from a restless sleep. Disoriented by unfamiliar surroundings, it took a few moments for reality to return. Someone moaned. Her first thought was that Ryder could be sick. Quietly, she crawled out of bed and tiptoed to the door, aware that he'd made his bed in the middle of the living room floor. The moan came again, only this time, louder.

When she'd seen him last, he'd been unfolding a sleeping bag. But this was frightening. She didn't know what to make of it. What if he was hurt, or sick?

Just as she turned the doorknob something crashed to the floor. An image of intruders made her hesitate, but only for a moment.

The door opened inward on well-oiled hinges. She peered into the living room, searching the shadows to make certain she and Ryder were still alone. The outer door was shut, as were the windows. As she listened, the hum of the central air-conditioning unit kicked on, changing the texture of the night. She took a step forward, then another, then another until she was behind the sofa and peering over it.

Ryder was stretched out in his sleeping bag there on the floor. Lying half in and half out of the faint glow from the security lights outside, he seemed more shadow than substance.

And while she was watching, he jerked and then moaned, throwing one arm over his eyes, as if warding off some unseen blow.

This explained the sounds that had wakened her. Ryder appeared to be dreaming. She moved closer, leaning over the sofa for a better view. And as she did, accidentally scooted it with the force of her body. The wooden legs screeched across the vinyl flooring like chalk on a blackboard. The sound was enough to wake the dead...and Ryder.

He came up and out of his sleeping bag and before Casey could react, he had grabbed her by the throat, and pinned her to the wall. His face and body were in darkness, but there was enough light for her to know to be afraid. The look in his eyes was grim, and the grip he had around her throat was all but deadly. She grabbed at his wrists before his grip tightened further.

"Ryder...Ryder, it's me."

"Oh, my God!" He jerked, moving his hand from her throat to the side of her face in a quick gesture of assurance. "Dammit, Casey, I'm sorry, but you startled me."

Casey closed her eyes as her legs went weak.

She rubbed at the tightness in her throat where his fingers had been. "It's okay. It was partly my fault for sneaking up on you like that."

Remorse shafted through him as he saw her fingering her throat. Dammit, he'd hurt her. He caught her hand, and then the moment they touched, wished that he'd kept his hands to himself. She was too close and too tempting.

Her focus suddenly shifted from her throat to him. They were face-to-face—body to body, and only inches from each other's lips.

Breath caught. Hearts stopped. First hers, then his.

She swallowed. "You were having a bad dream."

He inhaled slowly then spoke. "I'm sorry I frightened you."

Once again, she was struck by the size of him, of the breadth of his shoulders blocking out the light coming through the windows behind him.

"It's okay. It was partly my fault," she said.

She moved her hand and accidentally brushed the surface of his chest. His skin felt combustible. Muscles tensed beneath her fingertips and she jerked back her hand.

When he took a deep breath, she looked up. His eyes were glittering and there was a faint sheen of perspiration on his body. At that moment, she remembered what she was wearing, and realized what he was not.

He slept in the buff.

Her gown was short and sheer.

Seduction had been the last thing on her mind when she'd bought it, but from the way Ryder was staring at her now, it wasn't far from his. She could almost hear what he was thinking. He *was* her husband. This *was* their first night alone. But from her standpoint, what he was so obviously thinking could not—must not—happen.

Ryder was in shock. To wake up from the horror of reliving the crash that had killed his father to find a beautiful, half-dressed woman within reach made him want. He wanted to make love. He wanted to feel the softness of a woman's body—a woman's lips. To get lost in that certain rapture. To celebrate life because he couldn't forget death. That's what he wanted. But it wasn't going to happen, and because he knew it, his voice was harsh and angry.

"Go back to bed."

She tried to explain. "Look, I didn't mean to—"

He pinned her against the wall with a hand on either side of her head and leaned down, so close to her that his whisper was as loud as a shout.

"Either get the hell out of my sight or take off your clothes."

Casey bolted for the bedroom, slamming the door behind

her and then leaning against it, as if the weight of her body might add strength to the flimsy barrier that stood between them.

For several interminable seconds she stood without moving, listening for the sound of footsteps. When all she heard were a few muffled curses and then the sound of a slamming door, she relaxed and then panicked. What if he was leaving for good?

She opened the door with a jerk, but when she realized all of his things were still inside, she shut it again. She crawled into bed and pulled up the covers, again, erecting another puny barrier between them.

In spite of the cool air circulating throughout the room, it seemed stifling. And while she waited anxiously for him to return, she considered their temporary bonds.

Ryder Justice had promised to love and honor her, to take care of her in sickness and in health. She didn't know about the loving, but some part of her trusted that he wouldn't lie. He'd said he would stay the year and she believed him. It was that fact alone that gave her ease enough to go back to sleep.

When she woke again, the alarm on the bedside table was going off, and water was running in the shower.

Casey's first impulse was fear. He'd come into her room and she'd never known. Her second was picturing what he was doing. Remembering the condition in which he'd emerged last night, she jumped out of bed, grabbing for her robe and slippers as she ran a hasty brush through the tangles in her hair. This time when he came out of the shower, she had no intention of being anywhere in sight.

When she exited the apartment, she stood for a moment on the landing, savoring the Mississippi morning. It was going to be another hot one, she could tell. The thought of freshly brewed coffee and some of Tilly's hot biscuits and jelly drew her down the stairs with haste, across the courtyard, in the back door of the mansion, and into the kitchen.

"Something smells good," she said.

The woman standing at the stove turned in quick surprise. There was a faint flush from the heat of the oven staining her face and a warning in her eyes.

"Casey Dee, you scared me half to death."

"I'm sorry," Casey said, and went for her good-morning hug.

Tilly smoothed and fussed at the long hair hanging down Casey's back, then hugged her tightly to soften the accusation in her words. "Well now, girl, what are you doing over here without your man?"

She sighed. If only things were as simple now as they'd been back when she was a child.

"He's in the shower." Casey slumped in a chair with a pout. "Oh, Tilly, Delaney has made such a mess out of my life."

"No, ma'am. Delaney didn't do it, you did. He just went and made some silly rule, and as always, you're still running along behind him, trying to make everything right."

Casey was speechless. This wasn't the sympathy she'd been wanting. She tried to glare, but it just wasn't possible. Not at Tilly. And then she sighed. Tilly always gave her sympathy, but where Casey wanted it or not, it also came with the truth.

"So, he started it," Casey said, and managed to grin.

"And you sure did finish it, didn't you, girl? The very idea! Going down to the flatlands to find yourself a man."

Casey's eyebrows rose. "How did you know?"

Tilly snorted delicately and returned to stirring the eggs she'd been cooking. "I know, 'cause you're my baby," she said softly. "I know 'cause I make it my business to know."

The air in Casey's throat became too thick to breathe. She stood and slipped her arms around Tilly's waist, then laid her cheek in the middle of her back, relishing the familiarity of freshly ironed fabric and a steady heartbeat.

"And I thank God that you care," Casey said softly. "You and Joshua are all the family I have left."

Tilly set the skillet off the fire and turned until she and

Casey were eye to eye. "No, girl, you're wrong. You've got yourself a husband now."

Casey's laugh was brittle. "I don't have a husband. I have a stranger for a year."

Tilly took her by the shoulders and shook her. "What you have is a chance. Now make the most of it." Before Casey could argue further, Tilly waved her away. "Go tell your man my biscuits are about ready to come out of the oven. By the time you two get back, bacon and eggs will be ready, too."

"But I don't know if he likes..."

Tilly's stare never wavered. "Then don't you think it's about time you found out?"

Casey exited the kitchen with as much grace as she could muster. After her and Ryder's encounter last night, she was almost afraid to face him. The tail of her robe was dragging as she walked up the stairs. When she stumbled and came close to falling, she picked it up and walked the rest of the way with the hem held above her ankles.

Ryder met her at the door. She knew that she was staring, but she hadn't been prepared for the change in his appearance. Clean-shaven, smelling like soap and something light and musky, he seemed taller than ever. She tried not to gawk, but the new blue jeans he was wearing suited him all too well, and he'd left the top three buttons on his long-sleeved white shirt undone, revealing far too much of that broad, brown chest for her peace of mind. The only thing she recognized from before were his old black boots, and even they were shining. Still damp from his shower, his hair gleamed black in the early morning sunshine.

"Mornin'," he said softly, and stepped aside to let her in. "Someone from the house just called. Said they wanted a ride into the city."

Casey blinked, telling herself to concentrate on what he was saying instead of how he looked, but it was difficult. Today, those grey eyes of his almost looked blue.

"It isn't even eight o'clock," she muttered. "You haven't had breakfast, and they can wait."

A slight grin cornered one edge of his mouth and then slid out of sight. "I don't know what we'll eat. Yesterday I forgot to buy milk."

"It doesn't matter. This morning we're having breakfast in the kitchen with Tilly. She said to hurry."

"Who's Tilly?"

"The woman who raised me after Mother and Father were killed. She's Joshua's wife. You remember him from yesterday?"

He nodded, then reached for the broad-brimmed, black Stetson hanging by the door. "Someone else's cooking sounds good to me." When Casey moved toward their bedroom, he paused. "Aren't you coming, or don't you eat with the hired help?"

She spun, and there was no mistaking the anger in her voice.

"Don't *ever,* and I mean, *ever,* refer to Tilly or Joshua as servants again. Do you understand?"

Surprised by her vehemence, his estimation of her went up a notch. "Yes, ma'am, I believe that I do."

Again, Casey realized she'd overreacted. He must be as off-center as she felt. "Sorry. I didn't mean…"

"Easy now."

Her stomach tied itself into a little knot. If only he'd quit saying those words in those tones.

"I am easy," she said, and then groaned beneath her breath as a grin spread across his face. "Don't say it," she muttered. "You know what I meant."

"Casey."

A little nervous about what he would say next, she couldn't have been more surprised by what came out.

"Don't ever apologize for having a good heart."

After witnessing the dangerous side of him last night, his gentleness was the last thing she would have expected.

"Was that a compliment?" she asked.

He ignored her. "Hurry up and get dressed. I'm starving."

"Feel free to go on ahead. Tilly will be glad to…"

"No."

"No?"

"I'll wait for you," he said.

She inhaled sharply, and then shut the bedroom door behind her as she went inside. Her hands were shaking as she sorted through the closet for something to wear.

I'll wait for you.

His promise was echoing inside her head as she brushed and zipped and buttoned. Putting on makeup was even more difficult because she found herself looking through tears, but she refused to let them fall. She wasn't going to let that man get to her, not in any way.

Erica sauntered into the downstairs kitchen just as Tilly was dishing up the eggs.

"What's taking so long this morning?" Erica grumbled, picking a strip of hot, crisp bacon from the platter and crunching it between her teeth.

"Get on out of my kitchen," Tilly said. "Everything is right on time and you know it."

Erica hated this woman's uppity manner, and at the same time, respected her authority just enough not to argue.

"It's not your kitchen," Erica grumbled, taking one last piece of bacon with her as she started out of the room.

"It's not yours, either," Tilly said sharply, and banged a spoon on the side of the pan to punctuate her remark.

Erica glared. And then the back door opened and she forgot what she'd been about to say. She forgot she was chewing, or that she was holding her next bite in her hand. All she could do was stare—right past her sister to the man behind her. Almost choking, she managed to swallow, then dropped the other piece of bacon back onto the platter.

Casey didn't see Erica. Her focus was on the woman at the stove. Until Matilda Bass passed judgment on what she'd done, she wouldn't feel right.

"Tilly, this is my, uh…this is Ryder Justice. Ryder, this is

Matilda Bass. I consider her my second mother, as well as the best cook in the whole state of Mississippi.''

Upon entering the kitchen, he'd taken off his hat. He extended his hand in a gesture of friendship, which Tilly accepted with obvious reticence. But Ryder behaved as if he'd known her all of his life.

''Mrs. Bass, it's a pleasure. If everything tastes as good as it smells, I'd warrant Casey is right.''

Tilly's gaze wavered. She hadn't been prepared for someone like him, and he *was* someone, that she could tell. She frowned slightly. This man didn't look like any drifter out of the flatlands. He didn't sound like one, either. His words were sweet, his appearance sweeter. All she could think was, He'd better be good to my girl.

She nodded regally, accepting the praise as just. ''Call me Tilly, and I'm pleased to meet you, sir. You aren't from these parts, are you?''

He grinned. ''I don't answer to anything but Ryder, and no, ma'am, I'm not.''

Tilly nodded in satisfaction. ''I knew as much. I'd be guessing you're from Oklahoma…or Texas. Am I right?''

Startled by her perception, he didn't have it in him to lie. ''Yes, ma'am… Texas.''

Casey felt strange. Here she was married to the man and she'd been so caught up in her own agenda, she hadn't had enough curiosity about him to wonder where he was from, or how he'd gotten from there to here.

''Then sit,'' Tilly said. ''Food's ready.''

Only after they'd taken their seats did Casey realize Erica was in the room. She looked up at her and smiled, but when her sister sauntered over to Ryder and ran her fingertips lightly across his back, measuring their breadth from shoulder to shoulder, the urge to slap her away from him was almost overwhelming.

There was a cold, mirthless smile on Erica's face as she finally glanced in Casey's direction.

"Well, well, princess. Even when you fall, you land on your feet, don't you?"

Casey's hackles rose even further. "Let it go, Erica."

Erica's expression was bland, but her eyes glittered with envy. "Oh my, I guess that didn't come out quite right, did it?"

The antagonism between the two sisters was palpable. Ryder suspected it probably had more to do with old wounds than with his arrival into their midst. Nevertheless, whatever its roots, he seemed to be the latest weed to cause dissent. He took it upon himself to change the subject.

"Someone called me earlier for a ride into town. Do you know who it was?"

Erica's smile broadened. "It wasn't me, but that's not such a bad idea. I'll bet you give really good rides."

Ryder's expression blanked, and if Erica had been as astute as she believed herself to be, she would have backed off then, before it was too late. But she didn't.

"I'm even better at giving a hard time to people who tick me off," he said.

Erica's expression froze. A slap in the face couldn't have stunned her more.

If Casey had been the impulsive type, she would have thrown her arms around his neck and hugged him. But she wasn't, and the moment passed.

"Tell whoever it is that Ryder is unavailable until we've finished our breakfast," she said. "This morning, my husband and I just want a little peace and quiet and a meal to ourselves."

Ryder's eyebrows rose. Husband! Now she was admitting he was her husband?

Suddenly Ryder's mouth was only inches from Casey's ear. She could feel his breath—almost hear the laughter in his voice as he whispered.

"I thought we weren't using *that* word."

Casey glared.

Erica was left with nowhere to go but out. She walked

away, leaving Ryder with a contemplative stare that Casey chose to ignore.

"I guess if a person is observant, they can learn something new every day," he muttered.

Casey looked up. "Like what?"

"Never knew there were any barracudas in Mississippi."

"Excuse me?"

"Nothing," Ryder said. "I was just thinking out loud."

Tilly's back was to the pair, but her smile was wide as she added the finishing touch to her eggs before setting them on the table. She wasn't the type of woman to make snap judgments, but after the way Ryder had cut Erica Dunn off at the mouth, she was pretty sure he was going to do just fine.

She set the plates before them. "Now eat up before my eggs get cold." She set a full pan of steaming hot biscuits in front of them as well. "Fresh out of the oven, Casey Dee, just the way you like them."

Casey rolled her eyes in appreciation of the golden brown tops and reached for one to butter.

"Since you're a married lady now and have your own place, I guess you'll be needing to learn how to make these," Tilly said. "When you get time, I'll be needing to teach you."

Casey looked stunned. Ryder hid his grin behind a bite of scrambled eggs. Poor Casey. It would seem that her life had taken more changes than she was ready to accept.

"Making biscuits seems a bit of a leap for a woman who can't boil water," Ryder said.

Ignoring Casey's gasp, he scooped a spoonful of strawberry preserves onto his biscuit and then bit into the hot bread, chewing with relish.

"Well, I never," she muttered.

Ryder swallowed, took a slow sip of coffee, then fixed Casey with a sultry gaze. "I know that, wife. But one of these days you will."

The implications of what he'd just said were impossible to misinterpret. He hadn't been talking about biscuits, and they both knew it. Furious that he kept catching her off guard, she stabbed at the food on her plate with undue force, scraping the tines of the fork across the china and earning her a cool I-taught-you-better-than-that look from Tilly.

The rest of the meal passed in relative silence, broken only by the coming and going of Tilly and Joshua as they carried food into the breakfast room for the family who would now be living off the fruit of Casey's labors. It was Ryder who finally broke the silence.

"That does it for me," he said. "I guess I'd better go earn my keep." He winked at Casey, taking small delight in the fact that she didn't welcome it, and tweaked her ear for the hell of it as he passed.

"Do you know where you're going?" Casey asked, as he sauntered out of the room.

He paused, then turned, and once again, she was struck by the fact that his answer had nothing to do with the question she'd asked.

"No. But then it hasn't really mattered for months now. Why should today be any different?"

When he disappeared, she was forced to accept the fact that not only had she married a stranger, but it would seem one with more secrets than he cared to tell.

She took a last gulp of her coffee and tossed down her napkin. If he had her troubles, he'd have something to complain about. She glanced at her watch. It was a quarter to nine. Past time for the boss to be at work. But, since she *was* the boss, she was going to finish her coffee.

Meanwhile, Ryder was making his way through the maze of rooms and getting a firsthand impression of the atmosphere in which Casey had grown up.

The mansion itself was grand—with three stories of granite blocks that came far too close to resembling a castle rather than a home. The only thing Ryder felt was missing was a moat. The snakes and crocodiles were already in place, but they walked on two legs, rather than four, and hid their sharp teeth behind fake smiles.

His footsteps echoed on the cold marble floors as he made

his way toward the muted sound of voices coming from a room up the hallway and to the right. The breakfast room, he presumed.

As he entered the doorway, he paused, staring at the bright morning sun beaming in through spotless windows, through which an arbor of hot pink bougainvillea could be seen.

The crystal on the table was elegant. The china was a plain, classic white with a delicate gold rim, and the silverware gleamed with a high, polished gloss as the people in residence lifted it to their mouths. Flowers were everywhere. Cut and in vases. Growing from pots. In one-dimensional form, painted on canvas and framed, then hung at just the right level for the eye to see.

In spite of the heat of the day, Ryder shuddered. Such elegance. Such cold, cold elegance. He thought of the woman who'd come storming into that bar with her long hair down and windblown, wearing that bit of a black dress, and tried to picture her being raised in a place like this. For some reason, the little he knew of Casey didn't jibe with these surroundings. How could a woman with so much passion survive in a house with no joy—no life?

And Casey Ruban Justice had passion, of that he had no doubt. Most of the time she seemed to keep it channeled toward the business end of her world, but every so often her guard slipped, and had she known it, in those moments, Ryder saw more of her soul than she would have liked.

He settled his Stetson a little tighter on his head, as if bracing himself for a gale wind, and sauntered into the breakfast room as if he owned the place.

"Who wanted the ride?"

Three sets of equally startled expressions turned in his direction. Erica was still seething from his earlier put-down and chose to ignore him.

Miles stared, holding his cup of coffee suspended halfway between table and lips, trying to picture this clean-cut, larger-than-life cowboy as the same ragged derelict who'd come trailing in behind Casey yesterday morning.

Eudora gasped and set her cup down in its saucer with a sharp, unladylike clink.

"Why, it was me," she said. "But I'm not quite ready."

Ryder smiled. "I've got all day. Don't hurry on my account."

"For future reference, you need not come into the family area," Miles drawled. "Simply wait out front."

Ryder shifted his stance. It wasn't much. Only an inch or so. But to Miles, it seemed to make the man that much taller. And it made Miles distinctly uncomfortable looking up at so much man.

"Look," Ryder growled. "Let's get one thing straight. Like it or not, and I can't say that I care much for it myself, for the time being, I *am* part of your family. Therefore, do not expect me to scuttle around outside the back door like some damned stray dog looking for a handout. Do I make myself clear?"

Miles' face turned a bloody shade of red. All he could do was splutter and look toward Erica, who was usually the more verbal of the pair, for support. Unaware that Ryder had already put her in her place, he was unprepared for his sister's silence. He tried again.

"But Casey said…"

"Casey can say whatever she chooses," Ryder said. "However, you might want to remember that she's my wife, not my boss. And, you might also want to remember that while I mind my own business, I expect others to do the same." Then he touched the brim of his hat and winked at Eudora. "I'll be outside when you're ready."

He walked out.

When he was halfway down the hall, the breakfast room seemed to erupt into a cacophony of sound. Three separate voices, all talking at once in various tones of disbelief. Unable to remember the last time he'd felt this alive, he grinned all the way out the door.

Chapter 5

"Stop there!" Eudora ordered, pointing toward a boutique on the upcoming street corner.

Ryder aimed the gleaming white Lincoln toward a horizontal parking space and slid into it with nothing to spare. Before Eudora could object to the fact that he'd parked several doors down and she was going to have to walk, he had opened the door and was reaching in to help her out.

Smoothing at her hair and clothes, she began to issue her standard orders. "I don't know how long I'll be, but..."

"No problem," he said. "I'm coming with you," he said, and offered her his arm.

Ignoring the shocked expression on her face, he escorted her up the street and into the store. Eudora was so stunned by his actions that she let herself be led into The Pink Boutique.

The saleslady all but fawned as she met her at the door. "Mrs. Deathridge, please accept our condolences on your recent loss. Delaney Ruban will be missed."

"Yes, well, I thank you on behalf of the family," Eudora

muttered, casting a sidelong glance at Ryder who was still standing at her side. He was too big to ignore and seemed too determined to dissuade from accompanying her. She waved toward an overstuffed chair near the alcove where the dressing rooms were situated. "You may wait over there."

Ryder took his seat without comment. Eudora watched as he carefully lifted the Stetson from his head. Placing it crown-side down in his lap, he seemed to settle.

After that she relaxed, but only slightly. There was something about that man that unnerved her. Even though he was now across the room from her and sitting still, his presence was overpowering. Frowning, she turned away and began sorting through the garments on the racks, still conscious of his eyes boring into her back. He took up space. That's what he did. He took up entirely too much space.

Half an hour came and went, along with the saleslady's patience. Eudora had picked through and complained about everything the store carried in her size. It made no difference to her that Gladys was nearly in tears, or that the manager had made several pointed trips through the room, each time giving Gladys a sharp, condemning look for not being able to placate a customer, especially one from Ruban Crossing's foremost family.

Eudora was so caught up with the seriousness of her shopping spree that she'd completely forgotten Ryder's existence, so when he spoke, he had Eudora's...and the saleslady's...immediate and undivided attention.

"Take the blue one."

Eudora spun, still holding the dress in question. "Were you speaking to me?"

Ryder tilted his head. "It matches your eyes. Always did like blue-eyed women."

Having said his piece, he stretched, giving himself permission to take up even more of the floor space by unfolding his long legs out before him. While she watched, he locked his hands across his belly as if he didn't have a care in the world.

Eudora wasn't accustomed to having anyone, especially a chauffeur, give her advice on her choices of clothing, yet this man's entrance into their world had already changed their lives. She heard herself repeating his suggestion as if it had true merit and wondered if she was finally losing her mind.

"The blue?"

He nodded, then shrugged. "Yes, ma'am, but it was just a suggestion. My father always said it never paid to rush a woman."

"Oh, do quit calling me ma'am," Eudora said. "It sounds too elderly."

Ryder looked up and almost grinned. "Well, now, Dora, didn't anyone ever tell you that age is in the mind of the beholder?"

Eudora's mouth dropped. This man was positively impossible. Of course he should have known she meant for him to call her Mrs. Deathridge, not Dora! The very idea, shortening her name like that.

But the deed had already been done, and the name rang in her ears. Dora. That was what her husband, Henry, had called her, and Henry had been dead for all these many years. She gave Ryder a sidelong glance and disappeared into the dressing room with the blue dress in her hand. Dora. Dora. What would Erica and Miles have to say about this?

She shut the door behind her then looked up. Her reflection looked back. For a moment, she almost didn't recognize herself. Her eyes were bright—from shock, of course. But the glimmer did give life to her expression. Dora. She held the blue dress up beneath her chin. He was right. It brought out the true color of her eyes. She smiled. Maybe he wasn't so bad after all.

Only after he was alone did Ryder realize what he'd said. He'd actually thought of his father without coming unglued. In fact, just for a moment, it had felt damned good to remember him at all.

He jammed his Stetson on his head then pulled the brim

down low across his forehead and closed his eyes. Ah God, but he missed that old man. So much that it hurt.

Lash stood on the veranda, staring at the brake lights on the plumber's van as it slowed to take a corner. A soft, early morning breeze lifted the hair from his forehead, cooling the sweat that had beaded minutes earlier when the plumber had handed him his bill.

Despair settled a little closer upon his shoulders.

Impulsively, he walked down the steps and out into the yard, heading for the gazebo. As a child, it had been his favorite place. As an adult, it was where he went to hide.

Ivy clung to the latticed walls, crocheted by nature into heavy loops of variegated green. Inside, the air rarely moved and only the most persistent rays of sunshine were able to pick and poke their way through the dense growth.

He dropped onto the bench in a slump, then wadded the bill and tossed it into the gathering pile on the floor. Why bother to keep track if they couldn't be paid?

Minutes passed. He looked down at his watch. It was past time to open the office. With a sigh, he shoved himself off the bench, giving the pile of unpaid bills a final glance. Poor Graystone. She was so sick—in need of too many repairs for his meager pocket to accommodate.

His eyes misted as he walked across the yard. As he entered the house in search of his suit coat and briefcase, a continuing thought kept running through his mind.

It was Casey's fault. Casey had ruined it all. Beautiful, willful Casey who had so much, while he had nothing at all. He yanked his coat from a hook, thinking of the parties that would be given in her honor, coveting the priceless wedding gifts she would certainly be receiving as her due.

Despair fed anger. Anger fed hate. And something fell to the floor behind him with a clank. He spun in time to see a long, hairless tail disappearing beneath the cupboard. A rat. Another damned rat.

He grabbed a can of corn from the cabinet, firing it toward

the place where he'd seen it last. "What the hell are you still doing here? I thought rats abandoned sinking ships."

Several items had fallen off a low shelf and onto the floor as the door to the cupboard flew open. The sight of spilled salt sent Lash to his knees. Scrambling to regain his sense of balance in his superstitious world, he grabbed a pinch of the salt and tossed it over his shoulder. Even though one part of his brain told him that spilled salt did not bad luck make, he was too much a product of his upbringing to ignore it all now.

Still down on his knees, he set to retrieving the few family heirlooms he hadn't sold. It wasn't until he was setting his grandfather's sorghum pewter pitcher back on the shelf that he noticed a small, flat box at the back of the cupboard. Frowning, he pulled it out. When he opened the lid, his eyes widened and a delighted smile lit up his somber expression. Grandfather's letter opener! He'd completely forgotten its existence.

He ran a tentative finger down the thin, double-edged blade, remembering the hours he'd spent in Aaron Marlow's lap, remembering the first time his grandfather had let him use it without help. For all its beauty, it was still a small and deadly thing.

A brown shadow moved to the right of Lash's hand. He reacted without thinking. Seconds later, he rocked back on his heels in shock, staring at the carcass of the rat and the small silver dagger embedded in its body.

Bile rose, burning his throat and choking him as he scrambled to his feet and ran for the sink just in time to keep from puking on himself. When he was able to look back without gagging, all he could see was his family honor embedded in the belly of the rat.

In Lash's mind, it was the last and ultimate disgrace. Wild-eyed and looking for someone else to blame, he stared at the salt. Bad luck. Bad luck. It was all a matter of bad luck.

In a daze, he yanked the dagger out of the rat, wiping off the bloody blade on the kitchen curtain. His hands were shaking as he laid it back in the box. So, he'd come to this, and thanks to Casey Justice, this is where he would stay.

He shuddered then sighed as he closed the lid to the box. Casey. He'd lost everything because of her. The box felt warm in his hands as he slipped it into his pocket before picking up his briefcase.

A muscle jerked in his jaw as he walked out of the house. Once again, he glanced at his watch. There was something he needed to do before he went to the office. He didn't know where his manners had gone. He should have thought of it before.

Casey tossed her pen down on the desk and swiveled her chair to face the window overlooking the business district of Ruban Crossing. As she did, a flash of white caught her eye and she stood abruptly, searching for a glimpse of the family's white Lincoln.

Was that Ryder? She looked until her eyes began to burn and the muscles in the backs of her legs began to knot. Disgusted with herself, she turned away from the window to return to her chair.

The high gloss on her desk was obliterated by a mountain of paperwork to her left, which was only increments smaller than the mountain of paperwork to her right. She closed her eyes and tried to relax, playing her favorite what-if game. The one that went...what if she walked out of the office and never came back? In her mind, she was halfway out of town when her secretary, Nola Sue, buzzed.

"Mrs. Justice, you have a delivery."

The mention of her name change alone was enough to yank Casey back to reality.

"Just sign for it. I'll pick it up later."

"I'm sorry, Mrs. Justice, but the man insists on your signature only."

Casey sighed. "Then send him in."

Moments later, the door opened and a uniformed messenger

came into the room. Brief and to the point, he handed her a clipboard and a pen.

"Sign here, please."

Casey did as she was told, casually eyeing the flat, oblong package the man laid on her desk.

"Good day, Mrs. Justice."

And then he was gone.

My, how word does get around in this town, Casey thought, as she slipped a letter opener between the folds of paper. A glimmer of color began to emerge from beneath the plain, brown wrapping. The second layer of paper was a thick, pure white embossed with silver doves. An obvious allusion to the wedding that hardly was. Curious now, she abandoned the letter opener for her fingers and tore through that layer to a flat black box.

It was a little over a foot in length and no more than three or four inches in width. The lid was hinged by two delicate foil butterflies. Casey gasped at the contents as a card fell out and into her lap.

Inside lay a miniature rapier on thick, black velvet. She lifted it from the case, hefting it lightly. It felt heavy, even warm in her hand, and she knew before she turned it over to view the silversmith's mark that it was probably solid silver. It was the most elaborate letter opener she'd ever seen.

Curious, she laid it aside and picked up the card, all the while wondering who would send her such a thing. She read, "Casey, On your nuptials: You deserve this...and so much more. Lash."

She frowned at the oddity of the phrasing, then laid the card aside and picked the small rapier up again, eyeing the double-edged blade with caution. Something near the tip caught her eye. At first, she thought it was rust, and that the letter opener must not be silver after all, because silver did not rust. Even after she ran the tip of her finger across the spot, it didn't come off. But when she lifted it for a closer look, she suddenly shifted in her seat, making room for the unexpected sense of foreboding that swept over her.

She swiveled her chair toward the window and full light, tilting the blade for a closer look still, then tested the spot with the tip of a fingernail. It came away on her nail. Startled, she grabbed for a tissue and wiped at her finger, unprepared for the small, red stain that suddenly appeared against stark white.

She couldn't quit staring. The spot wasn't rust, it was blood—dried blood. But in such a small amount that it might have gone unnoticed.

Now her delight in such a gift was replaced with dismay. It seemed a travesty of something pure to receive a wedding gift with blood on it. The urge to put it out of sight was strong. She laid it back in the box, closing the lid with care, but the words on the card had now taken on a sinister meaning.

You deserve this...and so much more.

Deserve what? What did she deserve? The silver...the knife...or the blood?

The phone rang. It was the private line that only family ever used. She grabbed for it like a lifeline.

"Hello."

"Casey, darling, it's Erica. Have you seen Grandmother?"

For once, she was almost thankful for the whine in her half sister's voice. It gave her something else on which to focus besides Lash's gift.

"No, I'm sorry, but I haven't."

Erica sighed. "It's nearly one o'clock. She was going to meet me for lunch, and she's thirty minutes late. She's never late, you know."

Casey frowned. That much was true. Gran had a thing about being tardy.

"It's probably all his fault," Erica said.

"All whose fault?" Casey asked.

"Your husband...the family chauffeur...however you choose to define him. He took Grandmother shopping hours ago and no one's seen a sign of them since." The tone of Erica's voice rose an octave. "We don't know a thing about him. I can't believe you actually brought a stranger into this household, shoved him down our throats and then expected us to accept his presence as status quo."

Casey stifled a sigh. This was all she needed.

"Look, Erica. Nothing has happened to Gran. If it had, Ryder would have called. He is not a fiend. Besides, why didn't you call her instead of me? There's a phone in the Lincoln."

"I know that," Erica snapped. "But no one's answering."

Casey looked at the stacks of files on her desk and wondered how her grandfather had gone so wrong. She was beating her head against a thousand brick walls and all Erica had to worry about was a late luncheon date.

"I don't know what to tell you," Casey said. "I'm sure she's fine. I'm sorry she's late."

The connection between them was broken when Erica slammed the receiver back into the cradle. For a few wonderful moments, all Casey could hear were muffled voices from the outer office. With a dogged determination of which Delaney Ruban would have been proud, Casey dropped the gift into a drawer and buzzed Nola Sue.

"Cancel my lunch with Rosewell and Associates. Reschedule for sometime next week."

"Yes, ma'am," Nola Sue said, making notations as she listened to Casey's orders. "Do you want me to order you something to eat?"

"I suppose," she said. "And call home. Tell them I'll be working late and not to hold dinner."

Within seconds, she'd forgotten about Lash Marlow's present and Erica's phone call. Her entire focus was on the figures before her and the study she would need before she could make an offer for the acquisition of the Harmon Canneries near Tupelo.

A short while later, Nola Sue set a small, plastic tub of chicken salad, a cold roll, and a melting cup of iced tea on the corner of Casey's desk and tiptoed out without uttering a word.

It was sometime later before Casey even noticed that lunch had been served.

"Want some ketchup on those fries?" Ryder asked. Eudora poked the lingering end of a fast-food French fry into her mouth and then shook her head. Seconds later, Ryder handed her a fistful of paper napkins.

"Thank you," she said.

When she was certain Ryder's attention was otherwise occupied, she licked the salt from her fingers before drying them on the paper napkins he'd tossed in her lap, then leaned back against the seat, sighing with satisfaction.

She couldn't remember the last time food had tasted this good. Stifling a small belch, she lifted her cup to her lips and latched onto the straw poking through the plastic lid, sucking with all her might. A couple of swallows later, she began to suck air.

"How about another cherry limeade?"

"No, but thank you," Eudora said, and tossed a used napkin on the floor next to the wrapper that had been around her cheeseburger.

The food had been delicious. She wasn't going to think about the fact that it had all been served in recycled paper. There was something about reusing paper—in any form or fashion—that smacked of poverty. Eudora Deathridge had not suffered a day of want in her entire life, and had no intentions of starting now. She belched again, then sighed. This had been worth her impending heartburn.

Ryder hid a grin. He'd given her hell this morning and knew it. From the time they'd entered the first store, to the last one they'd exited just before lunch, he'd been on her heels at every turn.

He had been nothing but respectful. It wasn't in him to be anything else. But he figured the "family" needed to know right off that while he didn't mind driving them all over kingdom come, he was going to do it his way. And if that meant making himself a slight nuisance, then so be it. He was the best when it came to being a pain in the ass. If they didn't believe him, then they could just ask his...

Oh, God. He'd done it again. Micah's name kept hovering at the edge of his mind, popping out when least expected. He hated being weak, but guilt was eating him alive. No longer hungry, he began stuffing his leftovers back into the sack they'd come in.

"Here you go, Dora." He handed the half-filled sack over the seat.

Surprised by the gesture, she took it before she thought, letting it dangle between her fingers like something foul.

"What am I to do with this?"

"Trash. Put your trash in it."

She stared at the papers she'd tossed on the floorboard in disbelief. He was asking her to pick up trash? This time he'd overstepped his bounds.

"Now see here," she complained. "I don't think you..."

Ryder turned. Their gazes met. His eyes were dark and filled with a pain she hadn't expected.

"Need some help?"

"I don't believe so," she said quietly. "But thank you just the same."

She opened the sack and leaned down. A few moments later, she handed it back, watching as he tossed it in a barrel on the way out of the parking lot.

"Ryder."

He glanced up. Again, their gazes met briefly, this time in the rearview mirror.

"Yes, ma'am?"

"I'm ready to go home now."

He took the next turn, wishing he could say the same.

It was after eight o'clock. Ryder paced the small apartment like a caged bear—back and forth, from window to chair, unable to concentrate on the story on television, or eat the food congealing on his plate. Stifled by the presence of walls, he refused to admit that he was worried about Casey's absence.

Another half hour passed. By this time, he was steaming. He knew for a fact that Miles had packed up and left for a three-day trip to New Orleans to play. Erica and her grandmother had had a fight and Erica was sulking in her room because Dora had refused to grovel for forgetting their lunch date. Even Joshua and Tilly had finished up for the night and gone home. But Casey was still on the job. Something about that just didn't sit right with him, and his patience was gone.

He grabbed his hat on the way out the door. In a shorter time than one might have imagined, he had parked outside the Ruban Building and was on his way inside. A guard stopped him at the door.

"Sorry sir, but the offices are closed for the night."

Ryder shocked himself by announcing, "I'm here to pick up my wife."

"And who might that be?" the guard asked.

"Her name is—was—Casey Ruban."

The man took a quick step back, eyeing Ryder with new attention.

"You'd be the fellow Miss Ruban married."

Ryder nodded.

"Well, now, I might need to see some identification…just for the first time, you understand."

Ryder opened his wallet.

"Justice…yep, that would be you, all right," the guard said. "We heard Miss Ruban had married a man named Justice." He reached for the phone. "Just a minute, sir, and I'll let her know you're here."

"No," Ryder said, and then softened the tone of his voice with a halfhearted grin. "I was sort of planning to surprise her."

The guard smiled. "Yes, sir, I understand. Take the elevator to the top floor. Her office is the first one on your right."

"Thanks," Ryder said.

"You're welcome, sir," the guard said. "And congratulations on your marriage. Miss Ruban is a fine lady."

Ryder nodded. Even though she was a little hardheaded, he was beginning to have the same opinion of her himself.

By the time he got to her office, his sense of injustice was in high form. He walked inside and past the empty secretary's desk without pausing; his gaze fixed on the thin line of light showing from beneath the door on the far side of the room.

Casey's head hurt, her shoulders ached, and she was so far past hungry it didn't count. What was worse, she didn't even know it. Realization of her condition came only after the door to her office swung open and Ryder stalked into the room.

Startled, she stood too swiftly. The room began to tilt.

Ryder saw her sway and grabbed her arm before she staggered.

All she could think to say was, "What are you doing here?" before he took the pen from her hand, and turned out the desk lamp.

"I came to take you home. Your day is over. It's night. It's time to rest. It's time to slow the hell down. Do you understand me?"

He was mad. That was what surprised her most. Why should he be angry? It took a bit to realize that he wasn't angry at her. He was angry on her behalf. At that point, lack of food and exhaustion kicked in. Damn him, he wasn't supposed to be nice…at least, not like this.

She shrugged out of his grasp and reached for her purse. "I don't need you telling me what to do."

He stood between her and the doorway and once again, Casey caught a glimpse of the same man who'd come out of the shadows of Sonny's Place and taken a dare no other man had had the guts to take.

"Then consider it a suggestion," he said quietly, and reached for her arm.

This time she didn't pull away. They walked all the way to the elevator without talking, then past the night guard who grinned and winked. Silence was maintained all the way out to the car. It was only after Casey felt the seat at the back of her legs that she began to relax.

Ryder slid behind the wheel, then looked at her. It didn't take him long to make the decision. "Buckle up. You choose, but you're not going home until you eat."

Casey wrinkled her nose. "The car smells like French fries."

"Dora spilled a few. I'll clean it out tomorrow."

It took Casey a moment for the answer to connect. Dora? French fries? In the car? She turned where she sat, staring at Ryder in sudden confusion.

"Who's Dora?"

"You are bad off," he said, as he put the car in gear and backed out of the parking space. "She's your grandmother, isn't she?"

"You called her Dora?"

He shrugged as he pulled into traffic. "Said she didn't want me calling her ma'am."

"Why was Dora...I mean Gran...eating French fries in the car?"

"Because they went with her cheeseburger and cherry limeade."

Casey's mouth dropped. "She ate fast food?"

He grinned. "Ate it real fast, too. Never saw a woman so hungry."

Casey still didn't believe she was getting the story straight. "She ate her meal in the back seat of a car?"

Ryder gave her a sidelong glance. "Are you still faint?"

She covered her face with her hands and groaned. "My God, why did you take Gran to a fast-food restaurant?"

"Because she was hungry, that's why."

"But..."

He took the corner in a delicate skid, the likes of which the Lincoln had never seen. "You know what?"

Casey clutched at her seat belt, almost afraid to ask. "What?"

"You people are too uptight. You need to loosen up a little. If you did, you might find out you like it. Better yet, you might even live long enough to spend all that money you're so dead set on making."

There wasn't a civil thought in her head as Ryder turned off the highway and into another parking lot. But when he opened the door to help her out, the odor of charbroiled meat made her forget her anger. A few moments later, she realized where he'd brought her, and if she hadn't been so hungry, she would have laughed.

As he led her in the restaurant, she would have been willing to bet the last dollar she had in her pocket that, by tomorrow, it would be all over Ruban Crossing that Eudora Deathridge had eaten French fries in the back seat of a car. What was going to ice this piece of gossip was the fact that Casey and her honky-tonk husband had also shared a late-night dinner at Smoky Joe's. As restaurants go, it wasn't bad. It was Smoky Joe's sideline that gave him, and his restaurant, such a bad reputation.

Casey lifted her chin as they walked inside. She could tell by the sounds coming from the back room that the floor show was in full swing.

"Wonder what's going on back there?" Ryder asked, as he guided Casey to an empty booth.

"Mud wrestling," she said. One eyebrow arched as she waited for his reaction.

His interest sparked, he had to ask. "Women or 'gators?"

"Women," she replied.

She watched as the light in his eyes faded. She sighed. She should have known it would take more than naked women in a hot tub's worth of red clay to get him excited.

"I think he saves the 'gators for Saturday nights."

He handed her a menu. "Good. It'll give us a reason to come back."

Chapter 6

"I'm coming out. Are you decent?" Ryder yelled.

Casey pulled the sheet up past her breasts and tried to look relaxed as the bathroom door opened. He emerged, but she'd closed her eyes too late. My God! Doesn't he own a bathrobe? she wondered.

"I'll be through in a second," he said.

Casey could hear drawers opening and closing and clenched her eyelids even tighter. That damp towel around his waist was far too brief for her piece of mind.

Footsteps moved toward the doorway.

She opened her eyes. Too soon. She'd looked too soon. He was still there, standing in the doorway in a pair of white briefs. Lamplight spilled into the bedroom from behind him.

This time, his presence did more than unnerve her. Even though his face was in shadow, she knew he was watching her.

She held her breath.

He didn't speak.

In the bathroom next door, water dripped from the showerhead and into the tub. Then dripped again. Then again. Then again.

He started toward her, one slow step at a time. Casey stifled a moan, clutching at the sheet until her fingers went numb. Once she started to speak, and couldn't remember enough words to string together in one sentence. She went from panic to dismay to a calm she didn't expect. But when he walked past her and into the bathroom without saying a word, her calm moved to disbelief.

This time when he emerged, he didn't look back. The door swung shut between them with a firm thud and Casey was left with nothing but the sound of a racing heart. The drip no longer dripped. The man was no longer a threat. She was safe and sound and alone in her bed—and she didn't remember ever feeling as lonely as she did right now.

"What's wrong with me?"

She rolled onto her stomach, punching her pillow and yanking at her nightgown until she heard ribbons tearing. Finally, she closed her eyes, willing herself to sleep, and blamed her restless spirit on the barbecue she'd eaten at Smoky Joe's.

A chair scooted in the other room. He was obviously making his bed out on the floor. The comfort of hers as opposed to the one he was about to take made her feel guilty. She thumped her pillow and shifted her position. She just couldn't help it. He'd known from the start this wasn't going to be a normal marriage.

But no one told him he'd be sleeping on the floor for the next twelve months.

The long, unmistakable rasp of a large metal zipper being undone plucked at her conscience. The sleeping bag.

She rolled over on her back and opened her eyes. Although the king-size bed took up a lot of space in the bedroom, there was still ample room in which to move about. Their sleeping arrangements could do with an overhaul. Maybe if she traded the king-size bed for two twin-size ones—

Her nerves shifted into higher gear. That would be fair, but it would also increase the intimacy of their sleeping arrangements. She trusted herself to cope with it, but could she trust the man who was now her husband to stay in his own bed and on his own side of the room?

Well, why not? They were adults. Hopefully, two responsible adults. Nothing was going to happen. Having satisfied herself with what seemed a plausible solution, she sighed with exhaustion.

Lord, but it felt good to lie down. At the same time, she realized that she was here in bed, fed, bathed and resting because Ryder Justice had seen to it. She rolled back over on her stomach and burrowed her nose a little deeper into her pillow, savoring the knowledge that someone cared enough about her to make a scene. What she couldn't do was make a big deal out of it. Ryder Justice was simply passing through her life, not becoming a part of it.

Ryder couldn't sleep. The floor was hard. The covers hot. He kicked them back, leaving his body bare to the night, and still the cool flow of air blowing across his arms and legs could not ease the tension coiling within him.

Images kept popping into his mind. Casey alone at her desk. Casey in the other room, alone in that bed. He sat up with a jerk and reached for his jeans. *Get out. Get out now before you make a mistake you can't fix.*

Ryder didn't hesitate. He didn't need to know whether it was conscience or gut instinct warning him off. All he knew was he had to put some distance between himself and the woman who was his wife.

Grabbing his boots, he exited the apartment, then sat down at the top of the landing to put them on. The air outside felt thick, almost too warm and too stifling to breathe. Perspiration instantly broke the surface of his skin. He stood, then started down the stairs with no goal in mind other than to move.

Security lights dotted the grounds of the vast estate, highlighting the driveways, the doors to the house, and the area just inside the rim of trees circling the lawns. Down on the highway outside the city, he heard an eighteen-wheeler shifting gears as the driver maneuvered around a curve in the road.

Crickets rasped. A night bird called. A stringy cloud floated past the surface of a pale half-moon. Ryder lifted his head, inhaling the scents, absorbing the sounds. Ordinary sounds. But there was nothing ordinary about his situation, and there hadn't been since he'd walked out on his life six months earlier.

For lack of a better destination, he aimed for the trees at the far edge of the estate. It felt good to move, to be doing something besides lying in the dark and wishing for something he couldn't have. He glanced up at the mansion as he passed, trying to imagine what it would be like to grow up in such an austere environment. He'd had wide open spaces and brothers. Horses to ride and endless days of childhood where nothing ever changed and the status quo was your security blanket with which to sleep each night.

Music drifted to him from somewhere out beyond the ring of lights, probably from a passing car. It reminded him of the nights at home when he and Roman and Royal had been kids; of watching his mother and father dancing cheek to cheek out on the front porch while an old portable radio played nearby. He wiped a shaky hand across his face, remembering the night Barbara Justice had died leaving Micah to raise their three young sons alone.

Ryder paused, blindly reaching for the nearest tree as his composure crumpled.

You were the strong one, Daddy. You survived everything...except what I did to you.

Long, silent moments passed while Ryder stood in judgment of himself. Moments in which his heart broke and bled countless times over. And finally, it was the sound of laughter from another passing car that brought him to his senses.

Laughter. Proof that life does go on.

Angry that he was still part of that life, he moved deeper into the trees and away from temptation, unaware that he was being watched from the upper windows of the family home.

* * *

When Ryder moved out of sight, Erica stepped away from the window and flopped down on her bed, but the intensity of her conversation with Miles was still going strong. Although it was not necessary, she caught herself whispering into the phone.

"I said, I don't know what he's doing, but he's not sleeping in our dear sister's bed, that's for sure."

New Orleans at midnight was lively. More than once, Miles had given serious thought to never going home. He downed the last of the bourbon in his glass and then waved to a passing waitress for a refill before shifting his cell phone to his other ear.

"Look, sister darling, I already told you. It doesn't matter if he and Casey never get it on. The terms of the will have been met. She got married. She's living under his roof—under his protection. If it lasts a year, she's done her part."

Erica pouted. "It isn't fair."

Miles lifted his glass in a silent toast to a woman across the room before answering. "Who ever said life was fair?"

Erica kicked off her slippers and stretched out on her bed, absently admiring the color of polish on her fingers and toes. Practicing a pout she hadn't used in years, Erica's voice rose an octave.

"I can certainly vouch for the fact that life around here is deadly dull. When are you coming home?"

The woman in the bar lifted her own glass in a long-distance toast to Miles and smiled. His pulse reacted by skipping an anticipatory beat.

"Soon. Maybe tomorrow. The day after for sure."

Erica frowned. "Well, all I can say is you'd better hurry. Grandmother is beginning to waffle. In fact, if I didn't know better, I'd think she was quite smitten with Casey's honky-tonk man."

That wasn't something Miles wanted to hear. "You're kidding!"

"No, I'm not. She missed a lunch date with me and has been closemouthed about the reason why. All I know is, she scolded me for a comment I made about the chauffeur and then took herself off to her room.''

The woman across the room was smiling openly now. Miles knew an invitation when it was being sent, and listening to his sister whine about an old woman's bad attitude was ruining the moment.

"Look, Sis, I've got to go. When I know my flight, I'll call. Someone will have to pick me up at the airport.''

He disconnected in Erica's ear. She tossed her phone aside and picked up the television remote, but there was nothing on the tube that was as interesting as the man who was wandering through their woods. Curiosity won out over caution as she rolled out of bed in search of her shoes. She wouldn't go far. Certainly no farther than the back lawn. Definitely not into the trees. But she was going. She couldn't stand the suspense any longer.

Ryder walked until the darkness lifted from his spirit. When he came to himself enough to stop, he realized he could no longer see the house. In fact, he wasn't even sure which way it was and right now he didn't much care. Out here there were no walls to hold him back. He could run as far and as fast as his legs would take him, just as he'd been doing before he'd walked into that bar down in the flatlands. Casey had changed everything. And he'd let her.

Now his running days were over. Maybe he had no purpose on which to focus, but she certainly did. He'd never seen a woman so driven, so determined to succeed at all costs. He'd given her his word—and the Justice men did not go back on their word.

In the distance, a hound bayed and another answered. He recognized the sounds. They had keyed on a prey. At that moment, in the dark, alone in the woods, he could almost empathize with whatever creature was on the run. He knew what it felt like to be lost with nowhere to go. To run and run and then wind up at a dead end and facing destruction. That's where he'd been going when Casey Ruban walked into his life. In a way, he'd come to look upon her as his anchor, because without her, he had nowhere to go.

He turned back the way he'd come. A short while later he emerged from the woods to find himself within yards of the place at which he'd entered. Instinct and the need to get back to her had led him home.

He started across the lawn when a shadow moved between him and the bush to his right. Instinctively he doubled his fists, preparing to do battle when Erica stepped into the light.

"Sorry," she said. "Did I frighten you?"

He combed a shaky hand through his hair as adrenaline began to subside.

"No."

She giggled nervously and took a step closer, then another, then another, until she could feel the heat emanating from his body. Her eyes widened as a single bead of sweat pooled at the base of his neck, then spilled over onto the broad surface of his chest. When the sweat split the middle of Ryder's belly, she moved another step closer, tilting her chin until their gazes met. The invitation was in her eyes...in her voice...in the thrust of her breasts beneath pale yellow silk.

"Ummm, I didn't know little sister liked them this rough-cut. Poor Lash. He never stood a chance against a stud like you."

Like a moth drawn to a flame, she reached out, her intentions painfully clear, and found her arm suddenly locked in a painful grip.

Their gazes met. His dark and wary, warning her away; hers wild and frightened by what she perceived as an imminent threat.

"Let me go!" she gasped.

"Then back off," Ryder said, his voice just above a whisper.

She gasped, stung by the outrage of such an obvious refusal of her company, and yanked herself free.

"How dare you?" she said.

"No, sister dear, how dare you?"

Heat suffused her face. "I don't know what you mean," she cried.

His voice lowered, his words wrapping around her conscience, burning deeper and deeper with each angry syllable.

"Like hell. Don't tell me you only came out here to see if your sister's new husband would play hide-and-seek."

A sense of shame she didn't expect kept her momentarily silent. He was right, and she hated him for that and so much more. Unfortunately, Erica had never learned the wisdom of silence.

"I came out here because I thought I saw a prowler."

Ryder raked her with a gaze that left her feeling as if she'd been stripped and branded. If she hadn't been so afraid to turn her back on him, she would have dashed into the house.

"The only thing on the prowl out here is you," he said, and then walked away.

Her fear subsided as the distance between them grew, but it was obvious to Erica that Ryder wasn't afraid of the dark— or of anything else on this earth.

Erica clenched her fists and thought about screaming—actually thought about tearing her own nightgown, scratching her own face and arms and crying rape just to get the son of a bitch in trouble. But she was too vain to deal with marring her skin and too angry to fake being scared.

"Damn you," she muttered, and spun on one heel before stalking back into the house. "Damn you and that stupid wife of yours all to hell!"

She slammed the door shut behind her, her breasts heaving, her face flushed with a rage she hadn't felt in years, and suddenly found herself standing in a wash of white light.

She shrieked. "Tilly! My God! You scared me to death! What do you mean by sneaking around down here in the middle of the night?"

Tilly loomed over her like a dark, avenging angel. "Well, now, Miss Erica, I was just about to ask you the same thing."

At a loss for words, Erica pushed past her. She didn't have to explain herself to the help. She was halfway down the hallway when Tilly spoke, and her voice carried all too clearly in the quiet of the house.

"I saw what you did."

Erica stumbled, then picked up the tail of her gown, and started running toward the stairs. When she reached the safety of her room, she turned the lock and then threw herself on the bed and burst into tears. Somehow, she was going to have to find a way to make this right. It wouldn't do to make her baby sister angry. Not now. Not when she controlled the purse strings and everything else that mattered in Erica's world.

Ryder shut the door behind him, then stood in the darkness, listening. Casey was asleep. Even though the bedroom door was closed, he imagined he could hear the soft, even sounds of her breathing. The air-conditioning unit kicked on and the hum quickly drowned out all but the angry thunder of his own heart.

He looked down at himself, at the sweat running down his body, at the grass stains on the legs of his jeans, and took off his boots. He dropped his jeans by the bedroom door and kept on walking. Careful not to wake Casey, he closed the door to the bathroom before turning on the light.

Completely nude, he stepped beneath the showerhead before turning on the water, uncaring that the first surge came out fast and cold. He reached for the soap and began to scrub himself clean. This time when he was through, he knew he'd be able to sleep. His mind was as weary as his body.

He wrapped another towel around his waist before turning off the light, then opened the door, standing for a moment and letting his eyes adjust to the shadows. When he could see without stumbling, he started across the room.

Later, he would tell himself if he hadn't looked down...if he hadn't seen all that long dark hair strewn across her pillow and thought about what it would feel like to sleep wrapped up in its length, he might have made it out of the room.

But, he had looked, and the thought had crossed his mind,

and now he stood without moving at the foot of her bed, studying the face of the woman to whom he'd given his name.

She slept on her back with one arm flung over her head and the other resting on her belly. His first impression of her hadn't changed. She was truly a beautiful woman. But he'd learned since that first meeting in Sonny's Bar that the essence of Casey Ruban Justice did not lie in the strength of her features, but in the strength of the woman who wore them.

There in the quiet intimacy of a bedroom they had yet to share, Ryder realized he might not know the woman who was his wife, but he respected the hell out of what she stood for, and for tonight, that was enough on which to sleep.

He walked out, taking great care not to let the door bang shut behind him. The sleeping bag was right where he'd left it. He dropped his towel and crawled into it as bare as the day he'd been born, then closed his eyes, waiting for sleep to overtake his weary mind.

In the room next door and in the bathroom beyond, water dripped from the showerhead at a slow, methodic rate. And they slept, and finally, morning came back to start a new day.

Erica was playing it cool. In her mind, the incident with Casey's husband had never happened. She strode down the hall with purpose, heading for the kitchen, fully aware that was where Ryder would be eating his meal.

"There you are," she said, as if he'd been in hiding. "Miles called. You need to go to the airport and pick him up."

Tilly set a stack of dishes in the sink and wiped her hands on her apron as Ryder stood up from the table. "Oh, set yourself down and finish your food," she told him. "That boy won't be here any earlier than noon. He doesn't like to get up in the morning, so I dare say he won't be on any of the morning flights."

Erica refused to rise to Tilly's bait. "Here's his flight number and the time of his arrival. Don't be late. Miles doesn't like to be kept waiting."

Ryder slipped the note in his pocket without comment.

Erica pivoted, her duty done, and got all the way to the hallway before she got the guts to turn and ask, "Has anyone seen Casey this morning? I needed to talk to her about something."

"Board of directors meeting this morning. Been gone since seven," Ryder replied.

"Pooh," Erica said. "Business, always business."

"And that business keeps you off the streets, missy," Tilly told her sharply, banging a lid on a pan for good measure.

"And you in the kitchen where you belong," Erica retorted, and walked out, wishing she'd made a more ladylike exit by keeping her mouth shut. It seemed so common to argue with the help. Next time she wouldn't give the old biddy the satisfaction of a response.

"That woman makes my teeth ache," Tilly muttered.

Ryder kept silent, but he knew what she meant. A woman who would willingly seduce her sister's man wasn't the kind of woman who could ever be trusted. He took a long sip of coffee. Even if the sister wasn't sleeping with the man herself, it was still crossing a line no family member should ever cross.

Tilly topped off Ryder's coffee, then did something she'd promised herself years ago never to do. She meddled in family business.

"You watch out for that woman," Tilly warned.

Ryder glanced up, more than a little surprised.

"I know more than you think I know," she said softly. "I saw what she tried to do the other night."

Ryder's eyes narrowed as he braced himself for a retribution that never came.

"And I heard what you said."

He shifted uncomfortably in his chair and busied himself with adding sugar to coffee he didn't want.

Tilly put her hand on Ryder's shoulder and kept it there until he looked up.

"I have my notions about things," she told him.

"I'll just bet that you do."

Tilly refused to be swayed by the engaging grin he gave her.

"First time I laid eyes on you, I knew you were a good man. After what I saw the other night, I know you're going to be good for my Casey, too."

This time, Ryder was more than uncomfortable.

"Look, what's between Casey and me is strictly business," he said. "She asked for help. I offered. It's as simple as that."

Tilly lifted her chin and turned away, refusing to listen to what he had to say. "You're wrong, you know. Nothing is ever simple between a man and a woman."

Ryder set his cup down with a thump, sloshing the freshly sweetened brew out onto the white-tiled tabletop.

"I better be going," he stated. "The Lincoln needs gas, and I've got to find out where the airport is before noon."

Tilly turned. "You go on and get your gas. You find that airport and do your job and bring Mr. Miles on home. But you just remember this. It doesn't matter how long and how hard you work during the day, come nighttime, you and Casey Dee are going to be all alone."

Ryder reached for his hat. He damn sure didn't need anyone reminding him of that.

"Find yourselves some common ground," Tilly called out as he left the room. "You hear me? You have to start somewhere. Forget the gap and look for the bridge."

He was still thinking about that bridge Tilly had been talking about when he took the highway exit leading to the airport. A small, twin-engine Cessna lifted off directly in front of his view and he found himself stopping in the middle of the road to watch its ascent.

Even though the plane was a good half mile away and already several hundred feet in the air, his toes curled in his boots and he caught himself holding his breath until the plane leveled off. He lost sight of it when it turned toward the sun.

A car honked behind him, and he slipped his foot off the

brake and drove on. But the damage had already been done. The hunger to fly was mixed up in his mind with the fear of repeating a deadly mistake all over again.

Get it in gear, he reminded himself, and began looking for a place to park. He didn't have to fly. He was only here to give a man a ride home. No big deal. But his hands were shaking when he got out of the car, and the closer he got to the terminal, the slower his stride became. It was all he could do to make himself walk inside, but he did it.

Cool air hit him in the face, and he inhaled deeply, welcoming the change in temperature as his nerves began to settle. He paused while he got his bearings, then started toward the arrival gate of the flight on which Miles Dunn would arrive.

His nerves were strung so tight, he caught himself holding his breath. Twice he had to remind himself to ease up. And he should have known this would happen. Just because he wasn't piloting the planes didn't make this experience any easier.

He settled the Stetson firmly upon his head and gave the announcement boards a closer look. Being here brought back too many bad memories. That was all. Just too many memories. And no man ever died from memories.

"Flight 1272 from Atlanta and New Orleans is now arriving at Gate Three."

Buoyed by the announcement, Ryder took his bearings then started walking. Erica had claimed that Miles didn't like to be kept waiting and God knows he didn't have any desire to linger in the place himself.

Miles was hung over. His head throbbed and his belly kept lurching from one side of his rib cage to the other as he filed out of the plane along with the other passengers. Bile rose as he stared at the drooping diaper of the toddler in front of him. An all too pungent odor drifted upward, adding to the nausea he already had. That kid was carrying a load and badly in need of a change. When a sickly sweat broke out on his upper lip, he mumbled an excuse and shoved his way past them, desperately searching the waiting crowd for Erica.

He saw the Stetson first, then the man beneath it and groaned. Damn her, why didn't she come herself?

"Here are my claim stubs," he said shortly, slapping them into Ryder's hand. "I'll meet you in baggage."

Ryder took the stubs without comment and waited beside the men's room until Miles came out.

"I thought I told you I'd meet you in baggage," Miles muttered.

Ryder gave him a pointed look. "Wasn't sure you'd make it that far."

Miles's face turned red.

"Lead the way," Ryder said, and Miles did.

Luggage was just beginning to come through the round-about as Miles dropped onto a nearby bench.

"Rough flight?" Ryder asked.

Miles looked up from where he was sitting and belched.

Ryder cocked an eyebrow and stifled a grin. "Tell me which ones are yours," he said, pointing toward the varied assortment of circling suitcases.

"Four pieces. Brown-and-green alligator. Can't miss them."

Ryder nodded and a short while later, pulled the last one from the rack. Miles watched with a bleary eye, unwilling to move until he had to.

"That's it," Ryder announced, and lifted a bag in each hand. "I'll get these. You bring the rest," and started toward the exit without looking back.

Miles sat with his mouth agape while blood thundered wildly through every minuscule vein in his head. He stared at the remaining two bags in disbelief. The nerve of the man! Expecting him to carry his own luggage!

Miles staggered to his feet and hefted a bag in each hand before following Ryder's retreat.

"This just figures," he mumbled, as he staggered out of

the door. "You can't get good help these days no matter how hard you try."

When they started home, Miles began to relax, reveling in the cool, quiet ambience of the Lincoln's spacious back seat. But that was before the car phone rang. After that, Miles's homecoming took an unexpected turn.

Chapter 7

The car phone rang as Ryder was leaving the airport and turning onto the highway. He answered on the second ring.

"This is Ryder."

When that slow, deep voice settled in her ear, Casey breathed a sigh of relief.

"Ryder, where are you?"

He frowned. "Casey, is that you?"

She turned away from the noise behind her, trying to block out the paramedics' voices, as well as the police officer on the scene. "Yes, it's me."

"I already picked him up. Just a minute and I'll hand him the phone."

"Picked up who?" she asked.

"Your brother, Miles."

"I don't want to talk to Miles. I want to talk to you."

Ryder's frown deepened as her voice suddenly shattered.

"I have a problem. Can you come help me?"

Before he could answer her, the ambulance that had been parked behind her took off for the hospital with sirens running. Startled by the unexpected noises in the background of their conversation, it began to dawn on him that there was more behind her request for help than the obvious.

"Casey, what's wrong?"

He heard her inhale, and then she spoke, and her voice was so soft he had to strain to hear her answer.

"I had a wreck."

The car swerved beneath him and Miles began to curse from the back seat. Even though it was broad daylight and Ryder was driving down the highway leading into Ruban Crossing, in his mind, he saw light flash across a dark, storm-filled sky, heard the sharp crack of lightning as it struck the fuselage of his plane, and smelled smoke, even though the air inside the car was cool and clean.

His fingers curled around the steering wheel in reflex, and it took him several seconds to realize what he was experiencing was a flashback, and that everything was safe and under control. He took a deep breath and started over, asking what mattered most.

"Are you hurt?"

"No…at least not much."

An odd tension settled inside his belly. Her voice was shaking. If she wasn't hurt, then she'd at least scared herself to death.

"Are you at the hospital?"

He thought he heard a sob in her voice as she answered. "No, I'm still at the scene."

"Easy, honey. Just tell me where you are and how to get there."

She told him, and only afterward realized what he'd called her, but by then it didn't matter. He was already sliding to a stop at the intersection where the accident had occurred, and it would seem from the way the back door was flung open, he'd stopped just in time.

Miles leaned out and threw up on the right rear tire as Ryder jumped out of the front seat. After that, Casey didn't see anything but the look on her husband's face. She took a deep breath and started toward him.

Ryder felt sick. He could see a bump on her forehead that was already turning blue, and there was a small trickle of blood at the edge of her lip.

Wrecks. Damn, damn, damn, but he hated the sight of spilled fuel and crumpled metal. It reminded him of things he'd spent months trying to forget.

"Come here," he said softly, and pulled her close against his chest while he surveyed what was left of her car. The front half had been shifted all the way to the right, compliments of a one-ton truck that had run a red light. "Thank God for air bags," he said, eyeing the one that had inflated inside her car.

Her voice was shaking as she reached up, tentatively testing the size of the bump on her forehead. "It wasn't my fault."

Ryder caught her fingers, then lifted them to his lips in a quiet, easy gesture before cupping her face with his hand.

"It wouldn't matter if it was. What matters is getting you to a doctor. Why didn't they send an ambulance for you?"

"I told them I wanted to wait for you. Besides, I didn't think I needed…"

He missed whatever it was she said next. He kept hearing her say she'd been waiting for him. That did it. Whatever hesitation he'd had about holding her close was gone. He tilted her chin, carefully surveying the burgeoning bruises and angry red scrapes on the tender surface of her skin.

"I don't care what you think. You're going and that's that."

Casey rested her forehead against his chest. How long had it been since she'd had someone upon whom she could lean? When his grip around her firmed, for the first time in as long as she could remember, she felt safe…really safe. As she ran her tongue along the lower edge of her lip, tears began to well in her eyes.

She looked up at him for confirmation. "My lip is bleeding, isn't it?"

He wanted to kiss away the shock and the pain and the stunned expression in her eyes. He thought better of the urge and hugged her instead.

"Easy now. Let's get you in out of this sun. You can wait in the car with Miles while I tell that officer where I'm taking you."

"It's probably okay for me to leave," Casey said. "He already took my statement."

But she did as she was told, grateful for the fact that someone was taking over. It seemed her good sense and practicality was lost somewhere in the wreckage of her car and she couldn't think what to do next.

When she got inside, Miles was ominously silent. Casey glanced over her shoulder, wincing slightly as a strained muscle rejected the motion.

His condition would have been funny if it hadn't been too painful to laugh. He lay stretched out in the back seat with his arm thrown over his eyes, shielding them from the sun. He looked worse than she felt.

"Rough flight?"

He groaned and mumbled something she didn't understand. She turned around and closed her eyes, wishing that the world would stop spinning so she could get off.

Seconds later Ryder slid behind the wheel. He leaned over and fastened Casey's seat belt without giving her a chance to respond, then glanced in the back seat at his other passenger.

"Buckle up."

A brief, quick click broke the silence. It would seem that Ryder had made a believer out of Miles.

The trip to the emergency room was faultless, and it didn't take the doctor long to address Casey's bumps and bruises. They were minor. The injury that would take the longest to heal was to her peace of mind.

"While you're at it, you may as well give this one a going over," Ryder said, pointing at Miles who was slumped in a chair near the emergency room door.

Doctor Hitchcock frowned. "Was he in the accident, too?"

Ryder shook his head. "No. I had just picked him up at the airport when Casey called. He's a little the worse for wear. Guess his stomach's had a longer ride than it could tolerate."

Hitchcock gave Miles a judgmental look. He'd been doctoring the Ruban family for years, and it wasn't the first time he'd seen this one in a condition of his own making.

"Looks to me like he just needs a little of the hair of the dog that bit him."

It was the word *hair* that did it. Miles's stomach was too queasy for anything, including metaphors. He bolted for the bathroom seconds ahead of another surge.

Hitchcock snorted beneath his breath, but his eyes were twinkling as he glanced at Ryder.

"Casey will be ready to go by the time you bring the car around. Meanwhile, I suppose I can give the party animal something to help his nausea."

Casey tried a smile, but her lip was too swollen to do much about it, and her head was beginning to throb. "Thank you, Doctor Joe."

He patted her on the arm. "Don't thank me. Thank the good Lord for sparing you worse injury."

"Amen to that," Ryder said quietly, and went to get the car.

The doctor stared after him, then turned, giving Casey a long, intent look. "So, that's the new husband, is it?"

She sighed. "You heard."

He shook his head. "Lord, honey, who hasn't? Your sudden marriage has set the biggest piece of gossip in motion that Ruban Crossing has ever known. I don't know what Delaney was thinking when he pulled that stunt, but I can guarantee it wasn't these results."

Casey's eyes darkened in frustration. "I know what he wanted. He'd been after me for years to...let's see, how did he put it...marry well."

Hitchcock frowned. He'd known Delaney Ruban all of his life. In fact, they'd grown up together, and while Delaney had acquired more money in his lifetime than a man had a right to expect, he'd been obsessed about overcoming his upbringing as the son of a flatlands sharecropper.

"By that, I suppose you're referring to a socially acceptable marriage, such as to a fellow like Lash Marlow?"

Her shoulders slumped. "I couldn't do it, Doctor Joe. I couldn't marry a man I didn't love."

An odd smile broke the wrinkles in the old doctor's face. He looked toward the cowboy who was pulling that big white car to a stop outside the door.

"So, it must have been love at first sight for you two, then."

Casey looked startled. "Oh no! It was nothing like that. Ryder is a good man…at least I think he is. But we have an understanding. I'm just fulfilling the terms of Delaney's will. Nothing less. Nothing more. In a year, this will all be over."

Unaware that he'd been the topic of their conversation, Ryder came up the hallway, shook the doctor's hand, and all but carried Casey out to the waiting car.

Hitchcock had his own ideas about understandings. *That's what you say now, Casey Dee, but a year is a long, long time.*

As Miles Dunn staggered out of the bathroom with a wet paper towel pressed to his forehead, Hitchcock reminded himself of the vows he'd taken to administer to *all* who were sick or in need of healing and took him by the arm.

"Come with me, boy."

Miles looked out the door toward the car. He could see Casey was already seated inside. "But they're about to—"

"They'll wait." Hitchcock said. "Besides, this will make you feel better."

The doctor had said the magic words. Miles followed without further comment.

"Lord have mercy!"

If Tilly had said it once, she'd said it a dozen times since Ryder's arrival at the Ruban estate. And she was saying it again as Joshua passed through the kitchen on his way upstairs with an ice bag for Miles's head. The soup bubbling on the stove was for Casey. The tears running down her face were those of relief after she'd seen for herself that her girl was all right.

The house phone rang just as Ryder came in the back door.

Startled by the sound, Tilly jumped and the soup she was stirring sloshed over the side of the pot and splattered with a hiss onto the hot cooktop.

"Lord have mercy!" she muttered again.

"I'll get it," Ryder offered, and answered the phone before Tilly burst into a fresh set of tears.

Well aware that the call had to be from someone in the family, Ryder's answer was less than formal.

"This is Ryder, what's up?"

Erica's complaint was left hanging on the edge of her tongue. Somehow she didn't have the guts to say what she'd intended to say, at least not in the same tone of voice.

"Umm…I was wondering if someone was bringing up the ice bag for Miles's poor head."

Miles's poor head be damned, Ryder thought, but kept his opinion to himself. He glanced at Tilly.

"Erica wants to know about some ice bag."

"Tell her it's on the way up."

"It's on the way—"

"I heard her," Erica said. "Thank you."

"No problem," Ryder said, and started to hang up.

"Wait!" Erica shouted.

Ryder waited. It was her call. Her question. Her move.

"Is Casey all right? I mean, Miles said she'd had an accident."

"Come see for yourself," he offered. "She's at the apartment lying down, and I think she'd appreciate her sister's presence."

The thought of being in close proximity with Ryder gave Erica a chill. "Oh, I couldn't possibly leave Miles on his own. Grandmother isn't here and when she comes in, she's going to be beside herself that all of this happened while she was having her hair done."

A quiet anger he'd been trying to stifle suddenly bubbled over. "There's not a damned thing wrong with Miles. He's hung over, not hurt. Casey is the one who could have died today." He slammed the phone sharply onto the cradle and hoped that the disconnect popped in her ear.

Tilly hid her reaction, but she was secretly pleased. It was comforting to see someone else willing to champion her girl, especially a man who wasn't afraid to speak his mind.

Ryder turned, anger still evident in his voice. "Did Casey grow up in the same house with Miles and Erica?"

Tilly nodded.

"Then tell me something—how in blazes did she turn out so right and them so wrong? That pair must have been raised on ice water, not milk."

"They had each other," Tilly said. "After Casey's parents died, she didn't have much of anyone to baby her. Delaney loved her, but his intentions were focused on giving her the skills to run his empire, and truth be told, Mrs. Deathridge played favorites with the twins."

"Casey had you," Ryder said.

Tilly nodded. "Yes, that she did." She handed him a pot filled with the soup she'd just made. "It's vegetable beef, her favorite."

Ryder accepted the offering. "Thanks. Considering the blow Casey took to her mouth, that's about all she's going to feel like eating."

Tilly let him out the door, then watched as he crossed the courtyard, went up the stairs and into the garage apartment, carrying the hot pot of soup as if it were the crown jewels. When he was safely inside, she stepped back and closed the door. For the first time in weeks, she felt confident that things in this household were about to change for the better.

Not only did Ryder seem to respect Casey, but it looked as if he were willing to become her protector. However, just to be on the safe side, she might concoct a little potion. It wouldn't amount to much. Just a few herbs for good luck that she could sprinkle on their doorstep. Not a real spell.

* * *

Reclining in a nest of pillows, Casey winced as she reached for the phone, then had to shift the stack of papers in her lap to allow room for the smaller pillows beneath each of her elbows. Even though the accident had caused her to miss a stockholder's luncheon, it hadn't taken her long to regroup and bring the business to her.

At her request, her secretary had sent files on the most pressing issues and left the others that were pending back at the office. With a bowl of Tilly's soup for sustenance and the knowledge that Ryder was no farther away than the sound of her voice, she set up office in the middle of her bed and began going over the reports in question.

She read until the pain between her eyebrows grew too sharp to ignore and changed her tactics to returning the phone calls that had come to her office during her absence. It wasn't any easier. By late afternoon, it felt as if her lip was swollen to twice its normal size and the left side of her jaw was becoming increasingly sore. The last time she'd gotten up to go to the bathroom, she'd groaned at the sight of her face. The abrasion on her cheek was starting to scab, and by tomorrow, she was going to have one heck of a black eye.

Twice during this time, Ryder had appeared in the doorway. Once he'd frowned at the stack of work in her lap before disappearing without comment. The second time he'd come, the glare on his face was impossible to ignore, yet he'd still maintained a stoic silence about her behavior.

But the shock of the wreck was beginning to take its toll. Casey was near tears and wishing she could sweep everything off her bed, curl up in a ball beneath the covers and maybe cry herself to sleep. She heard footsteps coming up the outside stairs, then again inside the apartment. It was Ryder. She recognized the rhythm with which he walked.

He entered her bedroom without knocking just as the phone rang near her elbow. Before she could answer, he had it in his hands.

"Ruban Enterprises. No, I'm sorry, she is out for the rest

of the day. Call 555-4000 and make an appointment with her secretary.''

He tossed the portable phone completely out of her reach. Casey frowned. ''Hey! I wasn't through....''

''Yes, you are. Besides, I brought you a surprise.''

Casey sputtered in useless dismay as Ryder swept aside the files on which she'd been working. When he held out his hand, she sighed and took what he offered, using his strength to lever herself to an upright position on the side of the bed, then groaned when her muscles protested.

''Oh! I feel like I've been run over by a truck.''

''That's not funny,'' Ryder said, and scooped her into his arms before she had time to argue. ''Besides, if you think you hurt now, just wait until tomorrow.''

If it hadn't been so painful, she might have smiled. ''Thank you for such inspiring words of wisdom,'' she said, and slid her arm around his neck for balance as he carried her into the living room.

When he settled her down on the couch, she put her feet up on the footstool and eased herself into a comfortable position.

''Trust me, I know what I'm talking about,'' he said. ''By morning, every muscle you have is going to protest. At any rate, you should have been in bed hours ago.''

''I was in bed,'' Casey argued.

''I meant, alone. Not with a half-ton of papers and that damned phone. If you'd wanted company, you should have let me know. I would have been glad to oblige.''

When she blushed, Ryder knew he'd gotten his point across.

Refusing to give him the benefit of seeing how much his words had bothered her, she folded her hands in her lap and looked around the room.

''So, where's my surprise?''

He went to the kitchen, returning moments later with a handful of paper towels and a box he'd taken out of the freezer.

"What's this?" Casey asked, as he plopped it in her lap.

"Popsicles. Assorted flavors. Pick which one you want and I'll put the others back for later."

Her delight was only slightly more than her surprise. "Popsicles? You brought me Popsicles?"

"They won't hurt your mouth, I swear. In fact, it's going to feel pretty darn good on that swollen lip." He took the box out of her lap and tore open the top like an impatient child who couldn't wait for permission. "Which one do you want first? The red ones are cherry. The green ones are lime. The orange ones speak for themselves."

"I like grape. Are there any grape ones?"

"Grape it is," Ryder said, as he peeled the paper from a length of frozen purple ice.

Casey wrapped a paper towel around the wooden stick and took a lick, then another, then carefully eased her mouth around the end of the Popsicle and sucked gently. Cold, grape-flavored juice ran over her lips, into her mouth and onto her tongue. She closed her eyes, savoring the uniqueness of a childhood treat she hadn't had in years.

"Ummm, you were right. It tastes wonderful and doesn't hurt a bit."

Ryder caught himself holding his breath and squeezing the box of Popsicles until one broke inside the box under pressure. If someone had ever tried to tell him that women with black eyes and fat lips were sexy, he would have laughed in their face.

Unaware of the war waging inside her husband's conscience, Casey looked up. "Aren't you having any?"

Ryder shuddered then blinked. "I've had more than enough already," he muttered, and when someone knocked on the door, was saved from having to explain. "I'll get it. Sit still and eat your Popsicle before it melts."

Surprised by the unexpectedness of company, whoever it might be, Casey lifted a hand to her face. "I look so terrible."

Ryder's expression went flat. "I think your priorities got a little confused. Be glad you're alive to tell the tale."

The chill in his voice was only less intimidating than the look he was wearing. At that moment, Casey realized how little she really knew about the man who'd given her his name.

The knock sounded again and Ryder turned with the Popsicles still in hand and strode to the door, yanking it open with an abrupt, angry motion.

Outside heat swept inside, causing moisture to condense on the outside of the Popsicle box. Ryder was speechless. It was Eudora and she was clutching at the tail of her skirt with one hand and holding down her freshly done hair with the other as a hot, hasty wind blasted against the wall of the building.

"Are you going to ask me in, or am I to blow away?" Eudora asked.

He quickly regained his manners and stepped aside. "Sorry."

Eudora stepped over the threshold and into the apartment as if it were an everyday occurrence for her to be visiting the servants' quarters, when in actuality, she was quite curious as to the accommodations in which Casey had chosen to live.

The furnishings inside the garage apartment were simple compared to the elegance of the mansion, but to her surprise, the small rooms seemed comfortable…even homey. In fact it reminded her a bit of the first place she and Henry had shared.

Casey waved from where she was sitting. "Gran! Come in! I'm so glad you…"

Eudora gasped and clutched a hand to her throat as she walked toward Casey in disbelief.

"Oh my! Erica said you'd had an accident, but she led me to believe it wasn't…"

Eudora stopped talking, aware that whatever else she said was going to make Erica out to be thoughtless and uncaring. And while she silently acknowledged that fact from time to time, she wasn't willing to admit it aloud. Tears welled as she reached out to touch the side of Casey's cheek.

"Sweetheart, your face. Your poor little face. I'm so sorry. Is there anything I can do?"

Casey shook her head and then winced at the motion. "I'm fine, Gran. Actually, I look worse than I feel."

"I doubt that," Ryder said, and then extended the box toward Eudora. "What's your pleasure? We have orange, cherry or lime. We're saving the grape for Casey. They're her favorite."

Casey tried not to grin, but the shock on her grandmother's face was impossible to miss.

"Excuse me?" Eudora asked, eyeing the box Ryder had thrust beneath her nose.

"Popsicles. Want one?"

Casey held hers up to demonstrate, then realized it was melting and stuck it back in her mouth and sucked, rescuing the juice that would have dripped into the paper around the stick.

"Well, I don't think..."

Ryder dangled it under her nose. "Oh, come on, Dora. Have one."

When she almost grinned, Ryder knew she was hooked. "You're real fond of cherry limeade, so I'll bet you'd like a cherry one, wouldn't you?"

Without waiting for her to answer, he took one out of the box, unwrapped it as he'd done for Casey, and handed it to her with a paper towel around the stick to catch the drips.

"If anyone wants seconds, they'll be in the freezer."

Eudora stared at the icy treat he'd thrust in her hands and then straightened her shoulders, as if bracing herself for the worst. But when she lifted it to her mouth, the taste brought back sweet memories that made her heart ache. By the time she'd regained her sense of self, Ryder had made himself scarce.

"Well, now," Eudora said, and leaned back against the sofa cushions. "He's something, isn't he?"

There wasn't much she could add to what Gran had already said. "Yes, I suppose that he is."

"The question then remains, what are you going to do with

him for the next twelve months? Somehow, I can't see him playing chauffeur forever.''

Eudora ran the Popsicle in her mouth like a straw and sucked up what was melting with a delicate slurp while Casey thought about what Gran had said. What *was* Ryder going to do for the next twelve months? Even more important, what did she want him to do?

The clock on the bedside table stared back at Casey with an unblinking response. No matter how many times she looked, it seemed that time was standing still. It was midnight, and she'd been in bed for over two hours and had yet to relax enough to sleep. But it wasn't because she wasn't tired. She was. In fact, so tired that her bones ached.

She couldn't rest because every time she closed her eyes she kept seeing that truck coming out of nowhere—feeling the jarring impact of metal against metal—hearing her own scream cut off by the air bag that inflated in her face.

She rolled over on her side, then out of frustration, kept scooting until she was out of bed. If she could just get her mind into another channel, maybe she would be able to relax.

The bedroom door was slightly ajar, and she eased into the narrow opening like a shadow moving through space. Her body felt like one giant bruise, and every step she took was a lesson in endurance. As she started toward the kitchen, the room was suddenly bathed in light. She stifled a sigh. I should have known, she thought.

''What's wrong?''

She turned and then stammered on the apology she'd been about to make. Legs. He had the longest, strongest looking legs she'd ever seen on a man, and they were moving toward her. Casey made herself focus on his face.

''Uh...I couldn't sleep.''

His touch was gentle on her forehead as he felt for a rising temperature.

''You don't have a fever,'' he said, and cupped her face, peering intently into her eyes and checking for dilated pupils or anything else that would alert him to complications from her head injury.

But that could change at any minute, Casey told herself, and took a step back.

"I thought I'd get a drink of water," she said.

"I'll get it for you." He moved past her and into the small kitchen, sucking up the space and what was left of Casey's breath.

Moments later, he thrust a glass into her hands. Ice clinked against the sides as she lifted it to her lips and drank.

"Better?" he asked, as she handed it back.

She nodded and turned away. Ryder set the glass down and followed her awkward movements through the room with a thoughtful gaze. This was about more than a restless night. The tension in her posture and on her face was impossible to miss.

"You're afraid, aren't you?"

Startled by his perception, Casey turned and then couldn't hold the intensity of his gaze.

"It's okay," Ryder said. "Anyone would feel the same."

"How do you know so much about what I feel?" she asked.

"Let's just say, I've been there."

"You mean you've been in a—"

He interrupted, and Casey got the impression that it was because he didn't want to talk about it.

"Want me to sit with you for a while?" When she hesitated, he felt obligated to add, "No strings attached. Just one friend to another, okay?"

Her legs ached, her head was throbbing, and her eyelids were burning from lack of sleep. Maybe some company *would* help her to relax.

"Are you sure you don't mind?" she asked.

His eyes darkened and his mouth quirked, just enough to make her wonder what he was really thinking.

"No, ma'am, I don't mind a bit."

"Then, yes, I would like some company. But just for a while, okay?"

He nodded. "Okay." He followed her into the bedroom, leaving the door wide open between the two rooms.

A muscle pulled at the side of her neck and she winced as she started to crawl into bed.

"Easy," he said, as he helped her slide into a more comfortable position. "Want me to rub something on those stiff muscles? It might help you relax."

"Yes, please," Casey answered.

He disappeared into the bathroom and came out moments later with a tube of ointment. Casey's eyes widened as the bed gave beneath his weight and she rolled over on her side, her heart racing as she bared her shoulder at his request.

She was stiff and nervous and he felt her resistance to his touch as if he'd invaded her space.

"Easy...just take it easy," he coaxed, and laid his palm on the curve of her arm.

Casey flinched, and then when he began to move, she closed her eyes and let herself go. Gentle. His touch was so gentle. The ointment was a lubricant between his skin and hers, smoothing the way for the pressure of his fingers as he began to knead at the offending muscle.

"Oooh, that feels good," she said with a sigh, settling into the rhythm of his touch.

Ryder clinched his jaw and tried not to think of what else could be good between them.

The room became quiet and there was nothing to hear but the slide of skin against skin and the uneven breathing of strangers who just happened to be husband and wife. Several minutes passed and Casey had been lulled into letting down her guard when Ryder spoke.

"Casey."

Her pulse jerked, a little startled by the sound of his voice. "What?"

His fingers curled around her shoulder, his thumb resting at the base of her neck beneath her hair.

"I'm very glad you're okay."

Breath caught at the back of her throat and she squeezed her eyes shut as tears suddenly seeped out from beneath her lashes.

"Thank you, Ryder. So am I."

"Does your shoulder feel better?"

Her voice was just above a whisper. "Yes."

She heard him putting the lid back on the tube of ointment and felt the bed giving beneath the movement of his body. And then she thought of the loneliness of the night and the fear that kept coming when she closed her eyes, and asked the unforgivable.

"Ryder?"

Half on and half off of the bed, he paused. "What?"

"Would you mind—" She never finished the question.

"Would I mind what?" he finally asked.

"Would you mind staying with me? Just until I fall asleep?"

She couldn't see it, but a small smile tilted the corner of his mouth as he turned to her in the dark.

"No, honey, I wouldn't mind at all."

Casey held her breath as the mattress yielded to the greater pressure of his body.

"Easy does it," he whispered, and lightly rubbed her arm to let her know that he was there.

She closed her eyes and so did he, but not for the same reason. Ryder didn't want to think about the slender indentation of her waist so near his hand, or the gentle flare of hip just below it. He didn't want to remember the silky feel of her skin beneath his touch, or the way she sounded when she sighed. She had suffered much this day, and didn't deserve what he was thinking. But as time wore on, he couldn't get past wishing they were lying in bed for something other than rest.

Chapter 8

Sometime during the night it started to rain. It was a slow, heavy downpour that rolled like thick molasses off of the roof above where Casey and Ryder were sleeping, encompassing them within a dark, wet cocoon of sound.

Ryder woke with a start, the dream in which he'd been lost still so fresh in his mind that he came close to believing it was real. He looked down at Casey who lay sleeping with her head upon his chest and her hand splayed across the beat of his heart. Any man would consider himself fortunate to be in Ryder's place. The only problem was, she wasn't as awake and willing as she'd been in his dream.

The air felt close. The room seemed smaller. He ached. He wanted. He couldn't have. He moved, but only enough to brush the thick length of her hair that had fallen across her face. Her eyelashes fluttered against his chest. Her breasts had flattened against his side and she'd thrown her leg across the lower half of his body, pinning him in place. He swallowed a groan and made himself lie still when all he wanted was to be so far inside her warmth that nothing else mattered.

But lying still didn't help his misery, and finally, he slipped out of her arms and rolled out of bed, then stood in the dark looking down at her as she slept.

She trusts you.

Rain hammered against the roof as need hammered through him.

She's been hurt.

Hard. Constant. Insistent.

Justice men do not use women.

He turned and walked out of the room, grabbing his jeans from a chair as he headed for the door. He needed some air. Some distance. Something else on which to focus besides the thrust of her breast and the juncture of her thighs. He kept telling himself that this overwhelming feeling was nothing more than a result of proximity, that reason would return with daylight and distance, but his heart wasn't listening. He'd spent time with plenty of other women in his life and had been able to separate fact from fiction.

When he opened the door and stepped out on the landing, all he could see was a sheet of black rain falling directly before him. The security light was off. He reached back inside and flipped the light switch, clicking it on and then off again. The power was out.

The porch was damp beneath his bare feet, but it felt good to be concentrating on something besides sex. He combed his fingers through his hair and took a deep breath. The lack of electricity explained the sultry temperature inside the apartment, but it didn't excuse the sluggish flow of blood through his veins. That blame lay with the woman who'd interfered in his dream.

A soft mist blowing off the rain drifted into his face. He looked up. The small overhang under which he was standing offered little shelter, yet it was enough for him to get by. Right now, he couldn't have walked back in the apartment and minded his own business if his life depended on it. The dream was too real. She'd been too willing and so soft and he'd been halfway inside her and going for broke when something...call it conscience, call it reality, had yanked him rudely awake. Now he was left with nothing but a sexual hangover, an ache with no way of release. The muscles in his belly knotted and he drew a deep breath.

"Ryder?"

He groaned. She was right behind him.

"What's wrong?" she asked. "Is something wrong?"

"Go back to bed," he said harshly, unwilling to turn around.

A hand crossed the bare surface of his back on its way to his shoulder. He pivoted, and she was right before him.

Humidity draped the fabric of her gown to every plane, angle and curve, delineating a fullness of breasts and a slim, flat belly. Sticking to places on her body it had no business, taunting Ryder by the reminder of what lay beneath.

His fingers curled into fists and he took a deep breath as he reminded himself that she was bruised and battered and didn't deserve this from him. "Are you all right?"

"I just woke up and you were gone and I thought..." Her voice trailed off into nothing as she waited for an explanation that didn't come.

Silence grew and the rain continued to fall.

Casey sensed his uneasiness but did not immediately attribute it to herself. They were still strangers. There was so much they didn't know about each other. This mood he seemed to be in could have come from a number of reasons. And then suddenly the security light on the pole beyond the apartment came on. Although it was instantly diffused by the downpour, it was more than enough by which to see.

Dear God. It was all she could think as she shrank from the wild, hungry need on his face.

The moment she moved, he knew that he'd given himself away. Because he couldn't go forward, he took a reluctant step back and walked out into the rain before one of them made a mistake that couldn't be fixed.

Shocked by his sudden departure, Casey cried out, but it

was too late. He was already gone—lost in the downpour, beyond the sound of her voice.

Ryder didn't remember getting down the stairs. It was the rain that brought back his reason and calmed a wild, racing heart. Warm and heavy, it enveloped him—falling on his face, on his chest, down his body.

He began to walk, his bare feet sometimes ankle-deep in the runoff. He walked until a tree appeared in his path, then another, then another, and he realized he'd walked into the forest at the back of the estate. He paused at the edge, aware that he could go no farther in the state he was in, and found himself a place beneath the outspread limbs of an old magnolia.

Rain sounded like bullets as it peppered down on the large, waxy leaves above his head. But the longer he stood, the more the sound reminded him of hail. He drew a deep, shuddering breath and then cursed. It had hailed on them the night of the crash.

He closed his eyes, remembering the dead weight of holding his father's lifeless body in his arms. Someone moaned and as he went to his knees, he knew it was himself that he had heard. Pain shafted through him, leaving him smothered beneath a familiar cover of guilt.

"Ah, God, make this stop," he cried and then buried his face in his hands.

Back at the apartment, Casey stood on the landing, staring out at the night, anxiously watching for Ryder's return. The urge to go after him was strong, yet she stayed her ground, well aware that it was her presence that had driven him away.

Mist dampened her hair and her gown, plastering both to her face and her body and still she waited. Finally, she bowed her head and closed her eyes. "Dear Lord, help me find a way to make this right."

And the rain continued to fall.

Some time later, it stopped as suddenly as it had started— turned off at the tap with nothing but a leak now and then from a low-hanging cloud.

* * *

Ryder came up the stairs in a bone-weary daze, weary from lack of sleep and from wrestling with the demons inside himself. His bare feet split the puddle at the top of the landing and he walked inside without care for the fact that he would be dripping every inch of the way to the bath.

When he closed the door behind him, the cool waft of air that encircled his face told him the air-conditioning was back on inside. That was good. He'd had enough of close quarters to last him a lifetime and the night wasn't even over.

He walked quietly, so as not to disturb Casey's slumber in the other room, and was halfway across the floor when her voice stopped him in his tracks.

"I'm sorry," Casey said quietly. "Very, very sorry. I asked too much of you and you were too much the gentleman to tell me so." He heard her shudder on a breath. "I humbly beg your forgiveness."

A puddle was forming where he stood and yet the despair in her voice kept him pinned to the spot.

"There's nothing to forgive."

"Only me. I was selfish…thoughtless. I promise it won't happen again."

Why did that not make him happy? "Just let it go."

"I laid out some fresh towels. The bed is turned back. From this night on, we'll take turns sleeping in the bed."

The thought of her, bruised and aching and waiting up for him to come back from trying to outrun his devils made him angry, more with himself than with her; however, she caught the force of his guilt.

"Like hell. Go to bed and close your eyes. I didn't get mowed down by a truck. I don't have a busted lip or a black eye, and if I hurt, it's of my own making, not yours."

"But this arrangement isn't fair to you."

He almost laughed. "Hell, honey, there hasn't been two minutes of fair in my life in so long I wouldn't know it if it stood up and slapped my face." His voice softened. "Go to bed…please."

It was the please that did it. She stood, moving past him

in the dark like a pale ghost. Only after she was safe in bed with the sheets up to her chin did she sense him coming through the room. He paused at the bathroom door.

"If I'm gone when you wake up, call Tilly. She'll bring you some breakfast."

"I'll need a ride to work," she reminded him.

"No, you won't. I think you need another day of rest. Tomorrow is Friday. That will give you a long weekend to recuperate."

She totally ignored the fact that he'd just told her what to do, but at this point, it made no sense to argue with a sensible suggestion. "Where will you be?" Casey asked.

"Checking on your car that was towed. Contacting your insurance company." This time he managed a chuckle. "You know, doing stuff."

"Thank you," she said.

"For what?"

"For doing my *stuff.*"

This time, he really did laugh, and the sound carried Casey off into a deep, dreamless sleep.

Miles fought the covers beneath which he was sleeping as his dreams jumped from one crazy scenario to another. One minute he was flying high above the ground without a plane, flapping his arms like a gut-shot crow and trying to find a safe place to land, and the next moment he was standing in the middle of the intersection where Casey had had her wreck, watching in mute horror as her black sports car and the one-ton truck with which she had collided kept coming at him over and over from different angles. Each time he would escape being crushed between their vehicles, the scene would rewind and replay. On a nearby street corner, his grandmother kept pointing her finger and shouting. "I told you so! I told you so!"

He awoke bathed in sweat, only then aware that it was pouring down rain and the electricity was off. He cursed the bad taste in his mouth and got up with a thump just as the power returned. He could tell because his digital clock started blinking and the security lights outside came on all at once, returning a familiar pale glow to the curtains at his window.

He shoved them aside, looking down through the rain to the lawn below, and knew that the weather tomorrow would be miserable. The air would feel like a sauna and the bar ditches would be filled and overflowing.

''What the hell?''

There, through the rain, he thought he saw movement! He watched, staring harder, trying to focus on the shape. Just as he was about to reach for the phone to call the police, the figure moved within a pale ring of a security light and Miles froze, his hand in midair.

''Him.'' He stepped forward, all but pressing his nose against the glass for a better look. There was no mistaking who it was below. It was Ryder, half-dressed and moving at what seemed a desperate pace. He watched until the man disappeared from view before settling back down in his bed, his drink of water forgotten.

Long after it had stopped raining and he was back in bed, he kept wondering what would drive a man out of his bed and into a night like this? Had he and Casey fought? A twinge of guilt pushed at the edge of his conscience. She had gone through some hell of her own today. Tomorrow he'd send her some flowers. Having settled that, he turned over and quickly fell back asleep. It didn't occur to Miles that Casey would ultimately wind up paying for her own flowers, and if it had, he wouldn't have cared. To Miles, it was the thought that would count.

Lash awoke with a curse. Water was dripping from the ceiling and onto his left cheek. He got up to push his bed to a new location and stubbed his toe in the dark. The roof leaked. What else was new? The real problem lay in the fact that he was sleeping on the ground floor and it was still coming in through the ceiling. He didn't even want to think how the upper two stories of Graystone would be suffering tonight.

Cursing his wet bed and sore toe, he crawled back between the sheets, turned his damp pillow to the other side, and lay down.

Only sleep wouldn't come. No matter how hard he tried, his mind refused to relax. He thought of the phone call he'd had this afternoon from the police. Just for a moment before they'd completely explained, he'd thought they'd been calling to inform him of Casey's death, and then he realized that because he was the family lawyer, they'd called to tell him where they'd towed her car.

What bothered him most about the incident was the lack of emotion he'd felt at the news. He loved her. At least he thought he had. Wasn't a man supposed to cry at such a loss?

He closed his eyes, trying to imagine Casey dead, picturing the hordes of people that would come to her funeral, of the eulogy he would have delivered expounding her life. He saw her lying in the casket, beautiful even in death, and felt guilt that he was letting himself play so lightly with something as serious as her life.

He rolled over, taking the sheets with him as he turned on his side, still haunted by the sight of her face. As he tried to sleep, his thoughts began to unfurl like jumbled up scenes in an unedited movie.

In one scene, she stared at him, cool and patient, and he realized that he was remembering the way she'd looked the day of the reading of the will He tossed, rolling himself and the covers to the other side of the bed where Casey lay in wait for his arrival. There she stood again, her face a study in shock that slowly turned to a cold, white rage. He remembered that well. It was the way she'd looked when he'd announced the terms of Delaney Ruban's will.

He groaned. He could have talked Delaney out of the foolishness. *Oh God, if only I had.* But it was too late. Lash had presumed too much and he knew it. Who could have known? The Casey he thought he knew would never have gone into the flatlands and come out married to some hitchhiker, to some stranger she found in a bar.

And therein lay part of Lash's dilemma. He'd bet his life and the restoration of his family's honor on a woman who had never existed outside the realm of his imagination. In other words, he'd bet the farm on a woman who didn't exist.

"Casey."

The sound of her name on his lips made him crazy. He rolled onto his back, staring up at the ceiling. If things had gone the way they should have, she would be here, right now, in bed beside him. He closed his eyes and saw her smile, imagined he could feel the touch of her hand on his face, the breath of her laughter against his neck. He reached out, tracing the shape of her body with his fingertips, watching her eyes as they grew heavy with passion. He grew hot, then hard and aching, and when there was no one around to take care of the need, he reached down and dealt with it on his own, calling her name aloud as his body betrayed him.

"More flowers for little sister," Joshua announced, carrying another vase of cut flowers into the library and setting them on a table just out of the sunlight.

Casey smiled, more at the use of her childhood name than for the flowers he carried into the room. She started to get up when he waved her back.

"You stay where you're put," he ordered. "I'll be bringin' those cards to you."

Casey laughed. "You sure are bossy today."

Joshua lifted the card from the flowers and dropped it in her lap.

"No more than usual, I'd say."

He straightened the edge of the blue afghan covering her legs then patted her knee as he'd done so often when she was a child. His dark eyes searched the marks on her face. Her lip was no longer swollen, but the bruises were spreading and the scratches had scabbed over. The sights deepened the frown on his brow. He couldn't have cared for her more if she'd been born of his blood.

"You be needin' anything, you just give me a ring, you hear?"

Casey reached out and caught his hand, pulling it to her cheek.

"Thank you, Joshie...for everything."

He shook his head, embarrassed at emotion he couldn't hide. "Don't need to thank me for doing my job," he muttered, and stalked out of the room as fast as his legs would take him.

Casey glanced at the card, then back at the flowers. These were from Libertine Delacroix and they were pulling double duty: get-well sympathies and congratulations on Casey's recent wedding. She smiled. If Delaney were here he would be eating this up. Libertine was at the top of the county's social echelon. She had a summer home in Ruban Crossing and the family home on the river outside of Jackson.

The doorbell rang at the same time that the telephone pealed. Aware that Joshua couldn't be in two places at once, she picked up the phone.

"Ruban residence."

"Casey? Is that you?"

It was Lash. At that moment, she wished with all her heart that she'd let the darned thing ring.

"Yes, it's me. What can I do for you?"

She heard him clear his throat and could imagine the papers he would be shuffling as he gathered his thoughts. However, he surprised her with a quick retort.

"I heard about your accident and am so very glad that you're all right."

"Thank you."

"Yes, well...I know this may be an inconvenient time, but I was wondering if I might come by. There are some papers you need to sign."

She frowned. The last person she wanted to see was Lash and the last thing she wanted to do was think about her grandfather's death. But if there were more papers to sign regarding Delaney's will, she would have to do both.

"Well, I was just about to—"

"It won't take long."

She was honest enough to know that what she'd done by marrying Ryder had probably ended a lifetime of plans Lash must have had. Everyone knew that Lash's father had gone through the Marlow money as if it had been water and that his mother had run off with a trucker soon afterward. Everyone also knew what while Lash was a lawyer of the courts, his only ambitions leaned toward the restoration of his family name and the family home. And, if she'd married him as Delaney had planned, it could have happened. He would have had unlimited money at his disposal.

She shuddered. It was a wonder he didn't hate her guts. She thought of the wedding gift he'd sent that was still in her desk drawer at the office. In spite of his own disappointment, Lash had found it within himself to do the right thing and wish her well. She sighed. Guilty conscience won out.

"I suppose so," she said. "If it won't take long."

"Certainly not, my dear. I can promise that what I need won't take long at all."

"Then I'll be waiting."

She hung up the phone as Ryder walked in the room carrying a bright yellow, happy face balloon. The frown on her face disappeared.

"Oh, how sweet! Who sent me the balloon? I haven't had a balloon since I was little."

He leaned over and kissed the top of her head, then handed it to her.

"It's kind of pitiful compared to all these elegant flowers, but it seemed like a good idea at the time."

Although the kiss was as harmless as if it had come from a child, Casey felt her face flush. After last night, the word *harmless* did not mesh with the man who'd walked out of the apartment and into the rain.

"Is this from you?"

He stood at the end of the couch, absorbing the aftermath of yesterday's wreck on her face. Finally, he nodded, and then he grinned and Casey thought she would forever remember the way he looked, smiling down at her with the sunlight coming through the window behind him.

"With no strings attached." Then he laughed aloud when she dangled the one tied to the balloon. "Except the obvious, of course."

Casey grinned and handed him the balloon. "Will you tie it on the back of that chair for me?"

He did as she asked, then gave the balloon a final thump and set it to bobbing as he moved away. The big yellow happy face smiled down at her from across the room. Casey smiled back, then noticed that Ryder was leaving.

"Can't you sit down and talk to me?"

Ryder stopped at the doorway. When he turned, there was an odd, almost childlike hurt on his face.

"You don't need to pretend with me, Casey."

Suddenly, last night was out in the open. All the tension that had sent him out in the rain was back between them and there was nothing to say that would change what had happened.

Angry, she threw off the afghan and stood, unwilling to say this lying down. "The last time I played pretend, I was six years old. I pretended my mother and father weren't dead. When it didn't come true, I never tried again."

Ryder absorbed her anger as well as the passion with which she spoke, letting it flow over and then around him. Just when he thought she was finished, she came at him again. It would seem she wasn't through.

"There are things that need to be said between us. I would think that saying them in the bright light of day would be a hell of a lot smarter than waiting for dark. The world closes in when the sun goes down. Even with the absence of light, I've found it a difficult place in which to hide."

Stunned by the truth in her words, he couldn't find it in himself to walk away.

"So…is this our first fight?" he asked, and was rewarded by the red flush he saw staining her cheeks.

"Can't you be serious?" she muttered.

"Well, yes, ma'am, I can be serious as hell. However, I don't think you're one bit ready for that."

Casey paled. Just when she told herself he was a comfortable man to be around, that stranger came back.

"I thought you'd like to know that carpenters will be arriving tomorrow. I'm adding on a room to the garage apartment. Since we won't be sharing a... I mean we can't... We aren't going to..." She took a deep breath and started over, ignoring the heat on her face and neck. "You won't have to sleep on the floor much longer."

He thought about waking to find her wrapped in his arms. "That's real thoughtful of you, Casey."

"It is only fair."

His voice softened. "And you're always fair, aren't you, girl?"

Before she could answer, Joshua entered the room with Lash Marlow at his heels.

"Mr. Marlow is here. Says he has an appointment."

Willing herself not to flinch at what she perceived as accusation in Lash Marlow's expression, Casey eased herself back to the couch.

"Lash, it's good to see you. Ryder and I were just about to have coffee. Won't you join us?"

Lash pivoted, surprised that he and Casey would not be alone.

"That's all right," Ryder said. "I'll just leave you two alone to—"

"No!" Casey took a deep breath and made herself relax when she really wanted to scream. "There's no need," she said, softening her words with a smile. "It's nothing confidential. Only some papers to sign."

"She's right. Please don't leave on my account," Lash said and then smiled, and the sight made Casey shudder. It was the least happy expression she'd ever seen on anyone's face.

"Besides, I believe there should be no secrets between a man and his wife," he added.

Casey couldn't look Ryder in the face, and Ryder refused to sit down. Even after Joshua returned with the tray of coffee and Ryder had accepted his cup, the words kept ringing in his ears. *No secrets. No secrets.* Hell, there hadn't been more than ten minutes of honesty between them since he'd said "I do."

She thought he was a footloose drifter who'd wasted his life on the road. He didn't have it in him to tell her the truth because he was still trying to come to terms with some truths of his own.

There was a little matter of being responsible for his father's death and still finding the courage to live with it.

Every breath Ryder took was a reminder to him that Micah could no longer do the same. Every sunset he saw, every morning that came, came with the knowledge that, for his father, those simple pleasures had ceased. He carried his guilt with the ease of a man who's lived long with the shroud. Close to his heart. Selfish with the pain that shoved at him day after day.

Casey handed back the last of the papers. Lash took them from her, letting his fingertips accidentally brush the palm of her hand.

When she flinched, he had an urge to lean over and slap her face. How dare she have judged him and found him lacking? His family could trace their lineage back to the *Mayflower.*

Then he glanced at Ryder, careful to hide his thoughts. He would bet a lot—if he had it to bet—that this one didn't have two nickels to call his own. *At least I have my education— and several generations of a fine and noble name.* In Lash's opinion, Ryder Justice was nothing more than a stray, an alley cat of a man who'd been in the right place at the right time. That's what he was. That and nothing more.

Lash slid the papers into his briefcase and stood. "I'd better be going—let you get some rest and let your husband get on with his work."

The sarcasm was there. It wasn't obvious, but that wasn't

Lash Marlow's way. Casey chose to ignore the dig, and then she remembered the gift that he'd sent.

"Lash. I haven't had time to send a card, but I want to thank you in person for the lovely wedding gift you had sent to the office. It's stunning, truly stunning."

Lash turned, and there was an odd, satisfied smile on his face. "It's an heirloom, you know. It belonged to my grandfather, Aaron Marlow."

Casey looked startled. She'd had no idea. "Why, Lash, that's generous of you, but you really shouldn't have."

His gaze turned flat, almost expressionless. "Oh, it was nothing," he said. "After all, if things had been different, it would have been yours anyway. I thought you should have something to remember me by." He ventured a look at Ryder who had remained silent throughout their entire conversation. "I don't want you to think I'm treading on your territory," he said. "It's just that Casey and I have known each other for years."

Ryder set down his cup and then glanced at Casey before looking back at Lash. "I'm not worried. Casey is a woman of her word. Besides, I'm not a man who believes in boundaries."

Lash was more than mildly interested in the concept of what Ryder had to say. "So by that are you hinting at the fact that you believe in open marriages?"

Ryder took one step forward, but it was enough to back Lash up two.

"Not only no, but hell, no," Ryder said. "A man and woman stay together out of a commitment, not because there's a fence they can't climb."

Feeling slightly threatened by something he didn't quite understand, Lash started for the door. "At any rate, I hope you both get what you deserve."

Ryder thought about what the lawyer had said long after he was gone. There was something about him that didn't quite mesh.

Chapter 9

A month to the day from their wedding, the extra room over the garage was finished, and it was none too soon. There had been far too many times when Casey had seen Ryder's brown, bare body, and Ryder had spent way too many nights alone on a floor when he had a wife who slept alone in their bed. After thirty days of marriage, they were no longer strangers, but the strangeness of their situation was about to make them enemies.

"Just put the bed over here," Casey said, pointing at the wall opposite the sliding glass doors. "And the dresser here, the easy chair there... No, there I think, nearer the corner lamp. Yes, that's perfect."

A small, birdlike woman wearing a stiff blue uniform and high-top tennis shoes scurried into the room with an armload of Ryder's clothes, bypassing the deliverymen from the furniture store.

Her graying blond hair was pulled up in a ponytail reminiscent of the sixties. Her eyebrows were thick and black with a permanent arch, compliments of a number seven jet eyebrow pencil. The look was topped off with sky blue eyeshadow and frosted pink lipstick. Bea Bonnaducci's appearance hadn't changed since 1961, the year she'd graduated high school. The way Bea had it figured, if it had worked for her then, it should work for her now.

"Where would you be wantin' me to put the mister's things?" she asked.

"Put that stuff in the dresser and hang those in the closet. At last he has plenty of space."

Bea did as Casey directed and then scooted out of the room for a second load, leaving her to deal with the last of the furniture being carried in.

And in the midst of it all, Ryder strode into the bedroom, his nostrils flaring with indignation. He glared at the men who were setting the last pieces of the furniture in place, and when they left, he exploded.

"Damn it to hell, Casey! You waited until Dora sent me on some wild-goose chase and then you set Bea to digging in my stuff. I know you want me out of your hair, but you could have waited for me to get back."

Stunned, Casey stood mute beneath his attack, unable to find a single thing to say that would calm the fire in Ryder's eyes. She watched as he paced from one side of the room to the other. When he stepped inside the brand-new bathroom, he gave it no more than ten seconds of consideration before coming back out again.

"I thought you would be glad to have your own space," she finally said.

He spun, his posture stiff, looking for a fight that just wasn't there. "I didn't say I wasn't," he muttered. "What I said was…" He sighed, then thrust his hand through his hair in a gesture of frustration. "Oh hell, forget what I said." He stomped out of the room as suddenly as he'd appeared.

Casey plopped down on the side of the bed and knew she was going to cry. It wasn't so much the fact that he had yelled at her. It was the disappointment that did her in. He'd done so much for her over the past four weeks. All she had wanted to do was return the favor.

She doubled her fists in her lap, staring intently at a pattern on the carpet and telling herself that if she concentrated enough, the tears wouldn't come. In the midst of memorizing the number of paisley swirls in a square, a teardrop rolled down her cheek and into her lap. She drew a shuddering breath and closed her eyes. It didn't stop the pain or the tears. They rolled in silent succession.

Ryder walked back into the room carrying the last of his clothes that were on hangers and jammed them onto the rod.

"I sent Bea back to the house," he said, and then the bottom fell out of his world. Casey was crying, and it was all his fault.

"Oh, hell, Casey, please don't cry."

"I am not crying," she said, and hiccuped on a sob.

He stood, frozen to the spot by the pain in her voice and wondered when it had happened. When had she gotten under his skin? And there was no mistaking the fact that she was there. Why else did he feel as if he were about to explode?

"I am a total bastard."

It wasn't what she'd expected him to say. She looked up.

He groaned beneath his breath. Those big green eyes, the ones he'd come to know so well, were swimming in tears.

"I am the lowest form of a heel."

She sniffed and he dug a handkerchief out of his pocket and laid it in her hands.

"I do not deserve to see another day."

She blew her nose and then handed the handkerchief back. "Oh, don't be so dramatic," she said. "I suspect you were just being a man."

He stuffed the handkerchief, snot, tears, and all into his pocket and tried not to be offended by what she said. "Exactly what does that mean?"

Casey shrugged. "Tilly says when men don't want to show their emotions, they either curse or yell. You did both, which leads me to believe you were severely upset in a way I did not expect.''

He frowned. Damn, but that woman knew way too much about men for his peace of mind. ''At any rate, I am truly sorry. I'm sorry I yelled. I'm sorry I cursed. I will try not to let it happen again.''

She tried to glare. When angry, he was a force to behold, but when penitent, there was something about him that made her want to throw her arms around him and…

Her face turned red as she jumped up from the bed. ''Don't make promises you can't keep,'' she said, and stomped from the room.

Ryder groaned and followed her into the living room. She was fiddling with a stack of magazines. It made him nervous. He had a hunch she wasn't through yanking his chain, and when she spoke, he knew he'd been right.

''Ryder?''

If he was smart, he'd walk out right now before she dug in her heels, but where Casey was concerned, he wasn't smart, he was caught, and had been since that day in the bar down in the flatlands.

''What?''

''I don't understand. Why did you get so angry?''

''I wasn't really…''

''Truth.''

He sighed. Damn. Delaney Ruban had done a real good job on her. When she got a notion, she stuck to it with fierce intensity, and it wasn't in him to lie.

''I don't know. I walked in the apartment. Bea was going through my stuff. Too much was changing too fast.'' His voice lowered and Casey had to concentrate to hear what he said. ''I guess I'm uncomfortable with change.''

''But nothing has changed,'' she said.

''No, Casey, you're wrong. We're married.'' He held up his hand. ''And before you tie yourself into a little knot, I know it's not a *real* marriage, but dammit, I was just getting used to, to…things.''

He took a deep breath. What he was about to say was going to reveal more than he wanted, but she'd asked for the truth, and truth she was going to get.

"Even if we don't share anything but a name, there is a certain rhythm to our relationship that I was learning to accept." Then he thrust a hand through his hair and lifted his chin. She didn't have to like this, but it had to be said. "Dammit, I guess I wasn't ready to lose what little of you that I had."

Casey knew she was standing on solid ground, but for the life of her she couldn't feel it. Something inside of her kept getting lighter and lighter and she wondered if she was going to pass out...or fly.

"I didn't throw you away, Ryder. I only bought you a bed."

He took the magazines out of her hands and tossed them on the table, then pulled her into his arms. His chin rested at the crown of her head. His arms locked easily across her shoulders, holding her in place.

"I'm sorry I made you cry. I like my room. I promise to like the bed."

Casey closed her eyes and tried not to think of trying it out together just to test it for bounce. "And I'm sorry I keep bulldozing my way through your life."

His fingers itched to take down her hair, lay her across that bed and show her what bulldozing was all about. Instead, he counted to ten, pasted a smile on his face, and kissed the top of her head before letting her go.

"I suppose we should celebrate tonight," he said.

"Celebrate how?"

"You know, a room-warming. Maybe I should take you back to Smoky Joe's for some more barbecue." He grinned. "It's Saturday. That means it's alligator night, remember?"

She rolled her eyes.

"Well, then, maybe we could make it a christen-the-bed party, so to speak."

Casey's voice rose an octave. "Christen the bed?"

"Yeah, I always heard it was bad luck to sleep in a bed without breaking it in."

"Breaking?" She winced. She'd never heard herself squeak before.

"Yeah, come here, honey. I'll show you."

He dragged her across the room before she could argue and all the while she was moving she kept telling herself to do something—say something—anything except follow him across the room! But she didn't. She went where she was led as if she didn't have a brain in her head. When he leaned over the bed and picked up a pillow, adrenaline shot through her body like a bullet out of a gun.

Oh God, oh God, this is happening. It's really happening.

And then the pillow hit her square in the face.

She staggered, tasting fabric and feathers and reeling from shock. "Why on earth did you—?"

He sidestepped her and the question with a grin on his face and swung again. The blow landed on her backside, sending her sprawling facedown on the mattress. She grabbed the other pillow out of reflex, but it was instinct that made her swing and roll at the same time, crowing with delight as it caught Ryder up by the side of his head.

"That's nothing," he warned. "You're no match for me." He began to circle the foot of the bed.

"I'll make you eat those words," Casey cried, and leaped up on the mattress, using it as a bridge to get to the other side and away from Ryder's intent.

She was turning around as he drew back his arm and let fly.

The pillow shot through the air like a padded cannonball and stifled the jeer she'd been about to make. Within seconds, she found herself eating more feathers. But there was an upside to his latest attack. She now had both pillows.

"Aha!" she shouted, waving a pillow in each hand. The glee on his face made her nervous. When he started toward her, she began to retreat.

"Aha? What the hell is *aha?* I've never been hit with an *aha* before. Do they hurt?"

Casey panicked, threw both pillows at once and then ran. "No fair," she screamed.

He caught her in a flying tackle in the middle of the bed, at once mashing her face into the mattress and himself onto her. The weight of him was so great that breathing was almost impossible, and then just when she thought her lungs would burst, she found herself flat on her back and gasping for air. When she could talk and breathe at the same time, she looked up. Ryder was sitting on her legs with his arms above his head in a triumphant gesture.

"I hereby declare this bed has been thoroughly christened."

Casey doubled up her fist and thumped him in the middle of his belly.

"You cheated," she said, and tried to hit him again.

"Easy," he warned, and caught her fist before it could do any more damage. "Justice men never cheat. We just rearrange the odds."

Casey tried to stay mad, but the grin wouldn't stay off her face. "That's priceless."

"What's priceless?" he asked.

"Rearranging the odds. Delaney Ruban would have loved you."

Ryder's expression stilled. He couldn't quit looking at the woman beneath him. At the joy in her eyes. The smile on her face. Her hand on his leg.

He touched her. First her hair, then her face. And when she bit her lower lip and looked away, he heard himself asking, "What about his granddaughter? How does she feel?"

Casey felt as if all the breath had been knocked from her lungs. She was all too aware of his weight on her legs, his hand on her face, the need in his eyes.

"I..."

"Never mind," he whispered, and braced himself above

her with an arm on either side of her face. "I think I'd rather find out for myself."

She knew what the shape of his mouth felt like. They'd kissed before. Once, and just before dawn, in Judge Harris's front parlor on the day of the wedding. She thought she was prepared for what was about to happen. She couldn't have been more wrong. The man she'd kissed before had been a stranger. This time it was different. She'd seen this man wearing nothing but a towel—walked into his embrace on the day of her wreck—slept in his arms—laughed with him—cried with him—fought with him. She closed her eyes and tensed as his breath swept her cheek.

The gentle brush of mouth-to-mouth contact was familiar, even comfortable, and all of that changed when Casey's arms automatically wrapped around his neck. Ryder groaned and then rolled, taking her with him until she was the one on top and he was pinned beneath. She heard him whisper her name. Felt his hands in her hair—down her back—cupping her hips. Urgency sparked between them as their lips met again, then again, and then again.

Her pulse was racing, his body was betraying him. It was all there—from the wild glitter in his eyes, to the need coiling deep in her belly. She lowered her forehead until it was touching the space just above his heart. In spite of the heat between them she started to shake.

Ryder groaned. They'd gone too fast. But, dear Lord, who could have known they would go up in flames? They'd blindsided each other with nothing more than a kiss. He was almost afraid to guess at what might happen if they ever made love.

"Easy, Casey. Easy, honey," he said softly, rubbing his hands up and down her back in a slow, soothing motion. "That just got out of hand. I didn't mean to scare you, okay?"

She rolled off him and got as far as the side of the bed before covering her face with her hands. "Oh, my God. Oh, my God."

Ryder silently cursed himself for starting something they

hadn't been ready to finish. But he'd gotten his answer. Delaney Ruban's granddaughter might not love him, but she wasn't immune to him either. There was something there. He just wasn't sure what it was. He rolled over on his side and reached out, touching her back with the palm of his hand.

"Casey, look at me."

When she flinched, he got up with a curse and walked out of the room.

She couldn't think, couldn't move, couldn't speak. All she could do was remember his weight pressing her down and never wanting the connection to stop. Of feeling his mouth cover hers, of mingling breaths and racing hearts and resenting the clothing that separated her skin from his.

The phone rang, and the timing couldn't have been worse. Moments later, Ryder walked back in the room and tossed the portable phone near her leg.

"It's for you."

Casey looked up, but he was already gone. She picked up the phone with shaking hands and cleared her throat.

"Hello?"

"Mrs. Justice, this is Charles Byner, down at the bank. I just need your authorization to clear a check. It's quite a large sum above what's in the account and I need your approval to authorize the draw."

Casey swept a hand through her hair, trying to come to terms with reality. "I'm sorry," she said, trying to focus. "What did you say?"

"No problem," he said. "I'm really sorry to bother you at home, but Mr. Ruban had specific orders with regards to these particular accounts and since you're now the one in charge, I need authorization from you to clear the check, although it is more than a thousand dollars over the balance."

Casey sat up straight, her mind immediately jumping gears as she realized what he meant.

"Which account? Miles's or Erica's?"

The clerk lowered his voice. "It's the one in Mr. Dunn's

name. The check is for twenty-six hundred dollars. That's about eleven hundred dollars above the balance.''

Casey stood. "What is the balance, exactly?"

His voice lowered even more. "Let me just pull that up on the screen. Yes...here it is. The balance as of today is exactly $1,400.17.''

Casey gritted her teeth. "And was the usual amount of five thousand dollars deposited into that account at the first of this month?"

"Ummm, yes, ma'am, it was."

By now, Casey was livid. Delaney had set a precedent years ago that was about to come to a screeching halt. "Honor the check, Mr. Byner. I'll have enough money transferred into the account to cover it, but I'll be at the bank first thing Monday morning to make some new arrangements.''

"Yes, ma'am," the clerk said, and hung up.

Casey disconnected, then immediately rang the bank back through another department and dealt with the transfer in a no-nonsense voice. When she was finished, she headed for the house phone on the kitchen wall.

"Tilly, is Miles at home?"

"He's in the pool," Tilly answered.

"Would you please ask him to meet me in the library? There's something we need to discuss."

She hung up to find Ryder watching her.

"You okay?"

Casey's nerves were just beginning to settle. She hadn't expected it, but knowing that in spite of what had just happened between them, Ryder was still able to ask about her welfare, made her feel safe.

"No," Casey said. "But I will be."

"Need any backup?"

"Are you offering?"

The smile on his face was slight. "Are you asking?"

"It might get ugly," she said.

He dropped the clothes he was carrying onto the back of a chair.

"Honey girl, the last few months of my life haven't been anything but."

Surprised by the revelation, she would have given a lot to continue this conversation. Ryder was closemouthed with regards to anything about his past, and hearing him admit even this much was a definite surprise. But the confrontation with Miles was long overdue, and this latest stunt was, for Casey, the last straw.

"Then come if you want. For better or worse, you are part of this family."

"Unless I think it matters, you won't even know I'm around."

She nodded and started down the stairs, and it wasn't until they'd entered the house and were on their way to the library that she had fully accepted the impact of Ryder's presence in her life. The problems within her world were no longer just hers. They were theirs.

She entered the room wearing an expression the board members of Ruban Enterprises would have recognized. It was her no-holds-barred-don't-mess-with-me look. Ryder had disappeared somewhere between the library and the hall, yet she sensed he wouldn't be far away. Unlike Miles, he wasn't the kind of man who went back on his word.

And Miles wasn't far behind. She could hear the splat of bare feet on marble flooring as he made his way in from the pool. The careless smile on his face was no more than she expected as he sauntered into the library with a beach towel draped across his neck and water dripping onto the floor.

"I'm here. What's up?" he asked.

Casey schooled herself to a calm she didn't feel. "I just had a call from the bank."

If she hadn't known him so well, she might have missed the nervous flicker in his eyes.

He strolled over to the bar and poured himself a drink, even taking a sip before asking, "And what does that have to do with me?"

"Everything. It seems you wrote a check you couldn't cover."

He shrugged. "Oh, that. Delaney never used to mind when—"

"Delaney is dead, remember?"

Miles blinked. It was his only reaction to the cold, even tone of his half sister's voice.

"And in the grand scheme of things, exactly what does that mean?" he drawled.

"It means your glory days are over, Miles. I don't know what the hell you're doing with your money. I don't even want to know. What I will tell you is that your world is slightly out of sync, and as your loving sister, I intend to do all that I can to bring it back in order."

He set the glass down with a thump. "What are you getting at?"

"It's more a case of what are you trying to pull? Any unemployed, thirty-year-old man should not be spending in excess of five thousand dollars a month. Therefore, I am going to do you a favor. As of Monday, you will report to Princeton Hamilton in the legal department of Ruban Enterprises. You have a law degree. You're going to put it to work."

Miles froze. An angry flush began to spread from his neck, upward. "You bitch! You can't run my life."

Casey shrugged. "You're right. But I'm running Ruban Enterprises, aren't I? I covered this hot check, but I won't do it again. Also, there will be no more instant deposits into your account, because as of the end of this month, it will be closed. No more free rides, Miles."

Miles was so angry he couldn't form a complete sentence. His hands were shaking as he yanked the towel from around his neck and started toward her.

The urge to run was overwhelming, but Casey stood her ground as he shoved his way into her space and thrust a finger up against her nose.

"Don't let your power go to your head, sister dear. Someone might just have to knock you off that pedestal for your own damned good."

The anger on Miles's face was impossible to ignore and the knowledge that their relationship had come to this made her sick to her stomach. It hurt to know she was still the outcast when it came to family love. She reached out to him.

"I'm not trying to play God, Miles. You're my brother. I care for you very much, but don't you see? You're wasting the best years of your life."

He slapped her hand away and then grabbed her by the arm, yanking her sharply until she came close to crying aloud.

"You're going to be sorry for this," he said softly. "You're going to be very, very sorry."

He turned and walked out of the room, leaving Casey reeling from the venom in his voice. But his triumphant exit ended four steps outside the library door. Ryder had him by the arm and shoved up against the wall before he had time to call out for help. Miles had seen plenty of angry men in his life, but he'd never been afraid until now.

Ryder slammed his hand in the middle of Miles's chest, pinning him in place. "You son of a bitch. If I ever hear you talk to your sister again like that, you'll wish you'd never been born."

"It's none of your business," Miles said, and felt shame that his voice was shaking.

"That's where you're wrong. Whether any of you like it or not, she's my wife. What happens to her *is* my business. And I'm telling you now, so you'll be forewarned, if anything *ever* happens to Casey, I'm coming after you first."

So great was his fear that if Ryder hadn't been holding him up, Miles would have been on the floor.

"What the hell do you mean by that?"

"Exactly what I said," Ryder replied softly. "You better hope to God she doesn't have any enemies, because from this day forward, I hold you responsible for her welfare."

Miles's eyes bulged. "I would never wish Casey any real

harm. I was just mad, that's all. Hell's fire, man, she's my sister.''

"Then start acting like her brother."

Miles went limp as all the anger slid out of his heart. Truth hurt. "Let me go."

Ryder didn't move—didn't speak—and didn't turn him loose.

Miles saw himself mirrored in Ryder's eyes and didn't like what he saw.

"I didn't mean what I said to her. And I suppose in a way she's right."

Ryder turned him loose, but refused to move back. "Remember what I said. She hurts—you bleed."

Miles took off down the hall as if the devil were at his heels. By the time he got back to the pool, he'd convinced himself that putting his education to work was not only going to happen, but that it could have its benefits.

Ryder watched Miles until he was out of the house, and then stepped inside the library. Casey was at the window, staring out onto the lawn overlooking the back of the estate.

"Casey?"

She spun, and Ryder wished he'd given in to the urge and punched Miles right in the face before they'd had their little talk. She looked so hurt. So lost. So alone.

"I heard some of what you said to Miles."

Ryder could tell there was something serious on her mind. He waited for her to continue.

"I don't know how I got so lucky, but I am forever grateful for your presence in my life."

He wanted to hold her. He settled for a brief smile instead. "Oh, I don't know about that," he drawled. "I'd come near saying that I'm the lucky one. Besides, we Justice men don't take kindly to anyone messing with our women."

Casey swallowed a sigh. If only she was his woman in the ways that counted. "So, are you telling me that there's more than one of you that's been turned loose on the world out there?"

The smile slid off his face and she knew she'd said the wrong thing. "I'm not who matters," he said shortly. "I don't think Miles will give you any more trouble, but if he does, you know where I'll be."

He walked out and she had the strangest sensation that he'd just walked out of her life, rather than out of the room. In fact, the thought was so strong that she actually followed him through the house, then stood in the doorway and watched until he entered their apartment.

What did I say? What was it that turned him off and sent him running?

But there were no answers for Casey, at least not today.

However, when the mailman drove away from the Justice ranch outside of Dallas, he gave Royal Justice a clue to solving a mystery that had been worrying him and his brother, Roman, for months.

"Daddy, Daddy, I bwought you da mail."

Ignoring the trail of letters and papers she was stringing as she ran, Royal Justice swung his three-year-old daughter, Madeline, up in his arms and kissed her soundly.

"You sure did, honey. You're getting to be such a big girl."

"Gwinny helped," Maddie said, pointing at the baby-sitter who was coming behind at a fast clip, picking up the pieces that Maddie had lost.

"Good for Gwinny," Royal said. Gwinneth Anderson grinned, handed Royal Justice the rest of his mail, and took Maddie by the hand. "Come on, Scooter, it's time to feed the pups."

Maddie bolted, leaving Royal with a handful of letters and a smile on his face. He dropped into the nearest chair and began going through the mail with a practiced eye, discarding the junk and setting aside the bills to be paid. Every now and then one would be addressed to his brother, Ryder, and that one was tossed into a box with an accumulating stack that threatened to overflow. It was all he knew to do. It was Roman who'd saved Ryder's business from ruin.

Roman had taken over the charter service without batting an eye, claiming he could run his private investigation service and Ryder's charter business in the same location. He hired two pilots, an accountant, and then dug in for the long haul, convinced that Ryder would be back when he was ready.

Privately, Royal was a lot less optimistic, but that was just the difference in their personalities, not a lesser belief in the brother who was missing. He loved Ryder as much as Roman did and worried daily about his whereabouts, sometimes even wondering if he was still alive. It had been so long and they hadn't had a word.

He was down to the next-to-the-last letter in the lot, and he started to toss it in Ryder's box when he looked at the return address. MasterCard. No big deal. Everyone has credit cards.

And then he realized what he was looking at and took a deep breath as he tore into the flap. When he pulled out the itemized bill, he started to shake. Someone had used Ryder's card! Over the period of three weeks, someone had charged several hundred dollars' worth of men's clothing in Ryder's name.

Royal was as scared as he'd ever been in his life. Either Ryder was alive and well and buying up a storm, or someone was using his card. The implications of how anyone might come by Ryder's belongings was more than he could handle alone. He bolted up from the chair and headed for the phone. Moments later, a familiar voice growled in his ear.

"This is Justice Air and The Justice Way. State your business and we'll get back to you as soon as possible."

Royal groaned. That damned answering machine. When it beeped, he started talking.

"Roman, this is Royal. I just got a letter from—"

"It's me," Roman said.

"Well, hell," Royal said. "Why didn't you pick up the first time?"

"Wasn't in the mood to chitchat," he said shortly.

Royal cursed beneath his breath. That was so typically Roman. "The mail just came."

Roman snorted indelicately. "Don't tell me. You just won the Publisher's Clearing House Sweepstakes."

"Oh, shut the hell up," Royal muttered. "I'm serious."

"And I'm busy," Roman said. "Unless my favorite niece has done something utterly charming that I need to know about, I don't have time to—"

"Someone charged nearly a thousand dollars on Ryder's MasterCard. The bill came today."

Sarcasm was noticeably missing as Roman snapped, "Give me the dates. The store codes, anything that—no, wait! I've got a better idea. Fax me a copy of the bill."

"Oh, hell," Royal said. "You know I'm not good at making that damned thing work."

"Then get Maddie to help. She knows how," Roman said. "And do it now. If Ryder's alive, I'll find out soon enough. If someone is using his ID, they're going to wish they'd never been born."

"It's on its way," Royal said, and hung up the phone.

He turned, staring at the fax machine on the desk near the window, facing the fact that while he knew just about everything there was to know about ranching, the age of computers had him hanging in air. It was humiliating to know that a three-year-old could do what he had yet to accomplish, but this concerned Ryder, and it was no time to get macho about a damned old machine.

He headed for the back door at a fast clip. "Hey, Maddie," he yelled. "Come help me fax something to Uncle Roman."

Chapter 10

By Labor Day, Miles had become Eudora's fair-haired boy. Somehow, the fact that he was gainfully employed had become his idea and Casey's ultimatum had never happened. She couldn't have cared less who took the credit. His streak of ambition had even rubbed off on Erica. She kept making noises about pursuing a career of her own and spent hours each day pouring over *Fortune 500* magazines in search of ideas.

At night when it was time to go to bed, Ryder no longer wandered in and out of the bedroom in various stages of undress. Casey had her bathroom all to herself and began to realize why Ryder had become so upset when she'd moved him out of her life. The routine they'd been in had become normal, even comforting, and it was over. Because of the new bedroom, whatever connection they'd made between themselves was gone. In an odd sort of way, it was like being divorced.

But the awareness between them kept growing. It was there in the way Ryder watched her when he thought she wasn't looking—and the way his hand lingered on her arm long after the need for keeping her balance had come and gone—even the brief, sibling-like kisses they left on each other's cheek before saying good-night. They were wanna-be lovers, playing at being friends. And always, in the back of their minds, was the knowledge that the marriage they shared was a farce and the lie they were living was the very wedge that kept them apart.

It was just past noon when Casey turned off the highway and accelerated up the driveway into the Ruban estate, gunning the engine of her new car and taking the curve in a near skid. She pulled up to the garage and stopped just as Ryder slid out from beneath the Lincoln. His black hair was windblown and the grin on his face was too devil-may-care to ignore. His jeans were oil-slicked, his chest brown and bare. He was wiping his hands on a rag as he headed her way.

"Where's the fire?"

She wanted to throw her arms around his neck and beg him to crawl back under that car and take her with him, but she couldn't. At least, not today.

She bolted for the stairs. "I know, I was driving a little too fast, but I'm in a hurry." She hiked up her skirt and began to run up the steps, two at a time.

"Take off those damned high heels if you're going to run like that," Ryder yelled. When she didn't oblige, he threw down the grease rag. "Hardheaded woman," he muttered, and followed her inside.

She was in the bedroom. A suitcase was open and she was yanking clothes from a hanger and tossing them on the bed with abandon. Anxiety seized him. She was packing to travel.

"What's the rush?"

"I've got to be in Chicago by morning. I have less than an hour and a half to get packed and get to the airport." She turned in a helpless circle, then dived back into the bottom of her closet, muttering as shoes came flying out behind her. "I can't find my black heels."

Ryder bent down and picked up a pair from the pile in the floor. "Like these?"

She straightened. A smile creased her face as she yanked them from his hands. "Yes! You're a magician. Thanks a bunch."

His belly was starting to turn. He kept telling himself it was going to be okay, that the only reason this was bothering him was because the news was so sudden.

"So, what's in Chicago?"

"Digidyne Industries. We've been after them for years. Once before, Delaney had the deal all but done and they backed out. I just got a call that the CEO had a heart attack and died. The heirs are going to put it on the auction block and I want first dibs."

Ryder started to pace, sidestepping her trips from the closet and back as she packed what she needed to wear. "So, it's a big deal, huh?"

"Very! I'm lucky that Delaney's old contact even thought to make the call and let me know. Otherwise, we would have been out in the cold."

"Yeah, that was lucky all right." He sat down on the edge of the bed, staring at the toes of his boots.

Casey glanced up. "You need to hurry and clean up. We're going to have to drive like mad to make my plane." Then she grinned. "However, that should pose no problem for you." It was a joke within the household that the family chauffeur drove, as Eudora had put it, "Like a bat coming out of hell with its wings on fire."

"Yeah, no problem," Ryder said, and walked out.

A few minutes later, Casey burst into his room, her face flushed with energy, her eyes alight with excitement. "I'm ready."

Ryder walked out of the bathroom, buttoning a clean shirt. He didn't stop to analyze the wisdom of what he was about to do, he just knew that if he let her get on that damned plane without a piece of his heart, he wouldn't make it until she got back.

Casey went willingly as he took her in his arms and crushed her against his chest in a smothering embrace.

"Just be careful, okay?"

She laughed. "Tell that to the pilot. I'm afraid it's out of my hands."

He groaned and threaded his fingers through her hair, crushing the curls and dragging her closer. "Don't make light of fate, Casey Dee. Sometimes when you're not looking, it'll kick you right in the teeth."

The first thought in Casey's mind was that he wasn't kidding. Even more, he seemed panicked about the upcoming flight.

"I'll be fine," she said. "This happens to me all the time. Year before last, Delaney and I logged over seven thousand miles in the air. Of course we were in Europe three times, but that was an unusual year."

God, keep her safe, Ryder thought, then he lowered his mouth and drew her close. Casey closed her eyes, yielding, bending to his will and embrace, swept away by the unexpected demands of a kiss that left her breathless and more than a little bit stunned.

When he whispered against her cheek, she opened her eyes. His panic had become contagious.

"I want you back in one piece."

She shivered. She'd never seen him like this. It was almost as if he were in some kind of pain.

"I'll certainly do my best," she said, trying to lighten the moment. She grabbed at the undone buttons on his shirt and started buttoning them up. "I'm sorry to repeat myself, but we've got to hurry."

He tucked in his shirt and picked up her bags. His heart was pounding.

"Go get in the car," he grumbled. "I'll make sure you catch that damned plane. But when you get back, we need to talk."

Casey looked startled. An ultimatum?

She got in the car, watching as he dumped her bags in the

trunk and then slid behind the wheel. Something was wrong, terribly wrong. If only they had time to talk now. She looked at her watch. They would be lucky if they made the plane, never mind finishing a conversation.

He only glanced at her once. "Buckle up."

She'd ridden with him too many times before to doubt the necessity of doing as he'd asked. She did as she was told.

Casey was the last passenger to get on. She stood in the boarding area with her ticket in hand, waiting for the attendant to give her a boarding pass. Ryder stood beside her, pale-faced and stoic, yet his eyes never left her face. She reached out and touched his hand, wishing their circumstances were different, wishing she could throw herself in his arms and tell him he meant more to her than she could say.

"I'll call as soon as we land and let you know where I'll be staying."

Ryder nodded, trying to maintain his equilibrium, but he felt sick. The high-pitched whine of the jet's engines vibrated the windows overlooking the runway. In seconds, Casey was going to be up in that sky, and he knew only too well it was a hell of a long way down. He wanted to grab her and shake her until she listened to sense. Ruban Enterprises didn't need another Fortune 500 business. It was already a gargantuan conglomerate of its own accord. Why acquire more?

But he couldn't find a way to say what was in his heart. He couldn't say, I'm afraid I'll lose you like I lost my father. He couldn't say, I'm afraid I'll lose you before we ever make love. He couldn't say, I love you—because that wasn't part of the deal.

And then waiting was no longer an option.

"Take care!" Casey shouted, and started running down the gate toward the plane.

Ryder took several steps forward when the attendant grabbed his arm. "Sorry, sir, this is as far as you can go."

He groaned. God help him, but he'd missed his chance.

Just when he'd found a way to say the words without coming apart, she was gone.

He went to the observation deck, watching as the big silver plane started backing out of its slot. His fingers knotted around the rail as it rolled onto the runway. And when liftoff came, sweat was running down the middle of his back and he was praying with every breath. When the plane was no longer in sight, Ryder leaned his forehead against the vast expanse of glass, unaware of the heat against his brow. He closed his eyes, trying to picture her face.

"I love you, Casey." But when all was said and done, he was a case of too little, too late.

It was almost sundown when Ryder walked into the apartment. His heart sank as a red blinking light winked at him from across the room. He tossed the car keys on the kitchen counter and pressed the button, waiting for the sound of Casey's voice.

"Hi, there. Sorry I missed you. I'm staying at the Ritz Carlton. Here is the number." Ryder jotted it down as she spoke, then settled back to listen to the rest of the message. "The flight was fine, just a little bumpy. I'll be in meetings all day tomorrow, but I'll try to call you tomorrow night. Take care." She paused, and Ryder would have sworn he heard her take a deep breath. "Well...anyway...I'll miss you."

The machine beeped. The message was over. Casey was gone. He played it over once more just to listen to the sound of her voice, and wished to hell that Dora hadn't broken a nail. She'd had a fit the size of Dallas and nothing had satisfied her but to make an emergency run to her manicurist to get it fixed. He'd missed Casey's call because of a broken nail.

The house phone rang. "Now what?" he muttered, and shoved himself out of the chair. Tilly was on the line.

"I'm making pot roast. You come on over here and get yourself some food."

The last thing he wanted was to eat or to talk. Casey hadn't been gone four hours and already there was a hole inside of him that food couldn't fill.

"Thanks, but I think I'll just stick around here for the evening."

"If you change your mind, you know how to get here."

"Yes, ma'am, I do."

He hung up and then headed for the shower. After he cleaned up, maybe he'd watch a little TV, have an early night. After all, he had the whole place to himself. And it was the loneliest feeling he could ever remember.

By morning, it had started to rain. By the next day, and then the next, it alternated between gray skies and drizzle, with a downpour now and then in between. And as if the rain wasn't bad enough, a line of heavy thunderstorms was pushing its way into the state and today was the day that Casey was due to come home.

He sat at the window looking out at the rain, ignoring the fact that today he'd already angered Erica and caused Eudora to have to change her plans.

He didn't give a damn that Erica had a lunch date with a banker to discuss buying a business. He couldn't have cared less whether or not Dora was going to miss her bridge luncheon. Erica knew how to drive and Dora could take a cab.

Erica argued, then whined, then begged. When she realized that nothing was working, she started in with what she considered simple reasoning. If she drove herself, then there was no way she could keep from having to walk in the rain. At this point, Ryder had heard enough.

"Where are you meeting the banker for lunch?" he asked.

She sniffed. "The Tea Room."

"Take an umbrella, and use their valet parking."

Erica knew when she'd been had. She rolled her eyes and flounced out of the library, muttering beneath her breath about hardheaded men who did not know their place.

Eudora patted her hair and straightened her belt. She was

certain that the rapport she'd developed with this man would bring him around.

"Ryder, dear, it's Evadine Nelson's turn to play hostess for the bridge club. She lives right at the edge of town, remember? Hers is that big white house with the portico that I so admire."

"Yes, ma'am, I remember the house," Ryder said.

Eudora beamed. "Then you won't mind just dropping me off. It won't take more than half an hour either way. If Delaney hadn't insisted on building this place out in the middle of nowhere, we wouldn't be so isolated."

Ryder shook his head. "Dora, you weren't listening to me. I'm not budging until Casey calls. Dammit, look outside. There's a storm due in within hours. Chances are, her plane will be delayed, or the pilot will wind up trying to outrun it. Either way, I want to know what the hell is going on. I'll call a cab for you, but I'm not playing chauffeur today and that's that."

She rolled her eyes. "You know, things have been upside down ever since Casey brought you into this family. You're supposed to be the chauffeur. Chauffeurs are supposed to do as they're told." She tried to glare.

"So fire me," he said, and kissed her cheek, which brought a smile to her eyes that she just couldn't hide. "Go on with you then," she spluttered. "Go sit and wait for that phone call." She walked away, mumbling beneath her breath. "Land sakes, what will Evadine say? Me coming to her door in a cab, like some commoner."

Ryder followed her out the door. "Dora, you are a fine lady, but you are not the Queen Mother. Taking a cab now and then is good for the soul."

Eudora pivoted, giving him a cool, pointed stare. "I declare," she said, about to give him a piece of her mind, but Ryder didn't wait around to listen.

He ran from the main house all the way across the courtyard, then up the stairs just ahead of a cool gust of wind. Pausing at the landing, he looked up at the sky, judging the dark, angry swirl of clouds overhead. Today was not a good day to fly.

As soon as he entered the apartment, he turned on the television and flipped to a local station he knew would be broadcasting weather bulletins all day. With the phone at his side, he sat down to wait for her call.

A half hour went by. By this time he was pacing the floor. She'd promised to call before she left. She wasn't the kind of person who'd break a promise.

"A line of severe thunderstorms is blanketing the state," the TV announcer stated.

He turned toward the television, picked up the remote and upped the volume.

"Wind velocities have been measured at fifty to sixty miles per hour with gusts up to seventy and eighty. Authorities advise staying off of the roads and avoiding low-lying areas that are prone to flooding."

He glanced toward his bedroom. A sheet of rain splattered itself against the sliding glass doors that led onto the deck. His belly tied itself in a knot and he frowned, trying once again to focus on the weather man's report.

"The line runs from…"

Ryder groaned. On the map, the line of storms was virtually from the top to bottom of the state and moving eastward at a very fast pace. What was even more disturbing, the front extended across a large portion of the northern states, including Illinois. Maybe that's why he hadn't heard anything. Maybe her flight had been delayed and she was waiting for new information before she called.

No sooner had he thought it than the phone rang right near his hand. He jumped and then grabbed it before it had time to ring again."

"Hello?"

"Ryder! It's me! I'm in a cab on the way to the airport. Traffic is a mess, but I'll make my flight. I should get into Ruban Crossing around three. Can you pick me up?"

"What's the weather like up there?"

"Ummm, it's raining a little, but no big deal."

No big deal. "It's raining like crazy here. Why don't you just take a later flight, or better yet, take the first one out tomorrow?"

She laughed. "Now I know I've been gone too long. You are already making excuses as to why I shouldn't come back."

He got up and walked to the sliding glass doors and then jumped when a stroke of lightning tore across the sky right above his head.

"Did you hear that?" he asked, as the phone cracked in his ear. "A storm front is moving through. Today is not a good day to fly."

There was laughter in her voice. "It will be fine. You know they won't take off if there's any danger. Besides, the pilots usually just fly above the storms and land behind them."

He felt sick. Something inside kept telling him this was wrong—so wrong. "Casey, don't. I know what I'm talking about. Please, for God's sake, don't get on that plane."

The underlying fear in his voice was about to make her nervous. She decided to change the subject. "You didn't even ask me if the deal went through!"

He sighed and shifted the phone to the other ear. "Okay, I'll bite. How did the meetings go?"

She hugged herself, resisting the urge to giggle. She was pretty sure that CEOs did not giggle. "We got it!" she crowed.

"It's a done deal. I swear, Delaney is probably rolling over in his grave as we speak."

"Don't be talking about graves."

She laughed. "Just be at the airport. I can't wait to get home."

Their connection began to break up. "Remember," Casey said. "Flight 209. Three o'clock."

"Dammit, Casey, I don't want you to—"

The line was dead. Ryder hung up with a curse and sat

back down, staring at the television as if it were the lifeline between himself and sanity.

Ryder heard someone groan. That's when he looked up at the airport monitor, watching as the On Time notice of Flight 209 from Chicago was changed to Delayed.

His gut hitched itself into a knot. It figured. While it wasn't raining at the moment, the sky was black and the intermittent flashes of cloud-to-ground lightning could be seen for miles. It was an all too familiar scene. One right out of his nightmares.

He stood and walked to the observation point overlooking the runway. A couple of planes were waiting to take off, another was off-loading. Except for the weather, nothing seemed out of sync.

I'm just borrowing trouble.

Fifteen minutes passed, and then Flight 209 was a half hour late and before he knew it, an hour overdue. And, the information on the monitor hadn't changed.

He'd been up and down the terminal a dozen times, walking, trying to pass the time and ease the nervous tension that kept growing within him. Now he was back at the arrival gate, standing at the windows and watching the skies.

Suddenly, the skin crawled on the back of his neck and he turned. Nearby, a child was crying. A teenager was on a cell phone. A weary traveler had given in to exhaustion and was sound asleep, his head lolling, his mouth slack as every now and then a slight snore escaped. The attendant at the check-in desk was on the phone. Nothing out of the ordinary. Nothing to warrant the gut-wrenching instinct he'd had that he was about to be attacked.

He glanced up at the monitor and sighed, then out of curiosity, back at the attendant. But when her expression suddenly froze and he saw her look up in fright, the same sensation came over him again, this time pulling a kink in the knot already present in his belly.

Easy. It doesn't mean a thing.

Down the broad walkway, a small horn honked three times in succession. "Coming through. Coming through."

His focus shifted to the electric cart coming down the terminal. It stopped in front of the attendant's desk as she ran out from behind the counter. When she handed the driver a computer printout, the other man grimaced and wiped a hand across his face. Ryder stared as they scanned the list together. When the driver lifted his head and began to scan the waiting area, Ryder knew. He didn't know how, but he knew.

He started walking—past the crying child, past the teenager on the cell phone, past the sleeping traveler. He came to a halt directly in front of the cart and didn't wait for permission to interrupt.

"What happened?"

Both men looked up at him at once. But it was the glance they shared before one of them spoke that nearly sent Ryder to his knees. He'd been right. Something was worse than wrong.

"I'm sorry, sir? Were you speaking to us?" the driver asked.

Ryder leaned forward and pointed to the readout. "Don't play games."

Before either one of them could answer, an announcement came over the loudspeaker.

"All those waiting for information regarding the arrival of Flight 209 out of Chicago, please go to the VIP lounge in the west wing."

Ryder stared into the eyes of the man behind the wheel and felt the ground coming up to hit him in the face. He leaned forward, steadying himself on the cart.

"Are you all right?" the man asked.

Ryder took a deep breath and lifted his head. "Should I be?"

The man looked away.

Ryder's voice died on a prayer. "Oh, God...no."

"Sir, you need to go to the VIP lounge in—"

"I heard," he said shortly, and walked away, following the

small crowd of people who were making their way down the terminal. A few looked nervous, aware that the request was unorthodox. Some merely followed directions—like cattle on their way to a slaughter.

An official from the airline was waiting for them inside the door. And Ryder stood with the crowd, listening to the end of his world and wondering how a man was supposed to live with so damned much regret.

"We're sorry to inform you that Flight 209 has crashed in a cornfield just outside the Illinois border."

A few started to cry. Others stood, like Ryder, waiting for the miracle that would pronounce their loved ones okay.

"At this point, we don't know why this has happened, but there have been eyewitness reports that lead us to believe the plane might have been struck by lightning. We do know it was on fire when it went down."

Someone's perfume was too strong. The cloying scent drifted up Ryder's nostrils. From this day on, he would hate the smell of musk. A woman shrieked and sank to the floor while a man somewhere behind Ryder started to curse.

"On behalf of our airline, I am very sorry to have to tell you…"

Ryder tilted his chin and closed his eyes, waiting for the blow.

"…there were no survivors."

The wail that spread across the room began as a joint groan of disbelief. Ryder covered his face and then wished he'd covered his ears, instead. Maybe if he hadn't heard it, it wouldn't be true.

They were saying something about a passenger list and a verification of names, but he couldn't stand still. He knew if he didn't get out, he was going to come undone. He burst out of the lounge, even as someone was calling him back, and started the long walk back down the terminal.

One step at a time. That's how he would get out of the airport. But how would he get home? How could he face that apartment without Casey?

But as far as he walked, he knew he couldn't run away from the truth. He'd spent the last seven months trying to forget what he'd done to his father and now this? How far, he wondered, would he have to run to get away from Casey's ghost? And with every step that he took, the thing that hurt worst was knowing he'd never said, I love you.

Casey kept glancing at her watch, then out the window of the plane. Neither hastened the arrival time of her flight. She was going to be at least an hour late getting home. Poor Ryder. He would no sooner get back to the apartment and hear her message on the machine than he'd have to come right back to the airport again.

She leaned her head against the seat and closed her eyes, weary from the grueling three-day set of negotiations. But it was done! She'd proven her mettle in more ways than one. She'd been thrust into Delaney Ruban's shoes far earlier than she'd ever envisioned, and while she'd known *what* to do, it was the *doing* she'd accomplished that made her feel proud. Delaney had worked all his life to create his empire. She couldn't have lived with herself if she'd been the cause of its ruin.

Yet the glow she had expected to feel from her success was dim in comparison to the anticipation she felt in just getting home to the man who was her husband. She kept remembering their first meeting in Sonny's Bar, of how he'd come out of the shadows and into her life. Now she couldn't imagine what her life would be like without him.

Half an hour into the flight, the plane lurched, and she grabbed at her seat belt, testing the lock that was firmly in place. A few seconds later, it leveled back off and she relaxed. Ryder had been right. This wasn't a good day to fly. Intermittent turbulence had been nonstop since takeoff, and she told herself she should have seen it coming.

Right after she'd talked to Ryder, her cab had come to a complete halt on the freeway. Traffic had snarled itself into a knot that only time had been unable to unravel. She'd known then that unless a miracle occurred, she was going to miss her flight.

For Casey, the miracle did occur, but not in the way she'd envisioned. She arrived at the airport forty-five minutes late. Not only had she missed her flight, she'd missed her lunch and her mood was not getting better. Just when she thought she was going to have to spend another night in Chicago after all, an airline with a later flight into Ruban Crossing had a cancellation. At last she was on her way home.

"Ladies and gentlemen, we will be arriving in Ruban Crossing in about five minutes. Please turn off all electronic and computer devices and prepare for landing."

Casey did so with anticipation. If Ryder hadn't already received her call about the change in flights, she would call home as soon as she got to a phone. By the time she collected her luggage, he would be picking her up.

And then the plane touched down and taxied down the runway, then up to the gate to unload. It was one of the few times in her life she wasn't flying first class, but she didn't even mind having to sit toward the back of the plane, or being one of the last to get off. She was home.

Ryder moved aside out of instinct as a fresh swarm of passengers began to come out of the hallway to his right. His hands started to shake as he watched a man laugh and wave to a woman and child who were just arriving.

It isn't fair. That damned plane got here in one piece. Why not hers?

Twice he tried to move through the crowd and was unsuccessful each time, so he stood against the wall, waiting as face after smiling face moved past. Finally the flow was down to single file and he stepped away from the wall.

"Ryder!"

The hair stood up on the back of his neck and he stopped, but couldn't bring himself to turn. He had to be hearing things. Just for a moment, he thought he'd heard Casey calling his name.

He took a deep breath, clenched his teeth, and started moving again.

"Ryder! Wait!"

He groaned. God! He hadn't even been this bad after Micah was killed.

Someone grabbed his arm and he turned.

Casey dropped her briefcase and threw her arms around his neck. "I can't believe you're still here! This is fabulous luck! I thought I would have to—"

When her arms went around his neck, he started to shake. And when he felt her breath on his face, and her laughter rumble across his senses, he lifted her off her feet.

"My God...my God." It was all he could say as he buried his face against her neck, turning them both in a small, tight circle in the middle of the crowd.

His grip was almost painful, but Casey laughed as her feet dangled off the floor. This was definitely the way to be welcomed home.

"Maybe I should have stayed that extra day after all," she said. "If absence makes the—"

"You're alive."

The laugh died in her voice. "Of course I'm alive."

He set her down on the floor, then cupped her face in his hands, and the tears in his eyes were impossible to miss.

"You missed your plane, didn't you?"

She nodded. "You wouldn't believe the traffic jam my cab got in. I missed my flight, my lunch, my—"

"The plane crashed. There were no survivors. I thought you were dead."

She paled and then clutched at his arm, fixing her gaze on the shape of his mouth and the words coming out. She shook her head, finding it difficult to believe what he was telling her, but he was too distraught to ignore. Goose bumps broke out on her skin as the impact began to sink in.

"When my cab got stuck in traffic, the first thing I thought was if I missed my plane, I wouldn't get to go home, and if I didn't get home, I would have to spend another night away from you.''

Ryder's heart skipped a beat. "I missed you, too," he said softly.

"No, you don't quite understand," Casey said. "I did something selfish, very selfish, as I sat in that cab. I prayed for a miracle so I could get home. When I missed my plane, I was certain my prayer had not been answered." Tears filled her eyes. "Oh Ryder, why me? Why was I spared when so many others had to die?"

He crushed her to him. "I don't know, and I don't care. All I know is, five minutes ago I was trying to find a reason to take another damned breath and now…" Unable to finish, he held her close as a shudder swept through his body.

Suddenly, Casey felt like crying. "Ryder?"

He eased up, but was unable to quit touching her and began brushing the hair from her face. "What is it, honey?"

"Will you take me home?"

He held out his hand.

Chapter 11

Casey kept trying to focus on the familiarity of the country-side through which they were driving, but all she kept seeing was the look on Ryder's face when he'd turned around at the airport and seen her. It hadn't been filled with concern, it had been torn by devastation. To her, that meant only one thing. He cared for her as much as she had learned to care for him. Oh God, please don't let me be setting myself up for a fall, she thought.

"I'm going to let you out at the big house," Ryder said. "You need to let your family know that you're safe—just in case they've heard broadcasts about the crash."

Casey couldn't quit trembling. For some reason, her life had been spared and she didn't understand why. Ryder's presence was solid, unwavering; she felt a need to stay within the sound of his voice. "Where will you be?"

Just for a second he took his eyes off the road. "Right where I've been for the last three days. Waiting for you to come home."

She looked out the window and started to cry. "Oh Ryder, why? All those people. They'll never come home."

He saw Micah's face in his mind and as he did, suddenly realized that the pain of the last few months wasn't as sharp as it had been. Ever conscious of the woman in the seat beside him, he had to face the fact that if it hadn't been for a tragedy, he and Casey would never have met. He tried to imagine his life without her and couldn't. Something inside him clicked.

"I don't know, but I'm beginning to accept that everything that happens to us in life happens for a reason."

Her voice was shaking. "What could possibly be the reason for so many deaths?"

His voice was gruff as he turned off the highway. "Damned if I know. Maybe it was just their time to go."

Moments later, the gray slate roof of the main house appeared over the tops of the trees, and soon afterward, the house itself was visible.

"You're home," Ryder said.

Casey's gaze moved from the mansion to the small, unobtrusive apartment over the garage. "Yes, so I am."

It was the red blinking light on the answering machine that drew him into the apartment. He knew what it said, but he played it anyway, reliving his joy as he waited for the sound of Casey's voice to fill the room.

"Ryder, it's me, again. This day couldn't get much worse. I missed my flight."

He closed his eyes, listening to the rest of the message and feeling awed by the twist fate had taken on their behalf. When it was over he put her suitcase on her bed, then looked around. Some changes had taken place since he'd left to pick her up.

The apartment was clean. Bea had probably seen to that. A fresh bouquet of flowers was on her bedside table, more than likely thanks to Eudora. She was big on flowers. He walked out of the room and into the kitchen. There was a note on the refrigerator door. Thanks to Tilly, there was food inside, ready to be eaten.

He turned on the faucet and let the water run until it was cool, then filled a glass and drank it dry; filled it again, and did the same. When he put it down empty, his hand was shaking. He walked into his bedroom and sat down on the edge of the bed.

The intense quiet assailed him and for the first time since Casey had grabbed his arm in the airport and turned the light back on in his world, he let himself think of the brief period of time when he'd thought she was dead. Uppermost had been the overwhelming sense of pain and loss, but there'd also been regret. Regret that their lives had been so screwed up when they met. Regret that he'd never said aloud what he knew in his heart to be true.

A shuddering breath slid up and out of his throat. He'd been given a second chance, and he wasn't going to waste precious time again. Footsteps sounded on the stairs outside. He tensed. It was Casey. The front door opened and he heard her call out.

"Ryder?"

He stood. For him, there was no turning back.

"Oh, there you are! It was so quiet I didn't think you were here."

He paused in the doorway, staring at her and memorizing the way she looked and the way she moved. Her long, black hair was pinned up off her neck and slightly tousled from travel. Her eyes were wide and still a little shocked, her lips looked tender, almost bruised, as if she'd bitten them to keep from crying, which he supposed she had. He watched as she absently brushed at a speck on her suit. Red was a power color, she'd told him. He could definitely agree. She held a power over him he couldn't ignore.

When she stepped out of her shoes and bent down to pick them up, the hem of her skirt slid even higher up her legs, accentuating their length. His heart filled. That woman was his wife.

"Casey."

She glanced up, her shoes still in her hand.

"I need to tell you something."

That's right! He'd told her the day she left that when she got back they needed to talk. Her heart skipped a beat as she waited for him to continue. Instead, he started toward her.

"Today, when I thought I'd lost you, do you know what I regretted most?"

She shook her head, her eyes widening as he cupped her cheek.

"That I hadn't told you the truth about how I felt." His gaze bored into hers. "I know what I'm going to say wasn't part of our bargain, but dammit, sometimes things change. I am sick and tired of pretending I'm satisfied with being your husband in name only. I love you, lady. I want to lie with you, make love with you. I don't want another night to pass without holding you in my arms. If you can't handle this, then say so, because in about three seconds, it'll be too late."

Casey's eyes were full of tears as she dropped her shoes and put her arms around his neck. "Why waste three seconds when the answer is yes...a thousand times yes?"

Ryder reached behind her and locked the door, then her feet left the floor. "Your place or mine?"

"Anywhere, Ryder, as long as you're there."

He headed for his bedroom with her in his arms. When he put her down, his hands went straight to the buttons on her suit. His voice was shaking. "God give me strength," he whispered, fumbling as he tried to push buttons through holes.

"Let me," Casey said, and finished what he'd been trying to do.

She walked toward the sliding glass doors, pulling shut the drapes as she dropped the jacket of her suit on a nearby chair. On her way back to Ryder she stepped out of her skirt.

He wasn't prepared for the woman beneath the suit; not the wisp of red bra, the matching bikini panties, the long, silk stockings or the black lace garter belt holding them up. And this time, when he swept her off her feet, he wrapped her legs around his waist and sank down onto the bed with her still in his arms.

He nuzzled the curve of her neck, savoring the joy of being able to hold her, inhaling the faint but lingering scent of her perfume, testing the soft crush of her breasts against his chest, and knowing that the tight draw of his own muscles next to that wisp of red silk between her legs was becoming difficult to ignore. He held her close, savoring the joy of knowing she was still alive.

"Today I rode a roller coaster into hell and came out with an angel in my arms. I don't know why we were given a second chance, but I don't intend to waste it."

Her arms tightened around his neck as she rained brief, tiny kisses along the side of his cheek and his chin. He grabbed her face, gazing into her eyes and watching them fill with tears until he thought he could see all the way to her soul.

"I feel like I'm about to make love to a ghost. I can't believe I'm holding you, feeling your breath on my cheek, your arms around my neck. I must be the luckiest man in the world."

Casey's breath snagged on a sob. "I'm the one who got lucky. The day I got lost in the flatlands and found you in Sonny's Bar was the day my life began to change. You've stood with me. You've stood by me. I will never be able to repay you for what you've already done in my name."

"Hell, darlin', I don't want your money. I want your love."

"Then take it, Ryder. It's yours."

He rolled until she was lying beneath him in those bits of red-and-black lace. With an impatient snap, he undid the clasps on her garter belt and rolled down her stockings, silken inch at a time.

Longing to be one with this man was driving Casey to the brink of making a fool of herself. She struggled to help as he undid her bra. But when he hooked his thumbs in the waistband of her bikini briefs and started pulling them down, she moaned and closed her eyes.

Ryder leaned down and kissed the valley between her breasts.

His breath was soft against her face as he moved to her lips. "Are you okay?"

"No," she gasped, and tunneled her fingers through his hair. "Unless you hurry, I may never be okay again."

After that, he came out of his clothes with no regard to order, and when he threaded his fingers through hers and stretched out beside her, he closed his eyes and said a last small prayer of thanksgiving that he'd been given this chance.

Then Ryder Justice made love to his wife.

Casey propped herself on one elbow, looking at Ryder as he slept. She knew the shape of his face, the nearly square, stubborn jaw. Her gaze moved to his hands—broad and strong with long, supple fingers. She shivered, remembering what they'd done to her body in the name of love. Dear Lord, but he knew the buttons to push to make a strong woman weak with longing.

His chest rose and fell with each even breath that he drew, yet a short while ago, she'd felt the thunder of his pulse as he'd lain down upon her and driven himself into her, over and over, in mindless repetition.

Her body quickened in response to the memory and she glanced down to the bulge of him covered just below the waist with a sheet. Hers. He was hers. Before, they'd traded vows and made empty promises in front of Judge Harmon Harris. Today, they'd pledged their love in a way that would endure.

She reached out, gently laying her hand in the middle of his chest just so she could feel the steady rhythm of his heart, and as she did, he sighed and shifted in his sleep. She watched the thick brush of his eyelashes fluttering as some nameless dream pulled him further away from her. From his thick, black hair to those stormy gray eyes, she knew her man well. But she knew nothing of what made him tick.

Astute businesswoman that she was, she knew that in business, the swiftest way to achieve success was to know all there was to know about an enemy...or a competitor. And while Ryder was neither of those, he still had too many secrets for her peace of mind. He wasn't the type of man one would expect to find wandering the highways and byways of the Mississippi Delta. His education was obvious, his breeding even more so. Delaney would have called him a thoroughbred. Casey had an overpowering need to know this man who called her wife. There had to be more to him than a man who knew how to love and make love with a fine-burning passion.

She laid her head down on his chest and closed her eyes, smiling to herself as he pulled her to him. Even in sleep, his claim on her was strong.

Tomorrow. She would start the wheels of an investigation rolling tomorrow. But quiet. She'd keep it low-key and quiet. And it wouldn't be like she was snooping. She had a right to know all there was to know about the man she had married. Didn't she?

Royal Justice raced his daughter, Maddie, for the phone. He lost. Her tiny fingers curled around the receiver as she lifted it to her ear, speaking fast in order to get it all out before her daddy could snatch it out of her hands.

"Hello. This is Maddie. Is this you?"

Roman Justice kicked back in his chair and propped his feet on the top of his desk, absorbing the sweet sound of his only niece's voice.

"Well, hello, little bit. Yes, it's me. Is this you?"

Maddie giggled just as Royal got to the phone.

"Let me talk! Let me talk!" she shrieked, as Royal lifted it out of her hands. "It's Unca Roman. He called to talk to me!"

Royal shushed her with a finger to his lips and then lifted the receiver to his ear. "Roman?"

Roman flipped open a folder on the desk before him. "Brother, you're gonna have to get yourself some skates. If you can't beat a three-year-old to the phone, you're already in hot water. Just think what it'll be like when she's a teenager."

"Bite your damned lip," Royal muttered as Maddie danced

around his legs, begging to be put back on the phone. "I assume you have a reason for calling."

As always, Roman Justice did not waste words. "Ryder's alive."

Royal turned and sank into a nearby chair with a sigh of relief. "Thank the good Lord. What have you learned? Why hasn't he called? Is he all right?"

"Hell, you're just like Maddie. One thing at a time. Your guess is as good as mine as to why he hasn't called, but if I had to bet on a reason, I'd say he hasn't turned loose of the guilt."

"But it wasn't his fault. The FAA told him that. We told him that. Lord have mercy, even the preacher who preached Dad's funeral told him that."

"Yeah, well you know Ryder. The only person he ever listened to was Dad and he's—"

"Yeah, right," Royal said, and pulled Maddie onto his lap, whispering a promise that she could talk when he was through.

"So, what's the story?"

"Hang on to your hat, brother. He's married and living in some place in Mississippi called Ruban Crossing."

"He's what?"

"You heard me."

Royal shook his head. "Married! Ryder, of all people. His wife must be something to have talked a maverick like him into settling down. Do you think we ought to give him a call? You know—to wish him well and all that?"

A fly buzzed past Roman's ear. He never moved, but his gaze followed the flight of the fly as it sailed past his nose. Somewhere between one breath and the next, he snatched the fly in midflight, holding it captive in his fist while he finished his conversation.

"Hell, no. You know better than that. Ryder is the one who ran away from home. If we call him, it would be like that time Mama came after the three of us for sneaking off to the pond to go fishing when we were supposed to be in school, remember?''

Royal laughed. ''Remember? Lord, I had nightmares for years afterward. And you're right. If Mama had just given us time, we would have been home for supper and everything would have been all right. As it was, we were dragged home with our tails between our legs. It took weeks before I could look Dad in the face without feeling shame.''

''Just be glad we know where Ryder is.''

Royal sighed. ''Right, and thanks for calling.''

''No problem.''

Maddie tugged at Royal's arm. ''Your niece needs to tell you something, okay?''

A rare smile shifted the sternness on Roman's face. ''If it's Maddie, it's always okay.''

''Unca Roman?''

''What is it, little bit?''

''You pwomised to take me to the zoo.''

''I know.''

''So when is you gonna do it?''

The smile on his face widened. ''Whenever you want.''

''Now!'' she crowed. ''I want to do it wight now.''

The fly buzzed frantically against the palm of his hand as he glanced up at the clock. ''Put your daddy back on the phone and let me ask,'' he said.

Maddie handed her father the phone. ''It's for you. And you gots to say yes.''

Royal pretended to frown, but it was all a big fake. He nearly always said yes to his very best girl.

''What?''

''Your daughter and I have a date with the zoo. She wants to go now.''

''Fine with me,'' Royal said. ''Just remember, she can't have everything she wants to eat, even if she begs. The last time she threw up on your boots.''

''They were my boots. My problem. I'll be there within the

hour.'' He hung up the phone and then smashed his hand flat on the top of his desk, ending the fly's last bid for freedom.

Royal hung up. At least there was one uncle left upon whom Maddie could depend. He didn't know what he thought about Ryder getting married, and truth be told, didn't have time to worry about it. Ryder was alive and well. That was all that could matter.

Not even in Lash Marlow's worst nightmares had he envisioned the day that something this degrading would happen to him. But it was here, in his hands, on plain white bond, typed all in capitals in clear, black ink. He stuck his hand in his pocket, rubbing at the rabbit's foot over and over and the words still didn't change.

Foreclosure.

He'd slept with the knowledge all night, and when he'd awakened this morning, had almost convinced himself that it was all a bad dream. Until he'd come into the kitchen to make coffee.

The letter was there where he'd left it last night. He'd picked it up again, rereading it over and over until his stomach rolled and his heart was thundering in his ears.

One powerful word and it was enough to bring what was left of his world to an end. He tossed the letter back onto the kitchen table, forgot about the coffee, and went to the breakfront to pour himself a drink. The decanter was empty—just like his life. He stared around the room, trying to find some sense of reason for drawing his next breath when something hit the front door.

That would be the morning paper.

He waited until he was certain the paperboy was gone. Even the eleven-year-old boy who delivered the papers had quit believing the check was in the mail.

The rubber band broke as he was rolling it off the paper, snapping the palm of his hand and bringing a quick set of tears to his eyes.

"Ow! Dammit, that hurt," he muttered, and tossed the paper on the kitchen table next to the letter.

He'd make that coffee after all. At least he could have coffee with the morning paper. That was a civilized thing to do.

When the coffee began to brew, he sat down and began to unroll it, but the edges kept curling back toward the way they'd been rolled and he cursed beneath his breath. It should be against the law to roll up a paper. He remembered the days when his father had insisted on having the help iron his morning paper flat before bringing it to him to read. He grinned, also remembering the occasional times when it would arrive with one of the pages scorched. Such a commotion over paper and ink.

In the middle of pouring himself a cup of freshly brewed coffee, the phone rang. Still lost in memories of grander days, he answered without thinking.

"Mr. Marlow, this is Denzel Cusper, down at the bank. I wanted to call you early, before you left for the office. We had several checks of yours come in yesterday and I'm afraid your account is a little short of funds. You know, we value your business. Your grandfather banked with us. Your father banked with us. We value the Marlow name, and that's why I knew you'd want to take care of this right away."

There was a sick smile on Lash's face, although Denzel Cusper could not see it. He bit his lip and pretended he wasn't lying through his teeth. "Why, you're right of course! I don't know how I let that oversight occur, but I'll take care of it on my way in to the office." He could hear the Denzel Cusper's sigh of relief.

"That's just fine," Denzel said. "I'll just be holding these checks until your deposit clears."

"Thank you for calling," Lash said.

"No problem. Always glad to give a valued customer a helping hand."

Lash hung up the phone and poured his coffee down the sink. He didn't need caffeine. He needed money. He'd already spent his monthly retainer from the Ruban family, and the other clients he often represented were worse off than he was.

The foreclosure letter was still on the table right where he'd left it. Now this. Checks were going to bounce. He didn't even want to know how many. He had represented people who'd written hot checks, and he couldn't remember a one who'd gotten off without serving their time. The law was swift with regards to stealing, in any form.

Shame filled him. Thank God his grandfather hadn't lived to see this day. What his father hadn't lost, Lash had wound up selling to stay afloat. And now it was gone and Lash Marlow was sinking fast. In days gone by, there would have been only one honorable way with which to deal with this shame. Lash thought of the handgun in the drawer beneath the phone. He glanced at the paper he had yet to read. He could just picture the headlines.

"Local Lawyer—DOA."

Dead on arrival. He shuddered. There would be a scandal, but he wouldn't be around to face it. And while he was contemplating the virtue of an easy way out, his gaze fell on the corner of a familiar face pictured on the front page of the paper. He pressed the page flat.

"Ruban Heir Saved by Traffic Jam"

His eyes widened and he began to read, and when he was through, he stared down at Casey's picture in disbelief. Why? Why did someone like her keep getting all the breaks while everything he did threw him further and further off course?

"You bitch."

Startled, he looked up, expecting to see someone standing in the doorway of the kitchen. When he realized it was himself that he had heard, he looked back down and started to shake.

"You selfish, worthless, little bitch. I'd give my life to find a way to make you sorry for what you've done."

Casey's face smiled back up at him from the page, taunting him in a way he could not accept. He let go of his rage, giving hate full rein, and began to consider the wisdom of what he'd just said.

He knew people who would do very dirty deeds for very little money, which was exactly what Lash Marlow had. But if his scheme worked, when he was through, he would be the one in the dough, and that sharecropper's granddaughter would be sorry she'd thumbed her nose in a Marlow's face.

"Oh, my."

Casey's quiet remark got Ryder's attention. In the act of dressing for the day, he came out of the bedroom in nothing but his blue jeans. Casey was standing by the kitchen table, her morning cup of coffee forgotten as she stared at the headlines in disbelief.

"Ruban Heir Saved by Traffic Jam"

"How do they find these things out so fast?"

Ryder put his arms around her, reading over her shoulder as he cuddled her. When he saw the headlines, he sighed. Because of who she was, she would always be news.

"It doesn't matter. As long as they leave you alone, they can print your favorite recipe for toast for all I care."

She dropped the paper on the table and leaned against him. "I don't have a recipe for toast. I can't cook. Remember?"

He grinned. "Then you have nothing to worry about, right?"

She laughed and turned in his arms. "So it would seem."

His eyes darkened as he cupped her hips and pulled her close, letting her feel what was on his mind.

Her robe slipped open, revealing the clean bare lines of her body beneath. Ryder groaned and lowered his head, razing the tender skin on her neck with a series of nips and kisses that left her trembling for more than this sensual tease.

Casey shivered. "Make love to me."

With a flip of his wrist, her robe fell to the floor at his feet. He reached out, tracing the shape of her breast with the tip of his finger, then encircling her waist with his hands, holding her fast—wishing he could hold on forever.

"You are so beautiful, Casey Dee."

Her head lolled as his hands began to work their magic.

Skin tingled. Nerves tensed. Muscles coiled.

He lowered his mouth, trapping her lips and swallowing her sigh.

Heat built.

When his hand dipped between her thighs, she groaned.

Honey flowed.

She reached for his zipper, then for him, needing him—guiding him—to her—in her.

It happened fast. One minute she was standing, the next she was on the cabinet with Ryder between her legs. "Buckle up," he whispered.

Casey wrapped her arms around his neck and her legs around his waist. It felt as if everything inside of her was fighting to get out. Her heart was pounding against her chest. Her blood was racing through her veins. That sweet, sweet heat was building in her belly and she wanted the release. Clutching at him as hard as she could, she buried her face against his shoulder.

"Oh, Ryder, please now."

He began to surge against her in a hard, even rhythm. Over and over. Minute upon minute. Rocking. Hammering. Driving toward pleasure. Too close to hold back.

Casey's senses were swimming. There was nothing upon which she could focus except him inside her. And suddenly gravity shifted and she lost her sense of balance. Grabbing him tighter, she arched toward a thrust, crying aloud. "Ryder…Ryder…I'm coming undone."

Sweat ran down the middle of his back as she held him, encompassed him, pulling him deeper and deeper toward total release. He shifted his hands from her back to her hips—pulling her forward—moving faster. His voice was harsh, his words low and thick with oncoming passion.

"Then let it happen. I'm coming with you."

One cry broke the silence, then another, deeper and more prolonged, followed by soft, shaken sobs and gentle words of praise.

A short time later, Ryder picked up his wife and carried

her out of the room. The newspaper that had sparked the mood lay forgotten on the floor. Had Casey seen it again, she would not have disputed the claim. The traffic jam wasn't the first thing to save her life. It was the man she'd found in the flatlands down at Sonny's Bar.

Chapter 12

"This is all I have to go on. See what you can come up with. Oh, and I want this kept confidential, understand?"

"Yes, Mrs. Justice. Of course."

Casey hung up the phone then swiveled her chair until she was gazing out the office windows. Outside, sunshine beamed down on Ruban Crossing, sweltering the inhabitants with a humidity that left everyone limp and weary. A flock of seagulls swooped past her vision, then disappeared around the corner of the building. On their way to the river—on their way to someplace cool.

She told herself what she'd done was for the best, and that no matter what her investigator found out about Ryder, she would love him just the same. But in the following weeks since they'd first made love, she sensed he was holding something back and it made her nervous. What if the revelation of his secrets brought an end to their relationship? She closed her eyes and said a small, quiet prayer. That just couldn't happen. She couldn't give him up. Not when he'd become the most important thing in her life.

The intercom buzzed. She turned back to her desk.

"Yes?"

"Libertine Delacroix on line two for you."

Casey picked up the phone. "Libby, it's been a long time!"

"Yes, darlin', way too long," Libertine said. "I would have called about this sooner, but I thought that with Delaney goin' an' dyin' on us like he did, and then you gettin' married and all, well—I just thought I'd give everythin' time to settle."

Casey grinned. Libertine Delacroix's southern drawl was too thick to be believed, especially when Casey knew for certain that Libertine had been born and raised in Utah. The only thing south about her upbringing had been the window over her bed. However, after marrying Winston Delacroix and moving to their family home outside of Jackson, Mississippi, Libertine's speech had become as rich as southern fried chicken.

"How is that darlin' husband of yours, anyway?" Libertine asked.

An image of Ryder's face above hers as he slid into her body flashed through Casey's mind. She closed her eyes and leaned back in her chair, suddenly weak with longing.

"Why, he's just fine. Thank you for asking," Casey said.

"Good. I'm havin' a little party Saturday night. I want you two to come. You'll be the guests of honor, of course."

Casey opened her eyes and sat up straight. Libertine had never had a *little* party in her life.

"That sounds wonderful," she said. "But what do you mean by little?"

"Oh, no more than forty or fifty. It'll be fun! Come in costume of course and be prepared to be showered with belated wedding gifts as well."

Casey rolled her eyes. Good grief. A sit-down, costume party, wedding shower dinner? Only Libertine would attempt to pull off such a stunt.

"Thank you, Libby, Ryder and I will be looking forward to it."

Libertine giggled. "I do declare. I hear he's just the handsomest thing. Leave it up to you to pull the coup of the decade. I wouldn't have had the nerve, you know—goin' down in the Delta like that and callin' Delaney's bluff. Oh well, see you Saturday night, sugar. Eightish—costumes—prepare to have fun!"

Casey winced as Libertine disconnected. Lord have mercy! Costumes. She hadn't been able to get him in a chauffeur's uniform. What was he going to say about this?

A dragonfly darted past Casey's nose as she leaned on the fender of the Lincoln, watching while Ryder poured oil into the engine. Still in her work clothes, she was careful not to get grime on her suit. It was an original and one of her favorites.

Ryder didn't seem to have the same set of worries. He was minus a shirt, minus his hat, and as of moments ago when she'd unloaded the news about Libertine's call, minus his good humor.

"So, you're going to put me on parade. I was wondering when this might happen."

Casey winced. "That's not fair. I'm not the one hosting this party, therefore I am not the one putting you anywhere. Libertine Delacroix is famous for her parties. She was also one of my mother's closest friends—at least, that's what Tilly says."

Ryder tossed the empty oil can into the trash and wiped his hands. "Step back," he ordered, and slammed the hood shut with a resounding thump.

Casey followed him into the garage. "Her food is always fabulous. She has the best chef in the county, you know."

"Can't be better than Tilly's," he said shortly.

"They're giving us a belated wedding shower. I didn't know how to say no."

Ryder turned, and there was a light in his eyes she recognized all too well. "Oh, I don't know about that. You pretty much said a big loud no to the terms of your grandfather's will.''

She glared. ''That's different.''

He grinned.

''We're to go in costume.''

The grin slid off his face. ''Like hell.''

Casey groaned. ''Ryder, please. Don't be difficult about this. I love you madly. You can't blame me for wanting all of my acquaintances to meet you.''

''Yeah, right, and I'm supposed to remember these people the next time I see them when I've been introduced to them in costumes? Let's see, what would I say? Oh, I know. You were the pirate, right? And you—weren't you that Playboy Bunny?''

She grinned. ''I can heartily assure you that there will not be a single Playboy Bunny present.''

He yanked his shirt from a hook and pulled it on with a jerk. ''Well hell, you know that refusing you is impossible. However...just remember you're going to owe me, big time.''

Casey threw her arms around his neck and kissed him full on the lips. ''Thank you, thank you, thank you.''

The corner of his mouth tilted as he nuzzled the spot just below her right ear. ''You're very welcome.''

Before their play went beyond a point of no return, Tilly stepped out the back door. ''Casey, honey, telephone call for you.''

Casey waved to let Tilly know that she'd heard, then turned back to Ryder. ''So, what kind of costume do you want to wear?''

He cursed beneath his breath.

''Ryder, you promised.''

''You don't worry about what I'll wear,'' he muttered. ''I said I'd go, so I'll dress the part.''

It wasn't what she wanted to hear, but knowing Ryder, it was the best she was going to get.

''Want to go out to dinner?'' she asked.

''Want to go to Smoky Joe's?''

Casey groaned. She knew when she'd been had. "It's not alligator night."

He grinned. "I don't care. I have a hankering to see someone else's tail get slapped in the mud besides mine."

She made a face and then ran for the phone.

"Don't run in those damned heels," he yelled, but it was too late. She'd already done it. He frowned. One of these days she was going to break her leg pulling a stunt like that.

Casey leaned over the deck and waved at Miles and Erica as they came out of the main house. Erica's white antebellum dress floated just above the ground, billowing out around her and swaying with every step that she took. Miles looked dashing in black and quite reminiscent of a riverboat gambler. Eudora was sick with a cold and had declined the invitation with no small amount of regret. But she couldn't show up at a party with a box of tissues beneath her arm, no matter what costume she might wear. It just wasn't done.

"Hurry up!" Miles shouted, pointing toward a long white limousine pulling up in the driveway. "The limo's here."

"I'll be right down!" she called, and ran back into the apartment, closing and locking the patio door behind her.

Without Ryder, the apartment seemed too large and empty. He'd been gone for more than two hours, and although he called over an hour ago, claiming his costume had been undergoing alterations, he still wasn't back.

"Oh, Ryder, if you let me down at this late date, I'll never forgive you," she muttered, as she made a last-minute check through the apartment, making sure she had everything she'd intended to take.

She paused before the mirror then turned, glancing over her shoulder, making sure her own costume was in place, then smiling in satisfaction at the fluffy, white bunny tail right in the middle of her backside. She turned, ignoring the plunge of fabric barely covering her breasts and readjusted her long white ears. The black fishnet stockings made her legs look sexy, and her three-inch heels completed the picture. Yes, she

made a darn good Playboy Bunny, even if she did think so
herself.

As she started down the stairs to the waiting limo, she made
a bet with herself. *By the time I get to the bottom of the stairs,
Ryder will be driving up.* When her foot hit the last one she
looked up. The Lincoln was nowhere in sight.

"Damn and double damn," she mumbled, and started
across the courtyard. *Okay, by the time I get to the limo, he'll
be home.*

When she drew even with the limousine's black bumper,
she lifted her head to gaze down the long empty driveway.
Her expression fell. She couldn't believe it. He'd actually let
her down. What was she going to say to Libertine when they
arrived?

The driver hurried around the car to where she was standing, then opened the door.

"Watch your ears—and your tail, darlin'. Wouldn't want
either one of them to fall off before you got the chance to
shine."

She looked up, then gasped. "Ryder!"

"Your ride awaits. Now don't tell me you're about to
change your mind after I went to all this trouble."

She blinked. It was him. Resplendent in a dark, double-
breasted chauffeur's uniform with more gold braid and buttons than an admiral might wear.

He tipped his cap and held the door ajar. "Ma'am?"

She threw her arms around his neck. "You are going to
steal the show."

He held her close, patting at the fluff of her tail. "I'd a
whole lot rather steal me a rabbit."

"Oh, for Pete's sake," Miles grumbled from inside the car.
"Let's get a move on or we're going to be late."

Casey quickly took her seat, quite out of place beside a
riverboat gambler and an old-fashioned southern belle.

Erica glared. Leave it up to Casey. "I swear, little sister,
whatever you do tonight, don't bend over. You'll positively
spill out of that disreputable thing you are wearing."

Miles grinned, for once taking Casey's side instead of his twin's. "Oh, I don't know about that, Erica. Even if she is our sister, she looks rather stunning."

Erica sniffed. "You would say that. After all, you're just a man."

The glass door slid open behind Casey's head. Ryder's voice drifted out into the uneasy silence. "Buckle up."

"Have mercy," Erica shrieked, and grabbed for a seat belt as the limo took off, leaving a black streak of rubber to show where it had been.

Miles needed no warning. He was already strapped and waiting for takeoff when the limo accelerated. He'd ridden with this man before.

Casey laughed aloud, then blew Ryder a kiss as he turned onto the highway. Tonight was just about perfect.

Of the guests who'd come in full costume to Libertine's party, nine were in Rebel gray. Of those nine, only Lash Marlow wore the uniform of a southern general, and he wore it with pride. His great-great-grandfather Marlow had been a general during the War of Northern Aggression. It seemed fitting that he carry out the tradition, if only for the night.

But his pride in the past died a humiliating death when the Ruban party arrived. His gaze went past Miles and Erica Dunn. They were Rubans by marriage only. In the grand scheme of things, and blood being thicker than water, it was Casey who counted. But when he saw her and then the man at her side, it was all he could do to stay quiet. How dare she flaunt what she'd done to him?

Libertine Delacroix, who for tonight had dressed as Lady Liberty, was speechless for all of twenty seconds when she saw them, and then broke into peals of laughter.

"Casey, darlin', I should have known you'd outshine us all. And just look at this man on your arm! Introduce me this instant, you hear?"

Casey grinned. "Libby, this is my husband, Ryder Justice. Ryder, my very dear friend, Libertine Delacroix."

Libertine held out her hand. Ryder took it, then lifted it to his lips. "I'm real partial to liberated women, Mrs. Delacroix. It's a pleasure to meet you."

Libertine giggled at his play of words on her costume and name. "The pleasure is all mine, I'm sure," she drawled, then slipped her hand beneath his elbow. "Come along, you two. There's a ton of people who are just dyin' to meet you."

"I'll just bet," he muttered beneath his breath.

Casey pinched his arm. He looked down and winked at her.

"You promised to be nice," she warned.

"No, I didn't. I just promised to come."

She laughed at the sparkle in his eyes. Dear Lord, but she loved this man, so much that sometimes it scared her. She threaded her fingers through his, content for tonight to follow his lead.

An oblong silver tray glittered beneath the lights of the chandelier in the great hall as the wedding gifts were unwrapped before the guests. Crystal sparkled, fine china gleamed. Lash stood among the crowd, oohing and aahing along with them as each new piece was put up on display, and all the while, the idea he'd been fostering took deeper root in his mind.

Damn her—and him. He stared at the tall man in the chauffeur's uniform and resented him for not being ashamed. How can he hold his head high? By wearing that ridiculous costume, he'd all but announced to the world that he was nothing but hired help. Yet when Ryder casually tucked a wayward curl on Casey's forehead back beneath the rabbit ears she was wearing, Lash's stomach rolled. The look she gave him made gorge rise in his throat. *Damn her to hell. She never looked at me like that.* And that hurt, more than he was able to admit.

Out on the patio behind him, the band Libertine had hired was setting up to play. The thought of making small talk and pretending for another two or three hours seemed impossible to Lash, but he couldn't bring himself to leave.

Unaware of Lash's growing antagonism, Casey undid the

bow on the very last gift and then lifted the box lid, pulling out a crystal-and-silver ice bucket and tongs.

"It won't hold a six-pack, but it sure is pretty," Ryder drawled.

Casey grinned at him as everyone laughed. By now, the guests had figured out that Casey Ruban's husband had been one jump ahead of them all night. Instead of trying to be something he wasn't, he dared them to dislike who he was. They had tried and failed miserably. Ryder Justice was too intriguing to dislike and too handsome to ignore.

"This has been wonderful," Casey said. "Ryder and I thank you for your kindness and generosity."

Ryder took Casey by the hand and stood. "All kidding aside, it's been a pleasure meeting my wife's friends. Maybe one day we can return the favor."

Casey was surprised at his initiative, and more than a little bit pleased. He kept coming through for her, again and again.

Libertine waved her hand above the crowd. "This way, this way, my dears. We've dined. We've showered. The evening can't end without dancing."

The crowd followed her through open French doors and out onto a massive flagstone patio. People broke off into couples and soon the impromptu dance floor was crowded.

Inside, Casey wound her arms around Ryder's neck and leaned her head on his shoulder.

"What's the matter, Hoppy, are you tired?"

She tried not to laugh, but his jest was entirely too charming to ignore.

"Yes, but deliciously so." His hands were stroking at the small of her back, right where it ached the most. She wondered how he knew.

"Think you might have one good dance in you? I just realized I've never danced with my wife."

"If you don't mind dancing with a barefoot bunny, I'd be delighted."

He cocked an eyebrow. "It can happen. I like bare."

She ran a finger down the middle of his chest, stopping just above the spot where his belly button would be. "Yes, I know."

He waited. She kicked off her shoes. He took her in his arms just as the next song began. Drums hammered out a rollicking beat and a guitarist joined in, running his fingers up and down the frets as the strings vibrated beneath his touch.

"Oh darn," Casey said. "It's too fast."

Ryder took her hand and placed it in the center of his chest. "You're listening to the wrong rhythm," he said softly. "Feel the one in here. It's the one to follow."

He glanced down at her feet. "I'd sure hate to mash one of those poor little toes. Better hitch a ride on my boots, honey, then all you'll have to worry about is hanging on."

A lump came to Casey's throat as she stepped up on his toes. Sure enough, when Ryder started to move, she could almost hear the slow, steady beat of a loving man's heart. The ache in her feet disappeared. She laid her cheek on his shoulder and followed his lead as he circled them slowly up and down the marbled floors of Libertine Delacroix's great hall.

Out on the patio, Lash Marlow stood in the shadows, staring back into the house. The intimacy of the lady bunny standing on the chauffeur's feet was not lost on him, nor were the tender kisses he saw Ryder giving his wife.

Lash's hand slid to the long sword hanging from the belt around his waist. It would be all too easy to draw it now while everyone was otherwise occupied and slash those stupid smiles off of both their faces, but that wouldn't get him what he deserved. No, he had other plans for Casey, and it wouldn't be long before he set them in motion.

Bunny ears hung on one corner of the bedpost, a chauffeur's cap on the other. Clothing was strewn across the floor and the chairs. In the bed, Ryder and Casey slept as bare as the day they'd been born, entwined within each other's arms.

Outside, a wind began to blow. A cool front was moving in. Something clattered against the patio door leading onto the deck. Ryder shifted in his sleep and rolled onto his back as he fell deeper and deeper into the dream playing out in his head.

Lightning flashed and the plane bucked. Seconds afterward, smoke began filling the cabin. There was a whine to the engines as the plane began to lose altitude. Ryder pulled back on the stick, fighting the pull of gravity with all of his strength.

"God help us both," Micah said.

Ryder jerked, his head tossing on the pillow from side to side. He hadn't remembered hearing his father's voice—until now.

Lightning flashed again, illuminating the horizon and the tops of a stand of trees, but Ryder was hardly aware. It was all he could do to see the instrument panel through the thick veil of smoke. Muscles in his arms began to jerk from the stress of trying to control the plane's rapid descent, and still he would not let go. Yet no matter how hard he fought, it would not respond.

"I love you, boy."

Tears seeped from beneath Ryder's lashes and out onto the surface of his cheeks.

I love you, too, Dad.

One of the windows in the cockpit shattered. Smoke dissipated at an alarming rate. Visibility cleared, and then Ryder wished it had not. There was at least half a second's worth of time to see that they were going to die.

He sat up with a jerk, gasping for air, unaware that his cheeks were wet with tears.

"Oh, God."

He rolled out of the bed and reached for his jeans. He had to get out. He had to move. He couldn't breathe.

Casey felt the bed give. Suddenly she was no longer lying on Ryder's chest. She blinked, then opened her eyes. The sight of him jerking on pants and stomping out of the room was enough to yank her rudely awake. She didn't have to turn on a light to know something was dreadfully wrong. It was there in the shadowy movements of his body as he fled from the room. Seconds later, the front door banged, and Casey knew he was gone.

She crawled out of bed on all fours, searching for something to wear as she hurried through the house. One of his T-shirts was hanging on the doorknob. She grabbed it, pulling it over her head as she ran. It hung to a point just above her knees, but when she opened the front door, the fierce wind quickly plastered it to her body, leaving her feeling naked all over again.

She stood at the top of the landing, searching the grounds for a sign of where Ryder had gone. And then she saw him moving toward the trees at the back of the estate, and she bolted down the stairs after him.

Ryder moved without thought, trying to escape the dream clinging fast to his mind. It was just like before. No matter how fast he ran, he couldn't escape the truth. Micah had died, but he hadn't.

Wind whistled through the trees just ahead. It was an eerie wail, not unlike that of a woman's shriek. Without looking to the sky, he knew a storm was brewing. He stopped, then lifted his arms out on either side of his body like a bird in flight, and faced the force of nature for what it was. Unpredictable. Unstoppable. Uncontrollable.

The first drops of rain were beginning to fall when Casey caught him. She didn't stop to ask him why. She didn't care that she was getting wet. She just threw herself into his arms, becoming his anchor against the storm.

Ryder groaned and wrapped his arms around her, and although the wind still blew and the rain still fell, he knew a sudden sense of peace. He dug his hands through the wind-whipped tangle of her hair and shuddered as she bent to his will.

Rain was falling harder now and he couldn't find the words to explain the horror and guilt that he lived with every day.

Casey clutched at him in desperation. His gaze became fixed upon her face, and she could see his eyes. They were as wild and as stormy as the night. His fingers coiled in her hair. His body was trembling against her. A chill began to seep into her bones, and she knew she had to get them out of the weather. The gardener's shed was nearby. She pushed out of his arms, then grabbed him by the hand and started running. To her everlasting relief, he followed.

When she slammed the door shut behind them, the sound of the rain upon the metal roof was almost deafening, but at least they were no longer standing in the midst of it all.

"Lord have mercy," she said, and shivered as she lifted her hair from her neck and twisted it. Water ran out, then down her shoulder and onto her feet. She reached for the light switch.

It didn't work. It figured. In Ruban Crossing, if the wind blew or rain fell, inevitably, the power went out.

She turned, and knew Ryder was right before her, although she could barely see his face.

"Ryder?"

His hand cupped her shoulder, then her cheek. He stepped closer until their foreheads were touching and she could hear the ragged sounds of his breath. She lifted a hand to his face, and even though they'd just come out of a storm, she had the strangest sensation that what she felt were tears, not rain.

"Sweetheart?"

His lips found hers, stifling whatever else she might have said. They were cool and wet and softened upon impact, molding themselves to her mouth with tender persistence.

Casey sighed and when his arms encircled her, she leaned into his embrace. His hands were moving up and down her arms, across her shoulders, upon her hips. When he discovered she wore nothing beneath his shirt but herself, she felt him pause. His voice came out of the silence, little more than a whisper, but what he said made her blush in the dark.

Her hesitation was brief. There was nothing he could ask that would shame her. There was nothing she wouldn't do with or for this man who called her wife. She pulled the wet T-shirt over her head and dropped it on the floor. Her hands moved to his waist, then beneath the wet denim covering the straining thrust of his manhood.

When she took him in her hands, he groaned. When she knelt, she heard him take a deep breath. And she knew for the rest of her life, the sound of rain on a roof would bring back the memory of what she had done in the dark to bring Ryder Justice to his knees.

Joshua came into the kitchen. "Found this in the gardener's shed this morning."

Casey looked up from the kitchen table. Pink tinged her cheeks, but her expression remained calm.

Ryder glanced at Casey, then looked away. Even after the onslaught of emotions they'd shared last night, he'd been unable to explain what had sent him into the storm.

"It looks like one of my T-shirts," Ryder said. "I know I left one in the garage, but *I* didn't leave one in the shed."

Casey sighed. He hadn't lied. Not really. She was the one who left the shirt. Not him.

Joshua shrugged. "I think it will clean up all right. It's not torn, just wet and muddy."

"Thanks," Ryder said, and returned to the paper he'd been reading.

Tilly stared at the couple sitting side by side at her kitchen table. Everything seemed the same—except her instincts told her it wasn't.

"Is there something you'd be wanting to talk about?" she asked.

Ryder and Casey looked up, first at her, then at each other, before shaking their heads. Casey smiled. "No, ma'am."

Tilly glared. "I didn't get to be fifty-nine years old by being a fool." She banged a pot on the stove to accentuate her claim. "I know when something's not right. Did you two have a fight? 'Cause if you did, I'm telling you now, the best way to end it is talk it all out." She pointed a spoon at Joshua. "Tell them Josh! Tell them I know what I'm talking about."

Joshua rolled his eyes, thankful he was on the far side of

the room from that spoon. "My Tilly knows what she's talking about. She always does. If you don't believe me, then ask her."

Ryder grinned behind his paper as Tilly lit into Joshua for making jest of her claims. It was just as well. It changed the subject, which was fine with him.

He glanced at Casey. Worry was there on her face. He'd have to be a fool not to see it. But he'd give her credit. She hadn't asked a single question. She'd just been there, giving herself to soothe his pain.

He glanced at her face—at her mouth—at her hands. Dear Lord, but she had soothed much more than his pain. Impulsively, he leaned over, slid his hand at the back of her head and pulled her forward. Their mouths met. More than slightly surprised, she parted her lips. His were hard and unyielding, demanding that she remember what they were, what they shared.

She gave herself up to the kiss and felt more pain than passion behind the embrace. One day. One day he would talk. Until then, she would have to be satisfied with waiting for his answers—or with what she learned on her own. The private investigator she'd hired was due back on Monday with a final report. Surely she would have some sort of answer by then. Even if it didn't come from Ryder, she had a right to know.

Chapter 13

Last night's rain had washed everything clean. Lash took his morning cup of coffee out onto the veranda and gazed across the yard into the trees beyond. Although it wasn't visible from where he stood, he could hear the water rushing through the creek below. He smiled to himself and took a slow, careful sip of the hot brew, careful not to burn his lips.

It was all falling into place. The kidnapping of Delaney Ruban's heir was a brilliant plan. He knew exactly how it was going to happen—who was going to do the deed—even the amount of ransom he was going to ask for the safe return of Ryder Justice's wife.

The ideal location in which she would be hidden had all but fallen into his lap. An aging client had been admitted to a nursing home via letter and phone by a distant cousin. The law offices of Marlow Incorporated had been given power of attorney to see to her monetary needs, as well as prepare for the impending funeral that was bound to occur.

Lash had done as the family had asked. Fostoria Biggers was now residing in the second room on the right at the

Natchez Home for the Aged. Fostoria's money was in the bank, but Lash Marlow's name was on the signature card of her account. Her home out in the country was to be put on the market, and it would be—as soon as he no longer had need of it, which would be right after the Rubans coughed up three million dollars for Casey's safe return.

Friday he'd closed his office and gone to Natchez. The two men he'd hired with five hundred dollars he'd borrowed from Fostoria Biggers's account had come into town last night and were in a motel waiting for his call. The five hundred dollars was just a down payment on what he'd promised them when Casey's abduction was completed.

He took another sip of his coffee as he came down from the steps. He laughed to himself, and the sound caused a pair of white egrets roosting in an overhead tree to take flight. Fifty thousand dollars. Last month he couldn't have come up with fifty dollars, and now he had promised Bernie Pike and Skeet Wilson fifty thousand. And, compared to what he would have in his pocket before the week was over, it was a pittance.

The air was rich with the scent of bougainvillea that grew wild within the skeletal arms of a long-dead oak. The grass was still wet from last night's rain and by the time he reached the ivy-covered gazebo, the hems of his slacks were damp.

He stepped inside, then set down his cup and looked around. For the first time in more years than he cared to count, he could see light at the end of his tunnel of financial woes. It wouldn't be long before he could begin the repairs on Gray-stone and he could hardly wait. Even the gazebo was long overdue for a face-lift. And while it would have to wait just a little bit longer, there was one thing he could do.

He began gathering up the unpaid bills he'd been tossing on the gazebo floor, making a pile of them in the middle of the yard. Since the grass was damp, he had no qualms about what he did next.

He struck a match and gave it a toss. The papers were damp as well, but finally one caught—then another—then another, and while he watched, the ugly reminders of his past went up in smoke.

The folder from Childers Investigations lay on Casey's desk unopened. The private investigator was gone—had been for over twenty minutes, and Casey hadn't been able to bring herself to read the report. Fear overlayed curiosity as she stared at the name beneath the Childers logo.

Ryder Justice—Confidential.

Right now her world was just about perfect. But when she opened this up, it could reveal a Pandora's box of despair that no amount of money could buy, sell or fix.

She walked to the window overlooking the downtown area of Ruban Crossing and stared out onto the street without seeing the traffic or the flow of people coming and going into the Ruban Building itself. And because she was so lost in thought, she didn't see Ryder drive up and park, nor did she see him getting out of the Lincoln with her briefcase—the one she'd left in the kitchen chair during breakfast.

She glanced back at her desk, then walked to the far side of the room to refill her coffee cup. Another cup couldn't hurt. And it was as good an excuse as any to put off reading the report.

Her intercom buzzed, then Nola Sue's voice lisped into the silence.

"Mrs. Justice, your husband is here with your briefcase. He's on his way in."

A smile of delight broke the somberness of Casey's features as Ryder came through the doorway, dangling her briefcase from the ends of his fingers.

"Hi, darlin', sorry to interrupt, but I thought you might be needing this. I'll just lay it on your desk and get out of your hair."

Casey gasped. The report! It was on her desk! Before she could think to move, Ryder was halfway there.

Hot coffee sloshed on her fingers as she shoved the cup on the counter and made a run for the desk. "Ryder, wait!"

Startled by the urgency of her shout, the briefcase slid across the desk and then onto the floor, taking everything with it as it fell.

"Sorry about that," he said quickly, and knelt, intent on gathering up what he had spilled. But he froze in the act, unable to ignore the fact that his name was on every sheet of paper he picked up.

"It's not what you think," Casey said quickly, as she grabbed at the papers he was holding.

The look on Ryder's face had undergone a frightening transformation. The sexy smile he'd worn into the room had been replaced by a grim expression of disbelief. He stood, his words thick with anger.

"What does this mean?"

"I...uh—"

"You had me investigated?"

"You don't understand."

"So—you're telling me you *didn't* have me investigated."

Casey couldn't look him in the face. "I didn't say that."

"Then...what you're trying to say is that file is not a dossier of my life story."

Because she was so afraid, she took the defensive. "What I did was—"

"What you just did was stand there and tell me a lie."

She paled. The cold, hard glitter in his eyes was scaring her to death. Dear God, what had she done?"

"I did it for you," she said. "For us."

He pivoted, then picked up a cup full of pencils from her desk and flung them against the wall. They shattered and scattered like so much buckshot against a tin barn. Moments later, Casey's secretary burst into the room.

Ryder spun. "Get out."

Nola Sue gave Casey a wild, helpless glance and left at Casey's quick nod.

Ryder was so hurt, so betrayed by what she had done that he didn't trust himself to touch her. When she reached for him, he shoved her hand aside. "Well? Did you find what you were looking for?"

Panic-stricken, she wanted to throw herself into his arms and beg his forgiveness. But she couldn't weaken now, not when their future was at stake.

"I didn't read it."

The curse he flung into the air between them was short and to the point. Casey took it as her just due.

"But it's true. I was afraid to read it."

He grabbed at the scattered sheets he'd tossed on her desk and waved them in her face. "Why, Casey? Don't you know enough about me by now? Couldn't you trust that there was nothing in my past that could hurt you?" He groaned, and threw the papers on the floor. "Damn you. I would die before I let anyone hurt you—even myself."

This time she couldn't stop the tears. They spilled in silent misery.

He kicked at the papers on which he was standing, sending them scooting across the floor. "Then if you haven't read them, I'll save you the trouble. Depending on the depth of the report the investigator did, you will see that I'm the middle child of three sons born to Micah and Barbara Justice. They were ranchers. My older brother, Royal, still lives on the family ranch south of Dallas. My younger brother, Roman, is ex-military and is now a private investigator. I am a pilot. I own and run a charter service out of a private airport on the outskirts of Fort Worth. I also own a little under fourteen hundred acres of prime real estate on the outskirts of San Antonio, Texas, and unlike what you believed about me when we met, I am comfortably solvent. Before you, I had never been married, but last winter, I did something I'd never done before in my entire life."

Casey tensed.

"I ran away from home."

It wasn't what she'd expected him to say. Truth be told, she didn't know what she'd expected, but that certainly hadn't been it.

"I don't understand. What happened to make you turn your back on family and friends? Has it anything to do with the nightmares you have? The ones that drive you out of our bed? The ones you won't talk about?"

He started to shake, and Casey wished to God she'd never meddled.

"I was piloting a plane that crashed. I walked away. My father did not. He's dead because of me."

The look that passed between them was full of painful memories. For Casey, they were of the panic she'd seen on his face when he'd taken her to the airport. Of the plea in his voice not to fly in the storm. Of the desperation in his touch when he'd seen she was alive.

For Ryder, it was the death of a myth he'd been living. Of pretending that everything between them was perfect. Of hiding behind a marriage of convenience instead of facing the truth.

"You know, wife—I don't think you should be so judgmental about the terms your grandfather put in his will. From where I'm standing, you've picked up his manipulating ways all too well."

With that, he turned and walked out of the office, ignoring the sound of her voice crying out his name—calling him back.

It was all Casey could do not to cry. "Are you sure you haven't seen him all day?"

Joshua shook his head. "No, sugar, I'm sorry. The last time I saw him he was on his way to your office with your briefcase."

She groaned, folded her arms on Tilly's kitchen table and hid her face from the truth. *Please don't let him be gone.*

Tilly sat down beside her. "I knew something was wrong between you two the other day. I told Joshua so, didn't I?"

Joshua nodded.

Casey slammed her fist down on the table. "The other day was nothing." She stood, unable to sit still any longer. "If only I could turn the clock back to that morning, none of this would have happened."

Eudora came hurrying into the kitchen. "What on earth is wrong? I could hear shouting all the way down the hall."

"Mr. Ryder is gone," Tilly said, and then started to cry.

Eudora looked startled, then glanced at Casey for confirmation. "Is this true?"

Casey threw up her hands. "I don't know. He isn't in the habit of telling me anything important in his life," and slammed the door behind her as she left.

"Well, I declare," Eudora said, and dabbed at her eyes with a tissue as Erica came into the kitchen.

"What's going on?" Erica asked.

"Ryder is missing," Eudora said.

Erica looked startled and turned as her brother, Miles, sauntered into the kitchen with his hands in his pockets, as if he didn't have a care in the world. "What's everyone doing in the kitchen?"

"Ryder ran off," Erica said.

His expression changed from one of boredom to intrigue. "Really?"

Eudora frowned. "I don't believe it. I've seen the way he looks at Casey. I suspect they've just had an argument."

Miles scratched his head, as if a thought just occurred.

"If he's gone, I wonder what that does to the terms of Delaney's will?"

It was one of the few times in his life that his grandmother chose to slap his face.

Sometime toward morning, Casey cried herself to sleep. She would have been happy to know Ryder hadn't gone too far. But she didn't know, and because of the press it would cause, she hadn't called the police. If she had, though, it wouldn't have taken them long to locate that familiar white Lincoln. It was parked at the airport in very plain sight. And it wouldn't have taken all that much longer to locate the driver. He was standing outside of the fences that separated the highway from runway, watching as planes took off and landed, trying to exorcise the demon that had driven the wedge between him and the woman he loved. It had taken hours before his conscience would let him admit that while she'd gone about it all wrong, she'd had the right to know.

As he watched, a small private plane was taxiing for take-off, and he curled his fingers through the holes in the chain links, forcing himself to stand as the plane belied the laws of gravity. Since his arrival, over fifty planes had moved past his location, and not a one had crashed on takeoff or landing.

Then why spare me?

The question haunted him as much, if not more, than the fact that his father was dead. Weary in body and soul, he finally moved from the fence toward the car. He didn't know how, but he and Casey had to find a way to make things right. Living life without her wasn't worth the breath it would take.

But when he reached the car, it wouldn't start. The battery was so dead that jumper cables wouldn't even work, and because the battery was dead, the car phone was also inoperable. Ryder cursed luck and fate and everything in between, knowing that all he had to do was go inside the terminal and call home, but the idea of getting Casey out at four in the morning didn't seem all that wise, especially after the fight they'd had.

Forced to wait until daybreak when a mobile repairman could be called, he crawled into the back seat of the car, locked himself inside, and lay down and went to sleep. When he awoke, sun was beaming in the window on his face and it was long past nine. He groaned. Casey would be at the office. It would be tonight before they could talk.

"So," Miles said. "You're saying if Casey doesn't fulfill the terms of Delaney's will by staying with her husband for the entire year, it could still mean default?"

Lash leaned back in his chair and nodded, while his heart skipped a beat. This was his chance. This was the opportunity he'd been waiting for. Adrenaline surged as he contemplated the call he would make. Suddenly, he wanted Miles Dunn out of his face and he wanted it now.

"Look, Miles, it's simply a matter of wait and see. All married couples argue and they usually make up. I don't advise you to put too much hope in what you're thinking."

Miles looked slightly embarrassed as he stood. "Of course you're right. And I hope you don't think I was looking to gain anything by Casey's misfortune."

"Of course not," Lash said, as he ushered him out of his office.

When Miles was finally gone, Lash told his secretary to hold all his calls, then he slipped out the back door. He intended to make certain that the call he was about to make could not be traced back to him.

Casey was trying to concentrate on a stockholders' report when the phone by her elbow suddenly rang. It was the private line that only family used. She grabbed at the receiver, answering on the first ring. It had to be Ryder. Please God, let it be him.

"Hello?"

"Is this Miz Justice? Miz Ryder Justice?"

She frowned. The voice was crude and unfamiliar. "Yes, to whom am I speaking?"

"This here is Taft Glass. There's a fellow out here by my place who done went and had hisself a bad wreck. I found him myself when I went out this mornin' to check my trot lines. Looks like he'd been there all night. He's pinned in this big white car and all, and they're workin' to get him out, but he keeps callin' out your name. I told them medics I'd come up here to the bait and tackle shop and give you a call."

All the blood drained from Casey's face. She gripped the phone in desperation. Oh my God, she thought. I lay in bed and slept last night while Ryder was alone and hurt and crying out for help. Her hand started to shake and she gripped the phone tighter. This was why he hadn't come home.

She reached for paper and pen. "Give me the directions to

the scene of the accident," she demanded, and wrote at a furious pace as Taft Glass continued to speak.

She grabbed for her purse at the same time she disconnected. Her legs were shaking and she wanted to cry, but this was no time for her to be weak. Ryder's well-being was all that counted.

Halfway to the door, she thought of the wallet she'd tossed in the desk drawer this morning and raced back to get it. She reached in and grabbed, getting a handful of pens along with the small leather case. Without taking time to sift through the mess, she tossed it all in her handbag and dashed out the door.

"Nola Sue, cancel all of my appointments. I don't know when I'll be back, but I'll call. My husband has been injured in a wreck."

Nola Sue was still registering shock as the door slammed shut behind Casey's exit.

"It's got to be here somewhere," Casey muttered, glancing down again at her hastily written map, as she had more than once during the last half hour.

This part of the countryside was one she'd never been in. She was deep in the Mississippi marshlands and hadn't seen a house since she'd turned off the last gravel road.

She took the upcoming curve at a high rate of speed, skidding slightly as the road suddenly straightened. Suddenly, her nerves went on alert. A few hundred yards up ahead she could see a cluster of parked vehicles. She'd found them!

It didn't occur to her to wonder why there were no police cars in sight, and no medical units trying to get Ryder free. All she saw was the front half of a white car buried in a bayou and the back half sticking up in the air, like an awkward straw in a giant cup of thick, soupy mud.

Fear for Ryder made her miss the fact that the buried car was a '59 Ford and that it had certainly been in the water longer than overnight. Fact was, it had been there closer to a year, and it was still there because the owner had moved away soon after, leaving it stuck the same way he'd left owing rent.

But to Casey, the sight was appalling. Her heart nearly stopped. Dear Lord, the man hadn't told her the car had gone off into water. She couldn't bring herself to think about Ryder not being alive. She had to explain to him about the investigation. He had to understand that she'd done it because she loved him, not because she didn't trust him. In a panic, she braked to a skidding halt, unable to contemplate the idea of growing old without him.

A heavyset man separated himself from the cluster of vehicles and started toward her, while another man, tall and skinny with long, graying hair, watched from the tailgate of his truck. The man coming toward her was short and his T-shirted belly had a tendency to laze over the waistband of his faded blue jeans. The baseball cap he wore scrunched over his ears accentuated the fact that he was in dire need of a haircut. Unruly blond wisps stuck out from beneath the rim of the cap like greasy duck feathers.

A niggle of warning ticked off in Casey's head. This wasn't what she'd been expecting. When he leaned in the window and leered, she knew something wasn't right.

"Miz Justice?"

"Yes, I'm Casey Justice."

Bernie Pike grinned and yanked her out of the car. "Damn, lady. It took you long enough to get here."

Panic shafted through her as she struggled to pull herself free.

"Where's Ryder? Where's my husband?"

He laughed. "Now, that's probably about what he's going to be asking himself when you don't show up tonight."

"What do you mean?"

He slapped a rag on her face. It smelled of hospital corridors and science classes she thought she'd forgotten.

"Consider yourself kidnapped, honey, and hope that someone in your family thinks you're worth the price it's gonna take to get you back home."

She screamed and fought, tearing the cloth from her eyes

and kicking off her shoes as she tried to run. Something sharp pierced her arm, then the world opened up and swallowed her whole.

Ryder got as far as the edge of town and knew he couldn't wait any longer to see his wife. Night was too far away. In spite of the fact that he looked as if he'd slept in his clothes, which he had, he needed to see Casey now. He parked in front of the Ruban Building and told himself they would find a way to make things right.

Nola Sue gasped as Ryder walked into the office. "Mr. Justice, thank goodness you're all right!"

Casey's secretary wasn't making much sense. "What do you mean?"

"You know. With your wreck and all, we had no way of knowing how serious your injuries might be."

He frowned. "I wasn't in any wreck."

Her hands fluttered around her throat as his words sank in. "But Mrs. Justice said you'd had a wreck. She raced out of here in a terrible state."

Suddenly there was a knot in the pit of his stomach. He didn't want to think about what this might mean. "When?"

Nola Sue glanced at the clock. "Oh, at least an hour ago, maybe longer."

A muscle jerked in Ryder's jaw. "Who told her something like that?"

She shrugged. "I don't know. I just know that someone called her on the private line. You know, the one the family uses." She blushed. "I heard it ring. The walls aren't all that thick."

Damn, this doesn't feel right. "I want to look inside her office. Would you come with me? You'll know better than I would if something important is missing."

Nola Sue followed Ryder inside, and together they made a thorough search of the place.

"No, I'm sorry, sir, but everything looks the same."

Ryder tried a smile. "I'm sure we're just borrowing trouble. She's probably at home, cursing the fact that someone sent her on a wild-goose chase.''

Nola Sue nodded. ''I'll bet you're right.''

Even though he suspected it was useless, Ryder continued to stand in the middle of the room. He kept thinking that they'd missed something. He could almost feel it.

When they'd started their search, her top desk drawer had been half-open, but Nola Sue had said nothing was missing. There was a pad of paper and a pen right by the phone, just like—

He froze. The pad. Maybe she'd written something on there that would give him a clue. He raced to the desk, then dug a pencil out of the drawer. Carefully, he rubbed the side of the lead on the blank piece of paper, going from side to side as he moved down the page. Inch by inch, a set of directions was slowly revealed.

Nola Sue leaned over his shoulder. ''Oh my goodness. That's way out of town. In fact, if I remember correctly, that's out in the marsh.''

His gut kicked, reminding him that fate was not kind. ''Call the house. See if she's home.''

Nola Sue did as she was told and, moments later, gave him the bad news. No one had seen her since early this morning.

Ryder looked down at the pad, afraid to consider where his thoughts were leading, and picked up the phone.

''What are you doing?'' she asked.

''Calling the police. Something's not right. Someone has played a pretty sick joke on Casey, or her life could be in danger. Either way, I'm not waiting to find out.''

Casey woke up with a start. Several things became obvious to her all at once. She couldn't see. She couldn't move. Her arm was sore and there was a bitter taste in her mouth. And, she remembered why. She took a deep breath and heard herself sob.

''So, girlie, girlie, I see you're comin' around.''

She froze. *Oh God, I am not alone.*

"Please, let me go."

He laughed, and Casey felt like a fool. It had been a stupid thing to ask, but she'd had to, just the same.

"Now, we can't be doin' that. Not until your people come up with the dough. We went to a lot of trouble to set this all up, you know. Don't you think we ought to be paid for our time?"

Dear God, I've been kidnapped! "They'll pay," she said, and then choked on a sob.

He laughed again. "And why the hell not? It ain't like you're short on dough, now, is it?"

Something skittered across her leg and she kicked and screamed in sudden fright.

"Hey! Ain't no need for all that screamin'. If you can't keep your mouth shut, I'll just have to gag you, too—you hear?"

Her voice was still shaking, but there was just enough indignation to get the man's attention. "Something ran across my leg."

"Probably just a lizard. They's all kinds of water critters down here. Be glad it wasn't no snake."

She shuddered and thought of Ryder. Obviously, he hadn't been in any wreck. They'd used that excuse to sucker her right into their hands. If she'd had a foot free, she would have kicked herself. And along with that knowledge, came a question she was afraid to have answered. If Ryder wasn't in a wreck, then where was he? The thought of never seeing him again, of dying and not being able to explain to him why she'd done what she'd done was devastating.

"I need to go to the bathroom."

The man cursed. "I told 'em not to leave me out here. I told 'em somethin' like this was bound to happen. But hell no, did anyone listen?"

"Please."

He yanked at the cord binding her wrists to get her attention, then untied her ankles, dragging her up from the bed and standing her on her bare feet. A few steps later, he gave her a push.

"You got a couple of minutes, no more. And don't try nothin', either." His hand cupped her breast, and Casey could feel his breath on her face. "You'll be sorry if you do."

Casey wouldn't move, wouldn't let him know how scared she was, or how repulsed she was by his touch.

"Well, what the hell are you waitin' for?" he yelled.

She held out her hands. "For you to untie me."

He cursed, but moments later, she felt the rope come loose around her wrists and heard the door slam shut between them.

"No funny business," he yelled. "And remember, I'm right outside this door."

Her hands were shaking as she tore at the rag covering her eyes. When it fell free to the floor, she staggered from the unexpected glare of light. Quick to take advantage of the privilege she'd been granted, she did what she had to do, aware that it could be hours before he might let her get up again.

As she washed her hands, she searched her surroundings for something—anything, that might help her escape. But there was nothing in sight. Not even a window in the tiny, airless room.

The only remarkable thing she could see was a varied assortment of crocheted knickknacks sitting on floors, on shelves, even hanging from the walls. It explained nothing.

"Get out here, now!" the man yelled, and Casey jumped. "And put that blindfold back on your face or you'll be sorry."

She did as she was told, although she was already as sorry as a woman could be and still be breathing. If only she could start this day over.

Her hand was on the doorknob when the man suddenly yanked it open. He grabbed her by the hand, retied her wrists and ankles, and shoved her back down on a bed.

Loath to recline in a room with a man she could not see, Casey sat with her back against the bedstead, her knees pulled toward her chin. It wasn't much, but it was as good a defensive position as she could manage. The urge to come undone was almost overwhelming, but she refused to give way. She was going to need all of her wits to survive.

Chapter 14

Just as Ryder had feared, Casey's car was found at the location she'd written on the notepad. What broke his heart was learning they'd also found her shoes. For once, she must have heeded his warning and kicked off her shoes before trying to run.

Unfortunately, it had done her no good. There wasn't a clue as to where she'd been taken.

Now, just like before when she'd gone to Chicago, Ryder sat by the phone, again waiting for word. Only this time, the phone had been tapped, and when they heard—if they heard—he knew the request wouldn't be for a ride home. If Ryder's fears were correct, it would be for money in return for his wife.

Eudora had been given a sedative and was in her room asleep.

Erica was curled in a chair in the corner with her head on her knees, trying to come to terms with the fact that a member of their family was a possible kidnap victim and trying not to let herself think that if Casey didn't ever come home, everything that had been Delaney Ruban's would then belong to her and Miles. It shamed her to realize that she'd already envisioned what she would wear to her sister's funeral. She didn't want Casey to be dead. Not really. Right now, she would be perfectly satisfied if Casey were back and being the constant source of discord in their lives.

Before Mason Gant had become a detective on the police force in Ruban Crossing, he had been a star running back on his college football team. He'd planned on a career in the NFL, not one behind a badge. But a single tackle had changed his plans and the rest of his life. Before he knew it, fifteen years had come and gone and he was now Detective Gant, and carried a notebook and pen, not a pigskin.

Because of the identity of the missing person, he knew that this could very well be one of the most important investigations of his career and was not giving an inch as to protocol. He'd interviewed all of the hired help and the immediate family, except one. Miles Dunn had been the last to come home and the last to be apprised of his sister's situation. And as Miles slumped in a chair, it was Gant's opinion that Dunn wasn't nearly as bereaved as he would have liked.

"And where were you?" Gant asked, pinning Miles in place with a casual stare.

Miles raised his eyebrows in disbelief. "Why on earth should it matter where I was at? My sister is missing. Why aren't you out trying to find her?" Taking heart in the fact that several of Ruban Crossing's finest were present, he glanced at Ryder, confident that he could say what was on his mind without coming to harm. "Better yet, why aren't you questioning her husband? We don't really know a thing about him."

"Oh, but we do, and his story checks out clean. Besides, he has nothing to gain from her demise. On the other hand, you and your sister have several hundred million dollars at stake. Am I right?"

Erica stood up with a gasp of indignation as Miles shifted nervously in his seat. "Of course not. Casey inherited."

The detective persisted. "But what happens if she dies?"

Miles shrugged. "I wouldn't really know."

As the family lawyer, Lash was in attendance. At this point he interrupted, but seemed hesitant to do so. "That's not exactly true, Miles. You did come to my office this morning and ask what would happen if Casey defaulted on the terms of Delaney's will."

Ryder came to his feet, and if there hadn't been a desk and a chair between them, he would have put his fist in Miles's face.

Miles spun, his face livid with anger. "You're twisting everything. You knew I was asking because we all thought Ryder had flown the coop."

Lash looked repentant. "I'm sorry, Miles, but I felt obligated to tell the truth. If anyone needs me, you know where I can be reached." He picked up his briefcase and made a quick exit.

Ryder was shaking with anger. "You son of a bitch. Do you remember what I told you? If Casey hurts—you bleed."

The low, even tone in Ryder's voice frightened Miles far more than any shout of rage could have done. He scrambled to his feet and backed toward the door, looking frantically toward the police for protection.

"Sit down!" Gant said, and then glanced at Ryder. "While I can understand your indignation, this isn't getting us anywhere. A woman is missing and all you people seem able to do is fight among yourselves."

Ryder hunched his shoulders and stalked to the windows overlooking the courtyard, looking up at the small apartment over the garage. Precious minutes passed as pain twisted within him, drawing and pulling like a dull knife. The night before last, he'd slept in Casey's arms. They'd made love with an abandon that had surprised even him. And less than thirty-six hours later, someone had lied to Casey and stolen from Ryder the thing he cared for most—his wife.

And then suddenly the phone rang, and everyone jumped as if they'd been shot.

"You answer it," Gant directed, pointing at Ryder.

Ryder said a prayer and picked up the phone. "Hello."

"This is a recording. I will not repeat myself, so pay attention. Casey Justice is with me. At the moment, she is alive. If you choose to ignore my conditions, she will not stay that way long. For her release, I want three million dollars in small, unmarked bills, none of them larger in denomination than a fifty, none of them smaller than a five. I will call you at five o'clock, day after tomorrow, and tell you where and when to make the drop."

The line went dead, with the computerized sound of an altered voice still grinding in his ear. "Did you get that?" Ryder asked.

Gant nodded. "All we can do now is wait."

Ryder slammed the phone down. "Like hell. That's three days. In three days, anything could happen to Casey. Don't you have any leads? Didn't anything turn up when forensics went over her car?"

Gant was a man who believed in telling it like it was. "Forensics is still going over her car, and you know as well as I do that we don't have any other leads. However, we will actively be pursuing the investigation."

Ryder covered his face with his hands and turned away. He felt sick to his stomach and couldn't quit shaking. He kept thinking about Casey. Of how afraid she must be. "Dear Lord. Why is this happening?"

Gant briefly touched Ryder's arm. "Because someone got greedy, Mr. Justice. Now I suggest you try to get some rest. The next forty-eight hours will be crucial. The FBI should be here by morning." He grinned wryly. "You'll probably have to repeat everything you've told me to them. They're kind of partial to taking their own statements." His smile faded. "I think you should be prepared for the possibility that the kidnappers are going to want you, or another member of the family, to make the drop."

"I'll do whatever they ask, but I'm not very good at waiting.'' He exhaled slowly, as if the action pained him. ''There will be time to rest after Casey gets home.''

Gant looked away. He was too aware that the odds of that happening weren't all that good.

''If anyone needs me, I'll be at the apartment,'' Ryder said, and started down the hall when Erica caught up with him.

''Ryder.''

He stopped and turned.

Looking him straight in the face was the hardest thing she'd ever done. From start to finish, she was ashamed of the way she'd behaved, but she didn't know how to say it without admitting she'd been in the wrong.

''What do you want?'' he asked.

''If you don't want to be by yourself, I know Casey would want you to stay here in the main house. You could have her room.''

''I don't think so, but thanks.'' He turned away.

''Ryder, wait, please!''

He took a deep breath and turned around again. ''Yeah?''

''I'm sorry.''

He didn't respond.

''I have never regretted anything as much as I have regretted the stunt I pulled with you. All I can say is, I have envied Casey her place in this family all of her life, and it's not even her fault. She was born a Ruban. Our mother became one by marriage. Miles and I have been on the outside looking in ever since the day Mother said, 'I do.''' Her chin quivered as she continued. ''However, not even in my ugliest moment have I ever wished Casey to come to harm. I ask your forgiveness, and when Casey comes home, I will ask hers, too.''

Ryder knew truth when he heard it, and in his opinion, it was probably the first time in her life that Erica Dunn had been completely honest, with herself, and with someone else. And because she was Casey's sister, he held out his hand.

''Truce.''

She smiled. ''Truce.'' And she accepted the offer of friendship.

"Sure I can't change your mind?"

He shook his head and then hurried out the door. Erica watched as he ran up the stairs to the apartment, and although she couldn't hear it, imagined the thud as he slammed the door shut behind him.

Ryder grabbed the phone as soon as he came in the door, then sat down with it in his lap. Within seconds, he was punching in numbers, then waiting as it began to ring. Four rings later, the answering machine kicked on.

He closed his eyes as he listened to the message. It had been so long—too long since he'd heard the sound of his brother's voice.

"This is Justice Air and The Justice Way. State your name, your business, and if you want a call back, leave your number. Wait for the beep."

It didn't register to be surprised that Roman was now in charge of his business as well. Casey was foremost on his mind.

"Roman, it's Ryder. For once, pick up the damned phone."

A distinct click sounded in Ryder's ear, and he closed his eyes with relief.

"It's about damned time," Roman growled.

"Give me grief later," Ryder said. "Right now, I need you, brother, as I have never needed you before."

Roman sat up. Ryder was thirty-three years old and to Roman's knowledge, he had never asked a soul for help before in his life. "What's wrong?"

"My wife has been kidnapped. I want her back, Roman." His voice broke. "Dammit, I need her back. If anything happens to her, I won't—"

"Where are you?"

"Ruban Crossing, Mississippi."

"Hell, I knew that," Roman muttered. "I mean physical directions to your home."

Startled, it took Ryder a moment to reconnect his thoughts. Then he sighed. He should have known. After all, his brother *was* a private investigator.

"Got a pen and paper?" he asked.

"Does a bear—"

Ryder laughed aloud, drowning out the rest of Roman's remark. It made him feel good, almost normal, to hear Roman's ever present sarcasm. Some things never change.

He gave Roman directions to the Ruban estate, and when he hung up, for the first time since this nightmare had started to unfold, he knew a small sense of relief.

In a small, unused room in a forgotten part of Delaney Ruban's house, candles were burning, on pedestals, in cups, on plates, even on the floor. Candlelight flickered upon the walls and on the bare, lithe body of Matilda Bass, giving the cafe au lait colour of her skin a rich, golden glow.

Her hair was undone and hanging well below her waist and she moved as one in a trance, methodically unrolling a cloth she'd brought into the room. A handful of small, white bones fell out of the folds, arranging themselves in a crude sort of circle as they rolled to a stop.

She leaned forward, her bare breasts shifting, and she was barely aware of the thick, silken length of her hair against the skin on her back, blind to the candlelight surrounding her as she sat.

At her side lay a knife, the shaft, old and yellowed. The blade was long and thin, the kind that pierces and kills and leaves nothing behind but a tiny, red mark. The carvings on the handle were old and held a power all of their own.

When Joshua entered, Tilly sensed the air in the room stirring, and somewhere within her mind, she sifted through the change and knew that nothing threatened what she was about to do. Her focus shifted again as she went to her knees before the circle of bones, whispering in a language that she'd learned at her grandmother's knee.

Lash downshifted Fostoria Biggers's small white compact and turned into the overgrown driveway leading up to her house. It was nearly dark, and he knew that coming out here was risky, but he wanted to see for himself that the mighty Casey Ruban had been brought to her knees. Using Fostoria's car was just another way of blurring his trail.

The house was small and nearing total dilapidation. In fact, if possible, it was in worse condition than his beloved Graystone. Fostoria's porch had sagged some years ago, and was nearly rotted through from the wetlands upon which it had been built. Paint had peeled off all the siding except in a few sheltered places, and the curtains that hung at the windows were faded and limp. The grass in the yard was ankle high and Lash winced as he thought of walking through it. There was no telling what kind of reptiles were lying in wait.

He made it through the yard and onto the porch. Sidestepping the worst of the sag in the planks, he walked into the house as if he owned it. Bernie Pike spun toward the sound, his gun pointed directly at Lash's chest.

"Dammit, Marlow, you scared the hell out of me."

Lash frowned. "Point that thing somewhere else."

Bernie did as he was told.

"Where is she?" Lash asked.

Bernie pointed toward the first door on the right down the hall. "I put her in there. It was the only room that had a bed."

Lash nodded.

"When's Skeet comin' to relieve me?"

Lash frowned. "I told you two to guard her. I didn't think I would have to set up a work schedule for you as well. Call him and find out for yourself."

Bernie shivered and glanced nervously out the open door. "I'm ready to get my money and get the hell out of this swamp. There's snakes and lizards and all matter of critters out here. When is it all goin' down?"

"Day after tomorrow."

Bernie frowned and then cursed. "What's the holdup? I thought them people had plenty of money."

Lash glanced down the hall at the closed door and then

grinned. "Oh, they do, but I intend to delay the inevitable as long as possible. Why put her out of her misery—until she knows what real misery is like?"

There was an expression on Lash Marlow's face that made Bernie Pike shudder. He shifted his gun to his other hand, thankful that he was working for this man, not running from him.

"So, what do you want me to do?" Bernie asked.

Lash took a deep breath, his pulse quickening as he glanced at the closed door. "Get out. Get out and don't come back inside until I tell you to."

Bernie looked startled and then a slow grin spread across his face as he did what he was told.

When the house was quiet, and Lash could hear nothing but the sound of his own heartbeat in his ears, he gave his rabbit's foot a last quick rub, and started down the hall.

Casey's hands were numb and her throat was dry. She needed a drink in the very worst way, but calling attention to herself was the last thing she wanted to do. As long as her abductor thought she was asleep, he pretty much left her alone.

Something was crawling on the floor beside the bed and she prayed it stayed there. But the scritch-scratch of toenails on hardwood flooring was impossible to ignore. She kept telling herself that as long as she couldn't see what was making the noise, then she couldn't be afraid.

And then the air shifted, and another sound blended with those in her head and she tensed. That was the door! Someone was inside the room. Casey had learned a trick from Delaney early on in her life to take control of a situation by being the first to speak. She saw no reason to change her strategy now.

"I would like a drink of water."

A low, ugly chuckle centered itself within the waiting silence and Casey gasped. That didn't sound like her abductor. Someone else had entered the picture.

"Casey, Casey, ever the prima donna, aren't you? Tied up

like a sow going to market and still giving orders. Now what do you suppose it would take to bring you to your knees?''

''Lash?''

The blindfold was yanked from her face.

Casey blinked rapidly, trying to clear her vision as her eyes adjusted to the change in light. Lash leaned down and pinched the sides of her cheeks with his thumbs and fingers, squeezing and squeezing until speech was impossible and tears sprang to her eyes.

''That's it. Cry for me, honey. Show me you care.''

Casey jerked, trying to free herself from his grasp, and then to her surprise, he turned her loose and shoved her, sending her sprawling. Before she could think, he had untied her ankles and straddled her legs.

Panic shafted through Casey's mind. Lash's intentions were all too plain. And when he leaned forward, pressing the palms of his hands against the swell of her breasts, she groaned and wrestled with the ties still binding her wrists. They wouldn't give.

''Lash, for God's sake, don't.''

His slap ricocheted off the side of her jaw. ''You don't tell me what to do. I'm the one in control. I'm the one who calls the plays, princess, and right now, I'm going to take a little of what was rightfully mine.''

His fingers curled in the top of her blouse, and when he yanked, buttons flew, hitting the wall and scattering across the floor. Something scurried out from under the bed and Casey knew that one good thing had come from Lash's arrival. At least that creature was gone. If she only knew how to get rid of this one for good, she would never ask for anything again.

He laughed, and then grabbed at the hem of her skirt as adrenaline surged through him. This was power. He wished he'd thought of it sooner. At last he felt like a man.

Casey kicked and bit and screamed until her throat was hoarse. It served no purpose other than to arouse him more. His hands were at the juncture of her legs when the room began to grow dark before her eyes. A fresh sheen of perspiration broke out on Casey's skin as the sensation of fainting became imminent. Horrified at what he would do if she was unconscious and helpless, Casey thought of a prayer that didn't make it aloud. The darkness in the room was growing, and it was beginning to pull her in.

Her submission was so unexpected that Lash also paused, wondering what trick she was trying to pull. But she was far too limp and far too still for a joke. Frustrated that she would not be awake to suffer his touch, he thrust a knee between her legs, readying to shove himself in as well. And then Casey began to speak.

Surprised, he looked down. Her eyes were still closed. She was still limp—almost lifeless. And he would have sworn the voice that he heard was not her own.

Her breathing had slowed, and at first glance, she seemed to be asleep. But the words pouring out of her mouth were fluent in cadence, foreign in sound and speech, universal in intent. One brief, staccato sentence after another, she was invoking a curse of such magnitude upon Lash Marlow's head that he couldn't do anything but stare. Word after word, the curse continued, pouring upon every living person hereafter who might carry an ounce of his blood in their veins. Spoken in the old patois of French-speaking slaves, the threat became even more insidious as the promises continued.

Lash jerked his hand back from her legs as if he'd been burned. Pale and sickening, a cold sweat suddenly beaded upon his face. Lash was a true son of the south. He'd been born and bred in the ways of the past. He, too, spoke French like a native, and although he was a well-read, highly educated man, there was that part of him that had grown up believing in curses and superstitions and extremely bad luck.

"Shut up! Shut up!" His scream rent the air as he drew back and slapped her in the face.

It was after Casey tasted her own blood that she took a deep breath and opened her eyes.

Horror crawled up the back of Lash's spine. The woman looking out at him from Casey's face wasn't the green-eyed woman he'd known and coveted. This woman's eyes were black, and she was staring at him from hell.

He grabbed at his clothes, scrambling to get off of her legs and away from her body like a man gone crazy. When he was on the other side of the room, he pointed a finger toward where she lay and told himself it didn't matter. Words were just words. She couldn't stop the success of what he'd set in place. But everywhere he moved, her eyes followed him, staring—blaming—reminding him of what she'd just said.

"Say what you will, you stupid bitch," he growled. Then he laughed. But it was a nervous, jerky sort of bark. "Day after tomorrow it will all be over. I'll be rich, and you'll be dead."

And then he was gone, and while she lay on the bed, she came to an acceptance she didn't understand. Even though she was locked in this room and helpless in the face of her abductors, for a while, she had not been alone. Instead of being afraid, she took comfort in the knowledge. All she could remember was feeling sick and then falling into a deep, black hole. What had transpired after that, she could only guess, but she knew she had not been raped. And in the face of all that, it still wasn't the biggest horror of all.

Lash Marlow had purposefully let her see his face. She closed her eyes. She would never see Ryder again.

It was 3:00 a.m. when the knock sounded on Ryder's front door. Half in and half out of a weary doze, he staggered to his feet and made his way through the darkened rooms, turning on lights as he went. He grabbed the doorknob and jerked.

Roman walked inside, tossed a suitcase on the sofa and kicked the door shut behind him. Brother to brother, the two men looked at each other, judging the changes in each that the last few months had made. Finally, it was Roman who broke the silence.

"You look like hell."

Ryder walked into his brother's outstretched arms. Their embrace was brief, but it served its purpose. It was proof to

Ryder that the connection he'd tried to sever with his family was still as strong as it had ever been.

"You got here fast," he said.

Roman glanced around the room. "I figured I'd better."

Ryder hadn't expected to be so overwhelmed by the sight of his brother's face. It was all he could do to speak without breaking down. "Help me, Roman. Help me find her and get her back."

Roman's grasp was strong on Ryder's arm. "That's why I came, brother. That's why I came."

Like the sleuth that he was, Roman began to move about the room, picking up things and laying them down again, feeling, judging, absorbing the world in which his brother had been living. A photograph sat on a nearby table. Roman picked it up.

"Is this her?"

Ryder nodded. It had been taken the night of Libertine Delacroix's party. It hurt to look at it and remember how happy they'd been. "Yeah, minus the ears and tail," Ryder said.

One of Roman's rare grins slid into place. "Leave it up to you to run away from home and come out smelling like a rose."

"Well, I do declare!"

Eudora's ladylike gasp that accompanied her remark was in reaction to seeing the Justice brothers coming through the front door of the main house.

From the cold, handsome faces to the dark straight hair and those square, stubborn chins, they were alike as two peas in a pod. Their blue jeans were pressed and starched and their long-sleeved white shirts were a perfect contrast to the tan of their skin. The tilt of their Stetsons rode at the same cocky slant, and their steps synchronized as they stepped off space on the pale, marble floor.

"Dora, this is my brother, Roman Justice. Roman—Casey's grandmother, Eudora Deathridge."

Roman's expression never changed as he tilted his hat. "Ma'am."

A shiver moved through her as she looked into Roman's eyes. They were dark, and the expression seemed hard and flat. And she knew if he hadn't looked so much like Ryder, she would have been afraid of this man.

Ryder touched her arm. "We're going to use the library for a while, okay?"

"Why, yes, dear. Whatever you need," she said, and then made as graceful an exit as she could manage.

"There it is," Ryder said, pointing to the computer system in the far corner of the room.

Roman headed for it with unerring intent. Within moments, he was into the system and had it on-line.

"How did you do that?" Ryder asked. "I can never make those things do what I want them to do."

Roman looked up. "You just don't use the right kind of persuasion," he replied, then moved his eyes back to the screen.

Ryder found himself a chair and sat down. This morning, Roman had asked him for a list of names of people with whom Casey most closely associated. The question had surprised him. All this time he'd been thinking in terms of faceless strangers, not a betrayal from family or friend.

He'd asked why and was still shaken by his brother's cold answer. "Because trust will betray you every time."

It hurt him to know the depth of Roman's bitterness toward the human race. But his own life was in such a mess, he couldn't argue the point. All he could do was trust the fact that Roman had been in this business long enough to know what he was doing.

"Well, now, this is interesting."

Ryder came out of his chair like a shot. They were the first words that Roman had spoken since he'd sat down at the computer over an hour ago.

"What?" Ryder asked.

Roman leaned back in his chair. "Besides being the family lawyer, what is Lash Marlow to Casey?"

Ryder frowned. "Nothing, although I think her grandfather would have wished it otherwise. Remember what I told you about the will, and how we met?"

Roman nodded.

"Casey once mentioned that when Lash Marlow read that clause in the will, he was almost gloating. You know, like an I've-got-you-now look."

Roman stared at the screen. "He's broke."

Startled, Ryder moved to look over Roman's shoulder. "You must be mistaken. His family is old money. That's what everyone says."

"He has been served with a foreclosure notice, and up until two weeks ago, his accounts were all overdrawn."

Ryder frowned. "How the hell did you get that computer to do that?"

"That's privileged info, brother."

"Did you hack into the bank's computers?"

Roman spun his chair around as one of his rare smiles slowly broke across his face. "Now, Ryder, why would I do a thing like that? It's illegal."

Ryder started to pace. "Okay, so Lash Marlow is hard up for money. I'd venture to say at least half the people in Ruban Crossing could say the same."

He paused to look out the window overlooking the grounds. His gaze fell on the gardener's shed. Despair surfaced as he thought of holding Casey in his arms, and what they'd done that night in the name of love. It was all he could do to focus on what had to be done.

"Look Roman, there's no guarantee that whoever has Casey is even a local. In the business world, the Ruban name is known worldwide. Their holdings are vast. Casey's inheritance has recently been in all the papers…twice. Once when Delaney died. Again when that plane she was supposed to be on crashed and burned with all aboard."

Roman listened without comment, but when he turned back

to the computer, his gaze was fixed, his thoughts whirling. He kept thinking of what his C.O. used to say just before they'd go out on a mission. *Never overlook the obvious. It will get you killed every time.* In Roman's opinion, Lash Marlow had an obvious axe to grind. What remained to be seen was if he was the kind of man who could betray a client…or a friend.

The family was gathering in the main salon, and while they whispered among themselves as to the possible reason Detective Gant might have for calling them all together again, Ryder's thoughts were on something else. A few moments ago, he'd glanced up at the clock. Forty-eight hours ago to the minute, he'd walked into Casey's office a happy man. Within the space of time it took to spill papers from a desk, his world had come to an end. All last night he'd kept hearing the sound of her voice as she'd begged him to come back inside her office. If only he had.

A few moments later, the doorbell chimed and they heard Joshua directing Mason Gant into the room.

"Thanks for being so prompt," Gant said, waving away Joshua's offer of coffee. He glanced around the room. "I have some news," he announced, and when Ryder took a step forward, he held up his hand. "Sorry, I phrased that wrong. It is news, but not of Casey."

The doorbell pealed again and Joshua hurried from the room. Moments later, Lash Marlow followed him back.

"Sorry I'm late," Lash said, smoothing his hand over his windblown hair. "Had to be in court first thing this morning."

Gant nodded. "I just got here myself." He looked around. "Is everyone here?"

"Everyone but Bea. Today's her day off," Tilly said.

Gant pulled out his notebook. "I have her address. I'll catch up with her later."

"Detective Gant, before you start, there's someone I want you to meet."

Gant looked up, surprised by Ryder's remark. He thought he'd met everyone when he was here before. Suddenly a man walked into his line of vision and he realized that the fellow had been standing in plain sight all along, but had been so quiet and so still that he'd completely overlooked his presence.

His first impression was that the man was military. His second was special forces. And then he focused on his face and Gant knew before he spoke that this man was Ryder's brother...if not his twin.

"I'd wager your last name is Justice," Gant said.

Roman held out his hand. "Roman Justice, private investigator out of Dallas. I won't get in your way if you don't get in mine."

Gant grinned as they shook hands. He liked a man who said what he thought.

A coffee cup shattered, breaking the brief silence as everyone turned toward the sound. Lash was against the wall. He was pale and shaking and staring down at the floor.

"It slipped out of my hands."

Joshua ran to get a broom as Tilly fussed with the splatters that dappled the edge of a soft, moss-green rug.

Ryder stared at Lash, as if seeing him for the very first time. He couldn't bring himself to believe that anyone who knew Casey would want to cause her harm. And Marlow was, as usual, every inch the gentleman—from the cut of his clothes to the style of his hair. But why was Lash so upset over a spilled cup of coffee? Ryder kept staring and staring, remembering his brother's words and trying to see past the obvious to the man beneath. Suddenly, something about Lash's appearance struck a sour note.

"Hey, Marlow."

At the sound of Ryder's voice, Lash jerked as if he'd been slapped. He looked up. "Yes?"

"What the hell happened to your hand?"

He didn't have to look down to know they were referring to the row of skinned knuckles on his right hand and the long red gash that ran from one edge of his wrist to the other. Gorge rose in his throat as he struggled with an answer they all might believe. He could hardly tell them it was the remnants of his bout with Casey.

He managed a laugh. "I locked myself out of the house last night. Graystone may be past her prime, but like the lady she is, she does not easily part with her virtue. I broke a window trying to get inside. Lucky for me I didn't cut my own wrist, right?"

The answer was plausible enough. Ryder shrugged. If the man had cut his own throat, he couldn't have cared less. If there was news that pertained to Casey, he wanted to know now.

"Look Gant, let's get down to business. Why did you call us all together?"

Lash was counting his blessings that the subject of his wounds had been changed. But his relief was short-lived when Gant started to talk.

"Forensics came up with a print on Casey's car that doesn't match anyone else in the family."

Ryder stiffened. Was this their first break? "Do you have an ID?"

Gant nodded. "Belongs to a low-life hood out of Natchez named Bernie Pike."

Lash felt his legs going out from under him and slid into a chair before he made another social faux pas. By the time everyone present had assured the detective they knew nothing about the name, he had himself under control.

Although Gant's meeting with the family had been necessary, he hadn't really expected anything to come from this lead. At least, not from this quarter. He was gathering his things and readying to leave when he suddenly remembered another fact he needed to verify.

Lash Marlow was on his way out the door when Gant called him back.

"Marlow! Wait!"

Lash spun, his nerves tightening with every breath that he took. "Yes?"

"About the ransom. Will you be able to get it all together by tomorrow?"

He went weak with relief. "Yes, sir. The bank has been most helpful in this case. Some of it arrived today by armored car. The rest should be here before noon tomorrow."

Gant nodded. "Good. I don't want any last minute hitches. When that call comes in, I want to be ready to roll."

Lash stifled a smile. "I couldn't agree with you more."

Chapter 15

Now that Casey was no longer blindfolded, the thick layer of dust covering the floor in the room where she was being held was obvious. The footprints marring the gray-white surface were evidence of the degree of traffic that had come into Fostoria Biggers's home since she'd been gone. The absence of glass in two of the three windows of her temporary cell did little to offer an avenue for her to escape. They had all been boarded up from the outside. She couldn't get out and fresh air couldn't get in.

Last night when they thought she'd been sleeping, she'd dug and pulled and pushed at the boards until her fingers were raw and her nails were gone. Only after she heard one of the men stirring around had she ceased her futile bid for freedom.

Now, she thought it was some time after daybreak. The smell of morning coffee had drifted into the room. On the one hand, she felt justified in celebrating the arrival of a new day, but if Lash was to be believed, she would not celebrate another.

She stood at the door, holding her breath and desperately

trying to hear what the two men in the other room were saying. It was impossible. Their voices were too low and the door was too thick to hear anything other than an occasional murmur.

A plate lay on the floor near her feet. Remnants of the sandwich they'd given her yesterday to eat. She'd taken the food and a good look at the filth on their hands and decided she would rather go to her grave hungry.

Whatever it was that kept coming and going through a hole in the floor had made a meal of it last night. By now she didn't much care what she shared the room with, as long as it came on four feet instead of two.

In deference to her constant requests for drinks of water and bathroom privileges, her feet and hands were no longer tied. And, since Lash's departure yesterday, the blindfold had also been discarded. But while she now had an odd sort of freedom within the small, boarded-up room, the implications behind it were frightening. They no longer cared if she saw their faces because she would not be alive to tell the tale.

The sound of a chair being scooted across the floor made Casey bolt for the other side of the room. Ever since the arrival of Skeet Wilson, Pike's cohort, Casey had been afraid to sleep. Bernie had threatened her, but it was Skeet Wilson whom she knew would willingly do the deed. He was tall and skinny and walked with a limp. His hair was long and gray and tied at the back of his neck with a piece of shoestring. Some sort of blanket fuzz was caught in the knot and it was Casey's opinion that the shoestring had been there for a very long time. Skeet bore more scars on his face than teeth in his head, and he carried them all with a wild sort of pride. He had a face straight out of a nightmare with the disposition to match.

She stood with her back against the wall, holding her breath and praying that it would be Bernie who came in the door. If she'd been betting on the odds of that happening, she would have lost.

Skeet Wilson stepped inside then paused, carefully eyeing

the tall, slender woman with her back against the wall. Even though the blue suit she was wearing was filthy and torn and her legs and feet were bare and scratched, there was an odd sort of dignity to the way she was braced. In a way, he admired her. But it didn't matter what he thought. Skeet was a man who could be bought. And right now, Casey Justice wasn't a woman to him, she was fifty thousand dollars on the hoof.

"What?" Casey asked, as always, choosing to be the first one to speak.

Skeet grinned and smoothed his hand down the front of his fly, just to remind her who was boss. "Bed check."

Unless a miracle occurred, today was the last day of her life, but she refused to go out screaming and crying and begging for mercy they weren't capable of giving. She lifted her chin and squarely met his gaze.

"It's certainly obvious where you spent your last vacation."

It crossed his mind to be pissed, but her reference to the fact this his speech was peppered with penitentiary lingo was too good to ignore. He grinned, revealing his lack of a full set of teeth. And she was right. His world did revolve around the legal system. Just not on the side of law and order.

"Don't get too prissy, lady. You're real close to meetin' your maker."

Don't let him see your fear.

The thought came out of nowhere, and somehow Casey knew that at that moment, Ryder was with her in the only way he could be. Her hands fisted as she stared him down.

"That's what the mugger said before he snatched the old lady's purse and ran into the street."

Skeet's smirk froze on his face. Either she was losing her mind or it was already gone. He'd never known a woman with the balls to try to tell a joke to someone who was holding her captive. "That don't make much sense."

"It does if you know that, seconds later, the mugger was run over by a car. The old lady then walked into the street, lifted her purse out of the dead mugger's hands and bent over and whispered something in his ear.''

Skeet knew he shouldn't ask, but he was too intrigued to let the subject lie.

''So, what did she say?''

Casey grinned. ''To tell her maker hello.''

Skeet cursed and slammed the door shut between them. He wasn't all that smart, but it didn't take a genius to figure out what she'd been getting at and he didn't like it.

He and Bernie had gone through a lot these last two days. Marlow had threatened them with everything from murder to reneging on the last of their money if they so much as touched a hair on Casey Justice's head. Marlow had all but frothed at the mouth, claiming that right was to be his. Sick of his ranting, they'd finally complied. But Skeet wouldn't be sorry to see the last of her. She was too damned mouthy for her own good.

He kicked at an empty bean can in the middle of the floor and flopped back down in his chair. There wasn't any way this plan could fail. By tonight, he and Bernie would be rolling in dough. After that, he didn't give a damn what Marlow did with the bitch. Whatever it was, it was still less than she deserved.

''What are those?'' Ryder asked, as Roman sorted through a small case in his lap.

''Tracking devices, something like the ones the FBI will probably put in with the ransom money.''

Ryder nodded, although his opinion of the FBI left a lot to be desired. In his opinion, they asked too many questions and didn't give enough answers. They acted as if what was going on was none of his business.

''Won't the kidnappers be expecting something like that?''

Roman looked up. ''That's why I've got these. The Feds can do their thing. I'm going to do mine.''

''They're not going to like it,'' Ryder warned. ''You already ticked Wyandott off yesterday.''

Roman leaned back in his chair, remembering the confrontation he'd had with the special agent in charge. "No one dies from being ticked."

"You are a hard man, Roman Justice."

"Tell it to Uncle Sam. He took credit for making me this way. He can take the blame, as well."

If the situation had been anything else, Ryder could have laughed. As it was, he almost felt sorry for the man who got in his brother's way.

He glanced at the clock. It was almost noon. Where the hell was Lash Marlow with the money? He kept remembering what Roman had told him about Marlow's financial situation. It seemed to him that there was a fault in the theory that Lash should be responsible for its deliverance. It was like giving a starving man the keys to the cupboard.

The doorbell rang. Ryder jumped, then started down the hall, unwilling to wait for Joshua to let whoever it was in. Maybe there was news of Casey. But the Feds beat him to it. Lash was admitted carrying two large duffel bags.

"I've got it!" he crowed.

Two men in dark suits relieved him of the bags, leaving him standing in the hall with a jubilant smile on his face. Lash could hardly contain his joy. It was almost over.

"The armored car was late," Lash said, by way of an explanation for his tardiness.

Ryder listened without comment.

Lash smoothed a hand over his hair. "Any news?"

Ryder shook his head. "No."

What seemed to be a genuine grimace of dismay spread across his face. "You know, sometimes this all seems like a dream."

"More like a nightmare, if you ask me."

Lash nodded. "Of course, that's what I meant."

A man Ryder had never seen before came out into the hall from the main salon. Another Fed.

"Mr. Marlow, Detective Gant wants to speak with you."

Lash straightened his suit coat and followed the man into the room. Ryder was right behind.

Gant waved his hand toward the open bags. "It's all here, I presume?"

Lash nodded. "Three million dollars in unmarked bills. None of them larger in denomination than a fifty, none of them smaller than a five."

Gant nodded and turned back to the desk while Ryder struggled with a notion that wouldn't come. Something Lash had just said rang a chord of memory, but he couldn't figure out why.

Lash started toward the door. "If you have no further need of me, court awaits."

Gant paused and looked to Wyandott, who was officially in charge of the investigation. Wyandott didn't bother to look up. Gant shrugged. "I guess not. But if something comes up, I'll know where to find you, right?"

Lash chuckled. "One can only hope."

Ryder's hands were itching. The urge to grab Lash was overwhelming. It was all he could do to stay put as Marlow left. But at this point, Ryder couldn't pinpoint what it was that was bugging him.

The front door slammed behind Lash as Roman walked in the room.

"Who was here?" Roman asked.

"Marlow. He brought the ransom money."

Ryder pointed toward the bags on the desk and the men who were working on securing tracking devices within the bags.

It was when Roman started toward the desk that the notion hovering in the back of Ryder's mind started to take shape.

"Hey, Gant."

Gant looked up. "Yeah?"

"Marlow was gone when the kidnapper called, remember?"

Gant nodded.

"Then who told him how the money was to be paid?"

"I did," Gant said, then glanced at Wyandott, who had already expressed some displeasure in the way Gant had handled things thus far. "I knew it wouldn't be easy to accumulate that much money in small bills. Thought he needed as much time as possible."

But that wasn't what Ryder needed to know. "No...exactly what did you tell him?"

"I don't follow you," Gant said. "What are you getting at?"

Ryder's nerves were on edge. The more he thought about Lash, the more certain he became. "I want to know what you told him to bring."

"I said something to the effect that we needed three million dollars in small, unmarked bills by noon today."

"Did you tell him what denominations?"

"I told him no hundred-dollar bills. Everything had to be smaller than one-hundred dollar bills."

Oh, my God. What if Roman was right on target about Lash Marlow's involvement all along? "Then did you or any of your men ever play that tape for Marlow?"

"What tape?" Gant asked.

"The one you made when the ransom call came in."

Gant shrugged. "I don't know. I know I didn't." He looked at Wyandott. "Did you or any of your men?" All answers were negative.

The flesh crawled on the back of Ryder's neck. "Then can any of you explain to me why Marlow just quoted the kidnapper's exact terminology of the request he made for ransom?"

Roman pivoted, already following the line of his brother's thoughts. "I wasn't in here. What did Marlow say?"

Ryder stared around the room, daring the men to disagree. "You all heard him. He said, 'Three million dollars in unmarked bills. None of them larger in denomination than a fifty, none of them smaller than a five.'"

"Son of a bitch." Gant's epitaph was echoed in more than

one man's thoughts. "If memory serves, that's just about word for word."

Wyandott looked surprised, then began issuing new orders as Ryder turned and started running. Roman caught him at the door.

"You can't do what you're thinking."

Ryder yanked himself free. His words came out a cold, even tone. "You don't know what I'm thinking."

Roman tightened his hold. "That's where you're wrong. I know exactly what you're thinking, and I don't blame you one bit. But you've got to think of Casey. If Marlow is involved and he's alerted before the drop even goes down, what's going to happen to her? Better yet, how the hell would we know where to find her?"

Ryder hit the wall with the flat of his palm and then wiped a hand across his face. Every time he took a step he wanted to run, but to where? What had they done with his wife?

"My God," he said. "What the hell do you expect me to do? Wait until someone brings her back to me in a body bag?"

Roman got up in his face, and this time, he was the one on the defensive. "No, I expect you to let me do my job."

Ryder doubled his fists and refused to give an inch, even to his brother. Helpless in the face of so much logic, the urge to lash out was overwhelming.

Roman sighed. He didn't understand this kind of commitment between a man and a woman, but he'd seen enough of it to know it went beyond any blood ties. And as he gazed into his brother's face, he had a flashback of a little boy with mud in his hair and fire in his eyes. He remembered that same little boy had not only whipped the boy who'd beaten him up to take away his baseball, but he'd gotten the ball back, too. Even then, Ryder Justice had been a force with which to reckon.

"So, what's it going to be?" Roman asked.

Even though the urge to argue was overwhelming, Ryder

relented, slumping against the wall. "Then do it. Just know that every step you take I'm going to be on your heels."

"Wouldn't have it any other way, brother, but that will come later. Right now, there's one little thing I need to do before the day gets any older, and I don't want help in getting it done."

It felt wrong, and it hurt like hell to watch Roman going out the door without him, but Ryder stood his ground. Roman was right. He'd asked for his help. The least he could do was give him the leeway to do it.

"Give 'em hell, Roman."

Roman looked back, just as he started out the door. "Is there any other way?"

Lash was making himself a ham and cheese sandwich. He'd even gotten out his mother's good china on which to eat it. He slathered mustard on one slice of bread and mayonnaise on the other. *And why not? It's about time things started going my way.*

The sandwich was thick with meat, cheese, and lettuce. He pushed a toothpick into an olive, then topped his sandwich by stabbing the toothpick into the bread with a flourish. Now there was only one thing left. He opened the refrigerator and took out a bottle of wine. Chilled to perfection.

He walked out of the kitchen toward the old dining hall with china, wine and food in hand. When he stepped inside, there was a feeling of relief unlike any he'd ever known.

Spiderwebs draped the dust-covered chandelier above the table like torn and tattered lace. One of the panes was out at the top of a floor-to-ceiling window overlooking the back of the property and there was a bird's nest in the corner of the room. But Lash didn't see the ruin and decay. His jubilation was focused on former glory and future renovation.

The cork popped on the wine and he smiled to himself as he filled his glass. As he sipped, the chill of the grape and the dry, vintage taste of fine wine tingled on his tongue. He set the half-empty glass down in a patch of sunlight, admiring the way a sunbeam pierced the liquid.

He pulled the toothpick out of his food, popped the olive into his mouth, and chewed down. There was an instant awareness of an odd, unfamiliar taste as he gasped and spit the olive out into his hand.

And the moment he saw it, his flesh crawled. Somewhere within his mind, a drumbeat sounded. Then it began to hammer, faster and faster until he couldn't move—couldn't speak. He heard a cry, and then the faint, but unmistakable, sounds of a woman's soft voice. The language was French, spoken in the patois of the slaves his great-great-grandfather had once owned.

He jumped up from his chair and flung what was left of the olive onto the dust-covered table before running out of the room. The celebration and his meal were forgotten in the horror of what he'd just seen. And as the sounds of his footsteps faded away, the carcass of a small, white worm fell out of the olive and into the patch of sunlight beaming down through the wine.

Lash ran out of the house and into the woods, searching for a solace his mind couldn't find. To any other person, it would have been an unfortunate choice of an olive from a nearly full jar, but to Lash, it was the first step in a curse that had started to come true.

Decay. Everything around you will fall to decay. Flesh will fall off of your bones and be consumed by the worms.

Raised in a superstition as old as the land itself, in Lash Marlow's mind, the curse Casey invoked had begun. He thought about what would happen if he just called the whole thing off. If he could, he would have turned back the clock, stopped what he'd started before it was too late. As always, Lash's instinct for good was too little, too late.

Roman crouched beneath the low-hanging branches of a weeping willow, watching as Marlow came out of his house and ran into the woods bordering the backyard. He frowned.

Whatever it was that had sent him running couldn't have come at a better time. And still he waited, ever cautious, searching the grounds around the house for signs of other life. Except for the leaves in the trees, nothing moved.

Like a shadow, he came out from hiding, heading straight toward the dark blue sedan parked in front of the house. Within seconds of reaching it, he had secured a tracking device under the frame and was on his way back when he saw something that gave him pause. The fender of a small white car was just visible through the partially opened door of a nearby shed.

He frowned. According to the information he'd pulled from the Department of Motor Vehicles, Lash Marlow owned one car—a midnight blue, four-door sedan. He swerved in midstep and bolted for the shed, constantly searching the area for signs of Marlow's arrival.

The car was a small, white compact—at least eight, maybe ten years old. He glanced in at the gauges and whistled softly beneath his breath as he saw the odometer. Less than thirty thousand miles on a ten-year-old car?

What the hell, he thought. So, maybe Marlow just bought himself a second car and the change of ownership had yet to be registered. The mileage alone would make the car worthwhile. But he couldn't let go of the notion that he was wrong. This was a little old lady's car, not the type a man like Marlow would want to be seen driving.

And then it hit him. Little old lady! As in a woman named Fostoria Biggers? Her name had come up in conjunction with Marlow's when he'd been into the bank records and he'd thought little of a lawyer being an executor of an estate. It was done every day. But what if…?

He dropped to his knees. Regardless of why it was here, it was another vehicle that would be at Lash Marlow's disposal. Without wasting any more time, he affixed a bug to this car as well, and while he was on his knees, his attention was drawn from the car itself to the condition of the tires. He crawled closer. The treads were packed with mud and grass.

He picked at the grass. To his surprise, it still bent to the touch. He frowned. Someone had recently been driving this car. But where?

A door slammed. Roman's nerves went on alert. It was time to get out. He'd done what he'd come to do.

The call came in at exactly one minute to five. Every man in the room went on alert as Ryder reached for the phone.

"Ryder Justice speaking."

Like before, the voice had been altered. A mechanical whir was audible in the background.

"This is a recording. In fifteen minutes, Ryder Justice is to bring the money to the corner of Delaney and Fourth. There is a newsstand nearby. It will be closed. Set the bags inside the stand and drive away. If anyone attempts to follow the man who picks them up, Delaney Ruban's granddaughter will be meat for the 'gators. If you do as you're told, Casey Justice will be released."

The recording ended long before a trace could be made. Ryder cursed beneath his breath as he hung up the phone. He felt sick to his stomach. 'Gator meat? God help them all.

He started toward the front door. "Put the bags in the car."

"Wait!" Wyandott shouted.

Ryder turned. "Do what I said," he ordered. "Delaney and Fourth is halfway across town. I'll be lucky to get there in fifteen minutes as it is."

"I want one of my men in the back seat of your car."

Ryder grabbed him by the arm and pushed him up against a nearby desk. His voice was shaking. "I don't give a tinker's damn what you want. That's not your wife someone threatened to feed to the 'gators, it's mine. Now put the damned bags in the car or I'll do it myself."

Roman peeled Ryder's hands off of the agent's jacket. "Easy, brother. He's just doing his job."

Ryder spun, his eyes blazing with anger. "Don't push me, Roman. I've been hanging on the edge of reason for so damned long it hardly matters.'' His voice broke. ''If I lose Casey—''

''Put the bags in the car,'' Wyandott said. ''We won't be far behind.''

Ryder pointed at Wyandott. ''I don't know who will pick up these bags after I'm gone, but if one of your men even sneezes in his direction and my wife dies as a direct result, I will kill him...and then you for giving the order.''

Wyandott's face reddened, but he stepped aside.

Within seconds, Ryder was in the car and out of the driveway, leaving a cloud of dust and a group of men running for their cars to keep up. Roman watched from the step until they had all disappeared, and then he jumped in his car and drove out of the driveway in the opposite direction. He had his own agenda to follow.

Eudora watched from an upstairs window and then returned to her bed in tears. Downstairs in the library, Miles and Erica sat in uneasy silence, now and then venturing a glance at the other without voicing their thoughts.

Out in the kitchen, Tilly sat in a chair near a window overlooking the drive. Her posture was straight, her expression fixed. Only her eyes revealed her pain. They were wide and tear-filled as she watched for someone to bring her sweet baby home.

Everyone was waiting for a miracle.

Bernie Pike opened the door to Casey's room as his partner, Skeet, entered carrying another plate of food and a can of some sort of cola.

''Last meal,'' Skeet said, waving the plate in Casey's direction.

The urge to cry was almost more than she could bear. If only she was somewhere else and lying in Ryder's arms. But she didn't cry, and she wasn't in Ryder's arms, and she crawled off of the bed with undue haste. She wouldn't put herself in the position of giving Bernie and Skeet any more ideas than they already had. She didn't know that Lash had threatened everything but death to them if they so much as touched a hair on her head. She didn't know he'd saved that joy for himself.

"I thought prisoners were given a choice as to what they wanted to eat."

Skeet chuckled and dropped the plate at the foot of the bed and tossed the unopened can of soda beside it.

"Sorry, sweet thing. You get beans and weiners."

Casey glanced at the plate. The only thing good about it was that the small, lunch-size can of beans and weiners was still unopened. "And I was so hoping for your head on a platter."

Skeet slapped his leg and laughed, then elbowed Bernie and laughed again. "She's a hoot, ain't she Bernie? It's a damned shame Marlow is gonna 'do' her." Before Casey could think to react, Skeet reached for her breast. "I still think I'd like a little taste of what she has to offer. What Marlow won't know won't hurt him, right?"

Casey grabbed the can of beans from the plate and bounced it off of his head.

Skeet ducked, but it was too late. He yelped in pain when the can hit the corner of his temple. Seconds later, she was flat on her back on the bed with Skeet on top of her.

"You bitch! I'll make you..."

Bernie cursed and grabbed, pulling his partner off the woman and the bed. "Get away from her, dammit. You heard Marlow. You might want to part with your dillydally, but I don't. Besides, you asked for it."

Skeet's rage was slow to subside as he considered whether or not Lash Marlow was capable of castrating anyone. Finally, he decided he didn't want to test the theory enough to try again.

"You got about two more hours to play hell on this earth, then you can die on an empty stomach," he yelled, and out of spite, took the can of beans and weiners and stomped out of the room.

Bernie looked at Casey and shrugged, as if to say it was

all her fault, then shut the door behind him. The lock turned with a sharp, distinct *click* and when they were gone, Casey dropped to the floor and pulled her knees up close to her chest.

For the first time since the ordeal had begun, she was losing all hope. And the worst was in knowing Ryder would never know how sorry she was for betraying him by the investigation. They'd parted in anger and she would die with that on her conscience.

Despair shattered the last of her resolve. She slumped onto the floor, her legs drawn up against her chest in a fetal position, and she started to cry—slow, aching tears that welled and spilled in a continuous flow of pain.

Casey cried until she lost all track of time. Had it been two hours or two minutes since Skeet's warning that her time to die was close at hand? Was Lash already on his way? She remembered the wild expression on his face when last she'd seen him.

''God help me,'' she prayed, and then choked on a sob as she realized she was lying in a position to see directly beneath her bed.

The elongated neck and small, unblinking eyes of the creature beneath her bed were startling, but for Casey, who'd lived in imminent fear for the last three days of being eaten alive, it was a large relief.

''Well, my word,'' she said, and reached under the bed, pulling out a small, brown terrapin that had taken her move as threatening and disappeared into its shell. ''So it was you I heard all the time.''

Sympathetic to the fear that had caused it to retreat, Casey quickly set it free, and as she did, saw something else under the bed that made her heart leap. There, in the corner beneath her bed! It looked like—

She crawled to her feet and pulled the bed away from the wall just enough to reach behind. When her fingers curled around the butter soft leather, she pulled. She was right! It was her purse.

She clutched it to her chest as she crawled onto the bed,

then held her breath, listening to make sure that Bernie and Skeet were not about to come in.

Three days ago seemed like a lifetime. Casey couldn't remember what she'd been carrying in her purse, or even what she'd been doing when she'd gotten the call about Ryder's wreck. Her fingers were shaking as she undid the clasp. But when she opened it up, her hopes fell. Her shoulders slumped as she dumped the meager contents onto the bed.

Her wallet was gone, as was the compact cell phone she usually carried. She should have known this would be too good to be true. There wasn't anything left but a handful of tissues, some pencils and pens, her lipstick and small, plastic bottle of lotion.

Frustrated by the letdown, she slammed the purse down on the bed beside her and then winced when something within the purse itself hurt her hand.

"What in the…?"

She opened it back up. There was nothing inside but the black satin lining. She tilted it, then thrust in her hand, feeling within the bag itself. Something was there…but not inside…it was beneath…no, between. She pulled at the lining like turning a sock inside out, and saw the rent in the fabric near the clasp.

Curious now as to what was inside, she stuck her finger in the fragile lining and pulled. It ripped and then parted. Carefully, Casey thrust a finger inside, then another, and searched until she felt something cool and hard and sharp. And as she traced the object's length, realization dawned. Her hands were shaking as she pulled it out. She tried to think of how the letter opener Lash had given her as a gift had gotten out of her desk drawer and into her purse.

And then she remembered running back to grab her wallet on the day of the call, and of grabbing a handful of pens along with it as she dropped it inside her purse. That must have been it. She'd gotten the letter opener with everything else. And because it had been so sharp, it had gone straight through the lining and lodged in between.

She looked toward the door as her fingers curled around the miniature rapier's silver shaft. It wasn't much, but it was the first means she'd had of self-defense and she had no intention of letting it go to waste.

A laugh boomed out in a nearby room. Casey flinched, then shoved the dagger beneath her pillow. Not now, she told herself. Only when it was time. When it was time.

Chapter 16

Ryder pulled up to the newsstand with less than a minute to spare. He double-parked in the street and grabbed the two bags, moving in an all-out sprint. The stand was closed, just as the kidnapper had promised, but a small, side door stood ajar, and he shouldered his way inside.

It was little more than three walls and a roof. The half wall that opened up to the public could be propped overhead like a porch, shading the counter beneath. The concrete sidewalk served as its floor, and Ryder dropped both bags on it with a thump and walked out.

All the way back to the car, he had the impression that he was being watched. He didn't know whether that came from the Feds who had followed him here, or from the kidnapper waiting for him to leave. When he slid into the driver's seat and started the car, his instincts kept telling him not to leave—not to leave Casey's welfare up to kidnappers. But he ignored the urge and drove away, and had never been this afraid in his life—not even the night his plane had crashed—not even when he'd known that Micah was dead. He left with the knowledge that he'd done all he could do. The ransom had been delivered. Hopefully, his next point of contact would be the phone call telling him where to pick up his wife.

As Ryder drove away, Wyandott and his men began to slip into place around the area. A couple of blocks away, Gant watched from his car with binoculars trained on the door through which Ryder had come and gone.

And the wait began.

Five minutes passed, then ten, then twenty. In spite of the coolness of the evening breeze blowing through his window, Gant was starting to sweat. He could just imagine what was going through Wyandott's mind. The Feds must have been made. If the kidnappers got spooked and didn't pick up the ransom, he wouldn't give a plug nickel for Casey Justice's chance of survival.

Just when he thought it was over, an old man turned the corner and headed down the street, pulling a little red wagon behind him as he made toward the stand. Gant thought nothing of his presence until the man paused at the door, opened it up and then stepped in, leaving his wagon just outside.

Gant sat straight up in the seat, adjusting his binoculars for a clearer view as the man emerged. But it wasn't the bags Ryder had put inside that he was carrying out. It was a large black garbage bag. He tossed it into the wagon and started down the street when Wyandott's men suddenly converged upon him.

Gant threw down his binoculars in disbelief and started his car. In spite of the kidnapper's instructions, Wyandott was pulling him in. God help them all if this stunt got Casey Justice killed.

"You're under arrest!" Wyandott shouted, as two of his agents wrestled the old man to the ground.

The terror on the old fellow's face seemed sincere. "What did I do? What did I do?"

An agent slapped handcuffs around his wrists while another

tore into the bag. But they all stared in disbelief as a cascade of crushed aluminum cans fell onto the street.

"What the hell?" Wyandott muttered.

"They're mine, fair and square," the old man cried, as they pulled him to his feet. "Anthony gave them to me."

Wyandott turned. "Who the hell is Anthony?"

"The man who owns the newsstand. I pick them up once a week, regular as clockwork. Everyone knows. Anthony doesn't care. He saves them for me."

A knot was beginning to form in the pit of Wyandott's belly. He pivoted and pointed toward the stand. "Check it out!" Two of the agents were already running as Gant's car slid to a halt near the curb.

Gant strode toward Wyandott with murder in his eyes. "Have you lost your mind?"

Wyandott hunched his shoulders and thrust out his jaw. "Mind your own damned business."

"This is my city. That makes it my business," Gant yelled.

One of the agents came running. "Sir! You'd better come take a look."

Everyone converged on the stand, leaving the old man handcuffed and alone in the street near his cans.

The bags were gone!

"This is impossible," Wyandott muttered. "We didn't take our eyes off of this stand for a second. Not a damned second."

Gant stepped inside, and, as he did, caught his toe. He staggered, then looked down. A certainty came over him that they'd been lying in wait for nothing. Chances were that the bags had disappeared seconds after Ryder had left.

"He didn't take them out, he took them down," Gant said, pointing toward the slightly raised edge of a lid covering the opening that led down to the sewers.

Wyandott paled. "Hell." He grabbed his two-way. "Ambrewster...is that bug sending?"

The radio crackled, and then the man's voice came over the air loud and clear. "No sir. Everything is status quo."

Gant was on his knees and pulling at the lid when several of the agents followed his lead and began to help. A flashlight was produced, and even though they were yards above them, and it was black as a devil's heart down below, there was enough light to see two empty bags lying at the foot of the ladder.

And they had their answer. The signal wasn't sending because the bags were more or less right where Ryder had left them…minus the three million dollars that had been inside.

The radio crackled again. Wyandott jerked.

"Captain…this is Tucker…come in, sir."

"Go ahead."

"Sir, we've been following Marlow as you ordered. He parked his car and went into the courthouse at fourteen hundred hours. We have men stationed at every exit and he has yet to come out."

Wyandott was starting to worry. He kept thinking of the threat Justice had made to his face. This wasn't going down as he'd planned.

"I want to know if he's inside. Look for him, dammit, and don't stop until you do. He's mixed up in this somehow, I know it."

Ryder turned off of the highway without slowing down and skidded to a halt in front of the mansion. He was out of the car before the dust had time to settle.

But when Roman came around the house on the run, Ryder paused at the front door with his hand on the knob. He could tell by the look on his brother's face that something had happened.

"What?"

Roman grabbed him by the arm. "Gant just called me. The drop went sour. The kidnapper went underground into the sewers. He's got the money and all they've got left are those damned bags."

Disbelief, coupled with a pain Ryder couldn't name, nearly sent him to his knees. It was coming undone.

Roman grabbed him by the arm. "Don't give out on me now. We're going to plan B. Come with me. We don't have much time."

For the first time since Ryder had exited the car, he became aware of a loud, popping sound, but he was too focused on Roman to consider the source. "Where are we going?"

"Marlow is on the move," Roman said. "I've been tracking him, but he's moving out of range. You're going to have to help me, brother, or we're going to lose our best chance to find your wife."

They had just cleared the corner of the house in full stride, when Ryder stopped in his tracks.

"Son of a bitch."

Roman grabbed him by the arm, almost yelling in his face to be heard above the noise. "It's a Bell Jet Ranger, just like the one you have at home."

"I know what it is," Ryder said, staring at the helicopter's spinning rotors. "Where the hell did you get it?"

Roman almost grinned. "I borrowed it, so don't wreck the damned thing. I have to take it back when we're through."

Ryder started to sweat. Wreck? Hell, that meant making it fly first.

Roman grabbed him by the shoulder and jerked. "Are you going to stand there, or are we going to try to save your wife?"

Ryder started to run. "If you stole this, I'll break your neck."

"Just shut up and get in," Roman yelled, as he leaped into the passenger seat and grabbed at a laptop computer he'd laid on the floor.

A strange sensation swept through Ryder's body as he climbed into the seat. The sounds were familiar, even the feel of the seat at his back and the scent of fuel mixing with the dust and debris flying through the air caused by the rotor's massive pull.

Then he glanced at his brother and the moving blip on the computer screen in front of him. The tracking devices! Roman had bugged Marlow's car after all. His pulse surged. "Is that him?"

Roman nodded. "Yes, but I'm losing him. Take her up!"

Ryder stared. That blip kept blinking—blinking—blinking—like a pulse. Like Casey's pulse. He grabbed the seat belt. It snapped shut with a click he felt rather than heard. He took a deep breath and pushed in on the throttle and it felt as if the helicopter took a deep breath. Ryder glanced at the blip one last time and the guilt he'd been living with for the better part of a year simply disappeared.

"Roman."

Roman glanced at his brother.

"Buckle up."

Seconds later, the chopper went straight up in the air, then flew into the setting sun like a hawk flying out of a storm.

Lash was ecstatic. It had all been too easy. Just this afternoon, he'd driven Fostoria Biggers's little car to an abandoned garage near the downtown courthouse, then taken a cab back home. A short time later, he got in his own sedan, drove to his office, picked up some legal briefs, then drove to the courthouse and parked in his usual place.

Only when he got into the elevator, he didn't go up, he went down. Down into the basement. Down through a maze of heating pipes and furnaces, past the janitor's quarters where he picked up two large bags he'd hidden earlier, as well as a pair of gloves which he immediately put on. He was smarter than Pike. He wasn't leaving traces of himself anywhere to be found.

Down he went into a shaft leading straight to the sewers beneath the city. Counting tunnels and watching for numbers written on the walls beside the ladders with something akin to delight, Lash knew when he reached number seventy-nine that he was directly beneath the newsstand.

He waited, and minutes later, he heard the echo of boots against metal as Ryder Justice walked across the sewer lid and dropped the bags full of money...his money. A smile broke the concentration on his face. So far, so good.

He knew the bags were bugged. He'd watched the Feds planting the bugs himself. So he transferred the money from their bags into the ones he'd brought, and left the original bags and their bugs right where he knew they would eventually be found.

Once again, he was using the underground sewers of Ruban Crossing as a means by which to travel. With the narrow beam of a small flashlight for guidance, he began to count tunnels and ladders again until he came to ladder number sixty-five. This time he went up, coming out in the alley just outside the abandoned garage where he'd parked Fostoria Biggers's car.

When he drove out of the city, he was three million dollars to the good. As for the fifty thousand he was supposed to pay Bernie and Skeet, it was unfortunate, but he was going to have to renege.

It wasn't his fault Bernie had left fingerprints behind when they'd yanked Casey out of her car. Eventually the police would find Bernie Pike. And if they found Bernie, Skeet Wilson would not be far behind. Lash didn't trust them to keep quiet about his part in the crime. He couldn't leave witnesses. Not after he'd gone this far.

As he drove, he reached down and felt the outside of his pocket, reassuring himself that his gun was still there. Once or twice, as he pictured pulling the trigger and ending two men's lives, he came close to rethinking his decision. And then he would remind himself that, for three million dollars, he could live with a little bit of guilt.

All he had to do was walk in the house, pull the trigger two times and they would be out of the picture. At this point, his imagination began to wane. He kept picturing himself opening the door to the room in which Casey was being kept and pointing his gun at her as well. After that, the image faded. Would she beg? Would she cry? Would he be able to kill the woman he once thought he loved?

Fostoria Biggers's little car fishtailed in loose dirt as Lash sailed down the road toward her home. Only a few more miles.

"He's turning south," Roman said, and held on to his laptop as, moments later, the helicopter took the same turn, yielding to Ryder's skill.

Roman's gaze was completely focused on the screen before him. And the farther they flew, the more certain he was of where Lash Marlow was going.

"There's nothing out here but swamp grass and trees," Ryder muttered, as he banked the chopper sharp to the right, sometimes skimming so close to the treetops that the skids tore the leaves as they flew by.

Roman frowned, grabbing at the computer and leaning into another sharp turn. "If you were partial to driving there, you should have said so—I'd have gotten one of these things with wheels."

"Am I still on course?" Ryder asked.

Roman looked down at the screen. "Yes. We can't be more than a half a mile behind."

Half a mile. Would that be the difference between Casey's life—or Casey's death?

"I don't like this," Ryder said, glancing down at the blur of terrain beneath them. "There's nothing out here but snakes, alligators and wildcats."

"And the house where Fostoria Biggers was born and raised."

The helicopter dipped. Not much, but enough to let Roman know Ryder had been startled by what he'd said.

"Who is Fostoria Biggers?"

"One of Marlow's clients. I thought it was a little too convenient that Marlow has her car and her power of attorney. I checked land records at the courthouse. Would you believe that her house is just a little farther south...in the direction in which Marlow has been driving?"

Ryder looked startled. "How long have you known about this?"

Roman shrugged. "Bits and pieces of it since the first day. But it didn't all start falling into place until you caught Marlow repeating the kidnapper's demands, word for word. After that, we didn't exactly have time to talk. I figured you wouldn't mind if I took the initiative."

Ryder's expression was grim. "I don't care what you do. But when we get where we're going, Marlow is mine."

Roman nodded. That much he understood. He glanced back at the screen. "Read 'em and weep, brother. It looks like our runner is about to stop."

Ryder's heart skipped a beat as he looked down at the screen. For the first time since they'd gone airborne, the blip was stationary. He glanced out the windows, searching for a sign of the car and a place to set down.

It was Roman who saw it first. "There!" he shouted. "I see the top of a roof up ahead in that clearing." He leaned farther forward and pointed across Ryder's line of vision. "There's the road, just to your left."

"I see it," Ryder drawled. He gave his brother one last glance, and there was a wealth of understanding between them in that single look. "Hang on. We're going down."

It was getting late. Casey could tell by the temperature of the bare wooden floors beneath her feet. Every nerve she had was on alert. She'd said her prayers, and such as it was, her little game plan was already in place. The contents of the bottle of lotion she'd found in her purse was in a puddle on the floor just inside her door. Her letter opener was in one hand, held fast at the hilt, and an unopened can of beans was in the other.

Oddly enough, Bernie had had a change of heart, and sneaked them back in to her when Skeet wasn't looking. From the size of his belly hanging over his belt, she supposed he didn't think a person should die on an empty stomach. And, she was as ready to die as she would ever be, but not without a fight.

Just as she was about to get herself a drink of water from the bathroom sink, she heard a shout of jubilation outside her door. Her thirst forgotten, she stifled a moan. That could only mean one thing. Lash had arrived. Bernie and Skeet were about to get paid.

Lash pulled up to the house and put the car into Park, but left it running. This trip was going to be a real hit-and-run. He had to get back into the city and pick up his car at the courthouse. It was the final stage of his plan, and one that would tie up the last loose ends.

He was halfway up the steps when Bernie Pike met him at the door. "Did you get it?" Bernie asked.

Lash grinned and nodded as he put his hand in his pocket. "Where's Skeet?" Lash asked. "I want to pay you both at the same time."

"I'm right here," Skeet said.

"Hot damn," Bernie said. "My horoscope said this was my lucky day."

The gun was in Lash's hand before either man thought to react. Bernie went down still wearing his smile. Skeet had started to run and then stumbled and fell when Lash's second shot caught him square in the back. The echo of the gunshots beneath the roof of the old porch were still ringing in Lash's ears as he nudged each man with the toe of his shoe. Neither moved, nor would they ever again.

While Lash was staring down at their bodies, something fell on his sleeve. He looked down and then shrieked in sudden panic. Frantic, he brushed it off with the butt of the gun, then stomped it flat. What was left of a caterpillar lay squashed on the floor of the porch.

Another worm. A rapid staccato of drumbeats began again, ricocheting through Lash's mind as he backed away from the worm and into the house with his gun drawn. He was all the way inside and halfway across the floor before he realized he had his back to the door of the room in which Casey was being kept. He crouched and spun. Heart pounding and slightly breathless, he aimed the gun at the middle of the door.

It took a bit for him to calm down. And when he did, he went to the door, rattling the knob just enough to let her know he was coming.

The tone of his voice took on a high, singsong pitch. "Here I come, ready or not."

He opened the door, saw her standing across the room, and stepped inside, right into the puddle of lotion.

One second Lash was looking at Casey and the next he was staring at the ceiling and struggling to breathe. He clutched his chest with a groan and rolled as air began to fill his deflated lungs.

"Damn you," he gasped, crawling to his feet just in time to duck an object that came flying through the air. Although he knew it wasn't Casey, he pulled the trigger in self-defense, then gasped as something splattered all over his face. He looked down at himself in disbelief. Beans? He'd shot a can of beans?

For Casey, the two shots outside the door were unexpected. But when total silence followed, Casey suspected her worst fears were about to come true. Not only was Lash capable of killing her, but she'd bet her last dollar he'd just done away with Bernie and Skeet. It figured. He wasn't the kind of man to leave loose ends untied. Lash was nothing if not neat.

She backed against the far wall, and when his voice taunted at her through the door, she traded the dagger in her right hand for the can of beans, then held her breath and waited.

The door opened, and to her undying relief, Lash hit the oil slick of lotion and fell flat on his back. While he was struggling for breath, she hauled back and sent the beans sailing, then ducked when his shot went wild.

While he was still brushing at the thick sauce and beans splattering his coat, she came at him. It was only through an inborn sense of self-preservation that he looked up in time to see her coming, but he didn't move in time to save himself from the dagger's sharp thrust.

He swung at her head with the butt of his gun just as the pain began to burn through his chest. Casey went limp, slumping to the floor at his feet as Lash stared at the familiar silver shaft sticking out of his chest.

The drumbeat got louder. He kept thinking of the dagger sticking out of that fat rat's body, and now it was in him. The analogy was as sickening as the nausea rolling in his belly.

By now, the drumbeat was so loud in his head that he couldn't hear himself scream. And yet the soft patois of the French-speaking slave, warning—predicting—promising, could still be heard above the drum.

Sharp like a serpent's tooth, it will spill your blood and your flesh will be eaten by the worms of the earth.

In a wild kind of panic, he yanked at the handle, ignoring the pain, losing sight of the fact that, with Casey Justice unconscious and helpless at his feet, his goal was well within reach. Blood welled then poured out of the wound, and Lash staggered from the shock of seeing his life spilling on Casey's legs.

And then he heard her groan, and a certainty came upon him. *Kill her now, before it's too late.*

He wiped at the sweat beading on his brow and aimed the gun. He had to do it now while she was unconscious. He no longer had the guts to let her witness her own death. Not anymore.

He leaned down, jabbing the barrel of the gun at her head as the room began to spin around him. And then footsteps sounded on the porch outside and he turned and froze. A gourd rattled, like a rattlesnake's warning, and the drumbeat grew louder, hammering—hammering—in what was left of his mind.

Crazed with pain and the impending vision of his own mortality, he lifted his gun, his wild gaze drawn to the shadow crossing the floor ahead of the man coming in.

* * *

When the first two shots came within seconds of each other, Ryder panicked. He tightened his grip on the gun Roman had given him and picked up his pace as he moved through the marsh beyond the old house. Brush caught on his blue jeans and tore at his shirt. Limbs slapped at his face and stung his eyelids and eyes. Water splashed up his legs to the tops of his knees and he kept on running, assuming that whatever was in his path would have to move of its own accord. His focus was on the house just visible in the distance, and the small white car parked nearby.

A hundred yards from the house, he saw the bodies of two men sprawled upon the porch and fear lent fresh speed to his steps. That explained the two shots. Water splashed a bit to his right and he knew that Roman was there on his heels as they ran out of the marsh and into the clearing.

Another shot rang out and Ryder almost stumbled. Dear God, it wasn't possible that they'd come this far just to be too late. He couldn't let himself believe that God would do that to him...not twice.

Two seconds, then ten seconds, and Ryder was up on the porch. He cleared Bernie Pike's body in a smooth, single leap and came in the front door on the run.

"Dammit, Ryder, look out."

Roman's warning came late, but it would not have slowed his intent. He kept thinking of that blip on the computer screen.

Had his wife's heart stopped when it had, too?

He saw them both at the same time. Marlow was straddling Casey's body with his gun aimed at Ryder's heart. And the knowledge that he'd come too late filled his soul. Despair shattered his focus. Rage clouded any caution he might have used. His mind was screaming out her name as he pointed the gun at Marlow's chest.

"You lying son of a bitch."

They were the last words Lash Marlow would hear as Ryder pulled the trigger.

Lash's shot went wild as Ryder's bullet struck Marlow in

the chest. He bucked upon impact, and Ryder fired again, then emptied his gun in him just to see him dance.

Roman was only seconds behind. He came through the door with his gun ready, the echo of Ryder's last shot roaring in his ears. But hope died as he saw the woman on the floor and Marlow lying nearby. It looked as if Ryder would have his revenge, but little else.

Ryder's gun was clicking on empty chambers when Roman took it out of his hand. Ryder jerked, then groaned and let it go. The pain in his chest was spilling out into his legs and into his mind. He couldn't think past the sight of her battered and broken body lying still upon the floor.

Roman started toward the two bodies but Ryder stopped him. With tears streaming down his face, he grabbed his brother's arm. "No. Let me."

Roman ached for his brother's pain as he stepped aside, and Ryder walked into the room, absorbing the filth and degradation of the place in which she'd been kept. Dropping to his knees, he lifted her from the filth on the floor and into his arms.

Blood ran down her legs as her head lolled against his shoulder, and then he couldn't see her face for his tears. His heart broke as he cradled her against his chest.

His voice broke along with his heart. "No more! No more!" Laying his head near her cheek, he choked on a cry. "Ah God, I can't take anymore!"

His shoulders hunched as he bent from the burden of living when those he loved kept dying around him.

Roman knelt at his side, sharing his brother's pain. He glanced at the woman in Ryder's arms. Even through the bruises and dirt, her beauty was plain to see. Years ago, he'd shut himself off from this kind of loss. He'd seen so much death and too much misery to let himself be hurt by it anymore, but this was too close to home. This woman, Ryder's wife, was gone too soon. He reached out, lifted her hair from the blood on her face, and as he did, his finger brushed the curve of her neck.

His eyes widened as he tensed and shoved Ryder's hand aside. When he felt the pulse beating strong and sure, he rocked back on his heels. A miracle! That's what it was. A heaven-sent miracle.

Ryder choked on a sob. "Don't Roman. Just leave us alone."

Roman grabbed his brother's hand, his voice shaking as he pressed it at the pulse point on Casey's neck. "She's alive, Ryder. I swear to God, your wife is alive!"

At that same moment in the Ruban household many miles away, Matilda Bass heard a whisper. She froze, and then tilted her head, straining to hear. As suddenly as the whisper had come, it was gone, and Tilly's body went limp. She leaned against the cabinet as the bowl she was holding slipped out of her hands and onto the floor, shattering into a thousand tiny pieces, just like the weight that had been on her heart.

Joshua spun, wide-eyed and startled. And then he saw her face.

"Tilly?"

"They found her, they found her. My baby girl is alive."

Epilogue

From below, the shiny black helicopter flying high above the earth resembled an oversize dragonfly charging through the air. From up above, the earth resembled a vast crazy quilt in varying shades of greens and browns that covered the landscape over which they were flying.

As if at some unseen signpost up in the sky, the pilot suddenly shifted course and soon, a long black rooftop became visible in the distance, along with the roofs of several outbuildings, connected together with a chain stitch of holding pens and corrals.

Casey leaned forward, grabbing at Ryder's leg as her eyes lit with excitement. "Is that it? Is that the Justice ranch?"

Ryder grinned at her. "That's it, darlin'. All seven thousand acres."

Her smile was nervous as she glanced at him. "I'm a little anxious about meeting your family."

"Easy now, you know they're going to love you."

She sighed. "I wish I could have promised you the same thing when I took you home to mine."

Ryder laughed. "At least they like me now."

"Like! Oh, Ryder, in their eyes, you are the next best thing to sliced bread and you know it."

His grin widened. "Only because Miles's new girlfriend keeps him too busy to meddle in our affairs."

Casey nodded in agreement. "And who would have thought that Erica would go on vacation and come home with a husband?"

"Yeah, and he has a job, which was more than you could say for me when you dumped me in their laps. Dora is walking in tall cotton over the fact that they are moving to Atlanta and taking her with them."

Casey laughed aloud. "Gran will miss you. You were the best chauffeur we ever had."

"Dora and I understand each other," he said. "But let's be honest, I was the worst chauffeur, and you know it. However, now that I have moved my planes and the charter service to Ruban Crossing, I have become a bona fide, acceptable businessman."

She patted his leg in a tender gesture. "Tilly was right all along. Somehow she knew you belonged. You are the best thing that ever happened to my family." Her voice broke. "And to me."

Ryder gave her a quick, nervous glance. A few months ago he'd cradled her body on the floor of Fostoria Biggers's bedroom, certain that his world had just come to an end. Sometimes at night he still lay awake just to watch her sleep. What she had endured was beyond his understanding; that she had endured it at all was a miracle in itself.

Now, most of the time she was fine. But once in a while, when things got too quiet, he saw her soul slip into a shadow and he knew she was fighting a dark demon of her own. He knew from experience that it would take time, and a whole lot of love, for the memories of what she'd endured to recede.

"I love you," he said softly.

Casey shivered, as if struck by an unexplained chill, and

then she lifted her head and smiled and Ryder relaxed. For now, Casey was back in the light.

"I love you, too, wild man. Now take me home. I have a need to feel Texas under my feet."

Relieved that the moment had passed, he grinned. "Royal is going to love hearing you say that. He's a real homebody. He lives for his daughter and the ranch, and I can tell you right now that, except for a remarkable resemblance which we all share, Royal is nothing like Roman."

A small shudder rippled through Casey's body, but she refused to deny it access. Remembering Roman also meant remembering when they'd first met. Of waking up and seeing Ryder—of being lifted into the helicopter and looking up at an echo of her husband's face as Ryder laid her in Roman's arms—of helicopters and hospitals—of police and FBI. Of fearing the dark and doctors and needles. Of Tilly's hand on her cheek and Joshie's kiss on her brow. And always, overshadowing everything and everyone, was Ryder. Ever present, ever faithful, everlasting.

She turned to look out the other side of the helicopter, marveling at the size of the cattle herds in the far distance. From up here, the cattle looked like so many ants. Finally, she was able to say what she thought.

"Roman will always have a special place in my heart. I like him a lot."

Ryder's grin slid a little off center as his emotions betrayed him. "Oh, hell, honey, I like him, too. He's my brother. And I owe him more than I will ever be able to repay."

The look they shared was brief, but it was enough to remember they had a lot for which to be thankful.

Moments later, Ryder shoved the controls of the helicopter forward and it started to descend, aiming for a wide, flat area behind some barns like a horsefly heading for the rump of a steer.

That night, and long after Royal and Maddie had gone to bed, Ryder walked the halls of the house in which he'd been

raised, visiting the ghosts that had driven him away. Unable
to sleep, he'd checked on Casey one last time and then gone
outside to the wide front porch to listen to the night.

It was spring, and the air was sweet and cool. The scent of
flowers in the nearby flower bed reminded him of Casey. To
him, she would always be a fresh breath of spring. She'd been
his savior in so many ways that he couldn't begin to take
count, and they'd come too close to losing that which made
life worth living. That day in Fostoria Biggers's house, when
he'd touched her skin and felt the pulse of her life beating
beneath his fingertips, he'd known then that they'd been given
a second chance.

A night owl hooted from a nearby tree and Ryder paused,
listening to the familiar sound. A cow lowed in a nearby pasture, calling for her baby. Moments later, a plaintive bawl
announced the baby's location, and all was well. Ryder took
a deep breath, absorbing the peace of home and the assurance
that he'd done the right thing by bringing Casey here to visit.

A quick breeze came up, lifting the hair away from his
forehead and brushing against his chest like a lover's fingers.
He glanced up at the sky and then to the faint wisps of clouds
overhead, judging the possibility of a rain before morning.

And while he was looking at stars, the breeze seemed to
shift, and the skin on his flesh tightened in warning. A sound
came out of the night, like a whisper, or a memory, but it was
there in his mind. And he knew who it was that his heart
finally heard.

Welcome home, son.

He turned toward the house. But it wasn't Micah who came
out of the door.

Casey came off of the porch and out into the dew-damp
grass to stand beside him. She lifted her hand to his cheek,
feeling, rather than seeing the tears that had started to fall.

"Sweetheart, are you all right?"

Ryder wrapped his arms around her, holding her close until
he could feel the even beat of her heart. He buried his face

in the curve of her neck and took a deep breath. Flowers. She always smelled like flowers.

"Now that you're here, I'm more than all right."

Casey sighed, and held him even closer. "Come to bed, Ryder. I can't sleep without you."

He lifted her into his arms. "Then buckle up, darlin', and I'll take you to dreamland."

* * * * *

Roman's Heart

This book is about survivors.

No matter how difficult we try to make it,
life is simple. It's just a matter of identifying
our weaknesses and surviving the trials
and tribulations that come with them.
Some of us persevere. Some of us fail.

During my lifetime, I have met many people
whom I admire. People who've endured
and overcome great odds to become the person
God meant them to be.

I have been blessed in knowing a man like that.

To a man who has faced true and deep despair—
a man who knows better than most
what it takes to survive.

To Bobby.

This book is for you.

Chapter 1

It was the sensation of needles poking into the skin on her face that brought the woman to, and when she opened her eyes, the scream that came out of her mouth made a nearby hawk take flight. Framed by the panorama of majestic mountains clothed in the new green of spring, the view was breathtaking. But it wasn't the view that had caused her reaction. It was the binding sensation of the parachute strapped to her body, as well as the fact that she was caught in the highest branches of a towering pine and dangling far above the ground.

In terror, she grabbed for the straps. The sudden movement sent her swaying in the breeze like a flapping shirt on a clothesline. And the weight of her body, coupled with the abruptness of the motion, made the fabric of the parachute rip even more, sending her slipping through the branches to the ground below. She looked down in horror, knowing that if she fell now, it would more than likely kill her.

God help me.

At that moment the fabric snagged and then held on another

great branch, stopping her dangerous descent. With her heart thundering in her eardrums, she closed her eyes in a silent prayer of thanksgiving. In the blessed quiet that followed, a terrifying realization hit. Yes, she was stranded in a tree and dangling from a parachute, and as soon as she'd opened her eyes, a small part of her had accepted that fact without wondering why or how it had happened. But just now, when she'd been about to give thanks to the Almighty for still breathing, a great gap in her memory became fact.

"No! Oh, no!"

She reached for her face, testing the shape and texture of each feature, as if touching it for the first time. She wished for a mirror...or anything that would give back a reflection, because right now she didn't remember who she was.

Stifling a quick shaft of fear, she reminded herself that it wasn't a name she needed right now. What she needed was a way to get down.

She reached toward a nearby branch, and again the movement sent her into motion. Twisting and spinning like a yo-yo on a tangled string, she grabbed onto the straps, willing herself not to panic.

When she could think without wanting to shriek, she began another approach. Maybe she should consider her injuries. The ones she already had were miserable but minor. Adding more could be the difference between being able to walk away from this and dying.

Okay, where does it hurt the worst?

And then she almost laughed. As best she could tell, the answer was *everywhere*. The question shouldn't have been where does it hurt, but how much?

One thing was for certain. Her lower lip was throbbing, and there was a coppery taste in her mouth that made her stomach roll. She reached toward the ache with the tip of her finger, wincing when it came in contact with what felt like a cut.

She closed her eyes and groaned, then leaned to one side and spit, unwilling to swallow her own blood. And while her skin stung as if it had been flailed, the throbbing pain in her head was far worse. It was no surprise to discover a large knot just above the hairline. But when her hand came away bloody, as well, she jerked back in shock. Again, the motion sent her swaying precariously within the branches.

"Easy, easy," she muttered, deliberately taking deep breaths and exhaling slowly after each one. When the movement had ceased without her having fallen any farther, she relaxed.

As she continued to dangle helplessly above the ground, a stiff breeze came up, blasting its way through the pines and blowing her hair into her eyes. When she ventured another look at the sun sinking into the western horizon, panic returned. It would be dark soon. Time was running out.

And while she feared the act would be hopeless, she began to shout, knowing full well that there probably wasn't a human being within miles who could hear.

"Help!" she called, shouting over and over until the word was a scream and her throat was burning from the strain.

An eerie echo bounced back with each shout, and she felt helpless against the fear she heard in her voice.

A startled deer bolted from a nearby thicket. She groaned, envious of its mobility. Off to her left, a squirrel scolded, and something fell through the branches from above, hitting the side of her cheek as it passed.

"Ouch!" she cried, cupping her face.

Blinking through tears, she looked down, watching as a large pine cone ricocheted from branch to branch before hitting the ground. The sight sent a fresh wave of nausea rolling in the pit of her stomach. Quickly closing her eyes to reorient herself within the space in which she was hanging, she kept reminding herself that she hadn't been what was falling. It was only a pine cone that had taken the plunge.

Again, the squirrel's strident chatter broke the silence of her thoughts, and when she opened her eyes, she found herself at eye level and within feet of the bushy-tailed rodent. The little animal's aggressive behavior was unnerving.

"Get!" she said shortly, and the squirrel's pivot on the branch was as neat and swift as a square dancer's step.

With a flick of its tail, it scampered back the way it had come, and as she watched, truth dawned! The squirrel had just shown her the way down. All she needed to do was straddle a branch and then inch her way backward toward the trunk of the tree. After that, she could use the branches like steps on a ladder. In theory, it was simple. But there were the parachute straps to dispense with, and she reminded herself, she was *not* a squirrel. She had to find branches strong enough to hold her weight.

A few minutes later, she had maneuvered herself into position. Straddling a branch, she ignored the rough bark and sticky pine needles as she locked her legs around its circumference. And while she felt comfortable with the fact that the branch would hold her weight, the true test of her faith came as she unbuckled the parachute and let go of the straps. As they slipped through her fingers to dangle down through the branches, she saw that even they were pointing the way down. She began her descent.

The pale green pants and sweater she was wearing were no protection to her body. By the time she reached the last limb, her clothes looked as if she'd been carrying a panicked cat through a room full of barking dogs. There were snags, pulls and tears everywhere it mattered. And if that wasn't enough of an insult, she had run out of limbs a good ten feet from the ground.

Her hands were raw and the skin all over her body felt as if it were on fire. The throb in her head was making her sick, and she knew that the jolt of her landing would only make things worse. But there was no other way to get down. With one last look below, she let go of the limb with her legs, letting them dangle over the floor of the forest.

And then she let go.

The smell of rotting vegetation was suddenly strong in her nostrils as she hit feet first, and then pitched forward, falling onto her hands and knees and plowing through the mat of leaves on the forest floor. But she was down, and from what she could tell, still healthy enough to move.

She started to pull herself up when a bit of color off to one side caught her eye. It was a navy blue duffel bag that she'd seen.

Jump, girl! Take the bag and jump... and don't look back!

She spun, expecting to see...

But the moment she thought it, the name and face disappeared, and to her dismay, she was still alone. Curious, she reached for the bag, and as she did, the skin on the back of her neck suddenly crawled. She fell backward, as if she'd just seen a snake.

"Oh, God, what's happening to me?" she groaned, and sat back up, cradling her head against her knees until the feeling had passed.

But time was at a premium. There was a cool bite to the air that hadn't been there before. This time when she looked at the bag, she ignored her feelings and grabbed it. She pulled at the zipper, then rocked back in shock.

Money! It was full of money! Bundle upon bundle of one-hundred-dollar bills.

How could you? I trusted you, and this is the way you repay me?

Like before, the words came out of nowhere, and even though she knew there was no one there, she couldn't help looking over her shoulder. Without giving herself time to think, she zipped the bag and then stood, pulling the straps over her shoulders and carefully balancing the weight against her pain-racked body.

"Now to find shelter."

Ignoring her misery, she shifted the bag to a more comfortable position and began to walk, following the lay of the land down the side of the mountain. Somewhere below she would find help. She had to. Her endurance was just about gone.

Just as the last rays of sun were sliding behind the tallest of trees, she spied the rooftop of what appeared to be a cabin.

"Thank you, God."

Blinking furiously against tears of relief, she began walking faster, desperate for shelter before the impending darkness caught her out here alone.

Her legs were trembling from exertion. And although the rooftop was no longer visible, she'd gotten a pretty good fix on the direction. If she kept walking, she kept telling herself, she was bound to find it again.

The oncoming night was turning the deep green of the forest into a waning black. The ordinary became frightening; the unfamiliar brought terror. The night wind was still blowing, and a chill was seeping into her bones. Just as she feared another step would be impossible, she walked into a clearing and it was there. The cabin that she'd seen. But it, too, was quickly disappearing within the oncoming shadows. She began to move faster, frantically circling the building and searching for a door to gain entry.

By normal standards, the cabin seemed ordinary. An A-line roof. Log walls. A door and two windows in the front. But to her, it was magnificent. Within seconds, she was running, the bag bouncing against her aching body with every step. And when her fingers closed around the doorknob, it never occurred to her to wonder why it was unlocked. Staggering out of the night and into another sort of darkness, she slammed the door behind her and then stood without moving, absorbing the quiet—and the blessed sensation of safety.

There were shadows inside the room that appeared to be furniture, and just to her right, a light switch on the wall. Across the room was a narrow staircase leading to what appeared to be a loft. It was desolate and dark, and she wondered if she'd ever appreciated anything as much as she did this place.

Overwhelmed with a great weariness, she allowed the bag to slide from her shoulder. She realized, even as she was dropping to her knees and then stretching out on the floor, that there was bound to be a more comfortable place somewhere inside the cabin to rest, but right now she was too exhausted to search. Trembling in every fiber of her being, and hurting in places she couldn't even name, she cradled her head on her arm and closed her eyes.

"Just for a minute. I'll rest just for a minute."

It was her last conscious thought until morning.

Royal Justice had been mad at his youngest brother, Roman, plenty of times in his life. In their younger days, there had even been a couple of times when their arguments came to blows. But that was then and this was now, and Royal wasn't about to trade punches with the man his little brother had become. All he could do was state his position and hope that Roman saw the sense in it all. Unfortunately, Royal had a tendency to lose his cool under pressure, and yelling, which was what he was doing now, was getting him nowhere.

"Damn it, Roman! You are not indispensable. You aren't the only private investigator in the city. The citizens of Dallas will not suffer if you take some time off. God knows you can afford it. You are not a robot, and contrary to what you may think, you are not immortal." He took a deep breath and pointed a shaking finger in Roman's face. "If you don't take a vacation, you…little brother…are going to burn out! And I don't have time to pick up the pieces of what's left of you."

Roman folded his arms and leaned against the wall, listening to Royal's demands with an inscrutable expression on his face.

Royal continued without missing a beat. "So, here's the deal. Yesterday I called and had the utilities turned on in the fishing cabin. I even had some basic supplies delivered, although I suggest you take plenty of anything else you might want. All you have to do is get in your car and drive till you get there."

Having said what had to be said, Royal Justice stood in the doorway, determined not to move from the only exit out of the men's room at the Quesadilla Queen until Roman admitted he was right.

Roman considered his options. One, he could choose to

ignore his brother's less-than-subtle suggestion to go to the family cabin in Colorado. If he was going to take a vacation, the least Royal could do was let him pick the place. But then he'd never hear the end of it, and there was a slight truth to some of what Royal just said. He was tired. In fact, he was so tired of the whole damned rat race that for two cents he'd quit.

At that point, a thoughtful frown creased his forehead. But what would he do then? Inactivity was his hell. It brought back too many memories he'd spent years trying to forget.

Then he remembered the couple waiting for them at the table outside and shifted mental gears.

"Damn it, Royal, don't you think it's more than a little rude to invite Ryder and Casey out to dinner and then leave them alone while you pitch this fit?"

Royal didn't flinch. The fact that their brother and his wife were in town visiting from out of state was not as important as getting what he wanted from Roman. And the fact that he'd left them alone at the table to follow Roman into the bathroom was moot. He was on a mission to take care of his family, whether they liked it or not. But Roman was not co-operating as he'd planned. And the cool, absent tone in Roman's voice was adding to his frustration.

Royal glared.

"Ryder is fully capable of entertaining his wife for a few minutes without our presence," he muttered. "And you haven't answered my question. Did you hear a thing I said?"

Roman's composure slipped—but only a little. "Hell, yes, I heard you…and so did everyone else within a city block."

Royal flushed. He knew he'd been yelling, but he didn't have it in him to quiet down when he was on a roll.

"And," Roman continued, "you didn't ask a question. You made a statement. One, I might add, that is shot full of flaws. I never claimed I was indispensable to anyone except your daughter. I can claim to being Maddie's favorite uncle, and we both know it."

Royal almost grinned. "That's because you never tell her no."

Roman arched an eyebrow, but never cracked a smile. "She's only four. There will be plenty of people telling her no for the rest of her life. I see no reason why one of them has to be me."

The door opened behind Royal, and he spun, glaring intently at the man who just entered.

"We're full up in here right now, buddy," Royal drawled, and the glitter in his eyes sent the fellow scurrying back to his table.

Roman rolled his eyes in disbelief. "This is a public bathroom in a public restaurant. You can't commandeer the whole place just because you get an urge to play big brother. What if he was in a hurry?"

Royal's chin jutted dangerously. "When it comes to my family, I can do anything I damned well please if it means keeping them whole. Ryder is finally back on track. I don't intend to have you pull a similar stunt and disappear on me some day just because you let the pressure get to you."

Roman straightened. He'd let Royal blow off steam, partly because he *was* the oldest Justice, and partly because in a small, quiet corner of his mind, he knew Royal was right. But enough was enough. He took a step forward.

"Look, you bullheaded fool. Get out of the doorway before you get us both arrested. Let's go back to the table and enjoy the evening. Ryder and Casey will be leaving for Ruban Crossing tomorrow."

But Royal wouldn't budge, and as hard as Roman had let himself become, he knew he couldn't hold a candle to Royal Justice when it came to bullheadedness.

"Okay, I'll make a deal with you," Roman said. "I'll go to the damned cabin, but only after Ryder and Casey leave."

Royal started to frown. "You have to promise."

Roman threw up his hands. "I promise. Now are you happy?"

Royal gave him a long hard stare. "You swear."

Roman sighed. "Swear."

Royal relented. Roman was hard, but he didn't lie, and he didn't go back on his word. He grinned and held out his hand.

"Shake on it, buddy, and it will be a deal."

Given the fact that he might never get to order his food if he didn't comply, Roman cursed beneath his breath as he extended his hand. Royal's grip was as firm as the smile on his face. Moments later, they walked out of the men's room, sidestepping the line of men who'd been waiting to get in.

"Gentlemen, it's all yours," Royal said, waving his arm magnanimously.

"Big brother, you are a real charmer," Roman said, and knew that he'd been had.

A small sports car swerved into the passing lane behind Roman and sped past him as if he were sitting still.

"Crazy damn fool," he muttered, his eyes narrowing as he kept his four-wheel-drive vehicle to the inside lane of the narrow highway. There was a steep drop-off to his left that went straight down the side of the mountain. Speeding was not an option he was willing to consider, no matter how badly he wanted to reach his destination.

Not for the first time, he wished that he hadn't let Royal talk him into this trip. Hell, he didn't even like to fish, and from the looks of the sky, a storm was moving in. It would be just his luck to come all this way and then wind up stuck in the cabin with nothing to do.

He glanced at his watch and then shrugged. If he did get caught in the rain, it would be his own fault. He shouldn't have waited so long to start the trip. But Ryder and Casey had stayed and stayed, and by the time they'd left the ranch, it had been after 10:00 a.m. And then it had taken nearly thirty minutes more before Roman had been able to tear himself away from Maddie. For a four-year-old, she was a demanding little wench.

He glanced at the sky again. It was unusually dark for this time of day, even in the mountains. Normally it would be light for a couple more hours, but not this evening. The storm would take care of that. He shifted wearily in the seat and thought of his niece again.

Damn, but he loved that kid. It never ceased to amaze him how he'd let one small little girl twist him into knots. Thinking of one female only led to thoughts of another. And it was only in rare times like this that they came. An old pain tried to raise its ugly head, but he shoved the memories back into the past where they belonged. Twelve years had come and gone since he'd watched her die. Part of him had died that day, too, and he knew it. He'd buried what was left behind an impenetrable wall, and that's where he stayed. It was lonely, but safer.

A sound of distant thunder rumbled across the peaks. He looked back up at the sky. If he didn't hurry, he wasn't going to beat the rain. And that would mean unloading his vehicle in a downpour, or sleeping in a bed with no sheets.

As soon as he thought it, he snorted. Maybe Royal was right. Maybe he had needed to get away. He must be getting soft, worrying about where he was going to sleep. There had been plenty of times in his life when he would have settled...and quite happily...for a safe place to close his eyes, never mind whether or not there was a bed.

He'd taken far too many risks during his military career, although he rarely dwelled on the past. These days, he focused his energies on his job and the fact that he *was* still alive. Then he amended that thought. At least he was still alive, but that could change at any moment if he didn't start paying closer attention to this damnable road.

A few moments later, he began negotiating a nasty turn in the road, and out of habit, glanced up at the rearview mirror. Startled by the expression on his own face, he looked away.

Returning his focus to driving, he took the curve with cool skill, refusing to admit, even for a moment, that Royal could have been right. Roman knew himself. He wasn't about to break. It would take more than a few late nights on the job to wear him down.

Within a half hour, he had reached the cabin. The storm hit as he was carrying the last load inside. The rain began peppering against the windows as he kicked the door shut behind him.

He glanced around the room, trying to remember the last time he'd been here, and couldn't. The overhead light cast a dim yellow glow onto the brown leather furniture. He looked toward the loft, thinking of the king-size bed that was there.

And at that moment, the power went off, casting everything into darkness. With a muttered curse, he headed for the kitchen, trying to remember where he'd packed the flashlight and candles.

Yanked from a deep, dreamless sleep, she sat straight up in bed, her eyes wide and filled with fear. With a pounding heart, she listened, trying to discern what she'd heard. A nearby roll of thunder rattled the loft window behind the bed on which she'd been sleeping, and she wrapped her arms around herself and shuddered.

Thank God I'm not out in that.

A door suddenly slammed downstairs and she rolled from the bed, wincing as the movement sent fresh waves of pain shooting through her battered body. Shaking in every fiber of her being, she crept to the edge of the loft and gazed down through the railing, trying to pierce the darkness below. All she could see were more shadows, and yet she knew.

The owner! He's come!

Her first instinct was to believe she'd been saved. But then she remembered the duffel bag and panicked. She had visions of revealing her presence, only to find herself on the small end of someone's hunting rifle. People had been killed for far less than the money she was carrying. It would be very easy to hide a body in woods as dense as these, and whoever was down there could, quite literally, get away with murder. The instinct for survival that had gotten her this far kicked in again. She dropped to her knees and crawled across the floor, then shoved the bag beneath the bed and went in after it.

The floor was cold and hard against her belly, and the dust motes she'd unwittingly disturbed were tickling her nose. The duffel bag was against the wall at the head of the bed. Every time she flinched, the bulk of it pushed against her feet. Outside, raindrops were ricocheting off the roof like bullets against rocks. A cold draft was beginning to circulate around her legs and feet, while outside the thunder rumbled like a runaway wagon on a downhill ride.

She kept telling herself that maybe it would be okay. Surely God wouldn't let her survive all of this, only to let her perish at a stranger's hands. But she was too frightened to take a chance. And it would seem that the proper time for making oneself known had come and gone. In the midst of it all, she heard a sound that sent her into a panic. Someone was coming up the stairs!

Holding her nose to keep from sneezing, she scooted as far back as she could get and watched the landing, anxious to see his face.

The rain was coming down now in sheets. Roman could hear it running off the roof and down onto the hard-packed ground below. Out of habit, he flipped the light switch a couple of times and then shrugged. He wasn't the kind of man to waste time on things that were out of his control. At least there was dry wood by the fireplace. He'd build a fire. That would provide light and warm the place up, too.

Satisfied that he had something to accomplish, he began laying the kindling. A short while later, he stood before the fireplace, watching in satisfaction as tiny orange tongues of flame began eating their way into the dry wood.

His belly growled, but he ignored the complaint. Without power, he would have to cook over the fireplace and he wasn't in a Daniel Boone frame of mind. A gust of air rattled the door on its hinges. He thought of his apartment and of the well-stocked refrigerator he'd left behind.

"Damn Royal's meddling butt, anyway," he muttered, and

laid one last log on the fire before moving the fire screen into place.

Chilled from the weather and weary from the drive, he was immediately drawn to the loft. He reached for his suitcase and then changed his mind. To hell with sheets. All he wanted to do was lie down. He'd make the bed tomorrow in the bright light of day. With one last look behind him, Roman started up to the loft, taking care not to miss a step in the darkness.

Halfway up, he froze. He could feel the hair rise on the backs of his arms. Something wasn't right! Long ago, he'd learned not to ignore his instincts. He turned, gazing down at the scene below, and wondered what it was that he'd heard. Nothing seemed out of place. Everything was just as it had been when he'd come inside. A hard gust of wind hit the side of the house, rattling the windows, as well as the door.

Frowning, he retraced his steps to the door and turned the lock, relaxing only after the distinct click had sounded. Then he dug his handgun from a bag and started back up the stairs, satisfied that he'd done all he could. If someone wanted to try him, he was more than ready.

Heat was rising from the fire below as he dropped to the side of the bed and set the handgun on a nearby table. He looked down at his feet and then back at the bed. The mattress smelled a little bit dusty, but he was too tired to care.

In the back of his mind, he could almost hear his mother admonishing him to get his shoes off the furniture. With a rare smile, he bent down and pulled off his boots before dropping them onto the floor. With a weary groan, he lay down, folding his arms beneath his head and sighing as he looked up at the ceiling.

The rafters had taken on a warm, amber tinge from the glow of the fireplace below. His stomach rumbled again, but it was a small complaint he willingly ignored. He closed his eyes, inhaled slowly and never knew when he fell asleep.

Hours later, he awakened suddenly to hear the indistinct sound of fabric rubbing against wood. Without taking a breath, he reached for his gun.

Chapter 2

He's asleep.

For her, that fact had been too long in coming. The floor was cold and she hurt—hurt all over. If she didn't get out from under this bed and soon, she would never be able to move again. What's more, she needed to go to the bathroom.

Inch by painful inch, and using the duffel bag at her feet as a launch, she began to scoot forward. As she did, the stiff nylon fabric suddenly rasped against the hardwood floor. Although it was still raining, the sound seemed magnified by the quiet within the room. She froze, relaxing only after the soft, even sounds of his breathing could still be heard.

Easy does it, she told herself, and once again, began to pull herself out from under the bed.

The stairwell was only feet away when something—call it instinct—made her look back over her shoulder. Through the glimmer from the firelight below, she saw him, raised up on one elbow, the gun pointed straight at her head. A calm settled over her as she rolled over on her back, and for the first time since she'd regained consciousness in the tree, came face-to-face with the fact that she might not live through this after all.

"Don't shoot," she said quietly. "I'm not armed."

"But I am."

The words were harsh, the warning tone of his voice deep and angry, like the storm still raging outside. She took a slow breath and started to sit when his voice cut through the quiet again, this time in a manner she couldn't mistake.

"I didn't say you could move."

"Please," she said. "I need to go to the bathroom."

The request was so unexpected he laughed, and the short, angry bark brought goose bumps to the backs of her arms. She swallowed past a knot of cold fear.

"I never meant to deceive you," she said quietly. "I just needed shelter. I was asleep when you came. Your arrival startled me so that I hid before I thought. After that, it seemed anticlimactic to announce myself."

The bed squeaked as he stood, and when she looked up, fought back an urge to scream. He was so big...and so menacing.

"Get up."

His order was brief. As she rolled to her feet, it occurred to her that this man didn't waste energy on words.

Her movements seemed slow and measured, and once Roman believed he heard her groan. The thought crossed his mind to offer her help, and then he remembered that while she'd been hiding under that blasted bed, he'd been asleep on it. He rejected the notion. She got down on the floor; she could get herself up.

The muscles in his belly knotted at the thought of someone under the bed. It was a kid's worst nightmare come to life— a monster under the everlasting bed. It remained to be seen if she was really a monster after all.

"Downstairs," he ordered, waving the gun in her direction. "And take it slow."

"That I can do," she said briefly, unaware that her answer

deepened the frown on his forehead. With aching muscles protesting her every step, she bit her lip and began to move.

The floorboards creaked beneath his weight as he moved in behind her. At that point, the phrase *breathing down her neck* took on new meaning. A short while later, they were standing before the remnants of the fire, and staring into the bits of dying embers rather than at each other.

Roman pulled back the fire screen and then pointed toward a nearby stack of logs with his gun.

"You. Toss one on the fire."

The very idea of gripping anything with her hands was impossible to consider. She turned to him, holding out her hands in supplication.

"I don't think I—"

"Do what I said, lady, or we're right back where we started."

She turned toward the stack, gritting her teeth against the pain as her fingers curled around the rough, dry bark.

This time, her groan was loud and clear. Halfway to the fireplace, she lost her grip. The log fell to the floor with a loud, abrupt thump, rolling to one side as she dropped to her knees, cradling her hands against her chest.

"What the hell—?"

"My hands are hurt."

This time, he was forced to listen. He grabbed her hands and turned them toward the fire. In the light of the dying embers, he could see dark slashes and bloody stains. Guilt hit him belly high. He cursed beneath his breath and finished what she'd started.

Then without excuse or apology, he took her by the arm and pulled her to her feet. Within minutes, the room was aglow. And although they were still in shadows, they were finally able to see one another's face.

Even though she knew it was rude to stare, she couldn't help it. And, she reminded herself, so far he'd been anything but a gentleman himself. He was very good-looking, but the fact was lost in the fear rolling in her mind. In her entire life, she couldn't remember ever seeing such a cold, flat expression on a living man's face. And then she reminded herself that she was hardly in a position to be judging character. She couldn't even remember her own name.

Roman's gaze was hard and fixed. He had already schooled himself not to react to her condition until he had some answers he could live with. Yes, she was cut and bruised, and her clothing was bloody and all but in rags. And the dried blood matting parts of her hair to her scalp was further proof of her injuries. So at least part of her story had to be true. Problem was, he didn't trust pretty women. In fact, he didn't trust women at all.

"What's your name?" Roman asked, and saw a different kind of fear move across her face.

"I don't know."

That wasn't what he'd expected to hear. "What do you mean, you don't know?"

She reached toward the knot beneath her scalp. "Somehow I hurt my head. When I came to, I couldn't remember who I was or where I'd been going."

He almost sneered. "Amnesia is a lame excuse, lady. Try again."

Her gaze never wavered, nor did the tone of her voice. "Frankly, I don't care whether you believe me or not."

Reluctantly, he gave her points for attitude. Score one for you, he thought to himself. He shifted his stance. "You look like hell. What happened?"

There was no mistaking the anger in her eyes and it came through with the bitterness of her question.

"You're not married, are you?"

Roman was taken aback and found himself answering before he thought.

"No."

This time, she was the one who almost sneered. "Now, why am I not surprised? Your bedside manner leaves a lot to be desired."

His glare deepened. He didn't give a damn about her opinions of his manners or of anything else. In typical Justice fashion, he disposed of the subject by ignoring it.

"Lady, I don't waste my time on congeniality. In my line of work, it rarely gets the job done."

She stared pointedly at the gun. "I'm almost afraid to ask, but are you some sort of cop?"

"I'm no cop," he said shortly.

"Wonderful," he heard her mutter. "And where does that leave me...conversing with a hit man?"

A rare grin tilted the corner of his mouth. "I'm not a hit man, either. I'm a private investigator."

She sighed. "I wish I knew if I could afford you. I'd hire you to find out who I am."

The grin disappeared. She seemed bent on sticking to her story, and in spite of his better judgment, he was starting to believe her. He lowered the gun without comment, then pointed to her injuries.

"Did you have a wreck? I didn't see any signs of one on the road when I came up."

"I wasn't in a car. I think I was in a plane."

His eyes widened. "Are you saying your plane went down?"

She fought an urge to scream. The man was infuriating. But, she reminded herself, he was the one with the gun.

"No...maybe. Oh, I don't know. All I know is, I jumped out before it went down."

"Jumped?"

The room was beginning to tilt, and she reached out to steady herself, all but swaying on her feet.

"I regained consciousness in a pine tree. The parachute I was wearing was caught in the branches. Now, please. The bathroom. I need to go to the bathroom."

Roman hadn't missed a nuance of her expression. He had to admit she was good. But parachuting out of a plane and landing in a tree? The story was too far-fetched. He hated to let her out of his sight, even for a minute, but he could hardly ignore the request. Besides that, where the hell could she go? He finally relented.

"Down the hall, first door on your left."

"I know. I've been here since last night."

While he was absorbing the shock of that news, the power came back on, flooding the room in a sudden burst of light that left them both blinking...and in an odd, uncomfortable sort of way, slightly embarrassed.

"Thank goodness," she said. "At least now I won't bump into anything else." Her hand brushed across the surface of her belly as she turned away. "I don't have room left for another bruise."

There was no way Roman could ignore the truth of her condition now. In the light, the evidence of her injuries was overwhelming. He caught himself wincing in sympathy as she walked away. And as he stared at her backside, another, but far less serious, fact of her life began to emerge. She was missing a pocket on the seat of her pants. He grinned. Her choice of underwear was remarkable, to say the least. Daisies. Her panties had daisies on them—small white blossoms with bright yellow centers.

On a rare, mischievous impulse, he called out to her. "Hey, Daisy."

Startled by the unexpected and unfamiliar name, she pivoted. There was a tremor in her voice that hadn't been there before, but she couldn't help it. Did he know something about her that she didn't?

"Why did you call me that?" she asked sharply.

He shrugged. "Got to call you something. It's as good a name as any."

She frowned, waiting for him to continue.

"Wait a minute," he said, and stepped into the kitchen. Moments later, he came out and handed her a roll of toilet paper.

She blushed, but took what he offered with her head held high.

"Thank you," she said shortly, more focused on gaining relief than worrying about some fool name that he fancied.

Yet when she stepped inside the bathroom, the fact that she was still at his mercy hit her again, and she locked the door behind her. Considering his size and the fact that he was armed, it was a futile act of defiance, but it made her feel better, just the same.

Easing her aching fingers around the zipper, she pulled, breathing a sigh of relief as her pants dropped down around her ankles without fuss. But when she reached for her underwear, she stopped, staring intently at the fabric, and then down at the obvious hole in the back of her pants.

Daisy... It's as good a name as any.

A bright red flush crept up her face and into her neckline. He had some nerve. And then she thought of the look in his eyes and amended. An overdose of nerve wasn't the only thing he had. A complete lack of fear was more like it.

She caught sight of herself in the mirror and rolled her eyes in disbelief. He was right. She did look like hell.

Daisy. She said the name aloud, testing the sound on the tip of her tongue. "Daisy."

The name didn't ring any bells, but it didn't set off any alarms, either. She shrugged. He was right. For now, it was as good a name as any.

A short while later, she came out of the bathroom. Water was dripping from her hands and face, but the worst of the bloodstains were gone. To her surprise, the man was nowhere in sight. The urge to run was strong, but where could she go? She wrapped her arms around herself, shivering as she headed for the fire. The room seemed colder now than it had been a short while ago, and she was tired...so tired. The old sofa beckoned. It was four cushions in length, with just enough dignity to make a good bed.

Crawling onto it, she rolled herself into a ball, facing the fire. The heat emanating from the blaze seemed heaven-sent. In the next room, something hit the floor with a thump, but she didn't flinch. In a way, the sound was almost reassuring.

It was sort of like belling a cat. At least now she knew where he'd gone. She sighed and closed her eyes, only planning to rest. But moments later, exhaustion claimed her and she slept.

That was where Roman found her, curled up on the old leather sofa with one hand beneath her cheek and the other dangling over the edge of the cushion. Her vulnerability caught him by surprise. He found himself studying her in a way he would never have done had she been awake. He looked past his doubts to the woman beneath, realizing that he was more than intrigued. But he kept telling himself it was the mystery around her and not the woman herself that had caught his interest. And as he stood, he wondered how often he would have to remind himself of that to finally believe.

She was tiny, both in build and height. The top of her head was just below his chin, and she was a brunette. He preferred tall, leggy blondes. The cut on her lip broke the symmetry of her mouth in a way that made him ache. He winced, thinking about the blow it would take to split such a tender spot. There was a bruise on her right cheek and scratches down the side of her face and neck. Remnants of the tree, he supposed, and at that moment, realized that he'd bought into her story. It was far-fetched, but he knew crazier things had happened.

His gaze moved to her hands. They were ringless. So she wasn't married. He didn't ask himself if it mattered. He was simply following procedure—finding out all there was to know about a subject before he took him or her apart at the seams.

When she shivered in her sleep, his frown deepened. Her clothes were in rags, and even if they hadn't been, they weren't suited for this type of climate.

Well, hell.

A few moments later, he came out of the kitchen carrying a blanket. When he bent down to cover her up, a wave of emotion hit him that had nothing to do with the suspicion he'd had earlier.

She was so damned small and helpless looking. He pulled the blanket up over her shoulders, making certain that her back was covered. He watched as she grabbed the edge of the blanket, pulling it tight beneath the curve of her chin. It was an unconscious gesture, but an endearing one, as well. It reminded him of his niece, Maddie. Maddie was afraid of the dark and slept under covers, no matter what time of year. He wondered if Daisy was afraid of the dark, and then laid another log on the fire.

Outside, the wind continued to blow, although the rain must have passed. He hadn't heard it against the roof for some time now. Curious, he went to the front door to look out and was greeted by a blast of cold air. In spite of the darkness, the swirling snow eddying in the wind currents was impossible to miss.

"Son of a..."

He slammed the door shut and then turned, staring around the cabin and then at the woman asleep before the fire. At that moment, he made himself a promise. When he got home, he was going to punch Royal Justice in the nose. Not only had he let himself be bullied into taking a vacation he hadn't wanted, but if the weather didn't change, he was about to be snowed in, and with a woman he still didn't trust. He walked to the sofa and looked down, whispering more to himself than to her.

"Well now, Miss Daisy, we've got ourselves in one fine mess."

But Daisy didn't hear him, and if she had, at that moment she wouldn't have cared. Even though she was unaware of the snowstorm, she already knew there were worse things than being stranded inside this cabin. She could still be dangling from the limbs of that tree.

"Look, Holly-berry, look! See the bubbles. Now blow. Pucker up your mouth and blow!"

Daisy's mouth pursed slightly as she went with the dream, watching from inside the little girl's eyes as the bubbles flew from the wand and out into the air.

Laughter spilled from the child's lips as she gave chase,

waving her hands toward the bits of sunlight captured on the
surfaces of the bubbles.

"More," she cried. "Blow me some more!"

And they came, swirling through the air, dancing on wind
currents, sailing too high to catch and far out of sight.

Still drifting with the pleasure of the dream, Daisy opened
her eyes to a reality far removed. The log walls of the cabin
were an abrupt reminder of the past two days of her life. And
then she looked toward the window and amended that
thought. The past *three* days of her life. It was morning.

The scent of coffee was strong, as was the ever present
smell of the wood fire. She rolled over onto her back, contemplating the idea of moving farther, then abandoned the
thought for the comfort of the cover and the fire.

Cover!

She reached down, fingering the softness of the blanket. A
frown creased her forehead. Sometime between last night and
this morning, her reluctant host had tossed her a crumb of
kindness.

Humph. I didn't think he had it in him.

Guilt shafted as she reminded herself that, technically, *he'd*
been the one who'd been wronged. She'd infringed upon his
property and hospitality, and without notice or warning. She
sighed, trying to put herself in his place. What would she have
done had she awakened to find someone crawling out from
under her bed?

At that moment, a picture flashed into her mind—of a large
room done in shades of blue, with touches of white, and of a
great four-poster bed. The image came and went so quickly
she could have let herself believe it was still part of her dream,
but something told her it was not. Somewhere inside her
mind, she was waking up, and the room she'd just seen did
exist.

When tears spiked, she jutted her chin and gritted her teeth.
Crying would get her nowhere. If that memory had come, then
others would follow. For now, she needed to be concerned
with getting down from this mountain and getting to the au-

thorities. Then she remembered the bag full of money she'd left under the bed.

So maybe I don't go straight to the authorities. Maybe I do a little checking on my own before I announce myself to the world. I don't want to appear in public, only to find I'm on the FBI's most-wanted list.

With a reluctant grunt, she tossed back the blanket and rolled, first to a sitting position, then standing, looking down at her stained clothes with distaste.

"Oh, for a steed and a pot of gold," she muttered.

"And where would you go if you had them?"

Daisy spun. That man. How long had he been standing there?

"You startled me," she accused.

"Sorry," he said, but she knew he was not.

"You didn't answer my question," Roman said. "If you had that horse and money, where would a woman named Daisy go?"

"I'm sure you would agree, but for starters, out of your hair. You've been kind to put me up, but I think I've out-stayed my welcome."

Her reference to the fact that he'd kept a gun trained on her most of the evening was not lost on Roman, nor was the fact that she was keeping her distance. He didn't know whether she was still afraid of him, or if she was standing where she was because it was close to the door. And because he was the man that he was, he chose not to comment on either of her remarks.

Her eyes narrowed in anger. The man was inscrutable, as well as insufferable. She pitied the woman who—

"I just realized," she said. "I don't know your name."

"Justice. Roman Justice."

Justice…as in my way or no way at all? But she refrained from voicing her thoughts.

"Mr. Justice, I'd like to say it's been a pleasure, but we'd both know I'd be lying, so I'll stick to the facts. I don't know where we are, but I assume you had transportation up here, and I would appreciate a lift down to the nearest city. I can take it from there.''

Roman shook his head. "Afraid I can't do that just yet."

Her heart skipped a beat. "And why not?"

"Take a look outside."

She headed for the door. Even before she turned the knob, she felt the cold. Oh, no, this isn't going to be good. She looked outside. As far as the eye could see was a heavy layer of snow—cold and white, pristine in color and deadly in depth—and it was still falling.

She slammed the door and spun around. Her shock was evident.

"It's just a late-spring blizzard. They don't usually last all that long, but travel is out for the duration."

Daisy shuddered, partly from the cold and partly from nerves. Being trapped in this cabin, with this man—

She refused to think past being trapped. The possible consequences of the rest of it were too appalling to consider.

"Look at me," she muttered. "My clothes...my hair...I'm a mess...and I'm freezing."

He frowned. "Yeah, I figured when you felt better you'd start worrying about all of that stuff, so I dug around and found a few things you might be able to wear. They're on the bed upstairs."

Daisy had the grace to flush. Here she stood, worrying about the demise of her moral character, when for all she knew, she was an out-and-out thief.

"Thank you," she said shortly. "Is there a problem with the power?"

He shook his head.

"Then, if you don't mind, I would really like to take a bath and wash my hair." She shrugged by way of explaining. "The blood, you know. It's all dried in my hair."

Roman nodded, and when she started toward the bathroom, he felt obligated to add, "There's a clean towel on the back of the door, and you're welcome to use my shampoo. After you've dressed and had breakfast, I brought a first-aid kit. If you want, I'd be glad to look at your hands and that cut on your head.''

Daisy started to smile, but there was an expression on his face that stopped her intent.

"Thank you," she said. "I won't be long."

"Coming from a female, that would be a first," Roman muttered as he turned away.

"I heard that," Daisy said, and then shut the bathroom door behind her with a solid thump.

Roman looked back at the door and thought of the woman beyond, then reached for his coat and gloves. They'd be needing more wood and he needed to put some distance between himself and that woman.

Certain things about her were beginning to catch his eye. When she stood a certain way, he knew she was nervous. Something about the way she held her head at a dare-to-mess-with-me angle. And there was the way her eyes seemed to change color according to her moods. Sometimes they seemed dark, and more than once he'd seen them glittering with unshed tears.

He stomped out into the snow, kicking his way through the drifts to the woodpile and reminding himself that women were nothing but trouble. Oh, they had their place in his life, but nothing permanent. He'd learned the hard way about counting on women to stay the course. Granted, the ones he'd loved hadn't left of their own accord, but he was past trusting in fate, or in God, to give him one he could keep. He picked up the logs one by one, and when his arms were full, headed back to the cabin.

Chapter 3

The assortment of clothing he had laid out for her was, to say the least, eclectic. There were odds and ends that didn't match, and all of them smelled a bit like the cedar chest they'd been in, but Daisy didn't care. They were clean and, except for having to roll up the waistband of the gray wool pants she had on, almost a fit. The old red flannel shirt was soft and comfortable, and a welcome respite against her scrapes and bruises. And when she sat down to put on her shoes, she saw that he'd left her a pair of socks, as well. She pulled them on, savoring the warmth against her skin. They made her shoes a bit too tight, but she wasn't going to sacrifice warmth for comfort.

When she bent down to straighten her pants, a lock of her hair slid forward. Still wet from her shampoo, it felt cold against her cheek. Shivering, she headed for the stairs and the fire that was blazing below.

Roman looked up as he heard her coming, thinking he was prepared for the sight of a stranger in his mother's old clothes. She was shorter than Barbara Justice had been, but there was that same unmistakable air of fragility in their build. Just for a moment, he felt as if he were seeing a ghost. He stared at her, unaware he was frowning.

Daisy paused in midstep, with her hand still on the banister. If she was honest with herself, she would have to admit Roman Justice scared her to death. He was so big and his expression so cold. It was as if his very presence sucked the life out of a room. But there was something inside of her that refused to let him know how she felt. Instead of cowering, she lifted her chin and met his gaze straight on.

"Thank you for the clothes," she said quietly. "They feel warm and wonderful."

He nodded.

"Your sister's?" she asked, trying to make conversation.

He shook his head. "Don't have one."

"Oh."

Silence lengthened between them. Finally, it was Daisy who broke it.

"Do I smell coffee?"

Her question made him remember she hadn't eaten. "Yes. I left you a few strips of bacon on the back of the stove, and there's bread in the box. You better make yourself a sandwich to go with the coffee. I won't cook again until evening."

"Thank you."

Green. Her eyes are green. For some reason, he felt satisfied with having answered that question. A few moments passed before he realized that she'd spoken.

"What did you say?"

"Thank you," Daisy repeated. "I said thank you."

He shrugged. "You're welcome." Then he remembered her hands and the injuries she'd suffered.

He caught her by the arm as she started into the kitchen, then grabbed her hands, turning them palms up. They didn't look much better than they had before her bath. He knew they must be painful.

"I'll get your food. You dry your hair. It's bad enough that we're stuck here together. The last thing I need is for you to get sick.''

Daisy didn't know whether to thank him or kick him in the shins. His offer of help could be taken several ways, and none of them was particularly complimentary.

''Yes…well, I…'' Daisy said, and then gave up conversation as a lost cause when he walked away.

With a shrug, she turned toward the fireplace. No use talking to herself. And the fire did feel good.

When he came back in the room, Daisy was still running her fingers through her hair, using them in lieu of a comb to separate the strands so they would dry. He set the coffee and sandwich on the table at the end of the sofa and then took a tube of ointment from his pocket.

''After you eat, I'll doctor your cuts. You don't want to get an infection.''

Again, Daisy was forced into accepting his reluctant offers of help. She nodded, wondering what she'd done to deserve such a plight as she was experiencing now. If she *was* a crook, her justice was being meted out in a more effective manner than any the criminal system could have accomplished.

There is the money, she reminded herself. But until she knew where it came from, she wasn't the least bit comfortable about considering it as any sort of backup.

Uncomfortable at Roman's nearness, Daisy picked up her sandwich and then looked away as she took the first bite. But the wonderful flavor of crisp smoked bacon and sliced tomato, coupled with soft, fresh bread and some sort of sandwich spread came as a great surprise. She hadn't been expecting the garnishes he'd added, and made no effort to hide her appreciation.

''Mmm, this is good!'' she said, and then leaned back on the sofa and proceeded to down the rest of it like a starving pup.

Roman turned away, refusing to acknowledge her appreciation.

"Just a sandwich," he said shortly. "Let me know when you're through. I'll see to your cuts."

She looked up. "It's much warmer by the fire. You don't have to leave on my account."

Roman stood for a moment, staring intently down at the woman in his mother's clothes, and wondered what Barbara Justice would have had to say about her. Her hair was almost dry. The same length all over, the chocolate brown strands fell just short of her shoulders. A single strand of hair was stuck to her cheek near the corner of her eye. It startled him to know he'd thought of brushing it back.

"Oh, but I think I do," he said, and left her to make what she chose of the ambiguous remark. Besides that, he was still trying to get through to Royal, although none of his calls would go through. He supposed it was because of the storm.

So Daisy ate, alternating bites with slow sips of coffee as Roman finished unpacking. A short while later, he went upstairs with an armload of linens. When she heard him walking from one side of the bed to the other, she realized he must be making it up. A quick wave of panic came and went as she thought of the money hidden beneath it. What would he do if he found it? While he didn't seem like the type of man who would kill for money, she already knew that he *was* the type of man who, if he had to, wouldn't hesitate to kill. She set her cup aside and then leaned forward with her elbows on her knees, staring down at the floor and praying for insight that would help her get through this.

There was no sudden revelation—no bright burst of light holding badly needed answers—only the realization that she was on her own. Despair settled heavily on her shoulders as she buried her face in her hands.

And that was how Roman found her.

She looked so lost. He wondered if she was crying and was angry with himself for caring. He didn't want to be embroiled in anything personal, especially with a woman. When you got personal with a woman, emotions became involved, and Roman had learned long ago to keep his emotions in check. Life had aged him far beyond his thirty years. He didn't want to care. People who cared were people who set themselves up for a fall.

"Are you sick?"

Daisy jerked. She hadn't heard his approach, and that deep, angry voice startled her.

"No."

She refused to look up at his face. She was an unwelcome presence in his life, and she knew it.

Roman's conscience pulled. For a woman, she was being a trouper. Not once had she relied on tears or hysterics. His admiration for her lifted a notch.

"Let's take a look at those cuts," he said.

Daisy looked up, and although there were tears glittering in her eyes, she would have choked on them before she let one fall.

"Please do," she said. "I'd hate to be a larger burden than I already am."

Her sarcasm was impossible to miss, and Roman's guilt deepened.

"I never said you were a burden," he muttered, and reached for the ointment he'd laid on the table.

"Should I sit or stand?"

He glanced at her face. It was void of any expression, save that of waiting.

"Stay where you are," Roman said. "I'll come to you."

It was a poor choice of words. The moment he said them, they both knew there was another connotation that could have been taken.

She shifted farther back onto the sofa cushions and looked into the fire, telling herself that the flush on her face was from the heat and nothing else.

Roman stood behind her, waiting until she settled, then bent forward, carefully moving aside a lock of her hair above her eyebrow, then searching for the injury that had been the source of all that blood. Moments later, he felt a great lump beneath her scalp and frowned at the size of the cut on top of it. No wonder she didn't remember her name. Hell, it was a wonder she'd had enough sense left in her to walk.

"This might hurt," he said, squeezing a bit of ointment onto his finger before applying it to the cut.

She didn't flinch, but as he leaned closer, he heard the rapid and shallow breaths she was taking, and knew she was hiding her pain. Wishing there were a way to do this without hurting her, he touched her shoulder, feeling the rapid beat of her pulse pounding through her body.

"I'm sorry."

It was the quiet in his voice that calmed Daisy as nothing else could have done. At last, he said something she could believe.

She closed her eyes, taking a deep breath before she trusted herself to speak. But when she looked up, she found herself locked into a clear blue stare. She shuddered.

I don't know this man and yet I'm letting him call every shot about me, including my physical well-being.

The urge to bolt was strong, but there was something in his gaze—something strong and solid—that told her to stay, that it would be okay.

"It had to be done," she said, and held out her hands.

Roman circled the sofa, then sat on the cushion next to her. Again, the unexpected contact of her skin against his made him antsy, and he forced himself to focus on her injuries.

"You need a number on these," he said, turning them palms up, then palms down before applying ointment to both sides.

"If I'd been able to fly, it would have been easier to get out of the tree."

The unexpected bit of humor made him laugh before he thought, and a small smile played at the corner of his mouth as he finished the first aid.

But something had happened to Daisy she hadn't been prepared to withstand. In the short space of time between his laughter and his smile, she'd seen the man beneath the mask. In that moment, he'd become more than her captor, more than an unwilling host. He'd become human. For Daisy, that was a danger she couldn't afford. There were too many unanswered questions about her life to risk trusting anyone, especially a man who had her at his mercy.

"I think that's enough. Thank you very much," she said quickly. Before he could argue, she reached for her plate and cup and headed for the kitchen.

The smile died on his face as he watched her walk away. Everything in him was on alert. A woman with a past was always a complication. A woman with no past spelled trouble with a capital *T*.

He tossed the antibiotic aside and strode to the door, yanking it open with a jerk and then standing in the doorway, breathing in deep, cleansing drafts of the cold, sharp air. Tiny flurries of snow blistered his cheeks and burned his eyes, but he didn't budge. He stood, letting the wind and snow cleanse his mind in a way he could not.

By the time he stepped back, his focus was clear. All they had to do was coexist for a few more days. The weather would clear. He'd take her down off the mountain, and she'd be out of his life. The plan was a good one. It should have made him happy. It did not.

The scent of their supper was still in the air. Although Daisy's memory was as blank on food as it was on her personal past, she was pretty sure that she'd never had anything as good as the wieners he'd grilled over the fireplace and the beans he'd poured out of a can. For dessert, he'd opened a package of chocolate cookies filled with double helpings of white cream filling. When she saw them, she smiled in anticipation.

"Ooh, those are my favorites," she said, and then the smile froze on her face. "How did I know that?"

From his seat on the floor near the fireplace, he handed her a couple of cookies, then took one for himself.

"People with amnesia rarely forget everything about their lives," he said, twisting the cookie apart and then licking at the filling in a studied manner. "They will remember inconsequential facts. It's the big things that usually take time."

"Oh." It was all she could manage to say. Her gaze fell on the slow, steady lick of his tongue as it swirled around the cookie. There was something sensuous about the act that made her stomach pull. She swallowed nervously.

Look away. Look away. Don't let him see you watching.

Something crunched in her hand and she looked down. The cookie she'd been holding was in bits.

"I, uh—"

"Give it to me," he said, and held out his hand.

Embarrassed, she dumped the broken pieces into his palm and watched as he turned and tossed them in the fire.

"Here you go," he said, handing her another one. "Easy does it this time, Daisy Mae. You're supposed to put it *in* your mouth before you crunch."

There was a glimmer of jest in his eyes that she fought to ignore. Daisy Mae, indeed! She couldn't believe he was actually comfortable enough with her to tease, and she kept telling herself to lighten up.

Just eat your cookie, woman, before you do something you will regret.

Pretending great interest in which side to bite first, she turned the cookie around and around before she put it in her mouth. When the rich, familiar flavor of chocolate hit her tongue, she closed her eyes with pleasure and chewed slowly, savoring every bite. Then she proceeded to eat the two that he'd given her, and three others besides. When he offered her another, she shook her head.

"I couldn't possibly, but thanks," she said, daintily wiping at the edges of her mouth with the tips of her fingers.

Roman hid another grin. She'd be irked to know there was still a bit of cookie on her chin, but he wasn't going to tell her. With all her fussing and wiping, she was bound to come across it soon enough.

"Want a beer?" he asked as he got to his feet.

Daisy looked startled. "Uh, no. I don't drink. At least, I don't think I—"

Roman shook his head. "Don't apologize, and don't second-guess yourself. First instincts are always the best. How about some coffee, or maybe a pop?"

Daisy's interest returned. She'd seen the six-packs on the cabinet earlier.

"Too late for coffee, but I would like a pop. However, you don't need to wait on me. I can get it for myself."

Roman folded himself back up and sat down on the floor without arguing. "Fine. Bring me a beer when you come."

Her eyebrows rose, but she refrained from making a remark as she went into the kitchen. *He's been waiting on me all day. It's the least I can do,* she reminded herself. But she knew there was something inbred in her that resented like hell taking orders from a man. It made her wonder what her life had been like before.

As she was reaching into the refrigerator, the wind suddenly rattled the window over the sink and she looked up in fright. There was nothing beyond the glass but darkness. In a quick burst of panic, she grabbed the drinks and bolted for the living room, sliding to a halt as she reached the fire.

"Here's your beer," she said, still breathless from her sprint.

He'd heard her coming, her footsteps short and quick...all but running out of the kitchen. He took the can without comment as she settled onto the sofa. She was still fidgeting, even as he was taking the first drink. He stared at her without making any apology for doing so.

She stood up to him in ways that would have made his brothers laugh. She wasn't prone to hysterics and seemed to have a high tolerance for pain. Yet she ran from the night like a child afraid of the dark. Taking another drink, he tilted his head as the fluid slid down his throat, savoring the smooth tang.

"Tell me, Daisy, what *do* you remember?"

The question took her aback. But the images were quick to come to mind.

"Waking up in a tree—and hurting." She looked away for a moment.

Roman sensed she wasn't trying to hide her thoughts, but rather to gather them. He waited. It was her tale to tell.

She set the can of pop aside and then held out her hands.

"The blood. There was so much blood. I remember wondering if I was going to die."

Roman's gut knotted. He knew what that felt like.

She shuddered. "Each time I tried to move, the parachute ripped. I thought I would fall, you know." Then she looked at him. "The tree was very tall."

And you are very small.

Again, Roman was startled by the empathy he was feeling for her. It wasn't like him to be soft, not about anybody or anything—except Maddie. Where she was concerned, he was putty.

"But you got down," he said.

She nodded. "Yes. I got down." She thought of the bag and the money and looked away.

Her hesitation was obvious to a man of his profession. There was something she wasn't saying, yet he refrained from pressing the issue.

"Then what did you do?"

She looked back at him. "I started walking."

"How did you know where to go?"

"I didn't. I just followed the down slope of the mountain."

Smart girl. But he only nodded.

Her tone deepened as she continued, and he could hear the stress in her voice.

"It was almost dark before I saw the cabin." Caught up in the telling, she leaned forward. "You don't know how glad I was to see that roof. It was getting cold, and I'm afraid of the dark."

Again, saying that came as a surprise to her. She tried to laugh.

"This feels so weird. You know what I mean? It's the not knowing those little things about myself until they've snuck up on me that's driving me crazy."

Roman emptied the last of his beer and then set the can against the wall, giving her time to settle before he spoke.

"It's human nature to be in a state of constant change. I don't think it's unusual to not know everything there is to know about oneself."

Daisy leaned back, eyeing the big man with hard intent, trying to picture him in an unsettled situation.

"Somehow, I can't see you losing focus."

Roman had never felt as out of sync as he did right now. He tried to look away, but couldn't.

"Oh, I don't know. I think we all wear blinders from time to time. It's nature's way of protecting us from something we're not ready to face."

Daisy folded her hands in her lap.

"Roman?"

He hesitated to answer, wishing he was anywhere except pinned beneath that clear green gaze. Finally, he was forced to respond.

"What?"

"Are you running away from something, too?"

Only myself. But he chose not to answer her.

The wind subsided sometime during the night. Roman woke suddenly from a deep, dreamless sleep. He lay in the bed, listening for a sound from below, wondering if it was Daisy he'd heard.

But there was nothing but silence. He relaxed, telling himself to go back to sleep. Sleep wouldn't come. It took a few seconds longer before he realized that the quiet wasn't only inside the cabin; it was outside, as well.

The storm is over!

He rolled out of bed and reached for his jeans, telling himself he probably needed to put wood on the fire and knowing all the way down the stairs that he just wanted to see Daisy's face. He needed to know she was right where he'd left her—safe and warm by the fire.

He thought of trying the phone again. Maybe now that the winds had died down he would be able to get through to the ranch. Then he glanced at his watch. It was a quarter to three, which meant it was a quarter to four back home. No use waking everyone up now. There would be plenty of time in the morning to try the call.

He leaned over the sofa. Daisy was still there and rolled up in her blankets. Her hair was tousled and falling down on her forehead, as well as all over the pillow. Again, the urge to brush it out of her eyes was strong, but he stayed his ground, reminding himself not to get too close.

The fire was sputtering on a weak, dying flame, and he added some wood, taking comfort in the blaze that came forth. Then he stood, quietly moving the screen back in place and dusting off his hands, satisfied that they would be warm until morning.

He turned, glancing down at Daisy once more and making sure she was covered. Several seconds passed before he realized she was watching him. It startled him. He was the private investigator. He was the one used to doing the observations. He didn't much like being on the other end of the spectrum.

"Sorry," he said briefly. "I didn't mean to wake you."

She didn't speak, but her gaze moved over his body in a way that made him nervous. She stared, from the waistband of his jeans to the thrust of his chin and then down again. At this point, he clenched his teeth as a muscle in his jaw began to jerk.

Damn this impossible situation. "Are you warm enough?"

Her gaze locked on to his. "What's happening?"

Her voice was soft and sleepy, and the sound did a number on his heart. The barriers that he so prudently kept up were in serious trouble of shattering.

"The storm has passed...at least for the time being. I came down to add some wood to the fire."

"Oh."

Another lengthy silence ensued. The heat from the fire was warming his backside quite nicely, but it was the heat in his belly that was starting to burn.

"Go back to sleep, Daisy."

Like a child, she obeyed, and when she shut her eyes, he thought he heard her sigh.

He headed for the stairs without looking back, dropping into bed and closing his eyes, willing himself to sleep. But it took a very long time for nature to overtake nerves. It was almost dawn before it happened, and it was after nine when the smell of cooking food drifted into the loft and brought him into an upright position.

The knowledge that he'd overslept was only half as startling to him as the fact that Daisy had rummaged around downstairs long enough to cook. It was disconcerting to know he'd accepted her presence enough to sleep through the noise.

He swung his legs over the side of the bed and grimaced as he looked down at his jeans. They looked slept in, which figured, since he hadn't pulled them off after he'd gotten up last night. Then he shrugged and reached for his boots. The leather was cold and stiff as he pulled them on, and he wished he'd left them downstairs by the fire.

He grabbed a black sweatshirt from the back of the chair and pulled it over his head as he started down the stairs. By the time he came out of the bathroom, his hair was damp, as was the day-old growth of black whiskers still glistening from the water he'd sloshed on his face.

He entered the kitchen just as Daisy was taking a pan from the oven. The smell of fresh-baked bread hit him right where it mattered. His belly grumbled, but it wasn't all hunger that drew him into the room. Part of it had to do with the woman at the stove. There was a smudge of flour on the breast of her red plaid shirt, and a smaller one on the side of her cheek. Her hair was piled high on her head, but there were long, curling tendrils that had escaped from the knot, teasing the sides of her cheeks, as well as the back of her neck.

"I made biscuits." She held up the pan as if it were a seven-layer cake frosted with gold.

All he could manage was a smile and a nod.

Her eyes were alight with a joy he envied. "I wasn't sure I knew how," she continued as she set the pan on the old wooden table with a thump. "But you know, it was like you said. When I don't think about it too hard, I find I do things on instinct."

He took a deep breath and finally found the guts to speak. "You didn't have to cook."

"I know, but you've been so good to take care of me. It was the least I could do."

"Your hands…"

Still smiling, she held them up. "They're still a bit stiff, but that ointment you used worked wonders. Most of the soreness is gone." She turned and reached for the coffeepot. "Time's a great healer, you know."

The phrase had come to her from nowhere, but the moment she said it, the image of a short, gray-haired man flashed through her mind. She held her breath, certain that at any moment she would hear his voice and then know who he was. But the notion disappeared as quickly as it had come, and when she turned back around, some of the delight in her morning had faded.

Roman saw her shoulders tense and suspected she'd had another one of her "moments." When he saw her face, he knew he'd been right.

"It will get better."

Daisy blinked back tears of frustration as she poured out the coffee.

"Let's hope you don't have to say the same of those biscuits."

Again, her humor in the face of a serious situation caught Roman unaware, and he chuckled.

The transformation of his expression was startling—from cold to devastatingly handsome. Daisy busied herself with flatware and plates, and by the time the table was set, she had her emotions firmly in check.

They shared the food, but little else, each lost in troublesome thoughts. A short while later, their elation fell even further. Yes, the storm was over, but from the looks of the sky, another was impending. Twice Roman tried to use his cellular phone to call out, and each time, all he got for his trouble was static.

He kept thinking that if what Daisy remembered was true, there could be other people who'd gone down in the plane she'd been on. The authorities needed to be notified of the crash, and of her whereabouts, as well. But the snow was up over his knees, and the road he'd come up on was obliterated. Without the use of his phone, there was nothing they could do but wait for the weather to break.

Chapter 4

Davis Benton was standing on the roof of the Denver hospital when the medi-flight helicopter landed. He'd been waiting for this moment ever since he'd been notified of Gordon Mallory's plane going down. The terror of knowing his only daughter had been on the flight had been exacerbated by the snowstorm that had followed the crash. For a day and a half, search had been impossible. It was one of the few times in Davis's life when being rich didn't count. He could have bought this hospital and a dozen like it more than ten times over and never noticed a dent in his holdings. But he hadn't been able to beg, order or coerce even one pilot to take a chance on searching for the downed plane.

He'd been in Denver since the day before yesterday, waiting for a search to begin. Holly was his only daughter, in fact, his only child. They'd been close, but not unnecessarily so, and even though she was a grown woman, he was still dealing with the fact that she'd planned a trip with Mallory without telling him first.

He squinted, shielding his eyes and pulling the collar of his coat closer around his throat as the helicopter began to descend. All he'd been told was that they were coming in with three victims. Two were in serious condition. One of them was dead. His heart was in his throat as he watched the chopper descend. He kept thinking of death and how final it was.

Davis Benton had firsthand knowledge of such things. One day he'd been a happy, expectant father awaiting the birth of his first child, and before the day was out, his wife had gone into labor, delivered their baby and then died. Marsha had been taken from him without warning, yet he'd managed to survive. But if Holly was taken from him, there wasn't enough money in the world to make up for her loss.

The wind from the blades of the descending helicopter burned at his eyes as he tried desperately to focus.

Please, God, don't let Holly be dead.

When the chopper landed, his first instincts were to run toward it. But then the rescue team emerged and began unloading gurneys out of the helicopter's belly, and he found himself unable to move.

One group of hospital personnel raced past him, their expressions fixed with a purpose he didn't dare impede. His stare was blank, frozen with the horror only a parent could know as he gazed at the shape, then the face, of the first patient they pushed by him.

When he realized it was a man, his heart sank. That left only one other survivor. The odds in Holly's favor had just dropped.

"Please, please, please," Davis heard himself muttering, and blinked furiously to clear the thick film of tears from his eyes.

When the second gurney came out, even from here, he knew it wasn't his girl. The body was too long and the hair too light. They came closer, and he recognized the bloody but familiar face of Gordon Mallory.

At that point, his legs went weak. It was all he could do to stand upright as the last gurney was pulled out. When they began moving the covered body toward the rooftop entrance to the hospital, he became faint.

Hang in there, he told himself. You owe it to Holly.

"Wait!" he begged as they started to move past him.

The rescuers paused, their faces grim from the exhaustion and cold.

"Please," Davis said, reaching toward the body. "My baby...I need to see my girl."

"I'm sorry, sir," the nearest rescuer said. "But this isn't a woman. It's a man."

Davis's hand began to shake. "But Holly...where's Holly?"

The rescuer shook his head. "I'm sorry, sir, but there was no woman at the crash site. Only the three men we pulled out of the plane."

Davis was forced to step aside as they moved past him, but his mind was in a panic.

My God! They came back without her! How could they do that? Why didn't they stay to look for her?

He thought of her bleeding and disoriented, of wandering off from the crash site and then lying somewhere buried beneath the snow. Although it had been a long time since he'd bothered to pray for anything, he closed his eyes.

"Help her, Lord, because I fear right now she cannot help herself."

His mind was in a whirl. He had to get the rescue team back out there! But where to start? They'd obviously known there was a woman on board. He knew enough to realize they had probably searched as much as possible, but whatever clues would have been left had most likely been obliterated by the snow. A knot formed in his belly as the impossibility of the situation became real. What on earth were they going to do?

Then it hit him. Mallory was alive! And he would have answers. With resolve in his heart, Davis Benton bolted into the hospital.

* * *

It had been snowing since noon. As Roman had feared, the storm wasn't over. Being shut inside had made the day endless for both of them. They had done nothing but sidestep each other's presence, and now with the onset of the second wave of the storm, the cabin was closing in.

They spent the afternoon in near silence. Daisy tried to nap, and Roman pretended to read a book. He turned forty-four pages before it dawned on him that not only did he not remember what he'd been reading, but he didn't even know the title of the book. He gave it up as a lost cause and played solitaire until dark.

Then, while Roman was gathering in wood for the night, Daisy disappeared. When he heard water running in the tub, he knew where she'd gone. But an hour later, she had yet to emerge, and he was beginning to wonder if she was all right. Twice, he walked to the door with full intentions of calling to her, and for lack of a good reason, changed his mind each time.

He was in the kitchen when he heard her footsteps in the hall. A skitter of nerves danced their way down his back, but he made himself stay where he was. Instead, he reached for another potato and began to scrub it beneath the water running in the sink.

"Need any help?" Daisy asked.

"Nope."

"I took a bath and washed out a few things."

That made sense. Their choices of clothing were limited.

"I heard," he said, and scrubbed even harder on the hapless vegetable.

"It felt good to soak. Worked a lot of the soreness out in my muscles."

Soak? She was soaking. The hair stood on the backs of his arms as the image enveloped him.

"I changed clothes, too. I hope you don't mind, but you know how it is. Don't you just hate to put the same clothes back on once you've bathed?"

He turned, and the potato he'd been scrubbing fell out of his hands and into the sink while the water continued to flow.

"Uh…"

"It doesn't really fit, but it's so much warmer than the other shirt you loaned me. I know you have several, or I wouldn't have assumed."

"Fit?"

He wasn't making much sense, but Daisy thought nothing of it. The man was hardly a conversationalist. She pushed the rolled-up sleeves back up toward her elbows.

"I know it's way too long, but the cabin gets cold at night and I thought it would be warmer to sleep in."

"Sleep?"

"Yes. Your sweatshirt will be so much warmer to sleep in. You don't mind…do you?"

He shook his head, unable to tear his gaze away from what she held in her hands.

She turned away, her voice becoming fainter as she walked out of the kitchen, but he heard enough to know it was going to be a long night.

"I'm going to lay my underwear by the fireplace to dry, then I'll help you fix dinner."

Underwear. Those were the "few things" that she'd laundered. Every time he went to add wood to the fire, he'd be dodging lingerie. Well, hunky-damn-dory. Those blasted daisy panties and that bit-of-nothing bra were going to be the evening's entertainment.

He spun, turning off the water with a vicious twist of his wrist, then poking a couple of holes in the potato before tossing it into the oven with the other one he'd just cleaned.

Frustration mounted as he yanked a cast-iron skillet out of the cabinet and slammed it on the stove while considering the possibility of never speaking to Royal again.

She came back into the kitchen with that smile in her eyes, and Roman's temper fizzled like a wet match. If he hadn't come, what would have happened to her? Guilt hit him. She would probably have frozen to death, that's what. So what was a little inconvenience, compared to her life? It wasn't going to kill him to dodge a couple of unmentionables. And he was a very grown male, not some sex-starved teenager with a full set of raging hormones. So she didn't have a stitch on under his sweatshirt except those jeans, and they were so old and faded they clung to her skin like silk. So what? Now, if she'd been some tall, leggy blonde, this might have been a different story. He reminded himself again that she just wasn't his type. Daisy...or whatever her name was...was more than safe. Then she handed him a can of corn and the can opener and smiled. Yes, she was safe, but was he?

Daisy whimpered in her sleep, but the sound went unheard. High in the loft above, Roman tossed restlessly, trying to find ease, both in his mind and his bed, unaware that her dreams had taken her back into hell.

Heat waves danced just above the surface of the runway as Holly Benton got out of the cab. The private plane was there, right where Gordon said it would be. She glanced at her watch. She was early. But that was all right. It wouldn't take long to tell him she'd decided not to go. This was a step in their relationship she wasn't ready to take. In fact, she wasn't certain the day would ever come when she'd be ready to take a step like this with him. He was nice, and he treated her wonderfully, wining and dining her all over Las Vegas, but he didn't make her heart skip beats. All her life, she'd heard her father talking about how much he'd loved her mother and that the mere sound of her voice had made his heart skip a beat. She wanted that kind of relationship—that kind of love. But it wasn't going to happen with Gordon.

She turned to the cab driver. "Wait for me. This won't take long."

He settled back in the seat as she started across the tarmac. She could hear Gordon's voice inside the plane as she started up the steps. The tone was loud and threatening, and she wondered what on earth had angered him. Not once in the three months she'd known him had she ever heard him raise his voice, and because it was so out of character, she hesitated, thereby forever changing her fate.

"Damn it, Billy, it's too late to chicken out on me now."

"I don't care. I never signed on for murder."

Gordon Mallory sneered. "And it wouldn't have happened if you'd done what you were told to do."

"But I did what you said."

Gordon slapped his brother up the side of his head in frustration.

"Yeah, after the fact. This would have been an easy heist. Carl Julian had been skimming from the daily take at the casino for over six months. He had a million dollars of his boss's money in his safe. The last thing he would have done was report a robbery. What would he have said? 'Oh...by the way, the money I stole has been stolen from me.'" *He hit Billy again, only harder.* "If you'd done your job, Julian wouldn't have surprised us in the act."

"He wasn't gonna talk. You had no business killing him," *Billy mumbled.*

"I don't leave witnesses."

Holly froze. Her heart was in her throat. All she could think was that she had to get to the police. In her haste, the strap of her purse caught on the portable stairway. She gave it a yank, and everything inside went flying down the steps. Horrified, she looked up at the open doorway.

It was just as she'd feared. Gordon appeared in the doorway with his brother, Billy, right behind him.

Gordon took one look at her face and knew that she'd heard. When she began to run, he started down the steps after her, catching her by the arm before she'd reached the ground.

"Sweetheart, where do you think you're going?"

Play it cool, she kept telling herself, but her mind had gone blank. Where was a good lie when you needed one? Then she remembered the cab and tried a smile.

"I didn't have change for the cab," *she said.* "Then as I

*started up the steps, my purse caught on this stupid old railing
and look what happened.''*

Gordon frowned. She was good. He'd give her that. But he
could feel her pulse racing through her system and wasn't
buying a word of what she'd just said. Spilling the contents
of one's purse did not cause this kind of reaction.

Gordon pointed toward the cab. ''Billy, pay the man while
I get my sweet Holly out of this sun.''

Oh, God, now what do I do? She took a deep breath and
then pressed a hand to her forehead.

''No, Billy, wait,'' she said, trying to regain some control.
''I was coming to tell Gordon that I'd changed my mind. I'm
not really in the mood for Nassau after all.''

A dark smile broke the scowl on Gordon's face as he began
dragging her back up the steps. ''Oh, but Holly, I'll put you
in the mood.''

''But my things,'' she said, pointing back toward her scattered belongings.

''Where you're going, you won't be needing them,'' he
whispered.

''What are you going to do with her?'' Billy asked.

The smile on Gordon's face darkened even more. ''She
doesn't want to go. I thought I'd give her about an hour to
change her mind. Then—'' he tightened his grip on Holly's
arm ''—if she still wants out…why, far be it from me to force
a woman into anything she doesn't want to do. If she wants
out, then out she goes.''

Holly's heart dropped.

''But, Gordon, in an hour, we'll be in the air,'' Billy argued.

''Exactly,'' Gordon said, and then shoved Holly into the
plane before she could scream for help.

Daisy's head rolled from side to side on her pillow as she
struggled to breathe. Now she was caught in the darkness
behind a dirty blindfold and the rubberlike scent of duct tape
beneath her nose.

* * *

They'd been in the air for forty-five minutes, and in that time, Billy Mallory had hardly taken his eyes off of the woman Gordon had dumped on the floor between them.

"Damn it, Gordon, I still don't like this. Why can't we just drug her or something? It would be hours before she came to and we could be out of the country."

"You know me," Gordon said. "I don't leave witnesses."

But Billy stood his ground, desperately pleading his case. "Think what you're doing. Think who she is. Her old man has more money than Midas. If something happens to her, he'll tear up heaven and earth to find out who hurt her. If she dies, we'll never stop running."

Billy wasn't prepared for the blow, or the anger that came with it. When the fist connected with his jaw, he fell backward onto Holly's legs before dragging himself upright.

"You're going to be sorry," he said, wiping the blood from his lip.

Gordon cursed beneath his breath. "I already am. I should have known better than to let you get involved in something this big."

Billy spit blood as Gordon entered the cockpit, closing the door behind him. He could hear Holly Benton crying. If he hadn't looked down at her, he might have chosen a different path. But he did, and when he saw twin tracks of tears flowing out from beneath the blindfold, he snapped. Without giving himself time to rethink his actions, he yanked off her blindfold and tore off the tape before dragging her upright. He clapped his hand over her mouth and whispered near her ear.

"Keep quiet or we're both dead."

Her eyes were round with fear, but she did as she was told, watching in growing panic as he pulled a parachute from a nearby cupboard. The realization of what he intended seemed impossible to consider.

"What are you going to—?"

"You ready to die?"

She swallowed harshly, then shook her head.

"That's what I thought," he muttered, strapping her into

the chute and giving her a quick, thumbnail sketch of what to do.

"After you jump, count to ten and then pull this."

Jump? She looked nervously over her shoulder and then ran her hands across the front of the straps, feeling for the handle he'd just mentioned.

Billy glanced over his shoulder as the enormity of his betrayal sank in. His hands were shaking as he grabbed a nearby duffel bag and hung it around her neck.

"There, now," he said, adjusting the straps so the bag wouldn't interfere with the deploying chute when she jumped.

"What's in this?" she asked.

"The reason we're in this mess. I have no more stomach for crime. You can tell the authorities whatever you want, but when we land, I swear to God I'm going straight. I've pulled my last con, and that's a fact."

The roar of rage that came from behind startled them both. Gordon had come back, and God help them, she was still in the plane.

Billy threw his weight against the door, anxiously twisting the lever. The door popped, like a cork out of a bottle. Instantly, the cabin was engulfed in a blast of chilling cold. In the wild rush of wind that followed, the inside of the cabin became a maelstrom of everything that wasn't tied down.

A piece of newspaper hit Holly in the face as the pressure inside the cabin dropped. Between the weight of the parachute and the bag Billy had hung around her neck, she was helpless to stop the inevitable from happening. Along with everything else that wasn't tied down, she tumbled out of the plane and into the sky, falling head over heels like a broken doll. Hurtling toward earth, the bag around her neck was alternately choking her or pulling her down. Once as she rolled on her back, she looked up at where she'd just been. Things were flying out of the plane right behind her, fluttering like so much confetti that had been tossed to follow her down.

And then the rush of wind in her ears and the sight of the earth coming up to meet her brought her to her senses. She *closed her eyes, counted to ten, and then pulled the handle on the chute just as that damnable bag hit the side of her face. Blood was filling her mouth as the parachute deployed.*

Daisy rolled off the sofa and onto the floor just as the parachute ballooned, stopping the woman's descent with a jerk. The memory was gone the moment she opened eyes, but the instinct to run was still with her. Without knowing why, she crawled to her feet and ran out of the door and into the storm.

The brutal cold was like a slap in the face. Reality surfaced just as she fell off the porch and into a snowdrift that was over her head. She opened her mouth to scream and got a mouth full of snow instead. Choking and gasping for air, she inadvertently sucked snow up her nose, as well. The harder she struggled, the deeper she fell into the drift. Further disoriented by the engulfing darkness, she tried to dig her way out, unaware that she was upside down and digging the wrong way. When her hands hit solid earth, she panicked. Something was wrong! Fear cut deep, like the blistering cold surrounding her. There was nothing before her but blackness, and nothing to hear but the muffled sound of the wind.

The scream came at him in stereo, echoing within the cabin and then up into the loft. He came off of the bed within seconds, and was halfway down the stairs when she ran out the door. Even though he saw it happening, he couldn't believe his eyes. She'd gone out into that blizzard in her bare feet, wearing nothing but a sweatshirt that barely covered her knees.

"Daisy! No!" he shouted, but she kept on going and, moments later, disappeared from his sight.

In the seconds it took him to get down the stairs and across the room to the door, his heart had stopped and started twice over. If she got lost out there, she'd be dead before he could find her.

He paused in the doorway, shouting her name aloud. But

the wind threw it back down his throat. He reached back inside the house and hit the light switch, instantly flooding the porch with a weak but welcome glow.

And then he saw it, a dark indentation in the snow just off the porch. His heart dropped. She'd fallen into the drift! Without thinking of his own bare belly and feet, he stepped off the porch, only to find himself chest high in snow, and with more still falling.

With great effort, he began to move. Moments later, he stumbled upon something solid. To the best of his knowledge, there'd been nothing in this area but grass. What he was feeling had to be Daisy.

Thrusting deep, he began digging wildly, desperate to find her. The wind made the falling snow into a natural weapon, cutting his cheeks and stinging his eyes from the blast. And he was cold…so cold. Instinct told him to go back after some clothes, but he stayed. It was all he could do to keep digging.

When he felt fabric, then flesh, his heart skipped a beat. God help me, he thought, and went in after her, head first. When a hand suddenly closed around his wrist, he knew a moment of relief. At least she was conscious. In one motion, he scooped. When he stood, she was in his arms.

Staggering out of the snow and back onto the porch, he stumbled into the house. Clutching her close to his chest, he moved toward the sofa and the fire still burning in the fireplace.

"Daisy, can you hear me?"

When she didn't answer, his heart sank. Although her body was trembling, her eyes were closed. Snow clung to her skin, and her hair, and her clothing.

His hands were shaking as he laid her down. There was a panic in his voice that was relayed to his legs as they finally gave way. He knelt, and for a heartbeat, closed his eyes and leaned forward, resting his forehead on the sofa cushion and thanking God that she hadn't gone too far.

Daisy felt the heat first, then a pressure against her arm. When she opened her eyes, she saw him kneeling at her side.

Everything was mixed up in her mind. The dream that had sent her out on the run was gone. There was nothing left but the reality of a bone-chilling cold and the man at her side.

"What happened?"

Roman inhaled slowly, then looked up. "You went out for a little midnight stroll."

Her eyes widened. Only then did she notice the fact that they were both soaked to the skin.

"Dear God." She wiped a shaking hand across her face. "I must be going out of my mind."

She looked so small, so bedraggled, his heart went out to her.

"I know what you mean. For a moment there, I thought I was going to lose mine."

Daisy reached for him, touching the wet black hair plastered to his forehead and then grasping his wrist. His pulse was rock steady, just like the look in his eyes.

"I owe you my life."

He shook his head. "I don't believe in those kind of debts. Now, let's get into some dry clothes before we both catch pneumonia."

She started to get up.

"Stay by the fire," he ordered. "I'm going to run a hot bath. You need to get warm as quickly as possible."

"But what about you?" she asked, eyeing his bare feet and chest.

"I'll be fine," he said shortly. "I've been worse and survived. I will again."

Shuddering, she watched him walking away and knew how fortunate she was to have stumbled into his life. There was something about this man that demanded respect.

She rolled over and sat up, leaning toward the heat of the fire as melting snow puddled around her feet. And as she waited for him to come back, she kept thinking of the money hidden upstairs beneath his bed. He was taking good care of her now—but what would he think and how would he behave if he knew?

Leaning forward, she rested her elbows on her knees and covered her face with her hands as an old saying kept circling through her mind. ''Oh, what a tangled web we weave, when first we practice to deceive.'' All she'd done since they'd met was hide. And she was still hiding something from him—the truth as she knew it.

The fire was blazing. Daisy's underwear was dry and had been moved to make room for the wet clothes steaming on the hearth. By morning, the clothes would be dry. But to Daisy, the incident would never truly be over. She would never forget the panic of feeling buried alive, and then the overwhelming relief of his hand upon her thigh.

Cradling her cup of coffee between her hands, she stared into the fire, mesmerized by the flames slowing eating their way into the wood. It was thirty minutes past four in the morning. Sleep was over for her. The last thing she wanted to do was relive whatever it was that had driven her out into the storm.

Something banged in the hallway behind her. She didn't have to look over her shoulder to know it would be Roman, and not the wind. His voice cut through the silence in which she'd been sitting, sending her pulse into a swifter rhythm.

''Are you still cold?''

She shook her head, watching as he circled the sofa and then sat at the end, near her feet. She had a swift image of him stretching out beside her instead, and looked away before he could see it in her eyes. When he tucked at a loose edge of her covers, she took a quick sip of coffee, so as not to give herself away. The more she was around him, the more she wanted to be with him…in the true sense of the word.

Three days ago, she hadn't known he existed. And now, he'd become the most important thing in her life. She tried to tell herself it was all due to the predicament in which she'd landed. She didn't know who or where she was and she needed him for shelter and sustenance. And when the snow melted, she would need him to get her down off the mountain.

More than once, she'd seen the hard, unyielding side of him. But it was his gentleness and consideration that kept coming through, time and time again. That, and that slow, devastating smile. When she left, would he forget her? The thought hurt. She would never forget him.

Roman wanted to hold her. The feeling had been in the back of his mind for some time now. At least a day, maybe longer. Maybe as far back as the moment he'd seen daisies shining through the seat of her pants.

There was a knot in his throat that had nowhere to go. He'd done the unthinkable and let himself care for a woman he didn't even know. He tried not to think of the stupidity of the act, but it was almost pointless. There was nowhere he could go to escape her presence. Even when she wasn't in the room, the scent of her seemed to linger, like a fresh breath of the spring.

He kept reminding himself that she could be someone's wife—someone's mother. She could have a lover who was desperate to know of her fate. There was a selfish part of him that almost wished she would never remember—that her life would begin from the moment they met. At that point, his thoughts kept fading. What comes afterward? What happens when the snow melts? What do I do when the time comes for her to walk away? In his mind, he knew it was imminent. In his heart, the notion was abhorrent.

When Daisy stirred, he looked up. Their gazes met, then locked. A silence grew between them.

He kept looking at her eyes, then her mouth and the healing cut at the edge of her lip.

There was a muscle jerking at the side of his jaw. Daisy wondered if his belly was in knots. Hers certainly was. He inhaled slowly. When his gaze drifted down toward her mouth, she saw his nostrils flare. It wasn't much of a signal, but it was enough to let her know something of his mood. Unaware she was holding her breath, she waited for him to make the next move.

Roman's gut clenched. There was an unmistakable look in

her eyes, and he knew why it was there. More than once during the past couple of days, she'd come close to dying. When that happened to people, quite often they would turn to something to remind them how precious life really was. And what better way to do that than to lie in someone's arms, to feel the thunder of your own heartbeat rolling through your ears, to savor the feel of body-to-body contact in a never-ending embrace. With the right person, it could be heaven. But with the wrong person, it could be the biggest mistake of your life. He gritted his teeth and tried to shift the mood.

"Don't you want to try and get some more sleep?"

Her eyes never left his face. "I'm afraid to sleep."

He swallowed and tried to look away, but there was an energy between them he couldn't ignore.

"If you're afraid of a repeat performance, we could trade beds," he offered.

She shook her head, and there was a tone in her voice he'd never heard before.

"I don't need sleep."

He leaned forward. "Then what is it you need?"

Her breath caught. Say it. Tell him now. It's only three little words. I need you. That's what I need. I need you.

But the words wouldn't come, and although he could see her struggling, she remained silent.

He leaned back, only then aware he'd been holding his breath.

Daisy shuddered and then drew her knees up toward her chest, as if she'd come too close to a flame. She had to say something, do something, anything to break the tension between them.

"Then talk to me," she said softly. "Tell me all there is to know about Roman Justice."

He almost smiled. "Not much to tell."

"Then tell me the little bit."

He sighed. She was persistent. He'd give her that. Then he remembered. She'd fallen out of a plane, been up a tree and up to her eyeballs in snow, and he had yet to see her come unglued. Hell, yes, she was persistent, even tenacious, and talking should be safe.

"I'm the youngest of three brothers, and my parents are dead."

Daisy sighed, wishing she knew enough to reciprocate.

"Why did you become a private investigator?"

"I wanted to be my own boss and I needed a job that would utilize the skills Uncle Sam taught me."

Daisy frowned, a bit lost to the connection. "And that would be?"

"How to hide in plain sight."

"Can you teach me how?"

His eyes narrowed sharply. "Why would you want to hide?"

She thought of the money and then looked back at his face. If ever there was a time to trust him, it was now.

Chapter 5

"Roman?"

"What?"

"There's something I haven't told you."

His emotions went into shutdown. I knew this would happen. I let myself get too close to a stranger.

"So talk," he said shortly.

Daisy's heart dropped. The wariness was back in his voice, but it was too late to stop now. She got up from the sofa.

"Where are you going?" he asked.

She sighed. "Just wait here. You'll know soon enough."

When she started up the stairs, he stood.

She looked back just as she reached the landing, and he would have sworn there was true regret on her face. When she dropped to her knees beside his bed and then lay down on her belly and crawled under it, a knot began forming in the pit of his stomach.

Daisy came down the steps with the bag in her hand and dropped it at Roman's feet. Then she stepped back, waiting for him to make the next move.

"What's in that?" he growled.

"See for yourself. But don't ask me where it came from. All I know is, when I finally got down from the tree, it was lying nearby. I have a vague memory of falling out of the plane with it hanging around my neck."

"What's the big secret? If it's so all-fired important to you, why didn't you tell me about it sooner?"

She took a deep breath, gauging his reaction to what she was about to say.

"Men have killed for less. I didn't know you. I was afraid for my life."

"You aren't making sense," he said shortly, then knelt and unzipped the bag. The sides parted like an overripe tomato, revealing the contents all too clearly.

Roman's heart sank. Oh, hell. There was never a good or honest reason for someone to be in possession of so much cash. And she was right about one thing. Men had certainly killed for less reason.

Daisy held her breath. He was too calm. Then he looked up, and the blaze in his eyes seared her soul. All the doubt and mistrust that he'd had before was back—and a thousand times over.

"Is this yours, or did you steal it?"

The tone of his voice cut straight to her heart. Tears blurred her vision, but she wouldn't look away.

"I don't know." Her chin quivered. "I wish to God I knew, but I don't."

"There must be close to a million dollars in here."

She shrugged. "I didn't bother to count it."

He pulled the zipper and then kicked the bag toward her as he stood.

"Maybe I should have named you Bonnie, 'cause you can bet your little daisy behind that there's a Clyde out there somewhere who's wondering where you've gone."

She started to cry. Not sobs, but slow, silent tears that slid right down her face. She looked down at the bag and then back up at him and felt as if her heart were breaking.

"I don't want it. Put it somewhere, anywhere. Toss it out in the storm for all I care. I've had nothing but a bad feeling ever since I saw it."

Roman glared as she walked back to the sofa and lay down, pulling the covers up over her head.

"Hiding won't make it go away," he said shortly.

She didn't answer.

He looked back at the bag and cursed. He didn't want to be mad. He didn't want to distrust. But what the hell did she think he would do?

"I'll put it here in the downstairs closet."

She yanked the covers down long enough to get her message across. "You can throw it in the fireplace. Use it to start your next fire. Take it to the bathroom and use it for toilet paper. Just get it out of my sight."

He tossed it in the closet and then stuffed his hands in his pockets.

"Daisy."

There was a muffled answer from beneath the covers.

"Damn it, woman. Come out from under the covers and talk to me."

She emerged, her eyes red rimmed and swimming in tears, her lips quivering.

"You don't want to talk, you want to accuse. I may deserve everything you're thinking about me, but right now it doesn't feel like it, okay? Right now, I feel indignant as hell. Besides, how can I talk about this when I can't remember anything?"

"Look, I'm sorry," Roman said.

"Yes, and I'm..." The answer was right on the tip of her tongue. If she hadn't been listening to herself talk, it would have come out; she just knew it. "Oh, Roman, I almost had it," she said, and laid her arm across her eyes in defeat. "My name—it was right on the tip of my tongue."

He shook his head. If she was lying to him, then she was as good as it gets.

"It will come when it's time," he said.

A log fell off the stack and down into the ashes as sparks

flew up the chimney. Daisy shook her head, no longer able to believe in anything or anyone.

"Roman."

"What?"

"Why do I feel like I'm running out of time?"

"I don't know. Maybe your subconscious is trying to tell you something."

"Then I wish it would talk a little louder. I think I'm going crazy."

She turned over on the sofa with her back to the fire and closed her eyes.

He felt her rejection, both of him and the entire situation, and knew she was justified in feeling this way. The investigator in him kept trying to think of legal reasons as to why she could be in possession of so much money, but there were far too many illegal scenarios that kept coming to mind.

Frustrated, he shoved his hand through his hair, combing the short, dark strands in an absent fashion as he headed for the kitchen. He needed a drink. He would settle for caffeine instead.

A short while later, the rich aroma of freshly brewed coffee filled the room as he poured himself a cup. In the past few minutes, one thing had become patently clear. If Daisy hadn't trusted him enough to take him into her confidence, he would never have known the money was there. And what's more, she'd been right to hesitate in revealing the bag's presence. If the situation had been reversed, he would have reacted the same way.

Something blew against the outside of the kitchen door. He glanced toward it and then out the window. There was a faint glow to the east. Morning wasn't far away. There was another, less distinct sound behind him. He turned. Daisy was standing in the doorway.

"Roman."

"Yes."

"How much do you charge for your services?"

Although the corner of his mouth twitched, he responded with a straight face.

"Are you referring to personal or professional?"

"Do shut up," she muttered. "I'm serious."

"Enough," he said. "Although, from the contents of that bag, I don't think you'll have a problem with your bills. Why?"

"Because I want to hire you. I want you to help me find out who I am and why I have all this money."

He shrugged. "We'll see," he said shortly. "There's a real good chance that you'll remember everything on your own, you know."

But she wouldn't give up. "And there's a good chance that I won't. I have to know. Will you or won't you?"

He sighed. She reminded him of Royal, tenacious to a fault.

"I will."

"Then that's that," she said, and walked out of the room.

No, Daisy, that wasn't that, Roman thought. It was only the beginning.

Davis Benton prowled the hospital halls like a man possessed. While Gordon Mallory had yet to wake up, another stormfront had moved in right behind the first one, making further search of the crash site impossible. He kept thinking of his daughter. Holly hated the cold. And he kept mentally replaying the message she had left on his machine.

Daddy, Gordon and I are flying to Nassau for a few days. You know, a fun-in-the-sun sort of thing. I'll call you as soon as we get there so you'll have my number. Take care and I love you.

He stuffed a handful of coins into a vending machine and then wearily rested his forehead against it while waiting for the coffee he so badly needed. Although he hadn't completely given up hope, there was a part of him that had already begun making concessions with God. If he couldn't find her alive, he still needed to find her. He didn't think he could go through the rest of his life without at least laying her body to rest.

"Davis Benton?"

He turned, the hot coffee sloshing over the rim of the foam cup and onto his fingers.

"Yes, I'm Davis Benton."

"You're to come with me," the orderly said. "The patient you've been waiting to see just woke up."

"Thank you, God," Davis muttered, tossing the coffee in the trash as he went past.

A doctor emerged from Gordon's room just as they reached the door.

"Mr. Benton?"

Again, Davis nodded.

"You can't stay long," he said. "He's only just awakened, and he'll be groggy, so don't expect miracles."

Davis nodded again and started to push past him when the doctor took him by the arm, momentarily stopping him.

"If it weren't for the circumstances surrounding your missing daughter, I wouldn't be allowing this," he said.

Davis swallowed nervously. "I know, Doctor, and I appreciate your cooperation, more than you will ever know."

The doctor shrugged. "Ultimately, it's not my cooperation you need. It's Mr. Mallory's. Now, remember, don't stay long."

"I won't," Davis said, and then went inside.

Gordon Mallory's first thought upon awakening was that it felt good to hurt. After Billy had popped the door to the plane, all hell had broken loose. His fight with Billy had been put aside when the plane had suddenly gone into a nosedive.

Seeing the pilot slumped over the controls was the second-worst moment of his life. Seeing Holly sucked out of the door with his money was the worst. At that moment, he was certain they were going to die. And then Billy astonished him by climbing into the copilot's seat and taking control. The anger between them vanished, and it was anyone's guess as to whether they would make it or not.

The pilot continued to groan and clutch at his chest as the

plane kept losing altitude. Even Gordon said a few prayers. Twice they just missed going into the side of a mountain, and each time, Billy managed to keep them in the air. But when they began skimming the treetops, they prepared for the worst.

They went down in a tree-covered valley between two peaks, taking out a swath of trees and bushes with the under-belly of the plane before going nose first into the earth.

And when it was over, the silence was almost as frightening as the moments before had been. Where there had been screams and shouts, there was quiet. Great trees had snapped like toothpicks, and the fuselage of the jet was crumpled like used tin foil. Now there was nothing but the hissing sound of escaping steam and the frightening stench of spilled fuel.

He remembered trying to run and being unable to feel his legs. It was the next morning before he realized he wasn't paralyzed, only pinned down by the wreckage.

Billy was pinned in the cockpit, still alive, but from the sound of his voice, badly hurt. He answered Gordon's inter-mittent queries for several hours, but by morning, he became as silent as the woods in which they'd crashed. Gordon held out hope for a rescue up until the time it started to snow. After that, he lost all track of time.

When the rescue team broke into the cabin, Gordon thought he was dreaming. It was only when they freed him from the wreckage and he began to feel pain that he knew he was going to live. Then all his energies were focused on getting well and finding Holly, because where she was, his money would be also. He had a pretty good fix on where she'd gone down. With a little luck, he should be able to find her body.

And he was certain it would be her body they'd find. Billy had all but sealed her fate when he'd strapped a parachute to her back and then hung that duffel bag around her neck. Gor-don was convinced that the duffel bag would have interfered with the opening of the chute. And even if the chute had managed to open, the straps on the bag would have certainly strangled her. Either way, it was just a small setback. The snow couldn't last forever. All he had to do was get well and then recover what was rightfully his.

Then Davis Benton walked in the door. Gordon's first instinct was to panic, but he reminded himself there was no way Benton could know anything. There was no one left alive who could tell.

"Gordon, thank God you survived."

Gordon took a deep breath and then groaned with the pain of the motion.

"Don't move," Davis said. "Let me do most of the talking, okay?"

Gordon blinked that he understood. It wouldn't hurt to let Davis think he was worse off than he really was.

"They didn't find Holly. Do you know what happened to her?"

Gordon groaned. Hell, yes, he knew. She jumped out of the plane with his money.

"Don't know," he muttered.

Davis's hopes fell. The two small words were like a knife in the heart.

"Can you tell me what happened? Why did you crash?"

Gordon's mind was racing. Here's where he covered his tracks—just in case.

"We lost cabin pressure and I blacked out. I don't know what happened to Holly, or to the plane."

Davis wanted to cry. "Ah, God," he groaned, and covered his face with his hands.

If nothing else, Gordon Mallory was a realist. There *was* the possibility he'd never see his money again. And Davis Benton had just bought the entire story. It wouldn't hurt to add a bit to the scenario for good luck. He took a deep breath, aware that it would cause enough pain to bring tears to his eyes, and right now, he needed some tears in his eyes to say what he had to say.

The groan that came out of Gordon's mouth was not faked. The pain was real, as were the tears that followed.

Davis looked up. "Don't move," he said quickly. "I'll get a nurse."

"Don't want a nurse," Gordon mumbled. "Want Holly... my Holly."

Davis wanted to scream. "I know, son. I want her, too."

"You don't understand," Gordon continued, playing his role to the hilt. "We were eloping. She was going to be my wife and now she's gone." He closed his eyes and turned his face to the wall. "Without Holly, I don't want to live."

Davis rocked back on his heels, stunned by what Mallory had to say. Elope? He knew they'd dated. But he'd had no idea their relationship had gotten to this.

"Look, son, we need to think positive," Davis said. "I don't believe in giving up until someone else tells me it's over. And right now, I will have to see Holly's body before I quit hoping."

Gordon shook his head slowly from side to side. "It's hard to hold out for hope when you're the only survivor," he whispered.

Davis's eyes brightened as he suddenly clutched at Gordon's arm.

"They didn't tell you!"

"Tell me what?" Gordon mumbled.

"You aren't the only survivor. Your brother, Billy. He's still alive!"

The morning dawned bright and clear. Snow was anywhere from knee to chest high, but it had stopped accumulating. Roman stepped out of the cabin and took a slow, cleansing breath. Last night had, quite possibly, been the longest night of his life.

The money was still in the downstairs closet where he'd tossed it, and his accusations still hung in the air between them, although a semi-truce had been reached. When he thought about it, it was almost laughable. If he wasn't mistaken, Daisy had just hired him to solve the mystery surrounding her, and she was going to pay him with someone else's money. What was worse, he'd all but agreed to do it. If the legal system had a mind to pick nits, that probably made him an accessory after the fact to a possible crime.

He looked out into the clearing. The only thing visible of his vehicle was the roof of the cab and the upper portion of the windows. He shoved his hands in his pockets and frowned. Even if it started thawing right now, it would be two or three days before the roads would be passable.

He thought of Royal and went back inside for the phone. The air was clear, the wind almost nonexistent. Maybe now a call would go through. Knowing Royal, he'd be waiting.

Daisy was coming out of the bathroom when he came down from upstairs.

"What are you doing?" she asked, eyeing the cellular phone he was carrying.

"Going to try and contact my brother again. I just want to let him know I'm okay."

A nervous look came on her face. "Are you going to tell him about me?"

Roman frowned. "I'm going to tell him that there's a possibility a plane went down up here. Didn't you ever stop to think that there could be other survivors?"

The blood suddenly drained from her face. She could almost hear the urgency in the man's voice. *After you jump, count to ten and then pull this.*

"There *was* someone. I keep remembering a voice telling me to jump, then count to ten and pull." Her fingers fluttered around the middle of her chest, where the handle had been. "You know...the rip cord."

Another chink in the armor around Roman's heart just gave way. Every time he heard that frightened tone in her voice, he wanted to hold her.

"You did good, didn't you, Daisy?"

"What do you mean?"

"You're alive, aren't you?"

She shuddered and then sighed. "Yes, there's that." The

tone of her voice grew firmer. "Of course the authorities must know. Make the call. Do it now while I'm here."

"Then put on your shoes," he ordered. "I'm going outside. The reception should be clearer."

"Wait for me. I won't be a minute."

Roman stood for a moment, watching as she ran to get her shoes. She had put the old gray pants and the red flannel shirt back on, and even though she was dressed warm enough for indoors, the cold outside was quite bitter.

"I'm ready, Roman. Let's make the call."

He took his parka out of the closet and held it out. "Put this on first. It's cold as blazes outside. You'll freeze."

She was enveloped by its weight and warmth, as well as the scent of the man who wore it. Her heart told her that this was a little bit of what it would be like to be held within his arms.

There was laughter in Roman's voice as he leaned down to zip it up. "You're lost in there, but at least you won't freeze."

His head was close to her mouth. If she leaned just the least bit forward, she would have been able to feel the dark, springy strands of his hair on her face. She took a slow, deep breath, telling herself not to move.

Then he looked up.

The smile froze on his face as his gaze locked on to hers, and Daisy knew without words that he could see what she was thinking.

"Roman."

The sound of his name on her lips was little more than a whisper, and yet he would have heard it if she'd never voiced the word. His gaze drifted across her face, from those deep, expressive green eyes, past the natural pout of her mouth to the tremble he could see in her chin. His belly clenched with a longing that shocked him. He inhaled slowly, watching every nuance of her expression for a warning to back off. It didn't come.

"You know," he said softly. "You're not my type."

Her eyelids fluttered. "I don't like you much, either," she said softly.

"Liar."

She leaned forward and felt his breath upon her face. "I'm not."

Roman cupped the back of her neck. "Then prove it."

Daisy sighed as he came closer still. She couldn't stand it any longer. Their lips met. Someone groaned. Daisy broke their connection long enough to whisper, "Take that."

Then she kissed him again. "And that." She clung to his shoulders as he wrapped his arms around her and lifted her off of her feet. Once again, there wasn't enough room between them for a thought to pass through. "And that, too."

Roman groaned. He had more than he could take and still have good sense.

"Stop now, woman, while there's something left of me to recycle. You're right. You win. You don't like me one bit."

Roman nuzzled the side of her neck near the collar of his coat. She was the first woman he'd ever met who smelled sweeter than any perfume.

Daisy closed her eyes as her knees went weak. "I guess you'd better try that call."

Roman groaned. He didn't want to talk on a phone; he wanted to take her to bed.

"Yes, I guess you're right," he said, and reluctantly turned her loose.

"Still coming with me?" he asked.

"You couldn't lose me if you tried."

A rare smile broke the somberness of his face. "It scares the hell out of me to admit it, but I think I'm counting on that."

For the first time since Daisy's trauma had begun, she had a good feeling about tomorrow. No matter what happened now, she had Roman Justice on her side.

Roman pulled her beneath his arm as he punched in the numbers. Then he counted the rings. If Royal didn't answer before the fifth ring, the answering machine would come on. He didn't want to talk to a machine. He wanted to talk to—

"Hello! It's your nickel, start talkin'."

Roman grinned. As usual, Royal sounded annoyed. He hoped Maddie wasn't at the bottom of the problem.

"Royal, it's me, Roman."

Royal almost shouted. "Boy! It's about time you called."

"If you were so worried, you could have done the calling," Roman said.

Royal muttered a slight curse beneath his breath. "I lost the damned number to your cell phone. Maddie, I told you to take that mangy-ass cat out of this house and back to the barn."

Roman grinned. Unfortunately, his guess about Royal's mood had been right on the money. Maddie *was* the root of her father's ire. And he could hear the bell-clear tone of her little-girl voice in the background, still arguing her case.

"You heard me, girl," Royal roared. "And for Pete's sake, quit kissin' the damned thing. It's got fleas and God knows what else."

"Royal."

Royal paused in his tirade, as if he'd forgotten that Roman was even on the phone.

"Oh…yeah…sorry."

"You're going to be even sorrier if you don't clean up your vocabulary around her. Just listen to yourself. 'Mangy-ass.' 'Damned.' And who knows what else. You're going to be highly sorry when she goes to kindergarten this fall with those words on her lips."

Royal sighed. "I know. I know. Hell's fire, I need a keeper." Then he shifted gears. "Back to you. Are you snowed in?"

"Up to my chest."

Royal whistled. "You're kidding."

"No, brother, I'm not. And I have only myself to blame. Had I not given in to you in a weak moment, I could be home right now, enjoying a warm spring day, not shoveling wood into this fireplace like there was no tomorrow.''

Royal chuckled. ''Well, at least you 'got away from it all'.''

Roman glanced down at Daisy. ''Umm, not exactly.''

''What does that mean?'' Royal asked.

Roman changed tactics. There was serious business to discuss.

''Hey, Royal. I need you to do something for me.''

''Yeah, sure,'' Royal said.

''I want you to check with the FAA and see if there was a plane that went missing anywhere in this area, then get back to me.''

''Why?''

''Because I think one went down somewhere around here, and because we need to notify the authorities, if they don't already know.''

''Well, okay. But—''

Roman started to mention Daisy's presence, but he kept thinking of the money in the downstairs closet.

''Just do it,'' he said. ''And if there's one that went down, call me back with whatever information you can get and we'll go from there.''

''In the meantime,'' Royal said, ''enjoy the view.''

Roman looked down at Daisy. ''I am.''

Chapter 6

Gordon Mallory was in a panic. Billy was alive! Even if he was a screwup, he was still his brother and, in effect, had saved both their lives. But Gordon hadn't forgotten that Billy had also betrayed him. Not only had he helped Holly escape, but he'd also given away Gordon's money.

His thoughts kept turning in circles, with fear uppermost in his mind. Had Billy talked? He didn't think so, at least not yet. If he had, Gordon would have already experienced the consequences of the revelation. The fact that Gordon was flat on his back in a hospital bed wouldn't matter to the authorities if they knew he'd committed a crime. He'd never known the authorities to be particular about where they found the guilty parties, just as long as they found them.

Gordon also figured if Holly's father had talked to Billy, he would never have set foot in this room. All he could do was hope and pray that Billy had the good sense to keep quiet. If all else failed, there was the fact that Billy could still die.

Out in the hall, he could hear carts rattling. They were

bringing the food trays. He shifted on the bed, trying to find ease. Moments later, a nurse came in with a tray.

"Good evening, Mr. Mallory. Your meal is here."

He managed a smile, although how anyone could call this stuff edible was beyond him.

"I don't know why they call this food when everything is liquid."

"Now, Mr. Mallory, you're quite lucky to be alive, and I'm certain Doctor has his reasons for putting you on a liquid diet."

Gordon tried another smile. The last thing he wanted to do was antagonize his source of information. He sighed loud and long.

"I know, but it's just hard to be positive when I'm so worried about my brother. They won't let me see him and—" he let his voice drop an octave for effect "—he's all the family I have, you know."

The nurse's expression softened. "It must be rough," she said.

He nodded. "If only I knew how he was doing. Have you seen him?"

She hesitated. It was against hospital policy for a nurse to give out any sort of patient information other than affirming their condition.

Then Gordon added. "I know his condition is listed as serious."

That much she could say. "Yes, that's correct."

Gordon glanced down at his tray, as if contemplating where to start. He picked up his spoon and took the lid off a small cup to his right.

"Well, now, cherry gelatin. It's Billy's favorite."

The nurse frowned. "I'll be back later for your tray."

Gordon sighed again, hoping for a forlorn expression. When the nurse paused at the door and then turned, he hid his glee.

"Your brother is stable, Mr. Mallory. However, he hasn't regained consciousness, so that's probably why they have discouraged you from visiting. He couldn't talk to you anyway, so there's no need putting any stress on yourself by trying to walk.''

Gordon wanted to shout with relief. Instead, he maintained a calm demeanor.

''Nurse, I appreciate what you've told me. Rest assured I will keep the information to myself. And I will say a prayer for Billy's recovery.''

She slipped out the door, leaving Gordon with a lighter heart. In fact, he felt so good about the news that he jabbed the spoon in the gelatin and started to eat. He was halfway through before he remembered he didn't even like the stuff.

Davis Benton was in his hotel room and in the process of making a nuisance of himself, but he didn't give a damn. He was on the phone with search and rescue, and until they promised him what he wanted to hear, he wasn't going to go away.

''Look,'' he said, ''if it's a matter of money, I'll pay whatever it takes. The snow has stopped. The sky is clear. For God's sake, please reconsider! The least you can do is go back to the crash site and search the surrounding area. My daughter was on that plane, and even though she wasn't on board when you got there, she couldn't have gone far.''

As he listened, the frown on his face began to smooth out. The next argument he'd been planning wasn't necessary. It seemed they were already loading their gear.

''I'll be at this number all day,'' he said quickly. ''You will let me know if—''

Then he nodded as the man on the other end of the line told him what he needed to hear. Moments later, he disconnected, then dropped to the side of the bed with a thump.

The room was quiet. Too quiet. There was too much silence and too much time to contemplate his shortcomings as a father. The only thing left for him to do was pray, so he did.

Roman was shoveling a path to the woodpile. The exercise felt good, even though the air was so cold it hurt to draw a deep breath. More than once, he'd caught Daisy watching him from the window. There was a tension between them that he couldn't deny, and it had nothing to do with the weather. After what had happened between them this morning, the tension had increased. Everything he was about warned him to seize the moment—to go back into that cabin and take her to bed. He'd lived his life on the edge for too long and he knew all too well that for some people, tomorrows never came. The only certainty was the present, and even it could disappear in the space of a heartbeat.

It was the wisdom of getting close to Daisy that he questioned. Her amnesia and that bag full of money were two deterrents he couldn't ignore. He didn't want to fall in love with a criminal...or another man's wife.

He scooped the last bit of snow from the path and tossed it aside before glancing back at the cabin. Daisy wasn't at the window, but he would lay odds she wasn't too far away. He stuck the shovel in the ground and began to gather another load of wood. May as well make the trip back a useful one.

She met him at the door, holding it open as he came inside.

"Thanks," he said.

"I saw you coming," she said quickly.

He stood without moving, staring at the confusion on her face and contemplating the idea of pushing this further. His heart said yes. His instincts for survival said no.

"You're letting in cold air," she said, and slammed the door shut with a thump as Roman moved past her, dumping the wood on the hearth and then dusting the snow off his coat and gloves before hanging them nearby to dry.

She was standing so close that when he turned, he almost bumped into her.

"Sorry."

Her blush deepened. "My fault," she said, and turned away.

Roman hid a frown. They were caught in an emotional seesaw, and unless one of them had the good sense to stop it, something was bound to happen that they couldn't take back. And since his mind was supposedly sound, it was left up to him to be the one to practice good judgment.

She was busying herself at the sofa, brushing at a crumb that wasn't really there, then picking up a book. She looked as awkward as he felt.

"Daisy."

She jerked, and the book she was holding dropped out of her hands onto the sofa as she looked up.

"What?"

"About this morning…"

A faint flush spread up her cheeks.

"What about it?"

"What if you're somebody's wife?"

His meaning was all too clear, but giving up what she felt seemed a worse sin than persisting.

"And what if I'm not?" she countered.

"But you could be, and if it were my wife who was missing, I wouldn't want her in some other man's bed."

She bit her lip to keep from crying. "But I don't feel like I belong to anyone."

Her answer intrigued him. "Then what *do* you feel like?" he asked.

Like making love with you.

The thought stunned her, and she looked away, but not before Roman had seen the want in her eyes.

"Never mind," he said shortly, and headed for the kitchen, mentally cursing the size of the cabin and the snow outside. He needed to get away from her, and there was nowhere else to go but upstairs to bed. Since that was out of the question, then the kitchen it had to be. Only when he turned around, she was standing in the doorway. Her expression was grim, and there was a glint in her eyes he'd never seen before.

"I want you to understand something," she said.

He waited.

"I'm attracted to you, but I'm not stupid, and I can only imagine what you must think of me. Whether I'm married, or have a significant other, is immaterial to the fact that I am, quite possibly, a criminal.'' She drew a deep breath. ''If the situation was reversed, I wouldn't want me, either.''

Then she spun on her heel and stalked out of the kitchen, leaving Roman with the impression that she'd just thrown down the gauntlet. Whatever happened now was up to him.

It was almost midnight. Roman came out of the bathroom, towel drying his hair and glancing at the sofa. Daisy was already in bed. He looked toward the fireplace. There was plenty of wood on the fire, and the screen was in place. She should be fine until morning.

The sweats he was wearing were old, his T-shirt even older. And thanks to the bit of laundry Daisy had done this morning, the socks he was wearing were clean and dry. He tossed the towel on the back of a nearby chair and then used his fingers for a comb as he slipped past the sofa to check the lock on the door. Even though they were miles away from any sort of civilization, he locked it out of habit.

He was halfway up the stairs to the loft when Daisy's soft voice broke the silence.

''Roman.''

He paused in midstep, his heart suddenly hammering against the wall of his chest.

''Yes?''

''Good night.''

Only then did he realize he'd been holding his breath. He exhaled slowly.

''Good night,'' he said, and listened until she'd settled again.

He crawled into bed with an ache on his mind. All he could think was, damn the snow and damn this situation all to hell. He thumped the pillow several times in succession before shoving it to one side. Then he rolled over on his stomach and, using his arms for his pillow, fell fast asleep.

* * *

Locked in a nightmare, Daisy struggled to get free of her tangled covers. In her dream, they'd become the ropes around her wrists, and her sleep had become the blindfold across her eyes. She kept trying to scream, but nothing came out except sobs. God help her, she didn't want to die.

Roman opened his eyes with a jerk, his heart pounding. For a moment, he lay without moving, listening for the sound that had disturbed his sleep. Then he heard it. Daisy!

He kicked back the covers and rolled out of bed, afraid that she was about to pull a repeat performance of the night before. The last thing they needed was to take a midnight dip in another snowdrift.

He was halfway down the stairs before the sounds that he'd heard became distinct. And when he could see that she was still asleep on the sofa, his panic abated. Moving quietly, he circled the sofa to kneel down beside her. In the glow from the fireplace, the tracks of her tears had become thin silver threads stringing down her cheeks. Her forehead was knit in a frown, and she kept fighting the covers under which she lay. He hated to wake her, but watching her torment was worse.

In a voice he would have used with Maddie, he whispered her name.

"Daisy. Daisy. Wake up. You're having a bad dream."

Her eyelids fluttered, then her nostrils flared as she took a deep breath. Her forehead smoothed. The frown she'd been wearing disappeared with the dream, and as she opened her eyes, she swallowed a sob.

There was momentary confusion on her face as she focused on where she was and not where she'd been.

"Roman?"

He wiped at her tears with the balls of his thumbs. "You were having a bad dream."

Her lips were trembling as her gaze raked the contours of his face. Even in the dark, his strength shone through. The contours of his features were highlighted in the faint light from the fire. The familiarity of them gave her comfort. At last, something she knew. Something she recognized. Roman. Her Roman.

"Dear God," she whispered, and slipped her arms around his neck. "I'm so tired of this. I'm so everlasting tired of this. Ah, Roman, what if I never remember?"

Her gesture was unexpected, but the symbolic meaning was not lost on him. It was trust. Pure and simple. She trusted him, but did he trust himself?

"You will. You will," he said softly, and then pulled her arms from around his neck. "Easy," he urged when she would have fussed. "I'm not leaving you."

Instead, he sat down beside her and then pulled her into his lap before wrapping them both with her covers.

"Are you comfortable?" he asked.

Daisy shuddered on a sigh. Comfortable? The word was more like *content*.

"Yes," she said softly, and settled her head against the strength of his shoulder as he tightened his grip. She was certain that whoever she was, she'd never felt this safe. If the world—and that bag full of money—would just go away, she could be happy for life.

"Try to go back to sleep," he said.

"But you won't be able to rest sitting up."

He looked down at the crown of her head nestled beneath his chin. Considering the weight of the knot in his stomach, she felt surprisingly light in his arms. A slight grin broke the somberness of his face.

"I've been in a lot worse places."

Daisy tried to relax, but there were too many extenuating factors. As hard as she tried, she couldn't forget where she was—in Roman's arms—or where she was lying, next to Roman's heart.

The steady beat next to her ear matched her own pulse. She closed her eyes and tried to think of something else, only to become aware that one of his hands was cupping her bottom.

Afraid to move, and a bit afraid not to, she let her mind go blank. And then she felt the faint but unmistakable stirring of his breath upon her face and looked up. At that point, the inevitability of their circumstance took over.

Roman blinked, but not fast enough to hide what he'd been thinking. The impossible had happened. She'd seen through the wall behind which he lived, all the way to his heart.

"Don't," he warned her.

She pushed herself up until she was sitting in his lap, and facing him. There would be no more hiding.

"Don't what, Roman? Don't care? It's too late for that. I already do."

Her words hit him hard. And in that moment, he knew she was the stronger for having voiced the truth.

"And what happens tomorrow, Daisy? What happens after we make love? After you're embedded in every part of me? How do I give you up?"

Daisy knew what he said could happen, but there was a surge of need within her that told her to seize the moment, that tomorrow was never a guarantee.

"Then don't," she said. "Don't give me up. Ever!"

He took her by the shoulders and rolled, pinning her beneath him on the sofa as the covers slid off their bodies and onto the floor. His voice was a whisper against her cheek.

"This is dangerous, in more ways than one."

She wrapped her arms around his neck. "But, Roman, you forget. I can't remember living any other way."

He groaned and then lowered his head. Their lips met in a frenzy of need that never slowed down. He took the shirt from her body; she pulled his over his head. Piece by piece, their clothing came off until they were lying naked in each other's arms. He shoved a tousled lock of her hair away from her eye and then kissed the spot where it had been.

"Still hate my guts?"

Her eyes were alight with desire. "Clear to the bone," she said softly.

He brushed his mouth across the crest of a breast, before moving on to the other one. When she gasped and arched to his touch, he stopped and pulled back.

"Friendly enemies?"

She nodded and encircled him with her hand. "You know what they say about fine lines between love and—"

He thrust against her hand and when she felt him growing, hardening, pushing toward a promise of ecstasy, she knew this was going to be right after all. Then tears blurred her vision, leaving him slightly out of focus.

"Oh, Roman."

He thrust again, gritting his teeth against the need to hurry.

"What, baby?" he said softly.

"No regrets?"

A swift pain hit him right in the vicinity of his heart, but it was gone as swiftly as it had come. His head bent as he kissed an escaping tear.

"No regrets."

She wrapped both arms around his neck and pulled him down until all of his body weight was resting on her.

"Wait! I'm too heavy for—"

She soothed his concern with a touch of her hand to his cheek.

And then so it began.

A log shifted on the fire, sending up a shower of sparks that crackled and popped. Outside, the wind played with the last fall of snow, lifting it up into the air and then letting it go. Like the tides, there was a steady rise and fall, from without, and within.

Roman moved them to the floor. Cushioned by the covers they'd tossed aside, they made love with a frightening passion. Whispers sifted into the silence. There was a quick gasp—a soft sigh. Touch followed touch; kiss followed kiss. Each step of the loving continually moving them toward a certainty they could no longer deny.

And finally, there was a fever in the blood that demanded release. Roman shifted, moving between her legs and then holding himself suspended above her. He looked down into her face—that beautiful, beautiful face—and knew a moment of pure peace. And yet the man he was gave her one last chance to pull back.

"Still sure?"

The need to be with him was making her crazy. It was all she could do to answer.

"Yes, oh yes."

He slid inside.

For one brief, silent moment, neither breathed—neither moved. The suddenness of their joining was replaced by a familiarity that they'd done this together a thousand times before.

For Daisy, the world tilted. She grasped his forearms, needing to hold on to solid substance. Her body was shaking, her voice full of tears.

"Roman...oh, Roman."

He pulled back, but only a little. Just enough to let her feel him once more, and as he did, her eyes closed and her lips parted with a sigh. He thrust again—slower, deeper. When she arched beneath him, his world suddenly focused on the feel of being inside her.

"Ah, baby," he whispered, and the dance began.

Time lost all meaning. It could have been minutes. It could have been hours. They rode the heat, letting it build between them until it began to consume.

For Daisy, it came in a swift and blinding flash, taking her out of herself and then dropping her back into place without warning, leaving her weak and breathless and hopelessly in love.

But Roman was prepared. He'd felt it coming. That need to hurry on the edge of sweet pain. Each stroke bringing him closer and closer. And there was Daisy, beneath him, around him, begging, holding on to him because she'd already taken flight.

It was the heat of her body, and the tiny tremors within her that sent him over the edge. That and the fact he couldn't bring himself to let her go alone.

Muscles corded in his arms, in his neck, in his back. It

came over him in a wave, then spilling into her with a groan, shattering the last of the wall behind which he lived.

Their bodies were slick with sweat, their hearts hammering against their chests. But there was a knowing between them that hadn't been there before. He looked into her eyes and thought, So, woman…you may not know your name, but I know you.

"Have mercy," he whispered, and kissed the edge of her lips. Then he rolled onto his side and pulled the covers over them.

Daisy didn't move, couldn't move. She lay within the shelter of Roman's arms, waiting for her heartbeat to settle back into a normal rhythm.

Just before they fell asleep, Roman thought he heard her whisper.

"I take no prisoners."

He fell asleep with a smile on his face.

Chapter 7

It was just after dark when the phone rang in Davis Benton's hotel room. He came out of a deep sleep within seconds of the sound, grabbing for the phone.

"Hello."

"Mr. Benton. This is Lawrey, of search and rescue."

"Yes, Mr. Lawrey. Any news?"

"I'm sorry, sir, but no. In fact, the snow is so deep that any further searching is futile."

Davis's hopes fell. "But—"

"Understand that we will resume the search as soon as the snow melts. I don't know if you're aware, but the snowfall was well over four feet. With the drifts, it's often over six feet deep. She could be anywhere, and we'd be walking right past her...or on top of her. Do you understand?"

Davis groaned. Although the images were sickening, he understood all too well.

"Yes, and thank you for calling," he said.

When the line went dead in his ear, he started to cry. This was hell. If only he could wake up to find it had all been a dream. He thought of Gordon. If Holly had loved him enough to marry him, then he deserved to know the decision search and rescue had made. The last thing he wanted to do was get dressed and go out, but it was something that had to be done.

Gordon Mallory was progressing. It was unfortunate the doctors couldn't say the same for his brother, Billy. Billy Mallory's condition hadn't changed. He was stable but still in a coma. The head injury he'd sustained when the plane had crashed had been severe, and even though the doctors were doing everything possible, he had yet to wake up.

Gordon had made a public show of grief as he'd instructed the doctors not to put Billy on any sort of life support, claiming it would have been what Billy wanted. He didn't know that for certain, but it was definitely what Gordon wanted.

His entire focus was on getting out of the hospital and finding his money. Thanks to Billy, Holly had all the money. In a way, Gordon looked upon this judgment as fair. After all, if Billy had minded his own business, none of this would have happened...so it stood to reason that if someone had to pay, even with a life, Billy was it.

Lost in his own world, Gordon was startled when the door to his room opened, but when he saw who it was, he adopted the proper attitude of grief.

"Mr. Benton! Any news?"

Davis tried for a smile. It never came.

"Some, but it's not good. The search has been called off until after the snow melts."

"Oh, no!" Gordon cried. "Don't they know she could freeze to death?"

Davis's shoulders slumped, and his voice started to shake. "Actually, they didn't come out and say it in so many words, but I believe that's already what they think."

Gordon groaned and covered his face, but to hide his elation, not his grief. He had his own plans for finding the interfering bitch, and they didn't include mixing with a search-and-rescue team. If he had to, he was going to walk the entire area over which they'd been flying, and by damn, he'd find his money if it took the rest of his life.

"I'm so sorry," Davis said.

"I don't know what I'm going to do," Gordon said.

"Come home with me to recuperate," Davis offered. "It's the least I can do."

Gordon wanted to crow with delight. Although he had left a small nest egg in a Las Vegas bank, this was perfect. A free place to rest until he was back to full strength.

"That's very generous of you, Mr. Benton, but I can't leave my brother, Billy. He's going to need around-the-clock care. I'll have to stay here to—"

"We'll move him to Las Vegas, too. There are plenty of care facilities out there, and if he's able, he can stay at the estate. Now don't argue. I won't hear of you having to bear this on your own. In times like this, people need to stick together."

Gordon gathered his sheet around him, pretending to smooth out the wrinkles.

"I don't know how to thank you," he said. And it was true. He didn't know how to say thank-you. It was a skill he'd never learned.

Davis nodded. "I'm going back to the hotel now. If there's anything you need, please call. Meanwhile…"

Gordon smiled. It was a pious bit of playacting that would have made his old daddy proud.

"Meanwhile," Gordon echoed, "I'll be saying prayers for us all."

Davis left, assured that he'd done everything necessary to make things right. When he exited the hospital, it was almost dark. He flagged a cab, and the ride back to the hotel was one of the longest rides he could ever remember. He kept thinking that it wasn't fair, that a parent should not outlive his or her children. It was too much pain for a person to bear.

Roman had been awake for some time when dawn came to the mountains. After making love by the fire, they'd moved upstairs to his bed. Daisy had crawled into it, and into his arms without reservation. The crazy part was, it hadn't seemed strange to him, either. They hadn't known each other a week, and yet they'd made love with a familiar passion. Now here they were, sharing a bed as if they'd done this every night of their lives.

Part of Roman's restlessness was due to the woman in his arms, the other to a large dose of guilt. He kept thinking of what they'd done. Last night, making love to Daisy had seemed so right. Even more, it had *felt* right. She'd matched his emotions with a passion of her own that had surprised him. But in the light of day, there was a truth he couldn't deny. Daisy was a beautiful, loving woman, but she might not be free to give back that love. That was what worried him. That was what hurt. He looked down at her, wondering if, when the time came, he would have the guts to give her up.

She lay spoon fashion within his arms, her back to his chest, her head pillowed upon his arm. He held her close, his hand resting just beneath the softness of her breasts. In repose, she looked so innocent, but what the hell was an innocent woman doing with that bag of money?

She sighed in her sleep and then rolled over, burying her face against his chest. It was a gesture that didn't go unnoticed. He felt the burden of her trust and hoped when the time came he would have the strength to do the right thing.

The contents of the purse went flying, spilling everything that had been inside. Lipstick rolled off the edge of a step and fell to the pavement below. The faint shattering sound of the compact mirror breaking sent the woman into a panic.

Get away, get away! I have to get away.

Her legs felt weak, her body devoid of breath. No matter how hard she tried to move, she seemed frozen to the spot.

He'll find me here. I have to hide!

A shadow fell over her shoulder and onto the steps in front of her. Her mouth went dry. Someone grabbed her by the arm. Before she could scream, a hand clamped around her mouth while she was yanked up and backward. The last thing she saw was a patch of blue sky, and then everything went dark.

Daisy jerked and then gasped, trying to breathe for the woman in her dream. In the midst of her panic, someone caught her, holding her close and whispering words of comfort that set her heart back into a normal rhythm. She opened her eyes and then sighed as she remembered where she was, and who it was who was holding her.

"Roman."

"It's okay, baby," he said softly, smoothing the tangles of her hair away from her face. "I've got you. You're safe."

She shuddered, then slid her arms around him, holding him close.

"Something spilled, I think."

"What?"

"My purse…I think I dropped my purse."

He frowned. In the grand scheme of the mess she was in, that made little sense, but he let her talk, knowing she needed to get it all said.

"Then what?"

"I tried to run, but my legs wouldn't work."

He knew that feeling. It was pure, unadulterated fear. Only someone defensively trained would have been able to bypass that very human reaction. Gentling her in the only way he knew how, he held her close, letting her tell the story at her own pace. She continued.

"They heard me, you know."

"Who heard you, baby?"

Her mind went blank, and as hard as she tried, nothing else would come. She leaned her forehead against his chest in frustration.

"I don't know. Oh, God, I don't know."

Damn. Hiding his own frustration, Roman kissed the side of her face.

"It's okay. Look on the positive side. This is more than

you remembered yesterday. Just focus on the fact that things are coming back to you.''

She looked at him, and there was such terror in her eyes. ''What if—?''

He shook his head. ''No ifs. First rule—deal only in known facts.''

She tried to smile. ''Who's rule is that? The military, or some private-investigative thing?''

''Neither. It's something my father taught me. I guess you might say it's just the Justice way.''

The mention of his family made her think of the brother he'd called.

''Do you think your brother will call today?''

Roman tilted her chin with the tip of his finger and centered a hard kiss on the curve of her mouth.

''He'll call when he has something to tell me and not before.''

Daisy cupped the side of his face, remembering the way he made love and wishing they could stay like this forever.

''Is he like you? Your brother, I mean.''

''No one is like Royal. He's a law unto himself.''

A slight frown furrowed her forehead. ''Would I like him?''

Roman grinned. ''Probably. Most women do.''

''What does his wife think about that?''

''His wife is dead. He's been raising his daughter, Maddie, by himself almost from the start. Doing a good job of it, too. But don't tell him I said so.''

Daisy's expression grew solemn. ''How sad for him. How old is Maddie, anyway?''

''She's four, going on forty. She's definitely a female, just short.''

''She's probably resilient, too.'' Daisy said. ''I know I was. My mother died when I was…'' She paused in midsentence, a look of wonderment coming over her face.

Roman tensed. When she hadn't been concentrating, a truth had slipped out.

"Oh, Roman. I remembered something." Her voice was shaking. "My mother died when I was born."

"See," he said softly. "Like I said. When you're ready, it will come."

Daisy closed her eyes and turned her head, but Roman wouldn't let her hide, not even from herself.

"Daisy. Look at me."

She sighed, then did as he asked. "What?"

"Why did you do that?"

"Do what?" she said.

"Turn away from me."

Her hesitation was brief, but it was there all the same.

"Daisy…don't you think that last night moved us past the stage of keeping secrets?"

She nodded.

"You should be happy that things are coming back to you. Right now, they don't make much sense, but in time, they will. So what's the problem?"

Her lips were trembling as she looked into his face.

"I think I'm afraid."

He groaned and then hugged her close. "I'm with you on this all the way, remember?"

"But, Roman, what if you were right all along? What if I stole that money?"

"Then we'll give it back and deal with the consequences."

"What if the consequences aren't all I have to deal with?"

"What do you mean?" he asked.

"What if it's like you said? What if there's a man in my life?"

There already is a man in your life. Me. But he couldn't say it, and no matter how hard he tried, he couldn't ignore the fact that when her memory came back, the woman she would become might not like the man he was.

She slid her arms around his neck and pulled him closer. Her voice was soft, her gaze filled with tears.

"Roman?"

"What?"

"It's been a long time since last night."

The longing in her voice matched the one in his heart, but he was too attuned to what was still wrong between them to ignore how right this all felt.

"Have you faced the fact that getting more involved might make things worse?" he asked.

Daisy locked her fingers at the back of his neck.

"Right now, the worst thing I can think of is losing you."

He shook his head and grabbed her wrists. "Damn it, Daisy, you're ignoring the truth. You don't have me." And I damned sure don't have you.

Her voice started to shake as tears welled in her eyes. "Truth? You're my truth. You're my yesterday, and you're my tomorrow. Don't *you* understand? I can't remember anything or anyone but you."

Pain tore at his gut as he pulled her close again. "I understand more than you think. And I know something you aren't willing to face. Whatever you feel for me now is based on fear. You think you love me because I make you feel safe. You get your memory back, and then see how you feel. Until then, I think the less talk of making love, the better off we'll both be."

She tore free from his grasp. Tears were streaming down her face as she stood. Just when he thought she was going to stomp away, she spun, and there was a fervor in her voice he couldn't ignore.

"You speak for yourself, Roman Justice. Maybe you don't have the guts to trust your heart, but I trust mine."

Gordon was mobile.

He was a man who'd dreamed of traveling in style, and the gaping back of his hospital gown and the IV he was wheeling up and down the hall had never been part of the dream. But he was also not a man to stand in the way of progress, and getting off his back and onto his feet was progress indeed.

The nurse at his side was nothing like the elegantly dressed women he usually cultivated, but she would do until something better came along. At least this nurse had succumbed to his charms and his story. She'd taken him farther up the hall than he'd ever gone before, and that was just where he wanted to be. Up two more doors, and then the next room would be Billy's. It was simple. All he had to do was get there.

"You're doing great, Mr. Mallory, but I think we've gone far enough for today. We need to turn around and—"

Damn, damn, damn. Not yet. Not yet.

Gordon paused, pretending to rest while his mind was racing. And then a nurse burst out of a room up ahead and started toward them. When she drew near and realized it was Gordon she saw, without thinking, she burst out with her news.

"Good news, Mr. Mallory. Your brother is coming to."

The fact that Gordon paled was not lost on the little nurse at his side.

"Here, now," she said quickly. "You've been up too long. You need to get back to your bed."

Gordon shook off her hand. "No. I need to see my brother. That's what I need." And he started up the hall toward the open door.

"Wait, Mr. Mallory. You can't—"

He staggered inside, one hand clutching his broken ribs, the other dragging his IV. His gaze went directly to Billy, and had he not known for certain it was his brother in that bed, he would never have recognized him. Unprepared for the shock, all he could do was stare.

All those tubes. All those machines. And his face! My God.

"He's not as bad as he looks," the nurse said quickly, and grabbed Gordon by the arm, guiding him out of the room and back down the hall. "Most of that is superficial swelling, and the bruises will fade with time."

Gordon's stomach pitched, and it was with great effort that he made it back to his room before he heaved up the contents.

Long after the nurse was gone, the image of his little brother's face kept moving in and out of his mind. He kept remembering the days of their childhood, and hearing his mother reminding him over and over that Billy was his responsibility. That he was the big brother and to make certain that Billy didn't come to harm.

He closed his eyes, hoping sleep would help him escape the reality of the truth, but even then, it was with him. It was all Gordon's fault that Billy was in this mess. He'd needed a lookout at the casino. He'd talked Billy into doing the job, even though he hadn't really wanted to. And he hadn't planned on killing the casino owner. It had just happened. It was no wonder Billy had freaked out in the plane. It was no wonder he'd strapped a chute on Holly Benton and dumped the money out with her when she jumped.

Gordon accepted the guilt for the mess they were in. He hadn't meant to hurt anyone, but he'd gotten caught up in the power of having so much money in his hands. He'd been willing to do anything to keep it. Even murder...twice. If he had it to do over—

Then he cursed beneath his breath. It didn't pay to look back. What was done, was done. All he had to do was focus on getting better and, thanks to Davis Benton's offer, getting Billy out of this hospital and back to Las Vegas. The bottom line was, he didn't want his brother to die.

He tried to roll over, groaning aloud as he shifted position. It was no use. His ribs hurt too much for the effort.

"Well, damn, little brother. We nearly had it made."

There was little rest for Gordon that night. He was forced to lie in the bed, contemplating his sins and praying that whatever Billy might say in the future, the authorities would attribute to hallucinations, and not the truth.

It was beginning to thaw. From the loft where Roman was standing, he could hear water running off the roof. On the one hand, that was good. The supplies he'd packed were running low. But that also meant they would have to leave. The insular world in which they'd been existing was about to come to an end. Just the possibility of never seeing Daisy again made him sick. But if there was a man on the other side of this snowfall who had a prior claim on her, it could happen.

He leaned over the railing and looked down. She was sweeping up the bits of wood chips and ashes that were scattered on the hearth, oblivious to the fact that she was being watched. He glanced at the closet near the front door. There was a small fortune in that unassuming bag he'd tossed inside. As he looked back at Daisy, he kept asking himself, What's wrong with this picture? Experience told him to be wary until he knew all the facts, even though his heart was already committed. Instinct told him he already knew all he needed to know. She was innocent. She had to be.

He started down the stairs, suddenly needing to be near her, to see that look she got just before he touched her. A board creaked beneath his weight and Daisy turned with an expression of hope upon her face. Before either of them could speak, Roman's cellular phone rang, shattering the quiet with a rude reminder of the civilization they'd left behind.

Daisy froze as an overwhelming urge to hide came over her. Roman saw her fear and understood. It would be Royal. He ran the rest of the way to the phone.

"Hello."

"Little brother, how goes it?"

"It's starting to melt," Roman said. "What did you find out? Were there any reports of missing planes?"

"Yeah."

Roman's gut clenched. "So tell me."

"Some private plane went missing right before the snow. Took off from Las Vegas bound for the Bahamas."

The Bahamas. A good place to launder a whole lot of money.

"Go on," Roman urged, refusing to let his imagination get ahead of the facts.

"They found it before that second snow hit. Three on board. Two survivors, one dead. They are being hospitalized in Denver."

"Anything else?" Roman asked.

"Search and rescue is supposed to go back after the snow melts."

"Why?"

"To look for another body. It seems there was a fourth passenger in the plane, but she wasn't anywhere around when they pulled the others out. They're guessing she wandered off after the crash and probably froze to death. Have to wait until the snow melts to find her body."

The knot in his belly tightened. "She?"

"Yep, and are you ready for this. It was Davis Benton's daughter."

Roman frowned. The name was familiar. Benton? Benton? Where had he heard that name before? And then it hit him.

"Benton, as in the computer magnate?"

"That's what they said. I guess this was one of those times when being rich didn't help."

"What was her name?" Roman asked.

"Uh, Holly, I think the name was Holly."

"And the other passengers. Who were they?" Roman asked.

"Hang on a minute, will you? I have it all written down somewhere. Maybe in my other jacket. Here, talk to Maddie while I go look."

Roman winked at Daisy, trying to ease the tension on her face, and then covered the phone long enough to explain what was going on.

"Royal is looking for something. He's putting Maddie on the phone."

And then a sweet little voice piped in his ear. "Hello, Uncle Roman."

"Hey, Little Bit, what have you been doing?"

She sighed, and he could imagine the look on her face—the one she wore just before she unloaded a list of wants in his ear.

"Jus' nothin'," she said.

He grinned. "Nothing? You haven't done a thing since I left?"

Her voice grew smaller, more pitiful. "No, not a gol-durned thing."

He stifled a laugh. Royal was going to pitch a sweet fit when he heard that come out of her mouth.

"What about that cat you were playing with the other day?"

Her sigh deepened. "I can't play with it no more. It's flea-bit."

He chuckled. "Anymore. You can't play with it anymore."

"That's what I jus' said."

This time he had to laugh, and as he did, wished he could share the moment with Daisy. She looked as upset as Maddie sounded.

"Uncle Roman?"

"What, honey?"

"When you comin' home?"

"As soon as the snow goes away."

The moment it came out of his mouth, a loud clunk sounded in his ear. He could hear Maddie's footsteps as she ran away, and then he heard Royal yelling at her from across the room. Moments later, Royal was back on the phone.

"What the hell did you say to her?" Royal asked.

"Nothing."

"Well, you said something. She lit out of here, yelling at the top of her lungs that she was going to build a snowman before the snow was all gone." He snorted beneath his breath. "It's in the high eighties down here."

Roman laughed. Now he understood. "She asked me when I was coming home. I told her I'd come as soon as the snow melted. I guess she thinks when it snows, it snows everywhere."

"Oh, great," Royal muttered. "Now we'll be talking about weather patterns for the next week. I swear, I don't know where all that curiosity comes from."

"Royal…" Roman prompted.

"Oh, yeah. The notes. Now, what was it you wanted to know?"

"The other passengers. Do you know who they were?"

"Only names. The deceased was the pilot, Everett Bailey.

The two survivors are brothers. Gordon Mallory and his brother, Billy. My source told me they buy and sell real estate.''

Roman frowned. "Is that all?"

"Yeah, except…"

"Except what?" Roman asked.

"Well, not that it matters, since she never made it to the altar, but the missing woman was eloping with one of the Mallorys. Don't know which one. Hell of a thing, isn't it, to lose your sweetheart on the eve of a wedding?" Then he muttered, more to himself than to Roman, "In fact, it's hell losing her, no matter when it happens."

Roman's heart sank. Elope? That meant love—love strong enough to marry. Ah, God. Then his mind went back to the matter at hand.

"What about Benton?"

"What about him?" Royal asked.

"Is he in Denver, too?"

"Oh, yeah. They said he's been hounding search and rescue every day, and can you blame him? I'd be doing the same."

"Did they say where he was staying?"

Royal glanced down at his notes. "No, but if I was guessing, I say at the most expensive hotel in the city."

"Thanks, Royal. I'll be in touch."

"Take care, Roman. See you when I see you."

The connection was broken. Roman straightened and then looked at Daisy, trying to imagine her as someone named Holly. It didn't work.

"What did he say?" Daisy asked. "Am I a criminal?" Then her face crumpled. "Oh, please, Roman, tell me. I can't stand it any longer. Did I murder someone? When you take me back, are they going to put me away?"

He wanted to hold her, but considering what had to be said, keeping his distance seemed the wisest move.

"Does the name Benton mean anything to you?"

Chapter 8

Something nudged at the back of Daisy's mind, but it was too far back to remember. Her gaze was fixed and almost panic-stricken, her expression grim.

"No. Should it?"

Some of the tension Roman had been holding dissipated. He'd prepared himself for a revelation that hadn't happened.

"Maybe," he said, although he knew in his heart the answer should have been yes. The coincidence of her parachuting from a plane other than the one that had crashed would have been ludicrous.

Daisy staggered to the nearest chair and dropped. Her hands were in fists, her body shaking.

"Tell me," she said. "I have to… No, I deserve to know what was said."

Roman sighed. She was right.

"A plane did go down. The timing coincides with your arrival here. It went down the evening before the storm."

She swallowed once, but remained silent, her gaze fixed

upon the sternness of his expression. She was afraid—so afraid.

"They didn't find it until after the first snowfall had ended. There were three people on board. The pilot was dead, but there were two brothers on board who survived." Roman shoved a hand through his hair, while watching her every move. "As soon as the snow melts, they're going back out again to look for the woman who was supposed to be on board."

Her heart dropped. Oh God. It has to be me.

"Who was she?" Daisy asked.

"Her name was Holly Benton, the daughter of Davis Benton."

Again, something whispered in the back of her mind, but the voice wasn't loud enough to be heard. And then she focused in on the way Roman had spoken his name.

"Is he somebody? Davis Benton, I mean."

Roman nodded. "'Somebody' is hardly the word. The man is a megamillionaire. Controls a huge share of the computer market."

She thought of the money in the bag. Maybe that would explain why she had so much with her. But that didn't really make sense. No one, no matter how rich, carried hundreds of thousands of dollars around in a bag.

"Is that me, Roman? Am I Holly Benton?"

Roman shrugged. "Most probably. Royal indicated that her father was pretty upset about the fact that the search was called off without finding her."

She covered her face with her hands. "Oh, God. Why can't I remember something as important as a parent?"

Roman's belly was in a knot. Once he said it, there would be something worse between them than their earlier suspicions of each other. There would be the guilt. Hers for not remembering she was about to become a bride. His for taking what had been meant for another man.

"Do the names Gordon or Billy Mallory mean anything to you?"

Damn you, Billy! What have you done?

She jerked. The voice had come out of nowhere, and with it, an inordinate degree of fear. Her voice was trembling and it was all she could do not to cry.

"Why?"

Roman took a deep breath. "Because Holly Benton was on her way to the Bahamas with one of the brothers to get married."

She stood abruptly, her words running into each other like tumbling blocks. "No. That isn't me...wasn't me. I would remember something like that. I would remember loving—"

Roman took her by the shoulders, holding her until she was forced to look at him.

"Don't fight a truth we both knew could be there. We did what we did, and it can't be taken back. But—"

Daisy tore free of his grasp, her eyes huge and filled with tears.

"Don't you understand? I don't want to take it back!" She pressed the flat of her hand over the center of her heart as tears fell down her face. "It's not true!" she cried. "I would know it in here if it were so."

Roman reached out for her, but she spun and ran for the stairs. There was a pain in his chest that kept spreading, threatening to swallow him whole. He wanted to go with her, to run and hide, but there was nowhere to go. Once a truth had been spoken, it became impossible to deny its existence.

When he turned away, there was a stillness on his face that his family would have known, and for which they would have grieved. It was the wall behind which he lived. This woman hadn't died, but he was losing her just the same.

He picked up his phone and walked into the kitchen to hunt for a paper and pen. He had some calls to make. Somewhere in the city of Denver, one man believed he'd lost a daughter, while another believed he'd lost his future wife. Neither deserved to spend an added night living with such sorrow.

Davis Benton was coming up the hall to his room when he heard a phone beginning to ring. His heart began to pound.

It was coming from inside his room. He jammed the key in the lock and dashed toward it. Slightly winded, his voice was unusually curt.

"Hello. Benton here."

When Roman heard the man's voice, another knot was added to the others sitting in the pit of his stomach. This was one more step to the distance he was putting between himself and Daisy.

"Mr. Benton, my name is Roman Justice. I'm a private investigator out of Dallas, Texas."

Davis frowned. He'd had a few quack calls already, one from a lawyer offering to sue the dead pilot's family for the loss of his daughter, and another from a psychic who claimed she'd seen his daughter safe and sound and asleep in some cave. The urge to hang up was strong, but something made him hesitate.

"Look, Mr. Justice. I don't know why you're calling, but I can assure you that whatever services you think you can offer, I have more and better ones already at my disposal. So thank you, but no—"

"There is a woman standing beside me who doesn't remember her name. A few days ago, I came up to Colorado for a fishing trip and found her in my cabin. She claims to have parachuted out of a plane."

Davis froze. Please God, don't let this be a scam.

There was a distinct silence, and for a moment, Roman thought the man had hung up.

"Mr. Benton?"

Davis stuttered, trying to regain his composure. "If this is some hellish scheme to extort money from me, I swear I'll have you—"

Roman interrupted before the threat could be made. "Look, Mr. Benton. I don't want your money. I'm trying to help Daisy, not you."

Davis's heart sank. "It can't be my daughter," he said. "Her name is Holly."

If Roman hadn't been hurting so much inside, he would have managed a smile. "I told you, she doesn't remember who she is. I'm the one who gave her that name."

No longer able to stand, Davis dropped to the side of the bed.

"My God, my God," he whispered, and wiped a hand across his face.

"Mr. Benton?"

Davis shook off his shock. "Yes?"

"Will you describe your daughter to me?"

Davis frowned. He hadn't become wealthy by being stupid. "No, you describe this...this...Daisy person to me."

Roman swallowed past the lump in his throat. "Daisy, honey, come here, okay?"

When Daisy walked into Roman's arms, the fear on her face was almost palpable. Yet when his arms came around her, she knew that for a while, she was safe.

Roman gazed down at her face while talking to Davis Benton on the phone.

"She's not very big. In fact, the top of her head doesn't quite touch my chin, and I'm over six feet. Her hair is dark and shoulder length. Her eyes are green and there is a very small scar beneath her chin. When she laughs, her nose wrinkles just above the bridge and—"

Davis started to cry. "Oh God, oh God, that's my Holly. Please, let me talk to her. Let me hear her voice."

The weight around Roman's heart continued to pull as he looked down into Daisy's face.

"Just understand one thing, Mr. Benton. She doesn't remember her own name, so she's probably not going to remember you, either."

Davis nodded, and then realized they couldn't see. "Yes, yes, I understand," he said quickly. "Just let me hear. I'll know for sure if I hear her voice."

Roman handed Daisy the phone. "He wants to talk to you."

Her hands were shaking, but her voice was calm. As long

as Roman was beside her, she could handle anything that came her way.

"Hello?"

Davis choked on another sob. "Holly? Holly? Is that you?"

Daisy sighed. "I don't know, but I wish to God I did. It's very disconcerting to look into a mirror and see a stranger."

Davis's pulse leaped. That voice! That voice! He would have known it anywhere.

"Holly, sweetheart, it *is* you! Dear Lord, how has this happened? Why did you parachute from the plane? Why haven't you called sooner? Why—?"

Daisy paled. There were too many questions for which she had no answers. She thrust the phone back at Roman and hid her face against his chest.

Roman took the phone from her hands as he pulled her close.

"Mr. Benton, this is Roman Justice again. I don't know what you were saying just now, but Daisy is pretty upset. I think she's a little overwhelmed by all of this."

Davis took a deep breath. "I'm sorry. Of course. I don't know what I was thinking. But there are so many things I want to know."

"Yes, sir, and so does she. Unfortunately for her, she remembers nothing before coming to in the tree."

Davis's voice rose an octave. "Tree?"

Roman almost smiled. "Yes, sir. She dropped into a very wooded area, and the parachute got caught in a tree. She'll have to tell you all of that at a later date, but I'll say one thing for her, she's quite a survivor."

Davis could not contain his joy. "You must tell me how to get there. I can't wait to touch her. To hold her." His voice broke. "My God, I've been trying to face planning her funeral."

Roman understood all too well how Davis must have felt, because right now, he was facing a loss of his own.

"I understand, sir. But there's too much snow up here yet to drive down."

"To hell with driving down," Davis shouted. "I'm coming up in a chopper. Just tell me where you are from the nearest city. We'll find you."

Roman gave him directions, all the while knowing that within a matter of hours, Daisy would be gone from him forever.

"Do I have them down right?" Davis asked after reading the directions back to Roman.

"Yes."

Davis glanced down at his watch. "It's probably too late to get there today. We're about out of light. But I'll be there early tomorrow." His voice rose again, as the joy of his planning became obvious. "My word! I just realized during all of this time I never once thought of Gordon. He's going to be ecstatic. They were eloping, you know!"

Roman's arm unconsciously tightened around Daisy's shoulders. So, it was Gordon Mallory. He couldn't find the will to comment.

"Mr. Justice, you'll never know what this call has meant to me," Davis said.

And you'll never know what this call cost me. "Yes, sir. I can imagine."

"May I speak to Holly one more time?" Davis asked. "I want to tell her I'm coming."

Roman handed Daisy the phone. "Here," he said quietly. "And hang in there, baby. You've come this far. Don't quit on yourself now."

She took the phone from his hand and lifted it to her ear. "Hello."

"Holly, I'm sorry about before," Davis said quickly. "I was so excited that I didn't think about how you must feel."

She exhaled slowly, accepting the truth of her fate. Within days, Roman would no longer be a part of her life.

"I can understand that," she said.

"Good! I just want to let you know that I'm coming after you first thing tomorrow."

Panic hit again as she looked up at Roman. "But that's not possible," she said quickly. "There's still too much snow."

Davis laughed. "That won't stop me from getting to you. I'm coming by helicopter. By this time tomorrow, you'll be safe and sound back in your own home, and this will be nothing more than a bad dream."

Daisy couldn't comment. Her heart was breaking. What she'd endured had been all nightmare. With Roman, she'd had a very real glimpse of heaven on earth. Leaving him seemed impossible to consider.

"Oh," Davis added. "I'm on my way to the hospital now to tell Gordon face-to-face. I can't wait to see his expression when I tell him his future wife is still alive."

Daisy wanted to scream. This was the real nightmare. "I don't remember promising to marry anyone," she said quickly. "Please, Mr. Benton, I don't want to—"

Davis interrupted. "I know. I know. I just meant that Gordon should know. In no way would I shove him down your throat. Please don't be afraid. I can't bear to think you'll be afraid to come back to your own home."

Daisy sighed. Obviously, this was something that had to be faced.

"Just as long as you understand."

"Of course, of course," Davis said quickly. "Now, you rest easy tonight. I'll see you tomorrow."

"Yes," she said. "Tomorrow." She started to hang up when she heard him shouting. "Yes? Was there something else?" she asked.

Davis knew his voice was shaking, but he wouldn't let another moment of his life pass without telling her what was on his mind.

"Holly."

"Yes?"

"I love you, sweetheart. Very, very much."

When the line went dead in her ear, Daisy handed the phone to Roman. She took one look at the expression on his face, then turned and walked away.

* * *

Gordon's afternoon had been long. He'd gone over the events of the past couple of weeks so many times in his mind that he'd given himself a headache. Once he'd looked up in time to see a uniformed officer pass by his door. He broke out in a sweat, certain that Billy must have talked. When the officer passed without so much as a glance his way, his relief gave way to a hysterical fit of the giggles.

Guilt. That's all that was wrong with him. Just a case of the guilts. Everything would work out. It had to. He'd planned too diligently and done without for far too long to give it all up now. That money was his. All he had to do was find it.

He was halfway through his supper when he heard Davis Benton's voice out in the hall. He laid down his fork, preparing himself for a proper attitude of grief. What he got was indigestion instead.

Davis all but ran into the room. His face was wreathed in smiles, and there was a bounce to his step that didn't make sense.

Gordon frowned. What the hell was going on? This was no proper attitude for a man who'd just lost a daughter.

"Mr. Benton. It was good of you to come," Gordon said.

Davis laughed and clapped his hands. "This just couldn't wait," he said. "She's alive!"

Gordon froze. It couldn't be. He couldn't be talking about Holly. He'd seen her sucked out of that plane with that bag hanging around her neck like a deadweight. Even if she had survived the drop, there was no way she could have survived that blizzard.

"This isn't funny," Gordon said.

"No," Davis crowed. "It's a miracle, that's what!"

Gordon's voice cracked. "How do you know? Maybe it's a mistake!"

"No! No! No mistake! I talked to her on the phone." He turned in a circle, unable to contain his joy. "I heard her voice. Dear God, I heard her voice!"

Gordon jerked, sending the tray on his table to the floor in a crash of tin and plastic. Moments later, a nurse came running, followed by another.

Davis hugged one and patted the other one on the back. "Sorry about the mess. It's all my fault," he said, laughing at no one in particular.

They began cleaning up spilled food while Davis moved to one side, unaware that Gordon's quiet had nothing to do with shock and everything to do with pure, unadulterated fear. Gordon was convinced that any moment, that officer he'd seen earlier in the day was going to come into the room and place him under arrest. He kept trying to remember the name of that lawyer he'd played poker with back in Vegas, but his mind was blank. What he didn't understand was why Davis was so damned happy with him. If the situation had been reversed, he would have had murder on his mind. Then he stifled a laugh. The irony of what he just thought was not lost on him. Murder. That's what had gotten him into trouble in the first place.

Finally, the nurses were gone, and Gordon caught himself holding his breath, waiting for the proverbial ax to fall.

"Look, Mr. Benton, I never intended—"

Davis interrupted. "All this time, we thought she was dead. It wasn't ever said, but it's what we thought."

Gordon nodded. That much was right.

A slight frown dampened Davis's enthusiasm. "There is a small problem." And then the frown disappeared. "But nothing that time won't help, I'm sure."

Gordon flinched. Here it comes.

"She's suffering from amnesia. She didn't recognize me."

For the first time since Davis Benton had entered his room, Gordon knew a moment of true joy. Hallelujah, he thought. My luck hasn't all turned bad.

"Not even me?"

Davis frowned. "I'm sorry, but no. Not even you."

Gordon dropped back onto the pillow and closed his eyes. There is a God.

Davis read Gordon's behavior as despair. He couldn't have been more wrong.

"Don't worry, son," Davis said. "When we get her home—you know, back in her familiar surroundings—she'll be her old self in no time, I'm sure. But for now, you must realize her position. We're all strangers to her. We must restrain from pressuring her in any way. Her emotional state is very fragile."

Gordon's relief was so great that he felt like crying. A reprieve. It wasn't much, but it was enough to go on.

Davis left soon afterward, convinced of Gordon's love for his daughter. He'd seen the tears in Mallory's eyes himself. For the first time in days, Davis went to bed with his heart full of hope, while Gordon spent a sleepless night in hell, trying to console himself with the fact that if Holly was alive, then his money must be somewhere nearby.

Roman tossed another log on the fire just as Daisy came out of the bathroom. She was wearing another one of his sweatshirts, and from the looks of her, nothing else. The ends of her hair were damp from her bath, and her face was scrubbed clean. She could have passed for a teenager until he looked in her eyes. They held a look as old as time.

Roman wanted to hold her, but he kept remembering that she'd promised herself to another man. He set the fire screen in place and then looked away, kicking at a small piece of bark that had fallen onto the hearth.

Daisy took a deep breath, and then the words spilled out of her, like blood from a wound.

"I'm afraid of tomorrow."

He looked up, then nodded. So was he.

Her face crumpled as a sob tore up her throat. Doubling her fists and thumping viciously at the sides of her legs, she began to pace.

"I hate this. I hate everything about it. I thought I wanted to remember, but I was wrong. I don't want to remember anything but you." She collapsed on the sofa and buried her face in her hands.

Roman couldn't stand back any longer. He knelt before her and then took her hands away from her face.

"Look at me!" he demanded.

She turned her face away, unable to face what he might have to say.

Roman ached, for her and for himself, but several hours earlier, he'd accepted a truth about himself. If he had it to do over again, he wouldn't change one minute of their time together.

He cupped the side of her face, his voice softening.

"Look at me, baby."

She did, because he asked—because she didn't have it in her to deny him anything.

"Did you ever stop to think that when you see your father, your fears might go away?"

"But they won't," she sobbed, and threw her arms around his neck. "I know they won't."

Roman groaned and pulled her close. "You don't know that for sure."

"Oh, Roman, you don't understand. I keep thinking back to when I first saw you. I was so scared. I wanted to run away, but there was nowhere to go. And you were so angry with me and so distrustful." When he would have interrupted, she shook her head, refusing to give him the right. "No, don't argue," she said softly. "It's the truth, and rightly so. But something happened to me that I didn't expect. I fell in love with you, and when we made love, it sealed that fact in my heart. I am afraid to let you out of my sight. I am afraid I never see you again that I will die from this pain."

Roman's heart had been aching ever since he'd talked to Royal, but when he heard what she said, it felt as if he were coming apart at the seams. It hurt to draw breath. It was killing him to be touching her now and still know she belonged to someone else. In spite of his pain, he had to be strong for her. She didn't belong to him anymore. Hell, if he would be honest with himself, she'd never really belonged to him, except in his dreams. He grabbed her by the arms, shaking her to get her attention.

"Damn it, woman, you didn't die before. You're not going to die now," he said roughly.

"But, Roman, in a way, that's not true. I did die. I mean Holly died. You gave Daisy life, and she's all I know."

He lifted her fingers to his lips, gently kissing the palm of each hand. Her scrapes were almost healed. They'd been the last visible reminders of her accident. Soon she would be gone, just like the scars from her fall. It took every ounce of strength he had not to rage at the injustice of fate.

Daisy leaned forward. Her lips grazed the edge of his mouth, then centered on the curve of his lips.

"Roman, please don't let me go. Fight for me, damn it. Tomorrow, tell Davis Benton that I matter to you." Then her voice shattered, like splintering glass. "Or am I fooling myself? Am I the only one who cares this much?"

Anger darkened the blue in Roman's eyes to a thunderous shade of gray.

"Don't even go there," he said shortly. "I care." Then he took a deep breath. He was about to cross a line, but she'd bared her soul. The least he could give her was what was left of his heart. "I care." His voice softened. "But I made love to Daisy. Holly is marrying another man."

Daisy started to cry in earnest. "I'm not! I won't! And I wish tomorrow would never come."

He crawled onto the sofa beside her, then wrapped his arms around her, burying his face in the curve of her neck.

Daisy dug her fingers into his hair and pulled, forcing him to look her straight in the eyes.

"Today isn't over. Today I'm still Daisy. Make love to me, Roman, before it's too late."

Everything inside of him said no, but for once, his heart wouldn't listen. He inhaled sharply, breathing in the scent of her, then rolled, pinning her beneath him.

"This is only going to make the goodbye worse."

She shook her head. "Nothing is worse than goodbye."

There wasn't enough fight left in him to argue. And God help him, he wanted this, more than she could know.

Chapter 9

Roman's mind was telling him no, but his heart was shouting yes. He lifted Daisy from the couch and started walking toward the stairs that led to the loft. When he paused, she looked up. Before they went any further, he had to ask.

"No regrets?"

Blinded by tears, she shook her head. "Don't ask me that," she said. "Just take me to bed. At least for tonight, make this nightmare go away."

He could no more have refused her than he could have stopped breathing. He went up the steps, holding her close to his heart and wondering if she could hear it breaking. By the time he laid her down on the bed, his vision was blurred from unshed tears. For a moment, neither moved—neither breathed. They were lost in the pain on the other one's face.

Daisy reached for the hem of her shirt, and Roman moved.

"No, baby, let me," he said softly, and pulled it over her head, leaving her bare to his sight.

Daisy held up her arms. "Come lie with me, Roman. Make love to me now so that I never forget."

Her words tore at him in a way he could no longer ignore. Hit with the unfairness of it all, his pain turned to anger. He tore off his clothes and then moved on top of her, as if staking a claim. His words were clipped and low, his body shaking with unchecked passion. He grabbed her arms and pinned them above her head, branding her mouth with his, tasting the salt of her tears and taking away her breath.

"Don't you ever forget!" he said harshly. "You *were* mine. Even if it wasn't right. Even if it wasn't fair to those who knew you first. Even then...don't you *ever* forget!"

Daisy tore free from his grasp and wrapped her arms around his neck, pulling him closer, urging him with every ounce of her being to take her.

"Then give me something to remember you by."

Without foreplay, without warning, Roman slid between her legs and thrust, wanting to bury himself within her, wishing he could stay there forever.

Daisy arched to meet him, giving back as much as she took, and still it wasn't enough. She kept trying to concentrate on the scent of her man, on the way he held her close and the feel of his breath upon her face. But soon everything turned from thought to feeling as her body began to burn.

Time had no meaning. Focus shifted to the sound of flesh upon flesh, of quick gasps and harsh grunts, of soft, meaningless cries and deep groans of sweet joy.

Daisy left the earth first, taking flight on a hard, desperate plunge. Out of control, her body bucked beneath him, taking the last ounces of pleasure from the best of the pain.

Locked in the ebb of her climax, Roman gave up the fight and let go, spilling deep into the woman beneath him. One spasm after another, he shuddered, then groaned, holding back nothing, giving her all that he was. All that he would ever be. And when it was over, rolled her up in his arms and held her while she cried.

Roman hadn't slept a wink. Long after they'd made love for the last time, he lay quietly on the bed in the dark with

Daisy still in his arms, watching the contours of her face becoming more and more apparent with each passing hour. The tracks of her tears were still on her face when the day began to dawn.

There was a phrase that kept going through Roman's mind. Something about morning coming softly. He wanted to curse. This morning wasn't coming softly. It was ripping through the darkness, taking away the last vestiges of hope.

And while dawn was meant to signify new beginnings, for them it was the beginning of the end. Roman had walled himself off from all feelings, concentrating instead on what was to come.

A helicopter that would invade their solitude.

A father in search of a daughter.

A return to a past that Daisy couldn't—or wouldn't—let herself remember.

He kept trying to work the duffel bag full of money into the facts as he knew them, but no matter how many ways he considered them, nothing made much sense.

A child of wealth, as Holly Benton obviously was, had no need to steal, yet she was in possession of a king's ransom. As an investigator, he knew to never overlook the obvious, and that would also include the other passengers who'd been on that plane. Whatever the pilot had or had not known about the situation was now moot. He was dead and buried. That left the Mallory brothers. What was it Royal had said? Real estate? They dealt in real estate? Eloping with a million dollars, give or take a few thousand, wasn't standard procedure. Had the Mallorys been up to no good? And did Holly know, or was she somehow an innocent party to whatever had gone down? He frowned. Everything was supposition until she remembered.

Daisy stirred in his arms, and he tightened his hold, unwilling to turn loose of their last moments together. But then she opened her eyes and looked up at him without speaking. In the silence, he felt the pain of her withdrawal. The accusation was still on her face: if you loved me, you wouldn't let me go.

He cupped her cheek with the palm of his hand, silently pleading for understanding. It wasn't up to him to choose. Until she remembered everything from her past, they had no chance at a future.

She went limp in his arms and buried her face against his chest.

"Oh, God, Roman. It's here."

It took everything he had not to make love to her again. "What's here?"

"The morning."

There was such devastation in her voice, and he knew just how she felt. But delaying the inevitable was futile.

"I know, and I think we should be getting up. It would be better if you were dressed when your father arrives."

She groaned and clung even tighter. "It might be better for him, but not necessarily for me."

Roman gave her one last, long embrace and then crawled out of bed, giving her the space to do the same. He began pulling on his jeans.

"I'll make some breakfast."

"I don't want to eat," Daisy said. "I will throw up if I try."

His expression softened. "Then coffee. You can at least have some coffee."

She rolled to the side of the bed, then sat on the edge, staring down at the floor.

"Remember the night when I crawled out from under this bed?"

As he reached for his boots, he saw his hands were shaking. He sighed. That night was a lifetime ago. He dropped down on the side of the bed and began pulling them on.

"Yes, I remember," he said.

"I felt certain I was going to die." A small smile broke the somberness of her face, never quite reaching her eyes. "But I didn't, did I?"

He shook his head, letting her ramble, waiting for her to make her point.

"That's what you've been trying to tell me all along, wasn't it?" she said.

"What do you mean?" Roman asked.

"It's the uncertainty about all of this that scares me the worst. You, I know. You, I love. I don't remember loving Davis Benton, but maybe I did, and I know I have to give this meeting a fair chance."

"Good girl."

"But there's something I want you to do for me in return."

"Name it," Roman said.

"Hang on to that money for me. There's something inside of me that's afraid to let it be known it's in my possession. Call it instinct, call it lack of guts, call it anything you choose. But for now, I don't think anyone should know I have it."

He frowned. "I don't like it. I think you should show your father—"

"No!" Her vehemence was impossible to ignore. "Don't you understand? Until I remember everything, I don't know who to trust. The only person I know and trust is you." She stood, holding the sheet in front of her like a limp and wrinkled shield. "Will you help me?"

Against his better judgment, he agreed. "I'll help you, and you know it. But if I don't hear from you within a few days, I'll make my own decisions about the damned stuff."

She nodded. "Fair enough."

He finished dressing and stalked downstairs, telling himself he was probably getting into something way over his head. But there was no denying that Daisy didn't know whom to trust. And there was every possibility that someone had committed a crime to get that money. Until they knew for sure where it came from, he would keep her secret safe.

They stood together on the porch, watching as the helicopter descended from the sky. A good portion of the snowfall had already turned to runoff, leaving the ground beyond the cabin a mixture of mud, slush and snow. Daisy leaned closer against Roman's shoulder, then reached for his hand. Threading his fingers through hers, he squeezed gently, just to let her know he was there.

"Holly, they're here."

Startled, she looked up at him. "Why call me that now?"

It hurt to say it, but a truth was a truth. "Because that's who you are and who you have to be."

"And if I don't want to?"

He shook his head.

A short, stocky man emerged from the chopper. Ducking the downdraft of the blades, he started toward the cabin at a lope.

Something clicked inside of her. Although she didn't recognize him, there was a familiarity within her that eased part of the tension she was feeling.

"Easy, baby," Roman said softly. "It's going to be all right."

She looked up at Roman and shook her head. "Not from where I'm standing."

"I'm right here beside you," he said.

"For how long?" she muttered, and looked back at the man coming toward them. "You're sending me away, remember?"

Roman groaned beneath his breath. "I'm not sending you anywhere. You're going home. There's a difference."

Daisy wouldn't budge. Her chin jutted mutinously. "I'm standing on the only home I know."

"Damn it, don't make this any harder than it already is."

Her eyes flashed. "Then don't let them take me—"

Davis Benton heard the last part of what she was saying and interrupted before she could finish.

"Holly-berry, I won't take you anywhere you don't want to go."

She froze. Somewhere in the back of her mind, she could hear herself laughing at the name. She gasped as her belly drew itself into a knot, then stared long and hard into the stranger's face.

"Davis Benton?" she asked.

This was harder than Davis had expected. Knowing that the very sight of him brought fear to his own daughter's face was devastating. But he'd fought longer wars than this and won. Holly was worth whatever it took to get her back.

"Yes, dear, I'm Davis Benton. I'm your father."

Up until now, she'd refused to think of herself by that name, but now there was no denying it.

So, I truly am Holly Benton. She stepped forward and held out her hand.

Awkwardly, Davis grasped it, wanting to pull her to him, but settling for a brief handshake, instead.

"And you, sir. You would be Roman Justice?" Davis asked.

Roman nodded.

Davis's smile was wide and open. There was no mistaking his gratitude and joy.

"You've given me back a reason to live. How can I ever thank you?"

Roman glanced down. Daisy—he amended the thought— Holly was silent, too silent. There was a distant expression on her face, as if she'd removed herself from the both of them to preserve her sanity. He looked back at Davis. There was no mistaking the seriousness of the tone of his voice.

"By taking good care of your daughter."

"That's a promise," Davis said, then glanced at what Holly was wearing. The clothes were outdated and a little bit large. He glanced back at Roman.

"The least you can do is let me reimburse you for the use of your wife's clothing."

Roman's expression never wavered. "I'm not married, and I told you before, the only reward I want is Holly's safety."

Davis looked from Holly, to the man beside her and then back again. He glanced down. They were holding hands. In itself, that meant nothing. It was simply a gesture of reassurance for a woman who was afraid to let go. And then he looked at the expression on his daughter's face. Not once in the time she'd been dating Gordon had she looked at him like she was looking at the man beside her. A piece of anger turned loose in his mind. Had this man taken advantage of her when she was most vulnerable?

Roman could almost hear what was going through Davis Benton's mind, and it was the last straw in a day that had barely started.

"Benton."

Roman had Davis's attention. There was more than warning in his voice.

"What?" Davis asked.

"Don't even go there," Roman said softly.

Davis flushed. "I don't know what you—"

"You know exactly what I mean," Roman said. "Get that look off your face. Get that thought out of your mind."

Holly had been puzzled as to what was going on, and then suddenly grasped what was *not* being said. Anger spilled out of her in a rush.

"Mr. Benton, if you have something to say to me, then say it," she cried. "But don't start laying blame at anyone's feet." And then she laughed bitterly. "I realize I can't speak for Holly Benton, but I can certainly speak for Daisy, and she's a grown woman. She doesn't need anyone's permission to do anything she chooses."

When she called him "Mr. Benton," Davis began to worry. This woman looked like his Holly, but she was certainly more forceful than Holly had been.

"If it will make you more comfortable, I will call you Daisy. And you're right. No twenty-seven-year-old woman needs her father's permission to do anything."

Holly relaxed, absorbing the tiny bit of news that she was only twenty-seven. It felt as if she'd lived a lifetime after what she'd been through last week.

"You call me what you choose, but you will not judge me. I won't accept it."

"Fair enough," Davis said, exhaling slowly. That was close. He gave Roman a closer look. Whatever had gone on between them, his daughter was obviously ready to defend her right to do it.

"Mr. Justice, are you certain we can't give you a lift? From the air, it's quite obvious that the roads are still impassable."

Roman shook his head. "No."

Davis glanced at his daughter. "Is there anything you want to take with you?"

She glanced at Roman. Only him. When Roman's gaze darkened, she looked away and answered. "No, I guess not."

"Then we'd better be going," Davis said. "I chartered a plane to take us back to Las Vegas." He waved his hand toward the snow and mountains. "The sooner I get back to warm air and sunshine, the happier I'll be."

Holly tensed. This was it. She turned to Roman, begging him with one last look to stop this madness before it was too late.

"Holly."

Hope surged. He wasn't going to let her go after all. She took a step toward him, but the look on his face stopped her intent.

"What?" she asked.

"Find the truth, and the truth will set you free." Then he lifted his hand to her face, brushing a flyaway strand of hair from her eyes. "I'll be in touch."

She suddenly panicked. "I don't know how to reach you!"

Roman pivoted. "Wait a second. I'll be right back." He disappeared into the cabin, leaving the pair alone on the porch.

Davis fidgeted, knowing quite well it would be prudent to wait before he mentioned the rest of what he had to say, but prudence was not one of his strong suits.

"Your fiancé is in the hospital, anxiously waiting for your return. I'll take you to visit him before we fly home to Vegas."

Holly stiffened. "I don't have a fiancé," she said shortly.

Davis persisted. "But of course you do! You were eloping when the plane went down. Didn't Justice tell you?"

Her chin jutted mutinously. "Yes, actually, he did. And I'll tell you, just like I told him. I don't believe it. I don't feel it in here." She put her hand over her heart, but Davis ignored it, and her.

"You just don't remember, that's all. In time, it will all come back to you. You'll see."

She kept thinking of the money. Something was wrong with this story; she just knew it.

She glared at him, muttering to herself as much as to him. "Don't treat me like I'm simple. I didn't have a ring, so I wasn't engaged. How long had I known him?"

Davis looked startled. "Oh, uh, about three or four months, I believe."

"Was I an impulsive woman?"

He shook his head. "No, actually, you're pretty grounded in everything you do."

"Was I the kind of woman who would elope with a man I hardly knew?"

She was backing him into a corner, and he knew it. "Actually, I was a little surprised, but he said you were—"

Holly pounced. "Oh! Then we're operating on the word of a man who thought I was dead."

Davis frowned. Put like that, it sounded suspect. And then he discarded the idea.

"Holly, dear, you're just distraught, and I can understand why. Please believe me when I tell you that you're under no pressure from me or anyone else to do anything you don't want to do. Just come home. Give us a chance to prove we're right."

"I have little option," she said, and then turned to look as Roman came out the door.

"Here," he said, and handed her one of his business cards. "Call me any time, day or night. I check my messages regularly. I will get back to you as soon as possible, okay?"

Holly clutched the card tightly in her fist and, for the first time since the helicopter had landed, felt a small sense of relief. At least now she didn't feel as if she was losing him for good. Even though she was leaving him behind, he'd given her a way to reconnect.

Ignoring Davis Benton's presence, she threw her arms around Roman's neck.

"Thank you for everything."

Roman hugged her fiercely, knowing that when he let go, Davis would take her away.

"Like I said, I'll be in touch," he whispered.

To Roman's surprise and her father's dismay, she kissed him soundly before tearing herself away.

Davis took her by the arm and began leading her to the waiting chopper. She kept looking back, as if expecting some sort of reprieve.

And even after they were airborne and flying away, her gaze stayed fixed upon the man on the porch. It did her heart good to know that the entire time she was watching, he hadn't moved a step away from watching her go.

Holly exited the hospital elevator with a rebellious glare. Davis took her by the arm and began escorting her down the hall.

"Just for the record, this is entirely against my wishes," she said.

In spite of the fact they kept moving toward Gordon's room, Davis seemed sincerely apologetic.

"But what if it triggers a memory?" he asked. "Don't you want to remember?"

More than you can know. But she didn't say why. Until she could explain the money to herself, she wasn't about to mention it to anyone else.

"This is it," Davis said, and stepped aside, motioning for her to enter first.

At that moment, Holly wished Roman were at her side, not this man who called himself her father. She took a deep breath, bracing herself for the confrontation, and walked through the doorway.

Gordon was dozing. Roused by a touch on his arm, he heard someone calling his name and opened his eyes. The last person he expected to see standing beside him was Holly Benton. And the still, almost judgmental, expression on her face came close to stopping his heart. Afraid to move, he held his breath, terrified of what she might say.

Aware that things weren't going as he'd envisioned between the pair, Davis began the conversation.

"I know just how you feel," Davis said. "When I saw her, I was speechless, too. Aren't we blessed?"

Gordon nodded, trying to smile and hoping it didn't look as sick as he felt.

"My God," he muttered, looking back at Holly again and knowing he had to say something appropriate. "Holly...my darling, this is a miracle."

Holly didn't speak. She kept staring and staring into Gordon Mallory's face, and the longer she looked, the less she trusted him. He had yet to meet her gaze straight on, and he didn't seem glad to see her; he seemed scared. Why would her appearance cause him this type of concern? Her eyes narrowed thoughtfully as she took careful note of his injuries. He looked pretty good, considering the fact that he'd survived a plane crash.

Gordon was worse than nervous. That cold look on her face, as well as her silence, was unnerving. He cast a nervous glance at Davis, wishing them both to hell with no way back.

"What's wrong with her?" he asked. "Has her speech been affected by the accident, too?"

Holly answered on her own behalf. "There's nothing wrong with my speech, or my mind," she said. "The fact that I can't remember either of you does, in no way, mean I've lost the rest of my faculties. I'm sure you can understand how unsettling this is for me. I'm thrust into the midst of strangers who expect me to take their word for everything, which in fact, I cannot."

"Of course, of course," Davis said quickly. "No one expects you to—"

Holly interrupted, her patience worn well past the pretense of manners.

"I'm sorry, sir," she said. "But that's the problem. *You* do expect things from me I'm not willing to give, and I'm sorry if it hurts to hear that. I've promised to go back with you to Las Vegas, but I will in no way honor a promise I don't remember making. I have no intentions of marrying this man—ever." Holly turned to Gordon, fixing him with a cool green stare. "I'm sure you understand my position," she said shortly. "And while I wish you a speedy recovery, I have no intentions of trying to resume any sort of relationship."

Ire flooded Gordon's being. The infernal little bitch. How do I know she isn't pulling this amnesia stunt to get out of revealing the whereabouts of my money?

Davis took his daughter by the arm. "Holly, dear, I can see that coming here was a mistake after all. This could have waited until we all got home and in more comfortable surroundings."

She gave her father a startled look. "What do you mean, 'we all get home'?"

Davis looked a bit nervous as he explained. "Why, I've invited Gordon and his brother, Billy, to convalesce at the estate."

Holly felt as if the walls were closing in around her. Roman, damn you, why did you let them take me away? Then she remembered his card and felt in her pocket, making sure it was still safely intact. It was there. He was only a phone call away. She exhaled slowly.

"That shouldn't be a problem. The west wing is always reserved for guests. We..."

Stunned by what she'd just said, both men couldn't help but stare at her.

Holly shrugged. "That keeps happening to me. I don't

know what I'm going to say until it pops out. Roman says that's normal and that one day I'll remember everything.''

Davis was elated. What had just happened confirmed what the doctor who'd examined her had also said. He had to restrain himself from hugging her. This was such a positive sign and one he'd been praying for since he'd learned she was alive.

As for Gordon, he could only stare in horror. For him, it was another nail in his coffin. The more time passed, the less were his chances of escaping justice. Between Billy's revival and Holly's resurrection, he was another step closer to ruin.

Chapter 10

The temperature was in the high eighties when Roman pulled into the parking garage below the complex in which his office was located. He got out of his car, then stood beside it, giving the area a thorough sweep before he popped the trunk. The weight of the duffel bag he slung over his shoulder was nothing compared to the weight of responsibility he felt in having it in his possession. He headed for the elevator with his hand resting on the gun beneath his jacket.

The ride up to the fourteenth floor was swift, but for him, none too soon. Last night, before he'd left the cabin, he dumped the money in the middle of the living-room floor and started to count. When he passed the five-hundred-thousand mark, he began to sweat. When the count had risen to over nine hundred thousand, he'd gone into shock. By the time he had finished, the count was so close to a million dollars, the few thousand it was off hardly mattered. And he'd promised to baby-sit the damned stuff until further notice.

Within a few short minutes, it would be safe and sound behind lock and key.

His secretary looked up as he entered the office, surprised to see him.

"Mr. Justice! I didn't expect you in today."

"Afternoon, Elizabeth. And you still haven't seen me, okay?"

She smiled. "Yes, sir. I understand. If you don't mind my asking, when *am* I going to see you?"

Roman returned the smile. "Day after tomorrow. I'm going out to the ranch in the morning. Got to see a little lady about a cat. At last report, it was flea-bit and severely off limits."

Elizabeth's smile broadened. Her boss's fondness for his four-year-old niece was a well-known fact. She would have been stunned to know that another woman had gotten under his skin, as well, but in a different sort of way. She went back to her work as Roman entered his office, shutting the door behind him.

Roman paused inside, adjusting to the culture shock of civilization. This ultra modern high-rise was a far cry from the simplicity of the Colorado cabin he'd left behind. There was a stack of faxes on his machine and a small mountain of messages on his desk. A couple of packages had come in the mail that had yet to be opened, and a picture hanging on the wall over his desk was slightly askew.

But his focus was on the locked door across the room that led to a large walk-in closet. Inside were the classified files he kept regarding all of his cases, as well as a genuine reissue of an old Wells Fargo safe. More than once, he'd considered getting rid of the monstrosity. Now he was glad he had it.

In a few quick strides, he was inside the closet and down on his knees, working the combination. When the last tumblers clicked, he opened it, tossing the duffel bag inside. Only after the safe was shut, and the door locked behind him, did he breathe a quiet sigh of relief.

He dropped into the chair behind his desk and then swiveled toward the bank of windows, staring blankly out across the Dallas skyline. The view was lost upon him. He kept remembering the hurt on Holly's face and the fear in her voice.

Don't let me go. You are my world. Don't let me go.

He jumped up from the chair as if he'd been catapulted and stalked to the windows. The traffic on the streets below seemed to be moving in fits and starts, just like the beat of his heart. Guilt was a kicker. He closed his eyes and took a slow, deep breath. Damn this situation to hell and back.

Moments later, he found himself back in the chair with the phone in his hand.

"Elizabeth, get me the home phone number of Davis Benton in Las Vegas, Nevada."

"*The* Davis Benton?"

"Yeah. *The* Davis Benton. And if the damned thing's unlisted, you know what to do."

"Yes, sir," she said curtly.

A few minutes later, she rang him back. "Mr. Justice, I have the number for you. Shall I make the call?"

"No. I'm going to make the call from home."

"Yes, sir. I'll bring it right in."

"No need. I'm on my way out. I'll pick it up."

When he hung up, his pulse was racing.

A short while later, he pulled into his driveway and parked, glancing up at the front door of his house. Just for a moment, he let himself imagine what it would be like to know that Holly would be inside, waiting for him to come home. He felt in his pocket for the phone number Elizabeth had given him, then got out of the car and hurried up the walk to his house.

Even though the decor was definitely masculine, the burgundy upholstery with dark blue accents, as well as the jade vase on the mantel, retained a measure of casual elegance. Heading for the phone, he paid no attention to the gleaming hardwood floors and glistening windows, or the perfectly arranged throw pillows on the overstuffed sofa. And if he had looked, he would have thought little about it. Those were services provided by his cleaning lady, not by the love of his life.

He punched in the numbers and then caught himself counting the rings and holding his breath.

"Benton residence."

Roman frowned. It wasn't Holly's voice, although considering Benton's life-style, he hadn't really expected it to be.

"May I speak to Holly Benton, please? Roman Justice calling."

"Miss Benton isn't taking calls. Would you care to leave a message?"

"She'll take mine," Roman said.

"I'm sorry, sir, but Mr. Benton has left strict orders that Miss Benton isn't to be disturbed."

Roman's eyes narrowed angrily. The tone of his voice softened, but what he said could never have been misconstrued as compliance.

"Then you tell *Mr.* Benton that I called, okay? And you also tell Mr. Benton that I will call again tomorrow evening, at which time I expect to be put directly through to Holly or know the reason why. Got that?"

The maid hesitated, but just enough to let Roman know he'd gotten under her skin.

"Yes, sir, I will tell Mr. Benton you called."

"And who are you going to say called for Holly?" Roman asked.

"Mr. Justice?"

"That's right. I just wanted to make sure you were paying attention. You have yourself a nice day."

He hung up in her ear, then headed toward the front door. He had to unload the camping equipment and then let Royal know he was back.

Holly stood at her bedroom windows, gazing out across the carefully landscaped grounds. She couldn't help but compare them to the wild beauty of the Colorado mountains. Here, everything was laid out in geometric patterns. Dark greens became the backdrop for the early-blooming flowers, while variegated greenery had been interspersed among shrubs and bushes that had yet to yield their blooms. A complex irrigation system seemed to operate on some sort of timer. She'd noticed it coming on and going off at various times of the day and wondered how much money it took to keep a place like this in operation. Somehow, the luxury of it all seemed a terrible waste, considering the fact that, except for staff, she and her father were the only two people in residence. Then she frowned, amending that to four, counting Gordon and Billy Mallory, who were to arrive tomorrow by special plane.

Her shoulders slumped as she turned away from the windows to stare at the room in which she stood. It was decorated in shades of blue. A thick off-white carpeting covered the floor of the entire room. An elegant four-poster bed was obviously the focal point of the furnishings, with a matching dresser and armoire sitting on either side of it.

It was a woman's room—all whites and laces, accented with china and crystal figurines. There were a few pictures on the walls, none of which seemed remotely personal in nature. No family photos. No school mementos. Just understated elegance. Holly frowned. It was very, very beautiful, and she felt as if she were in jail.

As she looked around the room, it dawned on her that she'd seen it before—back at the cabin—during one of her fleeting moments of lucidity. She sighed. If this wasn't proof of her identity, then nothing would be. Just because she didn't remember it all certainly didn't mean it wasn't so.

But she was lonely here. The staff tiptoed around her as if she had the plague. No one seemed willing to talk to her, and she wondered if this was normal behavior or if her father had given them orders not to bother her with questions she obviously couldn't answer.

She dropped into a nearby chair. The term *heavy heart* had new meaning for her, because that's exactly how hers felt. A phone sat on the table, only inches away from her hand. She thought of Roman and wondered if he'd gone home, or if he was still in the cabin, waiting for the weather to clear.

Downstairs, she heard a telephone ringing and stared at the one beside her, wondering why it didn't ring in here, as well. Then it dawned on her that this was probably a private line. Testing the theory, she picked it up. The dial tone sounded in her ear. The urge to call Roman was almost overwhelming— to reconnect with someone she knew and loved.

Instead, she set the receiver back on the cradle and stood abruptly. Daydreaming would get her nowhere. She wanted this nightmare over, and the only way it could happen was to remember why it started. Davis Benton had brought her back to her roots. Maybe there was something here that would jar her memory.

The room around her beckoned by the very fact that nothing looked familiar. She kicked off her shoes and headed for the closet to change into something more comfortable than the dress she was wearing. A few minutes later, wearing shorts and a T-shirt, she began by going through the drawers in her dresser and praying for a miracle.

Billy Mallory was confused. He'd been so certain they were going to die that he'd expected to wake up in heaven...or hell, whichever the case might be. He hadn't been prepared for the pain, or the around-the-clock circus of needles, monitors and nurses, prodding, poking and talking about him as if he weren't even there. Just because he chose to keep his mouth shut didn't mean his brain was dead. The way he looked at it, he and Gordon were already in more trouble than they could say grace over. There was no use adding to the pot by spilling his guts in a drug-induced stupor. Choosing sleep over worry, he closed his eyes, willing the flow of painkillers in his system to take him away to that place where sound doesn't go.

"Hey. Billy boy, it's me, Gordy."

Billy opened his eyes. When he tried to speak, his tongue felt too thick for his mouth.

Gordon reached for a nearby cup and spooned up a chip of ice. "Here you go, buddy. Let's have ourselves a little ice."

Billy took the ice, grateful that someone understood his problem without his having to ask. The cold felt good on his tongue, and right now, the moisture it generated tasted better than his favorite cold beer.

"Umm," he mumbled, indicating his appreciation.

Gordon grinned and patted his brother on the leg. "You just rest. I'll talk. You listen."

Billy blinked an okay, anxious to know what had been going on while he'd been unconscious. But that was before he heard what Gordon had to say.

Gordon leaned close, whispering in Billy's ear. "Holly Benton is alive. Her father has taken her back to Vegas, and tomorrow morning, we're flying there, as well."

Billy's eyes bugged as a nearby monitor suddenly beeped.

"No, no, you're reading this all wrong," Gordon said. "You don't know the best part. She has amnesia. Not only does she not remember what happened to her, she also doesn't remember her old man, or even her own name. We're in the clear. And—" he almost giggled "—here's the best part. Benton invited us to recuperate at the estate because I told him Holly and I had been eloping."

Billy groaned and managed to mumble, "What about the crash? What are they saying?"

Gordon glanced over his shoulder, making certain they were still alone, and then continued. "As far as everyone is concerned, we don't know what happened other than the plane suddenly lost pressure. You were supposedly up front talking to the captain and that's why you were in the copilot's seat. And I conveniently blacked out, so I don't have to answer any awkward questions."

Gordon chuckled, more to himself than to Billy. "It's about as perfect as it gets." Then his smile slipped. "Except for that spoiled brat of a female. I'd lay odds she's still got that money and is playing it cagey, probably planning to keep it all for herself."

Billy grabbed at Gordon's arm. "No...not Vegas. Get away. We need to get away."

Gordon frowned. "Don't be foolish. I'm not going anywhere until I've got my hands on that money. And don't give me any grief about this, because this mess is all your fault. Just be glad you're my brother. Otherwise, I'd be inclined to break your fool neck."

Holly was down on her knees and digging through a closet when someone knocked on her door.

"Come in," she called.

Davis entered with a smile on his face. It didn't stay there long.

"My stars, girl! What on earth are you doing?"

She rocked back on her heels and gave him a long, studied look.

"Looking for Holly Benton."

Startled, Davis was at a momentary loss for words. Finally, he found the gumption to speak. "I'm sorry, but I don't—"

She pulled a stack of letters from a box and then sat down without looking up.

"This is my room, right?"

"Yes."

"So...everything in here would be mine, right?"

"I suppose so. I haven't been any farther than the door in years."

She glanced up. "Why not?"

The question startled him, and the longer he thought about it, the more he realized he didn't have a good answer.

"I don't know," he finally said. "I just haven't."

"Weren't we friends?"

Davis dropped down beside her, then reached out and brushed the side of her face with the back of his hand.

"Oh yes, Holly-berry, we're friends. And you are loved. Even if you don't remember that, please don't doubt it."

An odd sort of comfort settled within her. She nodded, then managed a smile.

"Just asking."

Ignoring the fact that he was still wearing a very expensive suit, Davis sat down beside her, curious as to what she was reading.

"What do you have there?" he asked, pointing at the letters in her hand.

"I don't know," she said. "Looks like they are from some-one named Shirley."

Davis laughed. "Your college roommate, Shirley Ponselle. You two were inseparable during those years."

Holly smiled. "Are we still friends?"

"I suppose, but it's been years since you two communi-cated other than by letters. She's an archaeologist and on a dig somewhere in South America."

"Wow, an archaeologist. I'm impressed!" And then she thought. "What do I do?"

"What do you mean?" Davis asked.

"I mean, I graduated, didn't I?"

"Yes, with honors," he said proudly.

"What was my degree? What do I do for a living?"

Davis looked a bit uncomfortable, but he managed to an-swer. "You have a degree in literature."

Holly's mouth dropped. "Really! Do I teach?"

He shook his head. "No, dear, you don't actually work in an official capacity. But you stay very busy, acting as hostess on my behalf and standing in for me at various functions when I'm unable to attend."

She frowned. "I have a degree in literature and I don't do anything but go to parties and spend money?"

Put like that, it sounded worse than it was, but Davis was unable to lie. "You make it sound worse than—"

She snorted beneath her breath. "A dilettante is a dilettante, no matter how you word it. No wonder you thought I was going to elope with that toad."

Now it was Davis's turn to look startled. "Gordon Mallory is no toad. He's a well-established businessman."

She stuffed the letters back in the box without reading them and got to her feet. From where she was standing, her father suddenly looked like a little old man and not the commanding figure he practiced to project.

"Whatever. I still say you're way off the mark with this eloping."

"Why?" Davis argued. "Just tell me why. You don't remember me. You don't remember living here. Why do you think you would remember Gordon?"

Holly offered him her hand, grunting as he pulled himself up. Then she picked a piece of fuzz off the hem of his jacket.

"It's hard to explain," she said. "Although it's true I don't exactly remember you, there are times when you say and do things that I know I've heard before."

Davis looked pleased. He hadn't realized she'd experienced any sort of progress.

"But that's wonderful," he said. "If one thing comes to you, then others will follow."

"That's what Roman said." Then her mood turned pensive, and she looked away.

Davis saw the look in her eyes. He knew how reluctant she'd been to leave the man. His first instinct had been to take her and run back to Vegas, but now that he'd had time to think, it would seem that the Justice man hadn't done her harm. In fact, it was entirely due to Roman Justice that he had his Holly back. And then he remembered why he'd come.

"He called today."

"Who called?" she asked.

"Roman Justice."

Disappointment filled her voice. "Oh, no! Why didn't somebody tell me? I was here."

"Because I left orders for you not to be disturbed."

Anger overwhelmed her, and it took everything in her not to shout.

"Without asking me first?"

"I'm sorry," Davis said. "I didn't think about him calling. I just thought about the people who might call that you wouldn't remember. I was trying to protect you. Not deceive you."

"Don't do that again," she said. "I want to talk to him. I have to talk to him. He's very important to me. Do you understand?"

Davis sighed. "I wish you could hear yourself. You are all but raving about a man you hardly know."

"I know enough," she said shortly.

"He said he would call again tomorrow night."

Holly relaxed, but only a little. The idea that she was being controlled in any way didn't sit well.

Davis knew when to push and when to step back, and right now, retreating would be wise.

"I suppose we'd better change for dinner," he said, and started out of the room. "We have about a half an hour."

She looked down at her bare feet and the shorts and shirt she was wearing. Roman wouldn't care what she wore to eat in. Then she smiled to herself. In fact, he liked her best when she wore nothing at all. And he would call tomorrow. It was enough for now.

"Okay," she said, and then a thought came out of nowhere. "Oh, Mr. Benton…"

He interrupted her. "Please. If you can't call me Dad, like you used to, at least call me Davis."

At that moment, Holly truly felt sorry for what he must be going through.

"I'm sorry…Dad."

The smile on Davis's face was startling in intensity. "Thank you," he said softly.

"You're welcome."

"What was it you wanted to tell me?" he asked.

"Oh, that's right," she said. "About Roman. I want you to leave him alone."

"But I had no intentions of—"

"You know how you are," Holly said. "Every time a stranger comes on the horizon, you call that stupid service of yours and have them investigated and you—"

Both of them stopped, their faces mirroring the surprise they were feeling.

"Oh, my," Davis said softly. "Oh, my."

Holly sighed. "That's the way it happens. Just when I think I can't find my way out of a paper bag, along comes this neat pair of scissors and snips away a little bit more of that stuff clogging up my brain."

"Okay," Davis said.

She looked up. "Okay what?"

"Okay. No investigation. If you vouch for the man, then that's good enough for me."

For the first time since she'd walked through the front door of this house, it felt right to be here.

"Thank you...Dad."

Davis retraced his steps long enough to hug her, and then left before she could object.

Even after he was gone, she still wore the smile on her face, and knew, somehow, it was going to be all right.

It was just after 3:00 a.m. when a siren broke the silence of the neighborhood in which Roman lived. Although the sound was common, it invaded his sleep and became part of his dream.

Holly was standing naked in the middle of a snowy field and crying tears that kept turning to ice. As soon as a tear would solidify, it would slide off of her face and onto the ground at her feet.

Roman called out her name, but she didn't seem to hear. And then it began to snow and he started to run, fearing that she would freeze to death before he could reach her. But it wasn't snowflakes that came out of the sky. It was hundred-dollar bills. They fell to earth, scattering with the wind wailing down the draw.

"Holly! Come to me! Hurry, hurry!"

Instead, she held up her arms, as if warding off the money

falling down around her head, and before he could reach her,
she disappeared before his eyes.

When he reached the spot where she'd been standing, all
he could hear was the echo of her voice crying, "Money,
money everywhere and not a cent to spend."

He woke up with a jerk to find himself drenched in sweat
and wrapped in a tangle of bedclothes.

"My God," he muttered, and rolled out of bed.

Sweat was running down the middle of his back, and his
heart was hammering as if he'd been running for miles. He
thought back to the dream and groaned. He *had* been running,
trying to get to Holly.

"This is crazy," he said, and headed for the bathroom.

Moments later, he was standing beneath the shower head
and washing away the sweat, as well as what was left of the
dream. By the time he came out, the only thing left from the
episode was a lingering reluctance to go back to bed. Instead,
he headed for the kitchen for something cold to drink, welcoming the feel of the cool air against his bare body as he
moved from room to room.

He opened the refrigerator and got a cold can of pop, rubbing it against his forehead for a few seconds before popping
the top. The metal was smooth and chill against his skin,
cooling the fever of the dream.

Roman.

Although the sound was only an echo in his mind, he instinctively shuddered, as if a ghost had just passed by. He was
hearing her voice because he'd been dreaming of her. That's
all. She wasn't in danger. There couldn't be anything wrong
because she was with her father. But the feeling wouldn't go
away.

Don't let them take me.

He spun, this time actually searching the shadows for form
and substance. Goose bumps broke out on his forearms, but
he turned away, disgusted with himself and what he viewed
as a weakness.

He popped the top of the can, listening to the carbonated hiss as the seal broke, then draining it in one continuous gulp before tossing the can in the trash. The sound of metal against metal broke the silence with an abruptness that made him blink.

Make love to me, Roman. I don't want to forget.

His heart was aching as he turned away. Forget? Only if he died. Right or wrong, when they'd made love, he'd staked a claim on a woman he wasn't willing to lose. What scared him to death was loving her now before she remembered her past. Then he sighed. But he'd known that from the start. It was a risk he'd been willing to take then. The least he could do was trust in her now and wait and see. And…he'd call her again tomorrow.

He glanced at the clock. It was already tomorrow. Too early to call anyone, even Royal, and too late to go back to sleep.

His belly growled, and he thought of the supper he hadn't wanted last night. There wasn't any food in the house, but somewhere out there was an all-night restaurant that had a steak with his name on it.

He reached for his pants.

Chapter 11

It was just after 10:00 a.m. when Roman got to the ranch. The worst was behind him, and knowing that he would be talking to Holly this evening had him in a better mood.

He parked and reached for the sack on the seat beside him just as the front door opened. Madeline Michelle Justice teetered out on the porch, wearing a bright green T-shirt that hung down to her ankles, with a pair of red high-heeled shoes peeking out from beneath the hem. There was a moth-eaten feather boa around her neck and trailing the ground behind her, as well as a lady's straw hat that had completely blocked all vision from her left eye.

He got out of the car with a grin on his face.

"Hello, madam, I don't believe we've met. My name is Mr. Justice, and who might you be?"

Maddie giggled, then slid into the make-believe with all the skill a four-year-old can muster.

"I am Miss Piggy and I'm waiting for my Kermie to take me to town."

Before he could answer, Royal appeared in the doorway,

grabbing at his daughter's arm just before she toppled off the side of the porch.

"Watch it, piglet, that first step's a doozie," he said, and aimed her back to the house.

"Piggy, Daddy! Not piglet...piggy. Miss Piggy," Maddie said, and clip-clopped her way inside.

Roman laughed out loud as Royal rolled his eyes.

"I never did learn what made women tick, and God gives me a daughter," he muttered, waving Roman inside. "Come on in. Coffee's on the stove. I have one more call to make, and then I want to hear all about your trip."

Roman shut the door behind him as Royal disappeared into the den. Still in her Muppet phase, Maddie moved down the hall toward her room, leaving a trail of feathers behind her.

As Roman stood, listening to the ordinary business of Royal's life, he was struck by the emptiness of his own. Unlike the orderliness of his own home, Royal's house looked lived-in. There was a pair of old boots by the door, and Maddie's pajamas and her precious blankie were slung over the arm of a chair. He picked up the blanket and then lifted it to his face, inhaling the faint but lingering little-girl smell. It was a mixture of talcum powder and soap, with something sweet thrown in. There was a sticky place down on one corner. If he was of a mind to guess, he'd say it was syrup, probably left over from her breakfast.

A longing for something like this of his own hit him hard, leaving him empty and aching and thinking of Holly. He set the sack on a nearby table and headed for the kitchen. He was going after coffee, but what he needed was his head examined. He'd fallen in love with a rich man's daughter who couldn't remember her own name. Added to that, he was in possession of enough unclaimed money to start a small war, and that summed up the mess he was in.

He was standing at the window with a coffee cup in his hand when Royal came in the room.

"Sorry about that," Royal said. "I've been trying to connect with that man for a week."

Roman turned and then shrugged. "No big deal. I wasn't going anywhere." He took a slow sip of the hot brew, savoring the kick of caffeine.

Royal's eyebrows arched. "You mean you're in Dallas and still haven't gone back to work?"

"Something like that," Roman said.

Royal grinned. "So, taking time off was good after all. Don't you hate it when I'm right?"

The thought of Holly hit Roman belly high. It was all he could do not to groan from the pain that came with it, but Royal was too busy congratulating himself to notice.

"You obviously didn't get to fish, but at least you got some rest," Royal said, and then glanced over his shoulder to make sure Maddie wasn't eavesdropping on their conversation. "I can tell you, if that had been me, I would have slept the clock around before I ever got out of bed. Between my daughter and the ranch, I can't remember the last time I overslept."

"Didn't sleep all that much," Roman said.

Royal frowned. "Why not?"

"I kept waiting for the woman on the sofa to snore."

Royal's mouth dropped open. Before he could speak, Maddie burst into the room, running barefoot and wearing blue jeans and a T-shirt that was inside out. Miss Piggy had obviously been laid to rest.

"Uncle Roman! Uncle Roman!"

He scooped her off the floor and into his arms, grinning as she threw her arms around his neck and plastered his face with kisses.

"I've been wondering where you were," Roman said. "Some strange lady met me at the door."

Maddie giggled. "That was me."

"No!" he gasped, pretending great surprise.

She giggled again, and began tracing the dark arch of his eyebrows with the tip of her finger, giggling even harder when he made them wiggle beneath her touch.

"Uncle Roman?"

He nuzzled the side of her neck, stealing kisses on a ticklish spot beneath her right ear.

"What, Little Bit?"

"You knew it was me, didn't you?"

"Knew who was you?" he asked, pretending to be puzzled by her remark.

She threw her arms into the air in a gesture of surprise.

"Miss Piggy! I was Miss Piggy!"

"No!"

"Yes, yes, I was!" Then she looked at Royal. "Daddy, isn't it funny? I fooled Uncle Roman."

"Yeah, it's real funny," her father said, as always marveling at the remarkable change that one small female could make in Roman Justice's demeanor.

Roman set Maddie down and then took her by the hand. "Come on, kid. We've got to see a cat about some fleas."

Royal frowned. "Hey, Roman. About the woman on—"

"Not now," Roman said. "Maddie and I have something important to do."

Royal followed them into the living room, grumbling all the way.

"Dang it, Roman, you can't just drop a bombshell like that on me and then expect me to ignore it."

Roman picked up the sack he'd brought and started out the door.

"First things first," he said. "If you need us, we'll be at the barn."

Royal thrust a hand through his hair in frustration. "What's at the barn?"

Roman turned. "A flea-bit cat."

Royal's face turned red. "Now, look here. Don't resurrect a mess that's already been ironed out."

Roman held up the sack. "No mess. Just flea powder and a cute little pink collar."

Royal groaned. "Damn it, Roman. I won't have a cat in the house."

"I didn't say anything about bringing it in the house,"

Roman said. "We're just getting rid of the fleas so she can play with it. Nothing wrong with that, is there?"

Royal was caught and he knew it. His eyes narrowed, and it was all he could do not to punch his brother square in the nose. Add to that, his daughter was clinging to Roman's hand like a cocklebur with a look on her face he couldn't bring himself to ignore.

"Fine, then," Royal muttered.

Roman grinned. "Come on, Maddie. Let's go find us a kitty."

She was so excited she tore free of Roman's grasp and bolted for the barn, her bare feet churning up the dust as she ran.

Royal stuffed his hands in his pockets. "Before you completely spoil my child, you ought to get one of your own."

"Been thinking about it," Roman said, and then went to catch up with his niece.

For the second time in the space of five minutes, Roman had stunned Royal into speechlessness. All he could do was gape as Roman disappeared into the barn. Snowbound with snoring women? Having children? What the hell had Roman been doing at the cabin anyway?

It was ninety degrees and climbing when the private jet Davis Benton had chartered touched down in Las Vegas. Gordon and Billy Mallory were about to embark upon the next phase of their lives. It was one that would either make them or break them. Billy was scared half out of his mind. Gordon was riding an adrenaline high. Within the hour, they would be housed beneath the same roof as a woman he'd intended to kill. They'd fled Las Vegas because of a murder he hadn't planned to commit. Now here they were, in essence, returning in style to the scene of the crime. Gordon had come to the conclusion that he was invincible. Somehow he would discover the whereabouts of his money before Holly regained her memory. And thanks to Benton's misplaced generosity, Billy was going to have the best of care while Gordon rectified the mistakes his little brother had made. It was a perfect plan. Nothing could possibly go wrong.

Medical personnel were on hand as they touched down, obviously waiting for their arrival. Before Gordon had time to disembark, they were on board, readying Billy for transport to the Benton estate. There, a special room and private nursing had been set up for his around-the-clock care. Gordon had been released from the hospital with the understanding that he would see his personal physician as a follow-up for his healing ribs. Gordon had willingly agreed. At that point, Gordon would have agreed to anything.

As they started to lift Billy from the stretcher onto the waiting gurney, Gordon laid a hand on Billy's arm.

"Take it easy, little brother. No one's going to hurt you. I promise."

Weary from the trip, as well as arguing with a brother who had visions of grandeur that would probably get them both killed, Billy closed his eyes, gritting his teeth against the pain of being moved. The problem with Gordon was, he dreamed big but thought small. Billy was too injured to fight the inevitability of the ax he expected to fall. He had nightmares about sleeping under Holly Benton's roof, of waking up to find her standing over his bed and pointing an accusing finger in his face. But as always, Gordon hadn't listened to him. Gordon was the big brother and, therefore, the one who must always be in charge. And like the follower he was, Billy hadn't enough gumption to strike out on his own. Instead, he continued to follow in Gordon's footsteps, no matter how deep the mud in which they walked.

Davis glanced out the library window as the ambulance pulled up to the estate.

"They're here," he said, and dashed out of the room before Holly had a chance to react.

Frowning, she followed her father out of the room. The closer she got to the front door, the slower her steps became.

She couldn't get past the notion that she was moving toward danger.

Damn you, Roman Justice. I don't want to do this alone.

But she kept walking, well aware that if he were standing by her side, he would expect her to make these last steps alone. I'm not welcoming anybody, she thought. I'm only finding my way to the truth.

Up ahead, she heard voices in the foyer. She recognized her father's, probably directing traffic—and then some people spouted jargon that branded them as medical personnel. But it was the loud, jovial male voice that made her pause in midstep. A memory of something dark, something awful, tugged at the back of her mind. The urge to turn and run was strong. Then she reminded herself that she was home, that nothing could hurt her here. And still she stood out of sight, listening and trying to remember.

"I say, Davis, this is wonderfully kind of you," Gordon said. "Billy's had a rough flight and is looking forward to rest, aren't you, Billy?"

Billy nodded, then pointed toward a small bag that a maid was carrying away.

"Those are my things."

Gordon laughed. "She's only taking them to your room," he explained. "Besides, you won't be needing them for a while."

Down the hall, Holly suddenly felt the floor beginning to tilt. The words she'd just heard had triggered an unpleasant memory.

Where you're going, you won't be needing them.

She reached toward a nearby wall for support as her legs threatened to give way. Swallowing several times in nervous succession, she closed her eyes and took slow, calming breaths, trying to rid herself of the terror that had swamped her. But as hard as she tried, she couldn't get past it. Somewhere before, she'd heard that same voice, saying nearly the same thing to her. But it hadn't been said as lightly as it had been just now. When she'd heard it, there had been a real and tangible threat behind every single syllable.

She could hear them! They were coming closer now, and every instinct she had told her not to let them see her fear. In the midst of her panic, Roman's words came back to her so strong, it was as if he were standing beside her, saying them again for the first time.

The truth will set you free.

She took a slow, calming breath and straightened her shoulders. When the men came around the corner, she was ready and waiting.

Davis knew Holly had been unhappy about the arrival of the Mallory brothers and was pleased she had come to greet them.

"Holly, darling, there you are! We're in the process of getting everyone settled."

"I heard," she said, and then turned her full attention to the man at her father's side.

The smile on Gordon's face slipped, but only a little. Play the part, he reminded himself. Play the part.

"Holly! Darling!"

Before she could react, Gordon had embraced her.

"The last time I saw you, it was so awkward. Me lying flat on my back in the hospital, and your dear little face so full of fear."

Holly withdrew from his touch as if she'd accidentally walked into something foul.

Gordon's face flushed with anger, but he refrained from comment, pretending he hadn't seen a thing.

"Well, now," he said heartily. "I'd better see Billy settled in before we make any plans."

Holly gave her father an angry glance. She'd warned him about pushing her into something that didn't feel right. If he thought she was going to knuckle under, rather than make a fuss, he had another think coming.

"We have no plans to make," she said shortly.

This time, Gordon made no effort to hide his displeasure.

He looked at Davis, as if waiting for him to smooth things over. But Davis had already seen Holly's mood for himself, and wisely, decided to make himself scarce.

"I'll just show them the way to Billy's room," Davis said quickly. "Lunch will be in thirty minutes. See you then."

He walked away, leaving Gordon and Holly alone in the hall to sort out their own affairs.

Forced to deal with the issue himself, Gordon turned his attention to Holly.

"It seems we've been left on our own. That was thoughtful. Your father knows we would have plenty of things to discuss."

Holly's expression never wavered. "He's mistaken. There is no 'we' and there's nothing to discuss."

Gordon wanted to shake her. He wanted to put his hands around her tiny white throat and squeeze until she admitted what she'd done with his money. But that was too premature. That might come later...if his other plans didn't work out.

"Holly, darling, you just don't remember. We meant everything to each other...you mean everything to me!"

Again, Holly recoiled as if she'd been slapped.

Gordon flushed and reached for her arm. "Damn it, you're not being fair."

She stepped out of his reach. "No, Mr. Mallory, you're the one who's not being fair. We have nothing to discuss, because I have no memory of you, or of us."

"We were on our way to Nassau! We were going to be married!"

She frowned. "So I've been told."

"Then how can you be so cruel as to ignore my feelings? Don't you know how much your withdrawal has hurt me?"

Now Holly was certain her instincts about him had been right. Hurt him? Didn't he know how much fear and confusion she'd been dealing with?

"You miss the point, Mr. Mallory. I can't ignore something I never knew existed. And if you cared for me as much as you claimed, you wouldn't be pushing me. Now, please excuse me. As my father said, lunch will be served shortly. I'm sure we'll see you then.''

She walked away, leaving Gordon alone in the hall with his thoughts. And while they were far from kind, it wasn't what bothered him most. It was that cool, assessing look in her eyes, as if she'd just taken his measure and found him lacking.

Royal was in the kitchen, finishing the dishes from their noontime meal. He glanced out the window, as always, checking to see where his daughter had gone, although with Roman still here, she wouldn't go far. He could hear the creak of the porch swing, and an occasional murmur of voices. That meant they were on the back porch, probably still playing with that damned kitten, although he had to admit that since Roman had given it a bath and a good dusting of flea powder, it was sort of cute. And Maddie was beside herself with delight. It had been all he could do to coax her inside long enough to eat lunch before she'd begged to go back outside.

He gave the last pan a good rinse and set it aside to drain before drying his hands. He still didn't have any satisfactory answers from Roman about what had gone on at the cabin, but he would have before the day was out or know the reason why.

''What's going on?'' he asked, as he stepped out on the porch.

Roman pointed. Maddie was dragging a piece of string behind her, while the kitten scrambled after it, trying to pounce.

''Frisky little beggar,'' Royal said, and sat down on the steps.

Roman nodded.

Royal sighed and gave his brother a studied look, then glanced up at the sky. The air was muggy. Far off on the horizon, a line of thunderheads was building.

''Probably rain before morning,'' he said.

Roman squinted up at the sky. ''Probably.''

Royal shifted gears. "At least we won't have to worry about this rain turning to snow."

The mere mention of snow made Roman think of Holly, which wasn't difficult since she'd rarely been off his mind. He glanced down and then quickly raised his feet as the kitten came racing toward him. It scampered beneath the swing, with Maddie not far behind.

As she started to run past, Roman scooped her off of her feet and into his arms.

"But, Uncle Roman, Flea-bit is going to get away!" she cried, struggling to get down.

"No, she won't," Roman said. "See, there she comes now. Why don't you sit here with me awhile. Flea-bit needs to rest. She's only a baby, remember?"

Maddie nodded. "But I could hold her."

"No, honey, it's too hot to hold her. She'll be cooler if you just let her be for a while."

Maddie sighed, but she knew better than to argue. While she sometimes talked her daddy into a compromise, when her uncle Roman put his foot down, it stayed put.

"Okay," she said, and leaned back in his arms.

Roman winked at Royal and then set the swing to rocking—not a lot—just enough of a gentle to and fro that lulled Maddie into a much needed sleep. The kitten was down at his feet, less willing to give up the play, but it, too, soon succumbed to the lazy afternoon heat.

Royal leaned back against the porch post, watching the ease with which Roman had put his daughter to sleep.

"Thanks," Royal said. "She needed that."

Roman looked down at the sleeping child in his arms—at the dark, flyaway hair and lashes so thick they made shadows on her plump cheeks.

"It was my pleasure," Roman said softly, and smiled.

Instead of breaking the mood by taking Maddie inside, Royal stayed put, aware that Roman could hardly bolt and run with Maddie asleep in his arms.

"Roman."

Roman looked up. Here it comes, he thought.

"What happened at the cabin?"

Roman sighed. As much as he wanted to keep Holly to himself, there were too many extenuating factors to ignore.

"There was a woman at the cabin when I got there."

Royal stiffened. "What happened? Did she break in? Was anything missing?"

Roman shook his head. "No, no, nothing like that."

"Then talk, damn it. I never did like guessing games."

"She'd been injured. There were scratches all over her and blood on her clothes. Had a hell of a knot on her head." He thought back to the look on her face when she'd seen him pointing the gun at her head. "And she was scared to death."

"Man," Royal muttered. "Car wreck?"

Roman shook his head. "Nope. Parachute."

"What?"

"Remember me asking you to find out if a plane had gone down anywhere in the area?"

"Yeah."

"Turns out she'd been a passenger on that plane. Only someone strapped a parachute on her and dumped her out a short while before it crashed."

"Good lord! Why?"

"We don't know."

"What do you mean, you don't know? Didn't she tell you anything?" Royal asked.

Roman shook his head. "She couldn't. She has amnesia. Right now, she's operating on instinct."

"What happened to her? Where is she at?" Royal asked.

"Back in Las Vegas, with her father."

Royal's eyes widened with sudden understanding.

"Are you telling me that you found Davis Benton's daughter? The one everyone thought was dead?"

"Yes."

Royal stared at his brother for a long, silent moment, and when he finally spoke, there was conviction in his voice.

"You fell in love with her, didn't you?"

Roman didn't answer, but he didn't have to. Royal could see it in his eyes.

"My God! I didn't think there was a woman alive, other than my daughter, who could bring Roman Justice to his knees."

"Shut up, Royal. There's nothing funny about any of this."

And then Royal remembered she'd been eloping with one of the men on the plane.

"Oh, hell, the fiancé."

Roman looked away.

"Damn, I'm sorry, Roman. I suppose when she regains her memory, they'll—"

Everything he'd been worrying about suddenly came to a head. "I'm going after her," Roman said.

Royal looked startled. "But I thought you said—"

"I know what I said," Roman muttered. "And I know what I told her when I sent her away. I told her it was for her own good, and that she needed to remember everything before she could make a decision about something this important."

Royal frowned. "Are you saying that she fell in love with you, too?"

"Yes. And I sent her back to someone else without a fight."

"So, what are you going to do first?"

"Put Maddie to bed and then catch the next plane to Las Vegas."

Chapter 12

It was fifteen minutes after 10:00 p.m. For Holly, the day had passed in snail-paced increments with everything moving toward a single, important conclusion—waiting for Roman's call.

She'd endured the entire day, including meals, with Gordon Mallory hovering over her every move, and every minute spent in his company made her increasingly nervous. If he looked at her, she found herself looking away. If he spoke, the very sound of his voice grated. And if he so much as reached in her direction, she had an instinctive urge to pull back. Whatever had been between them before hadn't been good, no matter what she'd been told. Just because she couldn't remember didn't make her stupid. Subconsciously, she knew she must be protecting herself.

Eventually, Holly had made her excuses and escaped to her room. And now, she was waiting. She'd had a bath. She'd washed her hair. She'd done her nails. She'd even suffered a small spurt of feeling sorry for herself and cried. None of which had produced the desired result. No phone call. No Roman.

She kept telling herself that, in his line of work, anything could have happened. He might have been called out on an important case. And she had to admit that he also might have changed his mind. While her heart wouldn't let her believe that he was an out-of-sight, out-of-mind kind of man, there was no escaping the fact that she'd known him less than a week.

Put in that perspective, the feelings she had for him could have seemed ludicrous. No one falls in love within a period of days, never mind falling into bed with a stranger. But she had done both and would do it again in a heartbeat.

She glanced at the clock, then rolled over on her bed and closed her eyes, making a bet with herself. It was twenty-two minutes after ten. He will call before eleven. It was a silly game, but it was a way to get through the next thirty-some minutes without going crazy.

Seconds later, she heard the faint, but unmistakable sound of the front doorbell. It seemed very late to be receiving visitors, but without any memory of her father's habits, she had no way of knowing if this was out of character for the household.

She reached for the blue silk robe draped over the end of the bed as she got up. It wasn't as if she would be expected to appear, but just in case...

Moments later, she heard voices, and much louder than they should have been. Curious, she opened the door and stepped out into the hall. And in that moment, she heard the familiar sound of a beloved voice.

Sweet music to her ears! Roman was here!

Forgetting that she was in her nightclothes, she bolted for the stairs.

Davis Benton was in a state of disbelief. Roman Justice had appeared on his doorstep and all but pushed his way inside. Angry with being disturbed, he had half a mind to call the police.

"Look, Mr. Justice, at any other time, I would be more than happy to receive you as a guest, but this is ridiculous. Do you know what time it is?"

"Couldn't get an earlier flight," Roman said, setting his bag on the floor at his feet. "And I'm not going to bed until I see Holly."

"Go to a hotel, get some sleep, come back tomorrow," Davis said. "She's already in bed."

Like Holly, Gordon Mallory had become curious and was halfway down the stairs when he heard Holly's name being mentioned.

"What's going on out here?" he demanded.

Davis turned. "Gordon, I'm sorry you were disturbed. Go back to bed. I'll deal with this."

But it was more than curiosity that made Gordon stay where he was. The stranger was looking at him in a judgmental manner, and like a herd bull sensing his territory was about to be invaded, he took the man's measure—and instant offense.

Although the man seemed ordinary enough, in Gordon's opinion, his style of dress left plenty to be desired. His clothing was entirely Western. Although he was wearing slacks, his white, long-sleeved shirt and Western-style sport coat seemed a bit too much. Added to that were black boots and a wide-brimmed gray Stetson. And then his attention moved from what the stranger was wearing to the man himself, and Gordon found himself wanting to bolt. He knows! But he took a deep breath, reminding himself there was no way he could know. No one but Holly knew and she couldn't—

A sudden burst of panic made his belly knot. Dear God, what if this had all been a ruse? What if Holly didn't have amnesia? What if they had planned this all along just to get him and Billy in a vulnerable position? What if...? He shuddered and grabbed hold of the railing for support. Get a grip, he reminded himself. Don't quit when you're still in the game.

* * *

Roman's attention was completely focused on the man on the stairs. This is the man she was going to marry? Granted, by present-day standards, the man was good-looking enough. A thick head of brown, wavy hair, large eyes and a trim physique. But there was something about him—a weakness about the chin and a reluctance to meet one's gaze straight on—that made Roman doubt. His eyes narrowed, his face becoming blank. Right now, Mallory was wearing a smug expression, but Roman couldn't help wondering how Gordon would have looked if he'd come in with the bag of money.

And then he heard Holly's voice and forgot about everything except her.

"Roman! You came!"

Davis turned and then groaned beneath his breath as Holly came flying down the stairs. From the look on his daughter's face, this mess was just beginning.

When she called out his name, Roman knew he'd been right to come. This woman was worth the fight and then some. He walked past Davis and headed toward the stairs.

Unprepared for Holly's sudden appearance, Gordon saw her run past him before he could stop her. When she threw herself into the stranger's arms, his stomach began to knot. This was worse than he'd thought. This man was obviously more than a stranger to Holly, and he was a threat to Gordon's plan. Now what should he do?

Holly leaped from the bottom step into Roman's arms.

"I thought you were going to call," she said, and threw her arms around his neck as he lifted her off the floor. Completely oblivious to the fact that she had an audience, she began hugging him, over and over.

Once he had her in his arms, every knot in Roman's body began to unwind. "I came to tell you that you were right," he said, and kissed the side of her cheek.

"Right about what?" Holly said.

"I shouldn't have let you go the way I did."

Her spirit soared. "So, are you saying—?"

Roman silenced her with a look, and then turned, still holding her in an embrace. His voice was strong and unwavering, his gaze clear and focused as he stared Davis Benton straight in the face.

"I came to tell your father something, too."

But Davis was in no mood for revelations. This type of behavior was unseemly, and completely out of character for the way he believed a daughter of his should behave.

"Now, see here, Holly," Davis cried. "This is extremely inconsiderate behavior in front of your fiancé. Have you no shame?"

"I keep telling you," she said. "I don't have a fiancé. I was never engaged. I was not eloping with that man, I just know it."

Roman's arms were around Holly, but his gaze never left Davis's face. "When you came to get her, she begged me not to let her go. I've been sorry ever since. I made a mistake. I came to fix it. Plain and simple."

Davis was floored. "Look here, Justice. Caveman tactics went out with woolly mammoths. People in our class don't behave in such a bohemian manner."

Anger settled deep in Roman's heart as his expression stilled. His voice was low and steady, but there was no mistaking his meaning.

"I don't come from class. I come from Texas. Down there, we fight for what's right, and right now, I'm the only familiar thing in your daughter's life." Then he looked at Gordon, waiting for him to argue.

Gordon was speechless. The truth be known, that damned Texan could have her. All he wanted was his money. But it was painfully obvious that all eyes were suddenly on him, waiting to see what he had to say about this. And to keep himself on the good side of safe, he knew he had to at least make a fuss. So he came down the stairs, hoping for the right tone of shock in his voice.

"Holly, darling, how can you do this? After all we meant to each other?"

Roman didn't give her time to answer. "You know something, Mallory, I'm beginning to believe Holly was right about you all along.''

A fresh spurt of panic shot straight to Gordon's heart.

"Right about what?" he muttered.

"That you two were not about to get married after all. If this situation was reversed, and some man had just interrupted my world and tried to take my woman out from under my nose, I would have punched his face. Then I would have taken said woman—and myself—into a room and locked the door. And I would have made damned sure I had changed her sweet mind before I let her back out.''

Gordon began to sputter. "All men aren't like you. Some of us are sensitive.''

Holly wanted to laugh at what Gordon just said, and she looked at him, her voice rich with indignation.

"You, sensitive? Really, Gordon. I saw you run over a dog without even looking back. To you, *sensitive* is a four-letter—''

When she stopped in midsentence, it dawned on them what had happened. Once again, a truth had come out when she least expected.

"Well," Holly said. "I believe I've done it again.''

Gordon pivoted and stalked upstairs without looking back. Davis threw up his hands and gave his daughter a long, hard look.

"I hope you know what you're doing," Davis said.

"I told you, Daddy. Trust me.''

"You're flying by the seat of your pants," he muttered.

Roman felt it was time to finish what he'd come to say.

"Please, Mr. Benton, hear me out.''

Davis shifted his glare from Holly to the man who held her.

"What more could you possibly have to say that you haven't already said?" he asked.

"I mean no disrespect, but your daughter is too important to me to just give her up without a fight. I've never backed down from anything in my life, and I'm not about to start now." Then Roman took a deep breath and looked at Holly. "But I take nothing for granted until she remembers who she is. I can't lay claim to a woman who doesn't remember her own existence. However...making her wait this out on her own wasn't fair."

Holly's heart began to pound, and her eyes began to burn. "So what you're saying is you came because you feel sorry for me? I don't need sympathy. There's too much in this house already. What I need is some faith. I need some-one...anyone...to believe what I do know!"

"And what would that be?" Davis asked.

Holly wanted to scream, but she stifled the urge, speaking instead in shaky and uneven tones.

"That I might not remember being Davis Benton's daughter, but I know who I am. I would *not* marry a man like Gordon Mallory." Then she pinned Roman with a piercing stare. "Unlike you, I don't have to wait for revelations and rainbows to know what's in my heart. However, I'm glad you're here."

Roman took a deep breath. "So am I."

She closed her eyes and leaned against his strength, gladly sharing the burden of her load.

Davis Benton hadn't become rich by being weak or inde-cisive, and he appreciated strength, both of body and char-acter, in others, as well. He hated to admit it, but the man intrigued him in a way Mallory did not.

Davis glanced at Holly and then shrugged. "As she re-minded me earlier, it's not up to me. This is Holly's decision. But I would ask you to give her some space. Don't pressure her into any decisions she's not ready to make."

Roman nodded. "Fair enough," he said, and held out his hand. Davis shook it.

Holly hugged her father, and then started to pick up Ro-man's bag.

"Holly, darling, what on earth are you doing?" Davis asked.

"Roman is staying here, of course."

"But—"

The smile on her face turned to ice. "Since you invited the Mallorys—people I don't even remember—I'm sure you won't mind Roman being here. At this point, he is the *only* person I do know."

Davis turned red with embarrassment. He had bullied her into accepting the Mallory brothers' presence. Put like that, he had no option but to accept with grace.

"Of course," he said quickly. "I was just thinking of the propriety of the situation."

"I fail to see the connection," she said. "I'm not in love with Gordon."

"But you were," Davis spluttered.

She shook her head. "It was Gordon who put that thought in your head. You told me you were surprised we were eloping. Why are you so dead set on believing a man you hardly knew?"

Davis threw up his hands. "I'm going to bed. Mr. Justice, I wish you a good night's sleep." He started up the stairs, muttering more to himself than to Roman, "And you're probably the only one who's going to get it."

Gordon was worried. Not only had that damned Texan just yanked his reason for being in the Benton mansion out from under his nose, but he'd been unable to regain favored status and he knew it.

Instead of going to bed, he headed for Billy's room. He didn't consider the fact that Billy was probably asleep, or that he needed his rest. There was a kink in the plan that he'd made. Billy needed to know—just in case.

He burst into the room, slamming the door shut behind him. Billy woke with a jerk and then groaned from the motion. Blinking sleepily, he looked up.

"Gordon? What's going on? What time is it, anyway?"

Gordon began to pace. "It's time to worry," he said. "That's what time it is."

Billy yawned. "I've been trying to tell you that for days."

Gordon frowned. "Shut up," he muttered. "I'm trying to think."

"That's what keeps getting us into trouble," Billy said. "Look, why don't we just move out tomorrow? We can get a place of our own and as soon as I'm able to travel, we could—"

"Get a place with what?" Gordon growled. "Thanks to you, we don't have any money."

"And thanks to you, I'm an accessory to a murder. Carl Julian is dead because of us," Billy muttered. "Besides, what about the ten thousand we left in the bank?"

Gordon ignored the reference to the money in the bank. Ten thousand was peanuts compared to the million he'd lost.

"Shut up. Shut up. I don't want to hear Carl Julian's name mentioned again."

"You could try getting a job," Billy said.

Gordon laughed, but it was a heartless sound, completely devoid of mirth.

"Doing what? I know how to run a scam, pick locks and cover my tracks. The openings for good con artists are few. I dare say my chances for employment would be better flipping burgers at a fast-food restaurant."

"At least it would be honest," Billy said.

Gordon's eyes widened in disbelief. "Since when have you grown a conscience?"

"Since I saw you cut a man's throat."

Gordon blanched. Even he had succumbed to a moment of weakness afterward. But it had happened so fast. One minute they were on their way to financial security, and the next moment Carl Julian had caught them in the act. Even after Julian had promised not to tell, Gordon had reacted without thought, cutting off Julian's pleas with the man's own letter opener. It had been easier than he might have thought, and they'd escaped without further detection. At least they had until Holly Benton had overheard their argument on the plane.

Gordon combed his hands through his hair in a gesture of frustration.

"Here's what we're going to do. I've still got a few friends here in the city. All I need is something to make Holly talk." When he saw the look on Billy's face, he quickly added, "Nothing that will hurt her. Just something to make her spill her guts."

Billy glared. "You mess with her again, and I'll tell everything I know. I'd rather go to jail than go to hell later on."

Shock spread on Gordon's face. "Since when did you get religion?"

"Since I woke up from the crash and found myself alive."

Gordon was stunned. He'd never heard his brother speak with such conviction. Now he was faced with the choice of doing what he wanted and leaving Billy behind when he ran, or changing his plans again. But he couldn't get past the lessons of his childhood. Take care of your little brother. Don't let Billy get hurt. Watch out for Billy wherever you go.

He glared. "Damn it, Billy, you're making this harder than it has to be."

But Billy wouldn't budge, and Gordon was forced to restructure his plans again.

"I'm going to bed," Gordon said. "You try and get some sleep. We'll talk tomorrow." He left, slamming the door behind him.

But for Billy, sleep was slow in coming. Doom was hovering on the horizon, and he didn't know how to stop it.

Roman woke to the smell of warm bread and creamery butter. He opened his eyes just as Holly was setting a breakfast tray on a nearby table. Her hair was piled high on her head, and the loose strands were still damp, obviously from a morning shower. The robe she was wearing was the one she'd had on when he'd arrived—sheer blue silk, with a matching gown beneath. It had taken every ounce of his willpower to leave her at the door to her room last night, but he'd done it. Now she was back, bringing temptation with her. There wasn't a Justice alive who'd ever been accused of passing up a good thing. He saw no reason to ruin the family's good name by starting now.

"Good morning, baby," he said softly, and then patted the bed. "Come here to me."

She did without hesitation, settling down beside him as if she'd done it a thousand times in the past.

"I can't believe you're here," she said softly, touching his arm, his bare chest, then smoothing back the hair on his forehead. "I kept telling myself this has happened too fast, that you would get home, take a deep breath and realize you'd made a mistake."

Roman frowned. "The only mistake I made was in letting you leave alone. I had nightmares." His frown deepened. "I haven't had nightmares in years, at least not since…" He stopped. That was a part of his life he'd never shared, not with anyone.

Holly waited, letting him decide how far this conversation needed to go.

Roman sat up in bed, pulling her close within the shelter of his arm. When she cuddled close, he settled her head beneath his chin and sighed. It was time to let go of a few ghosts of his own.

"I don't have a real good track record with women."

Again, she remained silent, giving him the freedom to pick and choose his words.

"My mother died when I was small. That left Dad to raise us three boys by himself. Considering the hell we gave him, he did a good job." He closed his eyes, remembering as a child the lonely, empty years of yearning for the gentleness of a mother's touch. "I decided at a pretty young age that I was too tough to cry. I don't know whether my older brothers drilled that into me with their constant heckling, or if it was my way of hardening my heart against any more pain."

Holly hurt for him. She had vague memories of her own empty years without a mother, of yearning to be held and rocked and fussed over, as only a woman can do.

"I'm sorry, sweetheart," she said softly.

He smiled and then stroked her hair, letting his thoughts drift. "I thought I could handle anything life dished out. After all, I'd already lost a parent, what more was there to lose except my own life?" Then he took a deep breath.

"That just shows how innocent and naive I still was. My senior year in high school, a new girl moved into town. Her daddy was the new head football coach at school, and her mother was my English teacher. Her name was Connie. For the next two years, we made plans. We dreamed dreams. We were inseparable. We were in love."

Holly held her breath, afraid to hear what came next, and at the same time, knowing it had to be said.

"She drowned the summer between my freshman and sophomore years at college. I stood on the shore of the lake, watching her as she skied past." He shook his head. "She was laughing and waving at me, so pretty and so full of life. Less than a minute later, a speedboat came out of nowhere and hit her. We couldn't get to her in time to save her. I watched her live, and I watched her die. After that, I just...well, I just quit."

Tears were running down Holly's cheeks. "Oh, Roman, it's a miracle that you even gave us a chance, isn't it?"

Roman looked down at Holly, at the tears on her face, at the love in her eyes, and knew a great sense of belonging.

"Naw, it wasn't a miracle," he said, trying to tease away the tears. "It was those damned daisy panties."

She laughed on a sob.

Roman cupped her face with the palms of his hands and then wiped away all traces of her sadness.

"I didn't tell you that for sympathy, baby," he said softly. "But I want you to understand that I do not—have not—given love lightly. Right now, there is a peace in my heart that hasn't been there in years, and I have you to thank. I've loved and lost two very different women in my life. I'm not looking forward to losing another."

"But you won't lose me. You can't! I love you, remember?"

"I remember a hell of a lot more than you do," he said shortly.

She looked away. "That's not fair," she muttered.

His expression hardened, and there was a warning in his eyes that she couldn't mistake. "You're right. It's not fair. None of this is fair. And telling you about my past when you're still lost from your own may seem selfish. But you need to know something about me right now, before it's too late. When it comes to love, I won't fight fair...but by God, I will fight."

Holly tilted her face for the kiss she saw coming. Just before his mouth touched hers, she whispered, "Then that's all I need to know."

Minutes later, when they had come up for air, Roman whispered against her cheek.

"Holly...baby?"

"Hmm?"

"Is the door locked?"

Drugged by the strength of his kisses, her eyelids fluttered sleepily.

"I don't know, why?"

"I'm going to make love to you. Didn't know whether you wanted an audience or not."

She turned the lock before he could change his mind.

There was an uneasy quiet during lunch that day. The only person unaffected by the silence was Roman, and that was partly due to the satisfying blush he'd put on Holly's cheeks and to the fact that he had metaphorically laid his cards on the table.

And while it was impossible to miss the dark, anxious looks Gordon Mallory kept slinging around the table, Roman couldn't help thinking it had nothing to do with losing Holly and everything to do with a bagful of money. The problem was, how to prove it. Since his investigator's license did not extend to the state of Nevada, he had a little networking to do.

A few hours later, Roman exited the court of records with a satisfied smile on his face. For a man who was supposed to be dealing in real estate, Gordon Mallory was sadly lacking in proof. There wasn't a single piece of property in the city— or the state—that was registered in either Mallory's name. Not only that, but neither one had ever been licensed to sell real estate.

There was another interesting fact that he'd turned up during his afternoon search. The Mallorys no longer had a Las Vegas residence. Just prior to the flight to Nassau, they'd moved out of their apartment and discontinued their utility services.

Roman could look at that two ways. Either Gordon had been planning on moving into the Benton estate after their marriage, or he'd never planned to come back from the Bahamas at all. With a million unclaimed dollars on board the ill-fated flight, Roman was leaning toward the last theory.

But these were still suppositions. There was still the matter of the money. If it hadn't been ill-gotten gains, someone would have reported it missing by now. Both Gordon and Billy should have been shouting to the heavens that it was gone.

In Roman's eyes, their guilt was confirmed by the simple fact that they hadn't said a word.

And he was honest enough with himself to admit that the possibility still existed that Holly had, in some way, been part of the scheme, but every instinct he had denied it.

For one thing, she had no motive. It was obvious that Davis Benton would give her anything she asked for, so she would have no need to steal money, except maybe for the thrill, and he ruled that out. She wasn't that kind of a person. That left the Mallorys as the prime suspects, but proving their guilt would be the kicker.

Chapter 13

Roman returned to the mansion just as they were about to sit down to dinner. Holly had been anxiously watching the driveway. When she saw the cab pulling up to the house, she breathed a sigh of relief. She'd been dreading sitting down to dinner with Gordon and her father casting mournful looks in her direction, as if it were all her fault she didn't remember her past.

As Roman walked in the door, Holly took him by the arm, pulling him toward the dining room.

"Where have you been? I thought you weren't going to get here in time to eat with us."

Roman grinned. "Hey, baby, I missed you, too, but give me time to hang my hat, will you?"

She rolled her eyes. "Sorry. In my other life...which I can't remember...I must have been a bit of a compulsive fanatic."

He bit the lobe of her ear and then whispered against her cheek, "If that has any bearing on the way you make love, I'm all for it."

Holly's face was still pink as she entered the dining room and took a seat to her father's right.

"What kept you?" Davis asked.

She picked up her napkin and then spread it across her lap. "Roman just arrived. He'll be right in."

Davis frowned and then gestured to a maid who was standing by with a tureen of soup, waiting to serve.

"No, don't serve it yet," he said. "We're not all here."

Gordon cast Holly a nervous glance and then laid his own napkin in his lap. He reached for her hand.

"Holly, my dear, how have you been? I see almost nothing of you during the day. Were you resting?"

She moved before he could touch her. "No."

He cast her a soulful look. "I can see that I assumed too much when I thought we'd at least be able to talk. If you'd let me, I'm sure we could work things out between us."

"When nothing is there, there's nothing to work out," she said bluntly.

Gordon flushed. "You've changed. You never used to be this cold. It's that man. He's brainwashed you, that's what."

After what I endured, I'm lucky I still have a brain. And then Roman came in and sat down beside her, saving her from having to respond.

Roman glanced at Davis and nodded.

"Sorry I'm late. You shouldn't have waited. Daddy always said if you can't get to the table on time, then don't complain about what you have to eat."

Davis laughed before he thought, and then motioned for the soup to be served.

"I think I would like your father. What does he do?"

A shadow crossed Roman's face, but he didn't hesitate to answer.

"He was a rancher all of his life. Died in a plane crash a little over a year ago. My oldest brother, Royal, now runs the family ranch."

Both Holly and her father looked startled. She had known he was dead, but not how he'd died.

"I'm sorry," Davis said.

"Was he flying commercial or private?"

Roman's mood darkened. "Private. Another of my brothers is a pilot. They were in the crash together. Ryder survived. Dad didn't." And then he shook off the feeling. "Ryder owns his own charter service out of Mississippi."

Davis nodded. "That's a long way from Texas. How did he wind up there?"

"He married Casey Ruban, one of Mississippi's finest," Roman said, and then winked at Holly.

Davis's spoon clinked against the bowl, a social faux pas that he rarely made. But the name startled him. Any businessman worth his salt knew that name.

"Any kin to Delaney Ruban?" Davis asked.

"His granddaughter."

"Oh," Davis said, eyeing Roman with renewed respect.

"I'm sorry to say I don't know the name. Is she anyone special?" Gordon asked.

"My brother thinks so," Roman said.

Gordon flushed. He'd like nothing better than to put his fist in that man's smug mouth, but the truth was, the man intimidated him. He was too physical...too animal. Give him a cultured crook any day of the week. At least he could speak their language.

"She inherited a megaconglomerate from her grandfather," Davis said. "Everyone expected her to fail at it, and instead, she's run it with an iron hand, just like the old man did before her."

Gordon couldn't help staring at Roman. He was far removed from the type of men he normally associated with and he couldn't quite figure him out.

"So one of your brothers is a rancher, another a pilot. What do you do?" Gordon asked.

"I'm a private investigator. I got my license about a year after I quit the military."

Gordon choked on a spoonful of soup. It took several moments and a glass of water before he caught his breath.

Perfect! This was just about perfect! A professional snoop had been added to the mess he was in.

"Sorry," he said, dabbing at his mouth with his napkin. "I choked."

Roman gave him a curious stare. "It happens."

"So, you're a private investigator," Davis said. "Who do you work for?"

Roman never cracked a smile. "Me."

Davis glanced at Holly, who seemed terribly focused on her soup bowl. This was so unlike the loquacious daughter he'd known before the accident. Like Gordon, he, too, wondered if she'd been brainwashed. It wouldn't be the first time a man had tried to get at Davis's money through his daughter.

"It takes a while to start up your own business," Davis said, expecting to hear a mouthful of excuses as to why it had yet to happen.

Roman frowned, thinking back to the first few months he'd gone into business.

"I suppose," he said. "But we were running in the black before the first year was out."

Davis's eyebrows arched. "My goodness."

Gordon had had enough of soup and of Roman Justice. It was time to put the man in his place.

"Don't you find that sort of work mundane?" Gordon asked.

Roman looked up, and if Gordon had known him better, would have been nervous about the look that came on his face.

"And what kind of work are you referring to?" Roman drawled.

"You know, cheating husbands, wayward wives, delinquent fathers and the like. It all seems so tawdry."

Roman's voice softened, but the glitter in his eyes was getting colder by the minute.

"I don't handle domestic disputes," he said.

Gordon sneered. "Then what do you *handle?*"

"Mostly corporate work relating to fraud, embezzlement

and industrial thievery. Sometimes, if the injured parties hire me, I work in conjunction with the authorities on a pending criminal case.''

Gordon's cocky attitude faded. This man worked in the big leagues, and the knowledge made him nervous. Stealing a million dollars was big; murdering to get it was about as big as it got. He glanced at Holly and then down at his plate. Damn, damn, damn her devious little hide. What the hell had she done with his money?

Davis eyed Roman with renewed respect. He knew all too well what fees that sort of work demanded. So, maybe Holly's instincts weren't so far wrong after all. And maybe he *was* a man to be trusted, but just in case… He glanced at Holly, remembering that he'd promised her no background investigation, but it wouldn't hurt to make a couple of calls.

Just then the maid came in with the main course.

"Ah," Davis said. "Prime rib, my favorite."

Holly smiled. "And lobster, and venison, and…" She caught herself. "Oh! I'm doing it again!"

Davis all but clapped his hands with delight. "Wonderful! Isn't this wonderful, Gordon? Billy is on the road to recovery. And my precious Holly, who we thought was lost to us forever, is getting well before our eyes!"

Roman looked at her and winked. "And the more time passes, the easier the memories will come."

Gordon tried to smile, but his belly was too full of panic to manage more than a weak grin. He had to do something to delay the inevitable. His mind was in a whirl as he forked a bit of the meat. Think, Gordon, think! You beat Carl Julian at his own game. You can do this, too.

He chewed thoughtfully, his eyes on his plate, but his mind on the business at hand. Suddenly, something occurred to him. He looked up.

"Holly, dear, I've been thinking about how frightened you must have been when you fell out of the plane, and how brave you were to find your way to shelter." He beamed at her, knowing he was on the right track. "Did you have to walk far after your parachute landed?"

She didn't bother to hide her surprise. In all the time she'd been home, this was the first time Gordon had showed any interest in the actual events that had happened to her.

"I don't know. Probably," she said. "I had no way of judging distance."

He looked suitably concerned. "I say, Justice, where is your cabin located as opposed to where Holly landed?"

Roman's mind was on something else. Something Gordon just said was bothering him, but he couldn't figure out what it was. It took him a moment or two to answer.

"Probably a good two or three miles downhill, although that's just a guess. I saw no need to retrace her steps to check her story. And even if I had wanted to, the snow prevented us from doing anything about it."

But Gordon wouldn't let go.

"Must be nice to have your own cabin. I might look into something like that as an investment." Then he added. "I'm in real estate, you know. Is it far from Denver?"

Now Roman knew he was lying about something. Mallory had no ties to the real-estate business.

"A couple of hours southwest, as the crow flies."

Gordon nodded, then proceeded to butter a piece of bread, letting the conversation drop. This was getting him nowhere. The man was too cagey, and he couldn't press the issue or they'd begin to wonder why he cared. However, he'd figured another way to eliminate a possibility. All he had to do was call in a few favors from some people he knew. After that, he'd know which way to proceed.

Roman sat without eating, still trying to work through what it was that kept niggling at him. *How frightened you must have been when you fell out of—*

Roman looked up, fixing Gordon with a calculated stare. All along, everyone had been assuming that Holly jumped from the plane. After all, she was wearing a parachute, which indicated planning on someone's part. But just now, Gordon said, "When you fell..." Those were two entirely different means of leaving a plane.

"Say, Gordon, exactly why did the plane go down?" Roman asked.

Startled, Gordon looked up. "Why, um, I was coming from the cockpit when I heard—"

Davis frowned. "I thought you told me you didn't know what happened," he said. "You said there was an explosion and then you blacked out, remember?"

Gordon blanched. Caught. Caught in his own lies. "Of course," he said quickly. "I was about to say, when I heard an explosion. I'm sorry to say I don't know anything else."

"Then why did you say Holly fell out?" Roman asked. "She was wearing a parachute, which indicates some sort of planning. And it's my understanding that no one else had one on. Why would she fall out if she'd been planning to jump?"

In the act of taking a bite of her food, Holly heard that same voice from her past.

Here. Put this on and be quiet. He'll hear us.

Staring at Gordon, she laid down her fork.

"Yes, Gordon. Why *was* I wearing a parachute? Why would you say I fell?"

Tiny beads of sweat began popping out on Gordon's forehead and above his upper lip. He shrugged and tried to smile.

"I'm sorry if I misled anyone," he said quickly. "It was just a figure of speech. As I said, I was in the cockpit with the pilot just prior to the incident, so I have no way of knowing why Holly was wearing a chute. I guess I just assumed she fell out during the explosion."

He was too nervous, and both Holly and Roman knew it. But why he would lie was beyond them. It was a small plane. They'd been on the same flight. Unless it had to do with the money in some way, this made no sense.

"Enough talk about that horrible event," Davis ordered, and the conversation moved to another topic. "On a different note, I saw in the paper that the police are still investigating Julian's murder."

"Who's Julian?" Holly asked.

Davis quickly apologized. "I'm sorry. I keep forgetting, sweetheart. Carl Julian was the manager of a downtown casino. He was murdered in his office a day or so before your accident."

"Did I know him?" she asked.

Gordon spoke quickly, too quickly for Roman's peace of mind.

"No! No, you didn't."

"But that's not so," Davis said. "She did know Julian. They chaired a fund-raiser together last year. A charity event for a local homeless shelter, I think."

Gordon hoped he didn't look as aghast as he felt. Everywhere he turned, his life was becoming more and more immersed in the Benton web.

"Sorry, Holly, I didn't realize. I suppose that was before we met."

"How awful for his family," she said.

"He doesn't have any," Gordon added, and then realized he'd given away too much knowledge about a subject he wasn't supposed to know anything about.

"That's true," Davis said. "He wasn't married. But he was a decent enough man. I heard the police had exhausted all of their leads."

Good, Gordon thought. At least one thing was still in his favor.

No one else at the table noticed the faux pas except Roman. He made a mental note of it, but let it slide without comment. Somewhere within all of this mess was the answer to the mystery surrounding the money. The sooner he found it, the better off everyone would be.

It was just after midnight when Holly heard footsteps in the hall outside her bedroom door. She'd been in bed for hours and trying without success to sleep. Every time she closed her eyes, her mind filled with images she couldn't identify. While she supposed it was flashes of her memory trying to return, instead of elation, she felt nothing but frustration. If her body was bound and determined to flood her mind with bits and pieces of her past, the least it could do was furnish subtitles to match.

The footsteps continued, and she thought nothing of them until they stopped just outside her door. She rolled over in bed and sat up, watching in sudden horror as the doorknob began to turn.

"Who's there?" she called, and the moment she spoke, whoever it was quickly hurried away.

The safety of her bedroom had suddenly become more of a jail than a refuge, and she got out of bed in a panic. Without grabbing a robe, she ran toward the door. Holding her breath, she eased it open just enough to make sure the hallway was empty. That was all she needed to know. She headed toward Roman's room, telling herself that as soon as she got there she'd be safe.

The same moment she burst into the room, Roman rolled over. He was out of bed and at her side within seconds.

"What's wrong?"

Holly couldn't quit shivering, although now that the moment had passed, she kept telling herself she'd made a big deal out of nothing.

"Someone was outside my room," she said. "When I called out, they ran away, as if I'd surprised them by not being asleep."

Roman shoved her toward his bed and then grabbed his pants, yanking them on in a rush.

"Stay here," he said. "Lock the door behind me when I'm gone and don't let anybody but me back in here."

His behavior startled her. "But, Roman, maybe I was just—"

He grabbed her by the shoulders. "Someone's missing a million dollars, remember? As you pointed out, people have been killed for a whole lot less. You stay here and do what I say. I'll be back."

Now she *was* afraid. She'd let herself believe that the

money was somehow going to explain itself and then disappear. And when Roman suddenly pulled out a gun and started toward the door, she grabbed him.

"Roman, I couldn't bear it if anything happened to you."

"Nothing's going to happen to me," he said shortly. "But I can't say the same thing for whoever the hell scared you. Lock the door behind me."

She did as she was told, then scurried to his bed, crawling beneath the covers and into the spot where he'd been lying, taking comfort in the fact that the mattress still held the heat from his body.

Roman slipped into his old military mode, moving without noise and listening and looking for anything out of place. He knew that what she heard might have been nothing. But then again, there was too much at stake to ignore the least sign of danger.

He paused outside each door, listening for sounds of life. He had no way of knowing who occupied which rooms, or how many were empty. But it was after midnight. If someone was still up, they were going to have to explain why to his satisfaction.

Just as he was about to start downstairs, he noticed a faint light beneath the door at the end of the hall. Whoever occupied that room was about to receive a visitor. Without knocking to announce himself, he pushed it open, recognizing Gordon, but not the man in the bed.

When Gordon saw the gun in Roman's hands, he gasped. "What's the meaning of this?"

Roman stepped inside and closed the door, then walked toward the bed without taking his eyes off of Gordon. When he reached the foot of the bed, he looked down. This must be the brother.

"I asked you a question," Gordon cried. "You have no right to come in here like this. Can't you see my brother is in fragile condition?"

Roman fixed Gordon with a cold, unwavering look. "Where were you about five minutes ago?"

Even by lamplight, Roman saw him flush.

"I was right here," Gordon cried. "I've been here ever since we retired."

Unintentionally, Billy Mallory gave away his brother's lie. Roman saw the surprise, then something that looked like concern, spreading across Billy's face.

Roman turned to the brother. "Is that right?"

Only then did Billy look away, but not soon enough to hide what he'd been thinking.

Gordon stood abruptly. "Don't question my brother as if he was on trial."

"Somebody tried to enter Holly's room. It scared the hell out of her, and I'm making certain it doesn't happen again…not even unintentionally."

The warning was there. All Gordon had to do was grasp it. And grasp it he did. At this point, he knew he'd do anything to get this man…and that gun…out of their room.

"I'm sorry I snapped," Gordon said, trying to smile. Then he pointed at Billy. "You can understand my concern."

Roman's voice fell to just above a whisper. "And you can understand mine. You know, for a man who was supposed to marry, you show damned little concern for the bride-to-be. That leads me to doubt your story. And when that happens, there's usually a reason behind the lie. I don't like to be lied to. And I don't like people threatening my woman."

He took another step forward until he and Gordon were face-to-face. As his voice became quieter, the threat behind it became more real.

"And I'm sure you can understand *my* concern."

Without giving Gordon time to answer, Roman turned his back on both Mallorys and stalked out of the room, shutting the door behind him with a very distinct thud.

Billy felt as if he might throw up. "Who the hell was that?"

Gordon's anger was about to erupt. "That, brother dear,

was Roman Justice, the man who pulled dear Holly out of the snow and saved her sweet behind.''

''I thought you said he was a nobody,'' Billy cried. ''Nobodys don't carry guns. That was a Luger, for God's sake.''

''So I was wrong,'' Gordon said.

Billy groaned. ''Why does that not surprise me?''

''Shut up!'' Gordon hissed. ''I've got everything under control.''

''That's what Captain Kirk said just before they blasted his butt into some far-off galaxy.''

Gordon spun. ''What?''

Billy rolled his eyes. ''Never mind. It was just a figure of speech.''

''This is no time to be fooling around,'' Gordon said.

Billy glared. ''Then try to remember that the next time you pass Holly's door. You promised me you'd leave her alone.''

''I wasn't going to hurt her,'' Gordon muttered, taking a syringe from his pocket. ''It's supposed to loosen inhibitions. I figured it might loosen her tongue, as well.''

Billy snorted beneath his breath. ''You weren't going to hurt her, huh? That's rich. It's probably what Julian thought right before you slit his throat.''

Gordon blanched, and then a dark, angry red spread up his face and neck.

''I told you not to mention his name again,'' Gordon said. ''Someone could hear you.''

''They'll hear a whole lot more than Carl Julian's name if you don't leave Holly alone,'' Billy said.

''I am, I will and I don't intend to discuss her with you again,'' Gordon growled. ''The way you act, anyone would think you were the one who'd been dating her.''

Billy was too quiet. When Gordon turned to look, he saw the truth on his face. For the first time since the entire fiasco began to unwind, now he understood why.

''You're in love with her.''

Billy didn't respond, but he also didn't deny. Gordon

wanted to slap him, but it would have done no good. The damage was already done.

"You little fool! You ruined everything for us because of a woman who doesn't even know you're alive."

"That remains to be seen," Billy said. "One of these days, she'll regain her memory. When she does, she will at least remember that I didn't want her dead."

Gordon pivoted angrily and stalked out of the room. He was so blinded by rage he didn't even notice the dark shadow of a man standing at the far end of the hall.

But Roman saw everything, including the anger Gordon had taken with him. A muscle jerked in his jaw. It was the only thing that gave away his emotion. He kept trying to think of a reason to get Holly out from under this roof without causing a scene. Because as long as Gordon Mallory was here, he knew she was in danger.

Two days later, and right in the middle of a busy intersection in downtown Las Vegas, Roman's cellular phone began to ring. He pulled into a parking space and then answered.

"Hello."

His secretary's familiar voice came over the line all too clear.

"Thank goodness," Elizabeth said. "I've been trying to get you for more than an hour. The darned call wouldn't go through."

Roman frowned. She wouldn't have called if there hadn't been trouble. He slumped down in the seat, trying to stretch his long legs. It was no use. Holly's car was too damned small to stretch anything but imagination.

"What's up?"

"The police just left, and Royal's been calling and leaving messages here since early this morning. Someone broke into the cabin and messed it up. Royal said a ranger discovered it after driving by and noticing the front door was ajar."

Roman frowned. "Damn. I locked it when I left—I know I did."

"Yes, the door had been kicked in," she said.

Roman sighed. "That's too bad, although I don't know how we could have prevented it. Do they have any leads?"

"No, but that's not everything," she said. Then she took a deep breath. "The police were here this morning because someone also broke into your house last night. According to what they told me, it seems to be in a similar condition as the cabin had been. They said it looked as if someone was looking for something, because there was a lot of valuable property that they completely ignored."

Roman sat up. "That's no coincidence," he said shortly.

"After Royal talked to them about the incident at the cabin, the police are inclined to agree with you. The detective asked me if you were working on any case that might cause such a reaction. I told them you hadn't taken on any new ones, and that as far as I knew, there was nothing pending that would indicate such behavior." She hesitated. "Was I wrong?"

"No, Elizabeth, you weren't wrong. At least not about the cases. However, I'm working on something here in an unofficial capacity that does."

"Oh! Well, should I call the police and—"

"No. I'll do it myself," he said, then he thought of the money he'd locked in the safe. "The office…was it untouched?"

He heard her gasp. "Why, yes, but is there a chance that—"

"Yes."

"Oh, dear. What should I do?" she asked.

"Call Texas Securities, tell them I want around-the-clock guards on my office, and I want it to continue until they hear from me."

"Yes sir," she said, making fast and furious notes.

"Oh, and Elizabeth…"

"Yes, sir?"

"Under no circumstances are you to go to the parking garage alone. Better yet, just close the office until I return."

"But your calls—"

Roman's eyes darkened. "Your safety is worth more than new business. If they're serious, they'll call back."

"Yes, sir. I'll get on this right away."

"Good, and give the authorities this number. If they have any more questions, they can ask me."

He disconnected, and then stared out through the windshield. But he didn't see the constant stream of pedestrian tourists. All he could think was that someone was looking for the money. Suddenly, the trip he'd been about to make to the newspaper archive seemed less important than getting back to Holly. Someone was getting desperate, and she could easily be their next target.

Chapter 14

Holly was coming out of the library with a book when Julia, the downstairs maid, called out to her.

"Miss Benton, your hairdresser is on the phone. Do you want to cancel your standing, or should I tell him you'll call him back?"

The question took her aback. Again, she was faced with how much of her life was lost. Somewhere within the city was a hairdresser who knew more about her than she knew about herself. And when the maid spoke again, Holly realized she must look as troubled as she felt.

"Miss Benton, why don't I tell him you'll call back?" Julia asked.

Holly nodded, mouthing a thank-you. Moments later, the maid was gone, leaving Holly alone in the hall and holding a book she no longer cared to read. She laid it on a nearby table and started toward the patio, thinking that sunshine and fresh air might lift her spirits.

As she was passing the ornate mirror in the formal dining room, she caught a glimpse of herself. There, framed in gilt and visible within the pristine reflection, she knew a moment of recognition and stopped. Her heart began to pound, and there was a long moment of anticipation as she looked down at her feet, at the white leather sandals she was wearing, and had the distinct memory of trying them on before she'd bought them.

"Oh God, oh God," she whispered, then closed her eyes and turned. When she opened them, she was facing the mirror and staring at the woman within.

For a long silent moment, she stared, analyzing the dark, shoulder-length hair, the wide, sea green eyes, as well as the woman's trembling lips. She stood without moving, waiting for that fleeting bit of recognition to expand. It never came.

Finally, she turned away, unaware that she was shaking. And that was how Roman found her. Standing in the middle of the room and wearing a look of defeat.

"Holly...baby...what's wrong?"

She walked into his arms.

"Oh, Roman, I thought..." She sighed and hid her face against his chest, relishing the feel of the soft white linen and the hard, steady rhythm of his heart.

"You thought what?"

"I thought I was going to remember."

His grip tightened. "You will."

"It was so close." She pointed to the mirror. "I saw my reflection, and for a fraction of a second, I almost knew the woman in there."

Roman had been wondering what excuse he would use to get her out of the house. Now he had it.

"You know what? I think you need to get away for a while. Let's take a drive. We'll pick up something later. Maybe have a picnic."

She sighed. "I'll go, but only if you promise I don't ever have to come back."

A wry grin tilted a corner of his mouth as he dug his hand through the back of her hair and pulled her to within inches of his lips.

"No promises," he whispered.

Tears came swiftly, but she blinked them away. "I know, I know, and no regrets."

"Where's your father?" he asked.

"I don't know, probably in his study. I heard him say something earlier about making some calls."

"Go change into something comfortable. I'll tell him we're leaving."

Now he had her attention. "Where are we going?"

He leaned down and whispered in her ear. "You'll see. Just hustle. I have this sudden and terrible need to get you naked."

Her eyes widened, and a small smile broke across her face. "An offer I can't refuse," she said, and took the stairs two at a time.

Roman watched her go, telling himself he was playing with fire. Day after day, he kept opening his heart to a woman who might one day give it back.

Ah, God, I've lived life on the edge before, but never to this extent.

All the way to Davis's study, he was wrestling with his conscience and trying to decide how much to tell her father about what was happening. By the time he got there, his decision had been made. Basically, he could tell him nothing without revealing the fact that she'd bailed out of a plane with a million dollars in her possession. The door to the study was open. He paused on the threshold.

"Mr. Benton?"

Davis was deep in a financial report and answered without looking up.

"Hmm?"

"I'm taking Holly out for a drive."

Now Roman had his attention. Davis dropped the report and looked up. There was a frown on his face, and Roman could already see the objection coming.

"She needs to get away for a bit. The pressure she's under is getting to her."

Davis stood. Anger was thick in his voice. "I do not pressure my daughter, and I'd rather you didn't take her off the premises."

"Mr. Benton, just because something bad happened to her once doesn't mean it will happen again. You can't keep her locked up. She won't get well until she regains a normal life." Then his voice hardened. "Don't forget what I do for a living…and I'm good at what I do."

Davis's shoulders slumped. "I overreacted. I'm sorry. But you have to remember that I thought I'd lost her. When you called and told me she was still alive, I felt as if I'd been given a miracle."

Roman turned to leave. "I understand. But it doesn't change what she's going through now."

"I know, and I'll try harder to give her space."

"That's good," Roman said. "If we're going to be late, we'll call."

"Fine," Davis said. "Have a good time."

Davis picked up his report and sat down, but Roman hadn't finished.

"Mr. Benton…"

"Please, call me Davis."

"Davis, then. Where is Gordon Mallory?"

Benton shrugged. "I don't know. He said something at breakfast about going to his apartment to get some more clothes for himself and for Billy. Why?"

"Just curious," Roman said, and left.

Now his interest was piqued. What apartment? According to the Las Vegas city billing records, Gordon Mallory no longer had one. He headed up the stairs to get Holly, but as he reached the landing, made a quick decision and went to Billy Mallory's room, instead.

He knocked. A private nurse he'd seen in the halls came to the door.

"Yes?"

"Is he asleep?" Roman asked.

"No, but he's—"

"I won't stay long. I was looking for Gordon and thought maybe he knew where I could find him."

She glanced over her shoulder. "I don't know," she said, still hesitating. She'd had orders straight from Gordon Mallory himself to keep people out. Still, it seemed cruel, keeping the young man all alone like this. In her opinion, a good frame of mind helped a body heal, so what could this hurt?

"All right, but only for a moment," she said.

"Thanks," Roman said. "Why don't you take the opportunity to take a break? I promise I won't leave until you get back."

She smiled. "Why, thank you. That's very kind. I did need to make a call."

"Take your time," Roman said. "I'll be here."

"Mr. Mallory, you have a visitor," she said. "Since it's nearly time to take your medicine, I'll go down to the kitchen to get it, rather than have staff bring it up. Would you like me to bring you a snack?"

Billy shook his head. "I'm not hungry," he said, wondering who his visitor could possibly be.

The nurse smiled. "I'll be right back."

She walked out the door as Roman walked in, and Billy had an urge to call her back. But he didn't. The worst thing he could do was give way to panic. As far as the world knew, there was no reason on earth why he should dread seeing anyone from this household. Right now, only he and Gordon were aware of their duplicity, and he wanted to keep it that way.

Roman stopped at the foot of the bed and nodded. "Mallory."

"Mr. Justice…isn't it?"

Roman nodded. "We didn't exactly get introduced last time we met."

"True," Billy said. "I saw more of that Luger than I did of you."

Roman refused to be intimidated by the remark. "Like I said before, I take a threat to Holly as personal."

Billy shifted his position on the bed, grunting painfully as aching bones and muscles objected.

"That's fine by me. I would never fault you for that," he said.

Roman frowned. That was a remark that Gordon should have made. He stared thoughtfully at the young man, judging him to be in his early twenties. He was smaller than Gordon, a bit fairer in hair and complexion than Gordon. One might say he was a faded version of the original. But Roman reminded himself that this man had been a passenger on the plane. He had to know more than he was saying.

"I assume you're healing," Roman said.

"Yes, but far too slowly for my peace of mind. If I had my way, I would be out of this bed and on my way to the Bahamas." And then he realized that he might have sounded a bit desperate and added. "I was looking forward to beaches and babes, if you know what I mean."

"If it was meant to happen, then it will happen," Roman said.

Billy's frown deepened. That was a rather cryptic remark.

"Did I hear you asking the nurse about Gordon?"

Roman nodded. "Where is he?"

"After waving a gun in his face the other night, I can hardly believe you want him for a tennis partner. Why do you ask?"

"Had some questions I wanted to ask him," Roman said. "Maybe you can help me, instead."

Panic returned twofold. Calm down, Billy reminded himself. All I have to do is play dumb. Gordon does it so well, surely I can handle a couple of lies on my own.

"I'll try," he said. "Although I don't remember much about the crash. In fact, I expected to die." He laughed harshly. "Imagine my surprise when I woke up in the hospital instead."

Roman didn't respond, but it occurred to him that, for someone who should have been thanking God that he was still in one piece and breathing, the man was rather bitter.

"So, what do you want to know?" Billy asked.

Roman strolled over to the window, giving the man a chance to relax. When he turned, his question caught Billy off guard.

"Everyone says that Gordon and Holly were eloping."

Billy's heart skipped a beat. He could tell by the tone of the man's voice that he doubted the story.

"Yeah, that's right," Billy said.

Roman kept baiting the trap, waiting for the man to give himself away. "That's odd."

"What's odd?" Billy asked.

Roman walked back to the end of the bed, pinning him with a hard, unflinching stare.

"You know the old saying—'Two's company, three's a crowd.' If they were eloping, then why were you there?"

Billy choked, and it felt as if all the air went out of his lungs at once. *Damn, damn, damn you, Gordon. I knew we shouldn't have come here. This man is too curious and he's asking questions no one else has thought to ask.*

"Every groom has to have a best man," he said, trying for a smile. "I'm Gordon's best friend, therefore the best man, right?"

"Oh, then you're saying that they were making a party out of eloping."

Billy relaxed. "Yeah, that's it. It was going to be a real party."

Roman shook his head. "Only three of you? Who was going to stand in for Holly? I find it strange that Gordon would insist on taking a witness, but Holly would not."

The smile stayed on Billy's face, but that's as far as it got. Panic continued to spread throughout his system.

"Don't ask me, ask them," he finally said. "I was just going along for the ride."

"Yeah, that's right. Babes and beaches, you said." Then before Billy could regroup, Roman fired another question that left Billy stuttering to answer.

"I'll bet you'll be glad to get up and about and get back

to your own home, your own things. Do you live far from here?''

He was saved from having to answer as Holly appeared in the doorway and waved at Roman.

''There you are,'' she said. ''I've been looking for you. I'm ready to go.''

Roman held out his hand. ''Come say hello,'' he urged.

She hesitated, and then entered. She knew this was Billy Mallory's room, but up to now had not paid him a visit.

''Mr. Mallory, I hope you're feeling better.''

It was hard for Billy to breathe normally. Of course, he knew about Holly's amnesia, but the total lack of recognition on her face was disconcerting. In a way, it lessened his perception of his own identity.

''I'm doing fine.''

He kept staring at her, taking careful note of everything about her, from the old Levi's she was wearing, to the tank top and tennis shoes. She was nothing like the stylish and perfectly manicured woman he'd been used to seeing, but he thought he liked this Holly better.

Suddenly embarrassed, she glanced at Roman. ''I guess I'll wait for you downstairs.''

She started to leave when Billy called out her name.

''Holly! Wait!''

She turned. ''Yes?''

''I'm very glad you are all right.''

His sincerity was obvious, and because it was unexpected, it touched her deeply.

''Why, thank you,'' she said, and then impulsively, walked to his bedside. ''I know this must be strange to you, but were we good friends?''

He sighed. ''Not as good as I would have liked, but yes, I'd say we were friendly acquaintances.''

Holly nodded. ''I thought so.''

Her answer surprised him. ''Why?'' Billy asked.

''I'm not uncomfortable around you.''

Billy smiled. "That's good. I would hate to think I made you afraid."

Dump her out if she doesn't change her mind.

A pervasive chill suddenly swept through her body. "I need to go now," she said, and bolted from the room.

Roman's eyes narrowed. Something had spooked her. He glanced down at Mallory. Billy's expression said it all. I'll be damned, Roman thought. The man's in love with her.

"Tell Gordon I was asking about him," Roman said.

Billy blinked, as if coming out of a trance, and then nodded. "I'll be sure and do that," he said.

"Here's your nurse," Roman said as the woman entered the room. "Wouldn't want to outstay my welcome."

As Roman left, Billy had the distinct impression that his and his brother's days were numbered. Roman Justice was no man's fool. Their story about the reason for the flight and explanation of the events leading up to the crash were weak, and he obviously knew it.

Billy rolled onto his side, testing his strength and mobility. A sickening pain hit instantly, and he fell back with a groan.

"Please, Mr. Mallory," the nurse cautioned. "You must not move."

Move, hell. Thanks to Gordon, I need to be able to run, and soon. I have a feeling our time is running out.

They drove west from Las Vegas, passing casino after casino until there was nothing to see except desert and the mountains in the distance. The closer they got to the foothills, the more relaxed Holly became.

"Roman."

"Yeah?"

"I'm so glad you thought of this. Thank you. I should have done it days ago."

Roman gripped the steering wheel a little tighter. She was so happy, and what he had to tell her was going to ruin the mood.

"You're welcome, baby."

She leaned back in the seat, completely relaxed and enjoying the lulling motion of the ride.

"When you left this morning, I expected you to be gone most of the day. Coming back was a nice surprise." Then it dawned on her that he had come back. She'd never asked why.

"Roman?"

He grinned as she scooted closer to him. "Now what?"

"I was so wrapped up in my problems I never did ask why you'd come back. You hadn't been gone an hour. Did you forget something?"

"No, I didn't forget anything."

There was something about the tone of his voice that alerted her to a problem. She sat up.

"Then why?"

He took a deep breath. There was no easy way to say what had to be said.

"I got a call from my secretary. The police had come to my office looking for me."

All the blood drained from her face as she straightened with a jerk. Clutching her hands in her lap, she was unable to look at him and afraid of what he was going to say.

"This has something to do with me, doesn't it?"

He pulled over to the side of the road and then stopped.

"Holly, look at me."

She turned and then waited.

"Someone broke into the cabin."

Her heart skipped a beat.

"They didn't take anything, just tore it up." He paused, then added. "As if they were looking for something."

She swallowed nervously.

"And last night, someone broke into my house back in Dallas and did the same thing."

She covered her face with her hands. "Oh God, oh God. It's the money."

He sighed. There was no use lying to her. "Probably."

"Probably? There's no *probably* about it. It's my fault this is happening to you. I asked you to hide that money for me. You tried to talk me out of it, but no! I wouldn't listen. And now your home and your property have been vandalized, and it's all my fault."

He took her by the hand and pulled her into his arms.

"Hush, baby, it's okay. It comes with the territory of my job."

She pulled back, unwilling to let him bear the burden of her mistake.

"But this is my fault, and it's not all right. What are we going to do?"

He traced the shape of her face with the tip of his finger and then grinned.

"I know what I want to do."

She grimaced. "Oh, Roman, be serious."

He bent his head until their lips were only inches apart.

"You want me to get serious? Here? In broad daylight? Where everyone can see?"

"You know what I mean," she said.

"Well, I might, then again, I might not. Are you saying you want to trade spit and hugs, or just talk about Gordon and Billy Mallory?" He grinned. "Personally, I'd a whole lot rather love you, but I'm a man of the nineties. I'm willing to let a female be boss."

She grinned, which was exactly what he'd been aiming for. "Trade spit and hugs! Where on earth did you ever come up with a phrase like that?"

"My daddy. That was his standard warning to all of us boys before we went out on a date. Boys, don't be tradin' nothin' but spit and hugs with your girl. You go any further than that, and you'll be changin' diapers before your time."

She laughed aloud. "He must have been quite a character. I wish I could have met him."

"I do, too," he said softly.

She looked at Roman. "Can we worry about the money later?"

A slow grin spread across his face. "You bet, baby. We've

got all night and all day tomorrow to worry about that damned stuff.''

"Good,'' she said. "Then let's go back to plan A. What was it you said earlier? Something about getting me naked?''

Roman threw back his head and laughed. Then he laughed some more. He couldn't remember the last time he'd felt this lighthearted, or this much in love.

"That's close enough,'' he said, and started the car. For today, he was willing to pretend that everything in their world was perfectly in place.

The Wild Horse Hotel and Casino was just off the highway and about a quarter of a mile from the foothills of a nearby mountain, although it wasn't the scenery that pulled in the customers. It was the luck of the draw…the game of chance…the opportunity to become rich from a throw of the dice. Even out here in the middle of nowhere, the place was packed.

Roman walked up to the desk with Holly beside him. It was all he could do to keep her still until they had checked in.

"You act as if you've never seen a casino before,'' he teased.

She grinned. "I'm sure I have, but for the life of me I can't remember where.'' Her eyes were alight with interest as she looked around. "However, I think I like them.''

He leaned down and kissed her square on the mouth. "Looks like I picked a hell of a place to talk you into getting naked. I may have to tie you to the bed to keep you away from those one-armed bandits.''

His reference to the slot machines was amusing, but not as funny as the notion that she'd rather gamble than make love to him.

She turned and slipped her arms around his neck, then whispered. "You can tie me to the bed any time you want, cowboy.''

His eyes glittered dangerously, but there was a go-to-hell grin on his face as he turned to the man behind the desk.

"We'll be needing a room," he said shortly. "Nonsmoking, king-size, for as long as it takes."

The clerk's mouth dropped. He took one look at the couple and reached for a key. Within ten minutes, they were in a room.

Roman locked the door and then tossed his hat on a nearby table.

Holly arched an eyebrow. "Is this going to be kinky?" she asked.

Roman grinned. "Why do you ask?"

"Well, you told me to wear something comfortable, so I was wondering…what, exactly, were you planning to do with me…besides tie me to the bed?"

He shook his head, and there was a distinct gleam in his eyes as he started toward her.

"Holly, baby, you are a caution and that's a fact. But I don't think I'll be needing that rope. I haven't had any trouble getting you in bed, and I'm not expecting any now."

Her heart was beginning to race. All she could think about was lying in his arms and coming undone.

"No trouble, I promise," she said softly, and pulled the skimpy tank top over her head.

"And no regrets," he said, tossing his shirt across the back of a chair, and reached for her.

Bare to the waist and aching to feel his weight on her body, she trembled beneath his touch.

"Ah, Roman, make love to me now."

Caught up in the heat of the moment, they discarded clothing, leaving it where it fell. The need between them was strong, the urgency mutual. She grasped his shoulders, pulling him with her. He followed willingly, pinning her to the bed with his weight.

Somewhere down below, the gamblers still played, sometimes staking their future in hot pursuit of a fast fortune. But there was no risk involved in what Roman and Holly were about to do. They'd been this way before. They'd danced this dance. They'd played this game. And all they had to do was bet on each other. He didn't have to be a gambling man to love his lady. She was a sure thing, all the way.

Holly looked up, imprinting every facet of him into her mind, wanting to remember this moment, to savor this feeling of certainty and of belonging for all time.

Roman felt himself falling, down into those eyes, past her soul and into infinity—and knew a moment of sheer terror. He loved this woman beyond anything he'd ever known before, but the mystery still surrounding her was escalating to the point of danger.

Lying beside her, he braced himself up on one elbow, and began tracing the shape of her face with the tip of his finger, measuring every feature by touch, as well as sight. Her eyelids were fluttering, trying to stay open, yet mesmerized by the slow, sensuous stroke of his hand. A muscle jerked at the side of his jaw. His voice was low and rough with emotion.

"Mine."

Her eyes flew open.

"Daisy...Holly...whatever you call yourself today or tomorrow, you're forever mine."

Swift tears filmed her vision. Her voice was shaking as she answered. "I wasn't about to argue the point."

His eyes narrowed, following the darkness of his thoughts.

"Right now, you don't remember enough to argue. It's afterward that I'm talking about. I don't know who you loved before, and I don't care. It's now and tomorrow that has to matter. You're mine now."

She laid a hand on the side of his face, settling the darkness back where it belonged—in the past.

"And I'll be yours tomorrow, and every other tomorrow that God gives me. I swear."

He tunneled his fingers through the back of her hair and then pulled her close. Her breath was soft on his face as he opened his mouth. When their lips met, he stifled a groan and let himself go, losing sight of time and reason in sweet Holly's arms.

Chapter 15

Holly lay still within the warmth of Roman's embrace, savoring the aftermath of his love. He had quite a way about him that she couldn't deny. He'd taken her high and let her down easy, and in spite of the time that had passed, was still trembling from the onslaught.

Footsteps passed their door, some hurried, others dragging. It was easy to tell who had won at the tables tonight and who'd lost. Holly pitied them for believing that money brought happiness. She'd obviously been born to money, and look what had happened to her. Added to that, there was a bag full of money that had nearly gotten her killed. Now the break-in at Roman's home, as well as the cabin. She was afraid. How was this ever going to end?

Roman stroked the length of her back, from the base of her skull to the curve of her backside, up and down, over and over, just like the way they'd made love. And even though passion had been satiated, he wasn't ready to let go of the motion. She was in his blood, in his heart, in his mind. And something else had happened during their drive out here. He had come to a decision she might not like. There was no time left to wait for her memory to return. He had to make something happen before something happened to them.

"Roman, what are we going to do?"

He paused in midstroke, with the palm of his hand splayed in the middle of her back. So the interlude was over. It was back to reality. He gave her a quick but gentle squeeze and then leaned back so that he could see her face.

"I have an idea, but it will involve how skilled you are at telling a lie."

She rose up, a startled look on her face.

"Lie? About what?"

"Remembering."

She frowned. "I don't understand."

"I know, baby," he said softly. "But when the time comes, you will."

She hid her face against his shoulder.

"I am afraid—for you, and for myself."

"Don't be," he whispered, and then pressed his lips against the crown of her head. "Trust me?"

She sighed. "Yes."

"Then let me worry about the details, okay?"

"Okay."

"That's settled, then," he said, and glanced at the time. "It will be dark before we get back to the city. I told your father that we'd call if we were going to be late."

"I'll do it," she said.

Ignoring her nudity, she rolled over to the side of the bed and picked up the phone, punching in the numbers without thought.

Roman watched her, waiting to see how long it took her before she realized what she'd just done.

"This is Holly. Let me speak to my father." She waited. Moments later, Davis picked up the phone. "Dad, it's me. We'll be late getting back, so don't wait dinner. We'll get something on the way."

Roman watched as she listened to her father's response. A few moments later, she told him goodbye, then hung up.

"That's that," she said, and then leaned back against him, reluctant to give up the body-to-body connection.

Roman ran a hand down the length of her arm, then pulled a stray strand of hair away from her cheek.

"Hey, you," he said, and tugged at her hair until she turned to look at him.

She grinned. "What?"

"What's your home phone number?"

The grin slipped. "Why, it's, uh..." She frowned. "I don't..." Then it dawned. "I did it again, didn't I?"

He nodded.

She thrust her fingers through her hair, combing it away from her face. "When I don't concentrate, I remember, but only the little things...the things that don't matter. Why can't I remember jumping out of a plane? Or why I had all that money? My God, Roman, this is crazy."

"No, baby. In a way, it makes a whole lot of sense. You aren't remembering that stuff because you don't want to. The more traumatic the event, the deeper your subconscious will bury it. It's simply a self-defense mechanism your body uses to protect itself."

She thumped the bed with her fist and then got out of bed, reaching for her clothes and pulling them on with angry motions. Roman hurt for her. He could only imagine how she felt, but within a couple of days, it should all be over. And the moment he thought it, his belly drew tight. He didn't want everything to be over. Not the love. Dear God, for his own peace of mind, let it go on forever.

Distracted and suddenly moody, he got out of bed and reached for his jeans, then began pulling them on. As he was dressing, he spied a small bit of color partially hidden beneath the fallen covers. When he bent down to get it, his mood quickly lightened. When he straightened, he was wearing a cocky grin.

"Uh, Holly?"

She had her tank top in one hand and a sock in the other. "What?" she asked, still looking about the room for her other sock.

He waved the lingerie above his head. "Forget something?"

She looked up. Her panties were dangling from his fingers.

"Oh, great. I'm not wearing my underwear!" She yanked it out of his hand and began unzipping her jeans. "Now I have to start all over."

There was a gleam in his eyes as he grabbed her hand, slowing her intent.

"Only if you insist," he drawled, and then slowly pulled the tab the rest of the way down.

Disgust left her, and in its place came a quick urge to be with him again.

"Are you sure?" she asked breathlessly.

He guided her hand to his zipper and the hard bulge behind it. "What do you think?"

Her voice was soft with longing. "That you're Superman?"

He shook his head and then smiled a slow, easy smile. "No, baby," he said softly. "Just a man." A man in love. But he didn't say it. He'd already said more than he should have. Besides, there was more than one way to say *I love you*.

After finding out that Roman had been in Billy's room, Gordon was livid. The urge to break something, preferably Roman's damned neck, was overwhelming. But it wouldn't give him what he wanted, so he let the urge slide.

Gordon was shaking with anger. "Why did you even talk to him?"

Billy glared. "You said to behave normally. You said not to raise suspicion. What did you want me to do, have him thrown out on his ear for paying a visit?"

Gordon picked up a pillow and threw it across the room.

Billy frowned. That only added to the decision he'd already made.

"I want to leave."

Gordon spun around, his face flushed with frustration and rage. "Then start walking."

Billy started to beg. "Please, Gordon. Let's get out. We've got some money, we can get more, but not if we're locked up in jail."

Gordon stalked to his bed, pointing a finger in his face. "We wouldn't have to get more money if you hadn't given mine away."

"You were going to kill her."

Gordon threw his hands up in the air. "So what were you thinking? That you would just give her the money as a going-away present?"

Voices sounded outside the door, and then faded as they moved away. Gordon lowered his voice.

"You wanted to save her so you put her in a parachute and let her jump. Okay, I can understand that." Then he started to shake, and a froth of spittle began forming at the corner of his mouth. "But why in the name of all that's holy did you give her the money, too? Tell me? Why did you do it?"

Billy's gaze never wavered. "It was blood money, Gordon. You killed for it. I wanted no part of that, just like I want no part of you now. Just help get me out of this place, then you can do whatever your heart desires."

"My heart desires vengeance," he grumbled. "She has something that belongs to me, and I think Justice is in on it. I had that cabin searched, as well as his place in Dallas. They came up empty, but that doesn't mean a thing. There are other options."

Billy paled. "Like what?"

"When I get everything worked out, I'll let you know."

"My God, Gordon, you've lost all reason. Did you know that?"

Gordon shook his head. "No, little brother. All I've lost is a million dollars." He turned on his heel and stalked out of the room.

Billy closed his eyes and swallowed past the knot in his throat.

"You're wrong, Gordon. That's not all you're losing. You're about to lose a brother, as well."

Morning was little more than a promise on the horizon when Roman picked up his cellular phone and headed for the door. After the events of the past few days, leaving Holly alone was no longer an option, but he was going no farther than outside the house. The patio overlooking the tennis courts was spacious. He had some calls to make, and he didn't want them overheard.

He walked down the hall to her bedroom door, then looked inside, making sure she was still asleep. When he saw her lying there, it was all he could do to stay put.

The temptation was strong to crawl in beside her and kiss her awake. He wanted to thrust his hands through that spill of dark hair on her pillow, to feel the swell of her breasts beneath his palms, to watch her eyelids fluttering as he entered her body. But now was not the time. With one last look around the room, he stepped out, closing the door behind him before heading for the stairs.

Downstairs, the staff was up and beginning their day, although they paid no attention to his presence as he passed. When he stepped out onto the patio, he took a deep breath and then closed his eyes, inhaling the morning day and comparing it to a new day back home.

Here, the air was brisk and drier, making the scents it carried more distinct. Spring in Texas usually brought thunderstorms, which gave free rein to the lush growth of anything green. In turn, the air would be filled with a damp, sweet aroma of everything that was in bloom. There was a beauty about this area that couldn't be denied, but he was a Texan born and bred, and it would forever be the place where his heart felt at rest.

At the thought, his eyes narrowed against a familiar spurt of old pain. Would Holly come with him one day? Or would he leave her behind when he left?

And then he shook off the mood and began to walk, moving

farther away from the house with every step. Right now, he couldn't think about his future until he was certain that Holly's would be safe. While his entire plan hinged upon his brothers' cooperation, he was in no doubt they would come to his aid. It was the Justice way.

Pausing beneath the overhanging branches of a nearby tree, he glanced back at the house once more before punching in a quick series of numbers.

Ryder Justice picked up the phone on the second ring.

"Justice Air."

Roman relaxed. "Ryder, it's me, Roman. I need a favor."

Ryder didn't even bother to think before answering. After what Roman had done last year to help save Casey's life, he would have walked on fire if asked.

"Name it," he said.

"Are you free to fly to the ranch tomorrow?"

"No, but I will be after I make a few calls. What do you need?"

"If it wasn't important, I wouldn't ask," he said briefly.

"Hell, little brother, I knew that," Ryder said. "Just tell me what you want me to do."

"I need you to fly out to the ranch, then bring Royal out here to Las Vegas."

Ryder grinned. "Las Vegas. What are you doing out there?"

"Sort of guarding a woman named Holly."

Ryder's grin spread. "Holly, huh? Is she a tall, leggy blonde?"

"No. She's a half-pint brunette."

Ryder chuckled. "Too bad. She's way off your course, right?"

"I wouldn't exactly say that."

Ryder stopped in the middle of a laugh. That wasn't the remark he'd expected to hear. If some woman could actually catch Roman's interest, then Ryder was curious, too.

"So, this…what did you say her name was?"

"It's Holly Benton, but I used to call her Daisy."

"Do I need to know why?"

"No."

Now Ryder was interested. "So you have a client named Holly, who's really Daisy, or vice versa, and you're guarding her sort of, but not really. Is that about it?"

Roman shifted the phone to his other hand and began to pace.

"Ryder, do me another favor, and shut up and listen, okay?"

Ryder chuckled. "Okay. Let 'er rip, although it's beyond me why you need to see Royal. Won't I do?"

"It isn't Royal I need to see, it's what he'll be bringing with him."

"And that would be?"

"A duffel bag."

"A duffel bag? You can't just go buy one out there?"

"Not one like this," Roman muttered. "For once in your life, I need you to listen."

It began to dawn on Ryder that his brother was serious.

"Sorry. I'm listening."

"After you and Royal get to Vegas, I need you to bring the duffel bag to the Benton estate on LaJolla Avenue. It's up in the hills. I'll leave word at the gate to let you in."

"You've got it," Ryder said. Then he paused. "Say, Roman, what's in this duffel bag, anyway?"

"A million dollars, give or take a few thousand."

Ryder took a deep breath and then swallowed twice in rapid succession.

"I'm not even going to ask."

"Good. See you tomorrow around noon."

"We'll be there. I'll see if I can talk Casey into taking the day off. She can stay with Maddie while we're gone," Ryder said, and disconnected.

Roman sighed in satisfaction. One down. One to go. He glanced toward the east and at the sunrise in progress. The vast cloudless sky was streaked with pink and gold. He looked at his watch. It would be after seven at the ranch. Maddie was a sleepyhead, so Royal would probably still be in the house. There was no use delaying the inevitable.

He made the call, again relieved to hear his eldest brother's voice on the other end of the line.

"Hello?"

"Royal, it's me, Roman."

"Where are you?" he growled. "I expected you to at least call after the break-in at the cabin."

"Didn't Elizabeth tell you we talked?"

Royal grabbed at a bowl of cereal and milk, just before Maddie pulled it off the side of the table.

"Yes, she told me. Madeline Michelle, you sit! I'll carry the cereal."

Roman grinned. As always, life with Maddie was never dull.

"Tell my favorite niece I said hello."

"Not until after she's through eating or I'll never get a bite in her mouth."

Roman laughed. "Fair enough." Then he got back to business. "About why I called. I need you to do me a favor."

"And that would be?"

"Do you remember a couple of years ago when I gave you the combination to that big safe in my office?"

Royal frowned. "Yes."

"Do you still have it?"

"Somewhere," Royal said. "Why?"

"Get a pen and paper. I'm going to give it to you again."

Royal took down the numbers. "Okay, got 'em," he muttered. "Now what?"

"I need you to go to my office. There will be an armed guard from Texas Securities on the premises. I'll call them ahead of time and clear you. There is a duffel bag in my safe. I want you to take it to the ranch. In the morning, Ryder will come and get you and fly you and the bag out here to Las Vegas."

Royal started backing up. "Las Vegas? I'm a parent, little brother. I can't just walk off and leave Maddie at a—"

"Casey is coming with Ryder. She'll stay with Maddie until you two get back."

Royal sighed. "Fine. So, I get this bag. We bring it to Vegas. Then what?"

"Ryder will tell you when he gets there. And the less said about the bag, the better. Put it somewhere where Maddie can't find it. I don't want her using the contents to cut out paper dolls."

Royal grinned. "What's in the damned thing, anyway?"

"A million dollars."

Royal cursed before he thought, then rolled his eyes when Maddie looked up with interest. This was great. Miss is-it-Maddie-or-is-it-Memorex? probably wouldn't forget a word of what she just heard. He turned his back on his daughter, lowering his voice so that only Roman could hear.

"Is it legal?" he asked.

Roman grinned. "I'm not sure. I'll find that out after you get here."

"Oh, fine," Royal muttered.

"Will you do it?" Roman asked.

Royal sighed. "Hell, yes," he grumbled. "You knew I would when you called."

"Thanks," Roman said. "See you tomorrow around noon."

Royal snorted beneath his breath. "I can hardly wait. What's for dinner?"

Roman's grin widened. "I'm not sure, but it may be crow."

Royal hung up in his ear.

All the way back to the house, Roman kept thinking of Holly and how she was going to play in the hand he'd just dealt. If he knew his lady like he thought he did, she was going to shine like a new penny. The secrets and lies within these walls were about to end.

It was just after lunch when a cab pulled up to the front door of the Benton estate. Billy was downstairs in his wheelchair, and had been watching for it for some time. His nurse came hurrying from the powder room, clutching at her purse and giving her hair a last-minute pat.

"I see our cab has arrived."

"Whose cab?" Holly asked.

Billy turned, unaware that she was there, and then sighed. He'd planned on leaving without anyone's noticing, but in a way, he was glad. It hurt to think that he would never see her again, but it was for the best. There never had been anything between them except what existed in his mind. To her, he was nothing but Gordon's younger brother.

"It's mine," Billy said, eyeing the white gauzy dress she was wearing and admiring the way it floated around her ankles, then clinging in all the right places. "Doctor's appointment."

Holly frowned. "I'm sure we could have had a doctor come here. Are you certain you're up to this?"

Billy managed a smile. Just like Holly. Always thinking of everyone but herself.

"Oh, yes. This was inevitable."

She thought nothing of his remark. Of course it would have been inevitable that one day he would be up and out of the bed. She had no idea he was referring to the split he was making with Gordon.

"Well, then," she said. "I hope your checkup is good, and you'll soon be able to join us at the table for meals."

His expression stilled as he let himself look at her one last time.

"Thank you, Holly Benton."

She smiled. "Why, you're welcome, but whatever for? I didn't do anything but wish you well."

"Yes, actually you did," he said softly. "One day you'll remember, but for now, let's just say that you were always kind to me. I won't forget it."

She laughed. "My goodness, you're only going to the doctor, not the moon. See you later," she said, and then waved them off as the cab drove away.

She thought nothing of their exit until a couple of hours later when Gordon stormed into the library.

"What the hell have you done with Billy?" he cried.

Roman was sitting at her side, and when Gordon burst into the room, he instinctively stood, putting himself between the man and Holly.

"Back off," he said shortly.

Still anxious, Gordon did as he'd been told. "I'm sorry, but Billy's not in his room."

"Oh, today was his doctor's appointment," Holly said. "He and the nurse left around—" She glanced at her watch. "My goodness, it was hours ago. I hadn't realized it had been so long. It's nearly five. They must have been delayed."

Gordon paled. Billy didn't have a doctor's appointment. In fact, they hadn't even connected with the doctor they'd been advised to see after Billy had been moved from Denver. Instead, the only medical personnel his brother had seen since their arrival was the nurse Benton had provided and a physician's assistant who'd come by a couple of times in the beginning. And while he knew it was possible that Billy had done so on his own and hadn't seen fit to mention it, he sincerely doubted it. Billy just wasn't the take-charge type.

He stuffed his hands in his pockets and then yanked them out, unintentionally scattering a handful of small change across the floor. Instantly, he was on his knees, gathering it up as if the coins were solid gold.

Roman frowned. There was more to this than a brother's concern. This man was about to come unglued, but why? Because they were a little bit late? He didn't think so.

"Why don't you give the doctor's office a call? I'm sure they can clear all this up for you," Holly said.

Gordon got to his feet. "Right," he said, and dropped the coins back in his pocket as he bolted from the room.

Holly frowned. "That was strange."

Roman stepped out into the hall, watching to see where Gordon had gone. A short while later, he saw a cab pull up, and then watched Gordon make a run for the door. Something was up, but what? As an investigator, he knew the best way to find out. Go see for himself.

"Get your purse, Holly. We're going for a ride."

"Maybe I'd better change," she said, brushing at a non-existent speck on the front of her skirt.

He grabbed her hand. "No time. And never mind about that purse, either."

Holly didn't stop to ask why. She could tell by the way Roman was moving that time was precious. Within moments of Gordon's exit, they were in her car and heading down the driveway, following the yellow cab that was disappearing down the street.

"What's wrong?" she asked.

"I don't know," Roman said. "But Gordon is in a panic about something, and I think it has to do with his brother. After everything that's happened in the last few days, I'd rather know than guess."

She nodded, then grabbed her seat belt and buckled herself in as he turned a corner, tires squalling.

Gordon was alternating between fury and fear. He kept telling himself that Billy *was* at some doctor's office, but his gut instincts were telling him different. He didn't want to believe that he had actually acted upon his threat.

A short while later, his cab pulled up at the bus stop. Leaving orders for the driver to wait, he bolted inside, staring at faces all the way into the ticket counter, hoping and praying he'd see his brother in one of them. But it wasn't to be. And after a brief inquiry, he learned that no one named Mallory had purchased a ticket today.

That left the airport. He glanced at his watch. It was getting late. He took a deep breath, telling himself to calm down. Maybe he'd just jumped the gun. Maybe Billy was back at the Benton estate already and wondering where he had gone. There was one sure way to find out. He headed for the phone.

As always, a maid answered. Gordon wasted no time on explanations, he just blurted out what he wanted to know.

"This is Gordon Mallory. Is my brother back from the doctor?"

"Just a moment, sir. I'll check," she said.

Gordon waited impatiently, cursing beneath his breath when someone ran past him, bumping his leg with a suitcase. He glared at the man who was standing in line behind him. If he wanted to use this phone, he was going to have to wait.

"Mr. Mallory?"

Gordon spun and then gripped the receiver a little tighter. "Yes? Who's this?"

"Your brother's nurse."

Gordon went weak with relief. It was true. He had overreacted after all. He felt like laughing and crying all at the same time.

"I was just checking on Billy," he said quickly. "I'll be a little late getting back and wondered how he was doing."

She frowned. "Why, I thought you knew! He's gone, Mr. Mallory. I just came back to pack my things."

The relief in Gordon's belly tied itself in a knot. Oh, God. I was right. It took everything he had to keep the tone of his voice at a normal pitch.

"Gone? Did he say where?"

"Why, no!" She started to worry. "Oh, dear, I felt bad about this all evening, but he was so insistent, and he said that you were aware of the trip."

Gordon managed a laugh, although if she could have seen his face, she would have known how insincere it really was.

"Oh, sure," Gordon said. "We were planning to leave all along, but I would have preferred that he wait for me. However, I should have known better. Billy has no patience, you know."

"Then it's all right that I let him go?" she asked.

"Of course," Gordon said. "I just hope he made all the proper arrangements to get help along the way."

"He certainly did," she said. "I heard him asking for wheelchairs and attendants at every stop."

"That's good," Gordon said, and then added as if it was an afterthought. "By the way, what flight did he take?"

"I don't know."

"But weren't you at the airport with him until he left?"

"Oh, no. When we left the Benton estate, we went straight to a travel agent. He made all of the arrangements with them. Of course, I was nearby, but I never overstep my bounds. Patient care and maintaining privacy are paramount in my book. I would never have eavesdropped."

"Of course not," Gordon said. "I didn't mean to imply—"

"Excuse me," she said. "But Mr. Benton is here now. Would you like to speak to him?"

Gordon panicked. The last thing he wanted Davis Benton to know was that his brother had skipped out on him.

"No, of course not," he said quickly. "Just tell him not to wait on dinner for me."

"Yes, sir, and may I say, it was a privilege to take care of your brother. He has a very kind heart."

"Thanks," Gordon said, then stood transfixed, listening to the buzz of the empty line, even after the nurse had disconnected.

His shoulders slumped. The nurse was right. Billy was too soft for the world in which Gordon lived. And while it gave him a lost, empty feeling to know that for the first time in his life he was on his own, he knew it was all for the best. Billy would just hold him back. He hung up the phone and walked away.

Half a block away, Roman watched from their car as Gordon came out of the bus station and got into the cab.

"Wonder what he was doing in there?" Holly asked.

"If he's smart, probably getting a ticket out of town," Roman muttered.

Holly looked startled. "What if he leaves before I remember everything? What if I never remember? How will we ever figure out where the money comes in?"

Roman waited a few seconds until the cab had passed them by before pulling out into the traffic behind it.

"Unless I'm wrong, he isn't going anywhere until he takes it with him." Then he added. "Besides that, remember what I told you. By this time tomorrow, it will all be over."

She sighed. "I hope you're right."

Roman glanced at her and winked. "Baby, it's time you realized I'm always right."

She rolled her eyes. "What have I let myself in for?"

Roman grinned. "If you're lucky, about seventy-five years of a real wild ride."

She laughed. "Then I hope I have the stamina of a cat," she said.

"Why a cat?" Roman asked.

"Well, they're supposed to have nine lives, and I've already used up a couple of mine. With you around for that long, I'm pretty sure I'll be needing more."

Up ahead, the cab was forced to stop for a stoplight. Roman reached for her hand as they, too, paused in traffic. There was a glint in his eyes as he lifted it to his mouth. Turning it palm up, he traced her lifeline with the tip of his tongue. He couldn't say what he was thinking. Giving life to his fears was dangerous. He kept telling himself that even when she remembered, their relationship would still be the same. But it wasn't Roman's way to lie...not even to himself. So when the light turned green, he accelerated through the intersection, channeling his focus back to Gordon Mallory.

Holly leaned back in the seat, for the time being, letting Roman do all the worrying about their future. It was after this mess was over that had her concerned. She didn't want to wake up one morning and become someone other than who she was now. Daisy had fallen in love. Surely God wouldn't be so cruel as to awaken Holly and then let Roman slip away.

Chapter 16

Gordon couldn't sleep that night, and Roman wouldn't. For the first time since coming to Davis Benton's home, Roman had seen Holly to bed and then stayed in her room. He couldn't get over the notion that Mallory was getting desperate. And desperate men had been known to do desperate things. With a million dollars at stake, anything could happen.

Breakfast was a stilted affair. Davis Benton knew something was wrong, but no one seemed eager to talk. He'd thrown enough conversational tidbits into the silence around the breakfast table to have started a dozen conversations and had yet to get one going.

Gordon was behaving strangely, and Davis had overheard the staff talking about Billy Mallory's sudden disappearance from his home. Roman was pretending to eat, but Davis was no fool. The man was spending more time observing Gordon Mallory's panic than he was chewing food. Added to that, his beloved Holly was pale and nervous. She'd dropped a spoon, as well as a fork, and at this point, had completely given up trying to eat.

Davis took a deep breath and set his coffee cup down. By God, this was his house and Holly was his daughter. These two men were all but strangers to him, and their appearance into her life had brought about drastic changes he didn't like.

"I want to know what the hell's going on."

His words shattered the silence in which they sat. Holly's cup clinked against the saucer. Gordon's heart skipped a beat, and he had a strong urge to run and never look back. Only Roman showed no reaction. Instead, he reached for a slice of toast and began buttering it as if Davis had never spoken.

"What do you mean?" Holly asked.

Davis glared. "Holly, I've known you for twenty-seven years, and you have yet, pardon the cliché, to pull the wool over my eyes. Something is going on, and I would very much like to know what it is. In fact, I think I deserve that much consideration, considering the fact that this is my house—and my table—and my patience that you are trying."

The urge to blurt out the truth about everything was strong, but now was not the time. She looked to Roman, silently begging for support, but he was spreading jelly on his buttered toast as if it had suddenly become the most important thing in his life. She wanted to scream at him. He had to know she was floundering. Why hadn't he come to her aid?

And then Gordon began to stammer and stutter, and glanced at Roman and then relaxed. Roman had known all along that, if for no other reason than guilt alone, Gordon would not be able to stay silent.

"I'm terribly sorry," Gordon said quickly. "I had no idea that my concerns were so obvious. It's just that I was thinking about my brother." He gave Davis a nervous smile and kept talking, almost without taking a breath. "We've been planning to leave, and soon. We couldn't presume upon your kind hospitality forever, but Billy got impatient and left yesterday without me. I will, of course, be following shortly, but there are a couple of things I still have to attend to."

Davis leaned back in his chair, listening without bothering to comment. He'd sat in on too many boardroom meetings not to know fast-talk when he heard it, but this made no sense. Other than the fact that Roman Justice has stepped into the picture and Gordon had been moved out, there was no reason for the man to be nervous. Angry maybe. Nervous, no.

"I see," Davis said. "So, where did he go?"

Gordon's face paled, and then a few moments later, flushed a high color of red.

"Uh, we've got a... There's a place we always went to.... It used to belong to—"

A maid came into the room, interrupting Gordon and unintentionally saving him from having to proceed.

"I'm sorry, Mr. Benton, but there's an emergency phone call for Mr. Justice," she said.

Roman stood. "Excuse me," he said, and left.

Gordon stood, taking the opportunity to escape Davis's third-degree. "And I'm afraid I must be excused, as well. I've got several calls to make. I'll be in my room if anyone needs me."

Holly watched both men exit and knew that her father deserved more than he was getting. When they were finally alone, she leaned forward.

"Dad, I know you're not stupid. And yes, something *is* going on, but I'm not sure what. All I can say is, Roman assures me that it will be over by tonight. I trust him. Will you trust me?"

Davis made himself relax. "I don't like this one bit," he muttered.

Holly reached for his hand. "Look at this from my point of view. I not only don't like it, but it scares me to death."

Davis frowned. "What do you mean, scares you? You're safe here. You have nothing to be afraid of."

She shook her head. "No, that's not true. In fact, Roman and I are convinced that there's something I should be remembering...something that had to do with the crash."

"I don't understand," he said.

"Neither do I." Then she, too, stood to leave. "Just make sure you're home for lunch, okay?"

Davis's frown deepened. "After what you just said, and the way everyone was behaving, I have no intention of setting foot out of this house. I'm not trusting your safety to anyone else until I know what's going on."

"It's your decision," she said. "But please know that if you need to, you could trust Roman Justice with your life. Believe me, I know. I already have."

She walked away, leaving her father to make what he chose out of the remark.

Gordon made it to his room without further incident, but the moment he got inside, sat down on the bed and started to shake. It would seem that Billy had the right idea all along. Everything was starting to come undone. Maybe it was time to leave. He'd been so certain that by staying close to Holly Benton, he would find a way to get back his money. But he could see it just wasn't going to work. Her memory was coming back faster than the headway he'd hoped to make. And so he sat, stewing in the juices of his own mistakes and planning his next move.

The longer he sat, the calmer he became. It's *his* fault, Gordon thought. If Roman Justice hadn't appeared on the scene, everything would have worked out all right. He'd had Benton's confidence, and simply by being under the same roof as Holly, he would have been able to gain hers, as well.

He stood and looked around the room. It had served its purpose, but now it was time to retreat. Several days ago, he'd noticed a small Pullman-type bag in the back of his closet. He didn't have many belongings here. Whatever it would hold would be all that he would take. If he had to leave something behind, he could always buy more. At least he still had the ten thousand in the bank. It would be enough to get a new start.

And then something hit him, and he wondered why he hadn't thought of it before. Billy! How had he managed to buy a plane ticket? What money he'd had on him had been lost in the crash.

"No, no, no. Please tell me no," Gordon mumbled as he reached for the phone.

A few minutes later, he slammed it down in disgust, unable to believe what he'd learned. Granted the account had been in both their names, but who would have believed the little weasel had the gumption to take advantage of him like this? Within the space of minutes, the ten-thousand-dollar nest egg Gordon thought he'd had was down to five. Billy had taken his half and run.

He yanked the bag from the closet and tossed it onto the bed, then began emptying the drawers of his belongings and dumping them inside. Something hit the side of the bag with a thump, and he frowned, wondering what it was that he'd heard. Underwear didn't thump.

As he dug through the pile, his fingers closed upon an oblong plastic box, and the moment he felt it, he remembered the drug-filled syringe. Using it on Holly that night would have been the perfect answer. She would have talked her head off and the next morning not remembered a thing. Gordon's hand clenched around the box. If she'd only been asleep, his troubles would already be over.

He dropped it to the side of the bag and continued to pack. But every time he tossed something else inside, he looked down at the box. By the time he was through, he'd convinced himself to give it one more try. Instead of leaving now, he would do it tomorrow. That would be the better plan anyway. He still had to close out his account at the bank. And there was always the chance that he'd have to travel to another location to retrieve his money. No need buying a plane ticket until he knew where he needed to go.

He laid the box on top of his clothes and then zipped the bag shut before stowing it out of sight. The fewer who knew about his plans to leave, the better. He glanced at his watch. It was just past 10:00 a.m. He grinned. Plenty of time to get to the bank and then back here for lunch. Keeping to a regular schedule within the family was the best way to maintain his innocence. If Holly started remembering too much, too soon, he could always claim that she was imagining things. After all, if he'd tried to murder her, wouldn't he have been long gone? Innocent people didn't have to run.

Pleased that he had all the answers worked out, he called a cab. A short while later, he announced to Holly and her father that he was making a quick trip to the bank and would see them for lunch. He didn't give a thought to the fact that Roman was nowhere in sight, nor would he have suspected himself of being followed. He was too locked in to the fact that his cover was impenetrable.

Roman had Holly by the hand as they came down the stairs. "Where did your father go?"

"I don't know," she said. "He was still in the library when I left him." She sighed. "I feel badly about keeping the truth from him."

Roman squeezed her hand lightly for assurance. "I know, baby. But it won't be much longer now. That phone call I had earlier was from Royal. He and Ryder are on their way. They should be here around eleven."

"And then what?" she asked.

"We made a plan. When they get here, all you have to do is follow my lead."

She glanced nervously around, making sure they were alone. "They're bringing the money?"

He nodded. "They're going to make quite an entrance." He leaned forward, lowering his voice so that he wouldn't be overheard. "This is what I want you to do."

She listened, her eyes widening with each word that he spoke. Only after he had finished talking did she realize she'd been holding her breath.

"Think you can do that?" Roman asked.

She nodded. "I'll do anything it takes to get this nightmare behind me."

He wrapped his arms around her and pulled her into a hug.

"That's my girl," he said softly.

"And don't you forget it," she said.

A shadow appeared in his eyes, as if an old ghost had just crossed his path.

"I don't willingly lose...or forget...what's mine."

Before she could speak, he'd captured her mouth beneath his, drugging her senses and her speech with a hard, swift kiss that stole the rest of her breath.

Her hands were shaking when he turned her loose.

"Trust me, Holly. I won't let anything happen to you."

She laid her hand against the beat of his heart. "I can do that, but it's time for you to trust me, too. There's only one thing I know for certain, and that is I would not wish to spend another day on earth without you in my life."

The expression on her face shattered his reserve. He pulled her off the last stair and into his arms.

Her heart was in her throat as he dragged her beneath the stairs and then pressed her up against the wall.

"Roman, someone will see."

"To hell with someone," he whispered, and wrapped his arms around her, then lifted her off her feet. "Right now, I have this overwhelming need to be deep inside you and am having to settle for this."

Her arms were around his neck, her feet dangling inches from the floor. She was holding on for dear life...and her love. She leaned forward, brushing the surface of his mouth with the tip of her tongue.

"Then take what you need, Roman Justice, because I couldn't refuse you if I tried."

He lowered his head. A soft, unintelligible groan slipped out from between his lips, and then he got lost in her spell. A few moments later, a sound came crashing down the hall, followed by a flurry of excited voices. With reluctance, Roman tore himself free and set her gently back down to her feet.

"Sounds like something just broke," he said, tracing the

edge of her mouth with his finger. "But as long as it's not my heart, I don't give a good damn."

She grabbed his hand and lifted it to her mouth before pressing a kiss into the palm.

"If it does," Holly whispered, "it won't be because of me."

"Then I'm safe," he said. "Because you're the only one who could do it. Now, let's go find your father. I need to let him know what's going to happen."

"Are you going to tell him about the—?"

"This has been your call from the first. It's not up to me. It's up to you. Do you want to?" Roman asked.

She thought for a moment and then nodded. "I think it's time."

"Then let's do it," he said.

When they walked into the library, they found Davis Benton standing at a window overlooking his estate. His shoulders were slumped, his expression grave.

"Dad."

He turned. "I wondered where you were." He eyed Roman without commenting on the fact that they were hand in hand. "Please, have a seat," he said.

"I'll stand," Roman said as he sat Holly down.

"More secrets?" Davis asked.

Holly heard the despair in his voice. "Don't be angry with Roman, Dad. He's only done as I asked."

Davis dropped into a nearby chair. "Anger isn't what I'm feeling."

Holly leaned forward. "Please, just hear us out. We don't have much time, and it's very important."

He frowned. "What do you mean, you don't have much time?"

Roman interrupted. "Baby, let me."

Holly nodded, relieved to have someone else trying to explain something she didn't understand herself.

"Then talk," Davis said.

Roman nodded. "I've been following Gordon Mallory, almost from the first day I arrived."

Davis straightened. "What on earth for?"

"Because we don't believe he and Holly were ever going to elope."

"Then why would she have been on that plane?" Davis asked. "She called me herself only hours before takeoff to tell me she was going with him."

Wait for me. This won't take long.

Holly stiffened. She could see herself getting out of a cab and walking across the tarmac to a waiting plane.

"I had changed my mind," she said suddenly.

She had their attention.

Roman had seen that faraway look on her face before. He knew that she'd just had another flash of memory.

"What are you remembering?" he asked.

She blinked, and the image was gone. There was a stunned expression on her face. "I told the cab driver to wait. I told him I'd be right back. My God, Roman, I wasn't going to go! Then why did I get on that plane?"

He shook his head. "I don't know, but you do," he said. "When it matters, you'll tell us."

She slumped back into her seat. "Where have I heard that before?"

He touched her lightly on the shoulder. "Easy does it, Holly. We're with you all the way."

Davis leaned forward. "He's right, sweetheart. Whatever's been happening, you must know you're not alone." Then he looked up at Roman. "So why the need to follow Mallory? Other than the fact Holly can't remember why she went, what's the big mystery?"

"Say it," Holly said. "You were right. I should have told him from the start."

Davis's voice was thick with frustration. "Damn it, people! Tell me what?"

"That Holly wound up with a duffel bag full of money when she bailed out of that plane."

Davis stood. "What on earth...?"

"It's true, Dad. It was at the foot of the tree when I finally freed myself from the parachute and climbed down. And I had a vague memory of someone shoving it at me and telling me to jump."

"Good lord," he muttered, and then started to pace. "But I don't understand. Why did you feel the need to keep it a secret? It surely belonged to Gordon. Why didn't you just—?"

"I was afraid."

He shook his head. "Afraid? Why? What was there to be afraid of?" And then a thought struck him, and he looked at Roman. "How much money are we talking about?"

"Just shy of a million dollars."

Davis's legs went weak, and he dropped back into the chair he'd just vacated.

"Sweet lord."

Roman gave his case another boost. "If it had been honestly earned, don't you think Gordon would have been bemoaning the loss loud and long?"

Davis wiped a shaky hand across his face. "He and his brother have been living under this roof at my invitation. If you suspected something was wrong, why didn't you say so? Why did you let it go this long?" he asked.

Holly reached out, needing to touch him when she said it.

"Because at first, I didn't know who to trust. Not you, Dad. Not even myself."

"What?"

Roman interrupted. "When we first met, she had convinced herself that she was a criminal and had come by the money illegally. It was only after we learned her true identity that we pretty much ruled that out." He grinned wryly. "Davis Benton's daughter would have no reason to steal."

"How can you be sure it was Mallory? It could have been the pilot. Maybe it was his brother, Billy! Yes, it could be him. He's the one who's run off, remember?"

Roman shook his head. "I can't explain it, but I doubt

that's the case. My guess is, Billy was an accomplice in something, but he doesn't come across as the stronger of the two.''

Davis nodded. "You're right. But just thinking they are involved is one thing. Do we have any proof other than guesses?''

"I did a little checking," Roman said. "Mallory doesn't have a real-estate license in Nevada, nor has he ever had one. And just before he and Billy left town for the supposed trip to Nassau, they gave up their apartment. If they were planning on coming back, they must have been counting on you to house them.''

"Which I did," Davis said with a groan. "What a mess. And what are we going to do?''

"I have a plan," Roman said. "Are you with us?''

"Anything," Davis said. "I'll do anything to make sure that Holly is safe.''

"Good. Now, here's what I want you to do.''

Davis listened, and when it was over, looked up at Roman with renewed respect.

"My boy, if this works, you're a genius.''

Roman shook his head. "It won't be genius that traps Gordon Mallory. It will be a guilty conscience.''

"Where is he now?" Davis asked.

"In his room," Roman said. "In fact, he's been spending a lot of time in there today. I'd lay odds that he's planning to leave, and soon. I followed him to a bank about an hour ago. He closed an account, in the process withdrawing a little over five thousand dollars. That's not pocket change, that's traveling money.''

Davis was furious to think that he'd unwittingly housed a criminal, never mind the fact that the man had lied about his relationship with his daughter.

"For two cents, I'd like to—''

Suddenly Holly waved to her father and then put her finger to her lips, indicating silence. They listened. Someone was coming down the stairs. It could only be Gordon. They glanced at each other and without missing a beat, Davis started to laugh, as if someone had just told a joke.

Gordon walked into the library with a smile on his face. "Sounds like I'm missing all the fun," he said.

Roman shook his head. "It hasn't even begun."

Before Gordon could comment upon the odd remark, Davis stood.

"You're just in time," he told Gordon. "We were about to sit down to lunch." He took Holly by the arm and winked at her. "The first course is cold shrimp salad, Holly's favorite."

Royal pulled up to the gates of the Benton estate, rolled down the window, then leaned out, pressing the small black button on a nearby call box. Moments later, an anonymous voice came over the line.

"Yes?"

"Royal and Ryder Justice to see Davis Benton."

"Just a moment, please."

Royal glanced at Ryder and shook his head. "Hell of a way to live, locked behind all this iron."

Ryder nodded as he looked around the estate. His wife had grown up almost the same way. Not behind walls and locked gates like this one, but within a world that certain members of society looked upon as fair game. The ultra-rich had their own set of problems, and in Ryder's opinion, having the money wasn't worth what came with it.

The gates began to open, and Royal glanced over his shoulder, checking for the umpteenth time to make sure the bag was still there.

"The sooner I get rid of that thing, the better I'm going to feel," he muttered.

"You forget," Ryder said. "The trouble hasn't even started. If Roman's theory is right, all hell could break loose after we get there."

Royal's eyes darkened and his jawline firmed. "I don't pretend to know what this is all about. Just remember...we watch Roman's back.''

"Goes without saying," Ryder muttered, and patted his jacket, making sure that the handgun holstered beneath it was firmly in place.

"Here goes nothing," Royal said, and took off down the driveway.

As they came around a long, winding corner, they both straightened in their seats.

"Son of a—"

"Wow! Roman's 'client' has herself quite a spread," Ryder said. "That doesn't look like a house, it looks like a castle. All it needs is a moat."

They pulled up to the front door and parked. "You get the bag, I'll get the door," Ryder said. "Hope this doesn't take long. I'm starving."

The doorbell rang in the middle of the first course. Holly's fork clattered against her plate as she glanced up at Roman. He winked at her and then continued to eat as if nothing had happened.

"Are we expecting anyone?" Davis asked.

Holly shrugged. "Don't look at me. I wouldn't know who to invite, even if the urge struck me."

The sounds of footsteps could be heard coming down the hall. The long strides and steady rhythm of their steps signified men.

"That's odd," Gordon commented. "They're coming without being announced."

Roman leaned back in his chair, his gaze fixed on Gordon's face, while everyone else was staring at the doorway.

They entered side by side, their steps in unison with equally imposing expressions on their faces. Even though Holly had been prepared for the fact that they were Roman's brothers, she was unprepared for the similarities in their looks.

Well over six feet in height, with thick, black, straight hair and piercing blue eyes, the men commanded attention. Both were wearing Levi's, shiny with starch and creases that looked sharp enough to break. Their shirts were Western cut, one white, one pale blue. The Stetsons they wore were pulled low, and she had the distinct impression that it was more to hide what they were thinking than to shade their faces.

Roman stood. "You're late." Then he added an introduction as an afterthought. "Everyone, these are my brothers, Ryder and Royal Justice."

Ryder glanced around the table and then grinned at no one in particular.

"I think it's okay, Royal. They look safe enough to eat behind."

Davis Benton started to grin. He'd be surprised if he didn't like these men as much as he liked their brother.

"We've just started," he said. "Please, take a seat."

"Not until I get rid of this blasted bag," Royal said, and plopped it in the middle of the table.

Gordon's ears began to buzz as an overwhelming weakness swept through him. If he hadn't been sitting he would have surely fallen. Wild-eyed, he grabbed the arms of his chair, ready to bolt.

That's my bag! That's my money! What the hell is going on?

Everyone's attention turned from the bag to Holly when she suddenly stood. For several long, heart-stopping moments, she continued to stare at the bag as if it were evil. And then she closed her eyes and groaned, clutching at her head as if in terrible pain.

"Holly, sweetheart! What's wrong?" Davis asked.

Roman grabbed her as she swayed on her feet.

"Holly, are you sick?" he asked, pretending great concern.

Gordon started to get up when she suddenly screamed. And even though the men had been prepared for her act, they hadn't been expecting anything as realistic as what they heard.

"You!" she cried, pointing a shaking finger in Gordon's direction. "It was you!"

Completely out of his mind, he jumped to his feet. "She's hallucinating," he cried.

"No!" Holly moaned, and began circling the table, moving toward Gordon with single-minded intent.

Roman's heart skipped a beat. This wasn't part of the plan. He motioned for Royal to block the door, just in case Gordon decided to run.

Holly started to shake. There was a terrible knowledge inside of her that wanted to come out. And it came like a flood, spilling over the dam in her mind and pouring into her consciousness in one horrific memory after another.

"You killed him," she mumbled. "And you were going to kill me."

Roman was starting to panic. She wasn't pretending. She was remembering!

"She's crazy," Gordon said, and started backing up. "When she hit her head, it messed up her mind. I didn't kill anyone and I wouldn't kill her. I loved her, remember?" He pointed at Roman. "We were going to be married until he came along."

"Shut up!" Holly screamed. "You lie! You lie! You always lied, but I was too bored with my life to pay attention to the signs. There wasn't going to be any marriage. It was just a long play-day weekend. But I was coming to tell you I didn't want to go to Nassau after all. Not with you. Never with you."

The brothers stood, frozen by the unexpected tableau being enacted before their eyes. They glanced at Roman. He was holding his own. They looked back at the woman. She was coming undone.

"I heard you and Billy arguing." Tears pooled in her eyes. "Carl Julian was skimming from the casino take. You said it was the perfect crime. You said he wouldn't report a theft of money he wasn't supposed to have."

Davis couldn't believe what he was hearing. In the middle of it all, a maid came into the room to serve the next course.

He gave her quick orders to call the police. Looking wild-eyed, she hurried to do as she'd been told.

"You're lying," Gordon said. "Why would I kill a man I didn't even know?"

"For that!" she cried, pointing toward the bag. "For Carl Julian's money."

Roman moved, putting himself between Holly and Mallory.

"That's enough, baby," he said quietly. "We've got him now."

"No!" she said, and pushed at Roman, trying to get past. When he continued to stand in her way, she started to weep. "He knew that I'd overheard him arguing with Billy. He dragged me onto the plane. He said he was going to kill me. He was going to dump me out of the plane after it was airborne."

Roman blanked out on everything except what she'd endured at this man's hands. Before anyone knew what was happening, he had Mallory pinned against the wall with his hands around his throat.

"You cowardly son of a bitch. For two cents, I'd—"

Royal grabbed one arm, Ryder the other. "Turn him loose, Roman! Turn him loose! Let the authorities take care of him."

Holly grabbed her head and then groaned. "Please, no more," she begged. "No more killing."

It was her soft-spoken plea that reached through Roman's rage. As it began to subside and reality began to return, he dropped his hold on Mallory as if he'd suddenly become a thing of great filth. He turned toward Holly, catching her as she began to slump toward the floor.

"It's okay, baby, it's okay. I've got you and no one's ever going to hurt you again."

Her legs were shaking, but her mind was still clear.

"Billy saved my life," she said. "He put me in the parachute. He's the one who shoved the money in my hands. If it wasn't for him, I would have died."

Roman held her closer. "Thank God one of them had a conscience," he said.

At the mention of his brother's name, Gordon broke. "Hell yes, he had a conscience," he cried. "Everything was perfect until he went weak on me." He glared at Holly, and when he would have taken a step forward, found himself staring down the barrel of Ryder's gun.

"I wouldn't be moving if I were you," Ryder drawled.

Gordon stared at the gun and the man who held it. Then he looked past Holly, to the bag that was sitting in the middle of the table. So close...and yet so very far away.

Spittle was running from the corner of his mouth as he turned.

"Damn you, bitch! You ruined everything. If it hadn't been for you, Billy wouldn't have betrayed me." His face was flushed with anger, and in the distance, the first sounds of sirens could be heard. The police were on the way. "He fancied himself in love with you, you know," Gordon said, and then laughed a dark, ugly laugh. "You didn't even know he existed, and yet he betrayed me, his own brother."

Holly shrank against the wall, only to find her father at her side.

"It's all right, sweetheart. He can't hurt you anymore," Davis said.

Roman pivoted, pinning Davis with a hard look. "Get her out of here. She's seen and heard enough for one day." Then he cupped her cheek as they started past him. There was a shell-shocked look on her face that made him nervous, but his pride in her overrode whatever fears he might have for their future. "You're a hell of a woman, Holly Benton."

She behaved as if she hadn't heard him speak. When she walked out of the room without looking back, he told himself not to panic. Then, before either of his brothers could stop him, he doubled his fist and turned. The punch he threw landed squarely on Gordon Mallory's jaw.

Gordon never saw what hit him, only an oncoming darkness, as if someone had just turned out the lights.

Royal took off his hat and scratched the back of his head. Ryder holstered his gun and then grinned.

"I'd say you got your point across, little brother. Now, let's get our story straight about what we're going to tell the cops."

The sirens they'd been hearing had suddenly stopped. It was obvious that they were here. There was a cold, hard look in Roman's eyes as he headed for the door.

"You don't have to tell them anything. If they want to know what happened to the son of a bitch, I'll tell them plain and simple. He messed with my woman."

All the way up the stairs, Holly kept reminding herself that her wish had come true. Now she remembered everything, including who she was, as well as who she'd been for the past few days. It was the latter that worried her more than the rest. Daisy had done things that Holly Benton would never have considered. But, Holly reminded herself, Daisy had done something in three days that Holly hadn't been able to accomplish in twenty-seven years. She'd found herself a man and fallen in love. In the face of that fact, Holly was a complete and utter failure.

With that on her mind, she fell into bed, barely aware of her father's presence.

Chapter 17

Gordon's worst nightmare was coming true, and there was nothing he could do to stop it. His jaw was aching and his head was still fuzzy. They'd handcuffed him within moments of his regaining consciousness, and now he was standing within feet of his precious money and it might as well have been on the moon for all the good it would do him.

Rage surged as an officer began to read him his rights. If he'd been free, he would have happily put a gun to Roman Justice's head and pulled the trigger, if for no other reason than to wipe the look he was wearing clean off of his face. Yet each time he looked at the man, Gordon found himself unable to withstand Roman's cold stare.

Gordon closed his eyes and turned away, momentarily focusing on the policeman's monotone voice.

"You have the right to…"

Gordon wanted to scream. Right? He didn't have any rights! What he had were handcuffs.

"If you so choose, one will be appointed…"

Choices? If it hadn't been so ironic, that would have made

him laugh. He'd been making choices for most of his life, and so far, very few of them had been right. Why break tradition and start now?

"Do you understand...?"

Gordon sighed. Hell, yes, he understood. He understood everything. Other than the fact that he was pretty much screwed, there wasn't much left to determine.

And then there was silence. He blinked, suddenly aware that everyone was watching him and waiting for some sort of answer.

"Sir!" the policeman said. "Do you understand these rights as I've read them?"

Gordon glared, first at the policeman, then at Roman.

"Yes, I understand. I understand everything."

Roman's stare never wavered. Again, it was Gordon who looked away.

"Book him," the sergeant ordered, then he turned to Roman. "Sir, as I told you before, we'll be needing complete statements from everyone."

Roman nodded. "We'll be down in a couple of hours. I want to make sure Holly is up to it."

The man nodded and left, taking the remaining officers with him.

The dining room was suddenly quiet, like the lull after a storm. Roman ran a hand through his hair, and then turned to his brothers. There was a halfhearted grin on his face, and his eyes were almost twinkling.

"Thanks for coming," he said.

Royal returned the grin. "Thanks for the invitation. I wouldn't have missed this for the world."

Ryder glanced toward the table. "Hey, Roman, where were you sitting?"

Roman pointed, then grinned when Ryder picked a shrimp from his salad and popped it in his mouth.

"Missed breakfast," he said, and then reached for another.

"Help yourself," Roman said. "I've got to check on Holly."

Roman stalked out of the room, leaving his brothers on their own. They looked at each other and shrugged.

"Looks like we're going to another wedding," Ryder said.

Royal nodded. "As long as it's not mine, it's fine by me."

Ryder picked up another shrimp. "Don't be too cocky, big brother. You know what they say. The bigger they are, the harder they fall. Besides, you're the only one left and you can't hold out forever."

Royal shook his head. "You're dead wrong, Ryder. I've already got a woman in my life, and she's just about all I can handle."

They looked at each other, then back at the table and the uneaten food.

"What do you think?" Ryder said.

"What was it Mom used to say about people starving in China?" Royal asked.

"Right," they said in unison as each reached for a fork.

Roman had been through every room downstairs that Holly would have been in. The only place left was her bedroom. He took the stairs up, two at a time, needing to see her, to hold her, to make sure she was all right. He would never have imagined that their plan to trick Gordon into revealing his guilt would also result in triggering her memory. His heart was pounding all the way to her room. For her sake, he was glad the amnesia was behind her, but now he was faced with his greatest fear. In the grand scheme of the rest of their lives, where did that leave him?

He knocked once on her door and then entered. Holly was lying on her bed with an arm thrown over her eyes and a damp washcloth in her other hand. Roman thought she was asleep.

Davis was sitting in a chair near her bed. He stood as Roman entered.

"She's fine. Just resting," Davis said, and started to shake Roman's hand and then impulsively gave him a quick hug instead. "I don't know how I can ever thank you. Thanks to you, I have my daughter back."

Roman shook his head. "I wasn't anything but backup. Holly is the one who deserves the credit. She had the guts to save herself, not once, but twice. It was my good fortune that she stumbled into my cabin."

But Davis would have none of it. "If you hadn't been there, she wouldn't be here, and we both know it."

Roman glanced toward Holly. He wanted to touch her, to talk to her, but he was afraid. Afraid to see the look on her face when she opened her eyes.

Davis looked at his daughter and then at Roman. "Well, now," he said briskly. "I'm sure there are a dozen things that need to be done."

"Are you going to call a doctor for her?" Roman asked.

"Yes," Davis said. "I was waiting for you to come before I left her. I'm sure she's all right, but I'll feel better if he checks her out."

Roman added. "You might want to check on my brothers. Last time I looked, they were giving the food on the table real serious consideration. There's a pretty good chance it's not there anymore."

Davis chuckled. "After the part they played in helping Holly, they can have anything their hearts desire."

"Don't tell them that or you'll be sorry."

Davis was still laughing as he closed the door behind him.

Now there was nothing in the room but Holly and a silence Roman couldn't ignore. His smile died as he turned toward the bed. Still lying with an arm across her eyes, she remained motionless. He took a deep breath and sat down beside her.

God help me. Please let this be all right.

He touched her arm. Her skin felt cold, almost clammy. He looked at her face. There were tears on her cheeks.

"Baby, are you all right?"

She turned without removing her arm, her voice sounded weak and just above a whisper. "My head. It hurts. It hurts so bad."

He stretched out on the bed beside her and then pulled her close, cradling her against the warmth of his body.

"Hang in there, Holly. Your dad is calling a doctor. He'll be here soon."

Holly hadn't been able to stop crying. The release of so much emotion had overwhelmed her. Yet the moment she felt his touch, the tension in her body began to ease. She shifted closer to him, taking strength from his presence.

"Roman?"

He pressed a gentle kiss at the back of her neck and then smoothed the hair from her face.

"What, baby?"

"Don't leave me."

As if he could. Pain tugged at his heart.

"I won't, I promise."

She sighed.

Minutes passed. Minutes in which Roman's thoughts went through hell and back. He'd held Daisy like this plenty of times, but this was the first time he'd held Holly in his arms. He loved them both enough to die for them twice over, and Daisy would have returned the favor. But what about Holly? He still didn't know her heart.

Just when he thought she'd fallen asleep, he heard her take a deep breath. She reached for his hand, threading her fingers through his and then pulling his arm a little closer around her.

"Roman."

"Yes?"

"I love you," she said softly, and then went to sleep.

God.

He closed his eyes, swallowing past the knot in his throat. Twice he took a long, deep breath, trying to gain control of his emotions. But it wasn't to be. Holly Benton had done to Roman's heart what no other woman had been able to do. She'd given him her trust and taught him to love.

Tears burned his eyes and at the back of his throat as he buried his face in her hair, inhaling the clean, fresh scent of her shampoo and the soft, sweet smell that was hers alone. He tightened his hold as his heart went free.

"That's good to know, baby, because I love you, too."

Epilogue

Night was looming as Roman took the last turn in the road.

"Are we almost there?" Holly asked.

He grinned. "Yes, Mrs. Justice, we're almost there."

Holly closed her eyes, savoring the sound of that name on his lips.

"Good."

"I hope you're not going to be disappointed. The cabin is a little rustic for a honeymoon."

She looked up. "It isn't rustic. It's romantic. Besides, it's where we started our relationship. It seemed only fitting that we should begin our married life there, as well."

Roman nodded. For the moment, speech eluded him. He loved this woman beyond words. Sometimes, it was easier to show her than to tell her. And if his brothers did as they'd been told, she would see soon enough.

"At least we don't have to worry about snow," she said, and then glanced at him and frowned. "It doesn't snow here in July, does it?"

He cocked an eyebrow and grinned. "I think we're safe."

She smiled. "Not that the fireplace wasn't cozy, but I have a new swimsuit. I want to go swimming."

"You won't be needing that suit."

Her smile faded. "Why not? Isn't there any place to swim?"

"You can swim all you want, but you won't be needing a suit."

She blushed, but the idea intrigued her. "I've never gone naked outdoors before."

His grin widened. "Well, now, you know what they say. There's a first time for everything."

When he began to slow down, Holly leaned forward in anticipation. It was strange, but in a way, this was her first visit. Daisy had been here, but Holly had not.

As they came around a curve in the road, he braked, giving her time to look. The last rays of sunlight were beaming upon the two-story A-frame cabin. The honey-colored logs seemed to be storing the fading sun's warmth. As she looked, her eyes filled with tears, remembering the relief she'd felt as she'd stumbled out of the forest and into the clearing. A place of safety.

She glanced at Roman. He was watching her. She tried to smile and failed. Her voice was shaking as she leaned against his arm.

"I'm glad we came."

He tipped her chin upward, then went to meet her, capturing her mouth with a slow, gentle kiss.

"I'm glad we came, too," he said softly. Then he glanced through the windshield toward the setting sun. "We'd better get unloaded. It's going to be dark before you know it."

"Yes. I remember."

He touched the side of her face. "Feels good, doesn't it, baby?"

"What does?"

"To remember."

She sighed. "Oh, yes. More than you will ever know."

They parked at the cabin and began to unload the car. As

Holly helped carry things inside, her thoughts kept returning to the events of the past months.

Of everything that had happened, one thing kept returning to haunt her. Billy Mallory. Was he all right or was he still running from his past?

As for Gordon, the evidence against him had been overwhelming. He'd been charged with theft, murder and kidnapping with intent to commit bodily harm. Holly's testimony sealed his fate. Spending the rest of his life behind bars without parole was a better sentence than he deserved.

His only saving grace had been denying that his brother had prior knowledge of any of his crimes until after they'd been committed. Gordon had maintained Billy's innocence throughout the entire trial. When asked, Holly had been able to answer truthfully that it was Billy Mallory who'd saved her life, as well as given her the stolen money to return. In the eyes of the world, Billy was a free man. It remained to be seen if he would ever forgive himself. Wherever he was, Holly hoped he knew she was grateful.

As they carried their things into the cabin, Roman sensed Holly's mood. She'd been through more hell in the past few months than most people would endure in a lifetime. Whatever it took for her to get through it was what she would have. He'd see to that.

Finally, everything was safely inside. It was only after Roman had closed and locked the door behind him that he began to relax. As he stood within the quiet, Holly came out of the kitchen. When she saw him standing by the door, she smiled. At that point, his heart took flight. It was true. She was here. And she was his for the rest of their lives.

Holly turned in a circle, looking up at the loft and then back at the kitchen.

"Oh, Roman, I feel like I've just come home."

"Come here, you," he growled, and then went to meet her, unable to wait.

He scooped her off of her feet and into his arms, then started walking toward the stairs.

Startled, she threw her arms around his neck for support and began to laugh.

"Shouldn't we unpack first?"

"It can wait. Now close your eyes."

She did as he asked.

He kept walking up the steps to the loft, holding her close against his chest as they returned to the proverbial scene of the crime. When he got to the landing, he stopped.

"Can I look?" she asked.

"Not yet," he said, and then set her on her feet.

"Now can I look?

He grabbed her by the shoulders and turned her around until she was facing the bed.

"Holly, baby..."

She was all but dancing with excitement.

"Yes?"

"Open your eyes."

The bed was the first thing she saw, and then what was on it.

"Oh, Roman."

She tried to say more, but the words wouldn't come. Her vision began to blur, but there was no way to mistake what she was seeing.

Daisies. They were everywhere. Hundreds upon hundreds of delicate white blooms with bright yellow centers. Scattered upon the bed, around the floor and across the pillows.

Roman pulled her close, letting his chin rest at the top of her head. His voice was low and filled with emotion, but there was no mistaking his intent.

"I'm going to make love to you there. And for the rest of your life, every time you see a daisy, you're going to remember this day...and me."

She turned. With tears streaming down her face, she reached for him.

"I told you once before that I might not remember my name, but I would always remember who loved me."

He nodded, silenced by the truth of her statement.

"The daisies will fade and the years will pass, but I will never...and I mean never...forget you, Roman. Do you understand?"

Nearly blinded by his own tears, he touched her face. "More than I would ever have imagined."

He picked her up and started toward the bed. Just before he laid her down among the flowers, he pressed one last, gentle kiss upon her mouth.

"No regrets?"

His tenderness was nearly Holly's undoing. Her breath caught at the back of her throat as she whispered against his lips.

"No regrets."

He'd been right after all. She would never forget the feel of silken petals sticking to her skin, or their clean, tangy scent filling the air as they crushed beneath the weight of their bodies. She wrapped her arms around him, holding on tight as he sent her to ecstasy.

It was forever a moment to remember.

Daisies in her hair.

Roman in her heart.

* * * * *

Royal's Child

With age comes wisdom. But in gaining this gift,
we often forfeit another. And that loss is
an unswerving belief in things unseen.
Oh, to be a child again. For just one day.
To walk in innocence and, on certain occasions,
to talk to angels who sit on our beds.
I dedicate this book to the child in all of us.

Chapter 1

The fat man on the floor was holding his crotch and cursing in at least two languages. But Angel Rojas was impervious to his threats. She'd heard them all before. Instead of cowering beneath his anger, she pushed at his foot with the toe of her shoe in a warning gesture.

"Shut up, Louie. You can't fire me. I already quit."

His face green, Louie groaned. "You bitch! Your days in this town are over. I'll make damn sure you never work around here again."

His threats didn't frighten her, and harsh words had long since lost their ability to hurt her. Angel Maria Conchita Rojas had learned early on that the only people who could hurt you were the ones you loved. And the last person Angel loved had been her mother, who died when she was seven. By the time she was nine she'd run away from home, weary of the beatings her father kept giving her. As a teenager, she had run from one foster home after another. Angel had been running all her life and was afraid to stop. If she had, the devastation of her life might have overwhelmed her. She'd become adept at surviving in a male-dominated world and even more so at protecting herself.

But at the age of twenty-five, she was still waiting to find a place to call home. Her entire existence consisted of what she called pit stops. Fat Louie's Bar and Grill on the outskirts of Tuscaloosa, Alabama, was about to become a part of her history.

Angel felt like cheering. Today she'd reached a breaking point and done something about it. Lewd innuendos and groping hands were a thing of her past. With a heartfelt sigh of relief, she tossed her apron aside.

"You owe me two hundred and fifty dollars for the last two weeks' work. Don't bother to get up. I'll help myself."

Louie cursed again. "I'll have you arrested for stealing."

Angel turned, and the look on her face was warning enough. Louie was silenced.

"I personally know six other women, besides myself, who are willing to file charges of sexual harassment against you. Are you interested in calling my bluff?"

Wincing with pain, Louie struggled to get up. But there was something in her words he couldn't ignore. His complexion darkened as he waved a fist in her direction.

"Just get your damned money and get out." Then he cupped his crotch again and groaned.

Angel counted out her money and then grabbed her jacket and purse. By the time she got to the door, Louie was on his feet and still cursing her name.

She never looked back.

Royal Justice rolled out of bed and stood within the quiet of his bedroom. His heart was hammering against his chest as he glanced at the clock. It was almost five. In an hour or so the sun would be breaking the cover of darkness. His four-year-old daughter, Maddie, was asleep in her room down the hall, and although he couldn't hear a thing but the intermittent drip from a leaking shower head, he knew something was wrong. Nearly five years of being a single parent had honed his instincts to razor-sharp perception. Without hesitation, he grabbed his Levi's, hastily dressing as he started out of his room.

Maddie was fine when he'd put her to bed last night, but he'd learned the hard way that time and children never stay static. Just as he reached the door of her room, the flesh crawled on the back of his neck. Shuddering, he paused, and it was as if a hand centered in the middle of his back suddenly pushed him forward. Frowning at his flight of fancy, he stepped in.

He knew before he touched her that she was sick. Maddie could tear up a bed faster than anyone he knew when she was healthy. When she was restless, it was impossible to tell head from foot. The covers were in a wad on the floor, and her pillow was nowhere in sight. He turned on the bedside lamp. When he brushed his hand across her cheek, her skin felt hot to his touch. She opened her eyes, but he could tell it wasn't him she was seeing. The image frightened him.

"I don't see her," Maddie mumbled.

"See who, baby?" Royal asked, but Maddie didn't answer. His hand was shaking as he cupped the side of her face. "Maddie? See who?"

"The lady. I don't see the lady."

He gritted his teeth and dashed into the adjoining bathroom, emerging moments later with a cold, wet washcloth. As he bent to wipe it across her burning face, she began to whisper.

"Daddy? Daddy?"

"Daddy's here, baby."

"I don't feel good, Daddy. My bed is spinning. Make it stop. Make it stop."

Royal clenched his jaw. He'd faced wild bulls, mad dogs and crazy hired hands without batting an eye, but anything regarding his daughter's well-being made him sick to his stomach.

"I know," he said softly. "Tell me where you feel bad."

She rolled into a fetal position without answering.

Royal's pulse shifted into high gear as he ran his hands

along her arms. Her entire body was so hot and dry it almost felt like paper.

"Angel," Maddie mumbled, weakly pushing against the restraint of her father's hands. "I can't find my angel."

Royal's heart nearly stopped. "No!" he groaned, and thrust his hands into her hair and turned her until she was facing him.

The mere mention of angels made him crazy. He'd watched his wife, Susan, die and had tried to die with her. But that was before they'd put Maddie in his arms. Within a week of bringing his baby girl home from the hospital, he'd been too tired and sleep-deprived to think of anything but the next bottle to heat and the next diaper to change. At that point, Royal Justice would have had to get better to die. But that was then, and this was now, and he wasn't giving up any more of his family without a fight.

"Maddie, tell Daddy where you feel bad. Can you do that?"

Instead of answering, she fell into a feverish sleep.

He turned on the overhead lights, trying not to panic. Her long, dark hair was damp with perspiration and was sticking to her neck and face. He threw back the covers, then inhaled sharply as his gaze centered on a large, inflamed area on her thigh. Stunned, he bent closer, rubbing the area, testing the size and the heat emanating from within.

"Damn."

There was little else to say. His hands shook as he quickly checked the rest of her body, making certain there were no more spots like it. There were not.

It hadn't been there when he'd put her to bed. He would have bet his life on it. And then he remembered how impatient he'd been with her and how cranky he'd been when he'd tossed her pajamas on the bed. He thought back. The phone had rung. He'd left the room to answer it. By the time he had returned, she was already in her pajamas and in bed, begging him to read her a story.

Pain wrapped around a big dose of guilt as he remembered

that he hadn't read her the story, either. Instead, he'd given her a quick kiss good-night and promised to read her two stories tomorrow. All he could think now was, *Please, God, let there be a tomorrow for her.*

He looked at the huge welt again. The only thing he could think of was that something had bitten her. Probably an insect. But what? She'd been bitten by mosquitoes, stung by bees, even stung by a wasp, and not once had she experienced a reaction like this.

When she began to shiver, he panicked. He had to get her to a doctor, and fast.

"Maddie, I'm going to get dressed and then I'm taking you to the doctor. He'll make you feel better."

The fact that she didn't even argue about an impending trip to the doctor was sign enough for Royal that this was serious.

He was down the hall and in his room within seconds, yanking shirts from hangers and socks from his drawer. Within moments, he was dressed and in her room.

As he lifted her into his arms, he noticed something on the sheets where she'd been lying. As he looked closer, he identified the tiny carcass of a brown spider. In spite of the fact that it was flatter than normal and its long legs were curled in upon itself, the mark on the dead spider's back was impossible to mistake. It was a fiddleback, a brown recluse spider, highly poisonous to all and deadly to some.

He looked in horror at her lifeless little body, then grabbed a blanket from the foot of the bed and wrapped her in it as he dashed from the room.

A short while later he was in his truck and flying down the darkened highway toward Dallas with Maddie beside him in the seat. Although he drove with one hand on the wheel and the other on his daughter, her covers were already trailing on the floor.

"Daddy, Daddy, I'm falling," she cried, weakly pushing at the quilt her father had wrapped around her.

He splayed his hand across her stomach, assuring her that he was there.

"No, baby, you're not falling. Daddy's got you. He won't let you fall."

"Angel...my angel," she whispered, and kicked at the covers on her legs.

"Son of a bitch," he muttered, quelling an urge to throw up. His voice was shaking as he glanced down. "Damn it to hell, Madeline Michelle, you do *not* see angels, do you hear me?"

In typical Royal fashion, he had reacted to fear with anger. And for Royal, the fear was all the greater for the fact that he had nothing on which to focus except his daughter's condition. He couldn't eradicate the spider. It was already dead. He couldn't blame Maddie for the incident. For once, his maverick child had been a victim of circumstance, not of rebellion. And his great strength was useless in the face of such overwhelming odds. It was all he could do to concentrate on the drive to the hospital. He wouldn't let himself think of life without her. He couldn't believe that God would be so cruel as to take away his wife *and* his child.

A short while later, he stood at one side of the bed where Maddie was lying. He was in shock and numb to everything around him except the rapid rise and fall of her chest as her little lungs struggled to cope with the ravages of a rising fever. It wasn't until they moved her into intensive care that he started to crumble. He headed for a phone.

Roman Justice glanced at the digital readout on his alarm clock as he reached for the ringing phone. When he saw the time, he frowned. It was seven minutes after six in the morning. This was his private line. Few people other than family had this number. Instinct told him this wasn't going to be good.

"Hello."

"Roman, it's me, Royal."

Roman heard the panic in his older brother's voice and rolled out of bed. He was reaching for his jeans as he spoke. "What's wrong?"

"It's Maddie. They just put her in intensive care."

Roman's heart dropped. It was all he could do to focus. Except for his wife, Holly, his niece was the most important person in his life.

His voice was rough and shaky as he buttoned his Levi's. "What the hell happened?"

"Spider bite. It was a fiddleback." His voice was shaky as he added, "It doesn't look good."

Roman flipped on the lights. "Where is she?"

"Dallas Memorial."

"Have you called Ryder and Casey?" Roman asked.

Royal took a deep breath and closed his eyes. "No. You do it. I don't think I can say this again."

Roman could hear the panic in his brother's voice. His hand tightened around the receiver. "Don't worry. I'll handle everything," he said. "Hang in there, brother. We're on our way."

Royal disconnected and leaned his forehead against the cool surface of the wall. The comfort of knowing his brothers were coming was small, but for now, it was enough. He straightened his shoulders, then lifted his chin and jammed his Stetson tighter on his head as he headed for intensive care. He didn't give a good damn about hospital rules. His daughter was only four years old, and he wasn't going to have her waking up in a strange place alone. There was no hesitation in his step. He wouldn't let himself believe Maddie might not wake up. She would get better. She had to.

He wangled his way through the closed doors of ICU and went to the nurse's desk.

"Please," Royal begged the nurse. "I won't move. I won't talk. I won't even breathe out loud. Just don't make me leave her."

The nurse was sympathetic, but the rules had been put in place for the benefit of the patients, not the family, and for the patients' sakes, they must be obeyed.

"I'm sorry, Mr. Justice, but visiting time is over. Everyone else has to leave, and so do you. I can't extend special privileges just to you, and you know it.''

"But what if she wakes up and I'm not here? What if she asks for something and no one hears her?"

"That's why we're here," the nurse said. "Now please."

"One more minute," Royal begged.

The nurse rolled her eyes then glanced at her watch. "I have to replace an IV. When I'm finished, you're out of here."

Royal went weak with relief. "Deal."

The nurse glared. "I do not make deals," she said, and walked away.

Royal didn't bother to watch her exit. He was too busy taking in everything they'd done to his daughter in his absence.

He looked at the needle in the back of her hand and winced. Maddie hated shots. He couldn't imagine how she was going to react when she saw it. He touched her forehead. It burned. His hands shook as he swept the hair from her face. Then he glanced up. The nurse was looking his way. He leaned down, desperate to get in one last word before he was forced to leave.

"Daddy's here, baby. Don't be scared. Daddy's here."

A soft sigh escaped Maddie's lips. Her fingers twitched, as if trying to grasp something just out of her reach. Then silent tears began seeping from the corners of her eyes.

"Can't find my angel," she whispered.

Royal's eyes widened in fear.

"Help me, Daddy. Help me."

He leaned his forehead against her arm, fighting the urge to weep.

"You just get better, sweetheart, and I'll help you find anything you want. Okay?"

Her eyelids fluttered as she drifted in and out of consciousness. Royal watched her struggling against the confines of the machines they had hooked her to and was almost glad she didn't know what was happening. As he watched, Maddie sighed and seemed to relax. He kept telling himself she was in good hands. And the longer he stood there, the more solid the belief became. His panic began to subside. She was in the hospital. The doctors would make her better.

"I love you, Maddie. Do you hear me? Daddy loves you more than anyone in this world."

"Mr. Justice."

He jerked. The ICU nurse was standing at his elbow, and the warning in her voice was impossible to miss. He straightened, giving her a hard look as he turned toward the door.

"Have you ever had a loved one in a place like this?"

The nurse blinked, taken aback by his anger.

"No, sir, I have not."

"Then I'll say a prayer for you that it never happens," he said shortly. "Because this is a parent's hell on earth."

When Royal exited ICU, Roman and Holly were waiting for him. Royal took one look at the fear on their faces and answered their unspoken question.

"As I said on the phone, it was a spider bite. They're pretty sure it was a fiddleback."

Holly pressed a hand to her lips and clutched her husband's arm. She and Roman had been married only a few short months, but in that time, Roman's niece had become as dear to her as if she was her own daughter. She couldn't bear to think of that tiny child suffering.

"Where did it bite her?" Holly asked.

"Her leg."

Roman looked toward the doors to ICU. The urge to see her was overwhelming. He couldn't believe such a lively child could be in such serious condition, and so quickly. He glanced at his brother, judging Royal's panic against his own.

"Royal?"

"Just pray," Royal said, and dropped into a chair. He stared at the floor, gathering the guts to say aloud what he'd been thinking for hours. His voice was shaking when he began to speak.

"She's pretty sick. Her fever keeps spiking. She's not out of the woods until they can get that under control."

Roman shook his head and slid into the chair beside his brother.

"I have never been this scared in my entire life," he muttered.

Royal managed a small grin. "Just wait until you have kids of your own."

Holly laid her hand on Royal's shoulder. "Is there anything we can do? If there's a specialist you need, all you have to do is ask. We'll get him here immediately."

Royal frowned as he glanced at the doors barring him from his child. "At this point, I don't think a specialist could help. Thanks for offering, honey, but there's not even anything I can do."

"Ryder and Casey are flying in," she added.

Royal leaned back in the chair and covered his face with his hands. He remembered last night and how Maddie kept begging him to read her a story. Guilt sat heavy on his shoulders as he took a deep, shuddering breath. Ah, God, if only this was just a bad dream and any minute he was going to wake up with Maddie begging him for breakfast. He bolted out of the chair and began to pace.

"I hate this," he muttered.

"Hate what?" Roman asked.

Royal wouldn't look at them, knowing they'd see panic in his eyes.

"The gathering of family. It makes Maddie's condition seem…"

He couldn't finish the sentence. He didn't have to. There was no way they could miss the point. Families gathered for various reasons. Births. Holidays. Illnesses. Deaths.

He shuddered. *Ah, God.*

All they could do was wait.

Seven hours into Royal's hell, his daughter woke up screaming. Royal was out of his chair in the waiting room of

ICU before anyone had time to react. He was halfway through the doors when his brothers stopped him.

"Wait," Ryder urged, nervously eyeing the bed at the other end of the ward where he knew his niece was lying. Already nurses were hovering around her. "Don't make matters worse."

"They can't get any worse," Royal argued, and would have pulled away but for Roman's terse remark.

"Yes, they could," Roman said sharply. "She could be dead. Now let them do their work. If they need us, they know where we are."

Royal slumped. He knew his brothers were right. Already the sounds of Maddie's panic were subsiding. But that didn't help him. He needed to see her—to reassure her that all would be right in her world. He stood in the doorway, staring long and hard down the ward until one of the nurses began ushering him out.

"For God's sake, let me see her," he begged. "You heard her. She's scared to death, and with good reason. She went to sleep in her own home, in her own bed, and she wakes up in this place attached to needles and tubes and machines, and I'm nowhere in sight. At least let me assure her that I'm not far away."

Maddie's plaintive cries wrapped around them. The nurse hesitated.

"Wait here," she said and pivoted.

Royal held his breath. The need to see his daughter was making him sick. He had never been able to bear hearing her cry. Knowing she must be frightened half out of her mind made him crazy. His fingers curled into fists as he watched the nurses in conversation by Maddie's bed.

And then one of them turned and motioned for him to come forward. His heart lifted. Within seconds he was standing at Maddie's side.

"Hey, baby girl, Daddy's here," he said. "Don't cry."

Maddie's wails dissolved into soft, gulping sobs. Careful

not to disturb her IV, he leaned forward and gathered her into a hug.

"I want to go home," Maddie sobbed.

"And I want you there, sweetheart," Royal said softly. "But you got sick. Do you remember?"

Tears were streaming down her face as her head rolled from side to side.

"I don't remember anything but the lady," Maddie said.

Royal frowned. "What lady, baby?"

"The one who was sitting on my bed."

Royal spun toward the nurses. The head nurse smiled and shook her head.

"She must have been hallucinating. We don't sit on patients' beds."

Maddie sniffed as Royal wiped tears from her face. "Not them," she said. "The pretty lady in the blue dress. The one who's sending me an angel."

Royal frowned. Even now, knowing that Maddie seemed over the worst, the talk of angels made him nervous.

"You were dreaming, baby. Sometimes when people get sick they have real crazy dreams."

Tears welled. "It wasn't a dream."

"Another minute, Mr. Justice, and then I'll ask you to leave. Even if your daughter is better, the other patients in here are not."

Royal nodded.

"Don't go," Maddie begged.

"I won't be far," Royal said. "See those doors?"

Maddie turned her head, nodding as her chin continued to quiver.

"Guess who's out there?"

Maddie clutched her father's hand even tighter.

"Uncle Roman and Aunt Holly and Uncle Ryder and Aunt Casey."

Maddie's eyes widened at the mention of her favorite people, especially Roman. "I want to see my uncle Roman."

"And you will, baby, you will. Just as soon as the doctor

lets me, I'll take you home. But you're going to have to take it easy for a couple of days. You've been a pretty sick little girl, okay?''

"Okay," she muttered, and her eyelids began to droop.

"Mr. Justice, please."

Royal nodded. The nurse was out of patience, and he was out of time.

"Close your eyes and take a nap, baby. I'll be back in an hour, okay?"

But Maddie's eyes were already closed. The medicine and her lingering weakness were taking their toll. Royal kissed her forehead and gave her cheek a last, lingering touch. By the time he got into the waiting area, there was a smile on his face.

Ryder stood up. "How is she?"

Royal nodded. "Better. The fever broke. I think the worst is over."

There was a general all-around hug between the Justice family, which lightened the mood considerably. But it was Roman who introduced some reality into the situation, reminding them that Maddie had a ways to go before being cured. His voice was quiet and filled with regret as he caught Royal by the arm.

"You know that bite is likely to leave a hell of a scar."

Royal nodded.

Holly frowned. "A scar? Surely a spider bite doesn't scar."

"This spider's bite does," Roman said.

Royal nodded. "It's a bitch, and that's for sure. Not only is it deadly, but the pain will be pretty severe and the flesh around the bite will probably rot away. But I don't give a good damn how it looks when it's over, because she will still be alive."

Casey slipped her hand in the bend of Royal's elbow and hugged him close to her. Her voice was sweet and low, filled with the accent of her native Mississippi.

"We will say prayers."

Royal was blinking back tears as he looked around the small waiting area.

"Thanks," he said gruffly.

"For what?" they all said.

"For being here," Royal answered.

"Where else would we be?" Roman said. "We're family. We're all we've got."

Chapter 2

Within days of the spider incident, the entire house had been fumigated, and Royal had hired two cleaning women from town to put the house to rights. He'd watched them with a wary eye, making sure that every insect and spider they swept up was dead. Maddie's room smelled of lemon-scented disinfectant and furniture polish. Her favorite teddy bear was on her pillow, awaiting her arrival. As soon as he got his baby girl back, his world would be on track.

He stood in the doorway to her room, remembering the day she'd been born. It had been a mixture of heaven and hell. Watching his daughter claim life and watching his young wife die. His emotions had run the gamut. But he'd survived, and so had Maddie.

Now, as difficult as it was for him to accept, she was growing up. This fall she would start kindergarten. That meant half a day of school. For years he had chosen to ignore the fact that the routine he'd adopted was no longer going to work. He wouldn't be able to yank Maddie out of her bed, toss her into the pickup with a peanut butter and jelly sandwich and take her to work with him. There would be no more fixing fence with her unceasing chatter in the background or hauling hay with her sitting by his side. Soon, her days would no longer be all his. Somehow, he was going to have to find a way to adjust.

Twice during his trips to the hospital, Roman had brought up the subject of a permanent housekeeper, and each time Royal had balked. He'd had a housekeeper when Maddie was a baby. She'd lasted through Maddie's third birthday and then moved away. The separation had been traumatic for them all. Royal had vowed not to put Maddie through such loss again. Over time they'd fallen into a routine that had suited them both. Just the thought of finding someone new to intrude into their world was an all-around pain-in-the-ass notion. Sharing space with anyone except his daughter, no matter how good and kind she might be, wasn't something Royal Justice did easily.

He glanced at his watch. It was almost seven. Holly had been at the hospital with Maddie more than three hours. They'd moved Maddie into a regular room, and she had not been left alone. Someone from the Justice family was with her at all times during the day, but it was Royal who stayed every night. His steps were light as he grabbed his keys on the way out the door. Tomorrow he was bringing her home.

Angel Rojas sat on the side of her bed, counting her meager stash of money. Rent on her apartment was due, and even though she knew truth was on her side, there would be no justice for her in this town. Not with Fat Louie's angry influence. She flopped onto the mattress, staring at the ceiling in quiet despair.

"Why do I keep getting myself in these messes?"

No one bothered to answer, because no one was there.

It was getting dark. One set of people were in the act of shutting themselves in behind closed doors while others were coming to life. And while the night called to some, there was nothing within it that called to Angel. She'd seen it all and committed a few more sins than she liked to admit, but turning tricks had never been an option.

She closed her eyes and rolled onto her side, then took a deep breath, making her mind relax. She was tired and heartsick and needed to rest. Today had been rough, but in the words of her heroine, Scarlett O'Hara, tomorrow was another day.

By sunrise she had made a decision. It had taken years for her to accumulate what constituted her worldly possessions, and parting with them was going to be painful. But she'd learned long ago not to dwell on a bad situation, and this was definitely one of her worst. If she had to leave town to survive, then she would do it. But there was no way she could take her things, too.

There was a living room suite bought at a yard sale. A bed and dresser that didn't match, and a table and three chairs she'd inherited from the previous resident of the apartment. Her entire wardrobe would fit in one small closet. The only thing she owned that she deemed of great value was a bookcase full of books she had spent years accumulating. She didn't own a car, she didn't have a credit card, and she didn't know where she was going. She gazed longingly around the small rooms, painfully realizing that this was no longer her home. Then she clenched her jaw, picked up the sign she'd made and walked outside. With a grunt, she stuck it in the lawn near the curb.

Moving Sale—Apartment Three

By five o'clock, she was sitting on the floor of an empty apartment and counting her money. Almost two hundred dollars to add to what she'd taken from Fat Louie, and she still didn't have five hundred dollars to begin a new life. Her hands were shaking as she folded her money and stuffed it in the bottom of her purse, then dropped the purse between her legs and closed her eyes.

"Please, God," she whispered. "Show me the way. All I want is a home."

That night she slept on the floor, and by daylight she was gone.

Later, someone remarked to Fat Louie that he thought he'd seen Louie's waitress hitchhiking west out of town.

Louie tongued his unlit cigar to the other side of his mouth, all the while cursing good riddance to the crazy bitch.

Meanwhile, Angel Rojas was doing what she knew how to do best—putting the past behind her and moving on.

"Maddie, want to come see the new kittens?" Royal asked.

"I guess," Maddie said, sliding off the sofa and dragging her feet as she followed him out the door.

Royal frowned. Ever since her return from the hospital, Maddie had been moping around the ranch like a calf that had lost its mother. Nothing seemed to interest her. Offers to let her cat, Flea Bit, into the house to play had fallen flat, and visits from her uncle Roman had failed to excite her. The doctors had quoted statistics, assuring Royal that some depression was normal after a hospital stay and that it would pass. But Royal didn't like statistics, and he wanted whatever was wrong with Maddie to be gone.

"What's wrong?" he asked, as they strolled toward the barn. He glanced at the angry red spot on her leg. Although it was healing nicely, it was far from well. "Is your leg hurting, baby? Want Daddy to carry you?"

"No," she said, and kicked up a cloud of dust without pausing.

Royal's frown deepened as he tried to find a topic that might excite her.

"Dumpling has a calico kitten with one blue eye and one brown eye, what do you think about that?" he asked.

Maddie paused and looked up. "Does that mean she sees blue with one eye and brown with the other?"

Royal grinned, scooped her off her feet and set her on his shoulders, careful to miss the sore part of her leg.

"No, it does not, and you know it," he said, chuckling as

they started toward the barn. "What color are my eyes?" he asked.

"They're blue," Maddie answered. "Just like mine."

"Right. And when you look, is everything blue?"

"No," she said, and he heard her giggle. The sound was music to his ears.

"Then there's your answer."

He heard her sigh and felt her hands gripping the crown of his Stetson. Carrying her like this was hell on the shape of a good hat, but he'd willingly sacrifice a truckload of hats just to get back the girl she'd been.

They entered the shade of the barn. He set her in the midst of the hay where a mother cat was busy grooming her two-week-old litter. Royal shook his head in dismay as he counted the kittens. Five more to add to the growing number already in residence on his ranch. And then he shrugged. A working ranch could not have too many cats. As long as they stayed in the barns and sheds where the mice and rats might be, they were fine.

But there was Flea Bit, the cat who, thanks to Roman's interference, had taken up residence in the house. That damned ball of fur was underfoot every time he took a step. Then he looked at Maddie, squatting in the midst of the hay, tenderly stroking the new babies while muttering her sweet talk to the old mother cat. His heart tugged. He hoped to hell Maddie didn't ask to bring any of these cats to the house. There wasn't enough spit left in him to tell her no about anything. He squatted beside her, and when he tuned in on what she was saying, his frown deepened.

"I'm sorry I didn't come see you sooner," Maddie said, stroking the old cat's head in short, gentle strokes. "I got sick." She leaned closer, as if telling the cat a secret. "I saw a lady," she said softly. "She promised me angels." Her lower lip drooped. "But the angel didn't come."

Ah, Royal thought. The reason for her depression.

He dropped to one knee, cupping the back of his daughter's head.

"Maddie, look at me."

Maddie continued to stroke the cat's head as if her father was nowhere in sight.

"Madeline Michelle, I'm talking to you," Royal said softly.

When Maddie looked up, there was a stubborn, like-father-like-daughter thrust to her chin.

"What?" she muttered.

"You don't need to worry about angels anymore, okay?"

Her face fell. "But Daddy, the lady promised."

Royal tipped her chin so she was staring at him eye to eye.

"Maddie, there was no lady on your bed and there isn't going to be an angel coming. Angels don't live with people, they live in heaven, remember?"

She nodded, but he could tell she wasn't buying his explanation.

"What you saw…what you thought you saw, that was all part of your illness. Do you understand?"

Her lower lip protruded. "I saw a lady," she said shortly, and turned away, pretending great interest in the kitten with one blue eye and one brown eye. She lifted it into her lap, carefully judging its odd markings with a practiced eye and then abruptly announced, "I'm going to name him Marbles."

In spite of the fact that his talk had gone nowhere, he had to grin. "Why Marbles?"

"'Cause his eyes are the color of the marbles in the bottom of Uncle Roman's fish tank."

Royal rocked on his heels and grinned. "Marbles it is," he said softly. "How about the other four? Don't they need names, too?"

Maddie looked them over carefully, then shook her head. "No, only this one."

"Why?" Roman asked.

She looked at him, as if surprised by the stupidity of his question.

"Because Marbles is a people cat, not a mouse cat."

Royal rolled his eyes. "Oh, no, you don't," he said lightly, and put the kitten with the mother before setting Maddie on his shoulders for the trip to the house. "We're not making a house pet out of another cat, and that's final."

There was a marked silence between father and daughter. They were halfway to the house when Maddie leaned close to Royal's ear.

"Daddy."

"What, baby?"

"Do you think Flea Bit will sleep with Marbles?"

"If we're lucky, no," he muttered.

"What did you say?" Maddie asked.

"I said, it's hard to know," he answered, and said a mental prayer for forgiveness for the small white lie.

Tommy Boy Watson was looking for whores. At the age of thirty-seven, he was old enough to indulge his baser instincts if he so chose, but it wasn't the sex he was after. Since the death of his father, Claude, the extermination of whores had become his quest. He'd watched his old man go from being a successful trucker to an invalid, fighting the ravages of AIDS. The irony of Claude Watson's disease came from the fact that he didn't even know who'd given it to him or how many he'd passed it to before he became ill. He'd been a notorious womanizer, often taking advantage of the prostitutes hanging around the parking lots of truck stops and rest stops along the nation's highways. After Claude had been diagnosed, it had taken a month shy of three years for him to die, and he'd died blaming the lot lizards and not himself.

At four inches over five feet tall, Tommy Boy was almost a foot shorter and one hundred pounds lighter than his father had been. His biggest disappointment in life had been his size. He'd compensated with attitude. He'd done the job well. Tommy Boy Watson wasn't just tough, he was mean. And since his father's demise, a little crazy, as well. His pale green eyes seemed innocuous until you looked beneath his smile. Pure evil dwelled there. He wore a long, unkempt beard and tied his thin and graying hair into a ponytail. He favored baseball caps and kept all his keys on a heavy silver chain hooked to a belt loop. He was fond of the clink the links made as they rubbed against the rivets in his jeans.

Six weeks ago, he'd stood at his father's grave with a bottle of whiskey in one hand and a switchblade in the other and made a vow to get rid of every whore to cross his path. In his mind, it was the least he could do to avenge Claude's death. No other decent man should suffer the way his father had suffered. He'd been on the road since then, leaving the mutilated bodies of fallen women in his wake.

Last night he'd crossed the state line into Texas. It was the first time he'd been this far south. He didn't know whether he liked it, and it didn't really matter. He hadn't come for his health.

His gaze was sharp as he watched the people coming and going from the truck stop parking lot. There were plenty of women, but so far, none looked as if they were surfing for business.

Today it was hotter than normal, even for Texas, even for the middle of May, but it gave him cool satisfaction to know that he'd left the state of Oklahoma with one less hooker than it had had the day before.

He wondered absently if they'd found her body yet. His pulse accelerated as he remembered how easily the flesh beneath her chin had parted under the blade of his knife. Like hot butter. He shifted his stance and giggled just a little, not because he was happy, but because it had been so easy.

He thought of his little house on the outskirts of Chicago and wondered what the boys in the neighborhood were doing. This was Saturday. Tonight they'd be gathering at the local bar, watching TV and laying bets, like whether or not Jimmy Riordan could chugalug six raw eggs in his beer without throwing up. They always bet on something. For Tommy Boy, it was what made life worth living.

Then his smile faded as he remembered what he'd set out to do. There would be time later for playing. After he was finished.

It never occurred to him to wonder when he might stop or how many dead women would be enough to assuage his anger over his father's death. All he knew was that his pain lessened with each slice of his knife.

Suddenly he straightened and pulled his cap tight across his forehead, shading his eyes from the blast of midday sun.

There. Just getting out of that old gray van. He saw her wave. He heard her laugh. He watched them drive away, leaving her standing alone in the parking lot. He watched her shift her duffel bag to her shoulder and start toward the restaurant. His pulse quickened. She was young, maybe mid-twenties. Her clothes were faded. Her legs were long. Her breasts... His breath caught at the back of his throat as he watched them bounce with the sway of her stride. His eyes narrowed. She looked Indian, maybe Mexican. He couldn't tell for sure, but there was all that soft-looking, warm brown skin, and enough black hair to strangle a man with. Resisting the urge to rub himself, he continued to watch her. It wasn't often that a whore excited him. Usually he felt nothing but disgust. His stare lengthened.

Yes. This was the kind of woman who'd tempted his father. This was a woman who could lead a man to his death with little more than a smile. When she disappeared into the restaurant, he smoothed a hand over the button fly of his jeans and started after her.

Angel was tired from the inside out. She'd been on the road for more than two days. It had been years since she'd done anything as foolish as hitchhiking, and although she'd started out apprehensively, so far her rides had been on the up-and-up. She glanced at the small sign near the restaurant door.

Bus Stop.

Lord, but what she wouldn't give for the money to travel in style. Not that bus travel was all that stylish, but from the backseat of a stranger's van, it was looking better all the time.

She rubbed her palm over the outside of her duffel bag, imagining she could feel the small stash of money secreted in the bottom. Her feet ached and her forehead felt hot. She hoped she wasn't coming down with something. She couldn't be sick. Not like this. Not without a place to call home.

A blast of cool air hit her as she entered the restaurant and she paused in the doorway, letting her eyes adjust in the dim interior. It didn't take long to see that she'd have to wait. There wasn't a seat available. With a sigh, she headed for the ladies' room to freshen up. Maybe when she got back, some of the places would have cleared.

Her stomach growled to protest being empty. The scent of food and hot coffee almost did her in, but she kept walking. She didn't see the man who came in behind her, and even if she had, she would have paid him little mind.

But Tommy Boy Watson saw her as she disappeared into the ladies' room. He cast a quick glance around and slid onto a vacated stool at the counter. From where he was sitting, he had a perfect view of the ladies' room door. A cold smile tilted the corners of his lips.

Go ahead and wash your pretty face, bitch. I can wait.

Angel leaned toward the mirror over the sink and stared at her reflection. Her scalp itched, and her skin was sticky with sweat and the dust of the road. She closed her eyes and let her chin drop toward her chest in disgust. She felt dirty from the inside out. All she'd ever wanted in this life was a place to belong, and here she was in her mid-twenties, on the road and still looking for rainbows. She turned on the water, letting it run hard between her fingers before leaning down and sluicing the dust from her face.

She turned off the water and reached for a paper towel. As she did, she caught a glimpse of herself in the mirror again, and this time almost didn't recognize herself. With water dripping from her eyes and face, she looked as if she'd been crying. It was a foreign thought. Angel Rojas didn't cry. Not anymore. The lack of expression on her face was frightening.

"God," she muttered. "Where have I gone?"

Then she shrugged off the thought and dried her face. There was no room in her life for regrets. Her belly growled again as she picked up her bag. Her feet were dragging as she walked into the restaurant. She found a seat and was soon immersed in reading the menu.

Tommy Boy was staring. He knew, like he knew his own name, that this woman was one who needed cleansing. He took a sip of coffee, picturing his father lying in this woman's arms, then picturing his father as he'd laid in his coffin. When he focused again, his face was filled with rage. Disease. Disease. They all spread disease.

"Want a refill, honey?"

He looked up. Startled by the waitress's intrusion, he glared. Realizing he had time to pass, he nodded.

He glanced at the woman in the booth again, watching her facial expressions as she studied the menu. When he heard the low murmur of her voice as she gave a waitress her order, his gaze snagged on the muscles working in her throat. And when she tilted a glass of water to her lips and drank, it was all he could do to wait. He had it planned. He knew just what he was going to say. It would be easy. After all, getting them into his truck was simple. They were bodies for hire. All he had to do was promise to pay for services rendered.

Angel stepped out of the restaurant and into the afternoon sunshine, wincing as the glare burned her weary eyes. She dropped her duffel bag and knelt beside it, digging in a side pocket for the sunglasses she'd put there last night.

"Hey, baby, did you lose something?"

Startled by the unexpected sound of a stranger's voice, she rocked on her heels and looked up. She had a moment's impression of long, greasy hair, a thin, straggly beard and eyes the color of a frog's belly. Her stomach knotted as she stood, but she refused to show fear. Instead, she slid her sunglasses up her nose, shouldered her bag and stared him straight in the face, taking momentary comfort in the anonymity.

"No, I didn't lose a thing."

The man grinned. "Just asking," he drawled. "Say, baby, I'm in the mood to party. How about it?"

The food she'd just eaten threatened to come up. "No," she said brusquely and turned away. To her shock, he grabbed her by the arm.

"Listen here," he said, running his hand up and down her arm. "I've got plenty of everything a pretty thing like you might need...including money."

It was impossible for Angel to misinterpret his intentions. His tone was suggestive, as was the way he smoothed his hand over his fly.

For Angel, it was shades of Fat Louie all over again. Her voice was full of anger as she yanked her arm out of his grasp.

"I've never been that hard up. Now get lost, mister, before I really get mad."

Tommy Boy was stunned. He hadn't expected a rebuff. The others had been all too willing to take some of his money. His lips narrowed angrily as he watched her stride away. It occurred to him that maybe he'd made a mistake, that maybe she wasn't a whore, after all. But a couple of minutes later, he watched her crawling into the cab of an eighteen-wheeler. He knew truckers weren't supposed to pick up hitchhikers. In his mind, the only reason that trucker had hauled her into his cab was to get a piece of tail.

"Damn her to hell and back," he muttered, and pivoted angrily.

By the time he got to his truck, he was in a blind rage. He gunned the engine, leaving a long black trail of rubber on the pavement behind him as he spun out of the parking lot and into the northbound lanes of Interstate 35, the opposite direction from the woman and the trucker. His head was pounding and his hands were shaking. The farther he drove, the more his head hurt. Sunlight bounced off the hood of his truck and into his eyes. He grabbed sunglasses from the dash and shoved them in place, cursing with every breath. Slowly, he became aware of a nagging little voice inside his head.

Go back. Go back.

He shook his head like a dog shedding water and focused on the highway traffic.

You let her get away. You promised to avenge me.

The familiar cadence of that voice gave him a chill. His father was dead. But it was still somehow Claude Watson's voice he heard.

Stop her. Have to stop her before it's too late.

Tommy Boy slammed on the brakes and made a sudden left on the interstate. Huge clumps of dirt and grass flew into the air as the tires on his truck tore through the center median. He bounced into the southbound lanes, barely avoiding a crash. Cars spun out of control, and a delivery truck full of bottled water skidded off the interstate and into the ditch to avoid a collision. Adrenaline rocketed into his system as he stuck his arm out the window and flipped off the cars behind him. Within seconds, he was out of sight, driving as fast as his black truck would go, desperate to find the whore who was getting away.

Chapter 3

Royal stood on the back porch, nursing a cup of coffee and planning his day. Sunrise had come and gone, and the day was bathed in light. Except for a couple of fading jet trails, the Texas sky was cloudless. He squinted against the glare of sun as he gazed east.

In the pasture next to the corral, the old cow he'd put there last week was bawling to be fed. He took another sip of coffee, contemplating the wisdom of hauling her off. It had been two years since she'd had a calf, her teeth were worn almost to the gums, and she had a monotonous tendency to jump fences. Then he grinned and discarded the notion. He admired an aggressive spirit, even in an animal, and he'd be damned before he sold her. She'd borne more than her share of calves over the years. So what if her fruitful days were over. She deserved a better ending than winding up in a can of dog food.

A door banged somewhere in the house behind him, and his attention shifted. Maddie must be awake. When the screen door squeaked behind him, he stifled a grin. One of Maddie's favorite pastimes was to sneak up on him. He braced himself for a great big boo. It never came.

He turned. Maddie was on her knees, cradling Flea Bit in her arms. Royal sighed. There would be cat hair all over her clean pajamas.

"Morning, sweetheart," he said softly, and set his cup on the porch rail. He knelt and lifted the kitten out of her lap and her into his arms. When she snuggled her nose against the curve of his neck, his heart tugged painfully. Even now, knowing that she was perfectly cured, he still hadn't recovered from the fear of almost losing her.

"You're awfully quiet this morning," he said. "Are you okay?"

Maddie nodded and wrapped her arms tightly around her daddy's neck.

"I had a dream."

Royal hugged her. "I'm sorry, baby. Did it scare you?"

"No."

"Then how did it make you feel?" he asked.

She hesitated, as if considering the question, then finally answered.

"Sad."

His frown deepened. "Want to tell me about it?" he asked. He sat in the porch swing and settled her in his lap.

She shrugged.

He let the question ride. In the past few weeks, he was coming to realize that Maddie was almost as hardheaded as he was. Instead of talking, they just rocked. The squeak of the chains from which the porch swing hung was persistent. But instead of an irritation, it was a comforting sound.

A light breeze had come up a short while ago and now it was slipping around the corner of the house, lifting the ends of Maddie's hair and cooling the heat of her warm little body as she cuddled against him. Royal glanced at the dark tangles they had yet to brush, then at the upturned nose she'd inherited from a mother she would never know. An emotion swelled within him, pushing up through his chest and tightening the muscles in his throat until it brought tears to his eyes. He jerked his head upward and closed his eyes, inhaling deeply to push back the feelings. Damn it to hell, but life just wasn't fair. Maddie was growing up, and the woman who would have rejoiced in it most was dead and buried.

Inside the house, the phone began to ring. And for Maddie, the sound was like magic. She came to life, bouncing off Royal's lap and heading for the door before he could even get out of the swing.

"I'll get it!" she shrieked. The door slammed to punctuate her announcement.

Royal grinned and got up to go inside. At least some things were back to normal.

In spite of the fact that the trucker Angel had accepted a ride with was well over six feet tall and pushing three hundred pounds, she felt safe. A priest had once told her the best way to judge character was to look in a person's eyes. When Angel had looked into the trucker's face, she hadn't seen a worn-out version of Grizzly Adams on uppers. She'd seen a friendly smile below a black handlebar mustache and warm brown eyes twinkling at her as he offered her a hand up in the cab.

"Where you headin', missy?" the trucker had asked.

"Where are you going?" Angel countered.

"South," the trucker said.

"That'll do," Angel drawled.

He laughed, and when Angel slammed the door shut, he began shifting gears. The big rig began to pick up speed. The farther they got from that parking lot, the better Angel began to feel. Even though the man who'd accosted her had only touched her arm, she'd known instant fear.

As the miles added up, she began to relax, although she kept glancing nervously in the rearview mirrors. She'd seen the man get in a new black truck, and although she knew it was silly to think he would follow, every time she saw a dark vehicle behind them, she tensed until she was sure it wasn't him.

"Lookin' for someone?" the big trucker asked.

Angel shook her head.

The man's eyes narrowed thoughtfully, although he gave her a smile.

"If you got trouble, missy, you'd best leave it behind you. That's what I always say."

With one last glance in the rearview mirror, she nodded.

"It is."

"That's good. That's good. Now then, we've got ourselves a decision to make. I'm pushing all the way to Houston tonight. You a mind to go that far?"

Angel blinked. Getting lost in a city that size wasn't what she had in mind, especially when she was still trying to find herself.

"No, I guess not," she said, although she was reluctant to give up the ride. "Just drop me off at the first convenient spot."

"What's your destination?" he asked.

"I thought maybe I'd try something on the outskirts of Dallas, around Arlington. It's summer. Maybe I can get work at Six Flags."

The trucker nodded. "Yeah, theme parks are the thing during vacation time, all right. You ought to do just fine."

A few moments later he pulled over. He pointed across her line of vision toward the west.

"See that highway off to your right?"

She turned and looked.

"Stay on that and it'll take you straight into Arlington."

Angel grabbed her duffel bag and paused at the open door.

"Thanks, mister."

The trucker's gaze quickly swept over the young woman, eyeing her feminine curves and old clothes. He knew what hard up looked like. He also knew what it felt like. His conscience kicked in as she began climbing down from the cab.

"Hey, missy."

Angel looked up.

"Hitchhiking is dangerous business."

She shrugged. "It's also cheap."

He laughed. "There's that, all right. Well then, be on your way, and Godspeed."

Angel watched until he was no longer in sight, then began making her way across the median to the other side of the highway. She glanced at her watch and was surprised to see she'd been riding with the man for almost an hour and had never asked his name. She saw a truck stop about a quarter of a mile ahead, and started walking. Her mind was on bathrooms and cold water and big, greasy hamburgers. For the time being, the pale, skinny man was forgotten.

Tommy Boy was sweating. The persistent whine in his head was eating into his nerves.

You let her get away. You promised to avenge me and you let her get away.

Tommy Boy's face was pale, and the pupils of his small, close-set eyes were fixed and staring. Every time he came to a crossroads on the highway, the knot in his belly gave another sharp tug. There were a dozen different highways the trucker could have taken. Without knowing his destination, he had no way of guessing where they had gone. But guilt rode him hard, and he kept on driving, stopping only to empty his bladder or fill up his fuel tank.

Once he spotted the back end of a rig like the one the trucker had been driving. Same company. Same color of trailer. He'd driven like a man possessed to catch up, only to find that he'd been chasing the wrong driver. Seeing the thin, bony face of a redheaded man behind the wheel had brought him to the point of tears. He'd eased off the gas and taken the first exit ramp off the highway, desperate to control his emotions. Moments later he was on the shoulder of the road, fighting the urge to throw up.

Time passed, and Tommy Boy was barely aware of the traffic. Finally he looked up. His mind was blank, his body, trembling. But the worst was over. To his everlasting relief, the voice had disappeared.

"Hell," he muttered as he started the engine. "What's one hooker? There's a dozen out there to take her place."

Having stated the facts as he saw them, he pulled onto the highway. Half an hour later, he realized the truck coming toward him on the other side of the road was the one he'd been chasing for nearly a day. When he saw the driver and that dark, bushy beard, he hit the steering wheel with the flat of his hand and laughed. The echo of his laughter was still with him when he realized the trucker was riding solo. Even though he knew the woman could be lying down in the sleeper, his instincts told him different. Somewhere along the highway, the trucker had dropped her off. Tommy Boy sneered. It figured. She was out there now, looking for another man to snare, another victim to infect.

Certain that fate was guiding him, he accelerated. He'd find her again. And this time, he wouldn't fail.

Angel entered the restaurant and paused in the doorway, eyeing the patrons and assessing the possibilities of her next ride. There were plenty of trucks in the parking lot, and every kind of traveling vehicle, including a half dozen fancy motorcycles parked off to one side. Surely someone would be going her way. But for now, all she wanted was a bathroom and food, in that order.

A short while later, she was finishing an order of fries and downing the last of her iced tea. She'd already spotted the people to whom the bikes belonged. With weather-worn skin as dark as burned toast, wearing denim, leather and boots, they were hard to miss. Some of them were with women. A couple were not. She'd already heard them talking about stopping in Arlington, so she knew they were going her way. When she noticed they were getting up to leave, her pulse kicked. It was now or never. She tossed some money onto the table to pay for her food, shouldered her bag and headed for the door.

The sun was bright in her face as she exited, but she waited to don her sunglasses. It was always better to ask for a ride when they could see your face.

"Nice ride," she said, as the group began to mount.

A couple of the women gave her hard looks. Another smiled. One of the men looked up. A long moment of silence passed between him and Angel, and finally he asked, "Need a lift?"

Angel stared hard and long at his face and at the expression in his eyes. Finally she nodded.

"Where you headed?" he asked.

"Six Flags. I'm looking for work." She paused and added, "And nothing else."

He nodded. "Fair enough." He turned and waved at the man to his left. "Juke, hand me your extra helmet."

In no time, Angel's bag was strapped on and she was settling in place on the Harley. The biker turned to look at her.

"I don't ride with strangers, so what's your name?"

Angel hesitated, but she could see no harm in the simple question.

"Angel," she replied.

The group broke into loud shouts of laughter as the biker got a silly grin on his face.

"What's so funny?" Angel asked.

"Your name," he said, and revved the engine.

She had to yell to be heard. "I don't get the joke."

"Hey, Demon, let's ride," someone called.

They pulled out of the parking lot in an orderly manner, two abreast. Angel caught a glimpse of herself in the windows of the gas station they were passing and knew a moment of panic.

Demon?

The man she was riding with was called Demon?

There was an instant when she started to shout at him to let her off. And then she caught a glimpse of something shiny and black from the corner of her eye and turned to look.

There. Pulling into a parking place at the pumps and getting out of the truck was the man from the diner. Instead of begging to get off, she found herself clutching Demon's jacket. Although she believed herself to be safely hidden behind the helmet's dark visor, she couldn't stop thinking about the coincidence of seeing him twice in one day and in locations that were so far apart.

Demon revved the engine.

It occurred to her that she could be putting herself between a rock and a hard place.

Dear God, please let this be all right.

She reminded herself that names could be deceiving. Demon was more than likely not a demon after all. Besides, she was called Angel, and she was about as far from holy as a person could get.

Royal got out of the truck with his arms full of groceries. Roman met him at the door, relieving him of part of his burden.

"Everything okay?" Royal asked.

Roman grinned, thinking of the can of shaving cream that had met an early demise. "If you're referring to your daughter, she's fine."

"I appreciate you coming to help me out," Royal said, as he set his sack on the kitchen cabinet. Roman followed suit.

"No big deal," Roman said shortly. "Besides, with Holly in Las Vegas visiting her father, I'd rather be here than in that apartment alone."

Royal grinned. "When you fell, you fell hard, didn't you, little brother?"

Roman arched an eyebrow but refused to be baited. "Don't be so damned smug. Your day is coming."

Royal snorted. "It'll be a cold day in hell before that ever happens," he muttered.

"Daddy, where's hell?"

Both men spun around. Royal had the grace to look shamefaced while Roman hid a grin.

"I keep telling you to watch your language around her," he said softly.

Royal glared at his brother, dug a package of Twinkies from the groceries and tossed it to Maddie.

"Here, squirt, take yourself outside to play while I put up the groceries, okay?"

Maddie caught her treat in midair and was out the door before her father could change his mind.

Roman rolled his eyes. "That's perfect," he drawled. "She curses and spits like a seasoned wrangler and now you're buying her off with enough sugar to keep her wired all night."

Royal sighed and looked away. "Yeah, yeah. Tell me something I don't already know."

Roman walked to the back door, watching as Maddie tore into the sponge cakes and broke off a piece for Flea Bit, who was scrambling around her feet. He smiled and turned.

"I'm sorry. That was none of my business," he said. "I don't know how you've done it—raising that baby all by yourself. You should be getting an award, not advice."

Royal looked away and frowned. "I know I'm not perfect."

"To Maddie you are, and that's all that matters," Roman said.

Royal shook his head. "Once I might have believed that, but no more. These days it's rare if I get a smile out of her. She's been moping around the house ever since she came home from the hospital. I can't seem to snap her out of it."

Roman stood, considering the reaction Royal was bound to have, and shook off the thought. Maddie was Royal's child. He had a right to know what was going on in her head.

"Come with me," Roman said. "I want to show you something."

Royal glanced out the door, assuring himself Maddie was still in sight, then followed Roman into the living room.

Papers were strewn all over the tabletop, the chairs and the sofa. A couple had drifted onto the floor.

Roman began picking them up and handing them to Royal one by one. At first glance, Royal took the drawings to be nothing more than something Maddie had done to pass away time. The longer he looked, the more obvious it became that his assumption was wrong.

"What the hell?" he muttered, shuffling them in his hands.

"She said they were angels," Roman said.

Royal's belly jerked. "I thought she'd gotten all of that out of her mind."

Roman shrugged. "From where I'm standing, it looks to me as if that's the only thing on her mind."

Royal looked up, his face haggard with worry. "What am I going to do? And don't tell me to take her to a shrink! Four-year-old children do not need to see shrinks."

Roman shrugged. "That's not entirely true. Some do."

Royal glared but didn't answer. His gaze was drawn to the pictures. They were all the same theme repeated over and over with different backgrounds. A childish rendition of a woman in blue, surrounded in colors of yellow, and a dark-headed woman with wings.

"Did she say who they were?" Royal asked.

Roman pointed to the woman in blue. "That's the lady who sits on her bed."

Royal groaned. "This is getting way out of hand."

"And the brown one is supposed to be her angel."

"Brown angels?" He sighed. "I suppose this could set a trend."

Before Roman could answer, Maddie burst into the room.

"Daddy, Flea Bit wants some more Twinkies."

"I don't think so," Royal said. "It will ruin Flea Bit's supper."

Maddie rolled her eyes and started to pout, but Royal side-tracked her by holding up the drawings.

"I thought we'd talked about this," he said gruffly.

Although she didn't understand why, she knew she was in trouble. She gave her uncle Roman an accusing stare and then dropped her chin.

Roman sighed. In Maddie's eyes, he'd let her down.

Royal laid a hand on Maddie's head. "Madeline Michelle, I'm talking to you," he said.

She looked up, her eyes brimming with unshed tears.

Royal relented and dropped to one knee. "I'm not mad at you, baby. I just want to understand."

One huge tear slid down the side of her face, followed by another on her other cheek. Her voice was trembling.

"They're pictures of my lady and the angel."

Royal groaned. "Maddie, there isn't any—"

Maddie took a step back. "You're wrong! You're wrong!" she cried. "She's my lady, and you can't take her away."

Royal reached for her. "I'm not trying to take anything away from you, baby," he said gently. "But you have to understand the difference between real people and pretend people."

Maddie's lips were trembling, but her chin jutted in a mutinous thrust. If it hadn't been so tragic, Roman could have laughed. At that moment, father and daughter had never looked more alike.

"They're not pretend. They're real!" Maddie shrieked. "You'll see. The lady said my angel is coming. Then you'll see I'm telling the truth."

She ran out of the room, the Twinkies and the cat forgotten.

"Well, now, I think that went real well," Roman drawled.

Royal stood and glared. "Just shut the hell up."

Roman nodded. "I'm out of here. Call me if you need me."

Royal was left with the handful of drawings and a growing certainty that the situation was out of his control.

Tommy Boy Watson slid behind the wheel of his truck and shut the door. Washed in the silence, he leaned his head against the back of the seat and closed his eyes, savoring the adrenaline high he was on. The feel of her flesh was still with him, soft and pliant. It had parted beneath the blade of his knife like warm butter.

Silently. Swiftly.

Opening for him. Bleeding for him. Cleansing the filth from her body...and stealing her life.

It was night. It would be hours, maybe even days before

her body was found. That suited him fine. He would be long gone before that could happen. He took a deep breath and opened his eyes. It was time to move on. Time to find the black-haired woman who got away. Maybe then it would be enough.

Angel was scared. The bikers she'd hitched a ride with were long gone, and twice since then she had seen a shiny black pickup truck like the one the skinny man had been driving. Each time, she'd been certain that she'd seen him behind the wheel. She kept telling herself she was being silly, that there was no way she was being stalked. But her instincts were telling her different. This was far beyond a coincidence. Fear was with her. The urge to run was overwhelming. But run where? Her plan had been to work at Six Flags. But instinct kept telling her to move on, to get as far away from Texas as she could.

The urge to spend some of her precious cash on a bus ticket was growing stronger, but her last ride had dumped her in the middle of nowhere. The highway stretched before and behind her like a flat gray ribbon. Added to that, the sky was darkening and threatening rain. She sighed. Rain. That would make this day just about perfect.

No sooner had the thought evolved than the first drops of rain began to fall. She rolled her eyes heavenward and hitched her duffel bag to her other shoulder, convinced that this day couldn't get much worse. And then a bolt of lightning split the sky with a crack, and she flinched.

"Okay, so I was wrong."

Hunching her shoulders against the sudden downpour, she started to walk.

Royal looked through the windshield to the darkening sky and frowned. "I was hoping we'd beat the rain."

Safely buckled into the restraints of a child's car seat, Maddie gave the darkening sky and the sudden downpour a minimal glance. She was too concerned with the free toy in the fast-food lunch her father had just bought her.

"What did you get?" Royal asked.

"Belle!" she crowed, holding it up for him to see.

He frowned. "Who's Belle?"

Maddie looked up in pure disgust. "Daddy, don't you know anything?"

He grinned. "Obviously not."

"Beauty and the Beast, remember?"

Recognition dawned. "Oh, that Belle."

Maddie rolled her eyes.

"Hey, you," Royal teased. "Give me a french fry and quit being so smart."

Maddie giggled and handed him two. "One for your mouth and one for your hand," she explained.

Royal was licking the salt from the ends of his fingers when he realized the dark shape he'd been seeing in the distance was a hitchhiker.

"Poor bastard. Hell of a day for a walk," he muttered, then stopped, remembering too late to temper his vocabulary.

To his relief, Maddie didn't bother to ask who the bastard was. She was busy craning her neck to look.

Royal continued to watch the hitchhiker as they drew closer. He hunched his shoulders against the downpour and ducked his head against the blast of the wind. He was almost upon him when he realized that the him was a her. A long black braid marked the middle of her back, and her clothes were plastered to her like wet tissue paper. She didn't have a spare ounce of fat on her body, and if it hadn't been for her womanly curves, he would have considered her far too thin. A fleeting notion of picking her up came and went, but then he thought of Maddie and moved into the left-hand lane to keep from splashing her as he passed.

Maddie jumped from her car seat and into the seat.

"Daddy! Daddy! Go back! Go back!"

Startled, he let off the gas. The pickup coasted as he looked in the rearview mirror. Had he hit something on the road and didn't know it? He searched for the hitchhiker through the pouring rain. To his relief, he could see her. Thank God, he thought. At least he hadn't hit her. He looked at Maddie.

"What's the matter with you?" he asked.

"That's her! You have to go back!" she screamed.

Royal stared at her, trying to fathom where the excitement had come from. She didn't get this worked up over Christmas.

"Sit down and buckle yourself up!" he ordered. "What's wrong with you, anyway? You're gonna make us have a wreck."

But Maddie was on her knees in the seat, looking through the back window.

"Hurry, Daddy, hurry. She's getting so wet."

Royal frowned. "I'm sorry, sweetheart, but it's not safe to pick up strangers. You never know when—"

"No!" she screamed, and started to cry in earnest. "She's not a stranger. That's my angel."

He hit the brakes before he thought, then cursed beneath his breath. The hitchhiker would take the red glow of brake lights as a signal. He looked in the rearview mirror again. Sure enough, she was jogging toward them.

"Now look what you've made me do," he muttered.

Maddie was almost hysterical with joy. It frightened Royal to see her elation. It was unnatural and out of control, and he didn't know how to stop it.

"Damn it, Maddie, you…"

She gave Royal a long, considering look. "Daddy, I don't think you should be cusping. My angel won't like it."

He rolled his eyes. "The word isn't cusping, it's cursing, and you're right. I shouldn't be doing it. But that doesn't change the fact that we do not know this woman. She's a stranger. Not an angel. Do you understand me?"

Maddie wasn't listening. She was busy gathering her food and making room for the woman to sit.

A chicken nugget rolled off the seat and onto the floor beneath Royal's boots. He clenched his jaw to keep from coming undone, and when the door suddenly opened, he pulled Maddie as close to him as he could, glaring at the woman in the rain as if this were all her fault.

"Where are you heading?" Royal asked, and before she could answer, a gust of wind blew a sheet of rain in the door. Maddie squealed and then laughed. Royal cursed and started waving his hand. "Get in, just get in!" he yelled. "We'll deal with destinations later."

The woman ducked her head and jumped inside, slamming the door shut behind her.

Suddenly there was nothing but quiet. Engulfed by the scent of chicken nuggets and french fries, they sat in mutual silence, each digesting a sudden change in circumstance.

Before a word could be spoken, Maddie leaned over and lightly ran her hand up and down the young woman's back.

Royal grabbed Maddie, scolding her as he moved her away.

"Maddie, where are your manners?" He glanced at the woman. "Sorry," he said.

She was soaking wet and minus any makeup, yet she was one of the most stunning women he'd ever seen. Hair as black as midnight, eyes so dark he couldn't see the pupils, and her skin was so smooth and so brown. He wondered if she was that brown all over, then jerked as if he'd been slapped.

"It's all right," Angel said. "I appreciate the ride…and the friendly gesture," she added, winking at Maddie.

Maddie beamed. "It's okay, Daddy. I was just looking for wings."

Water was running out of Angel's hair and onto her face as she threw back her head and laughed. The sound wrapped around Royal's senses like a warm quilt on a cold day. He shuddered, then glared.

"Sorry again," he said. "But it's a long story."

Maddie smiled at the woman and handed her the napkin from her lunch.

"You can dry off."

The woman smiled as she accepted the offer. "Thank you," she said. "You're a very pretty young lady. What's your name?"

"My name is Madeline Michelle Justice, but Daddy calls me Maddie."

Royal watched the woman make a futile attempt to dry off with the small piece of paper. He reached under the seat and pulled out a handful of clean paper towels he kept for emergencies.

"Try these," he said, then dropped them in her lap.

"Thank you," she said, and winked at Maddie, who was watching her every move in rapt fascination.

"What's your name?" Maddie asked.

The woman smiled. "Angel. My name is Angel."

Chapter 4

Maddie threw her arms around Royal's neck in wild excitement.

"See, Daddy? I told you! I told you!"

Royal was stunned into silence. How the hell had she known? He glanced at the woman who called herself Angel and gritted his teeth. There had to be a way out of this mess without insulting the woman or sending Maddie into a tailspin. Besides, he refused to believe that Maddie's search for an angel and this woman's name were anything more than a coincidence. A major one, he'd grant her that, but a coincidence nonetheless.

A little nervous about what was happening, Angel kept her hand on the door handle for reassurance.

"Why do I feel like I'm missing the punch line?" she asked.

Royal began unwinding Maddie from around his neck. He knew the truth, and it sounded crazy even to him. He could only imagine how anyone else would take it.

Maddie was so elated, he should have known she would

make matters worse, but he wasn't expecting her to transfer her affections so quickly. Before he could stop her, Maddie had gone from his lap to the woman called Angel in record time.

Surprised by the unexpected affection, Angel caught the little girl in her arms to keep her from falling to the floor.

"Easy, honey," Angel said gently. "I'll get you all wet."

Maddie wasn't so easily deterred. "You'll dry. That's what Daddy always says." Then she touched Angel's shoulders one last time, as if assuring herself they were truly bare.

"Damn it, Maddie, back off," Royal growled, and scooped his daughter out of the woman's lap. Maddie would have argued, but a sharp look from her father changed her mind. She slumped into her car seat and had to be satisfied with staring at her angel instead.

"I didn't mean to get her in trouble," Angel said softly, and then waved at her dripping clothes. "I'm just so wet."

A muscle jerked in Royal's jaw as he tried without success to ignore how wet she really was.

"It's not that," he said. "It's just...oh hell," he muttered beneath his breath.

"Daddy! I told you! You can't say bad words in front of angels."

Angel looked startled.

Royal grimaced. "Yes, you heard her right. She thinks you're an angel."

Maddie crawled to her knees and leaned forward. There was no mistaking the intensity of her expression.

"She is my angel, Daddy. The lady told me she was coming, and see? She was right. Now you have to believe me."

Angel felt as if she was treading water and losing ground. She ran her fingers along the cool metal of the door handle to reassure herself that she was still awake. If she had believed in its existence, she could have convinced herself that she had crawled into a twilight zone between fact and fiction rather than a pickup.

"I'm sorry," Angel said. "If there's a problem, then I'm

out of here and no hard feelings. I can't get any wetter than
I already am.''

"No!" Maddie shrieked, and threw herself into Angel's
arms. "You can't go. You can't. The lady said you would
stay. The lady said you would take care of me."

"God Almighty!" Royal muttered, and started to forcibly
remove Maddie from the woman's lap.

Their gazes met. The woman seemed to be begging him
for something. He hesitated. It was all the time Angel needed.

She set the child in her lap so they were facing each other.

"Maddie...your name is Maddie, right?"

Maddie nodded.

"So tell me, Maddie. Tell me about the lady and why you
think I'm an angel."

Maddie sighed with relief. At last. Someone who was willing to listen.

"A spider bit me." She pulled up the edge of her shorts.
"See, I have a scar."

Angel frowned. Scarring from an insect bite was rare. She
glanced at the father.

"It was a fiddleback. We almost lost her."

"No, Daddy," Maddie said. "I wasn't lost. Just sick."

Royal ran a finger along the curve of her cheek. "I know,
baby. You were very sick." He glanced at the woman. "She
had a very high fever. It was during the fever that she began
having hallucinations. She kept talking about a lady sitting on
her bed and telling her that an angel was coming." He sighed.
"I thought when we brought her home she'd forget about it,
but instead, it's gotten worse."

Angel felt the little girl's fingers curling around her thumb.
Touched by the trust, she looked at the small, grubby fist and
a smear of drying ketchup and felt a tightening in the back
of her throat. She blinked rapidly, then looked up.

"So a spider bit you. I'm glad you got well."

Maddie nodded. "The lady said I would. But she said you
would come to take care of me."

Royal was surprised. This was something Maddie hadn't

mentioned. He frowned, wondering about her sudden need to be cared for by someone other than him.

"What about your mother?" Angel asked.

"She's dead," Maddie said lightly, no more concerned than if someone had asked her the color of her hair.

Angel's heart went out to the child. She remembered what it felt like to be a motherless child.

"I'm sorry," Angel said. "My mother died, too."

That information brought a temporary silence into the confines of the truck cab. For a while, there was nothing but the sound of rain blowing against the windows and the underlying scent of cold food.

Royal wanted to dump the woman out and drive away. He wanted this to never have happened. But from the look on his daughter's face it was too late. Fate had interfered, and they were stuck with each other, at least for a time. The way he looked at it, the sooner he took the hitchhiker where she was going, the sooner his life would get back to normal.

He started the engine. "We're going about twenty miles west. You're welcome to ride that far."

Angel started to nod when Maddie came to life once more. Her lower lip was trembling, and her blue eyes were welling with tears.

"But Daddy, she has to come home with us."

Embarrassed, Royal started to argue when Angel took pity and said it for him.

"No, Maddie, you're wrong. I was on my way to—"

"No," Maddie said, as tears began to pour down her cheeks. "She said. She said you would stay with me."

"Who said?" Angel asked.

"The lady," Maddie sobbed. "The lady who sits on my bed."

"Sweet Lord," Royal said, and lifted Maddie into his arms. "Come here, baby. Don't cry. I'm sorry you're so confused, but I promise one of these days you'll understand."

"But, Daddy, I heard Uncle Roman tell you to hire another keeper. Why can't Angel be my keeper?"

A tender smile broke the somberness of Royal's face. "That's housekeeper, baby. Not keeper, although there are those who think I need one."

Angel grinned. There was something endearing about this big, tough man, although his piercing gaze made her slightly uncomfortable.

"Then you can hire Angel." Maddie turned tearful eyes toward Angel. "You can work for my daddy. He will pay you a lot of money."

Royal felt as if he was being backed into a corner. How do you explain to a child that you don't hire people off the street without insulting them? To his surprise, once again the woman relieved him of the burden.

"I'm sorry, Maddie, but that's not the way it works," Angel said. "Your father loves you very much, and he wouldn't let a stranger take care of his house...or you. Understand?"

Maddie's chin jutted. "I know that," she said loftily. "But you're not a stranger. You're my angel. I have pictures of you and everything."

Angel's eyes widened.

Royal sighed in disgust. "She's been drawing pictures."

"Oh, my," Angel said, eyeing the child with a new respect.

"We're having hamburgers for supper," Maddie said. "I like mine with ketchup and dill pickles."

Angel glanced at the drying smear of ketchup on Maddie's hand. "Ketchup is good. I like it on my french fries."

Maddie clapped her hands. "We gots fries. Daddy bought a big bag of them. You can have seconds."

"We *have* fries, Maddie," Royal said.

Maddie gave her father a disgusted look. "That's what I said. Now let's go home, Daddy. When my angel dries out, maybe then I can see her wings."

Royal groaned, and Angel was speechless. She was beginning to understand what this father had been going through.

"I don't know what to say," Angel said.

Royal knew he was going to regret it later, but he blurted the invitation before he could change his mind.

"According to the weather report, it's going to rain like this all night. I have never done anything this impulsive and foolish in my life, but I have an extra bedroom and a clothes dryer. You're welcome to both for the night."

"Yeah!" Maddie squeaked.

Angel felt as if she'd been pushed into a corner with no way out. In spite of the downpour and an overwhelming desire for hot food and dry clothes, her instincts were telling her not to get involved. Just as she was about to decline, a vehicle came flying past them, sending a spray of water onto the shoulder of the road and dousing Royal's truck.

"Crazy fool," Royal muttered, watching in disgust as the taillights quickly disappeared in the curtain of rain.

Everything Angel had been thinking came to an abrupt halt. She, too, watched as the shiny black pickup disappeared from sight. All she could think was that if she got out now, she would be at the mercy of the weather—and the driver of that pickup truck. This was past coincidence. That man was stalking her. She took a deep breath to calm her shaking nerves, and when Maddie's father looked back at her, she nodded.

"I accept your offer, but only for the night," she said, making sure that Maddie understood.

Maddie heard, but she let the warning go over her head. She wasn't concerned how it would happen. Her angel had come, like the lady had promised. Somehow, her angel would stay. She just knew it.

Royal nodded and started the engine. "Buckle up," he said. "It's time to go home."

Angel's heart tugged a little. Home. What a beautiful word. One of these days she would have a place of her own to call home, too. She glanced at the man as he pulled onto the highway and then focused her attention on the monotonous sweep of windshield wipers. A short while later, they began slowing and turned off the highway onto a blacktop road. Five minutes later, the rooftops of several buildings became visible through the rain.

Angel frowned. For some reason, this place seemed familiar, although she knew she'd never been here before. She glanced at the driver again, watching the expressions on his face as he drove on, checking fences, looking at cattle, pointing to an armadillo waddling through the runoff in a nearby ditch.

Angel flinched as if she'd been hit. There was so much power in his gaze and such a sense of pride in ownership. A vagrant thought drifted through her mind. Would he look at the woman he loved in such a manner? She let go of the thought as easily as it had come. Even if she was going to be angel for a day, she had no place in their world. She was only passing through.

She sighed. "So, Maddie's father... Since we're going to be sharing french fries tonight, I think it might be good if I knew your name."

Royal pulled the brim of his Stetson lower on his forehead, as if he was bracing himself for an unwelcome familiarity.

"My name is Royal Justice, and welcome to my home."

The steady rumble of the clothes dryer could still be heard toward the front of the house. But in the back, where the bedrooms were, it was silent. The rooms were dark, but Angel felt a measure of safety within their unfamiliarity that she hadn't known in years. She thought back to suppertime and the meal she'd shared with father and daughter, and smiled. Royal Justice was something else. At first glance, he gave the appearance of a big, tough cowboy. But she'd seen firsthand how easy his child could turn him to mush. Before the meal had started, the girl had let her cat in the house and smuggled it under the dining room table. It had been all Angel could do not to laugh. But when the cat, whose name she learned was Flea Bit, made the mistake of climbing up Royal's leg, Maddie's secret was out.

Royal let slip a mouthful of curses that even Angel hadn't heard as he calmly tossed the cat out the door. He'd given Maddie a hard, waiting stare, which she met with innocent silence. Angel lost it. Laughter bubbled up and out of her like a welling spring, surprising herself as well as Royal and Maddie. After that, the tension passed.

Angel sighed and rolled over on her back to stare at the ceiling. A faint glow of yellow from the night-light in the hall shone under the door to her room. She thought of the little girl sound asleep in her room down the hall, securely bundled within the confines of her favorite blanket. She couldn't imagine what it was like to feel that safe or that loved. Royal Justice was the king of his world, and Maddie was princess of it all.

Just for a moment, Angel let herself pretend she belonged in this place—with this man and his child—and then she snorted softly and discarded the thought. That sort of thinking was dangerous for a woman with no roots.

She focused on the sound of the rain pelting against the roof and gave a quick prayer of thanksgiving that she was sheltered, if only for the night. Soon she was sound asleep.

Hours later, she awoke to what sounded like an explosion followed by a roll of thunder so loud it rattled the panes of glass in the windows. She sat up in bed, her heart pounding wildly, and noticed that the light in the hall was out. But what panicked her more was the distinct scent of smoke in the air.

Instinctively, she reached for her clothes, too late remembering they were still in the dryer. The only thing she had on was a threadbare nightshirt that barely reached her knees. Before she could think what to do, she heard a child's terrified shriek. Her lack of clothes was forgotten as she bolted from bed and dashed into the hall.

She found herself up against Royal's broad, bare chest as he, too, came out of his room on the run. There was no time for embarrassment or apologies as they collided.

"Sorry," Royal said quickly, and grabbed her to keep from falling.

"What happened?" she gasped.

"That was lightning. Wait here."

She did as she was told, watching as he ran down the hall toward the sound of his daughter's cries. Seconds later, he emerged from Maddie's room, cradling his sobbing daughter against his chest.

Even though the house was in darkness, Angel could see enough to know that Royal was torn between fatherhood and responsibility to his property. The scent of something burning was still in the air. Obviously he needed to check on the house, but he didn't want to leave Maddie alone. Impulsively, Angel held out her hands.

"Give her to me."

Royal hesitated only briefly, then thrust Maddie into her arms.

"Here, baby, you stay with Angel while I check on some things. I'll be right back."

Maddie went without argument, clinging to Angel in trembling desperation and burying her face against Angel's neck.

"I'm scared," she sobbed.

"Me, too, sweetheart," Angel said, holding the small child tight. "But your daddy is big and strong, and he'll take care of you, just like he always does, right?" She felt the child nodding. "That's good, now let's see if we can find a flashlight or a candle. Do you know where the candles are?"

Another shaft of lightning shattered the darkness of the night. Angel flinched, but Maddie seemed calmer now that she had something on which to focus.

"There's a flashlight and some candles in the kitchen drawer under the phone."

"You show me," Angel said, and still holding the little girl in her arms, she made her way through the house to the kitchen.

"There," Maddie said, pointing to a cabinet drawer in the right-hand corner of the room.

Within a couple of minutes, the room was bathed in candlelight and the psychedelic pattern of a waving flashlight as Maddie aimed it about the room. The kitchen chair was cold against Angel's legs as she cuddled Maddie in her lap. Another roll of thunder rippled overhead, and she flinched, thinking of the man who'd run out in the storm. She pulled the child closer to her breasts.

"Are you cold, honey?"

Secure beneath her blanket, Maddie shook her head and snuggled closer.

The small child's trust was daunting. As she held her, the fragility of her body and the life that was just unfolding made her remember things she'd spent years trying to forget. She closed her eyes and rested her chin on the top of Maddie's head, thinking back to the time when she'd been four years old. If only she'd had a father like Royal, her life would have been different.

Her jaw clenched as she shook off the thought. Retrospection was not part of her makeup. She was practical, independent and more than a little antagonistic when it came to strange men. And she had not given motherhood much thought. Yet here she was, in a strange man's house, sheltering his child and wondering if the house was in danger of burning down around them. At that moment she knew that, given a chance, she would be good at the job.

She shivered as another gust of wind splattered rain against the windows. Even if lightning had hit the house, surely it would not burn in this weather.

The back door flew open and Royal ran inside, then slammed the door shut behind him.

Startled, Angel instinctively wrapped Maddie in a protective hold, and that was the way Royal saw his daughter— bathed in candlelight, swaddled in her blanket and a strange woman's arms. Breath caught in the back of his throat as he froze, stunned by the tranquility of the scene. He focused on the soft yellow halo of light behind them, and the thought crossed his mind that right now, Angel could very easily pass as a heavenly being. Then she spoke, and the moment was gone.

"Is everything okay? The house, is it...?"

Royal shook his head. "Everything's okay out there. I'm going into the attic to check on the wiring just to make sure."

Maddie frowned. "Make sure of what, Daddy?"

Royal hesitated. Lying to his daughter was not something he did, but at her age, she was still on a need-to-know basis.

"Oh, just to make sure that the storm didn't break any windows. We wouldn't want our Christmas decorations getting rained on, would we?"

A deep frown settled between her eyes. Christmas was her favorite holiday.

"Is it okay if we go back to bed?" Angel asked. "I think she's getting cold."

Royal nodded. "I'll put her to bed just as soon as I get back."

"I'll do it," Angel offered, and then felt as if she'd stepped over a line. "If you don't mind, that is."

The beam of the flashlight Maddie was holding suddenly stilled. Her voice shook.

"I don't want to go to bed in my room."

Royal cupped her cheek, tilting her face to his as he leaned down.

"You can sleep with me just as soon as I get back, okay, baby?"

She nodded and relaxed.

Royal's gaze slipped from his daughter's face to Angel. Her eyes were wide with unasked questions, but to his surprise, she didn't voice one. Her composure surprised him. She was the first woman he'd ever known who hadn't let loose with a barrage of questions in a situation like this.

"I won't be long," he said quietly.

Angel felt herself drowning in blue and then blinked. The notion passed, and Royal left. She shook off the feeling of lassitude and stood, still holding Maddie in her arms.

"Come on, sweetie, it's time to get some sleep."

Maddie sighed, but for once didn't argue. She bunched her blanket beneath her chin and laid her head on Angel's shoulder. By the time Angel laid her in Royal's bed, her eyes were closed, but she still clutched Angel's hand.

"Don't go till my daddy gets back," Maddie begged.

Angel hesitated. It made her more than a little uncomfortable to be in the man's room, let alone sitting on the edge of his bed. Even if he wasn't in it, his presence was impossible to ignore. The covers were thrown back, indicative of his hasty exit, and the pillow still held the indentation from his head. But the little girl's plea was impossible to ignore.

"Okay," she said softly. "Now close your eyes."

Maddie did as she was told, but moments later another bolt of lightning hit the ground somewhere between the house and the barns. Maddie shrieked and began to cry.

Angel slid into bed and wrapped her arms around her, shushing her as she cuddled her close.

"You're safe, little girl. You're as safe as you can be. Feel my arms around you, holding you tight?"

Maddie shuddered on a sob, but nodded.

"I promise I won't let you go until your daddy comes back, okay?"

"Okay," Maddie whispered, and scooted as close as she could get.

Angel smiled and pulled the little girl into the curve of her body. Above their heads she could hear the soft thump, thump of footsteps as Royal moved about the attic. Secure that someone else was taking care of business, Angel closed her eyes. Just to let them rest. Just until he got back.

And that was how Royal found them—wrapped in each other's arms and sound asleep in the middle of his bed. He didn't move and he couldn't speak. All he could do was stare at the image before him.

The woman's long black hair spilled across his pillow. His child lay within the shelter of her arms. Emotion hit him without warning, like a kick to the gut. He reached for the door facing, using it as a brace to steady his knees.

This was what it would have been like had his wife, Susan, not died. Tears burned the back of his throat. Was it the absence of a woman in her life that had caused Maddie's dreams? Could the yearning have been so strong that it had caused her to imagine the lady on her bed? And even if that was so, how did that explain the promise of an angel or of her arrival into their midst?

Royal drew a deep breath and stepped inside, staying only long enough to pull the covers over both of them. He couldn't look at the woman without wanting to stare, and he wouldn't let himself linger over Maddie for fear that he'd wake them both up. He paused in the doorway, looking back one last time before he closed the door.

The storm passed. Clouds were moving across the full face of the moon, dragging dark shadows along the moonlit ground as they blew. The sleepers were bathed in the luminescence of a heavenly glow, and for a moment, Royal could almost believe Maddie's claim of an angel come to earth. But then he shook off the notion and walked out of the room.

Angel woke up before dawn. The presence of a warm body beside her was startling, but only for a moment. She looked into the sleeping face of Royal Justice's daughter and remembered. She'd spent the entire night in Royal's bed.

This was just great. The thought of that man watching her sleep was unnerving. There was something about his unblinking stare that made her want to turn tail and run. It wasn't as if she was afraid of him. Angel wasn't afraid of anyone. She amended the thought. Except that man in the black truck.

Maddie sighed in her sleep. Resisting the urge to kiss her soft cheek, Angel pulled the covers over her bare legs and slipped out of bed, careful not to wake Maddie up.

For a moment, she stared around the room, searching for clues to the personality of the man who slept here. Nothing seemed obvious. It was large enough to accommodate the king-size bed. Except for an oversize picture of Maddie over the headboard, the walls were white and bare. But for a small wagon full of wooden blocks and a pink feather boa wrapped around the wheels, it was neat and orderly, just like the man who slept here.

She shuddered, as if coming out of a trance, and headed

for the door. She needed to get her clothes and get herself packed. If she was lucky, she might make Dallas before noon.

She moved through the rooms on bare feet, pulling at the hem of her nightshirt and hurrying as she neared the kitchen. Never had she felt as vulnerable as she did right now. Only a few more steps and she would retrieve her clothes. Dressed, she could face anything—even the man in whose bed she'd slept.

Royal was making peanut butter and jelly sandwiches when Angel entered the kitchen. She groaned. It had been too much to hope she would be the only one up. It had been bad enough last night to face the man in this threadbare nightshirt, but in the early morning light, she might as well have been naked.

Chapter 5

Royal was making peanut butter and jelly sandwiches when Angel entered the kitchen. She groaned. It had been too much to hope she would be the only one up. It had been bad enough last night to face the man in this threadbare nightshirt, but in the early morning light, she might as well have been naked.

"I'm just going to the dryer to get my clothes," she muttered, and darted toward the utility room.

"The electricity went off before they got dry," he said.

His announcement stopped her cold. She rolled her eyes, then folded her arms across her breasts as she turned to face him.

"Then I'll have to wear them wet. I can't leave looking like this. Besides, they'll probably be wet again before the day is over."

Royal frowned. For some reason, the thought of her out on a highway at the mercy of strangers made him angry. And then he reminded himself they were strangers to each other. She was a grown woman. She didn't need anyone to take care of her. He dropped a spoonful of grape jelly on a layer of peanut butter and smeared it around the slice of bread.

Angel watched in fascination, admiring the way the filling clung to the bread and wondering where he'd spent the night.

"Um, last night, the lightning…was anything damaged?"

"No, we were fortunate, but the phones are still out and so's the power," he answered.

She nodded and tried to think of something else to say.

"Mr. Justice…"

"Royal," he corrected.

Slightly embarrassed, she felt the need to apologize. "I didn't mean to fall asleep last night. Why didn't you wake me?"

He kept spreading jam. "It was late. You and Maddie were sound asleep. I didn't see the need."

"But I was in your bed."

He stopped and looked up. "And I was in yours."

The intimacy of that statement hit them at the same time, and neither moved or spoke. Royal was the first to break eye contact, and he did it by slapping a slice of bread on top of his gourmet creation and sliding it onto a plate.

"Since the power's out, this is going to have to serve as breakfast." He grinned. "Maddie won't care. Except for her uncle Roman's pancakes, this is her favorite breakfast, anyway."

It was his smile that did it. It changed everything about him in a way Angel hadn't expected. Just for a second she saw the boy he'd been and probably the man he could be with someone he loved, and she knew a swift moment of fear.

"I hate to ask, but I need something to wear," she said.

"I laid some things out in your room," he said shortly. "Wear whatever suits you until your own things are dry."

"But I thought you said the power was out," Angel said.

"It is."

"Then what…"

Royal interrupted. His voice was low and angry. "It's some of my stuff, damn it. Just get dressed." He stabbed the knife into the jar of peanut butter and reached for another slice of bread. "I think better when there's more between us than a few cotton threads."

Stunned, Angel alternated between punching him in the nose and laughing in his face. But then he looked up. Their gazes met and held. She was the one who broke. She bolted from the room as Royal dropped the knife into the jar of peanut butter and stomped out the back door onto the porch. There was a smear of peanut butter on the end of his thumb. He sucked it off as he stepped off the porch, intent on checking on the animals, when he heard a car coming down the driveway. It was Roman, probably coming to satisfy himself they had not blown away in last night's storm.

"Great," he muttered, thinking of what Roman would make of the half-naked stranger in his house.

"Hey," Roman called, as he got out of the car. "I tried to call. Your phones are out."

Royal nodded. "I know. So is the power."

Roman's gaze raked the familiar lines of their old family home. "Everything okay in there?"

Royal snorted. "About as good as could be expected," he muttered.

"What did you say?" Roman asked.

"Nothing," Royal said, and jammed his hands in his pockets.

Roman's eyes narrowed thoughtfully. Of all the Justice brothers, Royal was the most open with his thoughts. There was something going on Roman didn't understand. Royal was the kind of man who cursed when he was angry and laughed when he was glad. He wasn't given to hints, yet Roman would swear his brother was hiding something.

"Maddie all right?" he asked.

"Maddie's fine," Royal answered.

"No more visions of ladies and angels?"

Royal resisted the urge to roll his eyes. "Not anymore," he growled.

"Uncle Roman!"

Both men turned at the childish screech of delight. Roman grinned and held out his arms as Maddie bounded toward him. He caught her in midjump and swung her against his chest, nuzzling her neck and stealing kisses along the side of her cheek. Her giggles of delight brought smiles to both men's faces, but the smiles slid sideways when the back door opened again.

Royal groaned and gritted his teeth as Angel came out on the porch. She was wearing one of his T-shirts and a pair of his sweatpants. Everything was too long and too big. She should have looked like an orphan. Instead, those dark, bedroom eyes were wide and questioning, and her long, black hair was mussed and hanging to the middle of her back. She had the look of a woman who'd spent the night in a willing man's bed. Royal cast a quick glance at Roman and then looked away. Technically, that was exactly what had happened. The only problem was, the willing man had been sleeping elsewhere.

Roman glanced at Maddie, unconsciously tightening his hold in a protective gesture as he looked over her head at his brother.

"I don't believe I've had the pleasure," he drawled.

Royal's jaw clenched. Roman's sarcasm was too thick to stir.

"That's my angel!" Maddie shrieked, and wiggled to be put down.

Roman let her go, not because he wanted to but because she'd given him no option. To his shock, she ran and anchored herself to the woman's leg.

"She's going to be our keeper," Maddie said, smiling at Angel.

Angel cast a nervous look at Maddie's father and shrugged as she bent to pick Maddie up. This was his daughter, his problem. If he wanted to explain, it was his prerogative.

Royal frowned. He should have known Maddie wouldn't be happy to settle for one night.

"Roman, this is Angel Rojas. Angel, my brother, Roman."

Roman tipped his hat without smiling. "Miss Rojas."

She met his cool stare with one of her own. "Mr. Justice."

Maddie's next innocent remark only added to the furor. "We found her in the rain!" she said. "She came, just like the lady said she would."

Roman's eyes widened in disbelief as he turned to Royal. "You *found* her in the rain?"

Angel was tired and uncomfortable, and thanks to Fat Louie and that nut who'd been following her, she was pretty much fed up with men in general. The fact that Royal's brother kept looking at her as if she was a bug in need of squashing was the last straw.

"I wasn't lost," Angel snapped. "I was hitchhiking. They offered me a ride. The rest of this stuff about angels is over my head."

Her unexpected anger silenced whatever Roman had planned to say.

"But your name…"

"Is really Angel. Angel Maria Conchita Rojas, to be precise. I was born in Las Vegas. My mother died when I was small. I was raised in foster homes. I owe no man and no man owns me. And, as soon as my clothes are dry, I'm out of here."

Roman had the grace to blush. "Look, Miss, I didn't mean to—"

"Yes, you did," Angel snapped, then she looked at Royal. "I came out to tell you that the power is on. As soon as my clothes are dry, I will be out of your hair."

"No!" Maddie shrieked, and wrapped her arms around Angel's neck. "You can't leave! You can't leave! The lady promised you would stay and take care of me." She started to sob.

The words tugged at Angel's heart. In her anger, she'd forgotten to temper her words for the little girl's sake.

"But sweetheart, I told you yesterday that your daddy can't just hire a stranger to take care of you. He loves you more than anything in this world, and he would want only the best for you.''

''You're not a stranger to me,'' Maddie sobbed. ''I saw you in my dreams. I have pictures of you. Wait here. I'll show you.''

She wiggled out of Angel's arms and dashed into the house.

Angel glared at Roman without speaking while Royal shoved his hand through his hair in an angry gesture of defeat.

''This is one hell of a mess,'' he growled.

''It's none of my business,'' Angel said, ''but I'd watch my language if I were you. Especially around Maddie.''

Royal's face turned an angry red as Roman grinned. To his surprise, Roman found himself liking this woman for no other reason than her spunk.

Before anything else could be said, Maddie came running. The screen door hit the wall with a bang as she shoved a handful of pictures into Angel's hands.

''See! See? I knew you! I knew you!''

Angel glanced at the pictures, a little surprised to see that Maddie's childish drawings depicted what could only be described as a dark angel. Most people, and especially children, thought of angels having blond hair and long white robes. This angel had brown skin and long black hair. Angel frowned as she looked at them. One picture had the angel wearing braids. That was the way she most often wore her hair. She glanced at Royal, surprised by the understanding on his face.

''Well,'' she said softly.

He nodded.

''This is my favorite,'' Maddie said, pulling one out of the stack Angel was holding.

Angel smiled as she looked, then she gasped. The smile froze on her face. Her hands started to shake. Without thinking, she dropped to her knees and pulled Maddie close.

''Oh, my, little girl. Oh, my.''

Maddie looked at her father. ''See, Daddy. She likes my drawings a lot.''

Angel stared at the child, unable to tear her gaze away. It

wasn't that she didn't believe such things were possible, but she'd never expected to be part of such a miracle. And a miracle it was. She hugged Maddie gently, then got to her feet, handing the drawing to Royal without explanation.

"Wait here," she said, then took Maddie by the hand and went into the house.

Roman moved closer to look at the drawing Royal was holding. On one side of the page was the figure Maddie called the lady. She was the same in every picture. A woman wearing a long blue dress. On the other side was the figure Maddie called her angel. She was barefoot. Her long black hair was loose around her face, not in braids as in most of the other pictures, and she was wearing a bright pink dress with blue and green decorations around the bottom.

"What?" Roman asked.

"Don't ask me," Royal muttered. "I haven't been in control since yesterday when we were coming back from town. It was raining like hell. I saw a hitchhiker. Didn't even know it was a woman. Before I could pass her, Maddie was screaming for me to stop. I kept on driving. Maddie got hysterical, begging for me to go back. She said it was her angel, the one the lady said would come."

Roman inhaled slowly as the skin crawled on the back of his neck.

"Damn."

Royal grimaced. "You have no idea. Before I knew it, she was in the cab and Maddie was crawling all over her."

Roman's eyes widened. "Maddie doesn't like strangers."

"You forget," Royal drawled. "Maddie claims she's not a stranger. And then there's her name. Hell, when she told me it was Angel, I got a knot in my stomach that still hasn't gone away. While I was trying to think what to say, Maddie went berserk. The next thing I knew, I was inviting her to spend the night. At least until the rain had stopped."

Roman shook his head. "Man, Royal, what are you going to—"

The back door opened, and he never finished his question as Maddie and Angel came out hand in hand.

"Look, Daddy. Now do you believe me?"

Royal stared. First at the woman standing before him, then at the picture, then up again.

"It's still a little damp and needs a good ironing, but you get the picture," Angel said softly, as she smoothed the dress she had taken out of the dryer and slipped on.

Royal was stunned. "Oh, Lord," he whispered.

"Oh, Lord is right," Angel said. "I'm beginning to think He had something to do with this after all." She squeezed Maddie's hand as she continued. "I bought this dress with the first money I ever earned." Before either man could respond, she added, "It was honest work."

Roman couldn't think what to say. There was no disputing the fact that the pink dress she was wearing was old and fading, but the wide band of blue and green embroidery around the hem of the skirt was impossible to mistake. With her hair around her face and her feet brown and bare, she was the angel in Maddie's drawing come to life.

Royal looked at the drawing and then at Angel, shaking his head in disbelief.

"How?" he muttered.

She shrugged. "Ask your daughter. She seems tuned in to what's happening."

Maddie beamed. She didn't really understand everything that was being said, but she sensed her father's capitulation.

"Angel is going to be our new keeper, isn't she, Daddy?"

Royal didn't know how to answer. Common sense told him this might be the most foolish thing he'd ever done, but instinct was leading him in another direction. He didn't understand a damn thing that was going on, but in his gut, it felt right. He took a deep breath and then stared Angel Rojas straight in the face.

"Are you interested in the job?" he asked.

Angel's chin lifted defiantly. "Are you offering?"

Royal almost grinned. Damned if he didn't like her spunk.

Roman couldn't remain silent. Ever the private investigator, he interjected, "What about references?"

Angel's stare hardened as her gaze moved to Royal's brother. It was all she could do to keep her voice civil.

"Well, shoot," she drawled. "I must have left my résumé in my other pocket. However, I can give you names and places of where I've worked. You can call any or all of them about me."

Royal interrupted Roman before he could answer. "This is my daughter, my house, my business," he said shortly. "If there's any calling to be done, I'll be the one doing it."

Roman recognized the anger and authority in his brother's voice and took a mental step back.

"Well, now," he said softly, looking at Maddie. "I think it's time I went back to work. Come here, Little Bit, and give me a goodbye kiss."

Maddie giggled as Roman lifted her and swung her around before kissing her soundly on the cheek. Then he nodded to his brother and started toward his car. Just before he got inside, he paused and turned, as if he'd forgotten something.

To Angel's surprise, he was almost grinning as he tipped his hat to her.

"What was that all about?" she asked Royal as Roman drove away.

Royal gave her a long, considering look. "That was my brother's way of butting out of my business."

She nodded and then gave Royal a cool stare. "So, do you want those names and phone numbers or not?"

"Yes, I suppose I do."

His answer was just shy of rude, and Angel could have taken affront, but she chose to consider the source. Royal Justice seemed to be a man who made his own rules, and that she understood.

"I need a pen and some paper," she said.

"I'll get them!" Maddie cried, and bolted into the house, leaving Angel and Royal alone on the porch.

"Do you know what you're doing?" Angel asked.

A muscle jerked at the side of Royal's jaw. "Hell, no."

"Then why do it?" Angel asked.

Royal almost grinned. "I learned a long time ago that when it comes to dealing with women, I don't have to understand. I just follow my instincts."

His answer surprised her, and because she sensed it was an honest one, it compelled her to answer in kind.

"Look, Mr. Justice..."

"Royal," he corrected.

She took a deep breath. "Royal."

He nodded.

"As I was going to say...I am overwhelmed by your daughter's insight, and I promise I will not deceive you or let Maddie down. If the time comes when I think I should go, I'll tell you."

For a moment, Royal was silent. Finally, he nodded.

"Fair enough," he said. Then his features hardened. "But I warn you, mess with what's mine and you'll be worse than sorry."

A shiver slid down the middle of Angel's back. "Fair enough," she echoed.

Royal shifted, then headed for the house. "So, let's go see where Maddie has gone. If she found the peanut butter and jelly sandwiches, she's already forgotten what she went inside to do."

The city limits of Abilene were dead ahead when Tommy Boy Watson began to slow down. He'd been driving almost nonstop since passing through Dallas and points west. He'd seen the inside of more truck stop cafés than he cared to think about, and still no sign of that dark-haired whore. He had the beginnings of a headache, and his butt was numb from sitting so long in one place. His left leg, which he'd broken some years back, was aching in the place where it had healed. He hated to admit it, but he was going to give up the search. He kept telling himself it would be all right. That there were plenty of others like her out here on the highways for him to take out. Thanks to his efforts, the population of highway hookers was already down. Eight less, to be exact. He wiped his nose with the back of his sleeve and grinned.

And he was just getting started.

Ahead, the familiar sight of a Texas highway patrol car was visible. Tommy Boy admired cops. He often dreamed of being one. To Tommy Boy, there was power in packing a gun. He liked the look of bulletproof vests beneath their starched uniforms, thinking it gave them the appearance of wearing armor, like the knights of old.

He tipped his hat as he passed the parked patrol car. To his delight, the trooper nodded. Although the connection they'd made was impersonal, he was still grinning when he pulled into the parking lot of a small motel. In his mind, their occupations were similar. The police protected the public from criminals. Tommy Boy protected innocent men from the wiles of evil women.

All he needed was some food in his belly and a good night's rest. That would put that damned black-haired witch out of his mind once and for all. Besides, there were plenty of whores still left who needed cleansing.

Having decided on a plan of action, Tommy Boy paid for his room and strolled across the parking lot to a nearby café. To his delight, when he got inside, he saw two troopers sitting in a booth, eating their meal. Their clean-cut appearances and steely-eyed gazes gave him a sense of well-being. He shifted his stride to a swagger and nodded and smiled as he passed them by, then took a seat where he could watch them eat. Although he admired them, he also felt a sense of superiority. To his knowledge, only four of the eight women he'd killed had been found, and there wasn't a single clue pointing to him. There sat those cops, dressed to shine and legally packing, and they still had no idea they were within spitting distance of the man responsible. He grinned.

"What'll it be, mister?"

Tommy Boy looked up as the waitress slid a glass of water in front of him.

"What's good?" he asked.

"Me, if you're lucky," she drawled, and then giggled.

His hackles rose. Another pushy woman. Weren't there any decent women left in this world?

"I'll have a burger and fries and coffee. Plenty of coffee," he said shortly.

The waitress shrugged and walked away.

"Bitch," he muttered. Moments later she was back. She poured his coffee without comment and slipped away as quietly as she'd come.

His food came, and he ate it without relish, merely fueling his body. He gave the waitress another glance as he paid for his food, but she didn't bother to meet his gaze. He shrugged. It was just as well. He wasn't in the mood for cleansing. Not tonight. He craved sleep, not justice.

As he strolled across the parking lot to his room, he prayed that the night would be his and his alone. He didn't need any visions from Daddy. Daddy had to understand. He was doing his best. He was keeping his promise. It was all he could do.

Chapter 6

Royal stared at the list Angel Rojas had given him, taking careful note of each job she'd held. The dates went back as far as eight years, and he had yet to find a person who had anything but good to say about her. And yet each time he'd asked why she left their employ, none of them could give a clear answer.

It would seem that there was a bit of Gypsy in Maddie's angel, and he didn't like that. He didn't want to set Maddie up to get hurt. How would Maddie react if, one day, the angel up and flew the proverbial coop?

He looked at the list again. There was a discrepancy in the time frame. The two-year gap between her last job, at a sheriff's office in West Virginia, and her presence at his ranch bothered him.

The sound of laughter caught his attention, and he glanced out the office window. Maddie was in the porch swing, lying on her stomach and trailing a piece of rope between the slats, while Flea Bit did body flips trying to catch the frayed end.

Royal grinned, admitting only to himself that the damned cat did have its moments.

Then he remembered the list. Before he gave Angel the go-ahead to hang up her clothes in his house, he needed some answers. Two years was a long time to have been out of work. There were too many things that could have occupied her time. She could have been married…or living with a man. He frowned again, letting his mind wander into all the possibilities as to why a relationship fails. But he was guessing. It didn't have to be a man. For all he knew, she could have been in jail.

Angel's clothes were clean and dry and spread out on the bed. She didn't know whether to put them in her bag or hang them in the closet. Everything hinged upon the final nod from Royal Justice. She'd given him the list of her past employers over two hours ago. He'd taken it without comment and disappeared into his office. Now she waited.

It surprised her to realize how much she would really like to stay, but she'd learned years ago to do without things she couldn't have. Part of her had to admit that in spite of Maddie Justice's dreams, maybe this wasn't meant to be. Maybe Royal Justice would think she wasn't capable of caring for his daughter. She didn't have any experience in child care, but Angel didn't see that as a problem. Maddie was not a baby, she was a little girl—and Angel was a big girl. Somewhere within that concept there had to be common ground.

She stood with her arms crossed and her face blank, waiting for a man she didn't know to pass judgment on her past.

She stared out the window at the vast array of grassland that was the Justice ranch. Horses dotted the landscape, as did a herd of cattle on a distant hillside. The outbuildings were painted. The corral was in top repair. From where she was standing, there wasn't a single thing Royal Justice had left undone. He was a man in control of his world.

Then she thought of his child. Whatever had driven Maddie Justice to this moment was beyond his control. And Angel knew that scared him. She'd seen it in his eyes. The uncertainty, the lack of understanding for a child who had visions. In a way, she sympathized. For a man so obviously used to being boss, he was struggling to find his center with a daughter who conjured up angels in dreams. But she had to give him credit. Not many men would have stopped on a highway in a thunderstorm to pick up a stranger, especially on the word of a child.

Impulsively, she turned her back to the window and gazed around the room. It was without frills, but a place in which she could easily become comfortable. And then she sighed. She was past expecting miracles in her life, and even though she was at a loss to explain how Maddie had drawn a picture of her before they'd met, there was a feeling within her that said here was where she belonged. At least for the time being.

Yes, she believed she could come to love the child. As for the work—caring for the house would be simple, easier in fact than a lot of jobs she'd had. But caring for the man? She wasn't sure it was something she could do, or for that matter should do. He was obviously well-to-do, single and far too handsome for his own good. Not, she reminded herself, that she was an easy mark. It had been years since she'd been stupid enough to fall for a good-looking man's lies, and it would be a cold day in hell before it happened again. But that didn't change the fact that she was human—and lonely. As lonely as a woman could be.

Then a knock sounded at the door, and her thoughts scattered. She dropped her arms to her sides and lifted her chin, as if bracing herself for a blow.

"Come in."

Royal opened the door.

"Got a minute?" he asked. "There's something I want to ask you about your list of references."

"Ask away," she said. "I told you before, I have nothing to hide."

Royal leaned against the doorjamb, trying to find a tactful way to ask what amounted to a personal question. He reminded himself his daughter's welfare was at stake, took a deep breath and let go.

"So far, everything checks out," he said.

Angel exhaled slowly, unaware until he said it that she'd been holding her breath. But he stood staring at her with that cold, blue gaze.

"Why do I feel like you left out a but?"

Royal thrust the list in her hands. "You tell me."

She looked at it, frowning. "Tell you what?"

"Have you ever been married?"

Her eyebrows arched in surprise, but she answered without hesitation.

"No."

He glanced at the list, then at her. "The last name on this list is for a county sheriff in West Virginia."

She didn't see where he was going. "That's true. So?"

"So that was two years ago. What have you been doing since?"

Understanding dawned. Her attitude shifted from accommodating to defiant within seconds.

"Working at a place called Fat Louie's in Tuscaloosa, Alabama."

Royal frowned. "Then why didn't you put the owner's name and number on the list?"

"Because the only recommendation that bastard would give me is to go straight to hell."

Royal arched his eyebrows and remained silent, waiting for her to continue.

"Don't you want to know why?" Angel asked.

"Do I need to?" he asked.

Angel laughed, but it was a harsh, ugly sound that made the hair on the back of Royal's arms stand up.

"Who knows what men need?" she said, then she sighed and shoved her hands through her hair, combing the thick, dark lengths from her face. "Sorry," she muttered. "He's a bastard."

"What happened?"

Angel gave Royal a long, considering look. "Why don't you call him and ask? I'd be curious to know how he explains the fact that I left him rolling on the floor with his hands between his legs."

Shock swept through Royal, followed by a rage he hadn't expected. He kept staring at her, imagining her fending off the unwanted advances of some unknown man, and the thought made him sick.

"Why?" he asked.

Angel closed her eyes, picturing the endless months of fending off her boss's unwelcome advances. When she looked at Royal, there was a truth on her face that he couldn't ignore.

"Because I got sick and tired of getting caught in corners. Every time I turned around he was grabbing at me, running his big fat hands all over my body and making innuendos about what it would take for me to keep my job."

Royal's anger shifted to a darker, deeper place. "Did he—?"

Angel's face was devoid of expression. "I believe they call it sexual harassment. I called it quits. He crossed a line. I put him on the floor."

"But why didn't you press charges?" Royal asked.

She snorted beneath her breath. "And who would believe me? Despite reports to the opposite, don't you know that it's always the woman's fault for leading the poor man on? Besides, people look at me and think wetback. It doesn't matter that I was born in Nevada. My skin is not lily-white. My eyes are dark, my hair is black. I have no family—no permanent home. I might as well have *illegal* tattooed on my forehead. People like me rarely find justice in a white man's world."

Royal's face was flushed with anger. "Wait here," he said shortly. "I won't be long."

Before Angel could speak, he was gone. She dropped to the corner of the bed and closed her eyes. Wait here? Where else could she go?

A few minutes later Royal blindly punched in the numbers the long-distance operator had given him, trying to picture what a man named Fat Louie would look like. When the phone began to ring, he took a deep breath and tightened his grip on the receiver. A few seconds later, a man's voice rumbled in his ear. It sounded thick and harsh from lack of sleep or too much of something from the night before.

"Fat Louie's," the man said.

"I need to speak to the owner," Royal countered.

"That's me," Louie muttered. "Who's asking?"

Royal stilled. Had the men been face to face, Fat Louie Tureau would have known to back off. But they weren't, and the anonymity of a stranger's voice wasn't enough warning for Louie to hold his tongue.

"Royal Justice. I'm calling about a woman named Angel Rojas. I understand she used to work for you."

A string of profanity, coupled with a harsh cigarette hack, reverberated in Royal's ear. About the only distinguishable words he heard were "the bitch" and "her kind."

Although Royal narrowed his eyes, his voice remained calm.

"Exactly what do you mean by…her kind?" he asked.

Fat Louie spit. Royal heard the sound and almost hung up right then. Even if Angel had been lying through her teeth, this man was offensive enough to terminate the conversation. Still, Royal had Maddie to consider. He waited.

"Damn wetback," Louie growled. "Do 'em a favor and they just up and quit on you."

"I wasn't under the impression that she's an illegal."

"Well, maybe not," Louie muttered. "But it don't hardly matter. She's still a Mex, and she quit without notice."

Royal had known plenty of bigots in his life, and without ever having laid eyes on this man, Fat Louie from Tuscaloosa, Alabama, was about to win the prize.

"Did she give a reason she terminated her employment?" Royal asked.

There was a pause.

It was enough for Royal. And when Fat Louie suddenly

came back with a question instead of an answer, Royal knew she'd been telling the truth.

"What did *she* say?" Louie asked.

The corner of Royal's mouth turned upward just a little. "That she left you rolling on the floor and holding your crotch. Is that true?"

Another string of curses erupted. It was all Royal needed to hear. Without waiting for Fat Louie Tureau to answer, he hung up the phone and stalked out of the office. He went to her room and stood in the doorway. He glanced at her clothes laid out on the bed and then at the expression on her face.

"Do you have enough hangers?" he asked.

Her shoulders slumped, but only slightly, as if giving herself permission to relax. She glanced at the bed and then at the open closet door.

"Yes, I believe that I do."

He nodded. "Good. As soon as you get your things hung up, why don't you meet me outside? I'll walk you over the place. You need to know where things are located, especially Maddie's favorite hiding places. And we can talk money and days off then."

The urge to giggle was strong, but Angel nodded, waiting until Royal had walked away before allowing herself a small smile.

Royal wasn't as easy in his mind about what he'd just done as Angel had been in accepting it. All he could think as he walked outside to where his daughter was playing was that he hoped to God he wouldn't live to regret this.

Tommy Boy Watson pulled off the blacktop onto the graveled shoulder and got out. He stretched lazily then tilted his head to gaze at the stars. They were thick and bright: tiny pinpoints of white, blinking lights on a blanket of black velvet. The air was warm and humid. His blue and white striped shirt clung to his body like wet tissue paper to the side of a glass. But he didn't care about comfort. He didn't care about anything except that he was all right with the world.

A few miles north, the horizon was aglow from the lights of Abilene. He'd never been to Abilene before, but he was headed there. His belly growled, and he remembered he hadn't eaten a bite since early this morning. He rubbed a hand over his face, wincing at the two-day growth of whiskers. Tonight he'd get himself a room, then a steak. A great big steak. Sleeping in his truck was okay now and then, but tonight he was celebrating. Tonight he would shower and shave and sleep in a real bed. Tommy Boy liked a clean shave.

Somewhere to his right he heard a calf bawl, and he jumped. Then a few moments later a cow answered. He relaxed. No big deal, just a calf that had lost its mother. He shook a cigarette out of the pack in his pocket and lit one up, savoring the night, the silence and his smoke. When he was finished, he dropped the stub into the dirt, then ground it out with the toe of his boot until it was indistinguishable. He turned toward his pickup truck. It was time to get to business.

He let down the tailgate and pulled the tarp-wrapped body onto the ground as if it was so much trash. With a few quick tugs on the tarp, the lifeless body of Carol Jo Belmont, late of the Big Wheel Truck Stop, rolled into the ditch.

Anxious to be on his way, he folded the tarp and laid it in his truck, weighting it down with his spare tire to keep it from blowing away. He would need it again, of that he was certain. A few minutes later, he pulled onto the blacktop and drove away without looking back. By the time he'd reached the city limits, he was exhausted. But it was a good exhaustion. The kind that comes from knowing you've done a good day's work. He smiled. His daddy would have been proud.

By the time a week had passed, the trio at the ranch had settled into their routine. After a couple of days of hovering around the ranch house making certain Angel could cope with his daughter's antics, Royal began to relax. It would seem that Maddie's angel wasn't afraid of work. The house had never been cleaner. And coming in to hot meals, meals he didn't have to cook, and having clean clothes in his closet that he didn't have to wash were blessings he hadn't expected. But there was still the discomfort of living with a stranger.

On the other hand, Maddie had never been happier. And Royal was seeing a change in her he wouldn't have believed. His little tomboy was turning toward things of a feminine nature.

Royal glanced at his watch and cursed beneath his breath. In less than fifteen minutes, he was supposed to have Maddie at Paige Sullivan's birthday party, and he still had to change his clothes. Frowning, he screwed the lid on the bottle of leather cleaner and hung up the bridle he'd been working on. Life with Maddie had been a lot simpler when she was a baby. A female's maturation was difficult enough for a man to handle without all the added social events that seemed to come out of nowhere. Granted, she and Paige had been playmates and friends almost from the day they could toddle, but back then it hadn't been such a big deal. They played together when Royal and Tom, Paige's dad, had business to deal with, and that was that. But in the last year, Maddie had learned how to dial a phone, and to his disgust, so had Paige. At the age of four, Maddie had already been given a five-minute phone curfew. He was beginning to wonder what it would be like when she started school. More friends. More calls. And for a man who understood horses better than he did his own daughter, more worries. He didn't even want to think what his life would be like by the time Maddie was old enough to date. Then he reminded himself to concentrate on the present, and right now he was late for a date with his very best girl.

He entered the utility room, glanced into the kitchen and saw Maddie and Angel sitting at the kitchen table. Without paying attention to what they were doing, he bent to pull off his dirty boots.

"Hey, peanut, sorry I'm late. Just let me change my shirt and shoes, and we'll be ready to go to Paige's birthday party."

Oblivious to her father's presence, Maddie's gaze was fixed

on the still-wet, rose-colored polish gleaming on her nails. She mumbled okay.

Angel looked up. From where she was sitting, she could just see her employer's backside as he bent to pull off his boots. One soft grunt, then another. It would be fair to say her attention wavered.

She bit her lip and looked away, making herself focus on the last two tiny nails she had yet to paint.

"Just another minute and we'll be through," she told Maddie, and smiled at the intent expression on the little girl's face.

Maddie blinked and nodded, but only slightly. Angel's caution to remain still had turned Royal's child into a small, living, breathing statue. The female fascination of having her fingernails painted for the first time in her life had overtaken every outside stimulus. Except, of course, the completion of the project and gloating to her friend, Paige, about the acquisition of an angel.

Unaware that her presence was going to be Maddie's small coup, Angel dipped the brush into the bottle, then pulled it out, carefully removing the excess polish on the lip. Then she took Maddie by the hand and leaned forward, bent on finishing the task they'd started.

Sock-footed, Royal produced almost soundless steps as he entered the kitchen. Whatever he'd been about to say slipped out of his mind. He inhaled slowly, fighting an unexpected surge of tears as an errant thought came and went.

So this is what little girls do when left to their own devices.

Spellbound by the innocent beauty of their profiles as they bent to the task, it was all he could do to breathe. He looked at his daughter and saw her—really saw her—as the individual she was and not an extension of him.

She was wearing a dress he didn't recognize. It took a few moments for him to remember Ryder and Casey had given it to her for Christmas last year. To his chagrin, he realized this was the first time she'd worn it. His conscience pricked.

Her hair was in a braid. That made him feel better. He braided her hair, too. Then he looked closer. This was a fancy braid, with five plaits rather than three. And the ribbon in her hair…it matched the pink and white dots on her dress.

He knew a moment of loss, as if he'd stepped off balance. It was one of the few times in his life he could remember feeling helpless. He narrowed his eyes and shifted his gaze from his daughter to the woman who was holding her hand. Emotion hit him belly first. It was jealousy, pure and simple.

If it had been possible at that moment to turn back time, he would have done it. If only he'd taken a different road home that day in the rain, this wouldn't be happening. This woman wouldn't be giving his daughter things he couldn't. But Maddie looked up, and every selfish thought he'd been having died. He couldn't remember ever seeing such joy in her eyes.

"Daddy, look! Angel is painting my fingernails. I'm going to be so beautiful."

He shook his head as if coming out of a trance. And when he bent to kiss the top of her head, the smile on his face was only a little bit sad.

"You already are," he said softly. "Now hold that smile. I'll be right back." He started out of the room, then stopped. As difficult as it was to say, there was something he had to get said. "Hey, Angel."

She looked up.

"Thanks."

"For what?" she asked.

He cocked his head toward his daughter. "For that."

"It is nothing," she said quietly.

"Not to her," he said.

Angel could feel the power of his gaze even after he was gone. There was something in his eyes she kept dodging—a message she wasn't sure she should read. She screwed the lid on the polish and leaned back in her chair.

Lonely. That was what she'd seen. Royal Justice was just possibly the loneliest man she'd ever met. Although he had the love of his family and his daughter, this was a different kind of lonely. The kind that comes from not having anyone to share yourself with.

She wasn't sure he knew it. And if he did, she knew he'd never admit it. But it was there just the same. She knew because every time she looked in the mirror, she saw the same emptiness on her face.

A few minutes later he was back, and the indecision she'd seen in his eyes was gone. The take-charge man was back.

Royal breezed through the kitchen on his way out the door. "Come on, girl, you're gonna be late, and don't forget your present."

Maddie stood like a queen rising from a throne. Her pink and white dress belled around her legs, and the ribbon at the end of her braid was bouncing against the middle of her back.

"You carry it," she solemnly announced, pointing toward a neatly wrapped package. "My nails are still wet."

He stopped, flummoxed by the inability to cope with all this femininity.

"Oh…uh, sure," he muttered, and went to the cabinet to retrieve the present.

Maddie sailed out the door ahead of him as if she was going to war, marching with her head held high and waving her hands in the air to dry them as Angel had shown her.

As Royal was pulling the door shut behind him, he could have sworn he heard a snicker. But when he turned, Angel was busying herself cleaning up the cotton balls and polish.

"We should be back in a couple of hours," he said shortly.

Angel answered without looking up. "Yes, sir."

Royal frowned. "Don't call me sir," he growled.

"All right, Mr. Justice."

His frown deepened. "And don't call me mister, either."

Angel stopped. She knew she'd pushed him enough.

"Okay."

"Okay what?" Royal asked.

Angel flinched. Saying his name, even to herself, seemed too personal. But he was the boss.

"Okay… Royal."

Royal nodded. "Like I said, we won't be too long. Consider the next two hours free time for yourself."

She nodded.

He started out the door and realized she wouldn't know where they'd gone. He couldn't imagine why, but there was the outside possibility that she might need to reach him. But when he looked back, she was gone.

"Daddy! Come open the door for me! I'll mess up my nails," Maddie yelled.

Royal rolled his eyes. "Damnation, Madeline Michelle, you're pushing your luck," he yelled.

A magazine lay half open on the floor where it had fallen from Angel's lap as she'd drifted off to sleep. The digital clock in Royal's bedroom blinked, sending out a new number to indicate the passing of time. Outside, a light breeze blew, cooling the afternoon heat. Down in the barn, Dumpling, the old mamma cat, lay dozing in the hay while her babies nursed and slept. Peace pervaded.

Sonny French took the wrong road home, which was understandable considering the amount of liquor he'd been consuming. It did occur to him to wonder why his driveway had a curve he didn't remember, but by the time his mind had considered the thought, it was too late for him to miss the tree. He hit it head-on, bouncing his truck over a ditch and through the tightly strung wires of a five-strand fence and scattering the herd of cattle that had been grazing there.

It came through the depths of Angel's sleep. First the thud, then a crunching of metal, then the frantic bellows of animals gone wild. She came off the couch in one motion, staring in sleepy confusion and wondering if she'd been dreaming in stereo. But then she realized she could still hear the cows and ran to the window. Even from the house, she could see the crumpled front end of a vehicle jammed through Royal's fence. In the pasture beyond, cattle were bawling and milling in nervous congestion. She didn't recognize the pickup but was relieved to see it wasn't Royal and Maddie.

She ran for the phone, only to discover there were no emergency services in the area and wasted time looking up the police number. To make matters worse, when they asked her for directions to the accident, she realized the only thing she knew to tell them was Royal Justice's ranch. As luck would have it, the dispatcher on duty knew the place well, and promptly dispatched an ambulance and a sheriff.

Angel dropped the phone onto the receiver and dashed out of the house. By the time she got to the wreck, she was in adrenaline overdrive. The driver was slumped over the wheel with blood dripping from his forehead. Smoke poured from the crumpled hood of the truck, but Angel could tell it was steam rather than fire. Unwilling to move him for fear of injuring him more, she turned in a panicked circle, unsure what to do first.

To her dismay, the cattle had run to the opposite end of the pasture and were now coming toward her at a steady walk, curious to see what had invaded their space. She took one look at the length of fence that was down and groaned. She had no idea how to reach Royal and it would be several minutes at best before help arrived.

Panicked, she started toward the break in the fence. An expert on cattle she was not, but the least she could do was try to keep them from getting out until help arrived.

"My head," Sonny groaned.

Angel pivoted. One good thing. At least he was alive. She darted toward the cab.

"Don't move, mister. An ambulance is on the way."

"Don't need no ambulance," Sonny drawled. "Jus' need my bed. My good ol' bed." Then he groaned again and passed out.

Angel's eyes narrowed angrily. She'd seen the empty beer cans in the floor of his truck. Stupid man. She turned toward the pasture. The cattle were getting nearer.

"Now what?" she muttered, and once again started toward the broken fence.

But this time, as she circled the truck, she spied something in the pickup bed she thought she could use. Without hesitation, she crawled in on her hands and knees, grabbed a cattle whip from beneath a jumble of trash and jumped out.

The long handle was coated with a film of greasy dirt. The whip on the end wasn't much more than a yard long, but its tip was forked like a snake's tongue. She tried popping it over her head and almost popped herself in the butt.

Dancing sideways to dodge her own wrath, she began moving toward the converging herd with the whip over her head, waving it in the air and, when she got up the nerve, giving it a sharp crack to one side. After a few tries, the motion became easier. A flip of the wrist, then a sudden jerk back. That's all it took. She looked nervously at the cattle. Now if they just got the message, she'd be all right.

Chapter 7

The party was a huge success. Within five minutes of leaving Paige Sullivan's house, Maddie had slumped sideways in the seat and gone to sleep. Royal drove with one hand on the wheel and the other on her. The tires on his truck hummed as the miles sped away, and he thought as he drove that there was something inherently comforting about living in ruts. He'd been driving down this particular stretch of highway most of his life. He knew every bent tree and rusty fence post, every windmill, every owner of every acre he passed. He even knew the identity of the old fellow on the tractor in front of him.

Old Man Hargis drove, as his daddy used to say, like the dead lice were falling off him. Instead of being impatient with the snail's pace, he grinned. It was just as well the old fellow didn't drive much faster than he walked, because his eyesight was worse than his hearing.

Finally the road ahead cleared, giving him room to pass. He glanced at Maddie, giving her seat belt a tug to make sure she was still buckled in, then whipped out from the trail of

Hargis's diesel smoke. At peace with the world, Royal waved at his elderly neighbor as he passed, then slipped into his lane, leaving the old man far behind.

He thought back to the party. It had gone well. As always, he was the only male parent, but he'd long gotten over the oddity of being the only male present. In fact, there'd been times in his past when he'd secretly enjoyed all the female attention. Even if they were only friends. Even if they were all married to some of his buddies. A little fussing never hurt.

But that was before Maddie's blossoming. Today their appearance at the party had been the topic of conversation.

Maddie was wearing a dress.

The women couldn't believe it.

And Maddie's nails were bright with new pink polish.

Their eyes were round with wonder.

And then there was the hairdo and the fancy pink ribbon. The list went on and on. Add to that Maddie's announcement that their new keeper was an angel, and Paige Sullivan's fifth birthday had become the second most important event of the day.

Royal sighed, picturing the gossip around supper tables tonight, then leaned back and grinned. He had to admit, Maddie had dropped a bomb on them all with that one. He'd let her talk. And why the hell not? Her explanation was better than his. He still didn't know what to say about what he'd done.

Out of habit, he took a hand from the wheel and smoothed it over his daughter's head, then her shoulder, patting her gently before turning his attention to the road.

God, he loved her. More than breath. More than life. And today she'd glowed. He'd never seen her that way, so confident of herself as a female rather than just a child. He had Angel to thank. When he got home, even if it tied a knot in his tongue, he was going to do just that.

Four miles from home, he topped a hill. In the distance he could see the flashing lights of an ambulance as it dipped and disappeared into the valley below. He frowned and glanced at Maddie again, thankful she was asleep. If they came on a wreck, he didn't want her to see.

He accelerated slightly, as if being in his own space would give him a sense of safety from the outside world.

Three miles, then two, then one, and when he turned the curve in the road just above the ranch, his heart dropped. Damn it to hell, but that ambulance had turned down the drive to the ranch.

He thought of Angel, alone in the house. Of all the accidents that could happen. Of all the possible reasons for an ambulance call. His stomach did a flip-flop as he realized she could be hurt. The thought made him nervous, then guilty. If he'd been there, he might have prevented whatever had happened.

He turned down the driveway and topped the hill above the ranch. Nothing could have prepared him for what he saw. A wreck! Someone had run through the fence! Then he recognized the truck.

"Well, damn, Sonny French's truck. I'll lay odds he was drunk when it happened," he muttered, not realizing he'd spoken aloud.

Maddie stirred, then sat up, blinking sleepily. "Daddy, are we home?"

"Almost, sweetheart," he said. "But it looks like someone wrecked their truck in our fence. I'll have to stop and see. You stay inside, okay?"

By the time Royal rolled to a stop, Maddie was out of her seat belt and on her knees, bracing herself against the dashboard as she gazed through the windshield. She squealed.

"Daddy! Angel's in the pasture with the cattle. You told me never to get in the pasture with the cattle. You've got to go get her! Hurry!"

Royal's gaze shifted from the flashing lights of the ambulance and Sonny's wrecked truck to the pasture beyond. He could only stare in disbelief. The sight of one slender woman with a whip and a herd of milling cattle made him wonder what else she'd endured in his absence. As he watched, she raised the whip in the air. Although he couldn't hear it from here, Royal knew by the way the cattle moved that it had cracked.

"Look at her, Daddy. I didn't know Angel could do stuff like that."

"Neither did I," he said softly, then gave his daughter one last warning. "You stay in this truck and you do not get out until I say so. No matter what! Do you understand me?"

Maddie's eyes were round. "I promise, Daddy. I won't get out until you come and get me. Besides," she added, "I wouldn't want to get my new dress all dirty."

It was an amazing admission from a child who willingly shared bites of peanut butter sandwiches with a cat.

"Right," he muttered, jumped out and ran.

Angel's knee was skinned and bleeding from crawling into Sonny's truck, and her ankle was sore. She was limping, compliments of a gopher hole and an errant cow. There was fresh manure on her shoes and some mud on her shorts, but she'd done it. The ambulance was here, and not a single cow had gotten out.

The herd bull was standing between her and the herd. Every now and then he would lower his head and paw dirt, which made her nervous. The urge to run was strong, but she'd stayed this long. She wasn't going to run now. He took a couple of steps forward, then stopped and bellowed.

"Don't tell me your troubles," she muttered. "Just because you have a tail and long ears doesn't make you any different from the other males I've known, and I put the last one on the floor."

To make herself feel better, she popped the whip above her head. The loud, reassuring crack was enough to send the bull into the herd. She exhaled a shaky breath and then heard someone calling her name.

She turned. Royal was coming toward her at a lope. Relief flooded, along with the overwhelming urge to cry. He was home!

Then she froze. What in the world was wrong with her? She didn't need anyone to take care of her, and there was no need to cry.

So she watched him run toward her, and in that moment she began shaking from the sensation that she'd stood like this before, seeing the long stride of his legs and the way his body moved within his clothes. Feeling the air around her shifting to make way for his presence. Watching him silhouetted against the afternoon sun and knowing that when he reached her, her world would never be the same.

And then he was there, cupping her shoulders and staring intently into her face.

"Angel! Are you all right?"

She shaded her eyes and looked up, staring blindly into a dark, anxious gaze.

"Yes, I'm fine."

He squeezed her shoulders. The contact was brief and little more than one stranger to another, but her heart quickened as if waiting for more.

"I am so sorry you had to deal with this on your own." He moved past her to stare at the cattle.

"I managed."

It was her quiet, almost noncommittal tone that made him turn. And then he looked at her. Really looked. At the dirt smudge on the curve of her cheek and her skinned and bleeding knee. At her shoes caked with drying manure. At the mud splattered on her bare legs and the edges of her shorts.

He grinned. "Yes, ma'am, you sure as hell did." He looked at the whip. "Where'd you get the popper?"

She pointed with her chin. "Out of the back of that truck."

Royal's eyes narrowed thoughtfully. "You're one resourceful lady, aren't you, Angel Rojas?"

She shrugged. "What is that old saying? Necessity is the mother of invention?"

Royal nodded, then reached for the whip. "Give it to me," he said gently. "I'll handle it from here."

She relinquished the whip with a sigh and they both turned to look at the sound of another siren.

"That would be the sheriff," Royal said. "Why don't you go crawl in the truck with Maddie where it's cool? Wait for me there. I'll drive you to the house in a while."

She nodded and started to walk away.

"Hey, Angel."

She turned.

"Good job," he said.

She blinked, then shuddered. The sensation of déjà vu was even stronger.

"Thank you," she said, and started walking.

The closer she got to the wreck, the faster she went. By the time she reached his truck, she was running, her sore ankle forgotten in her need to get away. But she didn't get in the cab with Maddie. Pointing to her muddy clothes and dirty shoes, she let down the tailgate and sat on it with her legs dangling. A few minutes later the sheriff took her version of the incident for his records, and followed the ambulance and the wrecker as they removed Sonny and what was left of his truck from the ranch. There was nothing left but a large, gaping hole in Royal's neatly strung fence.

Angel glanced at the pasture, debating with herself about going out to help. But Royal seemed to have everything under control. A couple of minutes later, a red truck topped the hill. Behind it came a shiny new blue one. Then another and another. It would seem that word had spread fast about Sonny French's latest fiasco.

Before she knew it, several men were helping Royal fix the fence. Within thirty minutes, it was over. The men left, one at a time, tipping their hats and giving her polite but curious glances as they drove away. She felt like a fly in the icing on top of a big white cake. Noticeable—and not long for this world.

And then she heard Royal's deep, husky growl as he bid the last neighbor goodbye. He was on his way to the truck. Still shaken by her earlier sensations, everything inside of her coiled as she waited for his approach. Then he was standing in front of her, frowning, and her defenses went up.

"I thought I told you to get inside where it was cool," he growled.

"I was too dirty," she said.

He glanced at her knee, where the skin was peeled. The urge to tend it was strong. Instead, he found himself pushing when he should have been pulling back.

"Dirt washes off," he said shortly. "Next time do what I say."

Angel's chin jutted and her lips firmed as she slid off the truck bed and onto her feet.

"Now you listen to me, you—you...your royal highness. It'll be a cold day in hell before I do something I think is wrong just because a man told me to do it. And if you're going to have a problem with that, then let's just consider me fired."

Having said her piece, she started down the road toward the house, leaving Royal standing in the dirt, too stunned to speak. Not since his mother, God rest her soul, had a woman ever put him so neatly in his place.

Royal highness? He clenched his jaw. She had some nerve. But as hard as he tried, he couldn't get mad. Instead, he watched in disbelief as she strode toward the ranch with her head held high and that long black braid swinging like a pendulum down the middle of her back.

"Daddy, I want to walk with Angel."

His daughter's voice yanked him out of his shock. He inhaled sharply and turned toward the truck.

"Madeline Michelle, don't lean out the damned window!" he yelled. "You'll fall on your head! And you're not walking anywhere. You don't want to get dirty, remember?"

Maddie shrugged and dropped back in her seat as Royal slid behind the wheel and started the engine.

"Let's race her," she said, pointing to Angel.

A mental image of driving past Angel and leaving her

choking in their dust flashed through his mind. Royal looked at Maddie, then burst out laughing.

"Let's not," he said, then put the truck in gear. "I think I'm already in enough trouble. How about we just give her a ride?"

"Okay," Maddie said.

Royal pulled up beside Angel, letting the truck coast as he leaned out the window.

"Hey, lady, need a lift?"

Angel glared at him and stumbled when she saw the look of devilment on his face. She'd been expecting anger, not a challenge.

She stopped, forcing him to step on the brakes to stay even with her. There was nothing between them but the sound of a well-tuned engine idling smoothly.

"I can't," she finally said. "I'm fired."

He gritted his teeth, enunciating each word distinctly. "No, damn it, you're not fired."

Angel almost fainted with relief, but she'd die before she'd let it show. She waited. There was more he had to say.

Royal glanced at Maddie, who was listening to the conversation with far too much interest. He sighed and turned to Angel.

"How about if I said I was sorry?" he asked.

Her lips twitched. Her only sign of pleasure. Still she remained silent.

"Well?" Royal growled.

"Well, what?" Angel asked.

"Hell, woman, what do you want besides an apology?"

There might have been cow dung on her shoes and blood on her leg, but she wasn't lacking in attitude.

"The apology would do nicely…if I'd heard it. All I heard you ask was, would I like you to say you were sorry. I didn't hear you *say* you were sorry."

Royal didn't know whether to curse or laugh. Thinking of home-cooked meals and clean laundry, he grinned.

"My mistake," he drawled. "Miss Rojas, I am abjectly

sorry for behaving in an inappropriate manner. Would you accept my most heartfelt apology?"

She snorted as she started toward the back of the truck.

"Overkill is hardly your style," she announced, and slid onto the tailgate. When she was settled safely in place, she yelled, "I'm ready."

Royal glanced in the rearview mirror. All he could see was the stiff tilt of her head and shoulders.

"Hang on," he yelled, and then accelerated gently.

They rode the rest of the way to the ranch house in silence. Even Maddie was unusually quiet. After he had parked, Royal got out, then lifted Maddie out of the seat.

"Change that pretty dress before you go out to play," he warned.

"Okay," she said, and tore into the house, leaving Royal alone with the keeper.

Angel slid off the tailgate, wincing slightly at the jolt to her ankle. Royal saw it and caught her by the arm before she could escape him.

"Easy," he said softly, when her dark eyes flashed him a warning. "I'm just trying to help."

Angel sighed and nodded. "It's been a long day."

Royal resisted the urge to sweep her into his arms and carry her into the house. He offered her an elbow to lean on. She hesitated, then took it gratefully.

"Thank you again for all you did," Royal said.

Suddenly uncomfortable with the intimacy, she shrugged off his thanks.

"It happened. I was here. It was nothing," she said shortly.

"And you hurt yourself for me," Royal said. "Your ankle hurts, I think, although you don't seem to trust me enough to say so, and you have shed blood on my behalf." He pointed to her knee. "I think that deserves some special thanks."

She looked up and blushed, then looked away.

Royal stumbled. A man would need a blazing fire not to get lost in eyes that dark. And her skin—it looked like velvet, soft, brown velvet. Yep, he'd been right. That day in the rain…he should have kept on driving.

"Well, then," he mumbled. "Let's get you cleaned up, then we'll take a look at your bumps and bruises and see what we can do, okay?"

"I'm sure I'll be fine," Angel said.

Royal stopped. A frown deepened the grooves on his forehead.

"So am I," he said. "But indulge me…please."

Angel finally gave in. Not because he had weakened her resolve, but because he was so hardheaded it was easier to agree than to argue.

"Do you need any help?" Royal asked.

Angel bent, pulled off her shoes and left them on the front porch.

"No, but thank you," she said quietly.

She could feel the heat of his gaze between her shoulder blades all the way to her room. Before she opened her door, she thought about turning around just to see if he was still watching. But then she changed her mind and bolted inside. She didn't want to know.

A short while later, Angel emerged. Fresh from a shower, in clean clothes, she felt ready to tackle anything. When she walked into the kitchen, her opinion changed. Royal was waiting. Make that anything except Royal Justice, she thought. There was antiseptic on the table and a large box of Maddie's favorite bandages.

"Beauty and the Beast?" she queried, pointing to the box.

He never cracked a smile. "Maddie insisted."

"She does a lot of that," Angel said.

Royal's composure slipped, and he grinned. "Yeah, Roman says she's a lot like me. Now if you wouldn't mind, I will see to your knee and then get out of your hair."

Angel reached for the sack of cotton balls he was holding. "Oh, I can do that my—"

His fingers tightened around the plastic. "I know that," he said shortly. "Indulge me."

She sat, wishing she'd put on something other than shorts. They weren't tight, and they were completely modest, but his hands on any part of her body seemed a bit like waving a lit match over a dynamite fuse—just to see if it would catch.

Royal bent to the task, frowning as he dabbed an antiseptic-soaked swab to the wound on her knee. Even though it had happened some time ago, it was still seeping, evidence of how deep the abrasions were.

Although she hadn't moved, there was a muscle jerking above her knee. He was hurting her, and he knew it. Without thinking, he lowered his head and blew, just as he would have done for Maddie.

When his head dipped toward her knee, Angel froze, and when his breath touched her skin, whatever she had been thinking curled up and died. She groaned and he looked up, certain he'd caused her more pain.

"I'm sorry," Royal said. "It's deeper than I thought."

He was talking. She knew it because she could see his lips moving. But there was a roar in her ears that she couldn't get past. She swallowed twice, trying to think what to say, but the words wouldn't come. To save herself, she closed her eyes, blocking out the sight of his face. It was all that saved her.

When it came to a woman's pain, Royal was a pushover. Right or wrong, he'd been raised to believe that it was a man's duty to take care of what his father had called the weaker sex, although he had long since figured out that the only thing weaker about most women was their physical strength. When it came to endurance, they could beat a man hands down every time.

And he was living proof of that theory. Here he was, down on his knees and putting medicine on what amounted to a rather insignificant wound, and he was almost sick to his stomach. If she cried, he'd be lost.

His fingers were trembling as he gave the wound one last dab. His breath was shaky as he blew on it again. He rocked on his heels, waiting for it to dry, and reached for the box of bandages.

"Wanna pick?" he asked.

Startled by the question, Angel opened her eyes. The box of decorative bandages was in her lap. It was the icebreaker she needed. She smiled as she pulled a bandage out and handed it to him.

Royal managed a grin, opened it and pulled it out of the wrapper with a flair.

"It's Belle. Good choice."

Before he could stick it on, Maddie came running. "Let me. Let me," she cried. "I can stick it on."

Royal took one horrified look at his daughter and bolted to his feet. Her clothes, the ones she'd just put on, were dotted with fresh grass stains, and there was a dark, smelly smudge on the seat of her shorts. As she reached to take the Band-Aid, he grabbed her hands, turning them palms up and staring in disbelief.

"What the hell have you been doing?" he yelled.

A frown furrowed her forehead. "Playing with Flea Bit and Marbles," she mumbled.

"Playing what, the apocalypse?"

The analogy was over her head, which only deepened her frown.

"We wasn't playing any pocky lips. We played hide-and-seek. I won."

"I'd hate like hell to see those poor cats," he muttered, then handed Angel the Band-Aid almost as an afterthought and grabbed Maddie by the arm, intent on marching her to the bathroom to clean up.

Angel reacted before she thought. All she could see was a little girl in trouble for nothing but playing and a father who yelled before he talked. She grabbed Royal by the arm.

"Wait," she urged. "It's only grass and dust. It will wash...and so will she."

Her even tone was all the quiet Royal needed. Almost instantly, he calmed. He looked at Maddie. The obstinate look on her face was proof enough he'd reacted in exactly the wrong manner. Instead of arguing with Angel, he took a deep breath and dropped to Maddie's level.

"Sorry," he said gently, poking the end of her nose. "But you sure made a mess."

Maddie nodded in agreement. "I'm sorry, Daddy, but I was just having fun."

Royal hugged her then grabbed her hands, turning them palms up again.

"If you want to help doctor Angel, you have to wash your hands first. You don't want to get germs in her sore knee, right?"

Her eyes widened thoughtfully. "Right," she agreed, and gave Angel a nervous look, afraid the bandage would get applied without her assistance. "Wait for me," she begged. "I'll be right back."

"I'll wait," Angel promised as Maddie ran out of the room.

Again they were left alone. Royal ran a hand through his hair and exhaled softly.

"Thanks again," he said quietly, reached for his hat and walked out the back door.

The quiet slam broke the silence in which Angel was sitting. Down the hall, the sound of running water was evidence that Maddie was doing as she'd been told. Angel looked at the Band-Aid she was holding and set it on the table. She took a deep breath and exhaled slowly. Finally, she was alone.

Her knee still stung where Royal had applied the medicine. Her hands were getting sore, she supposed from gripping the filthy handle of Sonny French's whip for so long. Her ankle was throbbing, and her head was starting to hurt. But none of that was as bothersome as the unsettled feeling in her belly. She didn't know whether to start crying or throw up. Something was happening she didn't want—hadn't planned. She'd taken this job for a number of reasons, none of which included a physical attraction to the boss. But it was happening just the same.

She covered her face with her hands. "Oh, God, don't let this happen."

The sound of running footsteps warned that Maddie was on her way. She lifted her head and fought for composure.

"I'm ready!" Maddie announced, showing her clean hands as proof.

"Looks good to me," Angel said, and handed the little girl the bandage.

Chapter 8

Tommy Boy Watson had taken a liking to Texas, so much so that after he'd done the deed in Abilene, he'd moved toward the outskirts of Amarillo. Yesterday he'd stopped at a café to eat some lunch and overheard the two men in the booth behind him talking about a sweet little waitress named Darcy at the Little Horn Café. He'd listened absently until he'd heard them mention that twenty bucks would put her in a willing mood. At that point he stopped chewing. One added that he'd heard for fifty dollars, she could send a man to the moon.

Low laughter followed a couple of suggestive comments as Tommy Boy resumed chewing his food. He swallowed, washed it down with the last of his sweet iced tea and reached for his check. He had a sudden urge to see if this Darcy really was on the menu at the Little Horn Café. If she was, he figured it was time to do a little editing.

He tossed some money on the table and dug his keys out of his pocket. He strolled out of the café, picking his teeth and jingling his keys. He liked making plans. But he liked following through on them even more.

The Justice homestead had been in the family for over a hundred and fifty years. The original house, built by Royal's grandfather, had been little more than a bedroom with a cooking shed attached. When he married, they'd added two rooms downstairs and two up to accommodate his growing family. By the time Royal's father, Micah Justice, had taken over the running of the Justice ranch, the only thing left of the original building was the massive stone fireplace and the eight-foot hand-hewn log that was the mantel.

Angel knew the story. Royal had related it proudly after dinner one night. She listened with interest as he went through the generations, watching the pride on his face as he looked at Maddie, knowing she would be the link to keeping the Justice family alive.

Today, as Angel ran a lemon-scented dust cloth along the mantel, she was thinking of her history. Of the family she'd lost and the family she longed to have.

She moved to the tables, then the windowsills, applying polish and rubbing it in, savoring the rich sheen that came out in the wood and taking pride in her work. Some would look down upon work such as this. But to Angel, anything she got paid to do was worth doing well.

A week had passed since the wreck. Her knee had healed. Her heart had settled into its normal place. She'd chalked her emotional reaction to her employer as nothing more than the heat of the moment. She'd been slightly afraid of the cattle. Royal had come and taken the fear out of her hands. Gratitude. That's all it was. She'd been grateful, not attracted.

Having settled that firmly in her mind, she'd managed to stay in the background of Royal's world for the rest of the week. She cooked. She cleaned. She did everything a housekeeper should do except become a part of the family. As much as she enjoyed Maddie's company, she had an innate resistance to letting anyone get too close. In her entire life, the only person she'd ever loved without reservation was her mother. And she'd died, leaving Angel to the whims of a drunken father and a welfare system that didn't work. Angel had grown up the hard way, and in doing so had grown up hard.

Her appearance was attractive. Dark hair, dark eyes and the warm complexion of a sun worshiper. Some might even call her beautiful. Her behavior, while obstinate and willful, was never cruel. But she kept her feelings close to her heart where they would be safe. She'd learned the hard way that if she didn't give love away, then there could be no chance of rejection. And yet she'd agreed to stay with a child who believed she'd been sent from God.

It wasn't as if she really loved them, Angel told herself. They were good to her. It was easy to be good to them. It didn't have to mean anything.

She gave her cleaning rag another dose of lemon oil polish and knelt beside the massive dining room table to clean the legs. As she was working, she heard the back door slam and the familiar sound of Maddie's footsteps running through the house. She grinned. Maddie never walked when she could run.

"Angel! Angel! Where are you?" Maddie called.

"In the dining room," Angel called, and rocked back on her heels as Maddie burst into the room. She barely had time to register the fact that Royal was right behind her before Maddie thrust a handful of wildflowers toward Angel's face.

"These are for you!" Maddie said.

Angel looked at the wad of squeezed and broken stems in the little girl's fist, then at her face, then at the man behind her before looking at the flowers.

"Oh, my," she said softly, and reached for the wilting bouquet, inhaling the scent of crushed grass and sweet blossoms as Maddie thrust them in her hand.

"Do you like them?" Maddie asked, then before Angel could answer, she began pointing and talking. "These blue ones are my favorites. They're bluebonnets. Did you know that's a Texas flower? And these are Indian blankies.''

"Blankets," Royal corrected.

Maddie nodded without missing a beat. "Yeah, blankets. My daddy likes them best. They're not really blankets, you know. They're just flowers. I don't know why someone gave them that name. I think they look like clown flowers 'cause they're red and yellow like Ronald McDonald and he's a clown and—''

"Damn, Maddie, give it a rest," Royal growled, then tugged at her ponytail to take the sting from his words.

Maddie giggled, but she stopped talking, which was what Royal had intended.

Angel lifted the flowers to her nose, inhaling the separate scents. Some were sweeter than others, and the colors were as varied as a Texas sky at sunset. To her surprise, tears came quickly, blurring the colors and Maddie's face.

Maddie saw the tears and took a hesitant step back, leaning against her daddy's leg for comfort. She looked at Royal.

"Daddy, did I do something bad?''

Angel groaned beneath her breath and before she thought, reached for Maddie and pulled her into her arms.

"No, baby," Angel said softly, hugging the little girl close. "You did something good.''

"I did?''

Angel nodded. "Oh, yes, and do you know what it was?''

Maddie shook her head.

"No one ever gave me flowers before.''

"Ever?" Maddie asked. "Not even on your birthday?''

"No. Not even on my birthday." She hugged her again and kissed her on the cheek. "That's why these are so special. Thank you a hundred times. Maybe even a thousand times.''

Maddie beamed and spun out of Angel's arms. "We need water! Daddy said we need to put the damn things in water.'' She headed for the kitchen.

Royal's face turned red as he offered her a hand up. "I didn't mean that the way it—''

Angel eyed the wide, callused palm and the long fingers before getting up on her own.

"I know," she said, smiling slightly as she bent to smell them one more time. "I'd better help Maddie find a vase."

Royal shifted uncomfortably. "Yeah, Maddie can make a mess faster than anyone I ever knew."

"She's just a child," Angel said.

Royal nodded, watching the look of awe on Angel's face as she kept touching first one flower and then another. To him they looked like hell. Maddie had sat on part of them once and dropped all of them twice since they'd been picked. They were covered in dust, and if he wasn't mistaken, there was a small green worm climbing up one of the stems. A floral tribute it was not. But it had come from his daughter's heart. He kept thinking how close he'd come to ignoring Maddie's request for him to stop along the roadside where the flowers had grown.

All he could think was that this moment would never have happened and Angel would still have been waiting for her first bouquet.

"Angel?"

"Yes?"

"Was that true? Are these the first flowers anyone ever gave you?"

A wry grin tilted the corner of her mouth. "Yes. Doesn't say much for my popularity, does it?"

He frowned. "I'd come near saying the men you've known have been sadly lacking in class, that's what I'd say."

Then, embarrassed that he'd given so much of himself away, he pivoted, muttered that he'd help Maddie find that damned vase and stomped away.

Angel stood, staring at the stiffness in his posture and the haste with which he left, and tried to decide if he'd been angry with himself or with her. Finally, she shrugged. It didn't matter. Right now, nothing mattered but these flowers and the love in which they'd been given.

At that moment, a little crack began to form in the shell

around Angel's heart. But she didn't hear it, and if she had, wouldn't have recognized the sound. It would be a while yet before Angel Rojas became familiar with the sound of joy.

That night the flowers were the centerpiece for the dining room table, and long after the lights were out and everyone else had gone to sleep, Angel still lay, wide-eyed and sleepless, thinking about the way Maddie's arms had felt around her neck. Remembering the silky-soft texture of the little girl's skin against her cheek. Tasting the faint, salty taste of sweat as she'd kissed her.

A longing for something more than she had began burning within her. She felt empty and lonely in a way she'd never known. With a groan, she got out of bed and walked to the window. She stared across the yard toward the building beyond. The blue-white glow of the security light gave an icy appearance to all that she saw. She shuddered and spun to stare at the room before her.

Thanks to her sleepless night, her covers were in tangles, and although her shoes were near a chair and she knew her clothes were in the closet, the room had taken on an unfamiliar feel. It was as if she'd walked out of a nightmare into a place where she didn't belong.

She wrapped her arms around herself and closed her eyes, whispering a prayer her mother had taught her many years ago to take away bad dreams. But when the prayer was over and she opened her eyes, the feeling was still with her.

She bit her lip and sighed and headed back to bed. Just before she laid down, a thought occurred. She dropped the covers she'd been holding and hurried out of her room.

The red Spanish tiles in the hallway were cool beneath her feet. Out of her room, she felt vulnerable. Anxious not to be discovered, she hastened her steps, all but running to get to the dining room table.

Then she was there, sighing with relief when her fingers curled around the cool, smooth surface of the mason jar that doubled as a vase for Maddie's flowers. She scurried down the hall clutching the vase and her bouquet.

As she crossed the threshold to her room, her anxiety decreased. She sat on the side of her bed, lightly fingering the velvety petals. Peace settled. She gave the petals one last touch, then laid down, pulled the covers up to her chin and closed her eyes. The last thing she remembered was the hum of the central air-conditioning and the sound of her heartbeat in her ears.

The next morning began with a knot in her shoelace that she couldn't untie and went downhill from there. When she went into the kitchen to start breakfast, Royal was already up and the coffeepot was half empty. The anger on his face was evident as he talked on the phone, and although Angel did not know who he was talking to, she felt sympathy for them just the same.

"Look, damn it. I ordered that fertilizer over a month ago. You promised delivery last week, and it's still not here. I don't give a rat's ass who you're trying to blame. What I'm saying to you is, if it's not here today, then consider my order canceled."

Angel winced as he slammed the phone down. She was debating about leaving the room when he realized he was no longer alone.

"I'm sorry," she said quickly. "I didn't know you were—"

Royal shoved a hand through his hair in frustration, mussing the dark, spiky strands into instant disarray.

"No, I'm the one who should be sorry," Royal muttered and had the grace to look ashamed. "Sometimes I lose my temper."

Angel stifled a grin. That was the most obvious understatement she'd ever heard.

"Yes, I know."

Royal stilled and gave her a long, considering look. "Was that sarcasm I heard?"

She didn't flinch, returning his stare look for look. "Do you have a preference for breakfast?" she asked.

Royal tried to glare, but it was hard to get the point across when being ignored. He moved a step closer, taking some small delight in the fact that she took a step back.

"Yes, I have a preference," he said softly.

Angel's eyes widened and her heart started to pound. She wanted to run but couldn't find the will to break free of his stare.

"I'm hungry as hell," he continued, took another step toward her and lowered his voice to just above a whisper. "But I don't know what I want."

God give me strength, Angel thought, and wondered if she could deck him as she had Fat Louie. And then wondered if she would. There was something about the man she had tried without success to ignore.

"Do you have any suggestions?" Royal asked, knowing he was pushing every button she had and wondering, as he continued to bait her, why it mattered.

Angel doubled her fists and took a deep breath. But before she could react, he turned and poured himself another cup of coffee and strolled toward the back door as if she wasn't even there.

She went limp with relief and cleared her throat, thankful that her voice wasn't as shaky as her legs.

"Do you intend to eat breakfast or not?" she asked.

Royal turned, the cup halfway to his lips, and grinned. "Surprise me." He walked outside and let the door slam shut behind him.

The urge to throw something was strong within her as she stomped to the cabinets and yanked out a bowl. He wanted a surprise? She would give him a surprise. He'd think twice before he pulled that macho stuff on her again.

Royal glanced at his watch and then up the driveway, nodding with satisfaction as the man from Wilson's Seed and Feed circled the pasture, applying liquid fertilizer. It was almost two. His belly grumbled. He'd missed lunch, which was probably just as well. His mouth was still burning from breakfast. He knew the moment he'd started the game with Angel that he was taking his frustration out on her. But who would have known she'd take it so personally?

Hell, his lips were blistered and bound to peel, and he wondered if tongues peeled, too. He'd had hot food plenty of times in his life. In fact, he prided himself on being able to eat real Tex-Mex cooking with the best. But he'd never in his life eaten anything as hot as the omelette she'd put on his plate.

The first bite was already in his belly before he knew what had happened. He hiccuped and reached for his coffee, then changed his mind and poured himself some of Maddie's milk.

Maddie had continued to eat her cereal, unaware of the undercurrents between Daddy and her angel.

The milk had helped, but only slightly. He stared at the remaining omelette on his plate and then at Angel, who was shaking more pepper sauce onto hers. His eyes narrowed. Damn her. What was she trying to prove, that she was tougher because she could eat liquid fire? Infuriated that she was making him eat his words, he picked up his fork and took another big bite.

Angel didn't look up. Not because she was afraid of what she'd done but because she was afraid she'd laugh in his face. He was hurting, and she knew it. The hiccup was proof that his stomach had experienced an instant rebellion. But he was tough, she'd give him that. She heard the scrape of his fork against his plate and knew he'd taken another bite. She reached for a piece of toast and began to butter it with smooth, even strokes. Then she picked up the rack.

"Want some toast?" she asked.

Royal's eyes were running streams of pure tears, and he was in the act of digging a handkerchief from his pocket to stop the flow. He stuffed the handkerchief under his nose and yanked the rack of toast out of her hands.

"Thanks."

Angel met his glare with an innocent stare. "Don't mention it...again," she said softly.

He started to speak and choked and coughed instead. All

he could manage was a nod, but he'd gotten the message. He'd pushed. She'd pushed back. He wasn't sure, but he didn't think he would be pushing her again. At least not like that. When it came to revenge, Maddie's angel didn't play fair.

But Royal wasn't the kind of man to dwell on the past. So he'd made a mistake. It wouldn't happen again.

He glanced toward the house in the valley. Maddie was little more than a dot on the landscape, but he knew it was her. He could tell by the way she kept darting to and fro that she must be playing with one of those cats. He didn't see Angel anywhere. But that didn't mean she wasn't there. He'd seen the look on Angel's face when Maddie had given her the flowers. It was an instant friends-for-life gesture if he'd ever seen one.

And then he frowned. But where did that leave him? After the stunt he'd pulled this morning, were they going to be enemies forever? Something within him rejected the thought. He did not want Angel Rojas for an enemy. His frown deepened and he looked away. But what did he want from her? He'd hired her as a housekeeper. Why did he keep pushing her buttons? Why couldn't he just let her be?

Angel sat in the porch swing, watching as Maddie played with Flea Bit and telling herself she should go inside and get supper started. She'd baked a cake earlier and she knew it was cooled enough to ice, yet moving from where she was sitting was the last thing she wanted to do. It was peaceful here. Peace was something she hadn't known in years. She brushed a fly from her face and smiled, then laughed as Maddie held up the cat for her to see. It was wearing a pink bonnet from Maddie's Cabbage Patch doll, and Angel could see something that looked suspiciously like cotton balls running the length of the animal's belly. She bit her lip and sighed. Oh, Lord. So that's where the bag of cotton balls went. She didn't even want to know how Maddie had stuck them on. If the cat was lucky, it was with glue. At least that could be cut away. If she'd taped them on, poor Flea Bit might be wearing them for quite a while.

She stood and walked into the driveway where Maddie was playing.

"What have you done to Flea Bit?"

Maddie danced the cat on its back legs and waved a front paw at Angel.

"Flea Bit's a clown. See? He has a hat and little fuzzy balls."

Angel bit her lip to keep from laughing. That remark was priceless. Aside from the cotton Maddie had glued to the cat, Flea Bit did have little fuzzy balls and, she hoped, a sense of humor.

"Yes, I see," Angel said. "But don't you think he's played enough? It's getting awfully hot out here. Why don't you take the costume off Flea Bit and come up on the porch. I'll get him some milk and you an ice-cream cone, okay?"

"Yeah!" Maddie cried, and tore the hat off Flea Bit's head.

Angel winced and made a grab for the cat before Maddie started pulling at the cotton she'd glued to its belly.

"Be careful, sweetheart. Here, let me help you."

To Angel's surprise and relief, she saw the cotton balls had been stuck on with mud rather than glue. A little dab of water from the hydrant by the porch and Flea Bit was as good as new.

"Go wash your hands," Angel said. "Then you can have your ice-cream cone."

Maddie frowned. "The ice cream always melts on my hands. I wanna wash my hands after I eat."

Angel shook her head. "So we'll wash them twice. Now scoot."

Maddie started to argue, but the idea of ice cream was enough to snuff out the thought.

"Be right back," she yelled, and dashed into the house.

Angel held the cat in the air, giving it a careful inspection to make sure it had suffered no harm. Everything was still in place.

"Poor kitty," she said softly, and set it on the porch. "If you have the guts, hang around a minute. I'll get you some milk."

The cat must have understood, because it was waiting beside the door when Angel came out with the small dish of milk.

"I'm ready for my ice cream," Maddie announced, displaying her still dripping hands for Angel's inspection.

"You sure are," Angel said, and started inside to get Maddie her treat. Maddie surprised her by hugging her bare legs.

"What's that for?" Angel asked, a little surprised and a little bit touched.

"'Cause I love you," Maddie said, and left Angel standing as she dashed into the house.

Angel watched through the screen door as Maddie shoved a chair to the refrigerator, opened the freezer door and began digging through the contents for her favorite flavor of ice cream.

Angel kept telling herself to move, that Maddie would make a mess before they even started, but she didn't trust herself to speak. There was a knot in her throat and tears burning the back of her eyes and she could still feel the imprint of Maddie's body against her legs.

Love. Oh, Lord. This wasn't in the job description.

Something clattered to the floor, and Maddie ducked beneath the open door of the freezer to see if Angel was watching. It was all the jump start Angel needed.

"Wait, Maddie. Let me help," she said, and hurried inside.

Royal closed the last gate, then turned and watched as the truck from the feed store drove away. He glanced up, gauging the gathering clouds against the fact that all the liquid fertilizer had been spread. And by the looks of the sky, none too soon. It would be just about perfect if they got a good rain tonight. Not too much. Just enough to soak that fertilizer right into the ground.

Then he looked at the house in the valley, squinting against the glare of a setting sun and wondering where everyone had gone. Probably inside where it was cool. The day had turned out much hotter than predicted. He gave the darkening sky one last look and headed home. He should be just about able to finish the chores before anything hit.

Angel was swirling the last spoonful of white icing on her cake while Maddie was at the kitchen table, coloring in one of her coloring books. It was a quiet, homey scene, idyllic from a bystander's point of view.

The evening news was being broadcast, and Angel listened halfheartedly to the portable television on a nearby sideboard, trying to make sense of what the newsman was saying in conjunction with the running commentary being given by Royal's princess.

"Look," Maddie cried, and held up her book, waiting for praise.

Angel glanced at the picture. "Wow, Maddie. That's very good. I'll bet when you start to school this fall you'll be one of the best in the class at coloring."

Maddie nodded, as if to say, of course she would, and turned to a new page, anxious to begin her next masterpiece.

Angel's attention moved to the sixteen-inch television. She frowned as the picture of a young brown-haired woman was flashed on the screen.

"...found in a culvert by a passing motorist who'd stopped to change a flat tire. Amarillo authorities have identified her as Carol Jo Belmont, who was last seen at the Big Wheel Truck Stop. Her throat had been slashed and—"

The back door opened and Angel pivoted, the icing-coated knife clutched in her hand. It was Royal.

"Daddy!" Maddie squealed and abandoned her crayons for her father's arms.

The instant pleasure on Royal's face was, for some reason, difficult to watch. She turned and laid the knife in the sink then reached for a paper towel to wipe her hands. When she turned, her composure was firmly in place.

"You're already back. I'm afraid supper's not quite ready."

"That's all right," Royal said. "From the way the clouds are building, I think I'd better finish the chores first."

Maddie suddenly tightened her hold around Royal's neck.

"Is it gonna rain, Daddy?"

Royal nuzzled her cheek with his nose. "I hope so. The grass needs a drink."

She frowned and wiggled to be put down. "I'd better make sure Marbles and Flea Bit will be all right. Maybe they should come inside with—"

"No, ma'am, maybe they better not," Royal stated firmly. "But you can come with me if you want to. You can put them to bed and tell them good-night, okay?"

Cakes and coloring books were quickly forgotten as Maddie dashed outside. Royal gave Angel a tentative glance.

"That looks good," he said. "Is it safe?"

She flushed and turned away in embarrassment, but she knew what he meant. Obviously the Habenero peppers had gotten his attention. She lifted her chin and turned, refusing to let him know that he often intimidated her. Innocence dripped from her voice as she stared him straight in the face.

"Why? Shouldn't it be?"

Royal grinned and held up his hands, as if to say, I give up. "Just asking," he said, and glanced at the television. "Been giving any weather bulletins?"

She shook her head.

"Put it on channel four," he said. "They update better than the others."

Angel nodded and switched channels. The bulletin she'd been listening to was forgotten as she turned up the volume and turned on the stove. It was time to finish the meal.

Chapter 9

Supper was over, and Royal was giving Maddie her bath. Angel could hear the rumble of his voice and the childish squeals of Maddie's laughter as the evening routine played out. She knew that when it was over, there would be water on the floor and wet towels hanging from every hook, but it was something they both seemed to enjoy. While the hilarity was good, it reminded Angel that she was the outsider in this house.

At first she hadn't cared. In fact, she had welcomed the evenings to herself. The times when Royal was present and the duties of Maddie's keeper returned to the father, where they belonged, had been a welcome respite. But during the past few days, her feelings had begun to change. Instead of looking forward to the break in her routine, she began to dread it. Today was no exception.

She picked up a magazine and tossed it down, knowing she wouldn't be able to focus. Instead of turning on the television, she moved outside, choosing the old swing under a nearby oak tree rather than her usual place on the porch. She brushed off the seat, turned and sat, testing the length of her shorts against the wooden seat. Satisfied that they were long enough to prevent any splinters, she relaxed. Immediately, her shoes slid off her feet.

The rope from which the swing was hanging was thick but soft. Her fingers curled around its surface as she leaned back and pushed off. At once, the sensation of weightlessness took over, and she closed her eyes, letting herself go free. As she did, an old memory surfaced, one of standing at the side of a playground, watching as the other children in her class laughed and played. Even then she'd been set apart, by her ethnicity and the fact that the people she lived with were not her own. So she'd stood alone, wanting a turn on the swings but afraid to ask.

It had hurt then, not being one of the crowd. But now, after so many years on her own, it was her saving grace. She celebrated her differences. She did not mourn them. And she'd learned to appreciate her gifts rather than covet what she could not have.

Motion stirred the air, blowing bits of her hair into her eyes and then away from her face, plastering her T-shirt to the thrust of her breasts and caressing the backs of her bare legs as she continued to pump.

Back and forth.

Up and down.

Faster and faster.

Higher and higher.

When she opened her eyes, the world was flying past her in a blur of blue and gray shadows. She dropped her head forward and pulled up her legs, letting the momentum of her body move the swing.

Peace came then. With nothing but the soft whoosh of air against her ears and the beat of her heart for a rhythm, she began to slow down. Only after the swing was motionless did she become aware that she was no longer alone.

She felt his presence rather than saw him. When she looked

up, he was standing on the porch steps with his hands stuffed in his pockets, watching.

She shuddered.

Dusk hid all but the outline of his body and face from her gaze, and yet she sensed the intensity of his scrutiny. She didn't know whether to acknowledge his presence or make her excuses and leave. She did neither. When he came off the steps, her first instinct was to stand. And when he started toward her, the urge to run was strong. He moved quietly but with purpose, his strides certain and even. She tightened her grasp on the ropes and tried to tell herself that it was safe. But the closer he came, the faster her heart began to beat and the shorter her breaths became.

Lord help me. "Was there something you needed?" she asked.

Royal paused. Her question was a verbal stop sign if he'd ever heard one.

"Maddie wants you to read her a story."

Angel's voice rose an octave in pleased surprise. "She does?"

"Yeah," Royal said. "I told her this was your time to yourself, but that I'd ask."

Angel stared at him through the growing dusk, trying to draw a conclusion as to how he felt about his daughter's request. But it was getting too dark, and he was standing too still.

"I don't mind...if you don't," she said.

Her answer surprised him. "Why would I mind?"

She shrugged. "Well, I know how much you enjoy this time with her. That it's your special time together. I don't want to intrude or force myself into the situation."

Royal sighed, and Angel heard it. His voice was tinged with exasperation as he answered.

"Look, if it bothered me, I wouldn't have asked you. Okay?"

She nodded, and realized he probably couldn't see her.

"Yes, sir," she said quickly, then slipped on her shoes and started toward the house.

Royal stepped in her path, then cursed beneath his breath when he heard her frightened gasp.

"Damn it, woman, quit calling me sir," he said shortly. "And stop shaking like a cornered rabbit. I am not going to hurt you."

Before Angel could answer, he pivoted and stalked away. Thankful for the cover of darkness, she lifted a shaky hand to her face and started toward the house. When she got to the door, she turned and looked into the yard, past the illuminated circle beneath the security light. Motionless, she stared into the darkness.

Nothing moved, but he was out there somewhere. Was he watching her, as he had before? She breathed slowly, as if by doing so she could hear his approach. Then she sighed. Maybe she was reading more into this than was there. He had a right to observe her behavior. After all, he was her employer. Then why, she wondered, did every instinct she had tell her it was more than observation? Why did she feel as if he was waiting to pounce?

She shivered then stepped back, and without taking her eyes from the darkness, closed the door between them.

Royal stared at the house and the woman who stood in his doorway as he leaned against the hood of his truck. When he realized she was looking for him, the skin crawled on the back of his neck. The intimacy of such a search made him think of things better left alone. Half the time these days he didn't know whether he was coming or going.

The other day he'd gone to town to get horse feed and came home with everything but. He made appointments and then forgot to keep them. Even worse, he was getting short-tempered with Maddie for no reason at all. She was just a little girl. She shouldn't have to suffer for whatever was going on in her daddy's head.

As he watched, Angel moved. He took a deep breath, holding it as she took a step back—exhaling as she closed the door between them. The tenuous tie between them was broken. He shuddered. There was a hunger within him that was growing more and more difficult to control.

At the oddest times, her image would move through his mind and he'd catch himself thinking of the way her body swayed as she walked, of the way she chewed on her lower lip when she was thinking, of how her right eyebrow arched when she was about to let her temper fly.

He grinned. Damn, but she did have a temper. He was still trying to get over the slander of "royal highness" and had nightmares about Habenero peppers in his toothpaste. He ran his tongue over his lower lip. It was well now, but it had peeled, just as he'd predicted.

He'd learned a lesson that day. He still wasn't sure what kind of a friend Angel Rojas might be, but he could vouch firsthand as to how fierce an enemy she would make.

In a way, that was where their bond was strongest. He lived his life without following rules, railing against fate when it suited him and defying propriety to get something done his way. He respected independence. He admired passion. And from where he was standing, Maddie's angel had more than her share.

A faint rumble sounded in the distance. He looked at the sky, noting the absence of moon and stars. Clouds were gathering. Against the horizon, a single streak of lightning split the sky, like a fragile thread of silver. But it was soundless, too far away for worry. Chances were the rain would miss them.

He glanced at his watch. The luminous dial was a vivid reminder that morning always came far too soon. With a sigh, he pushed off from the truck and started toward the house. By now the story had surely been read. Maddie would be asleep. She always fell asleep in the middle of her bedtime story. And if he was smart, when he got inside the house, he'd go straight to his room and stay there. No more playing around with an angel's fire. Someone could get burned.

* * *

Amarillo wasn't all it was cracked up to be, at least not to Tommy Boy. It had been raining nonstop for the better part of two days. He'd been forced to stay holed up in this piss-poor room, waiting for the weather to clear. Yesterday he'd called his bank to check the balance in his checking account. It was getting low. Either he called a halt to his quest or he started working part-time jobs. He frowned as he considered his options. The promise he'd made to himself was getting out of hand. When he'd started this quest, the need to cleanse had burned within him. But with each woman who died, a little part of his anger died, too.

Nine women later, there was always the worry that the authorities might somehow connect the deaths. If that happened, his anonymity would be severely threatened. If the national media got wind of a serial killer, it would be over. He couldn't afford to let the FBI get involved. And yet there was a part of him that reveled in challenging the system, of getting away with the deeds. And the women who died had deserved it.

He'd traveled the same routes his daddy had taken. Unknowingly, he might have already taken out the woman who'd infected him. The possibility was remote, but it was there. He liked to think it had already happened.

He aimed the remote at the television set and clicked until he found a station broadcasting weather, then frowned. The northwestern part of the state was under a weather alert. There was a line of thunderstorms running from west of Amarillo all the way past the Fort Worth Dallas area and as far south as Austin. He cursed beneath his breath and aimed the remote, silencing the box. As long as this weather pattern held, the women in the business of selling sex would be somewhere else rather than the open lots of truck stops.

Since that was the case, he might as well make the best of it. Consider this a mini vacation. Bunching a pillow beneath his head, he rolled over and closed his eyes. The steady rhythm of raindrops splattering against the window soon lulled him to sleep.

* * *

Angel fought her covers as she dreamed her way toward morning. Lost in a nightmare in which Fat Louie played the lead role, she struggled to find her way out. One pillow was bunched beneath her cheek. The other had fallen to the floor. The lightweight blanket that had been covering her feet had slipped between the mattress and the footboard of her bed, and the sheet was wrapped around her legs. Sweat plastered her nightshirt to her body. The knit fabric clung to every curve, and her hair, still in a braid, had bunched at the back of her neck. In her mind, the sensations had translated themselves into Fat Louie's breath and Fat Louie's hands. She was fighting him now as she had fought him then. Closer and closer he came, pushing her into a corner, grabbing at her breasts and her backside. She doubled her fists to fight back—just as the light came on in her room.

"Get up!" Royal said quickly. "We've got to get to the cellar. I'm going to get Maddie. Meet me in the hall."

Angel was still trying to assimilate the fact that she was in this house and in this bed instead of stuck between Fat Louie and the wall of the restaurant kitchen when Royal disappeared.

"Wait!" she mumbled as she crawled out of bed, but he was already gone.

It was reflex that made her grab some clothes. What was it he'd said? Something about the cellar?

Then she heard it, the ominous howl of wind that comes with nature out of control.

Tornado.

It had been years since she'd heard the sound, and she'd been nineteen and living in Kentucky. That night a whole town had been destroyed, and eleven lives along with it. Now she had a real fear to face, not one of her dreams. Without hesitation, she began pulling on shorts and a T-shirt and looking for her shoes. Before she could find them, the power went out, plunging the house into darkness.

She turned. Guided by a slice of lightning that flashed outside her window, she headed for the hallway as Royal had told her to do. Her heart was pounding, her legs shaking as she called out.

"Royal!"

Suddenly he was there, coming toward her with a blanket-wrapped bundle in his arms.

"Here," he said, thrusting a flashlight into her hands. "Take this and lead the way."

Angel grabbed it and switched it on. She aimed the feeble beam of light ahead of them, mentally tracing the path they would take down the hall, into the kitchen and then to the cellar off the back porch.

She wished she'd been able to find her shoes, but it was too late to worry about that. Royal was at her heels. She could hear the rapid sounds of his breathing and Maddie's terrified sobs as they ran through the darkened house. The wind was louder, the howl a deep and eerie wail, like the sound of a runaway train.

She looked back once and almost stumbled.

"Hurry," he said.

He didn't have to say more.

Then they were at the back door and on the porch. Angel aimed the flashlight into the downpour and gasped as the wind blew the rain in her face. Royal was at her back, giving orders that she followed without thought.

"Trade," he said quickly, and shifted his daughter into Angel's arms before yanking the flashlight out of her hands.

Angel clutched Maddie with tender strength, sheltering her as much as she could as they dashed into the storm. Royal took her by the arm and dragged her toward the cellar, and she knew that, but for him, she would not have been able to stand. Another flash of lightning tore through the night, followed by a blast of thunder so loud it shook Angel's bones. Maddie started to scream. Angel wanted to join her. Instead, she stood with Royal, praying as he struggled to open the cellar door against the force of the wind.

Then it was open and he turned, bracing himself and shouting something to her that the storm took away. But she didn't need him to tell her what came next. Clutching Maddie, she ran down the steps and into another kind of darkness—one so thick that it felt devoid of any air. Before she had time to panic, Royal was behind her. The door slammed, and the sudden light from his flashlight was like the supernova of a star. She blinked and turned away, letting her eyes adjust to new surroundings.

Water dripped from the hem of her T-shirt onto her feet. A new fear arose as she remembered she was barefoot. Cellars were notorious for harboring scorpions and snakes. If they were here, she didn't want to know it.

Maddie fought against the covers over her head. Angel helped her emerge, then laid her cheek against the top of the little girl's head, rocking her in her arms as if she'd been a tiny baby.

"Ssh, ssh, baby, it's all right. It's all right," Angel crooned. "We're all together and we're safe. That's all that matters."

Adrenaline was starting to wane, and the muscles in Royal's arms were beginning to shake. There'd been a minute when he hadn't been sure he could get the door open. His fingers were trembling as he swiped them across his face to clear his vision. All he could think was thank God Angel had been here. He would never have been able to open the door with Maddie in his arms.

He looked at them, woman and child standing in the dim glow, and reacted without thinking. He moved. Seconds later he had them both in his embrace.

Surprised by the action, Angel flinched. But the feeling was so welcome. So right. They'd battled nature and won. They were protected from whatever was happening above them.

Maddie was still sobbing, but quieter. Angel ventured a look at Royal and knew she'd made a mistake. She was pinned by a smoky stare. Her mouth parted, but the words died on her lips.

Royal shivered. "Are you all right?"

"Thanks to you," Angel said, and looked away.

Royal cupped the back of his daughter's head. "Baby?"

Without looking up, Maddie held out her hands. Royal lifted her from Angel's arms and held her close against his bare chest.

"What's happening?" Maddie sobbed.

"It's a storm, sweetheart. But like Angel said, we're safe, and that's all that matters."

"What about Flea Bit and Marbles and Dumpling? What will happen to them?"

"They're probably safe and dry in the hay barn," he told her. "Remember, that's their favorite place."

Satisfied, Maddie quieted. The silence within the cellar lengthened as the storm continued to gather in strength.

Angel felt restless. She had questions, but unfortunately Royal Justice couldn't answer them as easily as he'd answered his daughter's. She kept thinking about the way it had felt to stand in his arms. His strength was evident, his compassion obvious, but something else had happened that she hadn't expected. Something she hadn't felt in so many, many years. Safe. She'd felt safe.

Needing to take her mind off of everything, including Royal's bare chest, she took stock of her surroundings. There were shelves directly before her with a couple of dozen empty fruit jars shoved to the back. There was a small jar of matches and a couple of empty lanterns on a lower shelf, which would do them no good. Three folding chairs leaned against the wall, and the concrete floor, while rough and damp against her bare feet, was clean—and as far as she could see, critter safe.

Before she had time to explore any further, the cellar door suddenly rattled on its hinges. Frightened, she spun around, looking to Royal for reassurance. She could tell he was battling some fears of his own.

"It's bad, isn't it?" she whispered.

He glanced at Maddie, who'd fallen back to sleep in his arms, then nodded.

She thought of the ranch and of his home. Of the barns and sheds and the miles and miles of fence. Of the animals, exposed to the elements. The loss could be devastating.

"I'm sorry."

"None of this is your fault."

"I know. That's not what I meant. I'm just sorry this is happening."

He nodded. "So am I."

Another blast of wind came, and to their horror, the heavy door began to lift. The sound of the storm was once again upon them. Wind funneled into the opening.

Angel screamed as the flashlight slid off the shelf.

Royal thrust Maddie into her arms and leaped forward, catching the door before it opened all the way.

"Get back!" he shouted, pointing to the farthest corner of the cellar. "Get back and get down."

Angel plastered herself into the corner and pressed Maddie's face against her shoulder to protect her from flying debris. She turned her face to the wall and began to pray.

Later she would remember momentary flashes of Royal straining to hold the door against the brunt of the storm. The pain of exertion contorting his features as his body threatened to give way. Of the wind drowning out the sounds of their screams. And just when she thought he might disappear before her eyes, that sudden and awful silence.

Royal dropped into the cellar as the door came shut with a thud. He sprawled on the steps. It was all he could do to stand.

"Oh, God," he muttered, and bent forward, clutching his knees and praying for strength.

For once, Maddie was too traumatized to speak. Her little blue eyes were wide with shock, her lips trembling as she clung to Angel's arms. She whimpered once and then was silent as Angel began to rock.

"Thank the Lord," Angel whispered.

Royal straightened and turned, fixing her with a weary stare.

"Keep Him on hold," he said. "It's not over."

Angel's eyes widened as a new fear began to spread. "But the wind...the sounds..."

"It's the eye."

Angel groaned. He was right! Already she could hear the wind beginning to pick up force. She looked at Royal, expecting to see defeat.

But she'd read him wrong. He wasn't defeated. He was mad. He grabbed the flashlight from the floor and began sweeping the darkened corners, searching for something, anything that might help. As the wind turned into another long wail, he spied a rusting crowbar on the lowest shelf. In a frantic lunge, he thrust it through the iron handle on the underside of the door, then jammed it into the groove between the door facing and the wall of the cellar.

Like Excalibur, it seemed to have pierced the stone, but it was enough of a wedge to give Royal added strength. It was an extra pair of hands. He held on to the crowbar and rode out the storm.

Maddie was silent, hardly moving, never taking her eyes from her father. Angel felt the child's tension, but there was nothing she could do except hold her close. Minutes passed. They felt like hours. Then finally the storm began to lessen. Angel didn't have to ask. She could see the answer on Royal's face. It was passing.

A few minutes later Royal let go of the crowbar and sat on the cellar steps, folded his arms across his knees and lowered his head. Angel could see the muscles shaking in his arms. Each breath he took seemed to come from deep, deep inside him, as if he had to search for its source and then draw reserve strength to claim it. Maddie wiggled to be put down, and Angel turned her loose, then watched as she walked to Royal's side and began to stroke his head as she did her kittens.

"Daddy...Daddy..."

Royal lifted his head. "What, baby?"

"Is it over?" Maddie asked.

He nodded, cupped her cheek and smiled wearily. "Yes, baby, it's over."

She leaned forward, as if what she had to say was a secret. "I want to go back to the house now."

Royal sighed, wondering if there was a house to go back to.

"I think you and Angel need to stay here for a minute while I go check on things, okay?"

It wasn't what she wanted to hear, but she nodded.

Royal started up the steps when Angel stopped him.

"Wait," she said, and handed him the flashlight, which he'd put on the shelf. "There will be damage. You need to see where you're going."

He frowned. "But that'll leave you two here in the dark, and Maddie's afraid of the dark."

Angel picked Maddie up. "So am I," she said softly. "But we don't want Daddy to get hurt, do we, baby?"

Maddie hesitated, and then shook her head.

Royal touched Maddie's cheek with the back of his hand, then he cupped Angel's shoulder. The look that passed between them was quick, but what Angel saw gave her strength. She nodded.

"I won't be long," Royal said.

Moments later, they were alone in the dark.

Chapter 10

Royal came out of the cellar braced for the worst. Although a steady rain continued to fall, the absence of wind seemed surreal. And it was dark. So dark. No security light. No intermittent flashes of lightning—just a curtain of water between him and what was left of his world.

Holding his breath, he lifted the flashlight, aiming the beam of light over the ground, then staring at broken branches, an uprooted tree, part of the pump house roof.

My God.

He clenched his jaw and aimed the beam toward the house, past the spiderlike roots of the upturned tree, past the roofless pump house. But it was raining hard, and the beam of light was too weak to pierce the darkness. He took a step forward, then thought of Angel and Maddie alone in the cellar. The idea of leaving them was repugnant, but he had no option. He stopped and turned, aiming the flashlight toward the cellar.

"You two okay?" he yelled.

Their voices echoed faintly in unison. "Yes."

"I'll be back soon."

Their answer was lost in the rain. Squinting against the downpour, he started toward the house, stepping around boards, over buckets, dodging whatever was in his path. He kept thinking of the generations of families who'd lived in the house before him, of the laughter and tears that had been shared behind those walls. Was it gone? Had it been damaged beyond repair?

He hadn't realized he'd been holding his breath until the beam of light caught and held on a corner of the house. He stopped, using the light to trace the angles of roof and walls. To his overwhelming relief, it was still standing.

"Thank you, God," he said softly, and moved up the steps into the house.

The first thing he stepped in was water. Expecting to see holes in the roof, he aimed the flashlight up. The ceiling seemed fine. He looked toward the porch and remembered running out of the house with Maddie in his arms.

The door! He hadn't closed the door behind him. The water had blown in with the storm. He aimed the flashlight to his left and started walking.

The living room had not fared well. A limb had blown off a tree and was half in and half out of the picture window. Sodden drapes hung askew, and the furniture near the window was soaked. The carpet squished as he walked across it, but it didn't matter. Things could be replaced.

He moved down the hallway, checking ceilings and floors, and entered Maddie's room. The window was broken, and the covers on her bed, as well as the floor around it, were covered in glass. He shuddered, then quickly moved away.

The door to Angel's room was standing open. Torn curtains and broken glass marked the beginning of the storm's entry there, as well. It was as if a madman had gone through the room, tossing things awry. Pictures had fallen off the walls. Lamps were on the floor. He aimed the flashlight to the ceiling, to the spreading water stain above Angel's bed.

He backed out and aimed the beam of light down the hall. One more bedroom to go. His.

Expecting more of the same, he was stunned when he pushed the door open. Everything was as intact as it had been when he'd left it, even the covers he'd tossed aside as he'd bolted out of bed. He whistled beneath his breath and shook his head. It didn't make sense, but he was glad to know there was one dry place they could spend the rest of the night.

The sound of glass breaking sent him across the hall. He shone the light. The big limb poking through Angel's window was closer to the floor. Everything was settling, including the weather.

He leaned against the doorjamb and sighed. Water was running out of his hair and into his eyes. Shivering from the cold, he swiped a weary hand across his face. There was plenty of damage, but nothing that couldn't be fixed. He shifted the flashlight to his other hand and started out of the house. It was time to bring his family home.

It didn't dawn on him until he started down the cellar steps that he had thought of Angel as part of his family. The ramifications of that simple acceptance didn't hit him until he shined the light in her face.

There in the dark, in the depths of the cellar, she sat—with his sleeping child in her lap and an expression on her face that stopped him cold. It was something he would have sworn he'd never see. But it was there just the same.

Trust. By God, she trusted him.

There had been times over the past few weeks when he'd pushed her too far, and he knew it. There were times she'd taken his guff without comment, but there were other times she'd given it back to him in spades. There had been times when he'd felt her fear, both of him and of the uncertainties in her life. He had not known how to make it better, and so they had kept their mental distances.

But tonight she'd done all he'd asked of her and then some. Because she had followed his lead so quickly, they'd gotten out of the house alive. He knew, as well as he knew his own name, that he could never have held Maddie and lifted the cellar door against the storm. And he could not have put Maddie down to do it, because the wind would have blown her away.

Royal's gaze blurred as he stared at his daughter's sleeping face. He couldn't begin to understand Maddie's dreams about a lady on her bed and the promise of angels, but by God, his doubts were over. Tonight Angel Rojas had lived up to her name. She'd been afraid of the storm and afraid of the dark, and yet she'd stifled her fears in order to protect his daughter, trusting him to take care of them both. Humbled by her faith, he shifted the light so it was out of her eyes. He started down the steps.

Angel knew her lips were trembling, but her composure had not shattered. All the while she'd been sitting in the dark, she'd been thinking of the path that had led her to this place. Only a few weeks ago she hadn't known these people existed, and now they were the most important people in her life. She thought of the storm that had raged over their heads and of the home they had abandoned. She saw the beam of Royal's flashlight as he started down the steps. He was back, and she was afraid to ask if there was anything left.

"Royal?"

"It's still there," he said.

"Thank God," Angel whispered, and then looked down as Maddie suddenly whimpered in her sleep. "Poor little girl," she said softly. "She's had a very rough night."

"We all have," Royal said and bent to lift her from Angel's arms as Angel looked up.

In the act of scooping Maddie and her covers, the backs of his hands slid the length of Angel's thighs. He clenched his jaw and closed his eyes. Her skin was warm and soft...so soft. Then he looked up. Their gazes met and held.

Even though the rain was still pouring down, he heard the rhythm of her breathing shift to an uneven gasp. He was close, too close to that sensuous mouth. All he would have to do was lean forward and he would know how she tasted. And then Maddie cried out in her sleep. He jerked and stood up, and the moment was gone.

An awkward silence ensued. It was all Angel could do to look at him, and Royal was at a loss as to what to say. It was the cold sifting into the cellar that prompted his return to sanity.

"Here," he said shortly, handing Angel the flashlight and then pointing to his sleeping daughter. "Trade me."

Angel stood. Once again the transfer was made. The moment Maddie was taken from her arms she felt weightless, as if the anchor holding her to earth had suddenly disappeared.

"Is it okay to leave?" Angel asked.

"Yes, and when we get out of the cellar, be careful where you walk. There's quite a bit of debris."

Angel nodded and thought of her shoes once more. Then she started up the steps, pausing at the top and aiming the beam of the flashlight into the cellar to light Royal's way.

The downpour had lessened to a drizzle. The thunder and lightning were moving away. As she waited for Royal to ascend, she shivered. She was wet and cold and about as tired as she'd ever been in her life.

"Do you want me to close the cellar door?" she asked as Royal cleared the top step with Maddie in his arms.

"Can you?" he asked. "It's pretty heavy."

"I'll try."

She laid the flashlight down, aiming it toward the opening. A few seconds later, the door fell shut with a thud.

Once again, Royal's estimation of this woman had to shift to make way for another fact. Angel Rojas was physically stronger than she looked. She stepped backward to pick up the flashlight, and he saw her legs, then her feet.

"My God, woman, you're barefoot! What were you thinking?"

The abruptness of his shout startled her, and she stumbled. Burdened with Maddie's sleeping body, he had to watch her struggling to catch her balance.

"Be careful!" he cried. "There's all kinds of debris out here. You could cut your feet to shreds."

She picked up the flashlight and turned, aiming it to the

right of his face, pinning him in the beam. The sarcasm in her voice was impossible to miss.

''I know that,'' she said, enunciating each syllable slowly and precisely. ''I'm not stupid.''

''Then why—''

''I couldn't find them. So I decided I'd rather be alive and barefoot than well-dressed and dead. Now for Pete's sake…and Maddie's…will you be quiet? You're going to wake her up.''

Without waiting for his permission, Angel waved the flashlight at him, indicating he was to follow, and took off across the yard.

Even in the dark, even in the rain, Royal felt the heat rising on his face as he followed her. All he could see was her silhouette, but it was enough to know she was ticked off. Maddie whimpered again, and his focus shifted to getting them all inside the house, into dry clothes and into bed.

''You might want to wait here,'' he said as they stepped on the porch.

''Why?'' she asked.

''Because there's broken glass all over the place. Give me the flashlight. I'll put Maddie in bed and then I'll come back for you.''

''But I…''

Before she could argue, he disappeared. All she could see was a faint trail of light and then nothing. Struggling against the urge to throw something, she folded her arms across her chest and slumped against the doorjamb. There were times when that man's attitude got on her last nerve, and this was one of them. She stared into the kitchen, peering through the darkness and telling herself she didn't see anything broken. Testing the theory of possible exaggeration, she took a tentative step into the kitchen and felt nothing but floor beneath her feet.

''Humpf,'' she snorted, and tried another step.

It took a second for the cold water to register, and when it did, she gasped and bolted outside. Her heart was pounding and she had the makings of a headache when she finally got her bearings. She hated to admit it, but it would seem that he'd been right. So she would wait. No big deal.

When she heard him coming, she braced herself for another confrontation. It never came. Before she knew what was happening, he handed her the flashlight and scooped her off her feet.

"I couldn't find your shoes, either," he said. "So don't wiggle. I'm too tired to argue."

Angel looked at him. At the hard angles of his face and the glitter in his eyes. She remembered how fiercely he had fought the storm to keep the cellar door shut and them from being sucked out into the storm.

"I'm sorry you have to do this," she said quietly.

As soon as she spoke, the tension on his face disappeared. He sighed. "And I'm sorry I snapped at you. I wasn't mad, just worried."

"I know. I shouldn't have been so defensive," she said. "I've depended upon myself for so long that I've forgotten how to accept help."

Royal nodded and kicked the door shut behind them after they entered the house.

"Aim the light straight ahead," he said. "And don't worry about what you see. There's nothing that can't be fixed."

She did as he said, absorbing the chaos of the house in the bits and pieces the light revealed. Although it was still standing, there was enough obvious damage for her to realize how dangerous it would have been had they stayed inside. She knew that most people killed in tornadoes were killed by flying debris, rather than by the twister itself.

"Oh, Royal," she said softly, and went limp in his arms.

He felt her shock. "Don't worry about it," he said quietly. "All that matters is that we're safe."

She nodded, but the images stayed with her. He passed her bedroom.

"Wait," she said. "You missed my room."

"You can't sleep in there," he said shortly. "The windows

are broken. There's glass and water all over the place, and it's the same in Maddie's room. But we got lucky. Somehow my room escaped being damaged. We'll be able to spend the rest of the night in there.''

Lucky? She was going to sleep in his room and this was lucky? Crazy was more like it.

''All of us?'' she asked.

He set her down just inside the doorway.

''All of us. Right there in my bed, with you on one side of my daughter and me on the other. And before you balk on me, consider the situation. It's after three in the morning. If you're as tired as I am, you won't care who the hell you're in bed with as long as they leave you alone.''

Angel bit her lip. A thousand questions were begging to get out, and she didn't have the guts to voice a one.

Royal leaned forward, pinning her with a cool stare.

''Do we have a problem?''

She glared at him. ''No.''

''Is there something you want to tell me?'' he asked.

She clenched her jaw. ''Like what?''

''Do you snore?''

''No!''

''Then we have nothing further to discuss.'' He thrust the flashlight in her hand. ''We need to get dry. I've already changed Maddie's clothes. My clean T-shirts are in the bottom drawer. Get one on and then get in bed. I won't be more than a couple of minutes behind you.''

''Uh, um—''

''On a practical note,'' Royal added, ''if you need to use the bathroom, don't flush. The power's off, and that means the tank won't refill.''

''Right,'' Angel said, and was thankful for the darkness because her face was flaming.

Having said all he needed to say, Royal stood, waiting for her reaction. When she neither moved nor spoke, he sighed in weary defeat.

''Woman, what the hell are you waiting for?''

She was as tired as Royal and probably twice as cold. Her feet felt as if they'd never be warm again. But she would have died before giving him a reason to complain.

"I guess nothing," she said shortly, and then turned her back to him and started pulling her wet T-shirt over her head.

"Oh, yeah, right," Royal muttered. "I was just leaving." He bolted out the door.

Long after they were both in bed, with Maddie sound asleep between them and the sound of rain falling softly on the rooftop, Royal lay without moving, staring through the darkness to the place where Angel slept. Even though the circumstances were extraordinary that had led to this event, he couldn't quit thinking that he'd never slept with another woman in his life except Susan. He'd had plenty of what he liked to call "encounters," but to lie down and sleep with someone was invoking a trust he held dear.

After a while, the uniqueness of the situation became less and less important. He closed his eyes. When he opened them again, it was morning.

Somewhere between a dead sleep and light slumber, Royal heard someone calling his name. He groaned and shoved his nose into the pillow. All he could think was that he ached all over and hoped he wasn't getting sick.

Then he heard it again and rolled over on his back. Whoever it was was persistent, he would give them that. He yawned and stretched, and as he did, felt the shape of little feet digging into his side. He frowned. Maddie? Why was Maddie sleeping in his bed? And then he remembered.

The storm.

He sat straight up in bed.

The door flew open. Roman's wife, Holly, burst in. Her short dark hair was loose and flying, her eyes filled with fear. When she saw them, the look on her face was somewhere between shock and relief. She turned in the doorway and shouted down the hall.

"Roman! In here! They're in here!"

At the noise, Angel woke with a start, and like Royal sat straight up in bed.

"What's happening? Is it storming again?" she asked, and started to reach for Maddie.

"No," Royal groaned. "It's my brother."

"Good Lord." Angel sighed and fell back to the bed with a thump, her hand plastered over her chest in dramatic fashion. "That probably shortened my life by a good year."

Royal grimaced. He knew just how she felt. But he should have known that Roman would come. The Justices had a way of looking out for each other. He was crawling out of bed as Roman ran into the room.

Roman's face was pale and his voice was shaking as he gave Royal a fierce hug.

"We heard about the storms when we woke this morning. Four people died and more than a dozen houses were destroyed. It's all over the news." He glanced over Royal's shoulder to the bed, and his eyes widened perceptibly.

Royal lifted a sleepy Maddie into his arms as she began to come to. "We're fine," he said. "Luckily this room escaped damage. The other rooms were uninhabitable."

Roman nodded. "We noticed," he said softly. "When I topped the rise leading to the house, I was afraid to get out of the car. And when you weren't in the cellar and you didn't come out when we called, we started to worry."

Holly leaned against Roman and sighed. "Actually, it scared us silly. I was afraid to look and afraid not to," she said, and started to cry.

Maddie frowned. "Don't cry, Aunt Holly. I don't like it when you cry."

Holly lifted Maddie out of Royal's arms and hugged her tight. "You've got quite a cleanup job ahead of you. Let us take Maddie. At least you won't have to worry about her getting hurt during the repairs."

Maddie's lower lip slid forward. "I want to go home with Uncle Roman and Aunt Holly. This house scares me."

Royal didn't bother to hide his relief. He glanced at Angel.

"It *would* make things easier for us."

Angel wished she could disappear. Nothing in her past had prepared her for the embarrassment of lying in her boss's bed, in full view of his family, while a disaster cleanup was being discussed.

"Is there anything you need?" Roman asked.

Royal nodded. "Yes, call the electric company and the phone company for me. I left my cell phone on the table last night. Needless to say, the tree limb and the rain didn't do it any good."

Roman whipped out his cell phone and handed it to his brother. "Use this one until you get yours back on. You'll need to make all kinds of calls. And as soon as I get Holly and Maddie into Dallas, I'll come and help."

"Bring breakfast when you come," Royal said.

Roman grinned. "Done."

"I want breakfast, too," Maddie said.

Holly grinned. "We'll stop at McDonald's, okay?"

"Yeah!" Maddie shrieked. "Beanie Babies."

Royal frowned. "I thought you were hungry."

In total female fashion, Maddie ignored the absurdity of her father's remark. Everyone knew that toys came with food at McDonald's.

Holly looked at Angel, feeling sympathy for the predicament she was in. "Are you all right?" she asked.

Angel nodded and ventured a look at Royal. "Thanks to him, we're all okay."

A little embarrassed, Royal shrugged off the compliment. "I'm glad I woke up in time. Just let me get my boots on and I'll get Maddie some clothes."

"Let me," Holly said. "I know where most of her clothes are kept."

"I'll show you!" Maddie said.

"No, baby. You can't go in your room until we get it all cleaned up," Royal said.

Maddie frowned. "I didn't mess it up, Daddy, honest I didn't."

Royal grinned. "I know that. Now let's get you to the bathroom and your hair brushed. As soon as Angel and I fix the house, Uncle Roman and Aunt Holly will bring you home, okay?"

Maddie shrugged. "Am I staying all night with them, too?" she asked.

Roman tweaked his niece's nose. "Yes, Little Bit, you're staying all night. Now quit worrying and do what your daddy says."

Royal and Maddie disappeared into the adjoining bathroom, and Holly went to Maddie's room to search for clothes. Angel was trapped beneath the covers and Roman's all-seeing gaze.

"Rough night?" he asked.

Angel glared. "I've had better." Then she added, "Maddie has some chigger bites on her leg."

Roman nodded. "We'll see to them."

"Don't forget to take her chewable vitamins. They're in the kitchen on the shelf to the right of the sink."

Roman nodded again, but his estimation of this woman had just gone up five notches. In spite of everything that had happened, her worries seemed focused on Maddie.

"Got some at the house," he said softly.

Angel sighed and looked away. "I just…"

"Don't apologize to me," Roman said. "I'm with you. Along with Holly, Maddie is one of the most important females in my life."

Angel almost smiled. "Well, then," she said softly, fidgeting with the covers and wishing someone would hurry up and come back. To her relief, Royal and Maddie emerged from the bathroom.

The silence in the room was impossible for Royal to mistake. He stared at the blush on Angel's face and gave Roman a hard-edged glare.

"Roman?"

Roman met the glare with a cool, unaffected stare. "Yeah?"

"Are you messing in my business again?"

Roman winked at Angel and grinned. "Nope."

Angel slid a little deeper beneath the covers and wished herself invisible.

"Surely there are more important things to dwell on this morning than this," she snapped.

Both men jerked as if they'd been slapped. Before they could respond, Holly was back with Maddie's clothes. A few minutes later they were gone, and Angel was left with the growing feeling that she'd just lost her safety net.

Wearing a pair of Royal's boots, she picked her way through what was left of her bedroom to find some clothes of her own. In the process, she stumbled. When she looked down, she saw the toe of her shoe sticking out from beneath the dust ruffle on her bed.

"Finally," she muttered, and gathered the shoes up with the rest of her things.

Dressed and shod, she began searching for Royal. She found him standing on the porch. She paused in the doorway behind him, absorbing his stillness. He stood with his feet apart, his shoulders back, as if bracing himself for a blow. She smiled. Just as she might have expected. The storm had passed, but if need be, Royal Justice was still ready to go to war.

Chapter 11

"What do we do first?" Angel asked.

Startled by the sound of her voice, Royal spun around. Separated by a yard of space and the screen on the door, he still felt as if she'd invaded his skin.

Do first?

He wondered what she'd say if he told her the truth of what he was thinking. With her, he didn't know where to start...or even if he should.

Angel pushed the door open and walked outside. His silence was unnerving, as was the look in his eyes.

"Royal? Is something wrong? Did the storm—"

"No," he said, and looked away. "My mind was somewhere else."

That she could understand. There was debris as far as she could see. One of the small outbuildings had completely disappeared, and others were missing roofs. There was a section of rafters lying across part of the main corral fence. The large tree at the edge of the yard was missing several large limbs, one of which had gone through her bedroom window. It was such a mess, and Royal seemed so solemn, her compassion overruled her head. She walked to where he was standing and took his hand.

"It will be all right," she said softly. "We'll have this place back to normal before you know it."

Breath caught in the back of Royal's throat as the scene before him suddenly blurred. He didn't look at her and couldn't bring himself to acknowledge her presence. Her tenderness was his undoing.

We? She said we?

He gave her a quick glance, nodded and looked away. The task of putting everything back to rights didn't seem as insurmountable as it had moments earlier.

"What do you want me to do first?"

Royal turned, and the urge to take her in his arms made him weak. He managed a grin.

"Hell, honey, even *I* don't know what to do first."

"Then we need to make a list," Angel said. "Wait here. I'll be right back."

She went into the house and came out with a pad of paper and a pen.

"Let's start with a tour," she suggested. "When you see something that needs to be fixed or replaced, I'll write it down. Then we'll go from there."

She looked up, waiting for his approval. "If that's okay with you," she added.

Royal hugged her. He knew it could be a mistake, but he didn't give a good damn. He'd made plenty of mistakes in his life, and if holding her this close was going to be another, then so be it.

Angel was taken unaware, but before she could think what to do, he'd let her go and turned away. She stood in silence while her heart hammered wildly against her chest, then watched as he bent to lift a small piece of corrugated tin from the flower bed and toss it over the fence.

"Machine shop roof," he said shortly, and turned to see if she was following. "Angel."

She blinked as if coming out of a trance, then managed to answer.

"What?"

"Machine shop roof. Write it down."

"Oh...yes," she said, and so the morning began.

By noon, the rural electric company had restored power and the phones were working. An insurance adjuster had come and gone, giving Royal leave to commence repairs. One of Royal's friends was a roofer, and he'd come within an hour of Royal's call. They were both on the roof assessing the damage to the house while Angel waited below. The inconsistent murmur of voices could be heard inside the house, and she knew Roman was on the phone talking to a contractor regarding other repairs. As she stood at the foot of the ladder, she heard a car coming down the drive. She turned to look.

It was a black pickup.

And just for a minute, her heart stopped. She was halfway up the ladder and heading for Royal before it dawned on her what she was doing. She stopped in midstep, took a slow, deep breath and made herself go back the way she'd come. By the time she reached the ground, the pickup was parked. The man who got out wasn't wearing a beard, nor was he short and skinny.

Well over the age of seventy, he rolled when he walked and was so bald that the sun reflected off of his head when he took off his hat. He gave her a wink and a grin, then glanced at the roof where Royal and the insurance adjuster were standing.

"Been up there long?" he asked.

"A while," Angel said.

"Then they oughta be just about through."

"Yes, sir."

He smiled and offered his hand. "Name's Waycoff, Dan Waycoff. I guess you'd be Royal's new housekeeper."

Angel nodded as her fingers were engulfed by a large, callused palm.

"I neighbor the Justice ranch to the west. Real pleased to

meet you," Waycoff said. "Been tellin' the missus that little Maddie is gettin' to be a handful for one man to handle alone, what with her startin' to school and all this fall."

"Yes, sir," Angel said.

"Hope you'll be happy here," Waycoff said. "Royal's a good man. Ain't many like him left in this world."

"That's true," she said, and looked up. To her relief, the men were coming down.

She held the ladder until they were clear, then started to make herself scarce. Royal stopped her with a look.

He was weary. She could see it in his eyes. And there was a smudge of dirt along the edge of his chin that she wanted to wipe away. Instead, she stood, waiting for him to make the first move.

Royal sighed, wishing he could call back that moment this morning when she'd taken him by the hand. He could still remember the softness of her skin and how firm her grip was. In a way, it was indicative of the woman herself. At first glance she seemed small and helpless, but he'd seen firsthand the strength, both mental and physical, that she continued to exhibit.

"Are you hungry?" he asked.

She started to lie, then knew it would serve no purpose. "Yes."

To her surprise, he grinned and tugged at her braid. "Then what are you waiting for?" He pointed at Dan Waycoff. "As soon as I get rid of this squatter, we're going to town to eat lunch."

Waycoff laughed. "You mean I'm not invited?" he teased.

Royal grinned. "Not unless you've taken a vow of fasting."

All the men, including Waycoff, laughed.

Angel smiled. She supposed it was a joke between old friends. Then she remembered that the man who was coming to replace the glass in the windows had yet to arrive.

"But what about the glass man," she said. "Shouldn't I stay and…"

Royal frowned. "Hell, no. I've already talked to him at length. The place is a mess. I told him to fix it. If he can't find the stuff that's broken on his own, then he doesn't need to be here. Now go do whatever you need to do, and tell Roman to finish what he's doing if he wants to come, too. We're leaving in five minutes."

"Yes, sir," she said, and started up the porch steps.

Royal frowned. She'd done it again.

"I thought I told you to quit calling me sir."

Angel turned. Her voice was steady, but there was an edge to it he didn't miss.

"When you quit giving me orders, I'll quit calling you sir."

Then she went inside, leaving him standing in the yard to make what he chose of her answer. He was muttering beneath his breath when he suddenly remembered he wasn't alone. He rolled his eyes and turned around. Both men were grinning.

"Quite a little lady you got there," Waycoff said.

Royal snorted. "She's something, all right, but I'm not sure *lady* is the right word. She doesn't pull punches, and the hell of it is, most of the time she's right."

Waycoff slapped Royal on the back. "Then you better be watching your backside, boy, 'cause that there's the kind of woman you don't want to play loose with."

Royal glared. "I'm not playing anything with her, including loose, and I'd better not hear anything to the different," he warned.

Both men looked suitably chastised and got to the business at hand. The roofer left with a promise to be back early tomorrow, and Waycoff left a couple of minutes later, after having delivered the news that his wife was bringing them food for their supper.

As the last man drove away, Royal felt the burden of rebuilding had lightened a bit. Plans were in motion. Decisions were being made. And friends were coming through for him in every way.

The main street of Alvarado was busy. Royal circled the block twice before a parking space became available. He wheeled to the curb, parked and pocketed his keys as he helped Angel out of the cab. Roman got out on the passenger side, and together the trio entered the local café.

The noise level was just below a roar. To Angel, it seemed that the customers all knew each other and no matter where they were sitting kept a running conversation going between bites.

Royal spied a table being vacated and started across the room with Angel behind him and Roman bringing up the rear.

It didn't take long for Angel to be noticed. A stranger's face was always fodder for comment, and when she was keeping company with one of the area's most eligible bachelors it was worth remembering. Royal felt the stares and knew, when the laughter shifted to whispers, that it was probably about Angel. He stopped at the table and pulled out her chair. She hesitated, then quietly took her seat. Roman dropped into the chair opposite hers and reached for the menus propped between the napkin holder and a bottle of steak sauce. He handed one to Angel with a wink, opened his own and began to read.

Royal lowered himself into his seat, grunting as his muscles protested. Angel heard him and looked up.

"I think I have some aspirin in my purse."

Because it was second nature to deny anything regarding weakness, Royal started to argue. But she'd offered without malice or jest, and his macho was just about gone, thanks to last night's wind.

"Don't mind if I do," he said shortly, and held out his hand, watching as she shook three tablets into it. When the waitress brought glasses of water and left with their orders, he downed the aspirins in one gulp.

"Hey, Angel."

She looked up.

"Thanks."

"It was nothing," she said.

"You noticed," he argued. "That's something."

Roman eyed his brother, then Angel, then his brother again. "Have I become invisible?"

Neither answered him.

Roman grinned. "Now I know how a boar hog feels about tits," he drawled.

Angel frowned. Royal narrowed his eyes to a condemning stare.

"I don't get it," she said.

"Damn it, Roman," Royal muttered.

But Roman wasn't through having fun at his brother's expense. He and Ryder had endured enough bossing from Royal through the years to last several lifetimes, and seeing his brother tied up in knots over a woman was too good to let pass.

Roman leaned forward. "Tits on a boar hog—out of place and completely useless?"

Royal's face turned dark red. Angel could tell his well-frayed emotions were about to explode. The urge to protect him came out of nowhere, and she reached across the table to Roman, her fingers curling around his wrist. She was smiling, but her grip on his arm was not friendly.

"Royal is your brother. And since I have no siblings, I can't say I know what sibling rivalry is like. But I don't like being the butt of jokes between you two. Added to that, you don't know how close you came to losing him last night. But for the grace of God and Royal's refusal to quit on us, you could have been planning his funeral today, not helping him clean up. So I suggest you shut up." She picked up her purse. "Now if you'll both excuse me, I'm going to powder my nose. When I come back, I expect peace and quiet at this table. If I have to eat my meal alone to get it, then I will do so. Do I make myself clear?"

Suitably chastised, Roman managed to nod.

It was hard to say who was more shocked, Royal or Roman. They sat in total silence, watching as Angel made her way through the maze of tables to the rest rooms near the front door. Anger was evident in the force of her stride. For a minute, neither of them moved.

When she'd lit into Roman, Royal had been too surprised to speak. Now he felt as if he'd been sideswiped. His ears were ringing, and he wondered if his face was as red as it felt.

"Well, damn," he said softly, and looked at his hands because looking at his brother was impossible.

Roman took a deep breath and grinned. "You're done for," he said softly.

Royal focused immediately. He spit his words out in short, angry jerks.

"Roman, just for once, like she said, will you shut the hell up?"

Roman lifted his water glass, making an anonymous toast, and took a deep drink.

"What was that all about?" Royal muttered.

Roman's grin widened. "Just drinking to your health. Like the lady said, I'm damned glad I'm not planning your funeral."

Royal leaned forward, making sure their neighbors at the nearest table didn't overhear what he said.

"If you don't shut that smart mouth of yours, you'll be worrying about your own funeral, not mine."

Roman laughed and drained his glass. Their food—and Angel—arrived at the same time. They ate their meal in total silence.

Angel was still shaking when she laid down her fork. Her plate was empty, and she had no idea what she'd just eaten. Her head was spinning, and all she could think was, *What have I done?* It had taken all her willpower to come back to the table and face them. She'd made a fool of herself, but she knew in her heart she would do it again. In her entire life, she hadn't admired many men. But after last night, Royal topped that short list by far. He'd put himself at risk time and again for her and Maddie. The way she looked at it, she owed him a debt she could never repay. Speaking up on his behalf was little reward, but it was the best she could do.

The waitress laid their bill at the edge of the table. Royal was reaching to get it when Roman slipped it from beneath his fingers.

"This one's on me," he said. "I'll meet you at the truck."

Royal nodded his thanks as Roman got up and headed for the cashier. He took a deep breath and ventured a look at Angel. She was fiddling with her purse and looking everywhere but at him.

"You ready?" he asked.

To his surprise, she met his question with a straightforward gaze.

"Yes."

He hesitated, distractedly chewing on the edge of his lip. It had to be said. There was no use waiting.

"Uh, Angel."

She froze. *Oh, no. Here it comes.*

"About earlier..."

She waited. All she could think was, *Please don't fire me.*

"It wasn't necessary...but thanks."

She went weak with relief. "It was no big deal. Just something I needed to do."

That was something he understood.

They exited the café, and the sultry air enveloped them. Angel dug in her purse for her sunglasses as Royal unlocked the truck. A few yards away, three men were leaning against the side of the building beneath a tattered awning, taking the offered shade for themselves with no regard for passersby.

"Hey, Justice," one of them called.

Angel looked up as Royal turned. She could tell by the expression on his face that he wasn't pleased to see them.

"Duke," Royal said, acknowledging the other man's presence as he sauntered toward them.

Duke looked from Angel to Royal and back again. The smirk on his face aggravated Royal even more.

"Well, now, I heard you got hit pretty hard last night," Duke said.

"We're still standing," Royal said shortly, and wished Roman would hurry.

Duke nodded and grinned at Angel. "You ain't too choosy about the company you keep, are you, darlin'? When you get tired of old Justice there, you come on into town and give me a try. I'm real partial to brown-eyed señoritas."

Angel froze. It wasn't anything she hadn't heard a thousand times before, but for Royal, once was obviously too much. One second Duke was grinning at her and the next he was sitting on the sidewalk with his hands across his face. Blood was oozing between his fingers, and there was a stunned expression in his eyes.

"Well, hell, Justice, I think you broke my nose."

"And you're damned lucky that was all I broke," Royal said softly. "She works for me, and she's proved herself to be a damned good friend, which is a whole hell of a lot more than I can say for you. And if I hear of you, or anyone else, saying anything off-color about this woman, that won't be all I break. Do we understand each other?"

Suitably corrected, Duke sat quietly, holding his nose and afraid to so much as look in Angel's direction.

But Royal wasn't through with him yet. "Don't you have something you'd like to say to Miss Rojas?"

Duke nodded, dripping blood all over his shirt and pants. "I'm real sorry, ma'am."

Angel stared in disbelief. Before she could answer, Roman came out of the café and stopped in midstride.

"What the hell happened?" he asked.

The two men who'd been standing with Duke shrugged. They wanted no part of Duke's folly.

Roman headed for Royal. "Is everything okay?"

Royal gave Duke one last look. "It is now," he drawled.

Then he turned, yanked open the door to the truck and stepped aside, waiting for Angel to get in. She slid into the middle of the seat, then watched as Royal circled the truck while Roman crawled in beside her.

"You okay?" he asked.

She arched an eyebrow and nodded as Royal slid behind the steering wheel. The door fell shut with a thud. There was a long moment of silence while Royal fumbled with the keys. Angel sighed. There was no use waiting. It had to be said.

"Uh... Royal."

He paused without looking at her.

"Yeah?"

"It wasn't necessary...but thanks."

He jammed the key into the ignition. "It was no big deal. Just something I needed to do."

Angel laughed.

The sound of her laughter was balm to his soul. Royal looked at her and grinned.

The shared moment bonded them in a way nothing else could have done. Resisting the urge to trace the smile on her lips, he started the engine.

Roman stared at them both as if they'd suddenly gone mad. "Have I missed something?" he asked.

"Yes," they said in unison.

He waited for an explanation that never came. "Well, then," he finally mumbled. "That's what I thought."

Angel was quiet all the way to the ranch. Satisfied with listening to the two brothers talking, she let her thoughts go free. It wasn't until later, when Roman and the workmen were gone and the sun was starting to set, that she realized it was going to get dark. And that meant going to bed. Without Maddie to lie between them, where would she sleep? Her mattress had been ruined by the rain, and Maddie's was still filled with shards of glass. Tomorrow new ones were being delivered, but tonight, the only place still in one piece was Royal's room...and Royal's king-size bed. Before her worry could fester, she heard a vehicle coming down the driveway. Royal was at the barn feeding Maddie's cats. She went to the door and recognized the black pickup from earlier in the day. That would be Dan Waycoff's wife with the supper she'd promised, Angel thought.

Hurriedly, she brushed wayward strands of hair from her face and smoothed the front of her shirt. There was no way to look good after a day like today. She'd been up to her knees in mud and water, and there was a small tear at the hem of her shirt from some of the branches she'd carried away. She sighed, hoping Mrs. Waycoff wasn't big on first impressions. When the woman crawled out of the truck, Angel began to relax.

Almost six feet tall and as thin and rangy as an old muley cow, the woman lifted a long arm in a friendly wave and hefted a box from the seat beside her. She started talking before the truck door was shut.

"Hello, there," she yelled. "I'm Myra Waycoff. Hell of a way to meet, isn't it, girl? Dan says you all were real lucky last night. We got side winds but nothing direct. Loosened a few shingles on the roof and rained in around the chimney, but shoot, I been tellin' that Dan for almost three years to fix it, and he hasn't done it yet. Do you like fried chicken?" She laughed and continued her spiel before Angel could answer. "Hell, what am I asking? Everyone likes fried chicken. Brought some potato salad and biscuits, too. And a pie. Royal likes my pies."

She was on the porch and walking through the door Angel held open. She set the box on the table with a thump, stood back and dusted her hands on the seat of her faded jeans.

Angel couldn't stop smiling. Never in her life had she met a woman as lacking in subterfuge as this one.

"It's nice to meet you, Mrs. Waycoff. My name is Angel Rojas."

"Have mercy, child. Call me Myra."

She enveloped Angel in a smothering hug, which Angel found strangely comforting. A combination of scents clung to her old plaid shirt. Angel recognized hay and sweet feed and, if she wasn't mistaken, ginger and cinnamon. Her grin widened as Myra launched into a barrage of questions she didn't seem to want answered.

"Angel, is it?" Myra said as she turned Angel loose. "Is that your real name? Lord have mercy, I'd never be able to live up to such a name. Dan says I'm hell on wheels." She threw back her head and laughed, making the short gray curls on her head bounce with vigor. "But when you get my age, if you're still kicking, I figure you ought to be able to be any damned thing you want. Know what I mean?"

The question wasn't anything more than punctuation, a way for Myra to catch her breath. She launched into another subject without batting an eye.

"You got hit hard," she said. "But not as hard as the Deevers down the road. Their whole house is gone."

Angel's heart went out to those people. Even if she didn't know them, last night they'd shared a terror no one should know.

"Oh, my," Angel said softly. "If they were as afraid as I was, then bless their hearts."

Myra beamed. "I knew before I met you that we were going to get along," she said.

"Why?" Angel asked.

"Because Dan came home laughing about how you put Royal in his place."

A slow flush spread up Angel's neck and face as she remembered. *I'll quit calling you sir when you quit telling me what to do.*

"I shouldn't have lost my temper like that," Angel said. "Royal is my boss."

"Pooh," Myra said. "He's still a man, isn't he?"

Definitely. But Angel kept the thought to herself.

Myra slapped Angel on the back. It was a comforting thud. The grin on Angel's face spread wider.

"Men are like range steers. They need boundaries or they'll run wild all over the place. Give 'em plenty of rope. Don't want 'em to feel like you've got 'em tied down. But for God's sake, make sure that rope is tied to something solid."

Myra Waycoff's analogies were priceless. Angel knew she shouldn't be discussing her boss like this, but she couldn't help herself. "Why?"

Myra grinned. "Because eventually they're gonna run out of rope, and when they do, they'll buck like hell before they realize they like being roped and they like being tied."

Angel was still laughing when Royal came in the back door.

He liked Myra Waycoff, but he was aware of her verbal tendencies. He shuddered to think what she'd been telling Angel.

"What's so funny?" he asked.

Myra gave him a hug similar to the one Angel had received. "You, boy. Just you."

Royal rolled his eyes and gave Angel a nervous look, wondering what family secrets the old woman had revealed. But Angel wasn't talking. In fact, she wouldn't even look Royal in the face. That was enough to make him worry, but he wasn't deterred for long. When he frowned at Myra, she slapped his rear. He grinned and kissed her soundly on the cheek before dancing her around the kitchen floor.

Angel was stunned. She'd never seen Royal so playful. A part of her rejoiced in the sight and a part of her felt guilty that she'd done nothing to make him happy. Even if he was her boss, their relationship should be comfortable. They should not constantly be at each other's throats.

"Quit, you damned fool," Myra finally cried, and thumped Royal on the arm. "I'm too old for such carrying on."

She grabbed Angel by the wrist and yanked her forward. Before either Royal or Angel knew it, they'd been thrust into each other's arms.

"Dance with her, boy. I'm going home. Nice to meet you, Angel, girl. I'll be back in a couple of days to pick up my dishes."

She was driving away before they had the good sense to move. Royal looked at Angel. Her eyes had the look of a doe caught in the headlights of an oncoming car. As much as he might like to explore the softness of her skin and the textures of the hair brushing across the backs of his hands, he knew it was time to let her go.

"She's something, isn't she?"

Angel swallowed, trying to find words in her brain that would make any sense. But coherence was lost to her. The feel of Royal's hands at the middle of her back and the solid length of his body pressed too intimately against her own was making her weak.

Then suddenly she was free and Royal was at the sink, washing his hands and whistling beneath his breath. Bereft by the abrupt abandonment, she turned and began taking out the food that Myra had brought. She didn't know Royal was standing at the sink and shaking or that the water he was using was deep-well cold to keep his mind off dragging her down the hall and taking her to bed. All she knew was that he'd let her go.

"Smells good," Royal said, as she began to take covers from bowls.

"Yes. If she cooks as well as she talks, it will be wonderful," Angel said.

Royal laughed, and the tension between them was broken. But all the way through their meal, she kept glancing outside to the ever-growing darkness.

Night.

What would it bring?

Chapter 12

The house was quiet. Only the sounds of running water from the adjoining bathroom could be heard. Angel sat on the edge of the cot Royal had set up. There were no words for the relief she felt when she walked into the room and saw it there, waiting to be made up. She'd done so quickly, claiming it as hers before Royal emerged.

She'd bathed while Royal had been on the phone. She stared at the closed door between them, then the few yards of space separating her cot from his bed and knew it would never be enough. Something was happening between them. Something she wasn't ready to face. Something she didn't know how to stop.

The water stopped. Her pulse skipped a beat and then accelerated. He would come out and she didn't know what to say. Too much had gone on between them to ignore. After the way Royal had decked that man on the street, people would obviously talk. She sighed. The only thing she had to her name was a good reputation. She didn't want to lose it. Not even for Royal. He'd hired her as a housekeeper, not a whore. She wouldn't be any man's whore, but dear God, she would be Royal's love.

Afraid to face him, she laid down on the cot, pulled the covers over her breasts and pretended to be asleep. The bathroom door opened. Willing herself to a calm she didn't feel, she heard him pause, then sigh. Her heart went out to him, but she didn't move.

Royal knew she wasn't asleep. And she was in the wrong bed. He hung his wet towel on the doorknob and turned back the covers on his bed. Without raising his voice, he calmly announced his intentions.

"I'm going into the living room to watch the evening news and weather. When I come back, you'd better be in this bed or I'll put you in it myself."

Angel's eyes flew open in sudden shock, but it was too late to argue with him. He was already gone. She heard the muted voice of a local newsman. She threw back the covers and sat on the side of the cot, contemplating his threat. His voice had been too calm, too matter-of-fact to ignore.

She stared at the wide, inviting surface of the bed on the other side of the room, then at the cot, and shook her head. He was too tall for the cot. He would be miserable.

"Fine," she muttered, and traded beds. She slid beneath his sheets with trepidation, but soon began to relax.

Her eyelids fluttered as she drifted in and out of reality. One arm slipped off the side of the bed as she rolled onto her stomach. She'd braided her hair to keep it from tangling in her sleep, and it was wrapped around the arm on which she pillowed her head. The room was quiet, so quiet. And she was so very, very tired. There was a light under the crack in the door, and every now and then she heard a phrase or two from the newscaster.

"...under an overpass in some weeds. The body has been identified as Darcy Petrie, a waitress at an Amarillo truck stop. Authorities have linked it to..."

Angel should have been listening, but she'd fallen asleep.

* * *

Royal came in and let his eyes adjust to the darkness. A slight smile broke the seriousness of his expression as he saw the way she was sleeping. Like Maddie, she was half in and half out of the bed. Carefully, he unwound her from the covers. His voice was just above a whisper as he leaned down.

"Angel, sweetheart, roll over."

Without waking, she sighed and did as he'd asked. As soon as she was in the middle of the bed, Royal straightened her covers.

Never in his life had he wanted anything as badly as he wanted to lie down beside her. Not to make love, just to hold and be held. He turned toward the cot, and seconds later was shifting the pillow beneath his neck to a more comfortable position.

A faint glow from the security light illuminated the room in shades of black and gray. He kicked at the sheet, trying in vain to lengthen the covers on his legs, but gave it up as a lost cause. He was too tall for the cot. But the code of honor with which he'd been raised had precluded him from taking the bed. He wouldn't have slept a wink if he had. Angel Rojas was tough, but only in spirit. There was a fragility to her stature that sometimes scared him. And then he remembered the way she'd stood by him through the storm and how she'd sheltered Maddie when he could not. He closed his eyes, trying to block out the images of dark eyes watching him…of her soft hands touching him…of her mouth and the way it looked when she smiled. A knot came in his gut as he admitted that his housekeeper meant more to him than she should.

When he heard her roll over, he turned until he was facing the bed, then lay watching her sleep. He stared so long his eyes began to burn and he told himself he'd close them. Just for a minute. Just to let them rest.

And then it was morning.

Tommy Boy Watson had been on the road too long. He was sick of getting lost and taking wrong turns. These days, the only face he recognized was his own when he looked in the mirror. He was tired of being a stranger in a strange place. It had been over a week since he'd performed a cleansing, and the voices were quiet inside his head. He hadn't dreamed about his daddy since that night in Amarillo. That had been a very close call. His first. He intended it to be his last. Tommy Boy was through with his mission and on his way home. He was satisfied his father would have approved of his final act of retribution.

The waitress who called herself Darcy had been all her reputation had promised. She'd taken his order and his measure at the same time. Between bites of his burger, he'd asked if she liked to party. She'd winked and she'd smiled and she'd named her price. He hadn't counted on the fact that she would tell anyone where she was going.

He was waiting for her in the parking lot under the broken security light when she got off at eleven. He watched the front door with interest, wondering if she would scream as the last one had or if she'd go mute with terror as he put the knife to her throat. His fingers curled around the steering wheel in anticipation. He would soon find out.

He saw her emerge from the café. To his dismay, she wasn't alone. Another woman was walking with her, and they were chattering away as if they hadn't a care in the world.

His first instinct was to leave. He was reaching for the keys to start the ignition when the two women veered away from each other. One went toward a small brown car parked a few yards from his. Darcy continued toward where he was parked. He sighed with relief. They'd taken the decision out of his hands.

A few sprinkles of rain were dotting the windshield of his truck as she opened the door.

"Still in the mood, honey?" she asked.

"Get in and find out," Tommy Boy said.

She giggled as they drove away.

He'd been wrong about her. She hadn't screamed and she hadn't frozen in fright. She'd fought him, and fiercely. His groin was still sore where she'd kicked. And when he pulled out the knife, she'd pulled out a gun. It was only by sheer luck that he'd slit her throat before she could pull the trigger.

Here he was, looking for a road that would take him north. He was heading home. Someone in a BMW whipped past him as if he was sitting still. But he didn't take it personally. Some people got high on fast cars. Tommy Boy preferred good music. He reached toward the dash and upped the volume on his stereo. The mournful wail of a sad country song filled the interior of his truck. He stroked his beard in thoughtful fashion and leaned back in the seat, uplifted by the music and the words.

About an hour later, he pulled off the highway to get some fuel and something to eat. By his best estimation, he was about seventy-five miles from the western edge of the Oklahoma border. The cloudless sky was a white-hot blue, and he reached for his cap before he got out of his truck. A stiff breeze lifted the edges of his untrimmed beard as he started toward the small café. As he crossed the parking lot, he heard a car pulling up behind him. He glanced over his shoulder, making sure he would be out of the way.

His heart skipped a beat. Texas highway patrol. He pulled the brim of his cap down and kept on walking.

Stay cool. Stay cool. It's no big deal. They have to eat, too.

A door slammed behind him. He could hear the crunch of gravel beneath the officer's boots. Tommy Boy hunched his shoulders and kept on going. Inside the café, Tommy Boy chose a seat at the counter. The officer sat in a booth. Tommy Boy reached for a menu, quickly gave his order, then downed the glass of water the waitress had given him. On the wall to his left, the noise from a small black and white television added to the busy hum of voices. He glanced up. A local anchorman was updating the latest reports on the aftermath of the tornado that had swept across the northern portion of the state, ending near Dallas. He remembered the night all too well. He'd been holed up in that Amarillo motel and had experienced moments when he'd believed the roof would go.

The waitress slid his order in front of him.

"Be needin' anything else?" she asked.

"Bring me a Coke. A large one," he added.

It appeared, along with a bottle of steak sauce and a bottle of ketchup.

Tommy Boy grabbed his fork and dug into his food like a starving man. Only after he'd taken a few bites did he think to slow down. He reached for a knife to butter his roll, listening absently to the broadcast still in progress. They flashed a picture onto the screen, and he didn't have to hear what the newsman was saying to know who she was. It was Darcy Petrie, and her body had been found. The knife slipped from his fingers and fell onto the plate with a clatter. The bite of food was still in his mouth, forgotten in his need to hear. There was a terrible fear in the pit of his stomach that hadn't been there before. But there had never been a witness before.

Calm down, Tommy Boy.

The voice came out of nowhere, and he gasped, then choked on his food. He took a big swallow of his drink and made himself relax.

I hear you, Daddy. I'm being calm.

But he couldn't help looking over his shoulder to the booth on the other side of the room. Just to make sure the patrolman was where he'd seen him last. Just to make sure this wasn't a trap. The officer was cutting into a piece of pie with relish, completely oblivious to Tommy Boy's anxieties. Tommy Boy sighed and turned to the broadcast.

"Last seen getting into a late model black pickup on the night of..."

"Son of a—"

The blood drained from Tommy Boy's face. It was just as he'd feared. Although they hadn't seen his face, they knew what he drove. The skin on the back of his neck began to crawl. Any minute now he'd feel the cold, hard press of a gun barrel. He stared at his plate, at the way the pea juice was running into his mashed potatoes and gravy. He wished he'd ordered a hamburger. He didn't like his food to touch.

He sat for a good two minutes without moving, without taking a bite.

"Somethin' wrong with your food, mister?"

He jumped, then looked up. The waitress was standing before him with a half-empty coffeepot in her hands.

"No," he muttered, and picked up his fork, trying without success to stop the tremble in his fingers.

She shrugged and walked away, leaving Tommy Boy with a sick, sinking feeling. He laid down his fork and turned, staring past the customers, past the booths lining the walls where the patrolman was seated, then through the windows to the parking lot.

His gaze went straight to his truck. A shiny black Dodge extend-a-cab with chrome running boards. His pride and joy. And it had been Darcy Petrie's last ride. His gaze shifted to the next row of cars, to a dusty black truck with a trailer. And then to his right, to a small black Nissan with a camper. And then to a large black four-by-four pulling a horse trailer.

See, Tommy Boy. I told you to relax.

"Yeah, Daddy, I see. I see," Tommy Boy muttered.

The man on the stool beside him looked up and stared.

"You say something to me, mister?" he asked.

Tommy Boy grinned and shook his head. "Nope. Just talking to myself."

The man shrugged and went back to his meal. Tommy Boy picked up his fork and cut off a big bite of chicken-fried steak. It was okay. He should have known it would be okay.

Three days after the storm, the house was almost back to normal. Angel had been relegated to the porch while new carpet was being laid. There were brand-new mattresses leaning against the south kitchen wall. Tonight she would sleep in her own room, and in her own bed.

Her eyes darkened as she gazed toward the barns and the men working there. Royal and two hired hands were still fixing fence. Even though they were a distance away, it was easy to tell which one was Royal. His shirt was bluer, and he was taller by half a head than the other two.

She sighed. Last night had been endless. They were both suffering the effects of close proximity. He'd fought the covers on his cot until two in the morning. She knew because she'd been awake. Finally, she had grabbed her pillow and rolled out of bed.

"I'm going to the bathroom," she said. "When I come back, I expect you to be in this bed and quiet. If you're not, I will put you there myself."

She dropped her pillow by the bathroom door and disappeared.

Royal yanked his pillow from the cot and threw it on his bed before falling onto it with a thump. The mattress gave only slightly, supporting his long length to perfection. He groaned in ecstasy and stretched. Covers were still on his feet, and he was not falling off of the sides.

The bathroom door opened. Angel picked up her pillow and headed for the cot.

Royal heard her straightening the covers, then heard the slight creak of wood as the cot gave to her weight. Guilt hit him. He sighed.

"Uh, Angel."

"Go to sleep," she said shortly.

He rolled on his side, bunched the pillow beneath his neck just right and did as she'd ordered.

And they'd finally slept.

Angel smiled, remembering what she'd found on the kitchen table this morning.

The note was still in her pocket. The flower, a lone purple iris that had miraculously escaped the storm, was in a vase and sitting in the kitchen window. She touched her shirt pocket, hearing the crackle of paper beneath her fingertips, then looked toward Royal, who was almost a quarter of a mile away.

You were aptly named.

A film of tears suddenly blurred her vision as she looked

away. She kept reminding herself not to make more of the note than it really meant. So he thought she was an angel. No big deal. It was a word often used lightly. But there was the flower. Society today kept advocating men to say it with flowers, and he had. Exactly what had he been trying to say?

The phone rang. She ran into the kitchen to answer. To her delight, it was Maddie, wanting to know if her room was fixed and if her kittens had all been fed.

And so the morning passed. As she prepared the noon meal, her gaze kept straying to the delicate petals on the purple iris. It had survived so much, and yet there had so much beauty yet to give.

It hit her then, with a paring knife in one hand and a tomato in the other, that people could be like that. That they could endure without breaking many times over, yet when it came time to give, those who had endured longest often gave the most.

I could be like that, Angel thought. *If anyone wanted me as much as I wanted them, then I would give everything…if anyone cared.*

Royal was at the kitchen sink washing his hands and Angel was putting the finishing touches on lunch when Roman walked in the back door.

"Come on in," Royal said dryly, aware that Roman always made himself at home.

"Thanks," Roman said, and winked at Angel, who was already setting another place at the table.

"How's Maddie?" Angel asked.

Roman grinned. "You talked to her this morning. She's in perpetual motion." Then he added, "What you don't know is since then she's been invited to a birthday party of some kid in the apartment across the hall." He glanced at his watch. "In fact, if I remember correctly, she and Holly should be in the middle of pizza with seven other kids and their parents. After that, someone said something about swimming."

Royal reached for a towel to dry his hands as he turned. "I don't think I packed her swimsuit."

Roman grinned. "I know. She and Holly have already been shopping."

"Lord," Royal muttered. "She won't be fit to live with by the time I get her back."

Angel interrupted. "Iced tea or coffee?" she asked.

"Tea," they both answered.

She started to get the glasses. Royal reached over her head and took them out of her hands.

"I'll do it," he said.

"But that's what you pay me to—"

Royal began putting ice in the glasses. "Something's burning," he said, ignoring her comments.

"Oh, great," Angel muttered, and grabbed a couple of pot holders.

Roman silently watched them in action. A slow grin began to spread on his face. It was like watching a mating ritual, but without any touch. He shook his head and sat at the place Angel had set for him. The way he figured, it was just a matter of time before one of them lost total control. And if he was a betting man, his money would be on his brother. He'd always been short on patience.

"Smells good," Royal said, as he set the tea-filled glasses at their places.

"Enchilada casserole," Angel announced as she transferred the hot dish from the oven to the table.

Royal stopped what he was doing and leaned over the food, giving it a long, testing sniff.

The gesture was so blatantly rude, Roman couldn't help but comment.

"For Pete's sake, Royal, Mom would have had your head for that. What are you doing?"

Royal sat and picked up his fork. "Just checking," he said.

Angel started to grin.

Royal gestured to Roman. "Guests first," he said, and

watched as his brother dished a generous helping onto his plate.

"It's very hot," Angel warned him.

Roman nodded and picked up his fork. "I'm letting it cool."

Royal looked at Angel. "Will it?" he said.

"Will it what?" she asked.

"Cool?"

She threw back her head and laughed, and the sound filled the room and Royal's heart.

"I don't get it," Roman said.

"Habeneros," Royal said.

Roman's nostrils flared as he looked at his plate in dismay. He could eat Mexican with the best of them, but over the years, he'd learned that Habenero peppers should be measured in voltage, not weight.

"Oh, that kind of hot."

"For very big men, you two are certainly concerned with your poor little tongues."

Royal snorted, "Well," he persisted, "will it cool, or should I just dig the hole now to save you the trouble, and crawl in before I die?"

"Have we been in disagreement?" she asked.

"Well, no."

"Then you have nothing to worry about."

Satisfied that she had not booby-trapped his food, Royal took a generous portion of the casserole, then filled her plate, as well.

"Is that enough?" he asked.

Angel was suddenly embarrassed that she'd been so unprofessional with her boss.

"Yes, sir," she said.

He frowned. "Hell, we've just spent the better part of three nights together. Don't go all prim on me now."

Her mouth dropped, and Royal knew if looks could kill, someone would be planning his wake.

Angel was on her feet, her voice shaking with anger as she stared him in the face.

"Listen to me, your royal highness! How dare you insinuate that anything has been—"

Ignoring Roman's snort of laughter, Royal grabbed Angel by the hand before she could bolt.

"Sorry," he muttered. "I don't know why, but you bring out the absolute worst in me. I didn't mean to be so disrespectful. And I didn't mean that the way it sounded. I was just trying to say that I thought we'd gotten past all the formalities. Okay?"

Angel glared, first at Roman, who was past being able to eat, and then at Royal, who looked as if he'd willingly shoot himself if someone would just hand him the gun.

She threw up her hands and sat, muttering in rapid Spanish.

Royal looked nervous as he picked up his fork. He didn't know whether to be relieved that she was still here or nervous that this would be his last meal. He glared at Roman, who was still laughing.

"Oh, shut the hell up," he muttered, then gave Angel another nervous look. "What's she saying?" he asked.

Roman wiped the tears from his eyes and shook his head in disbelief. "You don't want to know." He choked, then started laughing again. "Royal highness...Lord, that's a good one."

They ate in silence. Angel forked her food in angry jerks. Royal ate in nervous haste, and Roman snickered between bites. Royal noticed the time and got up to turn on the television.

"Weather report," he announced to no one in particular and poured himself some more tea.

But it wasn't weather that flashed on the screen. It was a picture of Darcy Petrie, late of Amarillo, and mother of two. After the first couple of sentences, they watched without speaking.

"Last seen with a man in a black late-model pickup truck. Darcy Petrie is survived by a four-year-old daughter and a two-year-old son. Authorities believe that her death is linked to the deaths of eight other women in four different states. If anyone has any information regarding the…''

''Oh, my God,'' Angel whispered, and stood with a jerk, spilling tea across the table and onto the floor. She kept seeing that bony face and those pale green eyes.

Roman grabbed a hand towel from the counter and began mopping it up, but Royal's attention was pinned on Angel. He reached for her a second too late. She slid to the floor in a slump.

Chapter 13

Angel came to in Royal's arms, but she couldn't remember what had put her there.

"What happened?" she asked, struggling to get up.

"Easy, now," he said gently. "You're all right. You just fainted."

A frown creased her forehead. "I've never fainted in my life."

"Except today," Royal said, and circled his thumb gently at a spot just above her ear. "You hit the floor pretty hard. Do you hurt? Are you sick?"

She winced at his touch. Her head *was* sore. Hurt, she supposed, when she'd fallen. Other than that, she didn't feel any different.

"I don't think so. I feel fine now. Please help me up."

"Fine does not faint," Royal said. "Lie still until you get your bearings." When she looked as if she might refuse, he added a small grin. "Please?"

It was too good an offer to ignore. Lifting a shaky hand to her forehead, Angel relaxed against the cradle of his elbow.

"This is so unlike me. I've never..." Memory hit. "Dear God...the man on TV."

Royal frowned. "Man? What man?"

Angel rolled off his lap and onto her feet. The abruptness of the motion made her sway unsteadily. Royal tried to pull her onto the sofa. She reached for his hand, trying to pull him up, instead.

"No, no, you don't understand. I think I saw him."

Royal glanced at Roman, who was coming into the room with a cold, wet cloth for her forehead.

"Saw who?" Roman asked. "What have I missed?"

"I don't know," Royal said. "Let her talk."

Angel was shaking as fear surfaced, reminding her how afraid she'd been and how certain she was that he'd been following her.

"In the kitchen when we were listening to that news bulletin—"

Roman interrupted. "Angel, honey, you're not making any sense. What news bulletin?"

But Royal remembered because he'd been thinking of Maddie, and that once upon a time, all the women who died had been someone's little girls.

"The murder victims in the interstate killings," he said.

Angel turned, her face alight with relief that someone was willing to listen.

"Yes," she cried. "That one." She pressed a shaky hand to the middle of her belly, making herself calm when she felt like screaming. "Oh, Royal, I could have been one of those victims. I saw him." She added, "At least I think it was him."

Royal undid himself from the sofa in slow, measured steps. Like a cat moving toward a cornered prey, he took her by the shoulders. "What the hell are you saying?"

Desperate that they believe her, she gave both men a beseeching look as she began to explain.

"When I was hitchhiking, before you and Maddie picked me up, a man at a truck stop offered me a ride." She blushed and looked away, suddenly ashamed to say it, although she had nothing to be ashamed about. "I think he thought I was a prostitute. He offered me money. When I turned him down, he got very angry."

The investigator in Roman began to take notice. Granted, her experience was frightening, but either there were huge gaps in her reasoning or she hadn't told them everything yet. He put a hand on Angel's shoulder. She jumped.

"Sorry," he said softly. He hated to push, but they needed to know everything. "Can I ask you some questions?"

Her chin was trembling as she nodded.

But it wasn't okay with Royal. Everything inside him was going haywire. He kept looking at her and trying to remember that he'd hired her to take care of his daughter and his home, not wring his heart into knots. But it didn't do any good. The longer he looked, the worse he felt. From the moment she'd hit the floor until he had her in his arms, he'd felt weightless. As if his world had suddenly come undone from its anchor. Only after he'd felt the steady beat of her pulse had he begun to relax. Her eyes were filled with tears and her lower lip kept trembling. It was more than he could stand.

"Come here, girl," he said softly, and wrapped her in his arms as he might have Maddie. "You're not in this alone."

His gentleness was her undoing. Silent tears slipped from her eyes, tracking the contours of her cheeks and then falling onto Royal's arms. Encircled within his embrace, her back against his chest, she felt capable of almost anything.

Roman gave her a long, steady look. "You okay?"

She took a deep breath. Bolstered by Royal's strength, she lifted her chin defiantly. "I am now."

He nodded. "Now then. This man, the one who tried to pick you up. Did he threaten or harm you in any way?"

Angel thought, slowly shaking her head. "No." Then she added, "But it was broad daylight and there were lots of people around the parking lot."

Roman frowned. "So what makes you think that he's the

one who's been killing the women? There are lots of crazies in the world. What makes you think this is the same man?''

Her stomach knotted as she remembered the fear and panic.

"Because after I refused him, he followed me. Every time I got a new ride, he was there. When I stopped to eat, he would show up at the same café.''

Royal flinched. "The sorry son of a—''

"Easy, brother," Roman said.

Royal clenched his jaw, swallowing a rage born of helplessness as he realized how close she'd come to dying. He thought of that woman's picture they'd flashed on the screen. He didn't even remember her face. Would he have noticed if it had been Angel's instead? He doubted it. He hadn't known she existed until she crawled into his truck, wide-eyed and nervous and soaked to the skin.

She stood within the shelter of his arms while her lifeblood flowed beneath his fingers, rapidly when she was frightened, more measured when she thought to take a breath and slow down. In a swift moment of revelation, he knew how spare his life would have been without her.

A false quiet descended upon him as his heart raged for revenge. As the eldest Justice, he'd been born to inherit what Anson Justice had started and what their father, Micah Justice, had continued to build. His values had been forged by men who believed in dying for what was right. He'd been raised with the knowledge that a Justice takes care of his own.

Granted, Angel was only the housekeeper, and technically that *did* put her under his concern. But she'd long ago become more than an employee. He just hadn't faced it until now.

After more questions from Roman, an uneasy silence fell upon the room. In the face of what Angel had told them, there wasn't anything left to say.

Angel was pacing between the sofa and the door, trying to remember everything. Although it was hot and sunny outside, she felt cold.

Poor Darcy Petrie. Poor little kids. Their mother was dead.

She stopped suddenly and turned, almost shouting as she remembered.

"His truck. I almost forgot to tell you about his truck."

"What about his truck?" Royal asked.

She was shaking all over, and Royal could tell that she was about to come undone. "It was a new one, and black. Shiny and black, just like they said on TV. And Royal, you know that day in the rain, the day you picked me up?"

Royal waited.

"He passed us while we were parked on the side of the road. That's why I agreed to go home with you. Right then, total strangers were more appealing than being on the highway with him."

Royal's fear for her grew. If he'd been a little bit later, they would never have met. That man would have gotten to her first.

"That does it for me," Roman said. "I'll be right back." He walked out of the room, leaving Royal and Angel alone.

She shuddered then moaned. "What if it's him? What if he's still out there looking for me?"

Royal held her, cupping the back of her neck and pulling her into a fierce embrace. Holding her close—but not close enough. His voice was full of anger, and Angel could feel the tension in his body.

"Look at me." He tilted her chin until their gazes were locked. "I won't let him hurt you."

She shuddered as his hand centered in the middle of her back. It was only a hand, but right then it felt like a shield between her and the world.

"I am so scared."

"So the hell am I," Royal said softly, and laid his cheek against the crown of her hair.

Slowly, her arms slid around his waist. His strength became her strength. The rhythm of his breathing her marker for survival. As long as he was with her, she would be safe. She kept seeing that woman's picture as it had flashed across the screen.

Darcy Petrie.

Mother of two.

She started to cry.

The tears tied Royal in knots. That she was crying was more than he could bear. She was his Angel of the laughter and the quick, hot temper. Not these deep, choking sobs. Not this blind, stark fear. He rocked her where they stood.

"It will be all right," he said. "I promise you, Angel, it will be all right."

Roman strode into the room. "I called the FBI."

Startled, she drew back from Royal's arms. "The FBI?"

"We're talking about a possible serial killer who's strung victims in several states. That drops him under the jurisdiction of the federal government."

Angel groaned. This was going from bad to worse.

Royal looked at his brother. "Murder is out of my league," he said quietly. "I'm asking you to stay with us on this."

Roman nodded, then gently patted Angel on the back of the head as he might have done Maddie.

"You couldn't drive me away," he said. "Now I'd better call Holly and tell her I'm going to be late."

Angel looked at Royal, wishing she could read his mind. He was her boss. He had a child to raise and a ranch to run. And because of her presence, something ugly had come into their world.

"I think it would be better for you and for Maddie if I left the ranch. You both need someone to depend on. This could get ugly," she said.

Royal tightened his hold on her, but his grip was far gentler than his voice. "Like hell." He looked at Roman and grinned. "And ugly doesn't scare me. I've been dealing with ugly brothers all my life."

Roman arched an eyebrow. Angel laughed. It wasn't much, but it was enough to make them all feel better.

A horn sounded. They jumped, and Royal strode to the window.

"Great," he muttered. "Finally. The plumber."

"What about the FBI?" Angel asked.

"If they show up on time, we'll give 'em a hammer and put 'em to work," Royal said.

Angel smiled. A few minutes earlier she wouldn't have believed it possible, but she was starting to relax. The shock of her discovery was settling in. The authorities had been notified. They would come. She would talk. And please God, they would catch the killer before anyone else died. It was simple…and it was out of her hands.

Roman stepped into the hall to make some calls. After he checked in with Holly, there were some things he needed to set in motion. He doubted it had occurred to either of them just yet, but if word got out that there was a witness, her life wouldn't be worth a damn.

Angel stared at the face on the paper, then took a deep breath. It was him. From the thin, angular face and pale eyes to his unkempt beard and graying ponytail. She could almost hear the nasal intonation of his proposition.

"What do you think, Miss Rojas?" the sketch artist asked.

She looked at Deaton, the agent who'd taken her statement, then at the face the police sketch artist had made.

"It's him."

"You're sure?" Deaton asked.

"Yes."

Deaton nodded at the officer who'd done the drawing. "I want this face on the evening news and every broadcast afterward until he's caught." He looked at Angel. "Down the road, we'll need you to identify him. Are you willing?"

She gave Royal a nervous glance. But when he winked at her and nodded, she knew it would be all right.

"I'm willing to do anything to help stop the killings," she said softly.

"Yes, ma'am. And if he turns out to be our man, you are one lucky lady to have escaped." Deaton's cool demeanor shifted noticeably as he remarked, "His victims did not die an easy death."

She flinched.

Royal saw her reaction. He'd had enough. He unfolded himself from a nearby chair. "You through with her now?"

Deaton nodded. "We'll be in touch."

Roman was leaning against the doorjamb, where he'd been standing and listening. "I can assume you have taken measures to insure that her identity is not revealed?"

Royal looked at his brother and froze. *Oh, God. I didn't think.* The bland expression on Roman's face was for him a dead giveaway. Roman had tuned into something neither he nor Angel had considered. If the killer knew there was a witness…

Deaton gave Roman a curious glance. "Of course."

"Just checking," Roman said.

Angel's back was to the men, but there was something in Roman's voice that made her turn.

"What?" she asked.

"There's nothing for you to worry about, Miss Rojas," Deaton added. "You've done your part. Now let us do ours."

"Like hell," Royal said. "She's just put her life on the line. You better make damn sure she's protected in every way, or I'll take care of it myself."

Deaton frowned. He had no patience with attitudes or loose ends. But there was something about Royal Justice that made him nervous. If ever there was a man less likely of following orders, he would be it.

"We don't need any unnecessary heroics," Deaton growled.

Royal wasn't about to be deterred by a man in a three-piece suit. He didn't budge an inch when Deaton pointed in his face.

"Keeping her safe is necessary to me," he said shortly. "Besides, we take care of our own."

"Speaking of own," Roman said, "I'd better head into Dallas. I promised Maddie and Holly I'd take them out to dinner tonight."

Royal sighed. He'd hated sending Maddie into Dallas, but it had been necessary after the storm. He missed his daughter like crazy. It was the first time they'd been apart for this long, and while Maddie wasn't having any problems, he was feeling rejected.

"Is she all right?" Royal asked.

Roman rolled his eyes. "Does a bear—"

"Never mind," Royal muttered, then grinned. "You can bring her home tomorrow. The house will be ready by then."

Roman nodded, then gave Angel a lingering look before leaving.

The last of the agents was getting into a car when Royal turned to Angel.

"Feel like getting some air?"

Air? After what he'd just said, she felt as if she were already flying. *We take care of our own.* She wanted to laugh. She wanted to cry. She did neither.

"What about the plumber?" she asked.

"He knows what to do. He'll leave when he's through."

She nodded, then followed him out the door.

Royal glanced toward the sky out of habit, checking the weather. It was hot, clear and cloudless—a good day to cut hay. Instead, he was dealing with federal agents and talking about serial killers, and he felt as if he'd walked into a nightmare.

The chains on the porch swing creaked as Angel sat down. He turned, his hands stuffed in his pockets, his gaze fixed upon her face. That beautiful face. Her lips were swollen from crying, her eyes red-rimmed and brimming with unshed tears. She was in shock, and he knew just how she felt. Hell, he'd been in shock for all of three hours now—ever since he realized that he'd fallen in love.

He kept staring at her, willing her to look up—to look at him. But she seemed bent on staring at the floor of the porch and the toes of her shoes. He sighed.

Angel knew he was staring. Her skin felt hot—her breasts felt achy and heavy. But she was afraid to look up. Afraid if she did he would see her true feelings. And that couldn't happen. She was nothing to him but the woman who took care of his child. It wouldn't do to let her imagination run wild. Yes, he'd been more than supportive, and yes, he'd comforted her in a way she hadn't expected. And yes, Royal Justice was possessive about things that were his. She kept reminding herself it was nothing but duty and honor that had made him say what he had to Deaton.

She worked for Royal. In a way, that made her part of the Justice family. He had given her plenty of grief, but he was a man who had honor. She couldn't deny him that. But love her? No way.

His family ties and family roots were deep and true. She had none. When he picked her up on the side of the road, she had no destination in mind. This ranch, this man and his child had become the most important things in her life. The last thing she wanted to do was lose them. And the best way to keep that from happening was to stay in her place. It was bad enough that she'd brought all this danger into their lives. Bringing shame to herself would be the last straw.

Royal wanted to shake her. She'd withdrawn into that damned expressionless shell again. He hated when that happened because he didn't know how to react. He could handle her fury. At least it was an emotion he recognized. Even her tears, as much as they tore at his heart, were easier to take than this wall of silence. He combed his fingers through his hair in sudden frustration and strode toward the swing.

"Talk to me," he growled.

She looked up. "About what?"

His control snapped. He yanked her out of the swing and into his arms before she could argue.

"About anything, damn it. You hide yourself from me behind those big brown eyes. You look at me, but you won't say what you're thinking."

Angel twisted out of his hold, her voice shaking with frustration.

"You know something, Royal? Not everyone has the luxury of saying what they think."

"And why the hell not?" he growled. "I never let anyone's opinion stop me from voicing mine."

She smiled bitterly. "And you're coming from a different place than most. You are your own boss. You don't have to answer to anyone to depend upon putting food in your mouth and a roof over your head."

He groaned. "That isn't what I mean." Then he turned and walked to the edge of the porch. "I didn't mean to make you angry. I don't want to fight. I know you're scared. Sometimes talking helps."

"Talking won't change what's happened," Angel said.

"You were a witness, for God's sake," Royal said. "Not a participant in the crimes."

Angel sighed and nodded. "You're right. I just can't get over feeling guilty about involving you in any way."

He wanted to hold her and settled for the olive branch she'd offered instead.

"So absolve your guilt and talk to me," he muttered.

She managed a smile. "Can we walk?"

He held out his hand.

By the time they reached the barn where Dumpling and her kittens resided, Angel felt better. But Royal was impatient. He didn't feel better. In fact, he was feeling decidedly worse. The closer they were, the harder he got. It was uncomfortable as hell and just that little bit disconcerting to know that a woman had that kind of hold over his emotions. Finally, he'd had enough.

"I'm still waiting," he said.

Angel paused at the granary door, where the sacks of horse feed were kept, then poked her head inside.

"Look. Flea Bit is sleeping with Dumpling and her babies."

Royal took her by the arm. "Look at me," he said softly.

Angel bit her lip and turned, meeting his gaze without blinking. It was the hardest thing she'd ever had to do.

Her skin was soft beneath his fingers, her mouth slightly parted and tilted upward as she looked at him.

"I'm looking," she said.

He exhaled softly. *God, so am I.* "What do you see?"

She answered without hesitation. "My boss."

"Is that all?" he asked.

Her gaze slipped.

"Don't do that," he said harshly, and laid the palm of his hand against the side of her face, making her look at him again.

"Don't do what?" she asked.

His voice lowered. "You know."

Her pulse skipped a beat. For a long, silent moment, they stared into each other's faces, taking comfort in the familiarities. Twice she tried to look away, and each time Royal forced her back. His gaze raked her face, and she could feel the warmth of his breath upon her cheek. There was a muscle jerking at the side of his jaw and a promise in his eyes she was afraid to believe. She moaned beneath her breath and then started to shake.

"What?" Royal whispered.

Her answer came out on a sigh. "You know."

He took a step closer. "I want to hear you say it."

Her nostrils flared in sudden anger. "Why?" she cried. "Why do you need to see my weakness? You already know my shame."

"There is no shame in loving, Angel, girl. Only in letting it go to waste."

She started to cry, soft, silent tears that spilled out of her eyes and onto his fingers as they cupped her cheeks. He lowered his head until their foreheads were touching and their lips were only inches apart.

"Angel Rojas, you're everything I ever wanted in a woman. You're beautiful and gentle and you have a temper that matches mine to a T. You make me laugh and you make me crazy. You may not be ready to hear this, but it has to be said. I'm in love with you, girl. And it's a damn good thing that your bedroom is going to be ready tonight because there's not enough willpower left in me to spend another night just listening to you sleep.''

Angel was stunned. Her ears were ringing from his words. She saw the truth in his eyes and still she couldn't bring herself to move.

Royal groaned. Her silence was his undoing. "I won't ever say this again,'' he said shortly. "But I won't say I'm sorry, either.''

"Thank you, God,'' she whispered, and moments later was in his arms.

Royal caught her to him. Burying his face against her neck and then brushing his mouth against the warmth of her skin, he groaned. It was just as he'd feared. She tasted as good as she smelled.

"Ah, God, I want to make love to you.''

His words were nothing but an echo of her emotions.

She leaned back in his arms until she could see his face and the fire blazing in his eyes.

"Then do it,'' she said.

His nostrils flared. It was his only response. Angel found herself in the hayloft, watching as Royal stripped off his clothes, making a bed on the hay for her to lie down. It was just as she'd dreamed. His body was beautiful in every way.

He turned to her. She pulled her T-shirt over her head. Already aroused, he gritted his teeth against a flood of emotion.

"Hurry,'' he growled.

"Then help me,'' she whispered.

She stood naked before him, waiting for the first steps of the dance to begin.

He reached for her, palming her breasts, then rubbing her nipples until they were hard, aching buds. She swayed on her feet, then gave up the fight and reached out to him.

He took down her hair, combing his fingers through the long, silken strands and letting it spill across her shoulders and upon her breasts. Her head lolled in silent ecstasy. Their gazes met and held.

He lowered his head.

Her breath caught. His mouth. God, his mouth. It was there on her lips, stealing her breath…and her heart. She wrapped her arms around his neck. She never knew when he pushed her down upon the bed he'd made in the hay. A pencil-thin ray of sunlight was shining through a small nail hole in the roof above them. After that, Royal was all she saw.

Chapter 14

The ranch had grown quiet. Everyone was gone. The soft mewling of Dumpling's kittens could be heard as the old cat left on a hunt. In the rafters above their heads, a roosting pigeon cooed softly to its mate circling the sky outside the barn. And in the loft, in the loose, sweet hay, a man and a woman were making slow, sweet love.

Their bodies were slicked with sweat, their hearts hammering against their breasts. Locked into the age-old rhythm, Royal rocked within the cradle of her hips. Lost in the sounds of her soft gasps and small cries, he kept driving them both toward a spiraling heat.

Angel moaned beneath her breath as a short burst of pleasure sent her arching toward his downward thrust. Good. So good. She bit her lower lip to keep from crying aloud and closed her eyes, concentrating on the feeling centered between her legs. Ah, God, she wanted more.

He gave her what she wanted.

And then it was coming.

Blasting through her body like a heat wave. Nailing her

where she lay and rendering her helpless to move. At that moment, willing to die from the joy, she felt it sweep through her system, leaving tiny aftershocks of the pleasure he'd given her to remember him by.

"Oh, Royal."

She felt empty and at the same time complete. She lifted her hands to him, sliding them up the sides of his face.

He was shattered by her complete capitulation. Her touch was the trigger that detonated the last of his control.

"Ah, God," he groaned. Thrusting in one last time, he let himself go, sliding deep inside her and spilling his seed...and his soul.

Afterward, they lay in silence, absorbing the enormity of what they'd done. For Royal, there was no turning back. He did not give his love lightly, and today he'd given his all.

As for Angel, she, too, had crossed a bridge. This wasn't the first time she'd shared her body with a man, but it was the first time she'd shared her heart. And while there was a part of her that feared this might not last, she was so much in love she was willing to take the risk.

Royal brushed his mouth against the base of her throat, then raised himself until he could look at her.

"Are you okay?"

Angel cupped the sides of his face with her hands. "I may never be okay again."

His heart skipped a beat. He knew just what she meant. And while he would still do what they'd done all over again, there was something he had to get said.

"This isn't over."

Her heart fluttered within her chest. "What isn't over?"

"The lovemaking...and the love. Today was a beginning, not an interlude."

She smiled and wrapped her arms around his neck.

He bit his lip and groaned when she pulled him to her.

"I have something I need to say to you," she said.

There was a gleam in her eye that was making him nervous.

"This isn't over," she said softly.

He started to grin. "What isn't over?"

"You." She rolled, pinning him to the floor and straddling his hips. "Me." He was getting hard all over again, pushing against her. She shifted quickly, impaling herself. "This."

Tilting her head and closing her eyes, she braced her hands against his chest and began her ride.

Royal watched her body undulating upon him until he began to lose focus. He fisted his hands into the long lengths of her hair and held on for dear life until it was time to let go.

Tommy Boy Watson's belly felt as if it was splitting in two. Twice in the past hour he'd been forced to pull off the highway to seek relief from the gripe centered in his lower regions. He didn't know whether it was caused by the food he'd been eating or the stress he was in. It was difficult to stay focused when he would have sold his soul for a roll of toilet paper and a bottle of Tums.

He'd been driving since daybreak, heading north on Interstate 35 through Oklahoma. He'd come this way before. It felt good to be retracing his steps. It felt right to be going home. Just as he topped a small rise, his belly knotted in a new fit of cramps. Frantic, he began searching the roadsides and the horizon for a place that would provide some privacy. There was none. The ache twisted deeper. Wild-eyed, he took the next exit, uncaring where it would lead, as long as it was away from civilization.

The speedometer was on seventy-five when he came over the hill. To his left was a large stand of trees and a herd of cattle grazing in the pasture beyond. A little farther down on the right, the roof and company sign of a rural gas station were just visible. His brain went in overdrive as he weighed his options. Stop now and brave the woods and the cows. Hold off a few seconds longer and opt for an outhouse with walls and a roof. He flew by the trees in a blur of black.

The station it was.

He saw the bathroom doors as he slid to a stop outside the station. One marked His. The other marked Hers. He headed for the one that was standing ajar. That it was the one set aside for the female sex no longer mattered. It was as far as he could go.

He emerged from the small, unlit room pale and shaken. For now, the pains were gone. But his legs felt as if the bones had turned to mush. He wiped a shaky hand across his face, feeling the wiry brush of facial hair against the palm of his hand. He sighed. His beard needed a trim.

"Anything I can do for you, mister?"

The unexpected voice made him jump. He turned, coming face to face with a teenage girl. He wouldn't have put her at more than fifteen. She was tall and gawky, her oversize clothes conveniently hiding the evolution of her femininity. Her hair was short and greasy, her skin marked with acne, both old and new. Tommy Boy looked at her and, except for the fact she was of the opposite sex, saw himself in her. A misfit. It was instant empathy.

"No. I was just resting myself a bit," he said.

She shrugged and started into the station.

As she reached the corner, Tommy Boy thought. "Hey, girl."

She stopped and turned.

"You happen to have anything for an upset stomach?"

She shrugged. "Just some of that pink stuff."

"That'll do," Tommy Boy said, and followed her inside.

She dug through a shelf behind the counter. Tommy Boy strolled to an old red pop box beside the door and opened it up. He grinned.

"Man, I haven't seen one of these in years," he said, looking at the cans of pop floating in the ice.

The girl didn't bother to answer. It didn't matter. Tommy Boy's remark had been more to himself than to her.

He thrust his hand inside, digging through the numbing water for a red and white can containing his favorite drink.

"Whoo, that's cold," he mumbled, as he pulled up his prize and carried it to the counter.

"Need any gas?" the girl asked.

Tommy Boy shook his head. "Nope, this'll do me."

"That'll be three dollars and twenty-seven cents," she said.

Tommy Boy reached into his pocket, pulling out a handful of bills and some change. A couple of quarters fell to the floor. He stomped on them quickly, trapping them beneath the soles of his shoes before they could roll under the counter. He tossed her some money and bent to pick up his coins as she began to make change. His gaze absently slid to a nearby newspaper rack. It took a couple of seconds for the face on the front page to register, and when it did, he stood with a jerk.

The girl was waiting. He held out his hand in a daze. She handed him his change.

"How much for a paper?" he asked.

"Fifty cents."

He laid two quarters onto the counter with quiet precision. His mind was racing as he watched her drop them into the register.

It was his face. The image was unmistakable. The headline beneath was even worse.

Have you seen this man?

His belly rolled and he broke out in a cold sweat, uncertain if it was nerves or another wave of peristalsis. Condensation from the can of pop was dripping through his fingers onto the floor. He kept staring at the young girl's face. At the expression in her eyes. Was she faking it until he drove out of sight? Would she tell? Did she know? His fingers twitched beneath the chill of the can. The switchblade in his pocket was heavy against his thigh. It would be an easy kill. Just set down the can and pop the blade. One swift, clean cut was all it would take. She wouldn't suffer, he'd see to that.

While he was thinking, the phone rang. He watched, his heart in his mouth, as she lifted the receiver. It still wasn't too late. He set the can on the counter and stuck his hand in his pocket. *Do it now, before she can tell.*

As his fingers closed around the shaft, a feeling of power came over him. He was in control. It was in his palm, the

weight of it making his pulse accelerate. He shifted from one
foot to the other, testing his balance, testing his nerve.

"Yes, Momma. See you in a little bit, and I love you, too,"
the girl said, and hung up the phone.

Tommy Boy froze. Her voice had lost its sullen tone. Her
acne-scarred face had taken on a beauty he wouldn't have
believed. When she turned, she was smiling to herself. He
saw the child she had been and the woman she could be.

"Anything else?" she asked.

He looked at the medicine on the counter beside his pop.
He rolled the knife in his palm one last time and then let it
drop into the depths of his pocket.

"Nope. I guess I've got everything here that I need."

"Come again," the girl said.

Tommy Boy dropped the medicine in his pocket, took his
pop in his hand and lifted a paper from the rack on his way
out the door. He never looked back.

Night came, and Tommy Boy was low on gas and afraid
to stop. The newspaper had been brutally frank about the way
the women had died, but he was angry they hadn't told all of
the facts. No one had seen fit to mention what they'd done
for a living. No one had seen fit to add that they had ruined
good men's lives. In his eyes, their deaths had been righteous.
They hadn't suffered nearly as long as his daddy had. It didn't
matter to him that their bodies had rotted before they'd been
found. At least they'd been dead before the rotting occurred.
His daddy's flesh had come away from his bones while his
heart was still beating.

But how? he wondered. Who had seen his face? Not the
other waitress at the Amarillo truck stop where Darcy Petrie
had worked. It had been raining, and dark. All she'd seen was
his truck. Then who?

Giving the gas gauge a nervous look, he pounded the steering wheel in frustration. Only a few miles from the Kansas
border, and he was running on empty. He was going to have

to chance a stop. The only satisfaction he had was that his looks had altered dramatically since this morning.

About an hour after reading the paper, he'd pulled to the side of the road and hacked off his ponytail with his knife. It had hurt like hell, but not nearly as much as when he'd tackled his beard. Two hours later, he was minus all but a thin, scraggly growth, nothing a good razor and a can of shaving cream couldn't fix.

The only decision he had left to make was what to do about his truck. The description in the paper fit his rig to a T. And while it wasn't the only black truck in the country, he felt like he was driving a big neon sign that said, Here I Am. Come And Get Me.

But he'd taken the risk and crawled inside. And here he was, still driving north and almost out of gas.

A green highway marker pointed east. Medford Blackwell exit. He took it without slowing down, rounding the sharp curve and sliding to a stop. He sat with his engine idling, reading the road signs and deciding where he would spend the night. Medford was twenty-two miles west, Blackwell only three east. Blackwell it was.

But first things first. He turned right and right again, coming to a stop at the self-service pumps of a busy gas station. He got out with a groan, stretching his legs and rocking his head from side to side on his neck. Bones popped. His head felt unusually light. He attributed it to the missing ponytail, which normally hung down his back. As he reached for the hose, a dark-haired woman walked into his line of vision. Her hair was long and pulled from her face with a thin, red ribbon. Her shorts and T-shirt were white, offsetting a well-oiled tan. He stared, trying to remember where he'd seen her before. Then he shrugged, stuck the nozzle into the tank and released the flow.

Gas fumes rose between him and the truck bed. He wrinkled his nose and stepped to one side, taking advantage of an intermittent breeze. It wasn't until he started inside to pay that it hit him. He stopped and spun, staring in the direction where the woman had been. But she and her car were long gone.

"Oh, man," he muttered. "Oh, man."

He'd just remembered why the woman had seemed so familiar. She looked like the whore down in Texas who had refused his ride. She'd seen his face. And she'd probably seen what he'd been driving. It had to be her. She was the only person who'd seen him up close and personal and then walked away. But where the hell was she now? He wanted to puke. Instead, he went in and paid for his gas.

Maddie burst into the house a few steps ahead of Roman. She flung her overnight bag aside and jumped into her daddy's arms.

"I'm back," she cried. "Did you miss me?"

He laughed and kissed her soundly. "No. Not me. I didn't miss you at all." Then he looked at Roman. "Thanks for everything."

Roman shook his head. "Don't thank me. And I'm sorry to dump and run, but I've got to meet a client in a couple of hours. See you guys later."

He was gone.

Maddie was unfazed by what she knew to be a monumental lie. She knew good and well that she'd been missed. She giggled and returned his kisses twofold. Everything was back in order. Then it dawned on her that her welcoming party was one person short. Her smile shrunk and a frown slipped into place.

"Daddy?"

"What, baby?" he asked.

"Where is my angel?"

"She's in the—"

Angel interrupted. "I'm right here," she said. "Do I get a hug, too?"

Maddie squealed and laughed as Royal pretended he wasn't going to give her up. By the time Angel got her kiss and hug, Maddie was weak from giggling. She leaned into Angel's embrace, melting against the loving welcome she knew was there.

"I missed you," Maddie said softly.

Angel's heart skipped a beat as her arms tightened. "Oh, baby, I missed you, too."

Royal watched them, his heart too full to speak. Maddie turned, her face alight with joy. Her world was back in its orbit.

"Did you take good care of my kitties?" she asked.

Royal rolled his eyes and pretended disgust. "If that isn't just like a woman."

Maddie giggled. "Daddy. I'm not a woman. I'm a little girl."

"Oh, well, then," he said. "I suppose it's still all right. And yes, I fed your damned cats, every morning and every night. They are so fat now that their bellies drag the ground. Are you happy?"

Angel arched an eyebrow at him, as if to say watch your language, but it was obviously a case of too little, too late. And it wasn't as if Maddie was paying attention. She'd heard his fussing too many times before.

"I want to go see them," Maddie shrieked. "I want to see if their bellies really do drag the ground."

"Why don't you take your bag to your room first?" Angel suggested. "You have a new bed and new carpet and curtains."

"Yeah!" Maddie shrieked, and darted toward her room.

"Your bag," Royal shouted, but it was too late. She was already gone.

Angel picked it up and handed it to him as he started out of the room. He took it without thinking and was halfway down the hall when he suddenly stopped. He dropped the bag where he stood and went to Angel.

"Did you forget something?" she asked.

"Hell, yes," he said softly, and scooped her up, leaving her feet dangling as he planted a hard kiss in the center of her mouth.

By the time he turned her loose, his ears were ringing and he had an itch he sure couldn't scratch.

Angel was reeling from the unexpected pleasure when she suddenly remembered that Maddie was just a short distance away. She glanced over his shoulder, making certain they were still alone.

"It doesn't matter if she sees," Royal said.

Angel looked startled. "But she will—"

"Look, lady," he said softly, and cupped the side of her cheek. "I wasn't playing games when we made love. I fully intend that it will happen again." He leaned down and kissed her. "And again." He kissed her again. "And again." Her sigh was warm against his face as he kissed her one more time. "And again."

Angel was still standing with her head tilted and her eyes closed when Royal lifted his head.

"Do you have anything to say?"

"Again," Angel whispered.

He obliged with a grin.

A week came and went without disaster. Maddie was in her routine, down at the barn with her kittens or begging Angel for afternoon treats. Royal had begun cutting hay, and only now and then when they happened to catch a newscast would either one of them remember what had transpired. The FBI had not called. Angel liked to tell herself that her part in the dirty business of murder was over. In the back of her mind, she knew there might come a day when she would have to pick him out of a lineup or even testify against him at a trial. But those days were so far out of the realm of her reality that she let the ugly thoughts slide.

At night, after Maddie was asleep, Royal would come to her room and lie beside her. The gentleness with which they made love was coupled with the growing bond between them. The times when he would just hold her brought tears to her eyes, and the nights as they planned the next day were the most precious to Angel of all. It was for her proof that she'd become a real part of his world.

On the days she was alone in the house, she let herself pretend this was her house she cleaned and her family for whom she prepared meals. Because even though she knew Royal loved her, he had yet to say the words she longed to hear. To belong, truly belong to this man and his child, she needed to be his wife.

And then the day came when she turned on the television and sat down to rest. She had a glass of iced tea in one hand and a freshly baked cookie in the other. Lunch was ready and waiting, but Royal and Maddie had yet to come back from town.

Condensation from the glass was making a wet spot in her lap, but she didn't care. She took a bite of the cookie, savoring the burst of brown sugar and chocolate chip in her mouth. The show in progress was interrupted for a bulletin. She listened absently, mentally preparing what would need to be reheated first upon their arrival, when the announcer's words began to sink in. Stunned, she laid her snack aside and leaned forward, focusing on every word.

"Today it was revealed that there may be a mystery witness to the interstate killings. Through unimpeachable sources, we have learned there was a woman near Dallas who narrowly escaped the killer's knife, and that she is working in conjunction with authorities to see that the killer is brought to justice."

Angel stood and screamed Royal's name. Only after she heard the echo of her voice in the silence of the house did she remember that he and Maddie weren't home.

"Oh, God, oh, my God."

Her hands were shaking as she locked all the doors. Before she could think what else to do, the phone began to ring.

Royal was at the feed store, arguing with Maddie as to why she couldn't have a grape sucker from the jar on the counter, when he heard the high-pitched beep that was the local television's signal of an upcoming bulletin. He looked at the small black and white television.

"Hey, Will, turn that up, will you?" he said.

The owner of the feed store picked up his remote and aimed it at the screen.

Royal's face turned pale and then a dark angry red. He heard enough to know that Angel's safety had been seriously compromised. Without asking for permission, he reached for the office phone and started punching in numbers.

"Daddy, who are you calling?" Maddie asked.

He yanked a grape sucker from the jar on the counter and all but stuffed it into her mouth.

"Here," he said. "Don't talk. Suck."

Her eyes alight, Maddie grinned. For one of the few times in her life, she did as she'd been told.

The phone rang once, then twice, then again, then again. Royal's belly was in knots. He didn't know what she would do if she saw it, but he kept remembering that once she'd offered to leave. Dear God, if she got it in her head that the killer would come looking for her, she might up and run.

"Come on, baby," he muttered. "Pick up the phone. Pick up the phone."

Angel closed her eyes and said a quick prayer as the phone continued to ring. It rang so many times the sound became human. But was it a warning—or was it a threat? Finally, she couldn't stand it any longer. Her hands were shaking and her throat was burning as she lifted the receiver to her ear. When she spoke, all she heard was her voice, high-pitched and tinny, and the fear coming out in a single word.

"Hello?"

Royal heaved a great sigh of relief. "Angel, thank God. Are you all right? Why didn't you answer the phone?"

She started to cry.

He cursed beneath his breath. It was just as he feared. She'd heard the broadcast.

"Angel...sweetheart, listen to me."

She choked on a sob. "What?"

"I'm on my way. No one's going to hurt you. I promised, remember?"

She nodded, then realizing he couldn't see her response, she said yes.

"That's a great big area they named. There is no way anyone could know it was you. Right?"

She shuddered. He was right. She'd panicked too soon. "I guess," she said.

A little of the tension went out of his body. Without missing a beat, he pointed a warning finger at Maddie to keep her sucker away from the feed store cat while adding a footnote to his call.

"Angel."

She sounded small and lost, and he wished to God he was there with her.

"We're on our way."

"Okay."

"I love you, baby."

A fresh set of tears spilled down her face. She squeezed the receiver tightly, holding on to her man in the only way she could.

"I love you, too," she said softly.

"You'd better," he growled. "We've got at least a good sixty years ahead of us, and some good loving, too."

She was smiling when she hung up.

The click sounded in Royal's ear and he hung up with a sigh. When he turned, he realized that Will had long ago hit the mute button, and every ear in the store, including Maddie's, had been trained on his end of the conversation.

"Uh..." Will began.

Royal's jaw slid forward in a mutinous thrust as he reached for Maddie's hand.

"If you want any more of my business, Will Smith, then you won't bother to finish what you started to ask." He looked around the feed store to the half dozen men gathered there. "That goes for the rest of you, too."

None had the guts to look him in the eye.

Will had known Royal Justice for more years than he cared to count. He'd seen him deck a man for raising his voice in front of his wife. But that had been before his wife died. After that, old Royal had kept to himself. He grinned. Maybe the gossip he'd been hearing was right, after all. Maybe Royal Justice *was* sweet on his housekeeper. And wouldn't that be fine.

"I ain't sayin' a word," Will muttered, pretending great indignation. "Alls I was goin' to ask was do you want to charge the feed you picked up?"

"Yes," Royal said, and started out the door. But he should have known his Maddie would have the last word.

"Daddy, are you in love with my angel?"

He groaned and slammed the door behind him.

Chapter 15

Angel heard Royal's truck coming down the driveway and ran out of the house. She was standing on the porch when it came to a sliding halt. He got out before the dust had settled, set Maddie on her feet with an order to go wash the grape sucker off her face and hands and headed for Angel with single-minded intent.

Angel met him at the steps. Within seconds, she was in his arms, her face buried against his neck. Safe. She was safe.

Maddie stared intently at the couple, drawing her own conclusions to what she was seeing. At that moment, Flea Bit came sauntering around the corner of the house with its tiny tail straight up in the air like a flag at full mast.

"Flea Bit," Maddie squealed, and held out her hands.

Royal turned. The word no was at the edge of his tongue when she picked the cat up. By then it was too late. Cat and girl were now stuck to each other with a thick, grapey glue.

"Well, damn," he muttered. But the look on Maddie's face was priceless. He couldn't help it. He started to laugh.

Laughter was the last thing Angel expected to hear, but when she turned to look, she started to grin.

Maddie was trying to let go, but every time she lifted her hand, a new patch of kitty hair got caught in the mess. The cat was squalling in pain and climbing the front of her shirt in a futile effort to get free. The closer it got to her face, the wilder Maddie's expression became.

"Daddy!" she screeched.

Angel was laughing as she ran to help. "Wait, honey," she cried. "Don't move. Let Daddy and me help you."

Maddie was considering the wisdom of a real good cry to offset the fact that she hadn't done as she'd been told, then decided it wasn't going to be necessary after all.

Her daddy was on his knees, trying to peel the cat's claws from the front of her shirt, while her angel was trying to unstick the hair from the palms of Maddie's hands.

"We're all stuck," she announced.

Royal paused and looked up. In every way that counted, Maddie was right. She was stuck to the cat. The cat was stuck to her shirt. Angel was getting sticky from both cat and Maddie, and intermittently, the cat stuck its claws into him.

"Yeah, honey, we sure are," he said, then grinned at the look on Angel's face as Flea Bit's little tail hit her square in the face.

Flea Bit hit the porch running and didn't look back. Maddie looked at her hands and sighed.

"Daddy?"

"Hmm?"

"Will the hair grow back on Flea Bit?"

Angel sat on the porch, folded her arms across her knees and dropped her head. Her shoulders were shaking uncontrollably.

Guilt hit Royal belly-first, and he started to panic as he realized he'd completely forgotten why they'd rushed home. He dropped to one knee and cupped the back of her head.

"Angel, honey, I'm so sorry. It's not that I didn't think of your feelings, but Maddie was...uh, well, the cat was so..."

"Oh, God," she gasped, and fell backward onto the porch with her arms out and her face streaked with tears. But they weren't tears of sorrow. She was laughing so hard she couldn't stop.

"If you could have seen your face," she mumbled, then rolled onto her side and laughed even harder.

Relief settled. All he could think was, thank God she wasn't mad.

Maddie started off the porch in the direction the cat had gone. Royal grabbed the tail of her shirt and gave it a yank.

"Inside. Now," he said shortly. "And don't come out until those hands are clean and shining."

She disappeared, leaving them alone on the porch.

"Here," Royal said. "I'll help you up."

Angel shook her head and held out her hands. "Don't touch me," she said, and laughed even harder. "I'm all catty, too."

He stood with a silly grin on his face, staring at her while the last empty place in his heart slowly filled. She had become his touchstone to sanity—his friend and his love. As he watched her, still trying to come to terms with her hysteria, she suddenly blurred before his eyes. It came to him then that without her beside him, his life would be far less than it was meant to be.

"Marry me."

The words silenced her as nothing else could have done. She rolled on her back, the last of her smile still fixed on her face.

"What did you say?" she asked, and heard the panic in her voice.

"You heard me," Royal said.

"Say it again," she whispered. "Say it while I'm looking at your face."

He squatted beside her. "Marry me."

She sat with a jerk. "Just like that? Without an I love you or I can't live without you? You say marry me just like that?"

His voice was shaking. "I love you. I can't live without you."

Angel started to cry. But not like she had before. Not because she was afraid of the killer. But because she was afraid she was dreaming.

"I don't know what to say."

Royal felt sick. He didn't know where this was going, but he would have liked a resounding yes.

"Say I love you. I can't live without you," he said.

Angel pressed a hand against her chest. The pain in there was so great that she thought she might faint. If this didn't work out, it would kill her.

"I love you."

He rocked on his heels and started to grin.

"I can't live without you," he prompted.

She bit her lower lip and took a deep breath. "I can't live without you," she echoed.

The grin widened as he stood and pulled her to her feet.

"My hands," she muttered, trying in vain to wipe the cat hair from her palms.

Cat hair was the farthest thing from Royal's mind. He lowered his head, nipping at the edge of her lower lip, then kissing the tears on her face.

"Angel, sweetheart…"

She felt rootless, as if she could take wing and fly. It was all she could do to answer.

"Hmm?"

"Isn't there something else you've forgotten to say?"

Her mind was racing. To the best of her knowledge, she'd said enough already.

"Like what?" she murmured, then groaned when he backed her against the wall of the house.

"Like yes."

If he'd just take his hands off her breasts, she might remember what they'd been talking about.

"Yes, what?" She sighed as her nipples peaked beneath his caresses.

"Yes, you will marry me."

"Yes, you will marry me," she echoed.

He lifted his head. There was a devilish grin on his face. "Well, now, Miss Rojas, don't mind if I do."

Royal was red in the face and way past congeniality. His last ounce of patience had run out the moment the federal agent had started to mouth weak excuses.

"Look, Deaton. I don't give a tinker's damn whose fault it was. The fact is that someone leaked the information to the media about Angel's existence. If you don't find out who did it and put a stop to it, the next thing will most likely be her name and address running on a crawl at the bottom of the screen. And if that happens, you better start running. And don't bother with a forwarding address because I'll be right on your ass."

Deaton winced. He'd known from the start that Justice could be trouble, but he didn't much blame him. He had no idea who'd leaked the information to the press, but he would find out. He'd already accessed the bank accounts of everyone who'd had seen to the files. If anyone tried to claim receiving a recent inheritance, they'd better have a dead body to back it up.

"Look, Justice, all I can say is I'm sorry. And you know as well as I do that it would be next to impossible to find Miss Rojas based on the information the media put out. There's what? A million people living in the Dallas area alone?"

"Hell if I know," Royal said shortly. "All I'm saying is, you screwed up. Don't let it happen again."

He slammed the phone down in disgust and picked up a paperweight from the desk.

"If you throw it, something will break," Angel said calmly. "And if it does, you're cleaning it up, not me."

Royal dropped the paperweight to the desk and reached for her, pulling her into his arms and hugging her close.

"Okay, okay," he said softly. "I hear you. I'm calm."

"And I'm Snow White," she said.

A frown creased his forehead as he gave her a cold, hard stare. "Was that a crude ethnic joke I didn't get?"

She grinned. "So I'm not lily-white and we're missing a few dwarfs, but there's still Maddie…and you."

This wasn't the first time he'd heard her make a remark about the color of her skin, something she should have been proud of. Then he remembered what she'd told him of her past. When life was a struggle, sometimes ethnicity got lost in just trying to survive.

"If I'd wanted lily-white, I could have had lily-white," he muttered. "Personally, I like my women like I like my toast. Hot and brown all over."

Angel's mouth dropped open. "Toast?" She started to grin. "Toast. Well now, you sweet-talking man, how can a woman resist after a compliment like that?"

Still grinning, she hooked her fingers in the belt loops of his jeans, pulling him closer and stealing a quick kiss.

Before he could follow through on the notion she'd put in his head, she spun out of his arms and headed for the door.

"Hey!" he called. "Where are you going?"

She stopped in the doorway. "To see if Maddie is asleep."

"Why?"

A wicked smile tilted the corners of her lips. "Because I can't seduce you if I don't have you all to myself."

All things considered, it was a long, eventful night.

Tommy Boy Watson sat on his motel bed, staring blankly at the television. A young, dark-haired man was walking the fields with a journalist, pointing out the recent damage done to this year's wheat crop. From what Tommy Boy gathered, Grant County had been hammered by the storm that passed through, and the current crop was shot. He sighed. If things didn't change, he was going to be next.

He closed his eyes and laid on the bed, trying to recall his daddy's face. It wouldn't come. All he could see was that dark-haired bitch turning her back on him and hitching a ride with that trucker.

It was her fault. Even though they hadn't said her name, he knew it had to be her. They'd talked about her on the six o'clock news, and he knew they would repeat it on this broadcast. Because of her, every lawman in the country would be looking for him. Then he reminded himself they'd be looking for the old Tommy Boy. He looked different now. He rubbed his hands up and down the length of his face, testing the baby-soft skin that had been underneath his beard. It made him feel strange, almost nude. His father, if he'd still been alive, wouldn't know him. When he looked in a mirror, he didn't know his face. They would never recognize him as the man in the sketch.

But there was his truck. The bitch had described it. And he had hauled the bodies in it until he found a place to dump them. He'd washed it out good, but with today's technology, if he missed so much as a hair or a drop of blood, his goose would be cooked. He frowned. As much as he hated to face it, he had to at least consider the wisdom of getting rid of his truck.

The sun was high in the sky the next day when Tommy Boy pulled into the street from the parking lot of Melvin's Used Cars. He adjusted the rearview mirror as he drove and fiddled with the radio stations until he had them all set to his liking. The interior of the little red Toyota pickup smelled like lemon oil and Armor-All. There was a cigarette burn in the seat, and one of the floor mats was missing. The right window was hard to roll down, and there was a faint scratch across the tailgate. The grudge he had against that bitch kept growing. Because of her, he'd had to give up his pride and joy— his new Dodge truck. His gaze slid to the dusty red hood. He narrowed his eyes. The paint job on this truck would never hold a shine.

He drove west out of Blackwell, heading toward the interstate. He'd been thinking all night about what he should do. He could go home. But if he did, he would spend the rest of his life looking over his shoulder, waiting for the day when that bitch would show up, pointing her finger at him and screaming, ''It's him.'' Or he could go to Texas and find her, like he should have done before. It would be a pleasure to shut her up once and for all.

He kept heading west. Either way he went, it was a long drive.

The interstate appeared. His belly knotted with uncertainty. Which way? A bridge was imminent. If he took the on ramp before he crossed it, he'd be in Kansas in less than half an hour. If he crossed the bridge and headed south, it would take a good day's driving to cross the Red River into Texas.

If he hadn't been so ticked off about the situation in general, he might have laughed at the incongruity of his dilemma. What was that old saying? Something about crossing bridges when you got to them? Well, here he was, facing the biggest bridge of his life and he couldn't make up his mind.

Make her pay. Make her pay.

Tommy Boy jerked when the voice echoed inside his head. A slow smile spread across his face as he gunned the little red truck across the bridge and took the southbound ramp.

''I hear you, Daddy. I hear you loud and clear.''

Maddie was digging holes in the dirt at the edge of the garden with a stick as Angel picked ripe tomatoes from the vines. Every now and then she would jump up and run down the row, pointing to one Angel missed. After the third time this happened, Angel set down her bucket.

''Come here to me,'' she said softly, then hugged the little girl tight. ''You know what, Maddie mine?''

Maddie grinned. She loved the nickname Angel had given her. It made her feel as if they all really belonged together.

''What?'' Maddie said.

''You are the best helper anyone could have. I don't know what I'd do without you.''

Maddie threw her arms around Angel's neck and closed her eyes in pure delight as Angel kissed her all over her face. Still giggling when Angel turned her loose, Maddie dropped to her knees and began fiddling with a bug running through the dirt.

"Angel?"

Angel stopped and turned. The plaintive note in Maddie's voice was unexpected.

"What is it, honey?"

"Are you and my daddy going to get married?"

Again, Angel set the bucket aside, but this time she sat down in the row and faced Maddie. She took her by the hands and pulled on the ends of her fingers until she had Maddie giggling.

"What would you say if we did?" Angel asked.

Maddie's eyes rounded, and her forehead wrinkled in a thoughtful frown. Finally, she answered.

"I do?"

Angel grinned, and then, ignoring the dirt and the proximity of the tomato plants, she lifted Maddie into her lap and pulled her close against her breasts. At that moment, the scent of little-girl sweat and freshly turned earth seemed sweeter than any flower could have.

"So you think it would be a good thing?" Angel asked.

Maddie nodded as she leaned against the softness of Angel's breasts. "The lady told me you would be my mama." She looked at Angel, testing her…judging her…waiting to see if she got that same look Daddy did when she talked about the lady who sat on her bed.

Angel shivered. There was so much going on with this child that neither she or Royal understood. But she had enough faith in herself and in God to know there were some things one didn't question.

"You still haven't told me what you think," Angel persisted. "I would live here for always. And your daddy and I would sleep in the same bed. But that wouldn't mean that your daddy didn't love you as much as he used to. It would mean you would have two people, not just one, who loved you most of all."

Satisfied with what Angel had told her, Maddie nodded,

then sighed. A few moments later, her eyes began to droop, then her head lolled against Angel's shoulder.

And so they sat between the rows of ripening tomatoes. A small sweat bee buzzed around a skinned spot on Maddie's knee. Angel waved it away as she bent and kissed the edge of her ear.

"I love you, Maddie mine," she said softly.

Maddie was silent for so long, Angel thought something was wrong. She looked down and smiled. Madeline Michelle was asleep.

Angel looked up. Royal was standing at the end of the row. She smiled and motioned him forward.

"She's been playing so hard," Angel whispered as he bent to lift his daughter out of her arms.

Royal nodded. At that moment, words were beyond him. When he'd first come out of the house and seen their heads above the rows in the garden, he thought someone had been hurt. The closer he'd come, the less his worry had been. He'd seen them laugh. He'd seen them hug. He'd watched Angel's tenderness as she'd settled Maddie close in her lap. And then he'd watched his daughter's eyes droop, secure in the knowledge that if she was with Angel, she was safe.

Angel watched Royal striding away with his child in his arms, then sighed and got to her feet to finish what she'd been doing. There was a satisfaction within her that hadn't been there before. An affirmation that what they were doing was right. Not just for the passion that bound her and Royal, but for the love she also felt for his child. She palmed a warm, red tomato and tugged, then set it in the bucket with the others she'd picked. She smiled. And her child, too.

By the time she looked up again, Royal was coming back.

"Look," she said, holding up the bounty for him to see. "You and Maddie sure know how to plant a garden. Just look at what you've—"

He took the bucket out of her hands and set it on the ground, then put his arms around her waist and lifted her off her feet. His face was buried against the heat of her neck, his body trembling against hers.

"Woman, you are breaking my heart."

Tears shattered Angel's vision as a burst of love for this man hit her square in the belly. One of her shoes dropped to the ground.

"Wait, Royal. My shoe."

He set her down, but instead of retrieving the shoe, he took the other one off, too. Then he scooped her into his arms and started toward the house, carrying her as if she weighed nothing at all.

Surprised by his intensity, she brushed her hand against the side of his face.

"Where are we going?"

He paused and closed his eyes, turning his face so his mouth was centered in the middle of her palm. The scent of the earth was on her—from the land on which they were standing to the pungent odor of crushed tomato leaves from the crop she'd been harvesting. He shuddered with longing.

"Inside. If I don't make love to you within the next five minutes, I might not come out of this day alive."

She smiled, then playfully rubbed her hand across the breadth of his chest.

"I never thought of myself as medicine before, but if I can help a good man with a great big ache..."

His eyes narrowed dangerously. There was a muscle jerking at the side of his jaw.

"You ever made love in the dirt before?"

She shook her head, her eyes widening nervously. All she could think was he wouldn't dare.

"Then don't mess with me, woman, until I get you behind closed doors."

Four days passed. Days in which joy came to the house in myriad ways and cemented Angel's presence in their lives. Angel hugged the memories to her, and each night before she went to bed, she stood before the mirror and looked at the woman she was becoming. Her hair was still the same. Long, thick, and black—sooty black. Her eyes were still large and brown, her brows finely arched. Her nose was still small and straight with a slight flare at the nostrils. Her lips had not changed. They were still shaped in a perpetual pout.

But the differences were there. In the glow in her eyes. In the tilt of her smile. In the tenderness of her touch. In the way her heart beat. Rock steady. Like the love she had for Royal Justice and his child.

The Angel Rojas who'd left Fat Louie rolling on the floor of his bar—defiant, disbelieving, distrusting of anyone or anything except herself—was gone. And each day that dawned brought a finer sense of purpose to her life. Since the day they'd put her mother in the ground, she'd been searching for a place to call home. It was now within reach. She'd accepted shelter from Royal, then a job. Now she was about to become his wife. Her life was full. Her heart was content. The only shadow on her horizon was the distant threat of having to one day face a killer. But it was so far removed from the life she was living that she gave herself permission to forget. Only now and then, when she happened to catch an update on the investigation and the drawing was flashed on the television screen, did she let herself remember the loose ends of her past.

But Royal hadn't forgotten a thing. When it came to the women he loved, he went all the way and then some. He had not forgotten that Angel was the only witness in a federal investigation, and while the chance that she would be in danger was remote, the fact that it was there was enough for him to act upon.

When a graying, middle-aged wrangler showed up on the Justice doorstep looking for a job, Angel thought nothing of it. His truck was old and rusting. Besides a suitcase, there were a couple of saddles and some tack in the truck bed. Nothing but a cowboy looking for work. When Royal hired him on the spot, she still didn't wonder. After all, he'd hired her with far less need and reason.

His name was Rusty. He tossed his meager belongings into the two-bed bunkhouse and went to work the same day. He ate meals with them, and in the rare times when there was nothing to do, he could be found sitting in a shady spot, whittling on a small piece of wood.

Maddie was fascinated with him…and with the knife. It took an entire day for Royal to impress upon her the trouble she would be in if she ever tried it herself. After that, everything settled. On August the first, just over a month away, Maddie would turn five. And before that month was out, she would be going to school. Everything was moving at an unstoppable pace.

Royal stood in the hallway with his Stetson in his hands. He'd been ready for the better part of thirty minutes waiting on women of all ages to get ready, too. Angel had poked her head out her bedroom door, blown him a kiss and waggled two fingers at him as an indication of how much more time she needed. His daughter wasn't any better. She'd dawdled on the porch with the kittens too long. And while he could have followed her in her room and done it all for her, it wouldn't have taught her a thing. So he'd taken a deep breath and calmed his frayed nerves and bellowed instead of screamed.

"Madeline Michelle, if I have to tell you again to brush your teeth—"

Maddie was running before he finished. She didn't have to hear the rest of it to recognize the implied threat. She'd never had the nerve to test her daddy that far and see what he *really* would do.

"I'm brushing. I'm washing. I'm changing my clothes," she shrieked.

He jammed his Stetson on his head and pivoted sharply. Out. He needed out.

"I'll be waiting on the porch," he yelled to anyone in general.

The door slammed behind him and hot air hit him in the face. Tomorrow was the first of July. He had hay on the field drying, and it looked like rain. And while he had some control over the women in his life, there was nothing he could do about the weather. Until the hay was dry enough to bale, there it would lay.

He caught movement out the corner of his eye and turned. It was Rusty coming from the back yard.

"We're driving into Dallas," Royal said. "Maddie starts school in a few weeks." He rolled his eyes and shook his head. "Buying clothes for school. My God, I knew this day was coming, and I'm still not ready."

Rusty nodded. "Mine are grown and gone for more than ten years now," he said. "But I remember how it was. It's hard to let go."

Royal glanced over his shoulder, making sure they were alone. "We should be back before three. If something happens, I'll call."

The older man's smile shifted. It wasn't much, but his expression had hardened.

"I suppose I'd better get at that tack," Rusty said. "There's a couple of bridles that need mending."

Royal nodded. "See you later. Oh, and don't forget. Angel said to tell you there's plenty of leftover roast and some of her chocolate pie in the refrigerator. Help yourself."

Rusty's smile shifted again, rekindling the light in his eyes. "I'll be doing just that," he said, and waved as he walked away.

The door opened behind Royal, and he turned. Angel was coming out the door, holding Maddie's hand. She was wearing gauzy white pants and a loose matching top, a recent purchase from a mail-order catalog. White backless sandals flopped against her heels as she walked.

Royal whistled appreciatively and winced when Maddie, wearing red shorts and a red and white top, put a matching sway in her walk as she headed toward the truck. It reminded him of the day she'd gone to Paige Sullivan's party with the nail polish still wet on her fingernails. He groaned beneath his breath and sighed as Angel slipped an arm around his waist.

"Poor Daddy. It's going to be all right."

"Oh, I know that," Royal said. "It's simple, really. She just won't be allowed to date until she's twenty-one."

Angel giggled and squealed with delight when he spun her off her feet and planted a swift, hard kiss upon her lips.

Maddie stopped in midsway and spun, her foray into adult behavior instantly forgotten. She was giggling and squealing along with Angel before she reached Royal's side.

"Do me next, Daddy! Do me!"

Royal laughed. His world was complete.

Chapter 16

The light was turning red as Tommy Boy braked to a stop on the outskirts of Dallas. He had seventy-five dollars in his pocket and less than four hundred in the bank back home. It was as close to broke as he'd ever been in his life.

For the last two days, he'd been so mad at himself for turning south instead of north that it was all he could do to keep driving. He'd never listened to his daddy all that much when he'd been alive. He didn't know why he was listening to him now.

The engine in his pickup coughed and sputtered, and he gunned the accelerator to keep it from dying right there in the street.

"Sorry ass piece of junk," he mumbled.

If it hadn't been for that black-haired bitch flapping her mouth, he would still have his good truck. Better yet, he would already be home. The engine sputtered again, and this time it died.

The light turned green.

Tommy Boy cursed.

Behind him, cars began to honk. He rolled down the window, stuck out his arm and flipped everyone off before popping the hood. His stride was short and jerky, evidence of his anger.

Waves of heat washed over his skin as he leaned inside. He turned his head, squinting to protect his eyes from a stream of escaping steam, and that's when he saw her. In the left-turn lane, sitting in the front seat of a late-model pickup. At first he thought he was dreaming. He'd looked for her for so long. He stood and stared. There was a child in the seat beside her, and a big cowboy behind the wheel. His heart leaped. It *was* her—the bitch who'd gotten away. By God, he'd found her.

He started to run for his truck and then remembered the piece of junk wouldn't start. He watched in horror as the light changed to green. They started to turn away from Tommy Boy, moving into a thick stream of traffic.

"No," he shouted, and clapped a hand over his mouth in shock.

He didn't want her to see him. He couldn't let her go. Frantic, he began to run behind the truck as it moved into traffic, ignoring the shouts and honks from other drivers as they swerved to miss him. He was looking for something—anything—that would tell him what he needed to know. A tag number wouldn't do. He certainly had no way to access the records. And he would have bet his life that wasn't the only blue Chevy truck in the state of Texas. Desperation kept him moving when the logical thing would have been to give up. But he couldn't. His life depended on ending hers.

He kept running. His lungs began to burn, and there was a stitch in his side. To make matters worse, the truck was stretching the distance between them. Out of nowhere, a man on a motorcycle roared past him. It was reflex that sent him diving into the grass in the center median. When he looked up, the truck was turning a corner.

"Oh, no," he groaned. They were gone.

And that's when he saw it. There on the side, in neat white letters on that dark blue paint.

Justice Ranch, Alvarado, Texas

He started to grin. Another car honked at him as he crawled to his feet. He grinned and waved, then started hoofing it toward his down-and-out truck. The smile on his face didn't fit his situation. But Tommy Boy knew something no one else did. His luck had just changed.

School clothes weren't all Royal bought at the mall. While Angel and Maddie were in the bathroom, he'd slipped into the jewelry store and bought Angel a ring. All the way home, one scenario after another ran through his mind about how he would give it to her. It had to be special. And the timing had to be right.

There was a smile on his face he couldn't control. After tonight, there would be no more misunderstandings about what Angel Rojas meant to him. The ring was his brand. The woman was going to be his wife.

He grinned again.

His wife.

They topped the hill above the ranch. Out of habit, his gaze raked the area for anything out of place. Roman's car surprised him. Although they talked on the phone every day, he hadn't seen him since the day he'd brought Maddie home.

"Uncle Roman's here," Maddie squealed.

"So I see," Royal muttered.

Surprised by his tone, Angel stared. "Is something wrong?" she asked.

Royal hesitated, then told himself he was just borrowing trouble.

"No, I doubt it. He usually calls before he comes, that's all."

Angel nodded, but she had picked up on the hesitation in Royal's voice and couldn't help but wonder.

Roman was sitting on the porch with Maddie's kitten in his

lap. He stood as they parked, and the cat scampered off the porch and under the lilac bush.

"Uncle Roman!" Maddie shrieked, and ran with her arms outstretched.

He caught her on the run and hugged her a dozen times over, kissing her between each embrace.

Madeline Michelle, princess of it all, soaked up the love like a sponge. It was no more than she expected.

"Aunt Holly sent you some brownies," he said. "They're in the kitchen. Ask Daddy if you can have some."

Maddie hit the door running and didn't look back.

Royal rolled his eyes and announced to anyone who cared to hear, "Yeah, sure, Maddie, you can have a brownie. Don't forget to wash your hands first."

Angel laughed. "She ate all her lunch, remember?"

He was smiling when Roman stepped off the porch.

"Rusty's gone," Roman said.

Royal pivoted. "Why and where?"

"Appendicitis. He called me over two hours ago. Said he was driving himself to the hospital." He glanced at his watch. "In fact, I'd be guessing he's probably going into surgery about now."

"Oh, no," Angel gasped. Her face fell. "Oh, Royal, he was all by himself."

Roman started to say more, but something made him look at Royal. Royal was frowning slightly and shaking his head. It wasn't much, but Roman realized Angel didn't know about Rusty's real identity or why he'd been hired.

"Well, I just wanted to let you know," he said.

"I guess I'd better get Maddie's packages," Angel said, and started toward the truck.

Royal caught her by the wrist, then cupped the back of her head in a tender gesture. "No, baby, I'll get them," Royal said. "You go check on Maddie. And if she's had more than two of those brownies, put the damned things away."

"Or maybe I'll get a glass of milk and join her," Angel said. "Chocolate sounds just about right." She started toward the house then stopped and turned. "Roman, tell Holly thank you."

"Sure thing, honey," he said, smiling. The moment she was out of sight, he turned. "What do you want me to do? I'll hire someone else today."

Royal sighed, stuffed his hands in his pockets and walked away from the house. Roman followed.

"What are you thinking?" Roman asked.

Royal turned. The wide brim of his Stetson was shading his face from the rays of the sun, but Roman could see the worry on his brother's face.

"About what I'd do if anything ever happened to her."

Roman stood watching Royal struggle with his emotions.

"You're in love with her, aren't you?"

Royal took off his hat and combed his hand through his hair. "Oh, yeah, big time," he drawled.

Roman grinned.

"If we didn't have bigger fish to fry, I'd say I told you so."

Royal set his Stetson on his head and then looked at the house. It was so familiar…so safe. He'd been born here. He'd brought his first wife here. And God willing, he would grow old and die here someday. And yet as comfortable as this place was to him, there was a pall on his soul. Something kept pushing at him to take his family and run. If he'd been another sort of man, he might have done so. But Royal had never run from a fight in his life, and he wasn't about to start now. He clenched his jaw and curled his hands into fists, then turned to Roman.

"Get someone else out here as soon as you can. If not tonight, then tomorrow at the latest. I've got a feeling in my gut that won't go away, and until that son of a bitch is caught and put behind bars, I won't feel right."

"Consider it already done," Roman said. "But how are you going to explain another hired hand to Angel? She's not stupid, you know."

Royal nodded. "It's her life that's on the line; I won't lie to her again."

A few minutes later, Royal was alone, watching the dust settle in the driveway and wondering where to go from here. As he started toward the house, the bulge of the ring box in his pocket reminded him of better things. When he entered the house, there was a grin on his face.

"Did anyone save me some brownies?" he yelled.

Two voices in the back of the house shouted no.

He was still laughing when he tackled them both on the bed.

All good plans and intentions were subject to change. Finding the right moment to give Angel the ring kept coming and then going without it having been done. Royal's frustration was mounting, and by nine o'clock, if he'd had a cage, he might have put Maddie in it. It was almost as if she sensed something was up and didn't want to miss it happening. They'd put her to bed twice already, and he could still hear her singing to her teddy bear.

He aimed the remote at the television and hit the mute button. "That little wart is still awake," he muttered. "Probably all that damned chocolate."

Angel looked up from a shirt she was mending. "Maybe I should read her another story."

He shook his head. "Knowing her, that's what she's angling for. How many did you read earlier?"

"Only two."

Royal grinned. "You, my love, are a pushover. I never read more than one."

"That's because you fall asleep first," Angel said.

He pretended to frown.

Maddie was beginning the second stanza of "Colors of the Wind," the theme song from the Disney video *Pocahontas*. It was loud and a little off key, but it was obvious by the way she was belting out the lyrics that she was into the moment.

Angel started to laugh. Not loud, and not at Maddie, just

at the situation. Here they were, two reasonably sensible adults, fitting their lives to conform to a child's.

Royal studied her face as she sewed, watching the dexterity of her fingers as the needle went in and out through the holes in the button she was sewing on his shirt. Her face was in profile, highlighted by the reading lamp beside her. He stared for so long his eyes started to burn. She was so damned beautiful.

Before he knew it, he was out of his chair and on one knee in front of her.

"Hey," she said, when he took the needle and shirt out of her hands.

Then he took the ring box out of his pocket and set it in the center of her palm and closed her fingers over it. His voice was rough with emotion as he looked at her.

"If you'll have me."

Angel's heart skipped a beat. Even though he'd already proposed and she'd said yes, this made everything official in the eyes of the world.

"Oh, Royal," she said softly.

"Open it," he urged.

She laid it in his hand. "You do it," she begged.

A little nervous, he took out the ring, then slipped it on the third finger of her left hand.

"If it doesn't fit…"

He needn't have worried. It slid down her finger like pearls against silk. He looked at the diamond solitaire shining on her finger like a piece of morning sky. His eyes darkened. "I love you, girl. Marry me soon."

The weight felt strange upon her finger as she slid her arms around his neck.

"Name the day, and I'm yours."

He groaned softly and leaned forward. "You're already mine, lady, and don't you ever forget it."

"Daddy, whatcha doin'?"

Royal rocked on his heels and stood up with a jerk.

"What the hell are you doing out of bed?" he growled.

But Maddie wasn't about to be deterred. She pattered across the floor and crawled into Angel's lap as if Royal wasn't even there.

"You and my daddy were kissing, weren't you?" she asked.

Angel was trying hard not to grin. "Yes, we sure were," she said. "Want to join us?"

The idea obviously had merit. Maddie giggled and threw her arms around Angel's neck and planted a kiss on the side of her cheek.

"My turn," Angel said, and kissed the little girl.

"Now you do it, Daddy," Maddie demanded, and lifted her arms to be held in Royal's arms.

He sighed and did as she demanded. After all, she *was* the princess of it all.

Four kisses and a giggle fest later, Maddie was in bed with her teddy bear tucked under her chin. Royal was about to turn out the light. Angel was sitting on the side of the bed with a book in her hand.

Maddie peeked out from beneath heavy eyelids, checking one last time to see if they were still there. Then she sighed.

"Angel."

"What, darling?" Angel asked.

"You're sitting beside my lady tonight."

It was all Angel could do not to bolt. The thought of sitting next to a ghost, however imaginary, was a little unnerving.

"That's nice," she said, darting a nervous look in Royal's direction. As she suspected, he was frowning.

"I'm going to sleep now," Maddie said.

"It's about damned time," Royal muttered, but not loud enough that anybody heard.

He turned out the light and stood aside, waiting for Angel. The night-light was on by Maddie's bed. Her teddy was tucked under her chin. Angel blew him a kiss as she headed for the kitchen to make them some coffee. Royal watched her go, savoring the comfort that comes from knowing that for once, he was doing everything right.

He turned and gave Maddie one last glance. And just for a second, before he focused and blinked, he thought he saw the silhouette of a woman, head bowed, hands folded in her lap, sitting at the foot of Maddie's bed and watching her sleep. But the moment was fleeting, and when he looked back, she was gone. Angry with himself for even thinking it, he strode away.

At four minutes after three in the morning, the wind began to blow. A low rumble of thunder could be heard in the distance, and Royal rolled to the side of the bed and sat up. Almost at the same moment, Maddie began to cry. Royal heard her first and was out of bed and halfway down the hall before Angel knew what was happening. She followed.

The light from Maddie's room spilled into the darkened hall. When she entered, Royal was sitting on the side of the bed with Maddie in his lap, and it looked as if there was no consoling her.

"What's wrong?" Angel asked, as she sat beside them and began stroking Maddie's hair. "Did you have a bad dream?"

Thunder rumbled again, closer. And then it dawned on Royal. The storm. Maybe she was afraid it would storm like it did before.

"Are you afraid it will storm?"

"No," she sobbed, and surprised them both by crawling from Royal's arms into Angel's lap. Angel held her close and rocked her where she sat.

"Don't cry, sweetie," she whispered. "Daddy and I are right here. There's nothing to be afraid of, right?"

"She said he was coming to get you," Maddie sobbed.

Angel's heart skipped a beat, and she tried hard to smile. But there was a part of her that already knew what the child was going to say.

"Who, darling?"

"The lady. She said the man was coming to get you. I don't want you to go. I want you to marry us and stay here forever."

Royal was starting to get scared. Between the look on Angel's face and Maddie's tears, it was more than he could handle.

"Damn it, Maddie, there is no lady. You're just having a dream."

Angel wasn't so sure. That sick feeling in the pit of her stomach was growing stronger.

"Royal, would you bring me a wet washcloth? We're going to wash away all these tears. And when they're gone, the bad dream will be gone, too."

Glad to have something to do, Royal stalked into the bathroom. As soon as they were alone, Angel cuddled Maddie close. It took her a minute to find the right words, but she knew they had to be said.

"Maddie, sweetheart?"

"What?" Maddie asked.

"What man is coming to get me?"

"I don't know," Maddie muttered, her eyes already closing in weary defeat. "Just the man. The man from the road."

Angel clenched her jaw to keep from screaming. When she looked up, Royal was standing in the doorway with the washcloth in his hands. Water was dripping onto the floor. He looked as if someone had unloaded a shotgun into his belly and he was waiting to feel the pain.

"Hellfire," he muttered, then turned and flung the washcloth into the tub. "Isn't this ever going to end?"

"Do you believe her?" Angel asked.

"Do you?" Royal countered.

Angel was too scared to cry. "Yes. God help me, I do."

Royal lifted Maddie out of her arms and started down the hall toward his bedroom. Angel followed. Maddie roused only slightly, settling as soon as he laid her down.

"What are you doing?" Angel asked as he set Maddie in the middle of his bed.

"Get in," he said, pulling back the other side of the covers and motioning for her to lie down.

"All of us?"

Royal's expression darkened. "Until I figure out what the

hell's going on, I don't want either one of you out of my sight.''

Angel crawled in beside Maddie, who was already asleep. Royal touched Angel's hand, gently fingering the diamond.

''Angel.'' His voice was quiet, just above a whisper.

''What?'' Angel's voice was low, too, so as not to awaken Maddie.

''I won't let him hurt you.''

She shuddered, drawing comfort in the warmth of his touch. ''I know.''

The thunder came and went. Not a drop came from the moisture-laden clouds. Sometime before daybreak, Royal slipped out of bed and went into his office. He unlocked his gun case, loaded a hunting rifle and carried it to his truck.

It was against the law to carry a loaded gun in a vehicle, but he didn't give a good damn about laws. All that mattered to him was keeping Angel alive.

It took Tommy Boy the rest of the day to get his truck fixed. When he finally left Dallas, it was getting dark, and from the looks of the sky a storm was brewing. He didn't care. In fact, he welcomed it. People died in the rain just as easily as they died on a clear day—and it was easier to hide the evidence.

When he drove into the outskirts of Alvarado, he realized he should have waited until morning. Everything in the small town was closed. He peered into one storefront after another, reading the signs.

Open at Eight.

Open at Nine.

He sighed. He wouldn't get anywhere until morning.

A police car turned a corner at the end of the block. His pulse accelerated. No need calling attention to himself. He got into his truck and started out of town. He'd seen a picnic area at a roadside park a few miles back. Good a place as any to spend a long night.

When the clouds rolled over and thunder rattled the windows in his truck, he rolled on his back and looked out the windshield to the dark sky above. Every now and then a periodic flash of lightning would show, but the rain never fell. When he looked up again, it was morning.

It was easier to find the Justice ranch than Tommy Boy would have believed. All he did was drive into Alvarado, order breakfast, then pump the skinny little waitress for information. He got more than he bargained for.

She said Justice, the man who owned the ranch, was well-to-do. People were saying the woman he'd hired as housekeeper was going to be his wife. And his little girl was starting kindergarten in the fall. He paid for his food and walked out of the café with one purpose in his mind.

So maybe the black-haired woman hadn't been a whore, after all. That would explain why she'd been so angry about his offer. Then he reminded himself she'd still taken a ride with a trucker. Maybe she was living a decent life and wasn't out infecting the good men of this world with her disease, but she'd still seen his face. She was the only witness who stood between him and safety. Tommy Boy was short on sympathy. She had to die.

He got in his truck and started out of town. All the way to the ranch, he kept discarding one scenario after another as to how he would effect what he'd come all this way to do. Maybe she'd be the only one in the house. If so, all he'd have to do was knock on the door.

Then he reminded himself there was the man to consider, this Justice man. Tommy Boy had seen him in the truck. He appeared quite large. Maybe even larger than his daddy had been. If the man was still at home…

Tommy Boy's fancy wandered. He finally decided he would play it by ear.

Royal was nursing his third cup of coffee and pacing the kitchen floor waiting for Roman to call. He could hear his daughter giggling as she and Angel made up the beds. His thoughts were on what was going on in Maddie's head, not what was happening in the real world, and how much, if at all, the two were connected. As much as he was opposed to the idea and as difficult as it was for him to believe, he would be crazy to ignore all the signs. Whether he understood it or not, something out of his control was choreographing his world. It was all he could do to keep up.

He drained the last of his coffee from the cup and turned to set it in the sink when the phone rang.

"Finally," he muttered, and answered. "Hello?"

"It's me," Roman said. "I've got a man on the way."

Royal went weak with relief. "Thanks, brother," he said softly. "I don't know what I would have done without your help on this."

"Don't mention it," Roman said. "Besides, I'll remind you of that next time I want a favor."

Royal grinned, and then got to business. "What's his background?" he asked.

"Retired undercover narc. He's a funny-looking little guy, but he knows his stuff. He'll be there before long and asking for work. Oh, yeah, you should know that he can't ride, so don't put him on a horse."

Royal laughed.

Roman added, "Just don't worry. You can trust him. He's the kind of man who blends into the background. You won't even know he's there unless it matters."

A phone rang in the background. Royal heard his brother talking to his secretary, then he came on the line.

"Look, Royal, I've got to take this call. If you have any concerns, don't hesitate to let me know."

"Thanks again," Royal said. It wasn't until they'd disconnected that he realized he hadn't asked for the man's name. Then he shrugged. What could it matter? How many funny-looking little guys were going to show up today on the pretense of asking for work?

Tommy Boy topped a low hill and whistled between his teeth as he slowed to absorb the size of the ranch in the valley.

Money. The man had money. He reminded himself why he'd come, and accelerated. The sooner this was over, the sooner he would be home.

He pulled up to the main house and parked. That blue Chevy truck was off to one side. He frowned. That probably meant the cowboy was home. A small delay, but nothing he couldn't handle. He got out and glanced in the mirror on the door of his truck, making sure his hair was slicked back and his cap was on straight. His narrow angular face was shiny in the early morning sun. He rubbed a hand over his chin, savoring the lack of whiskers, satisfied he was unrecognizable. He hitched his pants a little higher over his bony hips and started for the porch. The heavy weight of the switchblade bumped the outside of his leg as he walked. It was a good feeling to know that help was so near at hand.

He knocked, bracing himself for the moment of confrontation, practicing what he would say. A few seconds later, the door opened, and his first thought was that the cowboy looked even bigger without his hat, which seemed silly.

He yanked off his cap, revealing his thinning hair and high, shiny forehead.

"Mr. Justice?"

Royal glanced over the man's shoulder to the little red truck he was driving, then at him. He nodded.

Tommy Boy wadded his cap without thinking. That hard blue gaze was intimidating, and it was all he could do to stare him straight in the face.

"My name's, uh, Wilson, Fred Wilson. They said in town that you might be needing help. I'm a hard worker, and I need the job."

Royal frowned. Boy, Roman hadn't been off the mark on this one's description. He *was* a funny-looking little fellow, and if ever someone could blend into the background, he would be it. He glanced at the dusty red pickup and then stepped onto the porch. Time enough later to explain to Angel what was going on.

Justice's exit from the house was unexpected. Tommy Boy

took a step back and grabbed his pocket in self-defense. But when the man started talking, Tommy Boy let go of the knife. He felt as if he'd fallen down the rabbit hole with Alice. Nothing made sense.

"So when can you start?" Royal asked.

Tommy Boy looked startled. "Start?"

"Work."

"Oh, uh, now."

Royal nodded. "My brother filled you in on what's going on, didn't he?"

"Uh, yeah, right," Tommy Boy mumbled.

"Roman said you don't ride, which is just as well. I don't want you far from the house. Just find yourself some things to do around the barn and keep an eye on my family."

Tommy Boy didn't know what the hell was going on, but he'd landed on his feet with this one.

"Yeah, sure," he said quickly. "I can do that."

Royal nodded and pointed to a small, whitewashed building on the south side of the barn.

"That's the bunkhouse. Just unload your stuff. You're the only one who'll be staying there."

Tommy Boy nodded. Speech was beyond him.

"You'll eat your meals with us. Breakfast at seven. Dinner at twelve. Supper at six." Then he added, "I like to eat with my daughter, and she goes to bed around nine."

Tommy Boy's head was bobbing like a float on the end of a fishing line.

"Yeah. Right. Seven. Twelve. Six. Got it."

"Then I'll let you get at it," Royal said. "If you have questions, I'll be around."

Tommy Boy bolted for his truck and crawled inside. His hands were shaking as he started the engine and drove toward the bunkhouse. All he could think was that he must be dreaming and that he wanted to get this over before he woke up.

Chapter 17

"Hey, Angel," Royal called as he went in the house.

She came out of Maddie's room carrying a load of laundry in her arms.

"Yes?"

"I just hired a new man to take over Rusty's job," he said.

"Oh?"

"His name's Fred Wilson. He's an odd little duck, but don't let it worry you. Roman vouched for him."

Angel nodded and started toward the laundry room when something Royal said registered. She stopped and turned. Royal was still there, watching.

"Why would you need Roman to vouch for a man you hire?"

He hadn't meant to get into this now, but as he'd said before, he wouldn't lie to her again. Maddie came out of her room carrying a coloring book and a box of crayons. He frowned, trying to find a way to answer Angel without saying too much in front of Maddie.

"I hired him to, uh, take care of you two when I'm not around."

Her eyes widened. She would have asked more, but Maddie spoke.

"Daddy, come watch me color," she begged.

"I can't, honey. I've got to check on some cows in the north pasture. Want to come with me?"

"Yeah!" she yelled, pivoted and ran toward the door, still holding her crayons and book.

"I won't be gone more than half an hour or so," Royal said.

Angel nodded. "It will be all right," she assured him. "I know how to use a phone...and my fists."

Royal hugged her. With the laundry between them, it was hard to get close. She laughed when his hand got tangled in a sheet. He lowered his head, tasting the sweetness of her skin and breathing in the soft sigh that escaped her lips.

"You know something?" he whispered.

Mesmerized by the heat she saw building behind his eyes, she shook her head in slow denial.

"No, what?"

"The luckiest day of my life was the day you got caught in that rain." Then he kissed her.

Angel dropped the laundry. It fell on their feet as she slid her arms around his neck.

He groaned and pulled her close, then closer still, and it wasn't enough for what he wanted to do.

"Daddy!"

He groaned again. "Duty calls," he said softly, then brushed one last kiss against her mouth. "Hold that thought."

Angel sighed. "For how long?" she asked.

He grinned. "For as long as it takes. Trust me. I'll make it worth your while."

She was still smiling when the back door slammed. She bent, gathered the laundry she'd dropped and headed for the washing machine.

* * *

Tommy Boy never bothered to unload his stuff. It was risky enough just being here. He didn't plan to be around long enough to need a change of clothes. All he knew was that opportunity had been dumped in his lap. It was up to him to take advantage. He stood at the window, peering through a dusty pane and watching the house. Sooner or later the cowboy would surely leave. When he did, Tommy Boy would be in and out long gone before they knew what hit them. It did occur to him that he would be leaving more witnesses behind. But he'd figured that all out. After this was over, he was thinking of going to Canada. He'd lived in Chicago all his life. Maybe going home wasn't so good, after all. Maybe it was time for a change.

His persistence was rewarded. Justice and the kid he'd seen yesterday got into the blue Chevy truck. He didn't see the woman anywhere. He grinned. That meant she was in the house alone. When they headed his way, he stepped back from the window, unwilling for them to see him staring. To his relief, they kept on going, past the bunkhouse and the barns and up through some gates in a pasture above the main house. He patted the side of his pants, feeling the bulge of the knife in his pocket. No time like the present.

Royal's attention was divided between Maddie's chatter and the cattle he needed to move. But the farther he got from the ranch, the more anxious he became. He glanced at the picture she was drawing and managed a grin. He recognized Flea Bit. That was the one with a tail and four legs. The rest of them were up for grabs.

Sensing she was being observed, Maddie tried extra hard with what she was drawing, but the pickup was bouncing too hard to be very exact.

"Daddy, you need to slow down. I'm having a very hard time."

"Sorry, honey," he said. "But we're almost there. As soon as I stop, you can crawl in the truck bed and draw all you want, okay?"

"Okay." She sighed, set down her crayons, then got on her knees to look out.

A couple of unusually quiet minutes passed with Maddie staring intently out the back window and Royal growing more and more uneasy.

He kept thinking of last night and the dream Maddie had. The man on the road. She'd said the man on the road. Why would she have worded her warning exactly that way? It had to have been something she overheard. Something to do with Angel's testimony to the FBI or something he and Roman had said. But what? They'd been so careful every time the subject came up.

He glanced at Maddie. She was crying. Not loudly, just big silent tears running down her face. He hit the brakes and parked, then pulled her into his lap.

"Baby, what's wrong?" asked. "Are you sick?"

"I want to go home."

He frowned. Not once in her entire life had Maddie ever wanted to stay in the house in lieu of a trip to the pasture with him.

"But we're almost there," he said. "It won't take long to get the cattle moved into the other pasture. You know. You've watched me do it before."

But her story didn't change and her tears wouldn't stop. "I want to go home."

Exasperated, he made her look at him. "Can you tell me why?"

"I don't know," she sobbed and hid her face on his shirt. "I just need to go home."

He heard it then. It was a small change in words, but a whole different meaning from want to need.

"What do you mean, you *need* to go? Are you afraid Angel is going to bake cookies without you?"

"No, Daddy, no." Then she started to sob. "I can't tell you or you'll get mad."

Guilt hit him hard as he swiped at her tears with his handkerchief. "Baby, no. You can tell Daddy anything you need to tell him. I promise it will be all right."

She sniffed loudly and blew into the handkerchief when he held it to her nose.

"You swear?" she asked.

"I swear."

"It's the lady. She wants me to come back."

A chill made the flesh crawl on the back of his neck, but he made himself stay calm.

"How do you know?"

"'Cause I saw her. She waved at me."

"Saw who, baby? Who was waving at you?"

Maddie looked at Royal, gauging his mood. Then she sighed. "The lady who sits on my bed."

He couldn't think what to say.

Sensing she was losing his interest, Maggie began to beg. "It's true, Daddy. I swear it's true."

Royal set her on the seat. "Buckle up," he said shortly.

"Where are we going?" she asked.

He wouldn't look at her because to do that would be to admit she was right.

"Hand me the phone," he said.

Maddie opened the glove box and dropped the cell phone into his hand.

He punched in the numbers to Roman's office as he was turning, telling himself he was doing this for Maddie and not for himself.

"Roman, it's me," he said when he heard his brother's voice.

"Glad you called," Roman said. "I was about to call you. Nathan Dean called about an hour ago. His flight was delayed in Denver. It will be sometime this evening before he can get to the ranch."

Royal felt sick. "Who the hell's Nathan Dean?"

"The man I hired to replace Rusty," Roman said. "Why? Don't you still want him?"

Royal hit the brakes and shoved the truck into park. It was all he could do to breathe.

"My sweet Lord," he groaned.

"What's wrong?" Roman asked.

"About an hour ago a man knocked on our door wanting a job. He said his name was Fred Wilson. I thought it was the man you sent. I left him at the house with Angel."

Roman was out of his chair and reaching for the gun he kept locked in his desk. "It may be nothing, but I'm on my way."

"It'll take me a good fifteen minutes to get back to the house," Royal said.

"I'll call Deaton on the way out," Roman added.

Royal's voice was shaking. "Call me back."

The line went dead in his ear. Royal looked at Maddie. She was staring straight ahead, wide-eyed and silent. If he needed proof of his daughter's sincerity, he had it. She was never quiet for long.

"Hang on, baby. The ride's going to be rough."

When her coloring book slid onto the floor, she ignored it. When the box of crayons went bouncing after it, she never moved. Her gaze was fixed on something the rest of the world couldn't see.

Angel reached above the washing machine to the soap box on the shelf. The box was in her grasp when she felt a draft at her back. Her first thought was that the door hadn't latched when Royal and Maddie left. She turned and froze, her hand on the soap box and the beginnings of a smile on her face. Her heart dropped. She was supposed to lock the doors.

He was different, but she recognized him just the same. And when he spoke, she knew she was right. That voice and those washed-out green eyes. It was him. She didn't waste her breath on a scream. She just threw the soap in his face and ran.

He had expected, at the least, a hello. Instead, soap powder went up Tommy Boy's nose and into his eyes. He heard her running and leaped, rather than stepped, in the direction of the sound. He fell flat on his face. While he was struggling for a foothold in the tiny white pellets of soap, he could hear her getting farther and farther away. It was just like that day in Dallas when he'd watched from the grass in the center median as they turned the corner and disappeared. Only this time there wasn't going to be any sign on the door of a truck telling him where she'd gone.

Finally, it was rage that got him past the soap. He ran through the house, searching room after room. She was nowhere in sight. And while he knew there were probably places she could hide, instinct told him she was already gone.

He ran outside, the switchblade open and clutched in his hand. His eyes were burning unbearably, and there was a strong taste of soap on his tongue.

"You bitch!" he screamed. "You're gonna pay."

Angel was halfway up the ladder to the barn loft when she heard him shout. Even though the sound was far away, it startled her, causing her to miss the next step. Momentum slammed her body against the wall, and suddenly she was hanging by the tips of her fingers. Pain ripped through her leg as breath left her body. She bit her lip and groaned. Her grip began to slip. In panic, she clamored to regain a foothold. Only after she felt the wooden slat beneath her foot did she realized she could take a new breath. Desperate to get out of sight before he saw her, she resumed her climb. Blocking out pain, she made it to the top with less than a minute to spare.

In the loft, she frantically searched the flat, open spaces for a good place to hide. Except for a loose mound of hay toward the back and a dozen or so bales on her right, there was none. She glanced through a crack in the wall. He was coming this way. She stifled a groan. It was too late to find a new place. In another minute, he would be in the doorway.

She looked at the loose mound of hay. It was where she and Royal first made love, but there wasn't enough of it to hide in. Her only option was the bales. She darted toward them, crouched in the farthest corner and bit her lip to keep from crying. Her heart was racing, her muscles trembling from the massive adrenaline rush.

"You won't get away," he yelled.

She stiffened. He was here!

She closed her eyes, making herself focus until the sound of her breathing was almost nil. Then she waited, trying not to panic at the high-pitched, singsong voice of the man.

"It's all your fault, you know. If you'd just kept your mouth shut, no one would ever have known. But that's just like a woman. They never know when to shut up."

She shuddered and shrank into the shadows.

He was going from granary to granary, from stall to stall. She could tell by the sounds of slamming doors and muffled curses. And she was hiding above his head, trapped and weaponless. If only she hadn't climbed to the loft.

"They didn't matter. Not really," Tommy Boy called. "I only killed whores. Filth of the earth. Spreaders of disease. They destroy families, you know. If you'd left it alone, I would never have come back. But you saw me, didn't you?" He laughed. "You must have taken a good look at me then to have recognized me today. Not even my daddy would know me like this."

Something slammed. Angel winced. He was getting angrier, she could tell.

"Little Miss Do-gooder," he sneered, and threw a pitchfork across the aisle. It stuck in the dirt, swaying like a Saturday night drunk. "They deserved to die. They killed my daddy and lots of other good men like him. I made them sorry...then I made them pay."

Angel wanted to stand up and scream. The suspense of not knowing when or if he would appear was as frightening as the man himself. But she stayed. She couldn't give up on Maddie and Royal, and she wouldn't give up on herself.

Blood oozed from the wound along her shin, and she winced as she moved to an easier position. *Easy does it,* she thought, and made herself concentrate on something besides the pain.

"I never killed an innocent," Tommy Boy said. Then he chuckled. "Until you. Are you an innocent little Mex or are you a whore like the rest and just better at hiding your dirty little world?"

Angel shook her head. The man was crazy, and she needed a plan. It was silent. Too silent. She listened. Praying for the silence to continue, because she knew all too well that if he started up the ladder, she would know from the creaks and groans of the wood as it gave to the weight.

Tommy Boy had missed the ladder when he'd run into the barn. It wasn't until he was at the other end of the aisle and looking back the way he'd come that he saw it. When he did, he started to grin.

"Hey, missy, missy, missy," he called, giggling. He was calling to her like one would call for a cat.

He started to climb then realized that the open knife in his hand was a hindrance. Confident that he was in total control, he hit the lock on the switchblade and flipped his wrist sharply. The blade slipped into its sheath with a resounding click. He dropped it into his pocket.

"Now then," he muttered to himself and started to climb.

About halfway up he saw a dark splotch of red on the step. He touched it. It was wet. He grinned.

"Hurts, doesn't it?" he yelled, chiding her, goading her, feeling the power of total control. Then he looked at the opening above. Just a few more feet and he would be there.

Angel was shaking so hard her teeth were chattering. His taunts were like swords through her soul. As badly as she wanted to believe her life wouldn't end in this way, it was getting harder and harder to pretend.

She heard him calling out to her as if she were an animal. Kitty, kitty, kitty, as if she would have no better sense than to come running. Frantic, she looked around the loft, praying for an answer, for anything that would give her another way down.

Fur brushed her elbow, and it was all she could do not to scream. Her heart was pounding. She looked at the cat winding itself in and out of her arms as she braced herself on the floor.

Dumpling! It was Dumpling, probably searching for supper. With all those kitty mouths to feed, she was forever on the hunt.

She gathered the cat against her breasts and buried her face in the old cat's back, remembering the way Maddie would love her and talk to her as if any minute the old cat would stand up and talk.

A board creaked on the other side of the floor. He was here! Only God could help her now.

From the corner of her eye she saw a quick flash of gray and another of blue. Dumpling was starting to squirm in Angel's arms, and she realized the old cat had brought her kittens to the loft, probably teaching them to hunt. She hunkered down, waiting for Royal…waiting for a miracle.

Tommy Boy was getting antsy. He was tired of the games. He wanted them over, and now. The cowboy wouldn't stay away forever. He needed to be long gone before the cowboy came back. He palmed the knife and released the blade, taking comfort in the click as it locked into place. Once he realized she was in the loft, a new solution to his problem had come into play. He didn't have to cut her to kill her. He could break her neck. A headfirst dive through the opening in the floor would make her death look like an accident. He could leave in the middle of their grief and no one would be the wiser. It was perfect. All he had to do was get his hands on her, and it would be over.

"Here, kitty, kitty, kitty," he called, liking the way the words felt on his tongue.

He hadn't planned on getting the real thing, and in so many sizes. They came running out of the hay and out of the shadows. Two of them, then three of them, then five, crawling over his shoes and mewling at the top of their lungs. He didn't know they expected a treat.

"What the hell?" he shrieked, and kicked out, sending a kitten flying into the air. It landed with a squeak, then scampered away. "Get back! Get back!" he yelled, all the while moving to stay out of their way. It was an impossible feat.

He stepped on a tail first and then another's small paw. Two identical cries of pain sent old Dumpling scrambling out of Angel's lap and flying across the floor to her babies' aid. Snarling and spitting, she launched herself at the intruder, landing square in the man's bare face.

He screamed from shock and the sharp, ripping pains. The knife clattered to the floor as he reached for the cat with both hands. But it was too late. It was a hit-and-run affair.

He turned in a circle, screaming at the top of his lungs and looking for a cat to kill. Where there had been numbers, now there were none. At some silent message from Mama, every single kitten was gone.

Everything had turned into a blur of red as blood dripped from his scratches and into his eyes. He sank to his knees, trying to find the knife he'd dropped. Without it he felt undressed.

Angel stood as he screamed, quickly assessing his condition and her options for escape. He was on his knees between her and the opening in the floor. Her chance was slim, but thanks to Dumpling, it was better than it had been before.

She saw him searching for the switchblade while blood ran in both eyes.

God help me, she prayed, and bolted.

Tommy Boy heard her coming and started to stand. But she was too fast, and he was too blind to dodge what was coming. She hit him with her body, sending him sprawling again, and escaped through the hole in the floor.

"Son of a holy bitch!" he screamed, then saw the knife. Moments later, it was in his hand and he was flying down the ladder, half-blind and moving on instinct and rage.

Angel was running across the barnyard toward the back
pasture. The way she saw it, she just might outrun him. And
if she was lucky, she would run into Royal before the man
ran her down.

It felt good to no longer be trapped. She wanted to shout
from the excitement of the escape. Instead, she lengthened her
stride, felt the wind in her hair and the sun on her face and
knew that this wasn't the day she would die.

Royal was driving so fast, he wasn't even hitting the low
spots. Foreboding rode beside him like a ghost, reminding him
that he'd promised he would keep Angel safe. It had been
such a stupid thing to do—driving away and leaving Angel
with a man he'd never seen before. Rationally, he knew the
timing of the incident had been perfect for deception. But he
could have stayed. Should have stayed. He prayed as he drove
that he would get a chance to tell her he was sorry.

Maddie clutched the door and her seat belt with an intensity
he'd never seen. Her fear was palpable, but he already knew
it was not for herself.

About half a mile from the house, she started to cry again.
Royal groaned. Even if they survived this hell, would his
daughter ever be the same?

"Hurry, Daddy, hurry. The lady says hurry."

He cursed. Because something was happening that he still
couldn't see.

He came over the hill in the air, landing a few yards away
with a thump, and gave Maddie a frantic look.

"Are you all right, baby?"

Maddie was staring at the glove box as if it was a television
screen. Her eyes were wide and fixed and brimming with
tears.

"She's running now, Daddy. She's running."

Royal jerked and looked out the windshield. He groaned.
My God, Maddie was right! It was Angel, coming uphill toward him at an all-out stretch. Her hair was flying behind her,
and her arms were pumping frantically with every step. But

it was the look on her face and the man behind her that stopped his heart. He didn't know how and he didn't understand why, but Maddie had been right. They had needed to go home.

"Hold on, Maddie. I see her now. Everything's going to be all right."

He mashed the accelerator to the floor. There was a closed gate and less than a hundred yards between them when he came to a sliding halt. If he'd been alone, he would have crashed through the gate without hesitation. But he'd already put his daughter through hell. The possibility of putting her in physical danger wasn't something he could consider.

He unbuckled her seat belt and pulled her to the floor.

"Look at me, Maddie," he yelled.

She looked, her eyes wide with shock and fear.

"You get on the floor and cover your head and don't get up no matter what you hear. Understand me?"

"I promise," she said.

Royal got out of the truck and reached behind the seat for the rifle he'd stashed. He vaulted the gate without bothering to open it, then started running.

When Angel saw them coming over the rise, it had been all she could do to keep moving. But the man was too close and she was too set on living to take the chance. Her legs felt like rubber, and it was hard to take the next step. Her lungs burned. She needed a breath. *Keep moving. Keep moving.* The words became a chant that kept her going.

She could hear the man shouting and screaming, and she wondered how he had the breath to do all that and still run. Adrenaline, she reckoned. She could do with a burst of it.

Royal was out of the truck. She saw him jumping the gate and running. She needed to stop. She needed a breath. She heard a grunt of rage as the man reached for her. Her T-shirt tightened around her throat. With a last burst of energy, she sprinted away, giving herself some space. But it didn't last

long. She was at the end of her run. He would catch her, after
all.

Royal could see it clearly. The man called Wilson was almost upon her. There was no way he could get to her in time.
And there was no way he could take a clean shot without
hitting her. In the time it took him to take a breath, he'd come
to a stop and was waving his gun.

"Down!" he shouted, motioning for Angel to drop. "Get
down now!"

She lurched forward, sailing out and down like a swimmer
about to belly-flop. Royal watched it happening as he lifted
his gun to his cheek. The rifle stock was warm against his
face. The smell of gun oil and clover was in his nose as he
lined up the cross hairs on the telescopic sight.

Angel was almost on the ground, her face contorted in a
grimace in preparation for the pain of the fall. Her hair was
flying behind her like a widow's veil, long and black. Then
she was down. He saw the displacement of dust as she hit,
then the face of her killer as it suddenly appeared in his site.
The trigger was smooth against his finger. He squeezed off a
shot.

Tommy Boy never saw it coming. One minute the woman
was almost in his grasp, the next thing he knew she was on
the ground and his brain was coming undone. Just before the
lights went out, he thought he saw a quick flash of blue. Like
the blue from that damned Chevy truck. The thought died as
quickly as Tommy Boy Watson.

Angel was crying and couldn't stop. Royal rolled her over
and lifted her off of the ground and into his arms. He kept
kissing her face and wiping her tears and shaking so hard he
thought they both might fall.

"Oh, my God, oh, my God," Angel kept saying. "I
thought I would die. I thought I would die."

Royal held her. There was nothing he could say to take

away the shock. Only time would heal her wounds. All he could do was apologize over and over for leaving her alone with the man.

"I didn't know," he kept saying. "I swear I didn't know. I thought it was the man Roman hired to keep you safe." He buried his face in her hair. "Instead I nearly got you killed."

"But you came," Angel cried. "You still came."

It was then Royal remembered his daughter, who was still lying on the floor of his truck. It was because of her that Angel was still alive.

He cupped Angel's face. "It was Maddie. She made me come back."

Angel shook her head. "I don't understand."

"Neither do I," Royal said. "But she said the lady told her to come back. She said we needed to get home. All the way here she was crying and begging me to hurry."

Angel was stunned. "Oh, Royal, she saved my life, didn't she?"

It was still difficult for him to say it. "I wouldn't have come back if she hadn't begged me so hard."

She realized Maddie was nowhere in sight.

"Where is she?" she asked.

"On the floor in the truck." He put his arms around her. "Come on, sweetheart, let's go get our girl."

A few minutes later, they were on their way to the house, leaving what was left of Tommy Boy Watson for Deaton to clean up. Angel was sitting close to Royal's side and holding Maddie in her lap with the little girl's face pressed against her neck. They didn't want her to see the man sprawled on the ground or the grass beneath him turning red from his blood. It was enough that she would know her daddy had used a gun that day to save an angel's life.

As they turned the corner by the bunkhouse, they saw Roman coming down the driveway in a cloud of dust. He skidded to a halt a few seconds ahead of Royal.

Royal glanced at Maddie, then Angel.

"Wait here a minute, will you?"

She nodded. There were things that needed to be said that a little girl didn't need to hear.

Maddie clung to Angel as if she'd never let go.

"It's over, baby," she said softly.

Maddie nodded.

Angel could see the two brothers, heads together and deep in conversation. She watched as Royal pointed toward the hill above the barn, then saw Roman jerk as if he'd been punched and turn to look at her. Their gazes met and held. Then he headed for his car with Royal right behind them.

She watched them taking turns on the phone, then saw the look on Royal's face when he headed her way. There was such a sense of completion within her, as if every loose end in her life had finally been tied and clipped.

Royal opened the door. "Come here, punkin," he said softly, lifting Maddie out of Angel's arms, then transferred her into Roman's.

Roman headed toward the house, holding her close and whispering sweet little nothings near her ear, trying to coax a smile from his girl.

Royal reached for Angel, taking care not to hurt her any more than she'd already been hurt. But the need to hold her was overwhelming. He'd come close…too close to losing her.

"Can you make it?" he asked, letting her pull herself out of the cab.

Angel slid free and into his arms.

"You know what, Royal Justice?"

"No, what?" he said softly, cradling her close.

"It feels good to be home."

Epilogue

"**I** need to build a bigger closet," Royal muttered, as he pulled things off shelves and tossed old clothes aside to make room for Angel's things.

Angel grinned. They'd been married for all of a week, and he was determined her clothes should hang next to his, even if there wasn't room, even if the closet across the hall was nearly empty.

"I'm sure it will be fine," she said, and knelt beside a box he'd taken from the shelf.

She opened it, expecting something ordinary like maybe a hundred socks with holes or ties he didn't like. She found pictures instead. More than a dozen. All sizes. Some framed. Some in old cardboard folders.

"What are these?" she asked, lifting one out.

She turned it over. An odd shaft of pain came and went in her heart as she realized this must be Susan. Maddie's mother. Royal's wife. Then she reminded herself, that *she* was his wife now. But there was little joy in the knowledge that this pretty young woman with the smiling face and big belly had to die before that could happen.

"It's Susan, isn't it?"

Royal turned, then dropped the handful of shirts he'd been holding and knelt beside her.

"Wow," he said softly. "I'd forgotten these were even here." He rubbed the dust off one, grinning as he tilted it to the light. "She was eight and a half months pregnant here. See that dress? It was green. She was so sick of that dress— she called it a tent—swore she'd never wear green again." He stared at the image. "Seems like all that happened to another me...in another life. Do you know what I mean?"

Angel nodded. When Royal handed the picture to her, she laid it aside and watched as he resumed what he was doing. A long minute passed. Finally, curiosity got the best of her.

"I never thought of it before, but you don't have any pictures of her anywhere, do you?"

Royal leaned against the bureau. "They used to be everywhere," he said. "But after she died..." He shrugged. "I missed her so much, but there was Maddie. I couldn't grieve and raise our child. One day I just put them away. After a while I forget they were there."

Angel frowned. "Has Maddie seen these?"

A strange look crossed his face. "Well, hell. I don't know." He looked embarrassed. "That sounds awful, doesn't it?"

Angel shrugged. "Has she ever asked about her, like what she looked like?"

Royal shook his head. "Hardly ever. Maybe because she's still so little. Maybe because she's never known what it's like to live with a woman." Then he added, "Until you."

Angel smiled, but she set another picture aside as well. "Maybe we'll keep these out...just in case," she offered.

Royal pulled her to her feet and into his arms. "I knew there was a reason I loved you," he said softly, and proceeded to kiss her senseless.

As Royal was considering the wisdom of locking the door

and taking Angel to bed, Maddie burst into the room with Flea Bit under her arm.

"Daddy, can I take the meat scraps from dinner to Dumpling and the babies?"

After the part Dumpling had played in Angel's escape, Royal was all for buying the cat ground sirloin and serving it up on a platter.

"Yes, but don't stay long. As soon as we get this closet cleaned, we're going to the mall."

"Yea!" Maddie shrieked.

Disturbed by the noise, Flea Bit wiggled to be put down.

Maddie started to give chase and stumbled.

Angel caught her before she could fall. "Are you okay, honey?"

Maddie nodded, watching intently as Angel began moving the box on which she had stumbled.

"What's in there?" she asked.

Royal rolled his eyes. "You know what curiosity did to the cat," he muttered.

"Considering the fact that Flea Bit is about her best friend, I don't think that's a good analogy to use on her," Angel said.

Royal grinned. "Right. What was I thinking?"

Maddie dropped to her knees and peered into the box. Angel watched, curious as to what her reaction might be. But neither she or Royal was prepared for what came.

Maddie rocked on her heels, her eyes alight with joy as she held a picture aloft.

"Look!" she cried, waving it in the air. "Look at this, Daddy, it's her! It's her!"

Angel knew what was coming before Maddie got it said. She started to shake.

"What is it?" Royal asked, and took the picture out of Maddie's hand.

Even now, after all the years that had gone by and the love he felt for Angel, he felt sorrow that his first love had died so soon. It was Susan, taken on the day of their wedding, just before they'd left for their honeymoon. He remembered the way she'd smelled, like gardenias. And the silken feel of that dress she was wearing, as blue as the bluebonnets she'd had in her bouquet.

"It's her!" Maddie cried, and tugged at his hand until he gave her the picture. "It's the lady who sits on my bed."

Royal sat down because standing was suddenly impossible. Maddie's words were ringing in his ears, but they didn't make sense.

"I told you she was real," Maddie cried as she crawled in his lap. "Now do you believe me?"

Royal was shaken to the core. He kept looking at Maddie and then at Angel, remembering what Maddie claimed the lady had said. Sending them an angel. That was it. She was sending them an angel.

Angel sat on the bed beside him. "It all makes an odd sort of sense now, doesn't it?"

He stared at the picture until the face began to blur. Then he looked at Maddie—at the expectation on her face. He had to clear his throat before he could speak.

"Yes, baby. I believe you."

"Yea!" she shrieked, and bounced off his lap, going in search of the cat who'd slipped away.

Angel waited, accepting the fact that somewhere within this revelation was a miracle. For reasons she would never understand, she'd been led to this place, to these people, to this home. Not only had she been sheltered here, she'd been saved by an angel of her own.

Royal was shaking as he set the picture aside and pulled Angel into his lap.

"Tell me I'm not crazy," he begged, then rolled over, taking her with him onto the bed.

"You're not crazy," she said softly, and held him close, cradling his head upon her breasts.

Outside their window, they could hear Maddie scolding as she dug poor Flea Bit out from under a bush. A few feet away, a faucet dripped steadily, monotonously. The scent of dust was faint but unmistakable. Remnants of a past that had been disturbed. Royal sighed. She felt his body relaxing, heard his breathing shift as he drifted off to sleep.

Angel closed her eyes not to sleep, just to rest. With Maddie afoot, sleep was never an option. Quiet descended, followed by a peace unlike any she'd ever known.

It came then, faint, like a memory too old to retain but there just the same. Familiar, and yet hard to explain.

It was the scent of gardenia.

In that moment, Angel knew. She wouldn't look. Couldn't look, although she felt no fear. The communication was instant. Tears started to roll down her face and still she wouldn't look. There was no need. She'd heard in her heart all she needed to know.

"I hear you," she whispered. "Yes, I'll keep them both safe, just as you kept me."

And then the feeling was gone, and Angel knew that what had been left of Susan Justice would never come again. Not because she'd been replaced, but because there was no longer a need.

* * * * *

Available in November 2002!

#1 *New York Times* bestselling author

NORA ROBERTS

has cooked up two very special romantic concoctions
to tempt the most discriminating palate.

Table for Two

Containing SUMMER DESSERTS
and LESSONS LEARNED

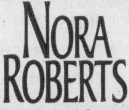

And coming in January 2003
TRULY, MADLY MANHATTAN
Containing LOCAL HERO and DUAL IMAGE

Available at your favorite retail outlet.

Where love comes alive™

EXPLORE THE POSSIBILITIES OF LIFE—AND LOVE—
IN THIS GROUNDBREAKING ANTHOLOGY!

Turning Point

**This is going to be our year.
Love, Your Secret Admirer**

It was just a simple note, but for the three women
who received it, it has very different consequences....

For Kristie Samuels, a bouquet of roses on her desk can mean
only that her deadly admirer has gotten too close—and that
she needs to get even closer to protector Scott Wade,
in this provocative tale by **SHARON SALA.**

For Tia Kostas Hunter, her secret admirer seems a lot like the man
she once married—the man she *thought* she was getting a divorce
from!—in this emotional story by **PAULA DETMER RIGGS.**

For secretary Jamie Tyson, the mysterious gift means her romantic
dreams just might come true—and with the man she least
suspects—in this fun, sensuous story by **PEGGY MORELAND.**

Available this December at your favorite retail outlets!

Where love comes alive™